Library
Western Wyoming Community College

NOBEL PRIZE LIBRARY

AGNON

ANDRIĆ

Nobel Prize Library

PUBLISHED UNDER THE SPONSORSHIP OF THE

NOBEL FOUNDATION & THE SWEDISH ACADEMY

S. Y. Agnon

Ivo Andrić

ALEXIS GREGORY, *New York*, AND

CRM PUBLISHING, *Del Mar, California*

The Nobel Prize Library is published under the sponsorship of the Nobel Foundation and the Swedish Academy. Essay on the life of Ivo Andrić by Vladimir Dedijer, and illustrations for *The Bridge on the Drina,* copyright © 1971 by Helvetica Press, Incorporated. Essay on the life and works of S. Y. Agnon, as well as essays entitled "The 1966 Prize" and "The 1961 Prize," and illustrations for stories by Agnon, international copyright © Éditions Rombaldi, Paris. Presentation and acceptance speeches originally published in English by the Elsevier Publishing Company, Amsterdam, copyright © 1969 Nobel Foundation; reprinted by permission. "Betrothed" and "Edo and Enam" from TWO TALES by S. Y. Agnon, translated by Walter Lever, copyright © 1966 by Schocken Books, Inc.; reprinted by permission of the publisher. THE BRIDGE ON THE DRINA by Ivo Andrić, copyright © 1959 by George Allen and Unwin Ltd.; reprinted by permission of The Macmillan Company.

Nobel Prize Library copyright © 1971 by Helvetica Press, Inc., New York City.

CONTENTS

S. Y. Agnon

1966

"For his profoundly distinctive narrative art with motifs from the life of the Jewish people"

Illustrated by PIERRE LEROY

PRESENTATION ADDRESS

By ANDERS ÖSTERLING

MEMBER OF THE SWEDISH ACADEMY

THIS YEAR'S Nobel Prize for Literature has been awarded to two outstanding Jewish authors—Shmuel Yosef Agnon and Nelly Sachs—each of whom represents Israel's message to our time. Agnon's home is in Jerusalem and Miss Sachs has been an immigrant in Sweden since 1940 and is now a Swedish subject. The purpose of combining these two Prizewinners is to do justice to the individual achievements of each, and the sharing of the Prize has its special justification: to honor two writers who, although they write in different languages, are united in a spiritual kinship and complement each other in a superb effort to present the cultural heritage of the Jewish people through the written word. Their common source of inspiration has been for both of them a vital power.

S. Y. Agnon's reputation as the foremost writer in modern Hebrew literature has gradually penetrated linguistic barriers which in this case are particularly obstructive. His most important works are now available in Swedish under the title *I havets mitt* (In the Heart of the Seas). Agnon, now seventy-eight years old, began writing in Yiddish but soon changed to Hebrew, which, according to experts, he handles with absolute mastery, in a taut and sonorous prose style of extraordinary expressiveness. He was only twenty when he left his native town in East Galicia, where, as the scion of an old and respected family, he had been brought up in a scholarly tradition. He felt drawn to Palestine, where now, as an aged classical author, he can look back on the long struggle for national re-establishment, and where the so-called cultural Zionism possesses in him one of its finest creative champions.

Agnon's unique quality as a writer is apparent chiefly in the great cycle of novels set in his native town of Buczacz, once a flourishing center of Jewish piety and rabbinical learning, now in ruins. Reality and legend stand side by side in his narrative art. *Hakhnasat Kalah* (*The Bridal Canopy,* 1922) is one of his most characteristic stories, in its ingenious and earthy humor a Jewish counterpart to *Don Quixote* and *Till Eulenspiegel.* But perhaps his greatest achievement is his novel *Oreach Nata Lalun* (*A Guest for the Night,* 1939), which tells of a visit to Buczacz, the war-ruined city of his childhood, and of the narrator's vain attempts to assemble the congregation for a service in the synagogue. Within the framework of a local chronicle we see a wonderful portrayal of destinies and figures, of experience and meditation. The lost key to the prayer house, which the traveler finds in his knapsack only after his return to Jerusalem, is for Agnon a symbolic hint that the old order can never be rebuilt in the Diaspora, but only under the protection of Zionism. Agnon is a realist, but there is always a mystical admixture which lends to even the grayest and most ordinary scenes a golden atmosphere of strange fairy-tale poetry, often reminiscent of Chagall's motifs from the world of the Old Testament. He stands out as a highly original writer, endowed with remarkable gifts of humor and wisdom and with a perspicacious play of thought combined with naive perception —in all, a consummate expression of the Jewish character.

Doctor Agnon—According to the wording of the diploma, this year's Nobel Prize for Literature has been awarded to you for your "profoundly distinctive narrative art with motifs from the life of the Jewish people." We should be happy if you would consider this international distinction as a sign that your writing need not be isolated within the boundary of its language and that it has proved to have the power to reach out beyond all confining walls and to arouse mankind's sympathy, understanding, and respect. Through me the Swedish Academy conveys its sincere congratulations, and I now ask you to receive the Prize from the hands of His Majesty the King.

ACCEPTANCE SPEECH

By S. Y. AGNON

OUR SAGES OF BLESSED MEMORY have said that we must not enjoy any pleasure in this world without reciting a blessing. If we eat any food, or drink any beverage, we must recite a blessing over them before and after. If we breathe the scent of goodly grass, the fragrance of spices, the aroma of good fruits, we pronounce a blessing over the pleasure. The same applies to the pleasures of sight: when we see the sun in the Great Cycle of the Zodiac in the month of Nissan, or the trees first bursting into blossom in the spring, or any fine, sturdy, and beautiful trees, we pronounce a blessing. And the same applies to the pleasures of the ear. Through you, dear sirs, one of the blessings concerned with hearing has come my way.

It happened when the Swedish Chargé d'Affaires came and brought me the news that the Swedish Academy had bestowed the Nobel Prize upon me. Then I recited in full the blessing that is enjoined upon one that hears good tidings for himself or others: "Blessed be He, that is good and doeth good." "Good," in that the good God put it into the hearts of the sages of the illustrious Academy to bestow that great and esteemed Prize upon an author who writes in the sacred tongue; "that doeth good," in that He favored me by causing them to choose me. And now that I have come so far, I will recite one blessing more, as enjoined upon him who beholds a monarch: "Blessed art Thou, O Lord, our God, King of the Universe, Who hast given of Thy glory to a king of flesh and blood." Over you, too, distinguished sages of the Academy, I say the prescribed blessing: "Blessed be He, that has given of His wisdom to flesh and blood."

It is said in the Talmud (Tractate Sanhedrin 23a): "In Jerusalem, the men of discrimination did not sit down to dine in company until they knew who their companions were to be"; so I will now tell you who am I, whom you have agreed to have at your table.

As a result of the historic catastrophe in which Titus of Rome destroyed Jerusalem and Israel was exiled from its land, I was born in one of the cities of the Exile. But always I regarded myself as one who was born in Jerusalem. In a dream, in a vision of the night, I saw myself standing with my brother-Levites in the Holy Temple, singing with them the songs of David, King of Israel, melodies such as no ear has heard since the day our city was destroyed and its people went into exile. I suspect that the angels in charge of the Shrine of Music, fearful lest I sing in wakefulness what I had sung in dream, made me forget by day what I had sung at night; for if my brethren, the sons of my people, were to hear, they would be unable to bear their grief over the happiness they have lost. To console me for having prevented me from singing with my mouth, they enable me to compose songs in writing.

I belong to the Tribe of Levi; my forebears and I are of the minstrels that were in the Temple, and there is a tradition in my father's family that we are of the lineage of the Prophet Samuel, whose name I bear.

I was five years old when I wrote my first song. It was out of longing for my father that I wrote it. It happened that my father, of blessed memory, went away on business. I was overcome with longing for him and I made a song. After that I made many songs, but nothing has remained of them all. My father's house, where I left a roomful of writings, was burned down in World War I and all I had left there was burned with it. The young artisans, tailors, and shoemakers who used to sing my songs at their work were killed in the war and of those who were not killed in the war, some were buried alive with their sisters in the pits they dug for themselves by order of the enemy, and most were burned in the crematories of Auschwitz with their sisters, who had adorned our town with their beauty and sung my songs with their sweet voices.

The fate of the singers who, like my songs, went up in flame was also the fate of the books which I later wrote. All of them went up in flame to heaven in a fire which broke out one night at my home in Bad Homburg as I lay ill in a hospital. Among the books that were burned was a large novel of some seven hundred pages the first part of which the publisher had announced he was about to bring out. Together with this novel, called *Eternal Life,* was burned everything I had written since the day I had gone into exile from the Land of Israel, including a book

I had written with Martin Buber as well as four thousand Hebrew books, most of which had come down to me from my forebears and some of which I had bought with money set aside for my daily bread.

I said, "since the day I had gone from the Land of Israel," but I have not yet related that I had dwelt in the Land of Israel. Of this I will now speak.

At the age of nineteen and a half, I went to the Land of Israel to till its soil and live by the labor of my hands. As I did not find work, I sought my livelihood elsewhere. I was appointed secretary of the Hovevei Zion (Lovers of Zion) Society and secretary of the Palestine Council—which was a kind of parliament-in-the-making—and I was also the first secretary of the voluntary Jewish Magistrate's Court. Through these offices it was my privilege to get to know almost every Jewish person, and those whom I did not come to know through these offices I came to know through love and a desire to know my brethren, the members of my people. It is almost certain that in those years there was not a man, woman, or infant in the Land of Israel whom I did not know.

After all my possessions had been burned, God gave me the wisdom to return to Jerusalem. I returned to Jerusalem, and it is by virtue of Jerusalem that I have written all that God has put into my heart and into my pen. I have also written a book about the Giving of the Torah, and a book on the Days of Awe, and a book on the books of Israel that have been written since the day the Torah was given to Israel.

Since my return to the Land of Israel, I have left it twice: once in connection with the printing of my books by the late Zalman Schocken, and once I traveled to Sweden and Norway. Their great poets had implanted love and admiration for their countries in my heart, and I decided to go and see them. Now I have come a third time, to receive your blessing, sages of the Academy.

During the time I have dwelt in Jerusalem, I have written long stories and short ones. Some have been printed; most I still have in manuscript.

I have already told how my first songs came out of longing for my father. The beginnings of my studies also came to me from my father, as well as from the rabbinical judge of our town. But they were preceded by three tutors under whom I studied, one after the other, from the time I was three and a half till I turned eight and a half.

Who were my mentors in poetry and literature? That is a matter of opinion. Some see in my books the influences of authors whose names, in my ignorance, I have not even heard, while others see the influences of poets whose names I have heard but whose writings I have not read. And what is my opinion? From whom did I receive nurture? Not every man remembers the name of the cow which supplied him with each drop of milk he has drunk. But in order not to leave you totally in the dark, I will try to clarify from whom I received whatever I have received.

First and foremost, there are the Sacred Scriptures, from which I learned how to combine letters. Then there are the Mishna and the Talmud and the Midrashim and Rashi's commentary on the Torah. After these come the *Poskim*—the later explicators of Talmudic Law—and our sacred poets and the medieval sages, led by our master, Rabbi Moses, son of Maimon, known as Maimonides, of blessed memory.

When I first began to combine letters other than Hebrew, I read every book in German that came my way, and from these I certainly received according to the nature of my soul. As time is short, I shall not compile a bibliography or mention any names. Why, then, did I list the Jewish books? Because it is they that gave me my foundations. And my heart tells me that they are responsible for my being honored with the Nobel Prize.

There is another kind of influence, which I have received from every man, every woman, every child I have encountered along my way, both Jews and non-Jews. People's talk and the stories they tell have been engraved on my heart, and some of them have flown into my pen. It has been the same way with the spectacles of nature. The Dead Sea, which I used to see every morning at sunrise from the roof of my house, the Arnon Brook in which I used to bathe, the nights I used to spend with devout and pious men beside the Wailing Wall—nights which gave me eyes to see the land of the Holy One, Blessed be He—the Wall which He gave us, and the city in which He established His name.

Lest I slight any creature, I must also mention the domestic animals, the beasts and birds from whom I have learned. Job said long ago (35:11): "Who teacheth us more than the beasts of the earth, And maketh us wiser than the fowls of heaven?" Some of what I have learned from them I have written in my books, but I fear that I have not learned as much as I should have, for when I hear a dog bark, or a bird twitter, or a cock crow, I do not know whether they are thanking me for all I have told of them, or calling me to account.

Before I conclude my remarks, I will say one more thing. If I have praised myself too much, it is for your sake that I have done so, in order to reassure you for having cast your eyes on me. For myself, I am very small indeed in my own eyes. Never in all my life have I forgotten the Psalm (131:1) in which David said: "Lord, my heart is not haughty, nor mine eyes lofty; neither do I exercise myself in great matters, or in things too high for me." If I am proud of anything, it is that I have been granted the privilege of living in the land which God promised our forefathers to give us, as it is written (Ezekiel 37:25): "And they shall dwell in the land that I have given unto Jacob my servant, wherein your fathers have dwelt; and they shall dwell therein, even they, and their children, and their children's children forever."

Before concluding, I would say a brief prayer: He who giveth wisdom unto the wise and salvation unto kings, may He increase your wisdom beyond measure and exalt your sovereign. In his days and in ours may Judah be redeemed and Israel dwell in safety. May a redeemer come to Zion, may the earth be filled with knowledge and eternal joy for all who dwell therein, and may they enjoy much peace. May all this be God's will. Amen.

BETROTHED

By S. Y. AGNON

Translated from the Hebrew by Walter Lever[1]

I

Jaffa is the darling of the waters: the waves of the Great Sea kiss her shores, a blue sky is her daily cover, she brims with every kind of people, Jews and Ishmaelites and Christians, busy at trade and labor, at shipping and forwarding. But there are others in Jaffa who take no part in any of these: teachers, for instance—and such a one was Jacob Rechnitz, something of whose story we are about to tell.

When Jacob Rechnitz had completed his term of study and been crowned with a doctorate, he joined a group of travelers going up to the Holy Land. He saw the land and it was good, and those that dwelt within it, they were calm and lovers of peace. And he said to himself, If only I could earn my bread here, I should settle in this land. Jaffa was his dearest love, for she lay at the lips of the sea, and Rechnitz had always devoted himself to all that grows in the sea. He happened to visit a school, and that school needed a teacher of Latin and German. The authorities saw him, deliberated on him; they offered him a post as teacher, and he accepted.

Now Rechnitz was a botanist by profession and expert in the natural sciences. But as the natural sciences were already in the hands of another teacher, while the post of Latin and German was vacant, it was this post that was assigned him. For sometimes it is not the position that makes the man, but the man who makes the position—though it must also be said that Rechnitz was a suitable choice.

So Rechnitz set to work. He met his duties faithfully. He chose the right books and did not weigh his students down with tedious topics. He was never bitter with his students; never too proud with his fellow teachers, most of whom were self-taught. His students loved him, his colleagues accepted him. His students—because he treated them as friends; his colleagues—because he allowed them to treat *him* as one. And, too, his tall bearing and full voice, his manners and his chestnut eyes that looked with affection on everyone, gained him the love of all. Not more than a month or two had passed before he had won a good name in the town. Not more than a month or two before he had become a favorite guest of fathers whose daughters had come to know him before the fathers themselves.

The fever of land speculation had already passed. The money-chasers, who had sought to profit from the soil of Israel, had gone bankrupt and cleared

---

1 *A glossary is printed on page 101.*

out. Jaffa now belonged to those who knew that this land is unlike all others; she yields herself only to those honest workers who labor with her. Some engaged in trade and some in the skills of which the land had need; others lived on the funds they had brought from abroad. Nor one nor the other asked too much of life. They left the Turk to his seat of power and sought protection in the shade of the foreign consulates, which looked on them more kindly than had the lands of their birth. The dreamers awoke from their dreams, and men of deeds began to dream dreams—of a spiritual center and a land of Israel belonging to Israel. From time to time they would gather and argue about the country and its community, and send reports of their proceedings to the Council of the Lovers of Zion in Odessa. And all the while, each man was father to his sons and daughters, and husband to his wife, and friend to his friends.

Life was unexacting, very little happened. The days slipped by quietly, people were undemanding. Their needs were limited and easily satisfied. The well-to-do were content to live in small dwellings, to wear simple clothes and to eat modestly. A man would rise early in the morning, drink his glass of tea and take a few olives or a little salad with his bread, work until lunch time and come home before dusk. By then the samovar was steaming, neighbors paid calls, tea and preserves were handed round. If some intellectual were present, he would make fun of the hotel-keeper who had misunderstood a Talmudic word, and called fruit preserves "jam." Or if a farmer were in the company, his conversation would be about the uprooting of vines and the planting of almonds, about officials and bribes. Or if a visitor from Jerusalem happened to be there, he would tell them what was going on in the City: if he were a cheerful type, he might amuse the company with a Jerusalem joke. But the people of Jaffa did not discuss news from abroad, since it was already stale by the time the foreign newspapers arrived.

Jacob Rechnitz was welcome and warmly received in every house. He appreciated people's efforts to speak German for his benefit, and pleased them in return with the smattering of Russian he had picked up. (Russian and Yiddish were still used rather than Hebrew; as for Rechnitz, he came from central Europe, where German was the common tongue.) Like most bachelors, he was glad to be brought into company; he fell in with his hosts' ways of thinking so completely that it seemed to him that their views were indeed his own. Every now and then he would be invited to an evening meal; and afterwards, when the head of the family settled down to reading the latest number of his Odessa journal, whether it was *Hashiloah* in Hebrew or *Razsvyet* in Russian, he would take a stroll with the daughters of the house. There was always light for such walks: if there were no moon, the stars would be shining; and if there were no stars, the girls' eyes did well enough. Another young man would ask for no more than such a life; but as for Rechnitz, another world lay in his heart: love of the sea and of research into her plants. Even at the season when Jaffa's air saps the marrow and the spirit of most men, he remained vigorous. From this same sea that brought profit to shipowners, carried vessels weighted with wares for merchants and yielded up fish for the fishermen; from these waters, Jacob Rechnitz drew forth his plants. Under the sea's surface he had already discovered certain kinds of vegetation that no scientist had ever seen. He had written about them to his professor; and his professor, glad to have a capable scholar stationed in such a region, had published his reports in the Vienna periodical brought out by the

Imperial and Royal Society for Botanical and Zoological Studies. Besides this, he urged his favorite pupil to persevere in his inquiries, since no investigation into the marine plants off that coast had been undertaken so far.

Rechnitz needed no urging. He belonged to the sea as a bay belongs to its shore. Each day he would go out to take whatever the sea offered him; and if the hour was right, he would hire a fishing boat. Yehia, the Yemenite caretaker, would haggle for him with the Arab fishermen; and off he would sail to where, as he told himself, the earliest ancestors of man had had their dwelling. Plying his net and his iron implements, drawing up specimens of seaweed not found along the beach, his heart beat like a hunter's at the chase. Rechnitz was never seasick; no, these mysteries beneath the waters, these marvels of creation, gave him fortitude. There they grew like gardens, like thickets, like shadowed woods among the waters, their eyes varying from the yellow of sulphur to Tyrian purple to flesh tints; they were like clear pearls, like olives, like coral, like a peacock's feathers, clinging to the reefs and the jutting rocks. "My orchard, my vineyard," he would say lovingly. And when he came back from the sea, he would wash his specimens in fresh water, which removes the salt that puffs them out, before laying them in a flat dish. (Anyone watching him might suppose that he was preparing a salad for himself, but he would forget his food for the sake of his plants.) Then he would take them from the dish and spread them out on sheets of thick paper; their slime was enough to make them adhere. Only a few of the world's botanists are concerned with marine vegetation, and of these few Rechnitz alone was at work on the seaweed off the coast of Palestine, investigating its qualities and means of growth and reproduction. Most scientists can only conduct marine research intermittently, on days when they are free from university duties; but Rechnitz was out every day of the year, in sunshine and rain, by day or by night, when the sea was warmed by the sun and when it was cold, in calm or storm, when other folk slept or when they were busy with their affairs. Had his concern been with the study and classification of plants on dry land, he would have become a celebrity, been made a member of learned societies and spent his time at discussions, meetings and conferences. But since his activities were in a sphere remote from the interests of the Jewish settlement, his name was unknown in the land and his time was his own. He carried on with his investigations and collected many plants. If he found a specimen he could not identify, he would send it abroad, hoping his teachers might know more about it. So it came about that they named a certain seaweed after him, the *Colorafa Rechnitzia.* It was not long before he was invited to contribute an account of the larger seaweeds for Professor Horst's famous work *Cryptograms of the Mediterranean.*

II

This is how Rechnitz's interest in his field began. When he first entered the university he chose no special subject but applied himself to all the sciences, and particularly the natural sciences, for these had drawn his heart. He already thought of himself as an eternal student, one who would never leave the walls of the academy. But one night he was reading Homer. He heard a voice like the voice of the waves, though he had never yet set eyes on the sea. He shut his book and raised his ears to listen. And the voice exploded, leaping like the sound of many waters. He stood up and looked outside. The moon hung in the middle air, between the clouds and stars; the earth was still. He went back to his book and read. Again he heard the same voice. He put down the book and lay on his bed. The voices died away, but that sea whose call he had heard spread itself out before him, endlessly, while the moon hovered over the face of the waters, cool and sweet and terrible. Next day Rechnitz felt as lost as a man whom the waves have cast up on a desolate island, and so it was for all the days that followed. He began to study less and read books about sea voyages; and all that he read only added to his longing, he might as well have drunk seawater to relieve a thirst. The next step was to cast about for a profession connected with the sea: he took up medicine, with the idea of becoming a ship's doctor. But as soon as he entered the anatomy hall he fainted; he knew then that this could never be his calling. Once, however, Rechnitz happened to visit a friend who was doing research on seaweed. This man, who had just come back from a voyage, showed him the specimens he had brought. Rechnitz saw and was amazed at how much grows in the sea and how little we know about it all. He had scarcely parted from his friend before he realized what he was seeking.

Perhaps this story about Rechnitz reading Homer, with all that followed in its wake, is little more than a legend. But after all it would seem to be less unlikely than other explanations of how he began his career. In any case, when he had finished his studies he left for Palestine; a prize received from the university and a gift bestowed on him by Herr Gotthold Ehrlich defrayed his expenses.

III

This Herr Ehrlich who assisted Jacob Rechnitz on his journey, and who had previously helped him to enter high school, was a wealthy merchant and the honorary consul of a small country which does not take up much space on the map. The garden of his villa adjoined the house of Rechnitz's father, and when Jacob was small he used to play with Susan, the Consul's only daughter. She was a capricious child, who took a special fancy to the boy and would not allow any of the other little girls to join in their games. "Jacob is all mine," she used to say, "and when I'm grown up I am going to marry him." To confirm this, she cut off one of her curls, as well as one of his, and mingled them together. She burned them and they ate the ashes and took a solemn vow to be faithful to each other.

Jacob was treated kindly by Susan's parents. She was an only child, so that whoever won her affections won theirs as well; besides which, the boy's own intelligence and good manners made him a favorite. Frau Gertrude Ehrlich, a lady whose health was delicate, took to him especially. She would give him presents that suited the occasion and so did not cause embarrassment; as for the Consul, he helped Jacob's father to meet the cost of his son's schooling, Rechnitz's income not being enough to educate the boy according to his talents. With the Consul's aid Jacob entered high school, and later on, the university.

In his first school year, Jacob spent a good deal of time with Susan. On summer days they made flower chains for one another, which they fitted out with butterflies' wings. In winter they went sliding on the ice-covered pond in the garden. Jacob helped Susan with her lessons, and she taught him to walk on tiptoe and like accomplishments. In the second year they grew rather more distant. This was chiefly because Jacob's father had sold his house to satisfy his creditors and rented an apartment in another neighborhood. All that year Jacob was much occupied with his studies, while Susan turned to the more usual pursuits of the daughters of the rich, to music and painting and outdoor sport. Even so, they were not truly separated, for the Consul's wife would invite Jacob to lunch on the first Sunday of every month, as well as on Susan's birthday. This continued until Frau Ehrlich fell sick, and the house was closed to guests, and Susan was sent to a boarding school for girls in another city.

After that, the Consul would invite Jacob twice a year to visit his office. The walls were covered with silk hangings, to which were attached two large portraits, one of his wife and the other of his daughter. Frau Ehrlich wore a long dress whose hem swirled all around the base of the picture. The color of the dress was sky blue, and it fell to the frame fold on fold, so that she seemed to move in a mist. On her head was a small bonnet made up like a kerchief, whose laces lay along the back of her neck. Susan's dress, however, reached only to her knees and her legs seemed to tremble lightly. When the sun lit up the picture she appeared to be on the point of running. Besides these pictures on the wall, two more stood on the table, again of mother and daughter, and before them was set a moist rose in a glass of clear water. The Consul was a man of tidy habits; before receiving visitors he would clear away all papers and notebooks not needed for the occasion, so that it seemed to Jacob, on entering, that the office was built solely in order to house the pictures, with the Consul like an old attendant seated constantly on guard. This impression was confirmed when, after Jacob had sat down, the Consul stood up from his chair and added water to the glass. The boy was always reluctant to raise his eyes above the level of his host's head, as if he had no right to look at the portraits. All the same, they imprinted themselves on his mind, and took on a life of their own: sometimes, he saw Frau Ehrlich vanishing into the mists, and Susan running on and on with a wet rose in her mouth. As for the Consul, he would greet Jacob kindly, remark how he had grown, and address him as if he were another grown-up.

In winter he would take Jacob to a coffee house where the tableware was of silver and the seats were soft. As soon as the waiter saw the Consul enter, he brought him his coffee, for the Consul was known there and everyone could anticipate his requests. "What shall we order for our young friend?" asked the Consul, beaming at Jacob; he would then call for cocoa with whipped cream and a tray of cakes. They would sit together until dark, and when they parted the Consul would bid him convey greetings to his father and mother.

In summer he took him riding in a jaunting-car with rubber wheels. They drove out of the city for an hour or so till they reached the Katharinenhof, which was fenced round with thick hedges whose fresh green shoots were beginning to darken. They entered a great park with circular flower beds and a statue of the Emperor. Somewhere about there were cows and cattle sheds, but you could neither see them nor smell them; behind the park was a view of mountain peaks, with the odor of pine trees drifting down, and the whole park seemed on holiday. They would sit down with the new-mown grass like mats at their feet and drink the excellent coffee for which this place was famous. The cream stood on it like a dollop of snow just ready to melt; and with the coffee there were little cakes to eat, made with cheese and poppy seeds and raisins; or else there was rye bread whose very smell made you hungry, and whose taste made you strong. They served it with fresh creamery butter glistening with drops of water. Afterwards, the

Consul lit a cigar and talked to Jacob about his studies; then, when the cigar was smoked, he lit a fresh one, rose from the table and said "Let's go," in a tone implying that enough time had been spent on pleasure, and now business called. Jacob got up hurriedly, watched the proprietor help the Consul on with his coat and blushed with embarrassment as the man came over to assist him too. He looked down at the ground, asking after the health of the *gnädige Frau.* The Consul removed the cigar from his lips and was silent for a moment; then he said, "I wish I could tell you that she is well." Since he could not quite say that, yet did not wish to leave Jacob sad, he added, "Susan, though, as I see from her letters, does very well." And Jacob, duly inclining his head, replied, "Please convey my best wishes to the *gnädiges Fräulein.*"—"I shall do that," Susan's father replied, in a tone suggesting that this was a task not lightly performed, but one which he would see carried out.

IV

In time Jacob left high school for the university. His father's financial affairs had improved, and he himself could now earn his keep by tutoring. He no longer needed the Consul's aid, but his affection for the older man still kept the twice-yearly meeting a fixture. When they parted the Consul would take out his pocket book, note down the next date and time, and remark, "So . . . in another six months! However, you must telephone my office beforehand." Lest that should sound like a veiled intention to put Jacob off, he would pause, add the months up, and conclude, "Well . . . in another half-year!"

Once, when Rechnitz telephoned on the prearranged day, he was told that the Consul was engaged and would not be available. Instead, he was asked to call a day or two later. Next day, when he was teaching one of his pupils, the youth's father asked Jacob to repeat the name of the consul he had once mentioned in conversation, and then showed Jacob a newspaper, pointing to an obituary notice. "Tomorrow," he added, "you will be going to the funeral of the Consul's wife."

All that night Jacob Rechnitz lay awake. Days that had gone now stood before him, days in and out of the Consul's house, when the Consul's wife had shown him so much kindness, in her ways and in her words. Jacob's mother, too, had loved him as a mother should love her son, and he had returned her love in a son's normal way; but his affection for Frau Ehrlich was something apart. It was a love that could be accounted for by no natural cause, though there was reason for it, no doubt, as there is reason for all things; yet the reason was forgotten, the cause was lost and only the effect remained. He had known, indeed, that Frau Ehrlich was an invalid, and this had troubled and saddened him; but never had he been so grieved as on that night, in his awareness of her death. Susan was now orphaned of her mother. That Susan's mother was dead, that she herself was an orphan, did not evoke in him any feeling of pity; it was rather like a new motion of the soul, when the soul attaches itself at once to one who is absent and another who is present, and is taken up into both as one.

Before daybreak Jacob Rechnitz had risen and made his way to the cemetery. In the press of his night time thoughts Jacob was sure that he had missed the funeral, though if he hurried he might yet arrive in time to see the last of the actual burial. The cemetery gates were open and he could hear the sound of digging among the graves. He ran forward between the trees and the tombstones in the direction of the sound. Two men were at work, standing up to their waists in the earth; a third was pacing out the length of the grave. When the diggers noticed Rechnitz, they looked up. "Do you want to see if it fits you?" they asked, indicating with their spades that he was free to step into the grave. Rechnitz did not understand them and did not move. The man pacing out the grave asked him what he had come for. Rechnitz looked at him in amazement: how could he ask such a question! When at last he realized that Frau Ehrlich's body still lay in the house, it was almost as if he had heard good news. Though she was dead, she was at least above ground.

Before the entrance to the Ehrlichs' villa men and women stood in silence. There are times and places when the tongue is tied even in company. Jacob's mother stroked his cheek and wiped away a tear; his father pressed his foot into the ground as though testing for a foundation. Suddenly the gates opened and men in mourning brought out the bier, laying it in a black hearse to which four black horses were harnessed. The scent of flowers floated across from the wreaths on and about the bier. The sound of muffled weeping mingled with the scent; an old servant had covered her mouth with a handkerchief so as not to be heard. While the hearse was being made ready for the journey, Susan and her father came out. Susan wore black, with a black veil over her face, her arm in her father's arm. Both walked as if set apart from this world. Involuntarily, Jacob took a step forward that she might see him, but then as quickly stepped back. Along that funeral way Susan did not once raise her eyes from her mother's bier. And since the bereaved had requested in newspaper notices that there should be no visits of condolence, Jacob sent a letter of condolence instead.

V

As we have said, Jacob Rechnitz set out for the Land of Israel, financed in part by the prize he had won from the university, in part by the Consul's aid; for when his course was completed and his doctorate granted, Ehrlich invited him to dine out in celebration, and presented him with a sum of money which saved him from the immediate necessity of seeking a post. The gift was made to seem not a matter of financial aid but rather a token of affection and esteem. It was in keeping with all that the Consul had done for him, and touched him so deeply that a refusal was out of the question. Rechnitz put the two sums together, and joined a party traveling to Palestine; there he found work as a schoolteacher, and settled in Jaffa.

He did not forget his benefactor. Twice annually, at the Jewish and the Christian New Year, Rechnitz sent greetings to the Consul. And when his first article was published, he sent him a reprint. But he never wrote to Susan, for the things that had bound them in childhood no longer counted, now that they were grown.

In brief, Jacob Rechnitz was now teaching at his Jaffa school, shaping the minds of many pupils and playing his part in meetings of teachers and parents. For there were already a few schools which encouraged parents to join in their deliberations, while the teachers in turn were given a chance to have their say in communal affairs—indeed, when it came to public meetings and discussions, there was not a man in Jaffa who neglected his duty. And yet Rechnitz found time to keep up his special study of marine vegetation, and occasionally to write an article on the subject. "There is a time for all, and a season for every desire." All the more so in the days before the

Great War, in Palestine; for then the days were many times longer than ours, and a man was able to do much more, with hours left over in which to take stock of his world. Ordinary people were tolerably contented, and since they were not obliged to give too much thought to themselves, they had time to spare for other matters.

Rechnitz would frequent the "enlightened" homes of the town, where he was given a warm welcome. If there was a pleasing daughter, that was good; if there were two, better still. There were in fact girls of breath-taking beauty who did not belong to such homes. These, who had come to the country by themselves, without their parents, had set their caps at poets and writers, whereas the daughters of the middle class preferred teachers and scholars, who could make a living by their occupations.

Jacob Rechnitz, as a teacher and scholar, thus came to be acquainted mainly with girls of this type; girls who, like most true daughters of Israel, were graced with good looks and comely bearing and winning ways. Jacob never spoke to them about his work. But he would tell them about other lands and seas, about strange peoples and tribes, their customs and habits, their poetry and myths. So it came to pass that if you heard a girl in Jaffa speaking of Greece and Rome, of Sappho and Medea, you could be sure that she had learned all this from Jacob Rechnitz. Until his arrival, no Jaffa girl had ever heard things of this sort, even though the town was full of men with university degrees who had learned of such matters in their time; for their minds had let it all slip, just as their minds had turned away from what they had studied before that in the yeshivas. But Rechnitz had gained his knowledge in childhood, when the things of the imagination and the works of nature go hand in hand, so that even with the passing of time and the growth of the mind they do not come into conflict. Furthermore, Jacob Rechnitz was a native of Austria, where one is less conscious of the Exile and where one's thoughts are drawn to happier things; and it is the way of these happier thoughts that they give pleasure not only to oneself but to others.

Many girls felt affection for Jacob, just as he felt affection for them. It may well be that some of them had marriage in mind, and Jacob perhaps thought of finding himself a wife, though he could not yet picture himself a married man, or decide who would suit him best. However, he would call upon Rachel Heilperin, or take Leah Luria for a stroll, or visit Asnat Magargot, or gossip with Raya Zablodovsky, or chat with Mira Vorbzhitsky, or now and then see Tamara Levi. Sometimes they would all walk out along the beach at night, when the waves kiss the sands and the sky caresses the earth. Because they were seven, that is, Rechnitz and the six girls, and because they walked together at night, the people of the town called them the "Seven Planets."

Their circle had come into being in the way of all circles. At first, Rechnitz had formed the habit of taking Leah Luria for walks. She had intended to go to Berlin on a visit to her relatives, and was therefore learning German from Jacob. Since conversational practice was all that she needed, they would take their lessons as they strolled by the shore. When her visit to Berlin was canceled, however, they continued their walks; and now Rachel Heilperin began to join them, for Rachel was Leah's friend, and her father was one of the trustees of Jacob's school, who would bring Rechnitz over to his home for "an olive or two." After that, Asnat Magargot attached herself, and then Raya Zablodovsky and her male cousin from St. Petersburg. But when the cousin began writing verses to her, she broke with him and brought Mira Vorbzhitsky instead, and Mira brought along Tamara Levi, who was previously acquainted with Rechnitz because when he first came to the country, he had lived next door. Thus the "Seven Planets" were constituted; and as seven planets they admitted no others, lest they lose claim to the title.

VI

One day before Chanukah a letter from Africa came for Jacob Rechnitz. It was from Herr Gotthold Ehrlich. For a year now the Consul and his daughter had been on their travels, and since they were returning by way of Egypt, they wished to visit the Holy Land, and Jerusalem the Holy City.

Rechnitz was delighted at the news. First, because he would see the Consul again. Secondly, because this would give him a chance to make some small return for much kindness. He did not want a great deal for himself, but one thing he desired was to show gratitude to his benefactor. Now, with the Consul's coming visit, Jacob could assume the role of a host and be of service to his guest.

He began to make all sorts of plans. First, he told himself, he would take a leave from school, so as to be free to show the Consul his country—Sharon, Galilee, the Jewish people tilling their soil. In his excitement, he forgot that the Consul had written expressly of his intention to spend only five or six days in Palestine; in five or six days one could scarcely take in more than the view a bird has of the sea.

In this time of waiting Rechnitz kept calling up memories of the Consul and his wife, their home and their hospitality. Again he saw himself walking with Susan, picking flowers in the garden and plaiting them together, or sliding on the ice of the garden pond. In his thoughts all the seasons merged, and all the goodness and grace in them became one. How many summers and winters had passed since then? Now the villa was locked up, the table was deserted, and the fruit and flowers of the garden were for no one to see. Frau Ehrlich was dead, and Susan was traveling about the world with her father, who since his bereavement had found no rest, but sought distraction in the very things that leave a man no peace, in constant journeys and wanderings from land to land. Rechnitz remembered the day of the funeral, the black hearse piled high with flowers, swaying slightly as it moved, and Susan following with the black veil over her face. Now, however hard he tried, he could not picture her as a grown woman. But sometimes the veil would lift to reveal her again as a child, running on tiptoe, chasing butterflies in the garden, and threading them into a chain of flowers around her head. How many years had gone, how many years had come, but Jacob still recalled her unforgettable caprices.

VII

The Consul did not disappoint Rechnitz. He came just when he was expected. One day as Jacob entered the school staff-room he saw awaiting him there a well-dressed, elderly man, accompanied by a tall and attractive girl. After Jacob had greeted his benefactor—or perhaps even before—Susan offered him her warm, finely-shaped hand and spoke to him as an old friend, using the intimate *du* and looking at him as if she still saw before her the boy he had once been. And yet in her glance there was inquiry as well as remembrance, as of a person seeking to compare present and past. He found himself embarrassed. It had never occurred to him that Susan might address him in terms of easy intimacy. With the beating of his heart and this sense of embarrassment he could not return her gaze. He too thought back to the past, yet without comparing the Susan of those days to the Susan who stood before him now.

Rechnitz had made so many plans for the day of the Consul's arrival; he had seen himself planning everything for the Consul's benefit and pleasure, informing the Consul of arrangements for this day and the next. But now, as he stood facing his benefactor, the plans were all gone from his head, and it was he who waited for directions. The Consul took his watch from his pocket, remarked that it was lunch time and asked Jacob if he were free to join them at their meal. So Jacob followed their lead, sometimes walking to the left of the Consul and sometimes behind Susan, until they reached the hotel.

This was situated in the German Quarter, not far from Rechnitz's school, where it stood in a wide, pleasant garden. There were shrubs and flowers and well grown trees as well as two large citrus groves that extended from the school to the edge of the quarter. Rechnitz had often walked in the garden, alone or with one of his girl companions.

Once again, Jacob was a guest at the Consul's table. And although this was not the old home, nor was Frau Gertrude Ehrlich there to preside, he behaved much as he had in the past. He took good care of his manners, and did not rush to speak until he was spoken to. When Herr Ehrlich asked how he was doing he raised his head, and, looking him in the eyes, replied, "I am an instructor in one of the Hebrew schools, where I teach a little German and Latin. The salary isn't high, but it's as much as I need since rent is low, food is cheap, and there's no need to spend much on dress: not even the rich do that. This country teaches people to be satisfied with very little and I am satisfied too. What is more, I have found a few intelligent people who, though not scientists themselves, have respect for a man of science." At this point Rechnitz blushed, for he had included himself among "men of science."

"And what of your research work?" asked Ehrlich. Rechnitz replied, "Here there is time for everything; even for useless things, such as my research."

Herr Ehrlich seemed pleased with his answer, which showed at once some knowledge of the world's attitude and a readiness to carry on with his work, and after all somebody ought to have a look into such matters, for Rechnitz's work might have its uses. Susan sat wrapped up in herself. She may or may not have been listening. At least her eyes did not question the value of Rechnitz's work.

Ehrlich poured a glass of wine for Rechnitz and took one himself, saying, "We happened to meet an old scholar on our travels, a professor with a lot of abstruse knowledge. Once I picked up a strange-looking plant from the sea and showed it to him. He said, 'This plant was unknown until a young Austrian research worker stationed in Jaffa discovered it. It's called after him *Colorafa Rechnitzia.*' Now you are an Austrian, you live in Jaffa, and Rechnitz is your name. Could you be that very man?—*Herr Doktor,* I am very happy that your reputation leads you to be mentioned in out-of-the-way places. Take up your glass, let's drink to your good health and the success of your research!"

Jacob lowered his head and fumbled for the glass, which Susan took up and placed in his hand. Again she sat back in her place. Apart from passing him some dish from time to time, she paid no attention to him. Jacob thought to himself,

Evidently she is sorry that she greeted me so warmly at first.

The waiter came up and set before each of them a small cup of black coffee. The aroma mounted. It reminded him of his room, where he would read alone over his drink with nobody's eyes upon him. He looked down at the coffee. A pale, brownish foam bubbled up on its surface. The foam was full of little eyes that flickered like sparks.

"Don't you take sugar?" asked the Consul.

"Oh yes," Jacob answered, but still forgot to take any.

Susan picked up the silver tongs, secured a lump and dropped it into his cup. "Another?" she asked, and caught a second lump.

"Thank you," he said, and began to wonder whether the instinct to recoil from what harms us would not hold Susan back; for if the sugar fell into the full cup, the coffee would spill over. Then again it seemed to him that this was the first lump after all, there was no need to fear, for when the coffee was poured allowance must surely have been made for the sugar.

The Consul took out his cigar case, offered a cigar to Jacob and chose one for himself. Taking Rechnitz's arm he strolled up and down with him, while the smoke rose up until their cigars were half burnt out, though ash still stood on the tips. The Consul halted in the middle of the lounge, removed his ash, and said, "So here we are, seated together again." Suiting action to word, he walked across to the sofa and sat down opposite Susan, settling Jacob beside him on his right.

He looked across at his daughter, then turned to Jacob, saying, "I'm sure you are busy in the afternoon, so come across this evening and we'll dine together. Wouldn't that be nice, Susan?"

Susan inclined her head in agreement. Evidently her mind was not on what she was doing, but all the same the gesture, however unaware, was pleasant to see.

Actually Rechnitz was free that afternoon, but since the Consul had declared him to be busy he could hardly contradict him. He recalled something he had read in a book of occult philosophy: how those motions of the soul that urge us on cannot bring us to act without the help of other, external factors. And if these external factors do not collaborate, all the motions of our soul are vain, and lead only to inner confusion. Rechnitz could indeed have consoled himself in the knowledge that he would be returning for supper; but he found no comfort in this, for the barren hours seemed to stretch on endlessly till evening.

Stripped of all cheer, he walked away from the hotel. He said to himself: Since they are here, I will do everything I can. But if they go, let them go. I will have a clear mind again. Why give myself needless cares? What is needless is not needed. I shall try to do what is right, and that is enough. Don't blame me, Susan, if you were mistaken in me, if you thought I still deserved the love you had for me once. We aren't children at play any more, but grown persons who have known the years. What a pity we aren't happy now!

VIII

A free afternoon. On free days, or at least on free afternoons, Rechnitz would stay in his room, make coffee for himself and read a book. When he had had enough of reading, he would get up to sort out his specimens, or take a walk by the shore in search of new ones. But today he felt no inclination to go home. He had already had coffee, and that deprived him of half his satisfaction, which lay in the pleasure of preparation. He would put the pot on to heat, watch the flames rise through the perforations in the burner and envelop the pot, while the water bubbled and boiled, rose and fell, and he would shake the coffee grains down on the water and smell the aroma that filled his room. The only alternative was to walk by the sea. Yet a walk by the sea did not appeal to him much. He had overeaten at the hotel; perhaps, too, he felt weighted down by the wine he had drunk. Some of the things he had said in the Consul's presence came back to his mind, and although he didn't exactly find fault with them, an unaccountable sadness took hold of him. His fancy wandered and returned, but he lacked the power to center his thoughts on one subject.

Leah Luria came by and saw Rechnitz alone. "Master, you stand in the markets of Jaffa as if the world were yours," she said.

Rechnitz buttoned up his coat and replied, "I feel more as if there were no place for me in the world."

Leah stared at him with her two fine eyes. "I hope to God that nothing has gone wrong, Doctor." Her voice was full of distress and concern, and a will to hit upon some good advice or suggestion. Her face, too, spoke of a longing to advise him, to save him from trouble.

Rechnitz shook his head. "Nothing's wrong at all, but when a man finds himself idle in the middle of the day, then he surely doesn't know what to do."

Leah said, "If a walk is something to do, we can walk for a while; only I promised to call on Rachel Heilperin. Let's go over to her place, perhaps she will come too." She looked at the watch on her wrist. "She must be waiting for me now. Would you come with me?"

Rechnitz answered with a Yiddish singsong, "And why not?"

She laughed. "Let's go, then."

"Come on." It hardly mattered whether he walked with one or with both of them, so long as it made his heart a little lighter.

Even though Leah Luria had given up studying German conversation when she gave up her trip to Berlin the year before, she and Jacob still kept to their walks. Anyone who saw them together would say that there went a perfect couple. And perhaps Jacob and Leah thought the same, each in his own way; except that Jacob thought similarly, or not very differently, about himself and Rachel Heilperin, and perhaps about himself and another, as we shall soon see. And perhaps these others, too, were of the same opinion, each in her own fashion.

Leah was not very young; she was already twenty-three or four. Her features were full, her face was neither too long nor too round, her forehead was smooth. She had ash-blonde hair and a full body, which she carried with such dignity as to impress everyone she met. She herself could never understand the attentions she received, and her manner suggested surprise; while, out of fear that she might bore her companions, she spoke little. Yet this very reticence added to her charm; for she gave the impression that if only she were to speak, one would hear words of wisdom. Her complexion was on the dark side; she wore a bright turquoise dress with a light chain round her neck, and thick-soled country shoes which added to her height and loosened her stride. Her arms were round and warm, her eyes seemed pleased at all you did. And even though these eyes might at first appear to be astonished, it was clear in the end that they approved of whatever you did. Why, you may ask, had Leah not found her partner in life? Because Rachel was the more beautiful girl. Tall and slender as a palm tree, to use the biblical image, she had not an ounce of superfluous flesh. Her eyes would light up occasionally, though for the most part they expressed chill indifference, and her lips would smile in such a way that you would gladly give her your heart, even before she took it for herself. Why then had Rachel not found her partner? Perhaps because of Leah, who demanded nothing of you, and in demanding nothing, led you to want to give her all. The reason for this is not as clear as it might be, but despite the confusion, it works strangely on the soul.

IX

Rachel and Leah were girls of good family, whose fathers had their place in the history of the Return. One of them was a correspondent of the great Ahad Ha'am, who addressed him as "My esteemed friend." The other's opinions carried weight with the Odessa Council, and even with Lilienblum and Ussishkin.

Much had happened in the lives of both men. Yehiel Luria, the father of Leah, had begun as a yeshiva student, devoting himself to the Torah in the traditional fashion; at times for its own sake, at times for the security afforded by a rabbi's life, at times for the prestige it carried, and at times because he could imagine no possible way of life without the Torah. But winds of change began to blow through the yeshiva walls; among them, a purifying wind that brought new promise of national revival. The students of the yeshiva began to speak of God's prophecies, of the return to Zion and the sprouting of the horn of salvation for the house of Israel in Israel's holy land. Some of them were later to belie their own words; others had the privilege of fulfilling in their lives what they sought after in their hearts. And when Yehiel heard that in the Land of Israel there were Jews who lived upon the soil, he resolved to go there and fulfill the Torah through work. He saw himself joining a settlement and becoming a farmer, sowing seed with one hand and holding his Talmud in the other; or following the plow with his copy of the Jerusalem Talmud resting upon it, thus at once fufilling the Torah of the Land of Israel and the working of its soil. When his time came to be drafted into the Tsar's army, he fled the country for Palestine and entered one of the yeshivas in Jerusalem. He had thus achieved the merit of following the Torah; but not of fulfilling it through toil, for the yeshivas were remote from the pioneer community in spirit, and work on the land was considered profane by the people of Jerusalem. He went on with his studies, much as he had done outside the country, except that there he had had great hopes for his life in the Land of Israel, whereas in the Holy Land itself half his hopes were gone. And now he was a married man and father of a daughter; he began to think hard of the practical future. He took what remained of his wife's dowry and went into business. The result was that he lost her money and was left with nothing but his Torah, and even that was not all it should have been. Once, however, he happened to accompany a collector of donations and tithes who was making his rounds of the settlements. He saw the Jewish people at work in the fields and vineyards, and although in those days the settlers were held in ill repute among the people of Jerusalem, Yehiel ignored all this and hired himself out to one of the farmers. He turned himself into a working man, and suffered what had to be suffered, and rejoiced that at last he had been privileged to till the holy soil. But not long afterwards, the farmers of the settlements assigned their land to Baron Rothschild's officials, and all the joy was gone from their work. Yehiel went away to another place, and then to yet another, until his wanderings brought him to upper Galilee, where he became a teacher. He spent himself in that effort, but received no satisfaction from it, for his pupils did not respond to what he tried to teach. So he left his school and went down to Jaffa, and with the help of his wife's relatives in Berlin started a shop for spades, pruning hooks and other tools needed on the land. Anyone coming from the villages found in him a friend and comrade and a good counselor.

Very different was the story of Boris Heilperin, Rachel's father. From early childhood he had received a modern education, and when he finished his studies, he became manager of a brickyard. His home was a meeting place for the Lovers of Zion, and later, for the "Political Zionists."

In the great Uganda schism, Heilperin suddenly resigned from his post in the brick works and left behind him both groups, the "Zionists" and the "Zionists of Zion." With his family he emigrated to Palestine and joined a pioneer settlement that had a number of members of the BILU group, with whom he had exchanged cordial letters. But not long passed before a dispute flared up among them. Heilperin said to himself, If I cannot live in harmony among these comrades, to whom I am bound in heart and soul, how much less so will I be able to live with the rest of my countrymen? So he went and rented fields from an Arab, and he and his household worked the land as ordinary farmers, until his children were grown to school age. Now there was no school within the village or anywhere near it; so he left his farm land and came to Jaffa, and opened a shop there for lime, cement and construction materials. There was no blessing on his business for the same reason that Luria had none: neither was accustomed to commerce, and it was a time of recession. Also, they gave their attention to the affairs of the Jewish Settlement rather than to their own. All the same they were content with their lot, and offered thanks, one to the Holy Name, the other to Fate, that they were privileged to live in the Land of Israel. Though their views differed, they respected one another. Luria held Heilperin in esteem for his determination, and Heilperin esteemed Luria for his integrity, while the newer generation respected them both, not only for these virtues but just because they were "respected." Their homes were open to all, teachers and writers were warmly welcomed. From four o'clock until ten at night the samovar was lit and tea awaited you. Both men had a liking for Dr. Rechnitz. Rachel's father forgave him for coming from the Hapsburg Empire and for not speaking Russian. Leah's father was even glad of this; he would not have minded, in fact, had Rechnitz come from Galicia, since he had married a Galician woman himself. Like the "enlightened" people they were, they did not try to rush Rechnitz into declaring his intentions, but waited patiently for that moment on which the fathers of daughters set so much store.

X

Rachel had already heard from her brother, who was a pupil at the school where Rechnitz taught, that important visitors had called on his teacher. There were an old gentleman and a grown girl. The old gentleman stooped, like all men of his age from abroad. But the girl was tall and lovely. The clothes she wore were not to be seen anywhere in Palestine.

Rachel said to Rechnitz, "I hear you have guests." He nodded.

"Who are they?" she asked.

"People from my city."

"And who is the girl?"

"She's the daughter of the old gentleman."

"Is she beautiful?"

"That depends on one's taste."

"My brother has told me about her."

Rechnitz looked up. "What did he say?"

"Why don't you tell us a little yourself? You're very silent."

"There's not much to tell. When I was a boy, our house was next to that of Herr Ehrlich, and I used to be in and out of his home, as happens with neighbors. When Frau Ehrlich died, and even before then, when my parents moved to another district, I gave up visiting, because of the distance and because we weren't on the same neighborly terms. Now it happens that the Consul and his daughter are traveling around the world, and on their way back from Africa they are spending four or five days in Palestine."

"And what about her?" asked Rachel. "I mean, the Consul's daughter?"

"She's with her father; and on their way home they have come to see the Holy Land."

Rachel smiled rather mysteriously; her eyes resumed their usual look of indifference. Rechnitz blushed. He thought of the many favors the Consul had done him; yet he had shown little gratitude by this offhand way of referring to him. He looked across at Leah.

"Leave him alone, Rachel," said Leah. "Can't you see that Dr. Rechnitz has nothing to say?"

"He may have nothing on his tongue," said Rachel, "but I think he has something on his mind. Tell us about it, Doctor."

"She is the daughter of my benefactor."

His tone of voice startled Rachel. She began to make some remark, reconsidered, and said instead, "If I may ask, how long have you been acquainted with her? You were neighbors, weren't you?"

Rechnitz answered, "We were neighbors when we were children, but I haven't seen her since I started high school."

"Interesting, *most* interesting," said Rachel.

"What's so interesting?" asked Leah.

"It is, don't you agree, Doctor?"

Leah said, "We'd do better to go for our walk. It's a shame to waste time indoors. Are you ready, Rachel?"

"Yes, ready."—"And so?"—"So, let's go."—"Where to?"—"Oh, wherever our feet take us. Doctor, what do you say? Shall we go to Mikveh? Or Sarona?"

Rechnitz said, "I'm invited to dinner, so I can't go very far."

Rachel laughed. "It's not an hour since he left her, and he already wants to be back."

Rechnitz looked at the clock. "Anyway," he said, "I have time for a short walk."

"I'll take it upon myself," said Leah, "to bring you back to the place you have to be at the time you have to be there."

They turned and took their way along the sea, as people in Jaffa do when they have no special destination.

XI

The sand, neither too loose nor too hard-packed, gave off a good smell. And above the sand, though not too far from earth, the sky was full of fresh clouds, half of them lead tinged with silver, and half, red gold. Over these were smaller clouds; some the shape of cattle or beasts or birds, and some like the smoke of sunrise. Mists of sulphur veiled them, mists that were torn, then opened, that wheeled and then moved on. The noise of the waves mounted, the sea was full, casting up numberless new conches and shells on the margin of the beach, like some being that lacked peace in its depths.

Rachel picked up a hollow shell and held it to her ear. Leah was about to make some remark but thought better of it and said nothing. She stooped to lift up a shell, whispered into it and threw it into the sea. Rechnitz picked up a plant that the waves had left, inspected it, and remarked, "I forgot to ask what time dinner is served."

Rachel looked at him as if she didn't know where things were heading. "Are you so hungry?"

"No, but . . ."

She laughed. "Well, let's ask."

He nodded. "Yes, of course; we had better go."

Leah gazed at the sea. "How lovely it is. It's a pity we have to leave."

"I can promise you," smiled Rachel, "that the sea won't run away between now and tomorrow."

"I suppose so," Leah answered, still looking out to sea.

"Don't you believe me?"

Leah laughed. "All right, let's go."

They walked back and reached the hotel. Susan was taking a walk on the grounds. Rachel halted suddenly and stared straight in front of her. Finally she pressed a hand to her brow and exclaimed, "How lovely that girl is! Who is she?"

Rechnitz silenced her and whispered, "That's she; that's the Consul's daughter."

"Oh indeed," answered Rachel in a different tone. "It's clear that she's haughty!"

"How do you know that?" said Leah.

"How do I know that she's haughty? Didn't you see that motion of her head when she returned Dr. Rechnitz's greeting?"

Jacob, however, recognized the gesture; she had inclined her head similarly when the Consul invited him to dinner. Such movements are unwilled: they do not come from our awareness, nor from the soul, which normally govern our gestures.

Leah glanced down at Jacob's hands. "You are going to your meeting empty-handed. Where can we get you some flowers to bring to your guests?"

Jacob was dismayed. He should indeed have thought of this, but he had made no preparations for his call. He looked hopefully at Leah, who gazed at the flower beds in front of the hotel entrance and commiserated with him.

Rachel suggested, "Mira lives only a few steps away; and if she's not at home, we can try Raya. Her Petersburg cousin just smothers her in flowers. Don't worry, Dr. Rechnitz; we shan't send you along without a gift."

Rechnitz glanced at her pathetically, then took off his hat in gratitude, crying, "Thank you!"

Rachel continued, "If it weren't for that fine lady in the garden, I might have fetched some flowers from the porter. There's nothing lovelier than white narcissus in the hands of a Negro. Why don't you speak, Dr. Rechnitz? Tell us a story, like that one about the African queen who used to come to her council of state riding on the back of one of her ministers."

Leah hugged her, exclaiming, "You are a good little girl, Rachel!"

"Aren't I? Taking the flowers that Raya's cousin brings her and sending them to that fine lady by means of Dr. Rechnitz! It would be still better if they were Mira's flowers originally, which *she* had given first to the cousin!—Forgive me, Dr. Rechnitz, I really don't mean any harm. Shake hands and let's make up.—Aren't you feeling cold, Leah?" Rachel slipped an arm around her friend's shoulder and kissed her on the neck. "Your neck tastes salty, Leah."

In return Leah embraced Rachel,

kissed her warmly and said, "I don't know what's the matter with me. I can't say that I am happy, but I can say that things feel good."

"If they feel good they *are* good," said Rachel. "For my part, I really don't know what's good and what isn't."

With her eyes on the ground, Leah pondered what her friend had said.

XII

Rechnitz arrived about half an hour before the meal. Susan was standing near the entrance, examining the picture postcards which the hotel clerk had set out before her. Seeing Jacob, she greeted him with a nod and returned to her postcards, laying some down for a second inspection. The Consul was below in the reading room, looking over a newspaper. He caught sight of Rechnitz, removed the cigar from his lips, put his paper down on the table, and extended his hand.

"I'm sorry to interrupt your reading," Rechnitz remarked.

The Consul took off his spectacles. "There's no news. The world carries on as usual, the newspapers likewise. They make us participate in the world's affairs according to their own notions. These newspapers unite mankind; they make opinions uniform. True, they may disagree among themselves, but their very disagreements prove that their outlook is basically the same and that they only differ on details. In the future, all human beings will be alike, except perhaps the savages in Africa—*they* may keep some of the individuality that God planted in the hearts of His creatures. Well, well! I'm philosophizing. All the same, there's a grain of truth in what I say, even if it sounds like armchair philosophy. But you, I am sure, have found interesting people here!"

At this point the Consul called a waiter and told him to reserve a special table for them at dinner, adding that if this were not feasible, they would wait until all the guests had finished their meal. Turning back to Rechnitz, he said, "That is to say, if you are not hungry. What were we talking about before? The press, was it? No, it was about people. Have you found interesting people here?"

"Where are people not interesting? It seems to me that every man has his appeal. Perhaps this is because I am not well acquainted with human nature and don't know many people. And perhaps it is because most of the people in Jaffa are Russians. And most of the Russians are lively—in mind and in body: they never get involved in one all-absorbing interest, with the exception of arguments; in that respect, of course, they are all alike."

The Consul flicked his cigar ash into the tray before him. "If you live another year among these Russians, you'll see that they, too, are like everyone else. What do they argue about? What is there that's worth arguing about?"

"It's enough for one of them to make a remark, and the other starts an argument at once. And even if they're both on the same side, there won't be a thing said without a grand debate."

"Most interesting," said the Consul.

Rechnitz watched him concentrate on trying to drop the unconsumed ash, and went on, "The facts in themselves may not be of special interest, but the process is interesting, since it repeats itself no matter what the circumstances may be, and one knows from the start that whatever Mr. Greenberg says will be contradicted by Mr. Berggreen."

Ehrlich smiled. "You made up those names, my dear fellow."

"Well," said Rechnitz, "it's true that nobody here is called Greenberg or Berggreen, but a number of people have names that are the reverse of one another."

"And what about the Sefardim?" the Consul asked.

"I'm not acquainted with them. They stay in their own homes and don't mix with the Ashkenazim. Perhaps they lack a social sense. Besides, they regard themselves as kings who have been deposed and are angry at us Ashkenazim for presuming to reign in their place. But I know the Yemenites a little. They're a nimble, quick-witted tribe, who love work and are very studious, and pious too. We have a Yemenite caretaker at our school. He has the face of a prince, and everything he sees sets his mind working. Once he asked me, 'Why is it that King David says: *Thou hast set a boundary, they shall not cross it, they shall not return to cover the earth; thou hast set a boundary to the waters of the sea, that they shall not go up on the dry land?* And yet we see that the waters of the sea do go up on the dry land.' "

"And how did you answer the Yemenite?"

"What could I reply?" said Rechnitz. "I didn't give him any answer, but I sighed deeply, as one does when regretting that things are not as they should be."

"That's the best answer of all," the Consul said. "But here I'm smoking, and I haven't offered you a cigar. Actually it's a sin to smoke tobacco in this wonderful fragrant air. But what can I do? It's my addiction. If I'm reading a newspaper or talking to someone, of course I smoke. And if I'm neither reading nor talking, I smoke out of sheer boredom." He laughed in the way people do who make fun of their own weaknesses and yet are quite contented with them. "Well, if you don't want a cigar, let's have a sip of brandy."

The Consul tasted some brandy. "Not bad, really," he commented. After a second glass he gave it fuller praise.

"This brandy," said Rechnitz, "is from Rishon le Zion. Shall we go there, sir? You will see a great wine press, without equal in Europe."

The Consul smiled a little patronizingly. "I doubt if I shall have time. After all, one can't visit the Holy Land and not go to Jerusalem, and we've only another four days. You must have been there already. Some tourists I met on the way were not impressed with Jerusalem, you know. Dirt and beggars, they said; nothing but beggars and dirt."

"Were they Christian or Jewish tourists?"

"What does that matter? It's a holy land for Christians, too."

"Yes, but they have lands of their own."

"What sort of conversation is this?"

Rechnitz blushed and said nothing.

"If the air of Jerusalem is as fine as that of Jaffa," said the Consul, "that will be good enough. I've not found the like of it anywhere. And the old Baron says so too. Do you know him? He was a general in Africa, or a governor for his king, or some such dignitary. What do you think, Jacob? Shall I settle down here? My late father's grandfather came to Jerusalem an old man, and passed away there at the end of a ripe old age. I remember when I was a child, a rabbinical emissary from Jerusalem came to the house and my father gave him money. And every year printed matter used to come from there, and every Rosh ha-Shanah eve my father would send a contribution. I was approached, too, on behalf of the Land of Israel; they tried to get me to buy shares in the Settlement Bank. I said to them, 'If it's charity you want, I'm ready to give you something; but what have "settlement shares" to do with the Holy Land? Old men go there to die, but what have young men to go for?'—I'm not referring to you, my friend; you came for the sake of your research, and science has its place everywhere!"

As Rechnitz was about to reply, the waiter came up to announce that their table was ready. The Consul nodded, and said, "We have been talking for a good while now, and all the guests should have had time to finish their meal. Waiter, see if my daughter is ready for dinner."

XIII

When the three of them were seated at dinner, the Consul turned to Susan and asked, "Well daughter, how did you spend your day? I don't think I've seen you since we finished lunch."

Susan replied, "Ask our guest that question: he will tell you."

"How should Dr. Rechnitz know?"

Jacob lowered his head as his host asked, "Well Doctor, how did our friend Fräulein Susan Ehrlich spend her day?"

What did Rechnitz know about Susan's doings? For a brief moment he had caught a glimpse of her in the garden while he was walking with Rachel and Leah, before she disappeared, leaving him nothing to remember but her nod. He looked at her in perplexity.

The Consul smiled. "Evidently you have a secret between you. Well now, let's ask Dr. Rechnitz how *his* day was spent."

Now, thought Rechnitz to himself, I suppose Susan will say, "Ask me." But Susan said nothing.

The Consul filled their glasses and drank a toast. As Rechnitz drank, he reflected on how tomorrow they would be traveling on to Jerusalem and he would return to his own affairs. And how they would come back to Jaffa, and leave again.

Susan was seated on the Consul's left, facing Jacob. Her spirit seemed to have sunk deep down into her being, or to have fled her body entirely. A light breeze was blowing in; the scent of lemon and orange trees filled the dining room. The lamp on the table shone with double brightness, and the sides of its white base grew red. From the gardens and the citrus groves came the cry of jackals, and the parrot in its cage stirred itself to echo their high-pitched screams. Suddenly the sea awoke; its waves pounded and a pleasant sea smell mingled with the fragrance from the gardens and groves that girdle Jaffa.

The Consul raised his glass: "Go tell my countrymen that while they're sitting over their cabbage with their blood congealing from the cold, we here take dinner by the open window! Are you cold, Susan? What are you bringing us now, waiter—black coffee? If I drink coffee at night, I can't sleep. Every age has its own customs: our forefathers used to take drinks that put them to sleep, but now we try to keep ourselves awake. After all, is there anything in the world worth staying awake for?—Those scents from the garden are most exhilarating: a mixture of jasmine and orange blossom, isn't it?"

Susan sat in silence. Those exhilarating scents were putting her to sleep. Without a word, she stood up from the table and kissed her father's brow.

"Are you going up to your room, daughter?" he asked.

"Yes, Papa."

Herr Ehrlich kissed her on the cheek and said good night. Susan gave her hand to Jacob, then left.

The Consul watched her leave and said, "Susan is rather tired; I don't think we shall go to Jerusalem tomorrow. What will you be doing?"

Rechnitz consulted his diary. "I am free tomorrow after midday."

"Then come and take lunch with us," said the Consul. "Susan and I are always glad of your company."

"How about our going to Mikveh Israel tomorrow?"

"Where is that?"

"About an hour's walk from here."

"Walk?" echoed the Consul in dismay.

"It's possible to go by carriage. And from there it's an hour's journey to Rishon le Zion."

"And what is Sarona?" asked the Consul.

"Sarona is a small village of Christian Germans."

"Where is it?"

"Very near here."

"I've heard," said the Consul, "that they are very good farmers and God-fearing people. Let's decide tomorrow where we shall go. We'll lunch at half-past twelve. Bring a good appetite with you—it will encourage us to eat, too!"

XIV

When Rechnitz came at noon, Susan was not there. She had spent most of the night looking over the pictures she had bought and had not gone to bed; in the morning she had been seen dozing at her window. Reluctantly she had let her father persuade her to lie down and take a short rest. "Susan won't join us for lunch today," the Consul said.

The meal passed in silence, the Consul eating little and showing no appetite. Evidently, thought Rechnitz, he is out of spirits. All the plans to show his visitors around Mikveh Israel and Rishon le Zion came to nothing because of Susan's fatigue.

Over coffee the Consul looked up and said, "I think you were about to make some remark."

Rechnitz had had no such intention, but since he was called on to speak, he considered for a moment and then said, "Would you like to go, sir, to Mikveh Israel, or to Rishon le Zion?"

"To Mikveh Israel or Rishon le Zion?" the Consul repeated. "After all the places we have been to, a little village like Rishon le Zion, or an agricultural school like Mikveh Israel, doesn't amount to much. Tell me, incidentally, why on earth do you give your settlements such long, double-barreled names? Our forefathers, who lived to a good old age, chose short, agreeable place-names, like Jaffa, Haifa, Acre, Gaza; and you people, who know that your time is brief, do just the opposite."

When Jacob was about to go, Susan appeared. Her face was flushed, her movements negligent. For seven whole hours, from eight in the morning until now, she had slept without a break, until the maid had brought lunch to her in bed.

"Are you leaving?" she said to Jacob.

"Yes," he replied in a whisper, as if afraid he would wake her.

Susan said, "Come back in an hour, perhaps we'll take a walk."

Jacob looked at the clock, took note of the time, and promised to come.

Within an hour he was back. Susan was seated downstairs in the hotel, dressed in warm clothes, gazing at a lithograph on the wall. When Jacob arrived she looked at him with the same gaze, as if he were part of the picture, or the wall itself on which the picture hung.

He bowed to her. "You wished to go for a walk, did you not?"

"For a walk?" she repeated, as if surprised.

"But surely you said you would like to take a walk?"

Susan stared at him as if he were trying to trick her, then stood up and said, "Very well, let's go."

XV

Susan walked in silence, and Jacob at her side was silent too. Words would not come for all the things he wanted to tell her. It seemed impossible, though, to go on walking in this fashion, and he searched for a subject to draw her attention. At that moment an Arab crossed their path. A member of some ascetic sect, he was barefooted and naked from the waist up. Two lances were embedded in his loins; his hair was long and unkempt; his eyes blazed with zeal. As he walked, he twisted the lances in his flesh, crying out *Allah karim;* while a great company followed him, repeating, *Allah karim!* Rechnitz halted and translated the words for Susan. She did not look at the ascetic and paid no attention to his cry. Soon they came to the "Nine Palm Trees," planted by Japheth, the son of Noah, when he founded Jaffa: one for himself, one for his wife, and seven for his seven sons. When Nebuchadnezzar laid the country waste he uprooted these trees and planted them in his own garden; but when the Jews returned from their Babylonian exile they brought them back and replanted them on the original site. This grove of nine palms, whose fresh green arch seemed to support the silvery clouds, made a crown of green and silver fronds that rustled and glistened, their colors alternating as the light breeze stirred them in their airy cavern, while the fibers of the fronds quivered like raindrops in a sunshower. The sight never failed to move Rechnitz, and especially now when he had the opportunity of pointing it out to Susan. He stretched out his arm, crying, "Look, Susan!" Susan nodded, without a glance either at him or at the palms.

Why am I showing her all this? he asked himself, distressed that he had taken her walking when she was so tired. Aloud he said, "Perhaps you would like to go back to the hotel?"

She nodded her head in agreement. "Yes. But first let's walk by the sea. It's quite near, isn't it?"

She raised her long skirt a little as they made their way.

The sea was still and very blue; the waves broke over one another, raising their crests as if held back from mingling with the waters beneath. Yesterday, the tide was full; now the sea withdrew from the shore, leaving a wide beach. No one was there, except for a single fisherman. Jacob would have given all the expanse of the earth in return for something that might draw Susan's attention. But nothing in the world could awaken this sleeping princess who walked by his side, insensible to his presence. Jacob called to mind the times when he had played with Susan in her father's garden, and they had fed the goldfish in the pool. But as he watched the sea and the lonely fisherman standing up to his waist in water, he could not bring himself to speak of things past.

Susan halted suddenly. "Do you remember how you and I used to play in our garden?"

He answered in a whisper, "I remember."

"Good," said Susan. "Let's go on."

Then again she stopped. "Do you remember what games we played?"

Jacob began to recount them to her as he walked. She nodded her head at every detail, saying, "That's right . . . That's right . . . I thought you had forgotten."

He laid his hand over his heart, as if to say, "How could anyone forget such things?"

Susan fell silent, but continued to walk, and Jacob followed at her side.

"Aren't you tired?" he asked.

Susan replied, "No, no. What's over there?"

"An old Moslem cemetery."

"Do they still bury their dead there?"

"I have heard that they don't anymore."

"Let's go there," said Susan.

When they reached the cemetery, Susan stopped. "Do you remember that vow we made together?"

"I remember," said Jacob.

She looked at him steadily for a moment. "Do you remember the words of the vow?"

"I remember them," said Jacob.

"Word for word?"

"Yes, word for word."

"If you remember the vow, repeat it."

Jacob repeated the substance of what they had sworn.

"But you told me," said Susan, "that you remember it word for word. Say it to me, then, word for word."

He hesitated, sighed, and at last said: "We swear by fire and by water, by the hair of our heads, by the blood of our hearts, that we shall marry one another and be husband and wife, and no power on earth can cancel our vow, for ever and ever."

Susan nodded her head in silence. After a while she said, "Now we can go."

They walked on; then she stopped again. "And what do you think, Jacob? Are we now exempt from that vow?"

His heart pounded so that he was unable to speak.

"Jacob," she said to him, "do you stand by your word?"

Still he stared at her without speaking.

"Are you prepared to keep your vow?" said Susan.

Jacob cried out loudly, "Yes, I am, I am!"

"Good," said Susan. "Let us go back to the hotel."

On the way she stretched out her hand to him, saying goodbye.

"Don't you want me to see you back?" said Jacob.

"It's not necessary."

"You may lose your way."

"I shall never lose my way," said Susan. "I never forget any place I have been; not even in my sleep."

A slight shudder ran through Rechnitz; the roots of his hair tingled. He whispered, "But still . . ."

"If you really want to come, then do so. But don't speak on the way. I want to do some thinking."

When they came to the hotel, she offered her hand to her betrothed and said goodbye.

XVI

Rechnitz shook himself out of a deep sleep. If you are told that people have a way of turning in their beds, you must not believe that this applied to Rechnitz, at least not that particular night. From the time he went to bed until the time he got up, he lay still as a post.

This fine sleep was the result of his afternoon walk with Susan along the beach. Now he put out his hand, picked up his watch and looked at it as if he were gazing through a soft curtain. "God above," he cried, "if my watch isn't playing tricks, I'll have to run all the way to school just as I am!"

But to run to school without dressing is impossible, and a man also has to wash himself. Accordingly, when Rechnitz had jumped out of bed he filled a basin with cold water, plunged his head into it, and after washing, shaved himself too. Aesculapius the god of health protected him, so that he escaped from slashes on the chin or cuts on the cheek. Finally, he put his wet shaving kit down on the bed, threw on his clothes and raced off toward the school.

The pupils were all gathered in the yard and the corridor. Some were munching at the snacks they had brought, some were improvising comic rhymes to set each other laughing. With all the noise, they overlooked the caretaker who was standing in the doorway ready to ring the bell. When they caught sight of him at last, they crowded around, taking hold of his arm, some to hinder and some to help in the ringing. In the meantime Rechnitz arrived and they followed him into the classroom.

Soon they were seated in their places. Rechnitz mounted the platform and took all in with a glance. Everyone was present. Rechnitz was in good spirits, as he always was when surrounded by his pupils. He began teaching in that resonant, cheerful voice which the boys and girls of his class liked so much, speaking or reading with a restrained ardor that awakened their enthusiasm, listing on the blackboard any words whose spelling might give them trouble. Had the bell not rung for the second time that day, he would have continued his teaching, and the class would have continued to listen attentively. After the lesson he ran the eraser over the board and went out. Only now did he notice his hunger, remembering that he had not had anything to eat either that morning or on the previous evening.

Rechnitz went into the staff room. The teachers were sitting together, drinking tea or eating the rolls which the caretaker's wife baked for them daily. They dipped the hard ring-shaped rolls into their tea and read the books set in front of them. Rechnitz drew up his chair alongside them and hummed the tune of the Hapsburg anthem, beating out the rhythm with his knuckles on the table. This fetched Yehia, who greeted him with "What would you like Rabbi?" The caretaker always called him "Rabbi," because he knew that Rechnitz was a great scholar in secular science; therefore, needless to say, he must also be greatly learned in the Torah; moreover, when he first came to Jaffa he had worn a beard.

"What would I like?" repeated Rechnitz. "I should like a full stomach for myself and happiness for you and all Israel."

"God willing," answered the caretaker.

Rechnitz looked up at Yehia's swarthy face and great black eyes. "Make it black coffee in a tall glass."

The caretaker brought it. Rechnitz clasped the sides of the glass in both hands and lowered his head as if he were trying to conceal his expression. He took a sip, added sugar to the coffee, and sipped again, while trying to think of what he had told the Consul about Yehia. Then he drained his glass. The teachers got up and went off to their classrooms, and he too made his way out.

Now my dear fellow, he said to himself, we can take a stroll in the school yard, or perhaps we ought to go over to the secretary's office and see if there's a letter addressed to the Herr Doktor.

Rechnitz went to the office. He had not been there on the previous day, or indeed on the day before that, for he was not a great letter-hunter like some teachers, who were constantly in and out of the secretary's room, rummaging and staring through all the mail for an answer to the crucial question of whether or not a letter had come for them. Even now he would not have entered had he not been at a loss for something to do between lessons.

The secretary sat at his little desk, his nose buried in a ledger, a pen in his hand, pretending to ignore the not inconsiderable presence of Rechnitz. And Rechnitz, having time to spare, and having also forgotten what he had come for, forgot the secretary's existence, too. He looked at the pictures on the wall, and at the space between the pictures. The secretary glanced up, then down again at his ledger, where he continued with his writing. Doubtless, thought Rechnitz, the celebrity whose portrait hangs on the wall believed a stern unbending expression suited him best. If not, he wouldn't have pulled such a face.—As for you, sir, you whose name I'm afraid I've forgotten, what exactly was the impression you were trying to make?

The secretary raised his nose like a divining rod, and their eyes met.

"Is there a letter for me?" asked Rechnitz.

The secretary stared at him contemptuously. "When do letters come from the post office—in the morning or afternoon? Since letters come in the afternoon, what is the sense in asking for them before people have properly digested their breakfasts?"

"I rather thought there might have been a letter for me from yesterday."

"From *yesterday?*" exclaimed the secretary in a tone of amazement. "Do you mean to tell me that a ship put in yesterday? Let me tell you there was no ship, or at any rate, no ship that brought any mail. But perhaps, Dr. Rechnitz, you mean *inland* mail? If it was inland mail, that is of course another matter."

"Yes, yes," said Rechnitz, grateful that this master of logic had put the subject on a reasonable basis. "Yes, indeed, I meant a letter from within the country; for example, from Jaffa itself."

The secretary laid his hand on a pile of letters and said, "The inland mail has indeed arrived, but I must inform you, Dr. Rechnitz, that no letter has come for you. That is to say, no letter from Palestine and none from Jaffa, which, as you may know, forms part of that country."

"Yes, of course," Rechnitz replied.

Why do you keep yessing at me? thought the secretary. If there's no letter for you, what's the sense in saying yes? A queer lot, these Germans. You can never get them out of the habit of conforming. And yesterday he took out some new girl from Austria, a Viennese she might well be, besides all the others. Now where did they go walking? By the sea. And what time did they choose to go walking? Just at the time when the sea turns cold and gives you a chill. A teacher with a cold!—Well!

The secretary sneezed.

XVII

The school bell rang again. Rechnitz stirred. It was the break between lessons and he was still free; he walked over to the book room, known as the "nature room" because it contained a number of minerals, plants, and stuffed animals and birds of the country.

The books were in a locked cabinet. He had no great desire to read, and certainly no desire to ask the secretary for the keys, so he stood and surveyed the stuffed creatures, which had been acquired from Ilyushin. These specimens are always a witness to Ilyushin's love for all living things; it was this love of his which gave them life even after their death. How beautiful, thought Rechnitz, is that swallow. She sits on her perch as if she were only dozing. When he went out he closed the door softly, as if he feared to wake the bird.

Finally he went back to the staff room. It was empty and the table was clear of rolls and cakes. Instead there were notebooks on it, and pamphlets and textbooks, including a new arithmetic manual. He picked this up and put it down, picked it up again and took a look inside, checked the figures given and wrote: "Duly checked and proved correct."

Again the bell rang, and Rechnitz murmured to himself that it was time to go. He passed a hand over his brow, as though to stimulate his memory. What do I want? he asked himself. But he had not found the reply by the time he was up on the platform facing the class.

Rechnitz raised his eyes and tried to keep them on his students. But his lids felt heavy and his knees were shaking. He crossed his legs, rubbed his eyes, and looked over the class again. The boys and girls sat in their usual rows; but above their heads a cloud seemed to hang, turning the class into something solid and opaque. Rechnitz began, "Boys and girls, yesterday we stopped at . . ." But he felt weak and wanted to cry. He closed his eyes and began again, "So yesterday . . ." The class could tell that their teacher's mind was far away, and everyone began to follow his or her private concerns. Rachel's brother took a novel out of his pocket, laid it on his knees and began to read. His neighbors to the right and left busied themselves drawing pictures. The girls were behaving even worse. Raya's sister twisted a paper dart and sent it flying at the nose of Asnat's sister, while Asnat's sister in turn held a little mirror up toward the sun and blinded her companions with the reflected rays. Rechnitz could see what was going on and his eyes ached with sorrow. How could these pupils, whom he treated as friends, disgrace him so?

"What are you reading over there?" he called out sharply.

Heilperin calmly exhibited his book and answered, *"Sanine."*

"What's that?"

"A novel."

"And what's it about?"

"I don't know, sir. I haven't read it yet."

"You don't know! You don't know anything, do you?—And you, what are *you* up to there?"

The boy trembled and pushed his notebook away.

"What's your opinion?" said Rechnitz. "Would you say it's worth my while to see what you have been drawing? Not worth my while? If so, why waste time on a thing that's not worth doing? As for you, my little friend, my dear Miss Magargot, if I had such a delightful mirror as yours, I should hold it up to your face and see two hard-working students instead of one. Yes, my friends, I suppose I *am* being sarcastic, and that's not what I am here for. But my dear friends, you're not here either just to read novels. Very soon Yehia will be ringing his bell and we shall be going home. What we shall do at home is a problem; because once a person doesn't do what he has to do, he doesn't know anymore what to do instead. And now Yehia, God bless him, is sounding the bell. So goodbye, boys and girls. Goodbye."

XVIII

What shall I do now? Rechnitz wondered. I can't go to the Consul's, because lunch time is near and I haven't been invited to lunch. If I went, Susan would think I was behaving as if I owned her and had the right to turn up whenever I liked. No, it's no good, he thought. It was half past twelve. In half an hour the restaurant would be full of regular customers; if he didn't hurry there would be no lunch left. He had not eaten there for two days and the proprietress would assume he was not coming.

Suddenly he remembered what he had been trying to recall in the break before his second lesson. Tonight, or last night, or even the night before, he had been invited to Susan's for dinner. Her room was small and pleasant. The table was set for a meal with bread and matzos, butter and milk, tomatoes and cucumbers, eggs and cheese. In the middle of the table stood a bowl of strawberries and on the strawberries was a red dusting of sugar. The room had a pleasant scent, and not only because of the strawberries: when Susan went out to bring in the tea, he looked at the wardrobe where she kept her clothes and saw a bunch of roses on top. He counted twelve roses, and was pleased, although he was not superstitious, to find that they did not add up to thirteen. What did they talk about, he and Susan? They talked about all sorts of people, including her father, the Consul. Oddly enough, Susan referred to him as if her were Jacob's father and not her own. And when she mentioned him she said, "Of course, I don't know him well, but I would suppose . . ." whatever it was she attributed to him. Jacob ate very little, and for that reason Susan refrained from taking much. Although he knew that she ought to eat more, still he did not force his appetite. After they had eaten and drunk, she went and sat down on the sofa and he sat on a chair facing her. She showed him a more comfortable place, saying, "Sit here," but he did not leave his chair, although he was feeling a pain in his shoulders from sitting where he was. In order not to tire Susan, he resolved to leave at nine o'clock. The time came, but he still stayed. They sat talking about Rachel and Leah, and about Frau Ehrlich, Susan's mother. And this too was strange, that Susan did not know where her mother was born until he told her. He glanced at his watch and found it was nearly ten. Time to leave, he told her; but Susan answered that it wasn't yet nine o'clock. "It's already ten," he said. "Is it really?" said Susan in surprise, and she corrected her watch. After a while he got up to leave and Susan went out to accompany him. When they had gone halfway, he wanted to turn back and see her home, but she would not allow this. She made her way home, while he waited for his streetcar. He bought a ticket and climbed in. The streetcar filled up and started to move. On its way it kept stopping to take on more and more passengers. Two young fellows got in and one sat on the other's knees. He heard them talking to one another about Otto Weininger and his book *Sex and Character*. The journey continued for an hour. And then, oddly enough, Jacob had found himself again sitting with Susan; and it was not yet eleven o'clock, although he had left Susan's house at ten, and she had accompanied him halfway, and he had even traveled for an hour on the streetcar, and spent an hour at home. How could it be, then, that he was with Susan at nearly eleven o'clock?

XIX

After his meal Rechnitz didn't linger in the little restaurant and didn't go back to his room. His habits had changed since the day of the Consul's arrival in Jaffa; the times when he used to relax over lunch, make his own coffee and read a book, seemed part of prehistory. He said to himself: The Consul will be taking his afternoon nap now. Susan will be sitting in her room arranging her photographs. If that's where she is, I can take a walk in front of the hotel; and if she is out in the garden, I can walk there, as I did the day before yesterday. But the day before yesterday I was with others, and today I shall be walking alone.

That stroll with Rachel and Leah on the day of Susan's arrival had given him a certain self-confidence in her presence, not because the stroll had made her jealous but for another reason, which was actually the same reason; it showed that Jacob Rechnitz was not isolated from the world and also that she, Susan Ehrlich, was by no means the only woman in that world. In fact he had not intended to take a walk that day, either with Rachel or with Leah, still less with both of them at once; it just happened that Leah had come across him. And so on, and so on. Yet if one looked more deeply into the matter, it seemed that there was another truth here; namely, that Rechnitz was quite in the habit of taking some girl out for a walk, whether her name were Rachel or Leah, or indeed Asnat or Raya or Mira or Tamara.

It is the way of people who have grown up in a beautiful place to take its charms for granted. But when they visit another lovely town, they not only note the new charms, but first become aware of the beauty they have always lived with. So for Rechnitz, the arrival of Susan in Jaffa served also to reveal the beauty of the girls with whom he was already familiar.

We have spoken of Leah Luria and Rachel Heilperin. Friends as they were, Rachel was the more sharp-witted and Leah the more sympathetic. Leah was older than any of her friends and yet her eyes shone with youth and good nature, as if they were the dwelling place of angels. If her talk was not too solid, still it gladdened the heart. When they were out on an excursion and sat down to rest, it was Leah who would arrange a meal for the whole group, seeing that everyone got his share and forgetting to look after her own needs in her concern for the welfare of others. As for Rachel, she was not to be measured by any standards of good or evil. If she did something wrong, you could not be angry with her; if she did a good deed, she did not think well of herself for it. She was also the kind of person you could speak to without any pretense. Yet this merit was also a defect, for nothing you did could help you, since all depended on her and nothing on you yourself.

And now let us consider Asnat Magargot. She came from Kirov, and it was said that her father had gone bankrupt and absconded to Palestine, much as most persons in that condition abscond to America. Bankruptcy and embezzlement are great transgressions, which cannot be atoned for until the ill-gotten gains are restored to their rightful owners, and even then it is doubtful if one is completely absolved. Magargot, however, was not very guilt-stricken; rather, he behaved as if he had done a great favor to the Land of Israel, proving by his action that the Settlement was a practical proposition, and that sudden departures from Europe need not have America for their destination.

Asnat, like Leah Luria and Rachel Heilperin, was a tall girl. She wore a greenish brown dress of fine smooth weave, with a silver belt whose roped ends fell below her knees. Though her dress was like the habit of a monk, Asnat's lips were eager—but not for kisses. You might be sitting beside her for two or three hours, my dear friend, almost crazy with the desire to take her in your arms; and she too might share something of the same idea. But that was all. You would merely pick up the two tassels that fell from her belt and go on talking about Ibsen's plays or something of the sort. The world has its set ways, and if it occurred to you to deviate from them, you would find this impossible with Asnat. Her steel-blue eyes cut your soul into little pieces. This was the more surprising because the kind of topics Asnat discussed—all those "problems of modern life"—were just the kind that create the greatest intimacy; and yet you could not so much as touch her with your little finger. What then did Asnat really want? She wanted much, and she wanted nothing; she wanted nothing, and she wanted much. On a summer night she would take a fancy to walking as far as Rishon le Zion and ask you to escort her. And you would walk along with her by the sand dunes for three hours in the darkness, going by night and coming back by night, without her letting you touch even the tassels of her belt, either on the way out or on the way back.

Raya Zablodovsky was a relative of Asnat, though you could hardly find two girls so unlike, either in stature or feature. Asnat was tall and her face bore witness to a quick wit; Raya was no taller than a child and her face testified neither to a quick wit, nor even to a slow-paced one. She had sandy hair and her lips pouted as if she had just tasted an unripe fruit. In disposition she was withdrawn, like a spoiled tame bird that covers its head with its wings. Some of her friends declared her too egotistic, others even thought her malicious. Yet they could not help being drawn to her, since both qualities, that is to say both the self-love and the malice, were cloaked in a humor that never failed to surprise. Thus, she might decide to seat herself on a boulder after spreading some fine silk scarf over it; if you remarked that this was strange behavior, she would say, "Not at all. It isn't my scarf, you see." Never in her life had Raya read a book through, neither in Russian nor in Hebrew, not even the books that everyone was talking about. She failed her examinations twice and left school before finishing, without any regrets. "In the end," she would say "you forget everything you have learned. As for me, I forget without bothering to learn it first." How, then, did she come to be one of the girls in Rechnitz's group? Simply because this is life's way: once you belong to a certain group, you belong, however different you are.

Raya's neighbor was Mira Vorbzhitsky, the daughter of Niuma Vorbzhitsky, who had been a guard of the Sharon settlements. He was the terror of bandits, and if he found any within his beat he was capable of picking a man up and using him as a flail against his companions like someone beating a garment with a stick. Mira had more agility than any girl in Jaffa, not excepting even Rachel Heilperin, for when she was little her father used to make her ride an unsaddled horse which he would set galloping over the hills, paying no heed to her frightened cries. She was still accustomed to riding bareback, and on occasion she would take a horse from between the shafts of a carriage and mount it and ride as far as Sarona. Although she had the graceful figure of a girl, she resembled a handsome youth. When she was a child and her father was still a guard, they had lived on the outskirts of the village away from other settlers, where her mother used to dress her in boys' clothes as a precaution against the Arabs. Her bearing still had something boyish about it, though her manners were those of a girl, and she was dear to her companions of both sexes.

Something has yet to be said about Tamara Levi. Her father had been a doctor. Once in the rainy season, on a dark overcast night, he was out riding on his donkey to visit a patient in the settlements. The donkey stumbled into a flooded wadi, and the doctor drowned. Tamara lived with her mother in a single room in a large apartment house. The mother was a rabbi's daughter and well aware of her standing, but she found it difficult to earn a livelihood. She would care for the sick, sometimes sitting with them all night. Her husband had left her nothing when he died; and now she had to make a living for herself and Tamara and to see that her daughter had the same education as other girls of good family. Mother and daughter loved each other much, but this involved them in serious conflict. For it happened that a certain school secretary, with quite a good income, was courting Tamara and her mother approved of the match. As for Tamara herself, she said that she had no objection to marriage but that she did not see why it should be with this man in particular, even though he did have a good position at the school where Rechnitz taught.

Tamara's hair, one supposes, was ash-gray; her eyes, it may be assumed, were blue; but the blue-tinted radiance that lit up her features and dazzled the eyes made these two colors seem interchangeable. At first sight she might have escaped your notice. Later, if not for the narcissus or carnation pinned on her breast, you might miss the presence of a heart underneath. Her real name was Tamar but she liked to be called Tamara, and since she was such a dear child, let us call her by the name she preferred. Her conversation was not notably wise; if one cared to say so, it even tended to silliness; but her lips caressed your heart much as the red flower on her own heart was caressed by the tip of her nose. Once Rechnitz had set his lips to hers; they had quivered slightly and just touched his in return. A touch that was hardly a touch at all. Heavens above, if that was the shadow of a kiss, what would a true kiss be like? No girl in the world had such lips as hers, and, besides this, every touch of her hand was like a kiss. But was there any man in Jaffa who knew it?

Tamara had this virtue too: she never used to complain or seem angry. She would look up at you admiringly and accept whatever you said as a gift of grace. So you would sit contentedly surveying the tip of her nose and letting the radiance of her face wrap you in a sweet blue mist. Only once had Rechnitz kissed Tamara and he did not repeat the performance; he was, after all, her teacher, and it was not proper for teachers to kiss their pupils. This applied even though there were teachers who permitted themselves such conduct and even though Tamara had now left school and belonged to his group of friends. At times Rechnitz regretted the kiss; at other times he regretted not having made a second attempt. However that may be, it was a good thing that he had no occasion to be alone with her, for more reasons than one. Since the school secretary had his eye on her with a view to marriage, it would not have been decent to spoil someone's life for the sake of a fleeting pleasure. That was a sufficient reason, but there was still another one which Jacob buried in his heart.

XX

A strange shriek interrupted the train of Rechnitz's thoughts. The parrot, which on the evening before last had perched in his cage at the hotel imitating the jackals' screams, was now in the garden answering the sound of the striking clock. Before him stood the old Baron, dressed in white, with a tropical sun-helmet on his head. The Baron was holding out an apple and the parrot, standing on one leg, extended the other, snatched the apple and pecked at it. *"Schmeckt's, Herrchen?"* the Baron asked. The parrot shook his hooked beak and cried, *"Schmeckt, Herrchen!"*

"A fine bird," said the Baron to Rechnitz. "I bought it from a hunter who had caught it to eat. There are places, you know, where they eat parrot-meat.—*Verflucht!*" he called to the parrot.

"Verflucht!" it answered back.

The Baron laughed and wagged his finger at the bird.

"Verflucht," he said to it, *"Verflucht,* you mustn't say *Verflucht!"*

The parrot replied with a shriek, *"Verflucht! Verflucht!"*

When Rechnitz had disengaged himself from the Baron, he went on to the hotel. But now, he reflected, the Consul will have awakened from his nap and lit the cigar he smokes out of boredom. I shall go across to him, perhaps he will be grateful to me for rescuing him from his ennui. And what will Susan have to say? She will say nothing because that is her way. There are some people whose silences are awesome; we imagine their minds to be full of great thoughts beyond our ken, thoughts which keep them from communicating, and this makes us shrink in their presence, believing that they hold in their hands the keys of all wisdom. Yet if we consider the matter well, we shall find that their silence grows out of overweening pride and that they don't surpass us by so much as the breadth of a parrot's claw. It is only because we shrink that they tower over us. And why do we thus belittle ourselves before them? This calls for investigation but I have no time for it. It is after four o'clock, the Consul is already up and having his ennui. I have extended my reflections too far and extended monologues are to be avoided in modern drama. *Verflucht!* I like the smell of baking in butter over there. Yehia's wife does all her baking in oil because the Jews here don't have any butter and because people in the East prefer olive oil to dairy products anyhow. It isn't a thing you can reason about but simply a matter of taste, just as the Sefardi teacher will say "a quarter-hour" instead of "a quarter of an hour." And now a quarter of an hour has gone by and I am still standing outside, delivering long monologues.

Rechnitz entered the hotel. Nobody was in the lounge, except the waiters setting the tables and brewing coffee. He walked through, glancing from side to side. The absent guests, he thought, the honored guests, are still sitting in their private rooms waiting patiently until the mere nobodies have prepared their food and drink. As for me, I'm one of the nobodies; and if I haven't the ability to prepare meals and drinks, at least the gods have given me the power to save somebody from boredom. *"Schmeckt's, Herrchen?"* And he looked around him again. The hotel clerk saw Rechnitz and said, "There's a letter for you, sir."

"A letter?" Rechnitz stammered, and his heart began to pound. The clerk brought the letter; Rechnitz took it and went outside. He walked through the garden, stopped under a tree, and leaned against it with the letter in his hand. A letter from Susan? Let's see what Susan has to tell me. Let's open the letter and see. But when he opened it he saw it was not from Susan but from her father. Again his heart began to beat fast, not the rapid heartbeat of a man awaiting some happy event, but such as one feels when expecting disaster.

Again he looked round. Seeing that no one was about, he reflected: Susan has told her father all that happened by the sea and he must be punishing me with a reprimand. Rechnitz was filled with rage. Does that old man think because he has thrown me a few crumbs from his table that he has the right to abuse me? Keep your crumbs, old man, for the dogs. I can provide for myself and, as for my name in the world of science, I don't owe it to you. *Verflucht,* these people with money! If you have taken the least scrap from them, they think they have bought you. I don't mind thanking you, Consul, for all you have done on my behalf, but you have not bought my soul. And if your daughter should be pleased to follow me, I shall take her from under your nose.

While he was saying this to himself, he looked at the words of the letter, and as he looked his eyes lit up. Here was no rebuke but instead a kind of apology. The Consul and his daughter had departed for Jerusalem without managing to take leave of him in advance. He saw too that the Consul sent his best greetings, as well as his regards, and added: "As soon as we are back in Jaffa, we shall be delighted to see you."

It was a good thing that Rechnitz read that letter. Even as he did so he put all the bitterness out of his heart. His soul returned and he reflected: All my life I never aspired to Susan. When I used to speak about her to her father it was with humility, and suddenly I've grown bold. If I were now to go to him and demand his daughter, he would be shocked. No, I shall not argue or pick a quarrel or talk big, but act modestly until he sees and understands for himself how much I love Susan. And if she is indeed to be my partner for life, as she pledged to be, I shall wait patiently for good angels to spread their wings over us and make our wedding canopy.

As he reflected, Rechnitz felt a lighter, calmer spirit. It is best for a man to act in character. What nonsense to think I had it in me to carry off Susan against her father's will—as if I had the power to do any such thing! At that moment Rechnitz saw himself as a man who has gone after an enemy, only to find that very enemy his friend. His humility gave him strength. He looked into himself and said, That is how I have been all my days and that is how I have come through. And so I shall be all my days and so continue to come through.

XXI

Herr Ehrlich stayed in Jerusalem longer than he had intended. The anniversary of his wife's death came around while he was there and he wanted to commemorate it in the Holy City. The day passed fittingly: he said Kaddish at the Wailing Wall, gave alms to the poor and visited various houses of charity. Certain things he saw met with his approval and he took due note of them. As for the rest, he looked the other way and ignored shortcomings, being mindful of the city and the occasion. He also paid a visit to the Shaarei Zedek Hospital, where he made the acquaintance of a certain doctor who sacrificed his sleep for the sake of his patients, not laying his head upon a pillow unless it were on a Sabbath or festival night and taking no reward beyond his simple needs. When Herr Ehrlich saw plaques affixed to the walls of the hospital and on each plaque the name of some benefactor who had contributed to the cost of the building or the care of the sick, he too made a contribution for the upkeep of a bed, to grace his wife's soul and serve as a lasting memorial in Jerusalem.

The Consul was very pleased with the city. True, what he had seen with his own eyes was unlike the Jerusalem of legend or the Jerusalem of his imagination. There were many things that could well have been dispensed with and also many things lacking that might well have been there. But since one did not really know where to make a start, or how to proceed in the way of reform, it was best to leave Jerusalem as she was.

Once again, Rechnitz is seated facing the Consul in the Jaffa hotel. The weather is chilly, the air damp; hot embers glow in the copper tray before them. The Consul has a thick cigar in his mouth and a woolen rug rests on his knees. He warms his hands alternately with the cigar and over the hot coals. Susan is some distance away, wrapped in her beaver coat. The coals whisper to themselves and the tray, reflecting their red glow, whispers back. The room grows warmer, the air more heated; a sweet languor seeps into the spoken word, like the languor that surrounds the body. From the sea outside the sound of waves mounts like the distant roaring of beasts of prey. The Consul shakes the ash from his cigar and remarks, "Today it's impossible to take a walk on the beach." And Rechnitz blushes; can the Consul be alluding to the walk he had taken with Susan?

But in fact the Consul was only referring to the stormy weather that had delayed his departure. What is more, he was glad that he did not have to travel, after wandering from country to country for over a year. He had seen so many lands: more than he could number, more names than he could remember. If he had not listed in his notebook the name of each place visited he would never have known where he had or had not been. Susan too was glad of the delay. She had taken many photographs and collected many souvenirs and now she needed time to arrange them.

On the day of her return from Jerusalem Susan had been very fatigued. Without finishing her meal she had left for her room and gone to bed. But on the next night she lingered over dinner. Unasked, quite of her own accord, she brought a portfolio of her photographs and souvenirs to show to Jacob. She was astonished at the way he recognized each object and gave it its proper name, and even more happy at the serious interest he took in her collection. And because she was grateful, she wanted to repay him by recounting various stories. That night, Susan told Jacob many tales. This was one of them: "Once upon a time there was a king who wished to marry me. This king had a fine palace made of palm fronds, and he also had two wives. One of these wives wore sardine tins in her earlobes to enhance her beauty; the other one looked just like the girl you were walking with on the day I arrived in Jaffa. But," added Susan, "you were out with two girls together and as I don't know which is which, I can't tell you which one looks like the king's wife."

The Consul laughed and cried in surprise, "What, do you take girls out for walks? I thought scientists were completely wrapped up in their work! It looks as though science is a complacent mistress who doesn't object to rivals. Tell me, Susan, are they pretty, these two girls?"

Susan looked at Jacob and answered, "That is for you to say."

"If," said her father, "he is thinking of his own reputation, he will answer that they are extremely beautiful; if he is thinking of yours, he will say they are not at all good-looking. And so, my dear daughter, *you* tell me—are they good-looking?"

Susan replied, "Whatever I may say, Dr. Rechnitz thinks they are."

"How do you know that?" asked the Consul.

"If it were not so, he would not have brought them along to exhibit to me."

"I did *not* bring them along to exhibit to you," Rechnitz protested.

"No?"

"No! It was like this, really. That afternoon after leaving here, I just happened to see them on my way and we took a walk together. And since I was invited to dinner and didn't know when it would be served, I went to ask the waiter, and they were good enough to come along with me."

"And the flowers you presented to me," said Susan, "were they given to you by one of them, or by both?"

"What you say is partly true," Jacob answered. "They both put themselves out to bring you flowers, but those I actually brought to you came from the gardener."

"They assumed," said Susan, "that I would be here today and gone tomorrow?"

"Quite possibly."

"But if so, they were wrong."

"Wrong indeed," answered Jacob, and he did not know whether to be glad or not.

Susan added, "Father intends to spend the whole winter here—don't you, Papa?"

The Consul, questioning, looked at his daughter, then nodded his head in agreement.

"Yes, daughter, I've been weighing whether it isn't worth my while to spend the winter here. You people don't realize how hard the European winter is, and all the harder now that I'm used to warm countries."

Susan stood up from the table, took her father's head in both hands and kissed his forehead. "Good Papa!" There were tears in her father's eyes.

XXII

That afternoon Rechnitz went to the post office and came across Susan walking about the market place. Her arms were filled with pottery. It was Susan's way to buy local wares at every place she visited, and here in Jaffa she had purchased various pitchers and clay vessels. What would she do with them? She might take a few with her or she might leave them all behind at the hotel, for next day, no doubt, she would find something more pleasing.

"May I help you?" Jacob asked her.

Susan glanced at him for a moment and held out two pitchers. "Don't worry about them too much; if they get broken, they get broken—the market's full of them."

"If that's the case, then give me more," said Jacob. "I'll be careful not to break them."

They left the market together by carriage. Susan said, "I always believed carriages were only invented to get in my way when walking, but all of a sudden you have put me into one and I find I am no longer afraid of horses and vehicles. Why do you look surprised?"

"I certainly am surprised. You are so used to traveling, yet you talk of carriages getting in your way."

Susan said, "I'm used to long journeys and forget that even short distances can be made easier with conveyances."

"Yet you seem more tired by these short distances than by long journeys."

"Great things add greatly to one's strength," she said. "Oh, how beautiful those palms are! How many are there?—Eight, nine?"

"Yes, nine," Jacob answered.

"I have never in my life seen such beautiful palm trees."

He wanted to say that he himself had already shown them to her but thought better of it and remarked, "Surely you have seen finer ones in the tropics?"

"Finer ones? Never in my life," she repeated. "Driver, stop a moment.—I don't know what has come over me, I could swear I have seen them before! No, not in a dream, Jacob, but awake!"

She blushed as she spoke; then, telling the driver to proceed, she said no more until they arrived at the hotel.

When the carriage came to a stop, she said to Jacob, "If you don't mind, let's go into the garden. Tell the driver he can leave the pots in the hotel. What language were you speaking to him? Hebrew, was it? And isn't Hebrew the language of the prayer book? So this driver speaks like the prayers; and you too, Jacob. How wonderful you all are here! Let's sit on this bench. I knew, Jacob, that you would agree with me. What a lot of good turns you have done me today. You have carried my pottery for me, and put me in a carriage, and brought me all the way back. It's good for a person to be good. We too ought to be good, not wicked. Do you think I am a wicked person? Sometimes I think so myself but it's not really true, I'm just too lazy to get people out of the notion of my wickedness."

Jacob said, "It would never occur to anyone to call you wicked."

"It may never have occurred to you, but how do you know what others think?"

"I judge the rest of the world by myself."

"But isn't it a kind of sinful pride to measure all mankind by your own standard?"

"On the contrary," said Jacob, "it's a virtue, because by so doing I can correct any mistaken ideas of yours."

"Please tell me, Jacob, what have human beings to be proud about?"

"You speak just like your father. He asks what have human beings to dispute about."

"I have never disputed with anybody in my life," said Susan.

"You have no need to, since everyone rushes to do your bidding."

"Everyone, that is, except myself. I sometimes think I have no will at all and whatever I do is done without any good reason. I am more frivolous than a child who makes his decisions by counting up the cherry stones. What does a girl like me want?"

The waitress set up a little table and asked, "What would madam like me to bring?"

"I don't want anything," said Susan.

"You see, Susan," Jacob remarked, "you have a very strong will. Since you didn't want anything, you said just that."

Susan blushed. "I really deserve to be scolded; it didn't occur to me that *you* might like something. But you don't? Well then, let's just sit and talk."

This was the most delightful meeting Jacob had known with Susan since the day she came to Jaffa. It had about it something new and something old and familiar; new, because she had not previously sat with him in this garden, and old, too, because it was thus in their childhood that they had sat together in that other garden of her father. The good gods give us more than we deserve. Here are Jacob and Susan among green boughs, and in winter time, when the garden of their childhood is covered with snow and the pond overlaid with ice. They talk about themselves and the world outside, which is no more than a small part of their own. At times, the good gods deal well with mortals, allowing them to see eternity in an hour. Let us then ask the gods to prolong this hour without end or limit.

Susan had laid her fine, delicate hands before her on the table. Jacob gazed at them, as he used to gaze at her mother's hands when she would place them on the table and his lips would long to touch them. We are so made that our memories lead from one thing to another; sometimes these lie close together, sometimes far apart. Jacob now recalled a time when he happened to be at Ein Rogel, at Ilyushin's, when Ilyushin was stretching an animal skin on a board; he had spread his hands out like that, or almost like that, in the course of his work. As Jacob sat there, surprised at the direction his thoughts had taken, the parrot suddenly made himself heard, crying out. *"Verflucht!"*

Susan shuddered and looked around her. Jacob laughed. "It's only the parrot," he said.

"Just this very moment," he went on, "I was thinking about a taxidermist I know called Ilyushin. I wouldn't say that bird is a mind reader, but all the same it's very queer—just at the moment when I thought of Ilyushin, the parrot called *Verflucht!*"

"Illusion?"

"Yes, Ilyushin."

Susan said, "Yesterday evening you remarked that you changed the flowers your girl friends gave you to bring me. What was the point in changing them?"

Jacob's cheeks flushed but Susan did not notice. She had closed her eyes, as she had a way of doing sometimes in the course of conversation.

"What was the point?" he repeated.

Susan nodded, her eyes still closed.

"I changed them because I'd found nicer ones."

"That sounds plausible," said Susan. "Now tell me the real reason.—Oh, I can see that just now you don't know; perhaps another time you will. What was the name of the taxidermist at Ein Rogel?"

"His name was Ilyushin."

Susan opened her eyes. "That's it—Illusion."

"And what has Ilyushin to do with us?" asked Jacob.

"Since you mentioned him, I wanted to know what he was called. Now that I know, you don't have to say any more about him. Cattle and wild beasts may enjoy a privilege granted to no man except the mummies in Egypt. Don't you smoke? I'll call a waiter to bring you some cigarettes. Let's honor the wisdom of Egypt, the land that gave eternal life to her sons, by ordering Egyptian cigarettes."

Then, forgetting all about the cigarettes, Susan went on, "Our days on earth are like a shadow, and the time of our affliction is the length of our days. How fortunate are those mummies, laid in the ground and freed from all trouble and toil. If I could only be like one of them!" Susan opened her eyes and looked up as if longing for release from the afflictions of the world.

"From the day of your mother's funeral, I have not seen you," Jacob said. "And even on that day I didn't really see you. You seemed so distant from this world, Susan."

"No, Jacob, I felt as if the world were distant from me. And now, here I am, still not part of the world."

"And in all those years, have you really had no happiness?"

Susan neither spoke nor moved. Looking across at her, Rechnitz took in her sadness. He wanted to speak but could not find words. Hesitantly, he said, "You are so troubled, Susan. What is it?"

She stirred a little. "What were you asking, Jacob?"

"I was asking what is it that makes you so sad?"

Susan smiled. "You ask, 'What is it?' as if there were one reason alone. There are many, and each is enough to make one sad, very sad indeed."

"But why?"

"I don't know—" she stopped short and remained very still.

"And yet you are—both of us are—young enough, with all our life before us."

"But that life before us—do you think it's going to be any better than the life that lies behind?"

"I haven't thought much about that," said Jacob.

"Neither have I," said Susan.

"Then what grounds have you for saying what you did?"

"What did I say?"

"You know what you said."

"Just idle talk," said Susan.

And Jacob too felt melancholy. This is the girl who wants to be my wife, he reflected. He felt restive as he considered her. This girl wants me to marry her, he thought again. And even while he pondered, he realized that without her the whole world would be lost to him.

Then human voices startled Jacob. "People are coming!" Susan nodded and replied, "It's Papa with the old Baron." As they approached, the Consul broke into a ribald laugh. Apparently the old man had just told him an off-color story. The laughter struck Jacob's ears unpleasantly; he had always known the Consul as a serious-minded man, yet here he was behaving frivolously. Susan stood up and said, "Let's go."

They walked away together. A little girl came by with a basket in her hand. Jacob turned to her. "What are you doing here?" he said. The little girl answered, "My Mommy sent me to get some lemons." He bent down and swung her in the air. "Sweetheart, I'd love to carry you off—you and your basket together. Tell me, what would your Mommy say if I carried you away?" The child answered solemnly, "Mommy wouldn't like it." Jacob laughed. "Tell your mother that you're a clever little girl." "Yes, I'll tell her," she replied.

"Whose charming child is that?" asked Susan.

"She's the sister of a girl I teach."

"One of those you were walking with here in the garden?"

Jacob hesitated a little. "You saw those two girls; how did they strike you?"

"They're very lovely," said Susan.

"Does that mean that you approve of them?"

"If you think well of them," replied Susan, "so do I."

"I don't know how to take that."

"I mean just what I said. But you have other friends besides, haven't you? Tell me about them."

Jacob began to tell her. When he had got round to describing Tamara, Susan looked at him rather closely.

The two old men were coming back, the Baron laughing raucously. This time, it would seem, the Consul had capped his story with a spicier one.

"So you're here, you two?" said the Consul.

"Yes," answered Susan, and went on to praise Jacob for his kindness in calling a carriage and bringing her back to the hotel.

"Happy is he who finds a good escort," said the Baron, and he cast a benevolent glance on Jacob.

"But aren't you cold, Susan?" asked the Consul.

"No, I'm neither too cold nor too warm. I'm quite happy, Papa."

The Consul looked at his daughter for a moment and went off with the Baron. At Susan's suggestion, she and Jacob sat down again together.

"Once," said Susan, "I dreamed that I was dead. I wasn't happy, I wasn't sad, but my body felt such rest as no one knows in the land of the living. And this was the best of it, that I wanted nothing, I asked for nothing, it just felt as if I were disappearing into blue distances that would never end. Next morning I opened a book and read in it that nobody dreams of himself as dead. If that's so, perhaps it was not a dream but wide-awake reality. But then, how can I be alive after my death? It's a puzzle to me, Jacob. Do you believe in the resurrection of the dead?"

"No, certainly not," Jacob said.

"Don't say 'certainly.' These certainties of yours bring me to tears." As she spoke, she closed her eyes.

At that moment, Susan seemed to hover over those blue distances she had spoken of. Then suddenly she answered Jacob's gaze. She took out her handkerchief, wiped her eyes, opened them and looked at him with absolute love. After a while, she said, "I am going to close my eyes and you, Jacob, are to kiss me on the eyelids."

Jacob's own eyes filled with tears. With the tears still there, he placed his lips on her wet lashes.

XXIII

Everything good happens when your attention is turned the other way. So it was with Rechnitz. An elderly scholar in New York, with whom Rechnitz had exchanged specimens of seaweed, had suggested the creation of an academic chair for him; the suggestion had been taken up and now Rechnitz received a written offer. Even though he had already won himself a high reputation, Rechnitz had not expected anything like this, for he was still a young man and aware that he had many superiors in the field.

He was lying on his couch that morning midway between sleep and waking. His thoughts went off in various directions without his knowing where they were heading. There are times when a man's limbs are still and his mind is at rest, and there are times when his mind goes wandering and carries back many thoughts. There are times when the limbs are still but find no rest or the mind goes wandering but carries back no thought and no idea. Yet again, both states may exist together: the mind goes wandering and the limbs are still, and a man finds neither rest in his limbs nor thought in his mind. Rechnitz wanted to get up from his couch but knew it would be useless. And so he had yielded to this kind of lethargy that brings no benefit, when he heard someone knocking on his door. He jumped up, opened the door, and there was the postman with a letter. Rechnitz received it with a groan, as if he had been interrupted in some important undertaking. The postman slung his bag over his shoulder and went away; Rechnitz opened his letter and read it. Certainly this was good news, and would have been so even if he had been expecting the appointment. All the more so when it came as a surprise.

Rechnitz always offered thanks for any benefits that came his way, sometimes to the good gods, sometimes to the Only One. Now he was silent and said no prayer, but whatever it was that had dulled his mind before now passed away completely.

He dressed and went to call on someone whose English was better than his. Actually there was no need, since he already knew what the letter was about. Nor did this man tell him anything new. But his eyes widened with surprise and he reached out his hand to Rechnitz, saying, "Congratulations, Professor!"

Perhaps Rechnitz was more moved by this response than he had been by the occasion for it. Possibly too, the man he consulted was more excited about the news than Rechnitz himself. Before the day was out all Jaffa knew that a young fellow who taught at the school had gained an unheard-of distinction. For in those days honor paid to learning still counted among ordinary people; all the more so when the honor carried with it a good salary. How many scholars were there who didn't even get as far as a university post, and here was an ordinary young teacher promoted to be a full professor!

In Rechnitz's time, a number of scholars had already settled in Palestine. Of these, some were engaged in research in Palestinology, others in biblical studies. They had this in common: they made their studies an adjunct to interests outside the field of pure learning, such as national, religious or social causes. Some of them were internationally famous and their opinions were generally accepted until the intellectual climate changed and new scholars came to the fore. As for Rechnitz, he subordinated his work to no other consideration. He took trouble and pains solely in the cause of pure knowledge. All seasons were the same to him. A storm outside or blazing sunshine never kept him back. Besides collecting marine plants from the sea off Jaffa, he collected them, too, off the coasts of Haifa, off Acre, Haderah and Caesarea, since the plants in the sea around Jaffa differ from those in other regions. And here we must remember that Rechnitz had found no professional colleague in the country and did his work in solitude. This isolation, which may lead to slackness, can prove a blessing to the true scholar, for if he makes some new discovery he clarifies its meaning all to himself and does not waste his time in superfluous discussions. With the strength of youth, with keen intellect and a discriminating eye, Rechnitz studied, investigated and assembled minute details as well as general principles, constructing from these a complete system. This ability to see and observe was matched by his ability to set out his observations in writing. His "Remarks on the Nature of Cyrenean Seaweeds," and even more so, those on Cerulean Seaweeds, made his reputation. And at the conference of zoologists and botanists, most of the lecturers referred to him; even those who disagreed with his views accorded him high praise.

Jaffa was getting more and more excited over the affair. People who had nothing to do with universities were talking about this young Ph.D. who had been appointed a professor. Everyone who came across Rechnitz, whether an acquaintance of his or not, would stop to congratulate him. His actual acquaintances invited him to take a drink in honor of the occasion, and wherever he went he found a holiday spread awaiting him. Here too we should remark that whatever people did was done in honor of science, for the parents of daughters knew well that now Rechnitz was a professor the Consul would never let go of him.

What is more, the daughters themselves knew that from the day of Susan Ehrlich's arrival in Jaffa, Rechnitz had made himself scarce, especially now that he was getting ready to leave. Nevertheless, they retained their affection for him. Leah sent him more flowers of the kind she had given him for the Ehrlich girl on the first day. Tamara baked a cake for him in the shape of a boat and set on it a little American flag made of sugar. Even Rachel Heilperin put herself out so far as to write him a letter of congratulation; and this was no small matter, for although she could speak with much fluency, when she sat down to write she stuck on the very first phrase. Should one write "My dear sir," or "Dear Dr. Rechnitz," or "My very dear friend Mr. Rechnitz"?

As for Rechnitz, the expression of people's good wishes moved him deeply. Imagine, even the school secretary, who had seemed to bear a grudge against him, was as pleased at this success as if it had been his own. Needless to say, Rechnitz's colleagues at school were delighted. In a sense they were happy for his sake, in a sense for their own; for here was one of their number, a fellow-teacher, who had gained this honor, so that it became theirs as well. And what an honor! From the time of Nietzsche until the time of Rechnitz, no young man in such a position had been appointed professor.

For the most part, Rechnitz left matters concerning his new appointment for time to settle. He returned to his normal life as though nothing had happened, except that now he began to learn English and to occupy himself with some matters which previously would not have received much attention.

XXIV

Rechnitz could see that Susan's father knew what had passed between the two of them. A girl like Susan was not used to concealing her actions. But it was doubtful whether her father knew just how things stood, since Susan's outlook was different from his own and she would certainly see the situation not as it was but as her heart pictured it. Even if she had told her father all, it was unlikely that he grasped the root of the matter. However that may have been, Jacob did not find a suitable pretext for speaking to him about what had happened, and he regretted this and yet was somewhat glad of it, since he feared that the Consul might call him to account. Just as he found no pretext for talking things over with the Consul, so he found no words to address to Susan. It was not that she avoided him, but that she showed him no overt sign of good will. Or if she indeed wished him well, she gave him no opportunity for speaking out. How was it that Susan managed to put him off; how was it that he could not bring himself to speak? Only because when they were together their conversation never led up to that principal point; when he parted from her, there he was in just the same position as the day before and the day before that. What should I do? he would think. What should I do? But since no answer was forthcoming, he would leave this for time to decide. It should be said that Rechnitz was not particularly passive, but since he knew the decision was not his alone, he left it for the moment when Susan would play her part.

The Consul and his daughter did not continue with their travels. It was clear that they meant to settle down, and now there was a coming and going of house agents carrying plans of apartments and houses. When Rechnitz saw these people he felt ashamed. He had boasted about the kind of person the Consul would find in the Land of Israel and now he had to admit that there *were* some Jews there who did not belong to the "spiritual center." But the Consul found no fault with them. A man had to live and what else could these poor devils do in a poverty-stricken country? When a bit of profit was coming their way, they would twist their words and tell lies whether they wanted to or not.

Meanwhile the Consul and his daughter stayed on in the hotel. Two or three times a week Rechnitz was invited to join them for a meal, sometimes for lunch, sometimes for dinner. When Susan was not present, her father would say to Jacob, "The child is tired, she has a headache." And his tone was sadder than the words suggested.

One day a strange thing happened. The three of them were seated together talking; Susan suddenly fell silent and dropped off to sleep in the middle of what she was saying. At first Rechnitz thought she had merely closed her eyes, as she sometimes did in the course of conversation. The next day Jacob saw old Dr. Hofmann walking out of the hotel together with Herr Ehrlich. After the doctor had taken his leave, the Consul noticed Rechnitz. "So you're here?" he said, and then, "Sit down Jacob, sit down," and then, "Today we shall take our meal without Susan. She has a headache." Many times before, the Consul had sat down to his meal without his daughter; now he behaved as if this were something new, and as distressing as it was new.

Over their meal, the Consul made a special effort to entertain his guest, as if Susan's absence imposed upon him a double duty of hospitality. When they had finished, he drew Jacob over to the sofa at the end of the lounge and talked to him about the United States and New York and the chair which awaited him there, as well as about Kaiser Wilhelm's project for teacher-exchanges between universities.

"I have never asked you," said the Consul, "what led you to your special field of interest?"

Jacob answered, "I was doing botanical studies and from botany I came to work on water plants; that's to say, I turned from higher to lower species of plants, and so to marine vegetation." As he spoke Jacob forgot that there had been another reason besides this.

"And do these plants," said the Consul, "also have their characteristic diseases?"

Rechnitz replied, "There isn't a single thing in creation that is not liable to disease."

Suddenly Jacob's eyes grew round with wonder. A new perspective opened up beyond the one he saw before him, like the vision of a painter struggling to apprehend what his eyes have never seen. The pond in the Consul's garden, whose water plants used to fascinate and amaze him, came back into his memory. Perhaps, after all, his heart had been drawn to these plants since those very days? Twenty years and more had passed since he had first gone down with Susan to the pond and drawn up the wet vegetation; the strange thing about it was that in all those years the thought had never come back into his mind. At that moment he saw before his eyes the same circular pond set in the garden among the shrubs and flowers, with Susan picking flowers and braiding garlands; now Susan jumped into the pond and disappeared; and now she rose again, covered with wet seaweed like a mermaid, the water streaming from her hair. As he thought of her hair, he thought, too, of how on that same day Susan had taken a curl from her curls and, with it, a lock of his forelock, and mingled them and burned them together and they had eaten the ashes and sworn to be faithful to each other. Like the ashes of her hair and of his own which Susan had intermingled, so the day of their vow was blended with the day by the sea when she had reminded him of it. As Jacob sat reflecting, the Consul took out his watch and said, "You look tired. No need to be ashamed of it. A young man like you needs plenty of sleep."

When Jacob got up to leave, the Consul said, "I can see that I shall not be staying here long. Perhaps we shall soon be leaving for Vienna. But as long as we are here we shall be happy to have your company any time at all."

Jacob asked in a low voice, "How is Susan's health?"

The Consul looked at him hard and answered, "If I only knew!" And again he looked at him as if he knew more than he would say.

XXV

What Susan's father did not tell him, others did. A grave affliction had overtaken her, a sickness which had not been heard of before in Palestine. Her head was dizzy and she had lost full control of her legs, which tottered as she moved about. When she spoke, her voice was indistinct and sounded like someone talking in his sleep; indeed, her only desire was for sleep. She would doze off at any time, on any occasion, in the midst of conversation, while walking or while taking a meal. Sometimes she would sleep for days on end, and after waking up would fall asleep again. Zablodovsky the doctor, Raya's father, said, "This disease seems so suspicious to me that I hesitate to call it by its name. The Ehrlich girl has come from a geographical region which leads me to fear that we have here a case of sleeping sickness. I could bring evidence to support what I say by means of a blood test, but from the symptoms themselves I should say that she has been bitten by a poisonous insect. The patient, I hear, sleeps a great deal, even for days on end; she eats and drinks after awakening, and there is a marked change in her disposition, for she was always full of life and is now apathetic. Perhaps you will say, 'But her appearance has not changed and she is no less beautiful than before.' But when I was a medical student didn't I see sufferers from this disease in its early stages who kept their normal appearance for several months without change? If we waste no time in treating the disease at its outset, we can still control it and cure her. There are certain mineral salts, derived from precious metals, which we can inject into the body until the poison is exhausted and the patient's health restored."

Susan's sickness caused no public alarm and her nursing gave rise to no difficulty, but she was in need of careful supervision. She was put to bed in her room with a nurse to watch over her, and everyone who passed by the room moved very softly, so as not to disturb the invalid and so as to catch something of her slumbering presence.

As for Rechnitz, he pays his calls on Susan's father, as he did years ago, except that then he would visit him twice yearly and now he comes twice a week. The Consul treats him even more cordially now and talks away on any topic that his mind prompts into words, or that words call up in his mind. So he describes his travels and the various kinds of people he has encountered. What extraordinary things he has seen. Even at the doorstep of his house, a man may behold such things as sometimes lead him to doubt his own eyes; how much more so when he travels into strange and far-off lands. At times the Consul repeats the same story, or confuses persons and places; for having known and seen so much, he is liable to substitute one person for another or this place for that. And when he says, "Now I am going to tell you something I have never talked about before," you may be sure that he will go over the same story he has related a hundred and one times already. Or he will stop in mid-course, look up alertly, and say, "Haven't I already told you this? It's hard on me, Rechnitz, the way you let me run on about things you've already heard." Then Jacob will answer, "Not at all, it's quite new to me." So the Consul returns to his story without misgivings. But even if he remembers having told it before, he continues just the same. It is like those songs we sing all our lives; they stir our spirits and remind us of the time we sang them first. The hotel servants come up and remove the loaded ash tray in front of him, replacing it with an empty one. In a deferential whisper they ask, "Would the Consul care for anything?" and withdraw as silently as they came.

Sometimes the Consul would call back the old days when Frau Ehrlich was still alive. When he spoke of those times his description was accurate in every detail, there were no slips; the miracle happened and the past was present once again. Jacob asked no questions about Susan and her father made no mention of her. But now and then he would clutch his head and say, "Any pain's better than a pain in the head," as if he had become a partner in Susan's suffering.

Once before Purim, Rechnitz was about to leave for one of those walking tours in which teachers and their students take part together at this season. There is no better time for them; mountains and valleys, hills and groves are covered with green and all the country blossoms like God's own garden. Before going away, Rechnitz came to say goodbye. The Consul gazed at him with admiration. "You look as fresh and blooming as a young god," he exclaimed. He took Jacob by the arm and led him out into the garden. The young man seemed to him a personification of spring, when all the world is made new. He, too, would gladly renew himself; if not in the mountains and the valleys, at least in the garden of his hotel.

The flowers were all in blossom, the lemon trees gave off their scent, the spikes of the palm trees reached up to the blue sky, and the sky itself seemed to blossom over every tree and bush. So deeply moved was the Consul that he could hardly find words to speak, beyond exclaiming at the beauty of this tree or that bush. Suddenly he reached out his hand in a gesture of helplessness, saying, "And there Susan lies, unable to see all the things that we can." A sigh broke from Jacob as he asked, "How is Susan now?"

The Consul took Jacob's hand in his. "Never," he said, "have I wished for a better husband for my daughter. But . . ."

Jacob lowered his eyes and waited. These was a pause, the pause continued, and still Susan's father did not speak. Jacob raised his head again and looked up. Susan's father became aware of him and said with a sigh, "Soon we are going to Vienna to see Notengel. Let's pray that he can find a cure for her disease. And you, my son," he went on, "here you are . . ." But the words failed him. He remembered a letter that Jacob's parents had written to him and tried to recall its contents, but could not bring them to mind. To Jacob he said, "Let me put it to you in this way. Suppose I am holding on to some valuable object, which I am about to return to its rightful owner. Suddenly the object slips from my hands before it has reached the owner and there we are, both left empty-handed; I who had it in my grasp and he who reached out to take it." While he spoke he looked down at his hands as if puzzling over how they had let it slip. Finally he extended his right hand to Rechnitz by way of farewell, and said, "Let's go now." Yet he held on to Rechnitz's hand, as old people do, clinging to the warmth that has come their way. And Rechnitz perceived this and was glad that he had this warmth to offer.

The Consul for his part became aware that Rechnitz still stood expectant. He saw in Rechnitz a healthy, fresh-cheeked young man in all his vigor, at a time when Susan was perhaps more seriously ill than the doctor would admit. His expression changed suddenly to resentment. What does he want of me? he thought. He let his hand fall and said briefly, "Goodbye."

Rechnitz parted from the old man feeling dejected, for never before had he been treated in this way. As he was going he heard the Consul call after him. Conflicting thoughts entered his mind; hope and expectation, and against this, anxiety and grief, which told him that if he turned back he would hear what was better left unheard. "Oh God," he prayed under his breath, "save me in your great mercy."

The Consul said, "I meant to tell you that when you are back from your walking tour you must not forget to come to us."

Rechnitz laid a hand to his heart and replied, "I shall come."

The Consul shook hands with him again, wished him a successful trip and showed by his expression that all his former affection had returned. Rechnitz, too, was calm again. Now, he thought, I must set about making the arrangements for my journey. He began reckoning up all the articles he must take with him. At first they came to mind in a confused jumble, but in the end they sorted themselves out of their own accord and there was no need to make a second reckoning.

XXVI

No change, no alteration in Susan's condition. She would sleep for days on end, or if she awoke, it was only to fall asleep again. What had the fates punished her for? What harm had Susan done? If it was for her haughty bearing, wasn't this an effect of the disease itself, which makes it harder to behave with normal friendliness towards others? Who would suppose that this charming girl, whose lids close over eyes so beautiful that no man seems worthy to behold them, whose figure has the stateliness of a solitary palm tree, is fated to sleep out her days?

Thus Susan lies in her bed and everyone who passes her room walks softly. Many days have gone by since Jacob last saw her; meanwhile her father has aged beyond his years. Although he has not been visited with the sickness of his daughter, he has lost his capacity for staying awake. When most men are fully alert, he is liable to drop off to sleep, even in the middle of speaking. Bestirring himself, he will sigh and say, "At night when I want to sleep I lie awake, and in the daytime when I want to talk to people I can't resist the desire for sleep."

Rechnitz saw his embarrassment and began to keep away from the hotel. Yet when he called to inquire about him, the Consul refrained from asking why he had not been round in the last day or two. There was no change in their relationship; in fact, the Consul felt a new kind of affection for Jacob, but the old age which had so suddenly fallen upon him inevitably left its mark.

When the university appointment was first made public, everybody showed even more friendliness towards Jacob than before, and this without any designs for themselves or their daughters. They recognized that Dr. Rechnitz was intended for Susan Ehrlich and there was nothing to be done about it. But when Susan fell sick, they again began to regard him in the old light. Sometimes the expectations of parents have a solid basis, sometimes not, and new hopes grow out of their very despair. The sleep into which Susan Ehrlich had fallen served to awaken such parental hopes. For their daughters, however, it was different. Of all their expectations nothing remained in their hearts but a sense of loss as they looked ahead to Rechnitz's departure.

Rechnitz now made his arrangements for the journey to America. On the way, he planned a stopover in Europe to visit his father and mother. Three years had gone by since he had seen them, for any holiday trips he had made were to the marine biology station in Naples, and not to his home. From the day he first hinted to his mother that he might be arriving, she had taken to sitting at her window reading his letters, one after another, or rereading the letter which the Consul had sent her from Jaffa. At this same time, Jacob in Jaffa was picturing himself as a child again with Susan. In her short frock, she chased butterflies, picked flowers and made a crown of them for her head. Actually, the Consul's house now stood desolate and untenanted and Rechnitz's parents had long since moved out of that neighborhood. But whenever his father's home came to his mind, he saw it still as standing next to the Consul's.

Meanwhile, Rechnitz turned back to his work. He was busy at his microscope, and happy, for sometimes small things give us great happiness, especially when they link together into something large. The humble sea plants with their tints of green, red, brown and blue, which have neither taste nor scent, and are without any counterpart on land, were dearer to Rechnitz than all the trees, bushes and shrubs of the earth. Out of the strength of his love, and his capacity to take unqualified delight in the smallest of things, his own soul grew and perfected itself ever more. And with this wholeness of spirit came tranquillity. Once again he surveyed, examined and tested, with an undistracted love, objects which he had set aside for many days, perhaps since the day when Susan Ehrlich came to Jaffa. Science is a complacent mistress who is not jealous of others; when you return to her you find what is not to be found in a thousand rivals. How many days and weeks had these sea plants lain, floating in salt water within their oblong trays of clear glass, exuding their salt water like tears! But now that Rechnitz had returned and wiped their tears away, they looked up at him so lovingly that in their presence he forgot any other concern.

Jaffa, darling of the waters, is crowded with men of all communities, busy at trade and labor, at shipping and forwarding, each pursuing his own ends, absorbed in his own task. There are others who take no part in any of these activities: such is Jacob Rechnitz. Yet even he is not idle; you might even say that he is busier than all the rest. What need is there for those plants he is so concerned with? The stars adorn the sky and provide light for the world and those who dwell in it, the flowers adorn the earth and give off their good scent; for this the stars and the flowers were created. But those weeds of the sea, which have neither scent nor taste—what good is to be found in them? Yet far away from Jaffa, from the Land of Israel, there are men who make a study of seaweed, just as Rechnitz does, men who value his activities and pay him honor and esteem.

XXVII

In honor of Rechnitz, all his colleagues, as well as the school trustees, got together and arranged a farewell party. At first they meant to hold it in the Semiramis Hotel, but finally they settled on the schoolhouse where Rechnitz had taught.

They seated Rechnitz at the head of the table with the two principals to his left and right and all the other teachers and trustees in order of precedence. The table was spread with an array of wines and cakes, oranges, almonds, pistachio nuts and various fruits of the season.

The first principal rose to his feet and said, "Gentlemen, we all know the reason why we are assembled here. One of our number, who has spent the last three years with us, is now leaving us. There is no need for me to say how much we regret this, but our joy is equal to our regret for we know that he is going to a great and honored position. We too gain credit from his advance, so I raise my glass and drink a health to him, to us all, and to our school—a school where we have such teachers as Rechnitz!"

After the toast had been drunk, the second principal began as follows: "My colleague has said that our joy is as great as our regret, since our friend here has been advanced to a great and honored position, namely, to a certain university abroad. But for my part, I admit to feeling sad. Why is Rechnitz departing? Because we have no university here. If there were one, he would not have to leave us; he would join our own university and teach there. My dear colleagues, I am raising an issue which, after all, needs to be frankly discussed. Why have we no university? Because we are content with too little and therefore get nothing at all. I know that people make fun of me for wanting a university. Why do they laugh? Is there any enterprise of ours which they don't deride? When we founded our school here, did they not laugh at us? Did they not call us charlatans? Now those who mocked us come begging for posts. I am not saying, of course, that a university is the same as a high school. No two things in the world are completely alike—except for the smart-alecks and scoffers, who are the same in all places and times. Today they laugh, tomorrow they are dumbfounded, the day after tomorrow they see what they can get out of it for themselves. Finally, they boast that it was they who suggested the whole idea. Let me say in conclusion that I hope we, too, will achieve a university before long to which we can invite our friend Rechnitz to come and lecture. What a great university that will be, when all the scholars of Israel, from all the universities of the world, gather in Jerusalem, on the Temple Mount, to teach wisdom and knowledge! Such a university, my dear friends, the eye has not beheld. But it follows of necessity that I mean no mere seminary for religious studies. We have enough already of this 'religious study' stuffed into us morning, noon and night. When I say university, I mean a real one, where all the forms of knowledge to be found in other centers of learning will be taught. And at this point let me turn to our colleague Rechnitz. My dear Rechnitz, just as we regret that you are leaving us, so shall we rejoice on the day you return here to our own university. 'Blessed be your going out and your coming in.' To your health!"

After this speech the hall rang with cheers. At last there was silence again, the toast was drunk, and speech followed speech until, when midnight had passed, the company went home quietly.

XXVIII

Ever since the Consul's coming to Jaffa, Rechnitz had given up visiting the homes he used to frequent. He had started by being available to the Consul at all hours; now he neglected him, too, and stayed in his room devoting himself entirely to his work. He would take up some piece of seaweed, cut it and examine it under the microscope, then attach it to a sheet of paper, fold the sheet, place it in his great album and note down its name, its habitat, and the date when he had drawn it out of the sea. Nearly two hundred separate species had been taken by Rechnitz from the sea near Jaffa, Haifa, Acre, Caesarea, Haderah, and elsewhere. It would hardly be an exaggeration to say that no one in all the world possessed as many sea plants of the Mediterranean as Jacob Rechnitz. Nowadays we are familiar with more than two hundred kinds of Mediterranean seaweed, and the specialists know of still more. But in his time, no one had a collection to match that of Rechnitz. There they were, dried, attached to their sheets, placed in the album. At first glance you would think you were looking into an artist's sketch book, each line was drawn with such exquisite care and beauty; for the way of seaweeds is to adhere to paper, become absorbed in it, and not protrude from the surface. But once you drop a little water on them, they grow soft and you see before you living plants, the work of the Creator who cares as much for each humble object as He does for what is high and mighty. There were times when Rechnitz dropped a tear in his rapture, which fell on the plant and brought it to life again.

The sea gave forth its daily harvest, and at night, under the moon, the daughters of Jaffa took their walks by the shore. The waves kissed their footprints and tossed up an abundance of plants such as Rechnitz had been used to gather. But you will not find Rechnitz there; he is well content with what he has taken to his room and laid out upon his table. Happy, at ease among his glass trays of saltwater, he sits with the great album before him, its pages full. That album is the bliss of his eye and soul.

This was all that Rechnitz did; he sat

in his room and devoted himself to his work. At times he was so preoccupied that he would forget to light the spirit lamp for his coffee or, if he lit it, to put coffee in the pot before the water boiled over and put out the flame. Needless to say, he no longer took tea with the parents of his pupils and girl friends; thus, he made himself a stranger in all those households and with all those good people who, though they seemed unimportant then, were to count for much in the days to come. For they dwelt in the Land of Israel and were among the first of its founders. The reasons for their coming were many and varied, but it may well be that the very people whose motives were most obscure will be remembered and inscribed for all time, while those who came specifically for their country's sake will be forgotten and ignored.

Rechnitz turned his thoughts away from these persons, and from their daughters too. This time was perhaps the best he ever knew. In his great desire for Susan he had put out of mind all lesser desires; now even that desire fell away. He knew that he must prepare for his journey, whether it be to America or to Europe, for now the Consul was about to leave and it was better to travel with him and Susan than to go alone. And yet work took his mind away from the journeys that lay ahead. People in Jaffa knew that he must get his lectures ready and took care not to disturb him. And Rechnitz too did not trouble himself with fancied needs. If he had found the time for it, he would have given praise and thanks to the gods for dealing with him so well.

XXIX

One night Rechnitz was alone in his room. The doors were closed and the blinds drawn, and the lamp lit up the table and the plants of the sea laid out upon it. This room had once been full of flowers and their scents; now he had in front of him only these odorless plants, together with the material for his course of lectures in America, which he was preparing in advance. This night, apparently so ordinary, was for Rechnitz singled out from all others, for in it he was experiencing what a man knows but once or twice in a lifetime. Having yielded his will to a single desire, the desire itself at last quits him and he is left free from any and all concerns. Never in his life had Rechnitz been so free a man as now; he had separated himself from Rachel and Leah, from Asnat, Raya and the rest, on account of Susan Ehrlich; he had come to despair of Susan because of her disease; his journey lay before him, and yet even this was put out of his thoughts in order that work might be his sole object and end.

We have intimated that Rechnitz was a modest young man and no woman-hunter; still, man is a social being and he may feel more affection for a group of charming girls than for the rest of the world. Sometimes his hidden thoughts may drive him beyond all reason; were he to consider them dispassionately he would be appalled. With the Consul's arrival reason resumed its proper place for Rechnitz, but at the cost of his tranquillity, which was only restored when he returned to his work. Were one to ask how it was possible for Rechnitz not to grieve at Susan's distress, the answer would be this: many factors for which language, however precise, has no name were operating to silence such thoughts.

So Rechnitz sat in his room, at peace with himself and free from all distraction, for he had come to accept the fact of Susan's sickness and distress. The good gods have favored Rechnitz, granting him peace and calm, together with joy in his work. But these favors were not to last long. The gods are envious, and when they see us prosper too much, they send their agents to change our lives. Every man learns this for himself; let those who have not yet done so now witness the case of Rechnitz. Enough, then, of the beauty of this night and the benefits of a tranquil mind; let us tell instead how Rechnitz lost his tranquillity.

As Rechnitz sat alone, he heard the sound of a light tap at the door; after the tap, the door opened and Tamara entered. Entered and stood still. Never before had she called upon Rechnitz; never, perhaps, had she been inside a young man's lodgings. One could tell this from her whole stance and from the dim glow that hung like a mist over her features.

Tamara paused on the threshold, waiting to be asked in. Her lips trembled like petals touched with morning dew. Rechnitz did not take her into his arms but he took her by the hands and seated her on the couch. Tamara was a girl of some humility. Never had she dared to think that people took notice of her, certainly not a great scholar like Dr. Rechnitz. No, the only reason for her coming was that she was planning to go abroad, and since he was also leaving, she had gathered up courage and come to visit him.

Tamara had been graduated from the Jaffa high school and was preparing to go to Europe, where she intended to study medicine, an interest she had inherited from her father the doctor. Meanwhile, she had taken up sculpture and clay modeling and now she was finding it hard to decide where her true inclination lay. The body contained so many secrets and her fingers were itching to create shapes; sometimes she dreamed of figures of flesh and blood, sometimes of figures in stone. Rechnitz found Tamara's conversation exciting, even though it contained no exceptional wisdom. He felt a sudden longing to grasp in his arms this body which was so uncertain about what it wanted, and to kiss Tamara full on the lips. It is quite possible that he would have done so, had he not heard footsteps coming up the stairs.

Again there was a sound at the door; this door, which had not opened to visitors for many days and nights, tonight opened twice.

XXX

Rechnitz pulled himself together and behaved as if there were no little Tamara seated in his room. Rachel and Leah came in. They had not intended to pay a call until, passing the house, they heard the sound of conversation and assumed that Rechnitz was not too busy with his work. In this they were certainly correct.

Tamara sat on the edge of the couch. She looked up at Rachel and Leah without animosity or envy; or if there were a trace of envy, it was only what a young girl would feel towards those older than herself who could talk to Jacob without being overawed. Now she lowered her head to sniff at the carnation on her blouse, pleased enough to take her place with Rachel and Leah, her seniors.

Rechnitz moved his basins and seaweed out of the way and transferred his microscope elsewhere. Only a few dry specimens remained on the table, which he did not need, as there were duplicates already mounted in his album. Now that his work was set aside and he had only his guests to attend to, he would gladly have offered them something, as was his usual way, but he could find nothing: no chocolate, no fruit—in fact, since the Consul's arrival he had felt no need for such things. But Zeus, who watches over guests, now intimated to the host that tea might be prepared, for tea is welcome on all occasions. So Rechnitz took out his spirit lamp and set it going. The alcohol lit up as it used to in the old days when Rachel Heilperin would drop in. Now Rachel sat and gazed, sometimes at the flame which flickered and mounted through the perforations, sometimes at its reflection in the looking-glass opposite, thinking to herself, Rechnitz is going to America and I shall not see him again. Probably he will put me out of his mind and not think of me any more, just as he never thought of me before he knew me. And probably this is the last time I shall ever sit in this room. She looked up towards Rechnitz but saw only his back, since he was occupied with getting out the tea and sugar. Pursing her lips, which had a way of pouting disdainfully, she picked up two or three of the seaweeds that Rechnitz had left on the table because he could not bring himself to throw them away. Holding them in her hands, she began to plait them together. At the same moment, or even a moment before, Leah Luria got up and took over the entire operation of tea-making, just as she always took every task upon herself.

The little burner stands between the door and the table; the water bubbles and rises, but when it reaches full boil there isn't enough for all the girls, as the kettle is too small. Let us leave the tea, then, and turn to other concerns. There is the burner with the water gradually heating. Opposite, Tamara sits on the edge of the couch. Rachel is at the table, plaiting herself a kind of garland. A song comes into her mind—

A lad sat by the spring,
Twisting flowers for a garland.

Then again she wonders at herself for bothering with such plants, whose smell is like that of iodine on a wound.

Leah said, "Here am I standing about as if I had nothing to do and I promised to go and see Asnat!"

Rachel answered, "You are nothing but a parcel of promises, Leah," and went on plaiting her garland.

"But since I promised her, what shall I do? How can I let her wait for nothing?"

"Oh, let Asnat wait until she's tired of waiting.—Where are *you* off to, Tamara?"

Tamara answered, "I am going to call Miss Magargot. That is, if Dr. Rechnitz has no objections."

"On the contrary," said Rechnitz.

Rachel laughed and said, "I knew that Leah and I would not be enough for you! Whom else shall we invite?"

But just as Tamara was about to leave, in came Asnat, and with her, her relative Raya. For Asnat, deciding not to wait any more, had gone for a walk with Raya Zablodovsky and while they were out they had passed by Rechnitz's house, heard the sound of conversation and decided to come in.

Asnat had not really intended to visit Rechnitz but she was glad now that she had come. And the same was true of Raya, who was not paying a visit for the sake of Rechnitz but to please herself; it was her own personality that guided her movements and so she made herself at home everywhere. Thus it came about that five girls were all met in the lodgings of Rechnitz, each for a reason of her own and all well pleased to be there.

"Is anyone still missing?" asked Rachel.

"If Mira were here," said Leah, "that would make a full session."

"Yes, but there wouldn't be a spare cup for her," said Rachel.

"I don't take tea," Tamara put in.

"My dear child," said Rachel, "yours is not the only mouth."

Tamara lowered her head and took another sniff at the carnation on her blouse.

"I didn't mean to mock you," Rachel added.

Tamara said, "I know that, Miss Heilperin, and of course I'm not hurt."

After tea, Asnat said, "How about going for a walk? All in favor, raise their hands."

"Better their feet," said Rachel, "so that we can get started."

"Let me first make our host's bed," said Leah, "so that when he comes back he'll find it ready for him. Where shall we go?"

"Where?" said Asnat. "By the sea, of course."

"And when we pass Mira's house," added another of the girls, "we'll call her out too. Who votes for that?"

So Rechnitz found himself again in the company of the six. Not long ago he had been glad that he had given them up, now he was pleased that they had returned. The envy of the gods works in devious ways, so that we ourselves cannot know what is for our good and what is not.

XXXI

The sea lay stretched on a bed as wide as the world, its nightshirt the moon-whitened waves. The shores had lengthened, moonlight lay on the sands and the sea. A beneficent spirit brooded over Rechnitz and the six maidens—for on the way they had called for Mira, who hurried to make up the quorum of the Seven Planets. When such a night as this and such a spirit are in conjunction, their power is complete, their blessing great.

Rachel, Leah and Asnat walked to the right of Rechnitz; Raya, Mira and Tamara to his left. Sometimes they changed places, those on the left wheeling over to the right, or those on the right passing over to the left, but they always took care to leave Rechnitz in the middle. And Rechnitz among his maidens was carried beyond himself, as he had been on those fine nights a year ago, and two years, and three years ago. At that moment, he put Susan entirely from his mind. But her memory formed a circle around his heart, like the golden lashes around her eyes as she slept.

Rachel Heilperin wore the appearance of being happy, while Leah Luria was happy indeed. "On a night like this . . ." she cried excitedly, and great untellable longings trembled in that lovely voice. Since she knew no way to sing the praises of the night, she stretched out her delicate arms and stared into the hollow of the universe. And night assigned that hollow its own starlit mightiness. "On a night like this . . ." she cried again, and again stopped short. But since she could not still the tumult within her, she called to the others, "Girls, girls, just look! Look!"

Sea and sky, heaven and earth, and all the space between were grown into a single living being; a luminous calm enveloped by azure, or an azure transparent as air. Up above, and under the surface of the sea, the moon raced like a frenzied girl. Even the sands were moonstruck and seemed to move perpetually. Like the sands, like all the surrounding air, the girls, and with them Rechnitz, were taken up into the dream. If they looked overhead, there was the moon running her race, and if they looked out to sea, there she was again hovering upon the face of the waters. Heaven and earth, land and sea, had become a single whole; and this was contained in yet another, greater whole that no eye could see.

Rachel took Leah's hand, Leah the hand of Asnat and Asnat that of Raya, and Raya took Mira's, and Mira Tamara's and Tamara took Rachel's; they encircled Rechnitz and danced around him—danced until Rachel broke from their ring and knelt down facing the sea with her eyes uplifted to the moon. Asnat stood still, stretched out her hands in the air and played inaudible notes on an unseen keyboard. "Listen, Tamara," said Mira, "if I had a horse, I would go galloping from one end of the world to the other!"

"Good people all," said Raya, "has anybody a horse in her pocket for Mira? Oh Mira, Mira, I've no horse in my pocket either, so what can I do for you, my dear? Could you possibly do without the horse and go on foot?"

"For your sake, Raya, I shall go on foot," Mira answered, laughing and putting her arms around Tamara. Tamara laid her head on Mira's breast and said, "You're a good friend." "Wait, little one, wait," Raya called to Tamara, "my shoe's full of sand." She leaned against her, took off her shoe and shook it empty.

Suddenly Leah called, "Look, good people all, just look! What's that out to sea? I swear there's a light burning on the water!"

They looked out to sea and at the light, which came from a passing ship. Only those aboard knew whether it was sailing to or from the Land of Israel, but to Jacob Rechnitz and his companions it made no difference where the ship was headed. They stood in silence watching the light floating on the surface of the sea. The spread of waters girdled both the ship and the light. Now the light sank, now it rose, again it sank and floated. On such a ship Jacob would soon be sailing over endless distances, and they, perhaps, would stand on the shore as now and see the light far off, while Jacob would not see them or be aware of their presence, even as the passengers on this ship were unaware of being observed. So the girls stood silent, looking out and clasping each other by the waist. At last they turned their thoughts from the ship and grieved for themselves, as if they had suffered some loss.

Once thoughts have entered the mind, words come to the lips, and Leah spoke aloud what they were all thinking. "I've been wanting to ask you, Dr. Rechnitz," she said, "when will you be leaving for America?"

Rachel said, "How could our doctor make such a long journey just as he is?"

"What do you mean by 'just as he is'?"

"I mean, all alone," said Rachel.

"And what does 'all alone' mean?"

"It means without a wife," said Rachel.

Leah took Jacob's hand and clasped it as a conciliatory gesture.

Rachel added, "What a pity it is we didn't settle among ourselves that whoever first took Rechnitz's hand won the privilege of going to America with him."

Leah withdrew her hand, remarking, "You're a wicked girl, Rachel!"

Asnat said, "But, Leah, doesn't taking his hand make you a wicked girl?"

Then Tamara came up and took hold of Jacob's hand.

"It will do you no good, Tamara," said Rachel. "We were talking about whoever *first* took his hand—which does not apply to you."

Tamara gave the hand a little squeeze and sniffed at the carnation on her blouse.

"I don't know why," said Mira, "but I feel as if I want to run—to run from one end of the world to the other."

"To run? What put that into your head?"

Mira said, "If I were to run, no horse and no rider would ever catch me." Even as she spoke, she started off on her light feet. Leah called after her, "Mira, Mira, don't go too far!" But Mira did not hear her; she was already some distance away and still running.

Said Raya to Tamara, "And you, my little Tamara, stand about like a hobbled bird. Don't you want to try your legs?"

Tamara raised her eyes and gazed up

at Jacob to see if her running would please him. Even as she looked, her feet lifted themselves of their own accord and she was off.

Asnat played with the tassels of her belt, swinging them back and forth as she said, "If Dr. Rechnitz doesn't take one of these mighty runners for a wife, I don't know whom he will take." As she spoke, the tassels slipped out of her hands and her legs began to quiver.

"Do you want to run, too?" said Rachel, taunting her.

"If you run, I will!" she answered.

"No," said Rachel, "you run.—What's this I am holding, a circle of thorns? Dr. Rechnitz, I forgot I had your plants in my hand and I've brought them out with me. Now listen to me, girls, listen. Whoever beats the others in the race will be crowned with this garland." She raised overhead the seaweeds she had plaited, repeating, "Whoever beats the rest takes this as her crown. What do you want to say, Leah?"

"That's not how the Greeks did it," said Leah. "What they did was this. The young men ran and whoever won the race received the crown from the most beautiful girl present. Isn't that so, Dr. Rechnitz?" And as she spoke she, too, felt her knees quiver. To Rachel she said, "Will you run with me?"

"Run, Leah, run!" said Rachel. "Perhaps you'll win the garland."

At this point the other girls returned. "Girls," said Leah, "if you'd been here a moment ago, you'd have heard a splendid thing."

"And what is this splendid thing we've missed?" asked Asnat.

"Do you see this garland?" said Leah. "We've all agreed that the fastest runner will win and wear this wreath, made of Dr. Rechnitz's weeds. Do you agree, Dr. Rechnitz?"

Rechnitz nodded, saying, "Yes." But his face grew pale and his heart began to quake.

Leah insisted, "The Greeks had the men run, not the girls."

Asnat answered, "But since all those young men are dead and we are alive, let's do their running ourselves. Do you agree, Dr. Rechnitz? Yes or no?—Why don't you speak?"

Rechnitz answered, "I agree," and his heart quaked all the more.

"Very well," said Asnat. "Stand in a line, girls. Now, where do we start from and where do we run to?"

She looked up in the direction of the Hotel Semiramis and said, "Let's start from the Semiramis."

"And where do we finish?"

"At the old Moslem cemetery. Dr. Rechnitz, you stand in line with us and call 'one, two, three.' At 'three,' we'll start. Raya, don't step out of line. Tamara, until Rechnitz gives the call you mustn't lift a foot, do you hear?"

"I hear," said Tamara.

"Stay in your place, then, and don't stretch your neck out like a camel's."

All the girls now stood together where the balconies of the Hotel Semiramis overlooked the sea. They faced the old cemetery, which they had taken as their finishing point. Each looked down at her feet as they made room for Rechnitz. And Rechnitz, standing in the middle, looked from side to side at the girls poised for the race, at the garland on Rachel's arm, and again at the girls, wondering which of them would wear it as her crown. His hands trembled and his heart beat so fast that he could hardly speak.

The sand was damp and firmly packed; the moon lay on the dim beach, and the dim beach was its mirror. Like drawn bows to which the arrows had not yet been fitted stood the six girls, each waiting for the word that would set her off.

But the word was still unspoken; it seemed that Rechnitz had forgotten all about their agreement of a moment ago, or perhaps he had not forgotten and that was the cause of his delay. One girl asked, "Why is he taking so long?" And another said, "Come on, Dr. Rechnitz, say the word!"

Then Jacob, in fear and trembling, called, "One!"—To left and right of them the girls quivered with excitement, so that the very sands beneath their feet quivered too. As for Rechnitz, he too was trembling, and perhaps more than they. Suddenly Rachel cried, "Wait, Jacob, wait!" She left her place, knelt down in front of Rechnitz, took the wreath from her arm and passed it to him before going back to stand with her comrades. "Now, Doctor," she said, "you can say, 'two, three.' " Rechnitz heard her but did not heed, or heeded her but did not hear. Then abruptly the words broke from his lips of their own accord and a voice was heard saying, "One, two, three!"

XXXII

Jacob held the garland that Rachel Heilperin had plaited from the dried seaweeds she had found on his table. He looked about him, uncertainly. The six girls raced side by side until one went twisting ahead, like a ball of twine that has dropped from the hands of the knitter. Then she was caught up and returned to the cluster of her companions. Again the rank was broken, by one here and one there, until one girl outpaced all the rest for a time, only to be overtaken; and again the group came together and again broke up. His eyes began to burn painfully; still he watched the running girls. He pricked up his ears to hear the sound of their feet, though this was difficult to catch, for now the tide was rising and the noise of the waves kept breaking through.

At the sound of the waves, at the sight of the limitless expanse of sea, Rechnitz closed his eyes. And now he saw his mother kneeling down before him. He was a small boy; she was threading a new tie round his collar, for it was the day Susan was born and he was invited to the Consul's house. But surely, thought Jacob to himself, she can't be my mother, and it goes without saying that she isn't Susan's mother either, because one is far from here and the other is dead; if I open my eyes I shall see that this is nothing but an optical illusion. The illusion went so far as to present him at once with his own mother and with Susan's; and since one object could not be two, it followed of necessity that here was neither his own mother nor Susan's. But if so, who was she? Susan herself, perhaps? Of course not, for Susan was ill in bed.

He opened his eyes and saw that all was but the image of an image, what a man compares to what he sees. Of course this was neither his mother nor Susan's mother nor Susan, but Leah and Rachel and Asnat and Raya and Mira and Tamara. Jacob shifted the wreath from one hand to the other and looked across at the girls who were racing side by side, or one close after the other, each trying to outstrip her companion. Rachel was as light-footed as a gazelle; it seemed likely that she would outrun the rest. But Leah, the deliberate one who measured all her movements, now passed Rachel, and Mira overtook Leah—naturally enough, since she was so accustomed to exercise and running. Finally she was left behind Asnat, with Rachel and Raya outstripping them both. Little Tamara vanished into thin air, she was swallowed up in space; but again she appeared, only to be swallowed up again and vanish from sight. Yet apparently she had managed to pass her companions. At first it had made no difference to Jacob who would outrun whom; now he felt some regret as he saw Tamara beating them all. At least there was some comfort in the thought that the old cemetery was far away and that one of her friends would probably get ahead before she could reach it. Indeed, a figure was now to be seen running ahead of Tamara, but since she was a good way off one could not tell quite who she was. Jacob shut his eyes and left it for time to decide. But time waited and did not defer to Jacob.

A good while passed. Rechnitz stood motionless. What has happened? he wondered. By now they should have returned, but they are not here yet. He looked around him. Heaven and earth, land and sea, were all confounded, and the waves of the sea were raised on high, the waves crashed like thunder, and the sound of the girls' running feet could not be heard. Why haven't they come back? he asked himself. The sea grew even vaster, its waves rubbed against the dry land, but there was no sound of the girls' feet, no sight of the girls themselves. Where had they gone, where had they vanished?

Rechnitz hung the wreath over his arm and began to run. He ran until he reached the place and found them all there, as well as one who had not been with them at the start. She was in her night clothes, like a maiden suddenly alarmed in her sleep. Silent and fearful stood the girls, and with them stood Susan Ehrlich, who had outstripped them all in the race. Neither Leah nor Rachel nor Asnat nor Raya nor Mira nor Tamara had seen her running, yet each of them had been aware in the course of the race that someone was ahead of her, without knowing this someone as Susan Ehrlich, Jacob's friend, who for many days and weeks had been asleep, never rising from her bed. With fear in their souls they forgot the garland and their agreement with Jacob. And Jacob, too, forgot all this as he stood before Susan.

Suddenly there was a voice calling him by name, a voice that came, as it were, from beneath Susan's eyelashes. Jacob shut his eyes and replied in a whisper, "Susan, are you here?"

Susan's eyelashes signaled assent. She put out her hands, took the crown from Jacob's arm and placed it on her head.

Here, for the time being, we have brought to an end our account of the affairs of Jacob Rechnitz and Susan Ehrlich. These are the same Susan and Jacob who were betrothed to one another through a solemn vow. Because of it, we have called this whole account "Betrothed," though at first we had thought to call it "The Seven Maidens."

EDO AND ENAM

By S. Y. AGNON

Translated from the Hebrew by Walter Lever[1]

I

Gerhard Greifenbach and his wife Gerda, both good friends of mine, were just about to go abroad. They hoped to rest awhile from the strain of life in our country and visit relatives in the Diaspora. But when I called to wish them well upon their way, it was plain to see that they were really troubled. I hadn't expected anything of the kind. After all, they lived a measured life, enjoyed a steady income, got on well together, and never did anything without first considering it carefully. If they had decided to go on their travels, they had surely managed to eliminate any obstacles and snags. Why then were they so dark and distracted?

We sat together over tea, talking about the countries they were going to visit. A good many lands are no longer accessible, for since the war the world has closed in on us and the countries that admit tourists are fewer in number. Even places which have not barred their doors do not exactly welcome visitors. Still, if a traveler goes about things sensibly, he can find ways of enjoying his trip.

All the time we talked, their anxiety never left them. I began trying to guess at the causes, but could not find any real grounds. These people, I thought to myself, are my friends; indeed I am almost one of the family. After the riots of 1929, when the Arabs had destroyed my home and I had no roof over my head, the Greifenbachs put me up. Again, in the bad times when people who had gone into town could not get back to their homes on account of the curfews suddenly imposed by the British, I had spent several nights at their house. Seeing them so worried, I felt I should ask the reason, but I found some difficulty in framing the question tactfully. I could see Mrs. Greifenbach staring straight ahead of her into the depths of the room. She was like someone looking at a beloved object in order to fix its image so firmly in mind that he will be sure of recognizing it again. Still staring at the room, she remarked, as if to herself, "It's hard to leave and hard to come back. I only pray that when we get home the doors won't be locked against us and we won't have to go to court with squatters."

Greifenbach made Gerda's words more explicit. "These are fine times," he said, "when we can't even be sure of a roof over our heads. You open the newspaper, only to read about people breaking into other people's homes. You go to the shops and hear of this person or that whose house has been broken into. A man's afraid to go out for a short stroll

---

[1] *A glossary is printed on page 101.*

for fear his house will be grabbed while he is away. And we've all the more reason to be anxious, because our house is so far from any others and a long way out of town. It's true that one room is rented to a Dr. Ginath, but that doesn't help us in the least; most of the time he's away from home, and when we go on our travels the house will be left with no one to guard it."

My heart beat fast as I heard this; not because of the Greifenbachs, but because they had spoken of Ginath as a real person. Since the time when the name of Ginath became world-famous, I had not come across anyone who could say he actually knew him. Nor had I heard any mention of him, except in connection with his books. And now here he was, staying in this very house where I came and went freely.

Even with his first published article, "Ninety-nine Words of the Edo Language," Ginath had drawn the attention of many philologists; when he followed this up with his "Grammar of Edo," no philologist could afford to ignore him. But what made him truly famous was his discovery of the Enamite Hymns. To discover ninety-nine words of a language whose very name was hitherto unknown is no small achievement, and a greater one still is the compilation of a grammar of this forgotten tongue. But the Enamite Hymns were more: they were not only a new-found link in a chain that bound the beginnings of recorded history to the ages before, but—in themselves—splendid and incisive poetry. Not for nothing, then, did the greatest scholars come to grips with them, and those who at first had doubted that they were authentic Enamite texts began to compose commentaries on them. One thing, however, surprised me. All these scholars affirmed that the gods of Enam and their priests were male; how was it that they did not catch in the hymn the cadence of a woman's song? On the other hand, I could be mistaken; for I am not, of course, a professional scholar, only a common reader who happens to enjoy anything beautiful that comes his way.

Mrs. Greifenbach could tell that I was excited, but could not tell why. She poured me another cup of tea and repeated what she had been saying before. I held my teacup while my heart pounded; at the same time, I could hear a kind of echo from my very depths. This did not surprise me; ever since the day I had first read the Enamite Hymns that echo had resounded. It was the reverberation of a primeval song passed on from the first hour of history through endless generations.

I held down the turmoil within me and asked, "Is he here?" Even as I said this, I was amazed at my own question. Never had I been inside a house where Ginath had been seen.

"Oh, no," answered Mrs. Greifenbach. "He's not in." Well, I thought, that's clear now. But since they've told me that he has rented a room, they must surely have seen him; and if they've seen him, they may very well have talked to him; and if they've talked to him, perhaps they can tell me something about him. With a great man who shuns publicity and lets nothing be known about himself, even the least bit of information is an unexpected find.

I turned to the Greifenbachs. "May I ask what you know about Ginath?"

"What we know?" answered Greifenbach. "Very little, so little it amounts to less than nothing."

"How did he turn up at your house?"

"That's easily answered," said Greifenbach. "He just rented a room and came to live in it."

"But how did he get here?" I insisted.

"Well, if you want to know the whole story, I can tell you, though there's really nothing to tell."

"Never mind that," I said.

"One afternoon in summer," he went on, "we were out on the veranda having tea, when a man with a walking stick and a knapsack came up and asked if we would rent him a room. We aren't in the habit of renting rooms. Besides, this man didn't so take my fancy that I felt like changing my ways in order to have him as a roomer. On the other hand, I was thinking, We do have a room that has been empty all these years. We've no use for it, and there's a separate entrance, a shower, and so on. Perhaps it would be worthwhile to rent the room, if not for the money's sake, at least to do a good turn to someone who wants to live in this modest neighborhood and is plainly a lover of peace and quiet. This fellow went on to say, 'I promise I won't give you much trouble. I travel about a great deal and only come to Jerusalem for a rest between one journey and the next. I shall not bring in any visitors, either.' I took another look at him and could see that it would be a good thing to rent him the room; not for the reasons he gave, but because by now I rather liked him. In fact, I was surprised at myself for not realizing at once what sort of man he was. I looked across at Gerda and could see that she agreed. So I said to him, 'Very well, the room is yours, on condition that you expect nothing from us; no service or anything at all except a bed, a table, a chair, and a lamp; and the rent will be such-and-such.' He took out his money and paid down a year's rent, and he has kept to his side of the bargain ever since, making no demands on us. That's all I can tell you, besides what I've seen about him in the weekly supplements to the newspapers, which I'm sure you have also read. I dare say you have read his Hymns, too. So have I, a bit here and a bit there, but I still don't see why they are so important. I'm not in the habit of expressing my views about matters on which I'm no expert, but I think I can say this: in every generation, some discovery is made that's regarded as the greatest thing that ever was. Eventually it's forgotten, for meanwhile some new discovery comes to light. No doubt that goes, too, for the discoveries of Dr. Ginath."

I let these remarks pass and returned to the main question, concerning Dr. Ginath himself. "My guess is that Gerda could tell me more," I said.

Mrs. Greifenbach looked at me, surprised that I should credit her with knowledge she didn't possess. She hesitated for a moment, reflected for still another, then said, "I really don't know any more than what Gerhard has told you. There's a separate entrance to the room, we don't have to keep it tidy, and our cleaning woman Grazia, who works hard, as you know, isn't keen on extra jobs. Since we gave Ginath the key to his room, I've not been in it, nor have I seen him; after staying here one night, he went off and didn't come back for months."

Having said this, Mrs. Greifenbach began speaking again about their intended journey, throwing in at the same time a sort of complaint. "Your head is so full of our tenant," she said, "that you don't listen to what we are saying."

"Possibly," I answered.

"Don't just say 'possibly,' " she went on, "you must admit that it's absolutely true."

"Heaven forbid that I should contradict you, but please tell me more about Ginath."

"Haven't I already told you, he only stayed one night and went away next morning?"

"And didn't you say, too, that he came back? Very well, when he came back what did he do?"

"Do? He closed the door and stayed in his room."

"What was he doing there?"

"Oh, he may have been drawing the pyramids to scale or writing a third part to *Faust*. How do I know?"

I looked hard at her for some time, but she only laughed and said, "I see you want to turn me into a detective."

"No," I answered, "I don't want you to be a detective. I simply want to hear more about Ginath."

"I've told you," she said. "Since we gave him his key, I've not spoken to him."

"But what did he do when he came back?"

"I'm sure he did one of the things I've mentioned. Which it was, I've not troubled myself to find out."

"Gerda," said Greifenbach, "just hasn't got that quality women are noted for. She isn't the least bit curious."

Gerda tapped her long, slender fingers on his hairy hands, saying, "*You* have enough of that quality for both of us. So you tell him."

"I?" Greifenbach exclaimed in surprise. "Even I can't tell him about things that never were."

"So you really want me to tell him," said Gerda. "Wasn't it you who said Dr. Ginath had created a girl for himself?"

Greifenbach laughed a long and happy laugh. "Do you know what Gerda's referring to? She's thinking of the legend about the lonely poet—I've forgotten his name—who was said to have created a woman to serve his needs. Are you familiar with that legend?"

"It was Rabbi Solomon Ibn Gabirol," I said, "and if you are interested, this is how the story ends. News of the affair spread about until it reached the king, who gave orders for the woman to be brought before him. The king saw her and fell in love with her, but she ignored him. They went and brought Rabbi Solomon Ibn Gabirol. When he came he showed the king that she was not a real creature, only segments of wood made up into the likeness of a woman. But what has this legend to do with Dr. Ginath?"

Mrs. Greifenbach said, "One night, Gerhard and I were sitting together reading Goethe when we heard a voice coming from Ginath's room. We knew that Ginath was back from his travels and that he was in there reading. We began our own reading again, and again the voice came through. Gerhard put his book down and said, 'That's a woman's voice.' But it wasn't only the idea of Ginath bringing a woman to his room that surprised us; it was the language she spoke, some strange tongue we had never heard before. Gerhard whispered to me, 'Ginath must have created a girl for himself, and there she is talking to him in her own language.' My dear, that's all I can tell you about Ginath. If you want to know more, ask Gerhard. He loves to make conjectures and treat them as proven facts."

Greifenbach, who had made a hobby of philology, began to speak of the mysteries of language and all the new discoveries in that field. I added something of what I had learned from the literature of the Kabbalah, which in this matter has anticipated academic scholarship. Mrs. Greifenbach interrupted us by saying, "The woman sang, too, in a strange language we knew nothing about. Judging by her voice, I'd say she was sad and bitter. Gerhard, where have you hidden the present our tenant gave you the morning after our anniversary?—What a pity you weren't there, my dear. Our wedding, you know, was a very simple affair, but we made up for it with our party ten years after.—Don't be lazy, Gerhard; get up and show him what Ginath gave you."

Greifenbach got up, opened an iron box, and took out two parched brown leaves that resembled leaves of old tobacco. He set them before me with pride and watched for my reaction. From the look on his face it was clear that he believed he was exhibiting a rare possession. I glanced at the leaves for a moment and then asked what they were.

"Look again," he said. I looked again but could see nothing except certain strange lines and markings which might be taken, if one were so inclined, for letters of a secret code.

"What is all this?" I insisted.

Greifenbach answered, "I know only what Ginath told me, and what he said was that they are talismans. What kind of talismans he didn't say, but he told me that he has a collection of such things, and these leaves are duplicates and come from a far-off country. It's a pity they have no power against squatters."

"Perhaps," said Gerda, "those that Ginath kept for himself do have that power."

Greifenbach lit his pipe and sat silent, as if preoccupied with his own thoughts. After a while he knocked out the ash and took a cigarette. He lit up and went on, "You see, whatever we find to talk about leads us back to our worries about the house. As for the squatters, it's even possible that right is on their side. A young fellow, let us say, comes back after the war. He needs a roof over his head and can't find one. What's he to do but break in somewhere? Let me tell you something. One Saturday evening I was standing at a bus stop. The bus was full up and passengers were still pressing in. The driver sounded his horn and drove off. All the people left behind stood about miserably as they waited for a second bus. But, of course, it never came; the more passengers there are, the fewer the buses, as is always the case in Jerusalem. A couple were standing together, a young fellow and a girl. The girl was looking at him with passionate longing. 'Günther,' she said, 'it's over a year since we were married and we've still not spent a single night alone together.' The fellow squeezed his young wife's hand, sucked his lips in and was silent with grief and anger. Günther and his wife haven't found a home for themselves. They live apart, wherever they happen to be. The landlords make difficulties about their visiting one another, hoping that they will get tired of their rooms and leave them, because meanwhile the number of people wanting apartments has increased and the number of rooms available has become less, and if they leave, the landlords can raise the rent. They meet each other in cafés and amusement places and separate to go back to their rooms at the opposite ends of the town, all because they have no place where they can live together. So now you know why we are so scared about our home. In fact, we got into such a state that one night Gerda woke me up because she thought someone was walking on the roof."

"You are always telling tales about me," said Mrs. Greifenbach. "Why don't you tell him what *you* said?"

"I said nothing. I don't remember saying anything."

"Do you want me to remind you?" said Gerda.

Gerhard laughed heartily. "And if I don't want you to, does that mean you won't tell him?"

"If it weren't so funny," said Gerda, "I wouldn't repeat it. Do you know what this master mind had to say? He said, in these very words, 'It must be the girl Ginath created, taking a stroll on the roof.' "

Greifenbach laid down his cigarette, took up his pipe again, and remarked to me, "Do you really believe I said that?"

"Who wouldn't believe a lovely girl like Gerda?"

Mrs. Greifenbach laughed. "A lovely

girl, indeed," she said, "whose wedding canopy has been pressing on her head for ten years now!"

"Have you two really been married for ten years?"

"Those leaves," said Gerda, "which Ginath gave to Gerhard were his present on our tenth anniversary. If they came into just anybody's hands he'd probably break them up as tobacco for his pipe. He wouldn't know there was magic in them. To tell the truth, we wouldn't have known either if we hadn't heard it from Ginath; and we believe him, because he's quite without guile. Well, tomorrow we start on our travels, and I don't know whether I should feel glad or sorry."

Without thinking about it much, I said to Gerda, "You've no need to feel sorry. I'll take it upon me to keep an eye on your house, and if I think it necessary, I'll stay here for two or three nights."

The Greifenbachs were delighted at this offer. "Now we can travel with an easy mind," they said.

"Surely you don't have to thank me," I added. "Really, it's I who ought to thank you; your house is a wonderful place for sleep, as I learned on curfew nights."

My remark brought back to mind that troubled time, when people who went into the city could not get home again because the Mandate government had suddenly proclaimed a curfew. Anyone out on the street who lived away from the center and couldn't find shelter in town would be taken by the police and locked up in jail for the night. His family, not knowing where he had disappeared to, would be worried to death. And this had led to other oppressive decrees against us, decrees which at the time seemed to be in the very nature of life in this country. So we talked on about the curfew nights. Yet, evil and oppressive as they were, some little good came of them. People were obliged to stay at home and as a result gave thought to their wives and children, which they had not been accustomed to doing when they spent their evenings at assemblies, councils, meetings and the like, all of which estrange a man from himself and, needless to say, from his family. You might even say that public affairs benefited; with fewer meetings and debates things worked out in their own way, and in spite of all turned out for the best. Another positive result of the curfew nights was that many bachelors, compelled to stay indoors, came to know the daughters of the house and ended up marrying them.

So we sat and talked, the Greifenbachs and I, until I said it was time for me to go. Greifenbach gave me the key of the house and showed me all its entrances and exits. Soon afterwards I parted from him and his wife and went on my way.

II

One day at sunset I went out to get myself some bread and olives. My wife and children had gone away to Gederah, and I was left to provide for myself. Carrying my bread and olives, I strolled about among the shops. I had no desire to go home, since no one was there and there was nothing I especially wished to do at the day's end. Walking on aimlessly, letting my feet carry me where they wished, I found I had come to the valley where the Greifenbach's house stood. In the stillness that fills the valleys of Jerusalem at sunset all manner of blessings abide. It is as if the valleys were cut off from the settled land around them; as if they contained in their depths the whole world. And this valley especially is ringed with a crown of trees through which beneficent vapors flow, keeping it free from the taint of malign airs. I said to myself, Since I am here, I shall go and see how things stand at the Greifenbachs' house; and since I have the key in my pocket, I may as well go inside.

I went in, put on the light, and walked about from room to room. The four pleasant rooms and their equally agreeable contents were all in good order, as if the mistress of the house had just given them her attention. Yet a month had already passed since the Greifenbachs left home. Truly, when a house has a good mistress it remains well kept even though she is far away.

Just then I was neither hungry nor thirsty, only tired. I put out all the lights, opened the window, and sat down to rest. Out of the secret places of the night, silence came and wrapped itself around me until I could see and touch the tranquillity. I made up my mind to spend the night there and so keep my promise to the Greifenbachs. I rose from my seat and lit the table lamp. Then I picked up a book to read in bed by a lamp already at the bedside, glad that I would not need to shift any article in someone else's house. Actually, so long as I held the key, I had the right to regard myself as in my own home; but the sense of strangeness we feel on such occasions makes us forget our privileges.

I sat in Greifenbach's chair and reflected. Just now, while I am staying in their house, perhaps they are looking in vain for a place to spend the night; or if they have found one, it is not the kind they are accustomed to. Why should they have left their beautifully furnished home to wander about in foreign parts? What reason, indeed, have all those who leave their homes and drift from place to place? Is it a first law of our experience or a mocking illusion that, as the ancient proverb has it, "Your happiness is where you are not"?

I took off my shoes, undressed, picked up my book, put out the table lamp and lit the one by the bed. I lay down and opened the book. I could feel myself dozing off, while an idea of sorts seemed to be thinking itself out on its own. Strange, I thought, that I, who on other nights can't get to sleep even after midnight, should now feel suddenly drowsy before the night has properly set in. I put the book down, switched off the light, turned to face the wall and closed my eyes. I told myself in silent speech: Here in this house, where not a soul in the world knows of your presence, you can sleep as long as you like and no one will come to seek you.

All around me was stillness and repose, such as one finds in the valleys of Jerusalem, which the good Lord hid away for lovers of tranquillity. The Greifenbachs had good reason to be concerned for their home: if any squatter were to break in, no one hereabouts would be aware of it. Little by little the run of my thoughts came to a halt, until nothing remained but the dim sensation that all my limbs were locked in sleep.

Suddenly I heard a sound of scratching and awoke. Since I had put my bread and olives away in a tin box, I was not afraid that mice might get at them; but I was afraid that mice might damage the carpet, the clothes or books, or those leaves that Ginath had given to Greifenbach. I pricked up my ears and realized that the sound was not made by a mouse, but by a man who was fumbling at the outside door. If it's not a housebreaker, I thought, then it must be Dr. Ginath, who has come home and is trying the wrong door. I'll open up for him, and so I'll see him face to face.

I got out of bed and opened the door. Someone was outside, groping for the bell. I pressed the switch, put on the light, and then . . . words failed me. After all, I had not told a soul that I would be spending the night at the Greifenbachs'—indeed, I myself hadn't known that I would be here—how then could Gabriel Gamzu have known my whereabouts?

"Is it you, Mr. Gamzu?" I called. "Wait a moment while I put on some clothes."

I went back and dressed, wondering why this visitor was here. He was not acquainted with either the owner of the house or his wife. Greifenbach was not looking for books in Hebrew, even less for manuscripts and first editions. The little Hebrew he knew had been learned with difficulty. Although he prided himself on his sound knowledge of the language and its grammar, all this amounted to was some biblical grammar he had studied in Gesenius' textbook on the structure of Hebrew. His wife managed better than he, for although her grammar was an amateur affair and she knew nothing of Gesenius, she could get on in Hebrew with her cleaning woman Grazia, and with the street traders too. All the same, Hebrew books were none of her concern. So the question still stood, what had brought Gamzu here? I had to conclude that he was here on my account. Gamzu knew that he was always welcome, to me as to all his friends and acquaintances, because he was a scholar, had seen the world, had voyaged to distant lands, and reached places where no traveler had been before. From these far-off parts he had brought back poems by authors about whom nothing was known and manuscripts and first editions of whose very existence we had been ignorant. But now he no longer traveled at all; he stayed at home with his wife. This man, so used to making journeys, had become in his prime the attendant of a sick wife who, it was said, had been bedridden since their wedding night. Whether or not the story was true, it was certainly a fact that he had a sick wife at home, that there was no earthly cure for her, and that her husband had to nurse her, wash her, feed her and attend to her every need. Nor was she grateful for his self-sacrifice, but would beat him and bite him and tear his clothes. Because of this he went about his business at night, being ashamed to show himself in the street by day with torn clothing and bruised face. Now he had come to me. And why had he come? He had saved twelve pounds to purchase a place for his wife in a nursing home; he was afraid to carry the money about on him in case he should spend it, and so he had left it with me. On the day he did so I had gone on a trip to the Dead Sea region and left the money behind at home. Thieves had broken in and robbed my house and taken Gamzu's money. I had sent him a message not to worry about it; all the same, he had come to hear from me directly whether I was really prepared to repay him what had been stolen. And since he had not been able to find me at home, he had come to see me here. This was my conjecture. I was later to see that it was wrong; Gamzu had not come on account of the money, but for another reason.

III

Having put on some clothes, I returned to Gamzu and said, "You've come for your money?"

He gazed at me woefully with an uncertain look in his eyes, imploring in a broken voice, "Please let me in."

I showed him into the house and offered him a chair. He looked around in all directions and deliberated for a while. At last he stammered out, "My wife." After another pause he added, "I went home and my wife wasn't there."

"So what do you intend to do?" I asked.

"Forgive me," he said, "for suddenly

bursting in on you. Just imagine: I came home after the evening service at the synagogue to get my wife settled for the night and found the bed empty. I went off in search of her. 'Going to the south, turning to the north, turning turning goes the wind, and again to its circuits the wind returns.' Suddenly I found myself in this valley without knowing how I came to be here. I saw a house; I felt drawn to enter it. I knew there was no point in doing this, but I did so just the same. It's good that I found you. Let me sit here for a short while and then I'll go away."

"Pardon me for asking, Mr. Gamzu," I said. "I have heard that your wife is bedridden."

"Bedridden she is," Gamzu replied.

"Then how is it that you found the bed empty? If she can't move, how did she get out of bed and go outside?"

He whispered, "She's a sleepwalker."

I sat for a while without speaking. Then I repeated his words in the form of a question, whispering back, "A sleepwalker?"

"Yes."

I looked at him as a man might who has heard a report and does not know what to make of it. Perceiving this, he said, "Every night when the moon is full, my wife gets up from bed and walks wherever the moon leads her."

I could not keep myself from saying reproachfully, "And don't you lock the door?"

Gamzu smiled slyly. "I lock the door."

"If so," I said, "how can she get out?"

"Even if I hung seven locks upon the door, and locked every one with seven keys, and threw each key into one of the seven seas of the Land of Israel, my wife would find them all and open the door and go walking."

I sat on, saying nothing, and he too sat in silence. At last I said, "Since when have you known that she is in that condition? I mean, that she's a sleepwalker?"

He clutched his forehead, dug his thumbs into his temples, and said, "Since when have I known that she is a sleepwalker? I have known since the day I met her."

I was silent again, but not for long. "Nevertheless," I said, "this did not keep you from marrying her."

He took off his hat, brought out a small skullcap and put it on, paused, and asked, "What were you saying?"

I repeated my words.

He smiled and said, "Nevertheless it did not prevent me from marrying her. On the contrary, when I saw her for the first time poised on a rock at the top of a mountain which not every man could climb, with the moon lighting up her face while she sang, *'Yiddal, yiddal, yiddal, vah, pah, mah,'* I said to myself, If she is not one of the angels of the Divine Presence who have union with the angels of the Divine Being, she must be one of the twelve constellations of the Zodiac, and none other than the constellation Virgo. I went to her father's home and said, 'I wish to marry your daughter.' He answered me, 'My son, you know of Gemulah's condition and yet you wish to marry her?' I said, 'The All-Merciful will be merciful to us.' He looked up to the sky, addressing the Holy One, 'Master of the World, if this man who comes from afar is filled with mercy towards her, how much more so will you, who are so near, show mercy to us.' Next day he called me and said, 'Come with me.' I went with him until we reached a mountain, the highest of the range of steep mountains that raised themselves up to heaven. I climbed with him, leaping with him from crag to crag, until he stood by a perpendicular rock. He looked about him in all directions. When he knew that no one could see us, he bent down and dug beneath the rock and lifted one stone. A cave opened up and he went inside. When he came out, he was holding an earthenware jar. 'Let us go back,' he said. On the way back, he opened the jar and showed me a bundle of dry leaves unlike any I had ever seen; and on them were the strange characters of a script unlike any that I knew; and the color of the characters, that is, the color of the ink in which they were written, was not like any color we know. At first sight I should have said that the scribe had mixed gold, azure and purple with all the primary colors of the rainbow and written with them. But as I stood gazing, the colors altered before my eyes and changed into the tints of seaweeds drawn from the depths, such weeds as Dr. Rechnitz drew up from the sea near Jaffa. Then again, they were like the silver strands we observe on the moon. I stared at the leaves, at the characters, at Gemulah's father. At that moment he seemed as if transported to another world. And then it became increasingly clear that what at first sight had seemed an illusion was the truth itself. If you ask me what it all meant, I can give you no answer. For my part it was clear, crystal clear, even though I wonder now how I am able to say this. And if I have no words to describe the experience, yet it was more distinct than anything one can explain in words. At that moment I had neither speech nor power to ask any question; and the cause of this was not the leaves or the characters on them, but the ecstatic state of Gemulah's father. As for the characters, all the colors which I had seen before faded later and underwent a complete change, but I have no clear knowledge of how the characters came to shed their colors and when this change came about. As I stood marveling, Gemulah's father replaced the leaves in the jar and spoke to me simply, with these words: 'They are plants of the earth, and they have been given power to influence the upper air.'

"A year later, on the night before our wedding, he said, 'You will remember those plants which I showed you on the mountain. You know what they are.' He stooped and whispered in my ear, 'There is a magic in them; what kind of magic I do not know. I do know that it has power to influence the atmosphere that surrounds the moon, and the moon itself. I now give you all these plants, and as long as they remain in your keeping you may control Gemulah's steps so that she will not go astray. Up to now, I have not taken them from the place where they were concealed. And why? Because, so long as Gemulah is calm and sheltered and wrapped up in her own wholeness, they serve no purpose. Now that the time has come for love and union with her husband, when she must draw upon her husband's strength, she is subject to a different influence and another mode of being. So, when the nights of the full moon come, take these plants and set them in the window facing the door, and hide them so that no man will notice them, and I assure you that if Gemulah leaves the house she will return to you before the moon returns to her proper sphere.' "

I said to Gamzu, "Tonight you forgot to follow all your father-in-law's instructions."

"I did not forget."

"Well then, how did it happen?"

Gamzu spread out his two empty hands and said, as if to himself, "Gabriel, your magic has gone."

"You mean it has lost its power over her?"

"Not at all," he answered. "It has gone from me."

"Has your wife rooted it out?" I asked.

"Not at all," he said. "I am the cause. I sold it. By mistake, I sold it. There was a gathering of scholars here, many scholars from all over the world came together in Jerusalem. Some came to my house to buy books and manuscripts. As they turned them over hurriedly, one man rummaging among the books I had set aside and another looking at those which his colleague had taken, in the midst of all this confusion some of the charms got mixed up in a heap of miscellaneous manuscripts and I sold them without knowing to whom. I don't remember, though I should have, for I can remember every manuscript I sold, but not this; and the money I got is the penalty I am paying, twelve pounds, which I left with you to buy Gemulah a place in the home for incurables."

Gamzu clutched his brow and pressed his temples. Then he rubbed his blind eye with one finger; for Gamzu had a blind eye, and when he was overcome by his thoughts he would rub it until it turned as red as healthy flesh. He wiped his finger and looked across at me as if he wanted me to say something. What can I say to him, I thought; I shall say nothing. So I sat facing him in silence. Again he spoke.

"Sometimes I think that Gemulah knows the man who bought it; that he is the Hacham from Jerusalem who appeared in her region when I was away in Vienna. And for this I have two pieces of evidence. First, all that same day she sang her *yiddal, yiddal, yiddal* song, a thing she had never done all the time she was here. Secondly, she began to speak the language they use in her parts, a thing she had never done since she left her country. I am sure that the man who bought the talismans brought this about; when she saw him she remembered the times when she lived in her own region and that same man had been a visitor. But then he was dressed like a Jerusalem sage; for anyone who visits those parts dresses that way so that the holiness of the city may protect him from the Gentiles."

Again Gamzu rubbed his blind eye, which seemed to be smiling between his fingers, as if mocking his distress, as if winking for me to laugh at this man who had sold an article on which his life and that of his wife depended. But I did not feel like deriding him. Rather, I was sorry for him. The thought suddenly came into my head that Dr. Ginath was the man who had acquired Gamzu's talismans; for had I not heard from Greifenbach that Ginath had a collection of magic articles and had given him some duplicates? I asked Gamzu, "About those charms, what material are they written on? Is it paper or parchment?"

Gamzu answered, "Neither paper nor parchment nor vellum; as I told you before, the charms are inscribed on leaves."

I correlated the times and saw that it was impossible for Ginath to have been the purchaser; indeed, that scholars' convention had taken place after the tenth anniversary of the Greifenbachs' marriage. And even if it had taken place before, was it conceivable that a European like Ginath would dress himself up as a Jerusalem sage, and be able to pass himself off as such?

Gamzu had read much, and studied much, and served many scholars; he had traveled through half the world. Truly there was not a community of Jews in which Gamzu had not been. Besides manuscripts and early printed books, he had brought back from every place he had been traditional tales and customs, wise men's sayings and proverbs, and stories of travelers. Whatever occurred, he would tell of similar occurrences as though recent events took place merely as the occasion for him to recall earlier ones; or he would pick up a word from those being spoken, and speak on it. Even now, he passed on from his immediate distress over the charms to an account of the way in which charms operate.

There sat Gamzu and rolled himself a cigarette and talked about the magic properties of charms, whose virtue is superior to that of drugs; for the drugs we find mentioned in ancient books cannot for the most part be relied on, since the ways both of nature and of man have changed and with these changes the effect of the drugs too has altered. But charms have undergone no change and still retain their first nature and condition, because they are yoked together with the stars, and the stars remain just as they were on the day when they were first hung in the firmament. And their influence is observed on all creatures, and especially on man; for according to the star of his nativity, such is a man's character and his fate. As it is said in the Talmud, "All depends upon one's star," and it is said, "Our star makes us wise, or makes us rich." The maladies of man likewise depend upon the stars, for the Holy One, blessed be He, gave the stars their power to work upon the lower orders of creation, whether for good or ill. The earth too is altered according to the stars, as Ibn Ezra put it in his commentary on Exodus, "For the regions of the earth change according to whatever star is above them"; and he also wrote, "And those who have the wisdom of the stars know this."

Yet we must not attribute to the stars in themselves any power or purpose, for all their power and purpose stems from that of their Maker and Creator, who keeps them employed. And what need, if one can so phrase it, has the Holy One of stars, except that, as Proverbs says, "The Lord hath made everything for His own sake." *L'ma-anehu.* This last word should be derived from *ma-aneh,* meaning song and praise, as in the verse, "sing out—*anu*—to the Lord in praise." And this is just what David said in his psalm: "The heavens declare the glory of God and the firmament declares His handiwork." All that the Holy One created was made for the sake of Israel, that they might know how to give honor to the Holy One and how to recount His praise, and the prophecy might be fulfilled, "This people that I have created, they will declare My praise." And the stars, like the angels, are half of them male and half of them female, in heaven as it is on earth, male and female; even so are the letters of the word "heaven" equal numerically to those of "male and female." And this being so, they yearn for each other, in heaven as on earth; and thus the way a man and woman are drawn each to the other is in accordance with their stars. What, then, gave the children of Benjamin such assurance, when they seized in the vineyards, each man a wife from the daughters of Shiloh? Were they not apprehensive that they might be unsuitably matched? But they knew that in the time to come the Temple would be built on the heights of their land, and that all Israel would have a share in it. For this very reason the color of the flag of Benjamin resembles the colors of all the rest of the tribes, and accordingly they were sure that the women they seized were their destined mates.

IV

As often happens with ideas, which you may develop as far as you wish or break away from at any time you please, so with Gamzu's account of the workings of charms and the functioning of stars: he went on until he chose to stop, and then began to tell me of his travels.

"If you wish to see Jews from the days of the Mishnah," said Gamzu, "go to the city of Amadia. Forty families of Israel live there, all God-fearing and true to the faith. They rise each morning to say their prayers; but they do not know how to pray, except for the verse 'Hear O Israel' and the response 'Amen.' They do not put on *Tefillin,* save for the rabbi and one old man. At times of prayer they sit in silence, and when the prayer leader says the blessings, they devoutly reply, 'Amen.' When the service brings them to the recital of 'Hear O Israel,' they shiver and quake, and recite it throughout in fear and dread, with trembling and terror, like men whose time has come to sacrifice their souls for God. And in the neighborhood of Amadia, shepherds move about, men of great stature with long hair; they sleep with their herds in clefts of the rocks, and do not know the laws of the Torah, not the least iota, and do not come to pray even on Rosh ha-Shanah. To them and to those like them that passage in the Mishnah refers: 'The case of a person who was passing behind the synagogue and happened to hear the sound of the Shofar.' Once a year a Hacham from Babylon comes to circumcise the boys who were born during that year." "Is your wife of this people?" I asked him.

"My wife is not one of them. My wife is from another region, from the mountains. At first, her ancestors were settled beside the good springs, where the pasture was also good. But their neighbors made war on them, and they retaliated and drove them back. Because of their great might some of their troops advanced into the lands of the Gentiles, for they misconceived the text: 'And to Gad he said, Blessed be he who enlarges Gad; he dwells as a lioness, and tears the arm, yea, the crown of the head.' For they have a tradition that they are of the tribe of Gad, but they did not know that the blessing refers only to the time when they lived in the Land of Israel, not to their exile in the lands of other peoples. All the Gentiles gathered together against them and defeated them and killed many and captured many as slaves. Those who were left took to the high mountains and settled there. They remain there still, and have no fear of the Gentiles; but once every few years collectors come to gather taxes from them. Those who are so disposed pay them, the others take up their weapons and hide in the mountains until the tax collectors have gone. Sometimes it happens that a man who has fled does not return, because he has been made a prey of the eagles who attack and tear him with their talons. And all this time they have looked forward to their return to the Land of Israel, as was promised them by God through Moses our Teacher, peace upon him, who said that they would all return, according to the text: 'Gad, a troop shall overcome him, but he shall overcome at the last.' All his troops shall regain their inheritance, which they took up beyond the Jordan, and no man of them shall be missing. Moreover they will come back with great possessions, as is written in the Aramaic Targum: 'And with ample riches they shall return to their land.' "

Gamzu went on to relate how when he first came upon them they were dejected, with many sick at heart because of their long exile and long-deferred hope. But Gevariah ben Ge'uel, his father-in-law, is remembered for good, for he read to them from the Midrash and the Jerusalem Targum, which they have in its complete text, and which he translated into their language, and so gave them new heart, till they began to remember all the promises and assurances given us by the Holy One concerning the time of the Messiah.

Gamzu continued, "Gevariah ben Ge'uel, my father-in-law, was a mighty man. His face was the face of a lion, his strength was that of a bull, and he was light-footed as an eagle in flight. High praises of God were in his mouth and a two-edged sword in his hand. He led his people in prayer, and he forged their weapons of war. He also healed the sick, wrote charms, and taught betrothed maidens the marriage dances and songs. For this he would take no fee; all his works were done for the sake of heaven. And Gemulah his daughter was his mainstay. She was accomplished in all their songs, those that they had once sung when they dwelt by the springs and also those of the mountains.

"If you had seen my father-in-law Gevariah when he stood on the peak of a rock, a sky-blue turban on his head, his complexion and beard set off by his flowing hair, his dark eyes shining like two suns, his feet bare and the color of gold, his big toes striking the towering rock while he raised a song from the depths as he led his troops onward and Gemulah his daughter sang at full pitch and between twenty-two and twenty-seven maidens danced, all of them beautiful and high born, then you would have seen a likeness of the festive days of ancient Israel, when the daughters of Israel went out to dance in the vineyards."

And how did Gamzu come to their land? "I had gone in search of manuscripts. I sailed the sea routes and walked for forty days in the wilderness. A sandstorm arose. But I failed to lay my head to the ground after the manner of those who cross the desert, who cover their heads when a sandstorm strikes, and when the storm has blown over stand up unhurt. The sand got into my eyes and blinded them; there was darkness all around me. The leader of the caravan saw my distress, and after some days brought me to a settled region, and to the house of a certain man, saying, 'He is of your people.' That man was Gevariah ben Ge'uel. He prepared charms and medicines for me, and his daughter Gemulah tended me as I lay sick.

"Gemulah was then about twelve years old, and her gracious bearing and lovely voice were the most beautiful things in the world. Even when she spoke of commonplace things, saying, for instance, 'Your bandage has slipped, Gabriel,' or 'Look down while I put ointment in your eye,' my spirit rejoiced as if odes had been chanted to me. And when she sang, her voice stirred the heart like that of the bird Grofith, whose song is sweeter than that of any creature on earth. At first I had difficulty in understanding their speech, even when they spoke to me in the Holy Tongue, because their Hebrew has more full vowels and fewer elided syllables than ours and they pronounce words differently. Their speech rhythms are strange, too, so that I was unable to distinguish between their Hebrew and the language they spoke among themselves, a language that no outsider has heard. Gemulah and her father had yet another language. Often I would find them sitting in the twilight, a white kid lying in Gemulah's lap and a bird hovering over the old man's head, while they conversed, sometimes in a leisurely way and sometimes in haste, sometimes cheerfully and sometimes with an expression of fear. I would listen to them but not understand a word, until Gemulah revealed to me that this was an invented language which they had made up for their own pastime. Since the day Gemulah was torn from her native soil all that speech has gone from her lips, nor does she express herself in any song, save on the nights when the moon is full and she takes her walks, singing as she goes. But on the day when I sold the magic text, she spoke in that language and let her lovely voice be heard in song. And in the evening she said, 'I want to eat *kavanim.*' This is a kind of flat cake which they bake on live coals. Now I must go and see if my wife has come back."

Gamzu took off his skullcap, placed his hat on his head, and stood up. But he had not got as far as the door when he

turned back and began to pace about the room, his arms folded behind him, the fingers of his left hand fluttering nervously. After a little while he said, "I can't understand why I came here, especially since I saw no light and didn't know you were in the house; but certainly there is some reason for my coming, and even if I don't know the reason, that doesn't remove it. Who lives here?"

"A certain Dr. Greifenbach," I said.

"And where is he?"

"He has gone abroad with his wife. Do you know them?"

"I do not know them," said Gamzu. "Is Greifenbach a doctor of medicine?"

"He is a doctor who has left his profession. Why do you ask?"

"Apart from these people, who else is here?"

"You and I. Before they went on their travels, I promised the Greifenbachs that I would keep an eye on their house. They were worried about squatters, since there are so many of them now among the soldiers back from the war. Tonight I have kept my promise and come to stay here."

Gamzu pricked up his ears. "And is no one else lodging in the house?"

"There is someone else," I said, "who is not at home. Why do you ask?"

Gamzu blushed and said nothing. After a while he asked again, "What is the name of that lodger?"

I told him.

"Can he be the famous Dr. Ginath?" said Gamzu.

"Do you know him?"

"I don't know him, though I have heard of his books. But I haven't read them. I don't look at books that are less than four hundred years old."

"Ginath's books," I replied, "go back four thousand years and more."

Gamzu smiled. "I am looking at the pot and not what is in it."

Smiling in turn, I said, "Well, then, in another four hundred years you'll be looking at Ginath's books."

"If in my third or fourth incarnation I am still interested in books," said Gamzu, "it's quite possible that I shall."

"Two or three incarnations," I replied, "are all a man goes through, according to the words of Scripture: 'And it is said, unto three transgressions of Israel, yea, four, I shall not reverse it.' No man of Israel passes through this world more than two or three times, unless he is obliged to fulfill some precept he has omitted from the six hundred and thirteen in the Torah; in which case he may even go through a thousand cycles of life, with reference to which it is said: 'He commanded it unto the thousandth generation.' But otherwise this is not so—yet you speak of a fourth incarnation."

"It was a slip on my part," said Gamzu. "You know my opinion, that no Jew is capable of saying anything for which the Bible gives no support, and especially that which is contrary to the plain meaning of the text. And do not answer me with those Bible critics who turn the words of the living God upside down. This they have learned from Gentile scholars, but in the depths of their heart they know that no text of Scripture has any other meaning than that which has been passed down to us by the Masorah. Yes, and the Hasidic leaders, they too twist the words of the Holy Writ; but the true *zaddikim,* because, as their name signifies, they are righteous, and study the Torah for its own sake, with the intention of serving heaven, these only have the right to read the Law beyond the text. But as for the Bible critics who have not the merit of studying the Torah for its own sake, their teaching is perverted in accordance with the emptiness of their own spirit. So you say that Ginath lodges here. Do you know him?"

"I do not know him," I said, "and I doubt if I shall get to know him. He hides away from people, and even the owners of the house do not see him."

"It is a good sign when people don't know a scholar. I like scholars who don't show up in every place and make themselves into a public spectacle. Let me tell you something. I once came to London and informed a certain scholar there that I had brought manuscripts with me. He got busy and came along with an escort of two, a journalist and a photographer. He took all the material I showed him and sat himself down in the pose of a great savant looking at his books, while the photographer stood there taking pictures. Two or three days later, someone showed me a newspaper. I looked at it and saw a face framed by books set between eulogies of that scholar, who, it seemed, had discovered precious works that were quite unknown until he brought them to light. What do you think of that?"

I said to Gamzu, "I think as you do."

Gamzu looked at me with an expression of annoyance. "You don't know what I think, so why say you think as I do?"

"Very well. I don't think as you do."

"Are you making fun of me?" he asked.

"Not of you," I answered, "but of that scholar, and of those like him, who waste their powers on externals to prop up their reputation. Whereas if they concentrated on their work, possibly they would become more famous."

"They would not become more famous."

"If so, they are right in behaving as they do."

"I must go," said Gamzu.

It was near midnight when he left, and I walked with him part of the way. The moon was full and the entire city glistened like the moon. If you have ever seen such a night, you will not find it strange that somnambulists leave their beds to go out and wander with the moon. When we reached the Georgian Quarter at the Damascus Gate I parted from Gamzu, expressing the hope that he would find his wife. He took out a handkerchief, wiped his eyes, and said, "God willing."

"If you want to get in touch with me," I said, "you will find me at my home. I mean to go back in the morning."

V

I returned to the Greifenbachs' house and went back to bed. Sleep came quickly, and I knew nothing until I was roused by the sound of train wheels. The train reached Garmisch and stopped there. The door of the compartment opened and their was a view of high mountains and streams; I could hear a voice singing *yiddal, yiddal, yiddal, vah, pah, mah.* I was drawn by the voice and wanted to follow it. The door was shut against me. The moon came out and covered me with her light. I smiled at her with one eye and she smiled back with a grin that covered all her face.

But there was no train. I was in bed at the Greifenbachs'. I turned over to one side and pulled the blanket over my eyes, because the moon was shining on my face. I was thinking of how the world has shut itself in so that none of us can go where he wishes, except for the moon, that wanders over all the earth, singing *yiddal, yiddal, yiddal, vah, pah, mah.*

After lunching at a restaurant in town, I had gone home to get on with my work. But when I broke off to make myself some coffee, I found there was not a drop of water in the tap. I went up to the roof and inspected the water tanks. They had become overheated in the sun and the water at the bottom of the tanks was barely an inch deep. Jerusalem, a dry place, was at that time badly in need of water. I left my work behind and went over to the Greifenbachs', for their house has a cistern, such as you find in the older houses of Jerusalem that were built when people drank rain water.

They had lived through many lives, the houses of Jerusalem. There is not one without a long story to it, especially the first ones to be built outside the walls. The Greifenbachs' house was no exception.

About seventy years ago, there came to the land a grandee of the grandees of Gallipoli, Signor Gamaliel Giron, to spend the close of his life in the Holy City. He found no house to suit his needs, for the Jewish population was confined to the old courtyards within the walls, and every courtyard was inhabited by many families, and each family was a large one. So he bought himself two thousand square cubits of land outside the city, below the Damascus Gate, and built there a spacious house and planted a garden. And because the house was a long way from the populated area, with no synagogue in the neighborhood, he set apart one room as a private chapel and hired men to come and make up a Minyan for prayer. On his demise he bequeathed the house to the charitable society *Gomlei Hasadim*. In time those in charge of the society's finances became pressed for money to pay the army tax, and mortgaged the house. The house remained under a mortgage for some years, they were unable to redeem it, and accordingly it was sold by those who had advanced the loan.

The house was sold to a German named Gotthold Gänseklein, who was head of the sect of Guardians, who had seceded from the sect of the *Gemeinschaft der Gerechten,* founded in the city of Gerlitz by Gottfried Greilich. Gänseklein, his wife and his mother-in-law lived in this house, and here he would hold prayer meetings and preach concerning the three true guards for redeeming the body and extending the limits of the soul. One night a quarrel occurred between Gänseklein's wife and her mother. The wife bit her mother's nose in order to disgrace her before the husband. People came to hear of this affair and Gänseklein was obliged to quit the country for shame.

Three Georgian brothers-in-law, who supported themselves by manufacturing Gouda cheese, now bought the house and made their cheese there. The Great War broke out, and Gamal Pasha expelled them from the country, because they were suspected of Zionism, the Star of David having been found stamped upon the cheese. After the war the Council of Delegates rented the house for their fellow member Georg Gnadenbrod. The house was repaired, the refuse heap cleared away, the garden replanted and the estate fenced in. Mr. Gnadenbrod had scarcely taken possession when his wife, Gnendlein, put her foot down and said that she did not wish to live in Jerusalem. They returned to Glasgow and the house was made into business offices. Then came the earthquake, which damaged the building and weakened the roof. For some years the house stood untenanted until Gerhard Greifenbach rented it and repaired it and decorated it and installed electric lighting and plumbing and other modern improvements. He and his wife had lived there until they felt a longing to go abroad and rest a while from the strain of life in our country, and I was asked to keep an eye on the house lest squatters break in and take possession. And now I was spending two nights there.

Cut off from the settled area, the house stood alone in the valley, surrounded by its garden gleaming in the light of the moon. And in that moonlight the garden and all that was in it, every tree, every shrub, seemed detached and unconcerned with its neighbor's affairs. Only the moon made no distinctions and shone impartially on all.

I stood at the window and looked out at the garden. Every tree, every shrub slept its deep sleep; but among the trees movements could be heard. If these were not the footsteps of Ginath returned from his journey, perhaps they were Gabriel Gamzu's. When I had gone along with him on the previous night I had asked him to let me know how his wife was; he had come back, then, to tell me. Or perhaps it was not Gamzu; after all, it could be anybody.

But that pure, perfect moonlight did not deceive me. It was none other than Gamzu walking this way. I went and opened the door and showed him into the room. Gamzu picked a chair and sat down. He took out some paper and rolled himself a cigarette. He put the cigarette to his lips, lit it and sat there smoking, paying no attention to me as I waited to hear if he had found his wife. I was annoyed, and in my annoyance said nothing.

"You don't ask me about my wife," said Gamzu.

"If you've anything to tell me, let me hear."

"Indeed I have something to tell you. Isn't there an ashtray?"

I went and brought him an ashtray. He groped about to deposit the stub of his cigarette. Then he looked at me with his healthy eye, wiped his ailing eye, rubbed his palm against his beard, licked his palm with the tip of his tongue, and remarked, "I thought I had burnt myself with my cigarette, but now I see that I have been bitten by a mosquito. You have mosquitoes in the house."

"Perhaps there is a mosquito here and perhaps there isn't a mosquito here. Who would notice a mosquito when he is honored by the presence of a dear guest like you?"

I do not know how Gamzu took this. What he said was, "I found her! I found her! Found her in bed fast asleep!"

It would be interesting, I thought, to know how Gamzu came to find his wife. But I shall not ask him outright. If he tells me, well and good; if not, I shall do without the information, rather than have him think that I am prying into his affairs. A few moments went by in which he said nothing; it looked as if he had put the whole matter out of his mind. Suddenly he passed his hand over his brow like a man stirring himself from sleep, and proceeded to tell me how he had come home, opened the door and looked into the bedroom without expecting to find anything. All at once he heard a steady breathing. Because he was so preoccupied with his wife, he thought he must be deceiving himself that he could hear her. He went over to the bed and found her lying there. He almost fainted with joy, and but for the reassurance her breathing brought, he would certainly have died there on the spot.

I was too amazed to speak. On the previous evening, I had told him distinctly that I was going back home, that I would not be staying at the Greifenbachs' tonight; so why on earth had he come here? And I was all the more surprised that he had left his wife alone on this moonlit night, after the moon had already shown him her power.

Said Gamzu, "You are surprised that I have left Gemulah alone?"

"Yes, I certainly am surprised."

Gamzu smiled with his live eye, or perhaps with his dead eye, and said, "Even if Gemulah wakes up now, even if she gets out of bed, she will not go walking."

"Have you found the talisman?" I asked.

"No, I haven't."

"If so, how do you come to leave your wife alone? Did the moon give you its personal guarantee that it would let your wife sleep in peace tonight? Seriously, Reb Gabriel, what makes you so confident?"

"I have found a cure."

"You consulted the doctors, did you, and got a prescription?"

"I did not consult the doctors," said Gamzu. "I am not in the habit of going to doctors, for even if they know the the names of all the diseases there are and the names of all the drugs for them, I do not rely on their kind. I put my reliance on one who has drawn his strength from the Torah, for he knows and can find a cure for every part of the body, and needless to say, I rely on him in matters that affect the soul."

"And have you found such a man, and has he provided a cure for Gemulah?"

"The cure was already at hand. When I was studying at the yeshiva of Rabbi Shmuel Rosenberg at Innsdorf, a woman came to the rabbi and told him that a certain youth was lodging in her house, who was sick in mind and moonstruck, so that every month at the new moon he would go through the window and climb along the roofs, endangering himself, for if he were to wake up in the course of his walking it was to be feared that he might fall and be killed. They had already consulted doctors and no remedy had been found. Rabbi Shmuel said to her, 'Take a thick garment, and steep it in cold water until it is well soaked, and leave the garment beside the young man's bed. When he has climbed out of bed and his feet touch the cold garment, the chill will wake him at once and he will get back into bed again.' She did this and he was cured. Tonight I too did this, and I am sure that even if Gemulah should wake and stand up, she would immediately go back to bed."

I sat there, still puzzled. If this was the cure, why hadn't Gamzu made use of it before? Gamzu sensed what I was thinking and said, "You are surprised that I have waited until now."

"I am not surprised. With all your great devotion to charms that are above nature, you paid no attention to the remedies that are in nature itself."

"I can give you two answers. One is that the charms you speak of are also in general to be thought of as medicines. Once, for example, I took sick while I was on a journey, and was cured by means of charms. And when I went to Europe and told the specialists, they said, 'The charms you used are known drugs, which used to be employed in treatment until better and more convenient drugs were found.' As for my waiting until now, heaven caused me to forget the remedy of the great rabbi as a token of respect for him, because I gave up attending his yeshiva and went on to others. And as for my remembering today, it was because the object was at hand. I happened to be mending a tear in my clothes, and as I sat holding the garment I remembered the whole affair. I got up at once and put the article into water, and when it was soaked I spread it out before Gemulah's bed."

"Now," I said, "I am going to ask you a simple question. Was it because you did not find me at home that you came here?"

"I did not go to your home and I did not think of coming here."

"And yet you came."

"I came," said Gamzu, "but not intentionally."

"You see, Reb Gabriel, your heart is truer than your conscious mind, and it sent you here so that you would keep your promise to let me know how your wife is."

"The fact of the matter is this," said Gamzu; "I was at home watching

Gemulah as she slept. I thought to myself, Now that Gemulah is asleep I shall go and pay a call on Amrami. I tested the garment I had left by her bed, soaked it in water again, and went out. As I walked, I reflected on Amrami. He was born in Jerusalem and grew up here. After spending forty or fifty years out of the country, he came back home, with nothing left of all he had acquired in those forty or fifty years, except for a little granddaughter and a few Hebrew books. Thinking of this I began to consider all those others raised in the Land of Israel who had left the country at about that time, rejecting the Land for the sake of a comfortable living abroad. Some of them were successful; some of them grew wealthy. Then came the Great Persecution, which took from them all they had, and back they came again to the Land of Israel. Now they complain and grumble that the country has become estranged from them. While I was thinking of how they complain, and while I gave no thought to their sufferings, I suddenly heard someone screaming. I went in the direction of the noise and saw a girl calling out to a young man: 'Günther, my darling! You're still alive, my darling! The Arab didn't wound you!' What was it all about? A young fellow and a girl were taking a walk in one of the valleys on the outskirts of the city. An Arab came up and began to annoy them. The young man shouted at him to chase him off. The Arab pulled out a knife and threatened the youth. The girl was in a panic because she thought he had been stabbed. In the meantime, I had gone out of my way and found myself down in the valley. I stood and wondered, Why am I here? I had meant to go to Amrami's, and instead, I have come to this house. Can you understand this? I cannot, just as yesterday I could not understand what had brought me here."

I answered, "Have not the rabbis said, 'To the place where a man is summoned, there his feet carry him?' But a man does not always know to what end he is summoned."

"So it is," said Gamzu. "To the place where a man is summoned his feet carry him. Whether he wishes it or not, his feet carry him there. Many have asked me how the hymns of Rabbi Adiel came into my possession. You too have asked me, if not in so many words, most certainly in your thoughts."

"Whether I have asked you or not, you have still not told me how it came about."

"If you wish, I shall tell you."

"If that is your wish, proceed."

Said Gamzu: "I came once to a certain village, and my feet would not allow me to go on from there. I said to myself, Nothing could be so patently foolish as to waste time in this wretched place, where the Jews have little knowledge of the Torah and are stricken with poverty. They can scarcely keep themselves by their work on the soil and by the fruit which they buy from the Gentiles straight off the tree and sell to the dealers in the city. Do you expect to find books among men like these? In the meantime I was overtaken by the Sabbath. I found a bed at the house of a man who packed dried figs and dates, and went with him to the synagogue, a structure of palmwood blackened with age. All the congregation assembled. They took off their shoes and kindled the earthenware lamp; they seated themselves and recited the Song of Songs; they stood and recited the Sabbath psalm and read the daily prayer 'And He is merciful' as on weekdays. And the prayers for the Sabbath were sung to their own melodies with which none of us is familiar, but which make their appeal to everyone who has a Jewish heart in his breast. So it was with their customs, which were handed down by their fathers, who had received them from their forefathers, as far back as the exiles of Jerusalem who were expelled by Nebuchadnezzar, king of Babylon. When he exiled Israel from Jerusalem, he ordered all the millstones in the land of Israel to be removed and loaded on to the shoulders of the young men. The young men went into exile laden with the millstones, and of them Jeremiah said, 'The young men carried a grinding mill,' and it is said, 'He weakened my strength on the way.' But the Presence saw their grief and poured life into the very stones, so that they mounted on high like wings and carried the young men away to a place where there was no oppressor. There the young men set down the millstones, and laid them as foundations for their synagogues, and from those that were left they built the foundations for their homes. And among these young men were some with a great knowledge of the Torah, who were learned in its mysteries and filled with the holy spirit. Many times have I pondered to myself whether their customs were not better received before the Presence than ours. So they set down the stones, and laid them as a foundation for the synagogues, and established a great settlement, virtually a kingdom. But still there was cause for anxiety, lest, heaven forbid, they should perish from the earth, for they had no wives. Then the Presence gave light to their eyes, and they saw maidens coming up from the sea, of whom it is written, 'From Bashan I shall bring them back, I shall bring them from the depths of the sea.' Each man took himself a wife from among them, and they bore sons and daughters, and passed their days and years in delight. So things continued for several generations, until—in their abundance of good—they forgot Jerusalem. And when Ezra wrote to them, 'Go up to Jerusalem,' they did not go, for they said the Presence had given them this place instead of Jersualem. Then there came against them the armed troops of the Gentiles, and went to war with them, and made great destruction among them, and few remained where once there had been many. Those who were left alive turned completely penitent and remembered Jerusalem and recognized, too, that those Gentiles had come against them only that they might be duly punished. Now I shall return to what I began to tell you.

"After the service they went to greet each other with kisses on the shoulder and beard, and wished each other a peaceful Sabbath and left for their homes after this exchange of Sabbath blessings. I went back with my host and dined with him, his two wives and his children all seated on the mat as they ate and drank and sang table hymns which were unfamiliar to me and which I had not come across in any collection. Before sunrise I awoke to the sound of singing, and saw the master of the house seated on his mat as he raised his voice in hymns of praise. I duly washed my hands and listened attentively to these poems which I had never heard in my life, never seen in any book of devotional verse. So moved was I by their sweetness and holiness that it did not occur to me to inquire who was their author nor how they had reached this simple villager. But even had I asked, he would have declined to answer, for in those parts they avoid speaking before they have said their prayers. After he had finished his hymn-singing, we went to the service, their custom being to pray at dawn.

"The entire community was gathered in the synagogue, seated round the four walls, singing psalms. Their way is for one of the congregation to recite a single psalm in a loud voice, word by word; after him, another takes his place, and then another. It is as if each man is given an audition to discover if he is fit to be an emissary of Israel before the Presence;

after finishing the psalm he lowers his voice, realizing that he is not fit for such a mission. When they reached the blessing for the daily renewal of light, the leader of the congregation came down from the dais and stood before the Ark, where he recited the call to prayer and the blessing for light, and then returned to his place. The congregation went on with the regular order of the Service through to the end of the Silent Devotion. For the repetition of the prayer, the leader again took his place before the Ark, while the congregation stood with willing heart, and responded 'Amen' with great devotion. While taking the scroll of the Torah from the Ark, their way is to say 'Happy is the people whose lot is thus' and 'The Lord will reign.' And their scrolls are of deerskin, the writing is in large letters, and they do not allow more than the prescribed seven readers of the weekly portion. To the reading of the Torah the women come, and sit down in the synagogue on each side of the door; and I heard that this was an ancient custom which not even the most righteous or saintly of men had ever opposed. For at the time when the Torah was given to Israel, no evil desire could prevail; and to this day it cannot prevail with those whose thoughts are wholly upon the Torah.

"After the Musaf Service I went home with my host. He seated himself on his mat and began with melodious hymns to the Presence, who had chosen His people Israel and given them the Sabbath day. Next he sang in praise of Israel, the people who had been so honored; and then in praise of the Sabbath, which, being holy, makes all who keep it holy. Afterwards we washed our hands and ate the chief meal of the day. The meal ended, but not the singing of hymns. I asked him about these hymns, about their origin. He said, 'I have them from my father. He was a great scholar and knew all that is in the books.' 'And where do the books come from?' He reached into a recess in the wall and brought out a bundle of writings, containing a great number of awe-inspiring devotional poems. Some were by Rabbi Dosa the son of Rabbi Penuel who originated the hymn *El Adon* and in his great humility did not sign his name to it, except in the fourth line, where he wrote of how the two great angels Knowledge and Understanding, who encircle the majesty of the Holy One, revealed themselves to him; and as he wrote of their works he introduced his name in an acrostic. In similar fashion I identified the poems of Rabbi Adiel, who composed the hymn, 'This people which Thou didst create, Thy holy commandments they shall keep,' and similarly those of other early poets who concealed their names. I broached the question of his selling me his book. He said, 'Even if you gave me an ox I would not sell it.' I asked him for permission to copy two or three of the poems. He said, 'Even if you gave me a sheep I would not let you.' He would not sell his book even in return for an ox, nor let me make copies even for a sheep. I went away despairing and came back to the city. Three days later he came to my home and presented the volume to me as a gift. I offered to pay him what it was worth; he would not agree. I raised the sum, and still he refused. I said, 'Even that amount, it seems, is not equal to the value you set upon it.' He answered, 'God forbid that I should take it. I am giving the book to you for nothing.' 'But why?' I asked. 'What concern is that of yours?' he said. 'You want it, and I am giving it to you.' I said, 'I do not wish to take it without payment. I shall give you what it is worth.' He put his hands behind his back and went away. It was hard for me to take a precious article like this from a poor man. I went to the learned men of the city to seek their advice; as soon as they saw me coming they hastened to meet me and greeted me with great deference. I said, 'My masters, why have you seen fit to do me such honor?' 'How else could it be,' they said, 'seeing that you are favored by heaven?' 'I do not deserve to be addressed in this way,' I said. 'Why do you think that I am favored on high?' They answered, 'There came a villager, who told us that he was instructed in a dream to give you a holy volume in manuscript which he had inherited from his father, who had it from his father, and so back for many generations.' I said, 'I have come to you because of this book. Set a value upon it and I shall leave the money with you.' They answered: 'God forbid that we should take money from you.' I said, 'I swear that I will not budge from here until you tell me how much I must pay.' When they saw that I was determined, they agreed to take from me a certain sum of gold dinars, and I left the sum with them. I do not know if the poor villager took what I left for him or not. Possibly he was told in his dream to give the money to charity, and did so. That is the story of the collection of devotional poems which came into my possession not long before I became acquainted with Gemulah."

VI

Perfect as the moon was Gemulah; her eyes were sparks of light; her face was like the morning star; her voice was sweet as the shades of evening. When she lifted up her voice in song, it was as if all the gates of melody were opened. She knew, besides, how to bake *kavanim* and how to roast meat on hot coals. Though Gemulah was only twelve years old when Gamzu first chanced upon her home, her wisdom shone out like that of a mature woman, for her father had passed on to her the secret knowledge laid up by his ancestors. She was his only child, his wife having died in giving birth to her. He had taken no other wife, and since he could not bear to think of so much wisdom perishing, he had handed on what he knew to his daughter.

Gamzu spent about a year in her father's house, until his strength began to return to him. Then he went his way and traveled to Vienna to have his eye treated. He spent a year in Vienna and left with one eye only. All the time he was in the hospital he consoled himself with the thought that his sight would return and he would then go back to Gemulah. When he left the hospital he had no funds for travel; all his resources had been eaten up in doctors' fees. Akibah Amrami met him and said, "Obadiah and Obadiowitz are seeking a man like you, who would be willing to travel on their behalf to distant countries and bring back rare books." He went to see Obadiah and Obadiowitz; they marked out all the places he was to go to, paid his traveling expenses, and authorized him to spend on their account as much as he needed. God prospered his way and Gamzu gave satisfaction to his employers. He was able to save some of his earnings, and so he set out for the land where Gemulah lived.

In the meantime something had happened in Gemulah's country, the like of which hardly occurred once in a jubilee cycle. A holy man, a Hacham of Jerusalem, had appeared there and stayed for six months. Six more months had already gone by since his departure, yet his name was still on everybody's lips. Those who had been sick spoke of how Hacham Gideon had relieved their suffering. Others told of how Hacham Gideon had taught them ways to ease the burdens of life. He had also shown how all kinds of illnesses might be avoided, even without incantations, even in the case of infants who normally die of the evil eye. He had taken no fees from them, and if they had given him a present he had made them a gift in return. Gamzu was of the opinion that this Hacham Gideon was no Jerusalem Hacham, but a European man of learning, an ethnologist or something of the kind. He saw as evidence of this the fact that Gideon had recorded in his notebook all the songs he had heard from Gemulah and even her conversations with her father in the language they had devised for themselves.

So Gamzu returned to Gemulah's home, and when Gemulah saw him, she rejoiced as a bride over her bridegroom. She roasted a kid for him and baked *kavanim* and sang for him all the songs that Hacham Gideon had liked. Nor did she concern herself with the affairs of Gadi Ben Ge'im, her neighbor, who insisted that Gemulah had been betrothed to him since the time when they were nursed together at his mother's breast; for Gemulah's mother having died in giving birth to her, the mother of Gadi had reared her as a daughter.

At this time evil fell upon Gevariah, Gemulah's father. He had gone up to the mountaintop to learn from the eagles how they renew their youth. There an eagle had attacked him, not heeding the fact that Gevariah came in peace, without any weapon, not even a stick. Gevariah fought back, and had he not managed to beat off the eagle, he would have been mauled beneath its talons and torn to pieces and devoured. Even so, the eagle injured his left arm, lacerating the flesh. Gevariah neglected the wound until he took sick and died.

Before his death, he appointed a night of dancing, for his own and Gemulah's sake, for such was the custom in their country. Seven nights before a betrothal they appoint a night of dances, and it is usual on such occasions for the young men to come, and each snatches a wife for himself from among the girl dancers. Gamzu was aware that Gadi Ben Ge'im intended to snatch Gemulah, but he anticipated him and won her and made her his bride.

For seven days and seven nights they held the wedding feast. Gevariah lay upon his mat and conducted the dances with his uninjured hand. Seven different dances he conducted each night, and eight kinds of dances each day, that Gemulah might give birth to a son who would be circumcised on the eighth day. With the end of the seven days of feasting, Gevariah's life ended, too.

Gemulah mourned her father for seven days and nights, with songs of lamentation every day and night. At the end of her first week of mourning she made him great obsequies, with songs and dances full of dread and wonder. After thirty days had passed, Gamzu began to speak to her of the journey they must take. Gemulah heard him out, but could not grasp what this meant for her. When she understood she protested strongly. Little by little she was persuaded, until she consented to leave, but she put off making the journey from week to week and from month to month. All this time the moon did not affect her; it seemed that because of her grief at her father's death the moon had no power over her. She was also protected by the charms, though there was no change in her condition, and she was like an unripe fig that is still closed up, on the tree, her sweetness all stored within. At the end of the year of mourning, she said of her own accord that she was ready for the journey. Gamzu hired two camels, and they rode until they came to the edge of the desert, where the caravans go out. They joined a caravan, journeying for forty days until they came to a settled region. Gamzu bought shoes for her feet and dresses for her to wear and a kerchief for her head, and they rode on until they reached a port. There he hired a ship, and they sailed to the Land of Israel. And because they were traveling to the Land of Israel, the Name preserved them from all evil. But it was not so in the Land itself. As Rabbi Alshekh wrote, concerning the dispute in the Talmud as to whether a man is judged every day or on New Year's day only: the latter applies outside the Land, but in the Land of Israel one is judged daily; each single day the Holy One sits in judgment upon His people. The beginning of the judgment was that Gemulah no longer sang her sweet songs. Later, all speech was withheld from her. Next, she was possessed by melancholy. Lastly, she fell seriously ill. With her sickness she began to torment Gamzu. His plight grew worse from day to day.

As Gamzu was relating this, I heard a sound like the opening of a window. At the same moment I could hear spoken words. I was not afraid, but I was certainly astonished, since besides myself and Gamzu there was no one in the house, and neither he nor I had opened a window. I began to recollect the dream I had had on the previous night, the train I saw and the window that opened. And again I was amazed at the power of dreams, which come back to us when we are awake as if they were real happenings. Once more I heard the same sound. I listened attentively and thought, Ginath must have come home and opened a window. But how could one explain the sound of spoken words? Gamzu saw I was distracted, and said, "You are tired. Do you want to sleep?"

"No, I am not tired, and I don't want to sleep."

"Are you troubled about something?"

"I can hear footsteps."

"If I can trust my own ears," said Gamzu, "there has not been a sound or the slightest suspicion of one."

"If that is so, I must be mistaken. Let us go back to what we were talking about."

Gamzu began to speak again about his experiences with Gemulah in Jerusalem. Many a time her life had hung by a thread, and had not the Holy One helped him, he would not have been able to endure his distress for a single day. But God's mercies are great. He sends a man afflictions, but He also gives him the strength to withstand them.

I do not remember the exact sequence of Gamzu's remarks, but I recall that he told me again about the garment, and in bringing this to mind made mention of his teacher. Having spoken of him, he also mentioned the time of his youth, which he had spent as a student in yeshivas.

You know Gamzu as a man with many connections, in demand among scholars of the East and West alike for books and manuscripts. But he had begun as any other yeshiva student, boarding out on the charity of the local townspeople. Once a certain householder sent him to buy a copy of the concise *Shulhan Aruch.* At the bookseller's he came across a book quite different from the rest. Every other line of print was indented, and every word had vowel points; some lines resembled the Great Hymn of Praise sung by the ministering angels, some the confession *Al Het.* He looked at it for a long while, full of wonder; never in his life had he seen a book like this.

The bookseller watched him, and told him he could have it for forty kreutzer. For a yeshiva student, forty kreutzer was a large sum; even if he sold his long coat, he would not get that amount for it. But he had a box which a carpenter had made him in return for giving lessons to his son. It was something of a luxury, since all his possessions, apart from the clothes which he stood up in, could be wrapped in his shirt; but it gave him the kind of pleasure one feels in owning an article of intrinsic beauty. He gave his box to the bookseller and received the book. It was the *divan* of the poems of Judah Ha-Levi, edited by S. D. Luzzatto. He read it again and again, until he knew all the poems by heart. And still he was unsatisfied. He began to pore over festival prayers and penitential hymns and elegies and old prayer books, reading and transcribing for himself. He could not afford the paper to copy down all the things he liked, so he noted down only the opening lines as reminders. Because he was so fastened to poetry, he came unfastened at the yeshiva. Accordingly he went and hired himself out to a bookseller. The shopkeeper could see that he knew a great deal, and sent him out to widows with the books of their husbands left on their hands, as well as to the "enlightened" rich who were clearing their homes of sacred literature. In time he began to make his own purchases. Later, he started traveling to far-off countries, and still later, to lands which no European had ever crossed. He reached the farthest edge of the desert and brought out books and manuscripts of which the most eminent bibliographers had no knowledge, as well as *divans* by anonymous poets who in their holiness and humility had left no record of their names.

Gamzu rolled himself a cigarette and laid it down. He rubbed his dead eye, smiled out of his good eye, and again took up the cigarette, holding it unlit between his fingers and saying, "When I pass over to the next world, they will lead me to the place where carcasses like me belong. I shall lie there in my shame, justifying the divine decree that I have been left exactly where I am, telling myself I have no right to expect anything better, naked as I am of merit and good works. At that moment, rank upon rank of demons will be massing against me, created out of my own sins. They will rise on high before the seat of judgment to accuse me and make hell deep for me. While waiting for the sentence, what shall I do? I shall say over from memory the hymns I know, until I forget where I am, and become so excited by them that I shall start shouting them aloud. The holy poets will hear me and say, 'What noise is that from the grave? Let us go and see.' They will come down and see this wretched soul and take me up in their hallowed hands, saying, 'You are the man who rescued us from the depths of oblivion.' And they will smile at me in the humility of their virtue and say, 'Gabriel Gamzu, come with us.' So they will bring me to dwell with them, and I will find shelter in the shade of their holiness. That is how I console myself in my misery."

Gamzu sat there smiling, with the expression of a man who knowingly deceives himself and is aware that he is only joking at his own expense. But I knew him very well; I understood that he believed in what he had said, more completely, perhaps, than he would admit to himself. I looked at his face, the face of a Jew out of the Middle Ages, reincarnated in this generation in order to procure manuscripts and early prints for scholars and investigators, enabling them to write observations and annotations and bibliographies, so that men like me might read these works and delight in the beauty of their verse.

Thus Gamzu bore his sufferings and solaced himself with the thought of better things to come. Meanwhile he was fully taken up with the troubles of his wife, an incurable invalid. I began to speak to him about nursing homes where the sick receive some degree of attention. "It would be a good idea to place Gemulah in a nursing home," I said. "As for the cost, I have here the first payment of twelve pounds; the rest will surely come."

Gamzu blew on his skullcap. "Those twelve pounds," he said, "are what I received for the manuscripts I sold to whoever got the talismans." I asked if he suspected this person of taking the magic objects by deceit.

"I am not a suspicious man," he said. "It is possible that whoever took them did not notice them at first, and when he did so, told himself that since they had come into his possession they were his. Or perhaps he believed that the charms were part of the lot he had bought. He may sometimes have thought one way, and sometimes another. Morality admits of compromise, and a man can still be moral even if he compromises according to his need; especially where books are concerned."

"Do you suppose," I asked, "that he knows the properties of the charms?"

"How should he know? If an article of that kind came into my hands by chance, and no one told me what it was, would *I* know? Besides, all these scholars are modern men; even if you were to reveal the properties of the charms, they would only laugh at you; and if they bought them, it would be as specimens of folklore. Ah, folklore, folklore! Everything which is not material for scientific research they treat as folklore. Have they not made our holy Torah into either one or the other? People live out their lives according to the Torah, they lay down their lives for the heritage of their fathers; then along come the scientists, and make the Torah into 'research material,' and the ways of our fathers into—folklore."

I listened carefully to what Gamzu said, and thought of those scholars who acquire what their original owners regarded as articles of magic, but which for those who have bought them are only so much bric-à-brac; and I thought, too, of this poor Gamzu, afflicted and dejected, whom the Holy One had crushed with sorrow. If we are allowed to judge a man by his deeds, surely it was not for the deeds Gamzu had done in this incarnation that he had been so doomed. But who was I to involve myself in these issues? Such as I was, I should be satisfied that the Holy One had, in a manner of speaking, not looked in my direction for some little while. I passed my hand over my forehead as if to set these thoughts aside, and gave all my attention to my companion.

There he sat, in a strange posture, his head bent to one side and an ear turned towards the wall. After a considerable lapse of time, in which he still kept his ear averted, I said, "You look as if you can hear what the stones in the walls are saying to one another."

He stared at me without reply and went on listening, his ear concentrated on the wall and both eyes aflame. There was no difference between his good eye and his dead eye, except that one was full of amazement and the other grew more and more irate. I took it that he was listening to matters which made him angry, and asked, "Can you hear anything?"

He stirred as though from sleep. "I can hear nothing, nothing at all. And what about you? Do you hear anything?"

"No, nothing," I answered.

He rubbed his ear. "Well then, it must be a hallucination."

He began to feel about in his pockets, produced some tobacco, and set it down. Then he extracted a handkerchief and laid that down, too. Next he stroked with his fingers the space between his nose and beard, then passed his hand over his beard, and finally said, "Didn't you say you could hear footsteps?"

"When did I say that?"

"When? Just a little while ago you said it."

"And didn't you answer that there was not a sound, nor the slightest suspicion of a sound?"

"So I said," he replied, "and so I am still inclined to think. But if you were to tell me now that you can hear something, I should not contradict you."

"Then you did hear something?"

"No, I didn't," he answered.

"Very well," I said, "let's return to our previous subject. What were we talking about before?"

"I swear, I don't remember."

"Does what you say count so little to you," I asked, "that you don't even try to remember it?"

"On the contrary."

"Why 'on the contrary'?"

"Because talk between two men of Israel is important, just as songs and hymns are; when you try to repeat them, the tune is never the same. Listen, I have just had an idea. I shall take Gemulah to the village of Atruz."

"To Atruz? Why?"

"Atruz is the name for Atroth Gad, which is in the territory of Gad, and Gemulah is of the tribe of Gad. She will breathe the odor of her own land and recover her health. I shall never forget how glad she was of my presence when Gadi Ben Ge'im was about to snatch her and I anticipated him and seized her first. I would give all the vastness of the world only to hear Gemulah laugh again as she laughed at that moment. But now let me ask you about that doctor, not Dr. Greifenbach, but Dr. Ginath. Everything you have told me about him pleases me. Our sages of blessed memory have said, 'Who is wise? He who knows his place.' If it were not wrong to add to their words, I should continue, 'when others do not know it.' At any rate, I am surprised that you live with him in the same house and have not come to know him. Is he old or young? How do you like his books? You have made me curious about matters I have not given any thought to. Why is this?"

I said, "See how many of our savants have been given high positions, and the journalists hang on to what they say and make them into worldwide celebrities, yet we ignore them. But this great scholar has no post, no articles are written in his praise; yet we wonder at him and try to know more about him. Even you, Mr. Gamzu, have undertaken to read his books in your second or third incarnation, and already in this one he arouses your curiosity."

Suddenly the colors began to change in Gamzu's face, until at last all color left it, and there remained only a pale cast that gradually darkened, leaving his features like formless clay. Within that clay without form, I read a kind of horrified amazement. Contemplating it, I was so shocked that my hair stood on end, for never in my life had I seen a living man so completely divest himself of his own likeness. Gamzu took hold of my hand and said, "What's the matter?"

I sat speechless. When I withdrew my hand from his, he did not even notice. "What happened to you?" I asked.

Roused from his trance, he smiled in an embarrassed fashion, waved his hand and said, "Idiot that I am, I've been fooled by my senses."

"What is your answer, then?" I asked.

"I don't know what you are referring to," he replied.

"To the suggestion of the nursing home."

He waved his hand again. "My mind is not on that now."

"And when will you put your mind to it?"

"Not now, at any rate."

I began to describe to Gamzu how much he would benefit if he sent his wife to the nursing home. "It would certainly be good for Gemulah to be there, and you too, Mr. Gamzu, would take new heart; then perhaps you would go on your travels again and discover new hidden treasures. These days, it is as if the earth had opened up and brought forth all that the first ages of man stored away. Has not Ginath discovered things that were concealed for thousands of years, the Edo language and the Enamite Hymns? But why should I mention Ginath? Haven't you yourself discovered ancient treasures that were unknown to us?"

Gamzu looked at me, but his ears were inclined elsewhere. Sometimes he turned them in the direction of the door, sometimes toward the window, and betweentimes toward the wall. I was irritated with him. "What a brain you have, Reb Gabriel. It is not enough that you listen simultaneously to what the door, the window and the wall are saying to one another; you even take note of every word spoken by a mere man like me."

Gamzu stared at me. "What did you say?"

"I didn't say anything," I replied.

"I was convinced that I heard people speaking."

In my annoyance I answered, "If so, tell me in what language they spoke. Was it in Edo, or Enam?"

Gamzu realized that I was angry. In a broken voice he said, "Believe it or not, they spoke that very language."

"What language?"

"The language that Gemulah used to speak to her father, the language they made up to amuse themselves. My nerves are in such a state that I believe I hear things impossible to hear; and I am not far from saying that what I hear sounds like Gemulah's voice."

I sat quiet, making no reply; for what indeed should I say to a man whose spirit has been broken by his troubles and who seeks to console himself with that which gave him pleasure in the days when he enjoyed peace of mind? Gamzu's blood had drained away from his face; only his ears seemed to be alive. He sat there and hearkened with those ears which were all that was left to him of his whole motionless being. In the end he waved his hand in dismissal and said, "It is all mere fancy." He smiled with embarrassment, adding, "When a man's imagination gets the better of him, the merest shadow of a wall seems like a substantial thing. What is the time? It is time for me to go back home. I am worried that the garment I put down before Gemulah's bed may have dried up by now. In the Land of Israel even the moon gives off more heat than the sun in other countries."

He stood up, then sat down again. Seated, he stared straight ahead and muttered sorrowfully to himself, " 'And a word was secretly brought to me, and mine ear received a whisper thereof.' "

"You are sad," I said.

He smiled. "It is not I who am sad. Those words were spoken by Job. He was the sad one."

I surveyed him and tried to think of what I could say. I felt in my pocket, like a man who has been searching in the recesses of his heart and ends by rummaging through his possessions. In so doing I brought out a picture postcard that had reached me from Greifenbach and his wife. I looked at it and saw depicted there a kind of moon shape resting on a roof. Gamzu took out some paper and tobacco, and rolled himself a cigarette. He licked the edges of the paper and put the cigarette between his lips and lit it. "Won't you smoke?" he asked. "Let me roll you a cigarette."

"Don't trouble, friend," I said, and taking out a pack of cigarettes, I lit one for myself.

We sat smoking together; the smoke of the cigarettes rose in the air, and our conversation came to a halt. I looked at the smoke and began to reflect in silence. If Gamzu gets up to leave, I said to myself, I shall not tell him to sit down again; and if he goes, I shall not call him back. When he has left, I shall make my bed and lie down. And God willing, tomorrow I shall write a letter to Gerhard and Gerda saying, "Your house is being well looked after." As for my own home, I am not worried, for after the thieves broke in I had strong new locks made.

Now my thoughts turned to my wife and children, who were staying in the country. Away from the city, they would certainly be asleep by now, for village people go to bed early. I too should be asleep were it not for Gamzu. As for Gamzu, wasn't it strange that he had come here? What would he have done if he had not found me? I reached out and tilted the lamp over to the other side. The moon came and shone straight into the room. My eyelids closed involuntarily, my head began to nod. With an effort I looked up to see if Gamzu had noticed that I was falling asleep. I saw that his fist was clenched and laid against his lips. Saying nothing, I thought: Why should he have put his hand over his lips? If he wants to hint that I am not to speak, I am not speaking anyhow. From so much thinking my head grew heavy; my eyelids were heavy too. My head sank down on my breast; the lids closed over my eyes.

Both my eyes were closed, craving a little sleep. But my ears were not ready for sleep, because of the sound of bare feet on the stone floor of the nearby room. I bent my ear and heard a voice singing, *"Yiddal, yiddal, yiddal, vah, pah, mah; yiddal, yiddal, yiddal, vah, pah, mah."* I am back in my dream again, I thought. The moon shone straight upon my eyes. I said to the moon, "I know you. You are the one, aren't you, whose face was on the picture postcard." Again the voice sang, *"Yiddal, yiddal, yiddal, vah, pah, mah."* The moon lit up the voice, and within the voice was the likeness of a woman. If that is so, I said to myself, then Greifenbach spoke the truth when he said that Ginath had created a girl for himself. But this pain in my fingers, where has it come from all of a sudden?

I opened my eyes and saw Gamzu standing beside me pressing my hand. Taking my hand out of his, I looked at him in amazement. Gamzu sat down again. He closed his live eye and let it set in sleep, but his dead eye began to burn. Why did he squeeze my fingers, I wondered. Because he wanted me to listen to the song. So there really was a song, a song in waking and not only in dream. What song, then? It was a woman's, and she was beating time with her feet. I laughed inwardly at my having been ready to think of her as a girl created by the imagination. And to rid myself of all doubt, I made up my mind to ask Gamzu what he thought. Gamzu had closed his dead eye together with his live eye, and his face wore a smile of delight, like that of a young man who hears his true love speaking. It was hard to break in upon his rapture. I lowered my eyes and sat in silence.

There was the sound again, no longer the sound of singing now, but of spoken words. In what language? In a tongue that was unlike those we know. I wanted to ask Gamzu about it. I opened my eyes and saw that his chair was vacant. I looked all around but could not see him. I stood up and went from room to room without finding him, and came back and sat down again. About ten minutes passed, but he did not return. I began to feel anxious lest something had happened to him. Getting up from my chair, I went out into the hall. Gamzu was not to be found. I shall wait for him in my room, I thought. Before I could manage to return, I entered a room which had been built as a *sukkah* for the Tabernacles festival and was now serving as an anteroom to that of Ginath. I looked around me, and saw Gamzu standing behind the door; I wondered what on earth he was doing there. The palm of a hand reached out and touched the door. Before I could decide whether what I saw was really seen or not, the door opened half way and the light in the room shone out brightly. It drew me and I looked inside.

Moonlight filled the room, and in the room stood a young woman wrapped in white, her feet bare, her hair disheveled, her eyes closed. And a young man sat at the table by the window and wrote in ink on paper all that she spoke. I did not comprehend one word of her speech, and I doubt if there is any man in the world who could understand a language mysterious as this. Still the woman spoke and the pen wrote. And this was clear, that the man writing down the woman's words was Ginath. When had he returned, when had he gone to his room? He must have come back while Gamzu and I were sitting in Greifenbach's room, and the woman must have gotten in through the window. That was why I had heard a window being opened and the sound of bare feet. With all the things I was seeing in quick succession I forgot Gamzu, and did not notice that he was standing beside me. But then Gamzu—yes, Gamzu!—did a strange thing. He forgot all manners and proprieties. He flung himself into the room and twined his arms around the woman's waist. This chaste man, who had devoted his entire being to his wife, burst into a strange room and embraced a strange woman.

And now things began to get confused, and I am surprised that I can remember their sequence. These events all happened in a short time, yet how long it seemed. I stood with Gamzu facing the room of Ginath, and the door was half open. I peeped into the room, which was lit up by the moon. The moon had shrunk in order to get inside, but once in, she proceeded to expand until the whole room and its contents were visible. I saw a woman standing there, and a young man seated before the table writing. Gamzu suddenly rushed in and clasped the woman's waist with his arms. The woman drew back her head from him, and still in his embrace, cried out, "Hacham!" Her voice was that of a maiden whose love has fully ripened.

The young man answered, "Go, Gemulah, follow your husband."

Gemulah said, "After all the years that I have waited for you! Now you say, 'Go, Gemulah.' "

"He is your husband," the young man said.

"And you, Hacham Gideon," said Gemulah, "what are you to me?"

"I am nothing."

Gemulah laughed. "So you are nothing! You are a good man, you are a lovely man, in all the world there is no man so good and so lovely as you. Let me stay with you, and I shall sing you the song of the bird Grofith, which she sings only once in her lifetime."

"Sing," said the young man.

Gemulah said, "I shall sing the song of Grofith, and then we shall die. Gabriel, when Hacham Gideon and I are dead, dig us two graves side by side. Do you promise you will do that?"

Gamzu put his hand over her mouth and held on with all his might. She struggled to escape from his arms, but he held her tight and shouted to Ginath, "Do you know what you are? A sinner in Israel, that's what you are! You are not even afraid to steal another man's wife!"

"Don't listen to him, Hacham Gideon," cried Gemulah. "I am not any man's wife. Ask him, has he ever seen me naked?"

Gamzu let out a long and bitter sigh. "You are my wife," he said, "my wife, my wife! You are consecrated to me by the law of Moses and of Israel."

The young man said, "Go, Gemulah, go with your husband."

"So you reject me," said Gemulah.

"I do not reject you, Gemulah," said the young man, "I only tell you what you must do."

With that, her strength left her, and were it not that Gamzu still held her she would have fallen. And once Gamzu had grasped her, he did not let go of her until he took her up in his arms and went away, while Ginath and I looked on.

VII

The moon went her way, completing her journey of thirty days. Thirty days had now passed since Gamzu took his wife back from the house of Ginath, and all this time I saw neither Ginath nor Gamzu. I did not see Gamzu because he did not come to my home, and I am not in the habit of going to his; as for Ginath, he went away immediately after that affair. I came across him once in an Arab coffeehouse, with Amram, the son of the Samaritan high priest. Since nothing came of it, I shall not dwell on it. Once again I found him in Giv'at Shaul, at the parchment workshop belonging to Hacham Gavlan and Hacham Gagin. Again, nothing came of it, and I shall not dwell on it.

My wife and children have returned from their holiday; the water has returned to the tanks, to the pipes, and to the taps. I stay at home and rarely go out, nor do I know how Gemulah has been faring with Gamzu since he took her back. Since, on balance, goodness outweighs evil, I assume that she has made her peace with him, and that having done so, her own language has returned to her. Perhaps she even allows herself to sing, and once more her voice stirs the heart like the voice of the bird Grofith; and as you know, Gamzu loves nothing so much as Gemulah's voice lifted in song. Why then did Gamzu lay his hand over her mouth to silence her? Because songs are conjoined, they are linked up one with another, the songs of the springs with the songs of high mountains, and those of high mountains with the songs of the birds of the air. And among these birds there is one whose name is Grofith; when its hour comes to leave the world, it looks up to the clouds and raises its voice in song; and when its song is ended, it departs from this world. All these songs are linked together in the language of Gemulah. Had she uttered that song of Grofith, her soul would have departed from her, and she would have died. For this reason Gamzu stopped up her mouth and preserved her soul that it might not depart.

I stay at home, then, and continue with my work, whether it be little or much. But when the sun sets I lay my work aside. "Behold that which I have seen: it is good, it is comely"—and so forth—"to toil under the sun," for so long as the sun shines upon the world, it is good, it is comely in the world. If I have a little strength left when my work is done, I go for a walk. Otherwise, I sit alone in front of my house or stand in the window and watch how the day passes and the night comes, how the stars take their places in the sky and the moon rises.

The moon and stars have not yet come out. But the sky gleams with its own light, burning from within, and a blue-gray glow, like the bloom on a ripe plum, hovers between heaven and earth, while the whole world is alive with the chirping of countless crickets. Not far from my house there is a commotion among the trees. It continues until it sounds like a forest on a stormy night, like a sea in tempest. I wonder if something is not astir in the world.

I have stood alone and looked behind the back of the world; and because so much has already happened, I have looked away from events that are at present taking shape. One of those past happenings was the affair of Gamzu and Gemulah: the story of a man who comes home and does not find his wife; "going to the south, turning to the north, turning turning," he goes on, and at the last finds her in a house where he chances to be. But what truly amazed me was this: with my own eyes I had seen Gamzu snatch his wife away, and yet it seemed to me that it was only a story, like the one he himself had told me, of how on one occasion dances were held, and Gadi Ben Ge'im was about to seize Gemulah, and Gamzu forestalled him. There is no event whose mark has not gone before it. Such is the parable of the bird: before it flies, it spreads its wings and they make a shadow; it looks at the shadow, raises its wings, and flies away.

The moon has not yet appeared, but she is about to rise, and a place is set aside for her in the sky. Clouds that seemed a portion of the sky itself are parted now, moving this way and that on their course, while the moon ripens towards her rising. Happy is he who can make use of her light without being touched by it.

My thoughts turn to those who long for the moon. And from thoughts of the moon, to thoughts that are bound up and conjoined with the way earth binds us. And from earth to man. To those whom the earth welcomes, and those who wander about like the shades of night. I do not refer especially to that young couple who had not found a home for themselves; nor especially to those who left the country and, on their return, found that the land had become estranged from them. Nor do I mean in particular Greifenbach and his wife, who went abroad to take a rest from the strain of life in our country. I refer to all men who are in the grip of this earth.

Greifenbach and his wife are about to return. Their cleaning woman, Grazia, told me this; a picture postcard from Mrs. Greifenbach had come for her. I know this, too, from the contents of a card they wrote to me. And since they are about to arrive, I have been to see how their house is faring.

Their house is locked up. No one has broken in. I do not know if Ginath is in his room or not. At any rate, the window that opened for Gemulah is now closed. When the Greifenbachs return to Jerusalem, they will find everything securely in its place.

Next morning when I picked up the newspaper to see if the Greifenbachs' return was announced, I read that a Dr. Gilath was dead. Since I was not acquainted with any person of that name, I did not linger over the news. But my heart sank, and when a man's heart behaves irregularly, evil things begin to take shape. I began to wonder if there was a misprint and "l" had been substituted for "n." Once a man enters into evil speculations, they do not leave him. I took up the paper again and saw the letter "l" standing out plainly in the dead man's name, yet my eyes which could see the "l" also saw "n," as if the "l" had been twisted and turned into an "n." The matter troubled me so much that I got up and went out.

I looked at the announcements on the walls but found no declaration of his death. Ginath did not hold an official post and was not known in town; there was nobody to publicize his death on the billboards. But I learned from another source that he was indeed dead, and how his death came about.

I shall start at the beginning. I was walking the streets and reflecting to myself: If it was Ginath, why was the name as Gilath? And if it was indeed Gilath, why do I have these forebodings?

Old Amrami, leaning upon his granddaughter, came across me and said, "Are you going to the funeral?"

I nodded and said that I was.

"What a strange case!" he said. "A woman who can't move from her bed meets her death on a roof."

I looked at him long and hard without knowing what he meant.

He went on to say, "Wonderful are the ways of God; who can understand them? A man risks his life to save another life in Israel, and the end of it is, he falls and is killed. So now we are not going to one funeral, but to two. To the funeral of Gamzu's wife, and to the funeral of Dr. Ginath."

Amrami's granddaughter Edna added, "The newspapers didn't report this, but eyewitnesses say that last night a gentleman went out of his room and saw a woman climbing up onto the roof. He rushed up to save her from danger, the parapet collapsed, and they both fell to their death."

So we walked, Amrami and Edna and I, until we reached the hospital where the bodies of Gemulah and Ginath had been brought. The hospital was closed. At the gate sat the porter, looking at passers-by, daydreaming that they were all asking his permission to go inside and were all being refused. But his luck was out; not a man asked if he might enter the hospital, but all went into the open courtyard where the mortuary stood.

At the side of the courtyard, standing apart, was the patients' laundry. Small as it was, it performed a service to the dead, for it fulfilled the obligation of hospitality by admitting visitors. Alongside it, on a broken bench, sat three professional watchers of the dead, while a fourth stood up behind them and rolled himself a cigarette. He saw Amrami and me and attached himself to us, telling us that he had sat all night beside the corpse, reciting psalms for the dead. And who, he wanted to know, was going to pay him for saying those psalms? He could tell I was an honest man; he would grant me the *mitzvah* of paying him.

A family of mourners came and sat down on the bench opposite. A woman detached herself from the group and walked in front of them, raising her voice in loud wailing and laments, swaying her shrunken body to the rhythm. She was sad, very sad, and so was her voice. Not a word that she uttered could I understand, but her voice, her bearing, and the expression on her face moved all who saw her to tears. The woman took from her bosom the picture of a young man and gazed at it intently. Again she sang, in praise of his beauty and his grace, recounting all the years he would have have had for life, had not the angel of death come for him too soon. All the mourners wept bitterly, and all who heard them wept in sympathy. Just so Gemulah must have wept for her father, just so she must have mourned him.

As I stood among them, I saw Gamzu coming out of the mortuary. The perplexity of soul that always accompanied him had left him for a while; in its place came two new companions, amazement and sorrow. I went up to him and stood by his side. He rubbed his dead eye with his finger, then took out a handkerchief and wiped his finger, saying, "He was the one. He was the Jerusalem Hacham, and he was the scholar I sold the talismans to."

One of the mortuary attendants came over to us. He looked once at me and once at Gamzu, like a dealer who has two customers and wonders which he should attend to first. While trying to make up his mind which of us was the more important, he asked for a cigarette. Gamzu searched in his pocket and took out cigarette paper and tobacco. In the meantime they brought out Ginath's coffin. Gamzu lifted his finger to his dead eye and said calmly, "Ginath is the one who bought the talismans."

The coffin bearers moved on; about half the necessary Minyan, I and three or four others who were at hand, followed to perform the last rites. A beggar with a tin box approached. He banged on his box, calling repeatedly, "Charity saves from death." Each time he looked behind him, lest in the meanwhile other bodies had been brought out and he should stand to miss what the accompanying mourners might give him.

On the way back from the Mount of Olives, Gemulah's funeral procession caught up with me. And on the way back from Gemulah's funeral I was stopped by an automobile in which sat the Greifenbachs, just returned from their travels.

Greifenbach saw me and called from inside the automobile, "How nice to see you! How really nice! How is our house getting on? Is it still standing?"

Mrs. Greifenbach asked, "Has nobody broken in?"

"No," I answered, "no one has broken in."

Again she asked, "Did you get to know Ginath?"

"Yes," I said, "I got to know Ginath."

Both of them said together, "Get in and ride with us."

I answered, "Good, I shall get in and ride with you."

A policeman came along and shouted that we were holding up traffic. The driver started up the car, and the Greifenbachs went on without me.

Some days later, I went to the Greifenbachs to return their key. On the same day officials had come to examine Dr. Ginath's room, but they found nothing except his ordinary utensils and two tins full of the ash of burnt papers. The ash was probably made up of his writings. When had Ginath burnt these? On the night when Gamzu took Gemulah back? Or on the same night that Ginath went out to save Gemulah and was killed with her?

What induced Ginath to destroy his own work, to burn in a few minutes the result of years of toil? As is usual in such cases, the question is disposed of lightly: It was psychological depression, they say; grave doubts brought him to this deed. But what led him to such a state of depression, and what were those doubts of his?

To these questions no answer is forthcoming. For surely there is no way of estimating, no way of knowing or understanding such a matter, especially where one is dealing with an enlightened spirit such as Ginath, and with works of wisdom and poetry such as his. No explanations can affect the issue, no accounts of causes alter it. These are no more than the opinions people put forward in order to exercise their ingenuity in words without meaning on cases that cannot be solved, on happenings for which there is no solace. Even if we say that events are ordained from the beginning, we have not come to the end of the chain, and the matter is certainly not settled; nor does any knowledge of causes remove our disquiet. They found this, too, in Ginath's room: a deed of annulment, in which Ginath canceled the rights of the publishers to bring out his books, forbidding them to reprint his vocabulary—that is, the ninety-nine words of the Edo language—and his book of grammar—meaning the grammar of Edo—and his book of Enamite Hymns.

As usual, the dead man's orders were not carried out. On the contrary, his books are printed in increasing numbers, so that the world is already beginning to know his works, and especially the Enamite Hymns with their grace and beauty. While a great scholar lives those who choose to see his learning, see it; those who do not, see nothing there. But once he is dead, his soul shines out ever more brightly from his works, and anyone who is not blind, anyone who has the power to see, readily makes use of his light.

Glossary

AHAD HA'AM, pen name of Asher Ginzberg, 1856–1927, major Zionist thinker; in his writings he envisioned the Jewish homeland as a center for spiritual revival.

AL HET, a long prayer of confession of sins.

ALLAH KARIM, *God is noble.*

RABBI ALSHEKH, 16th-century teacher, preacher, and casuist, disciple of Joseph Karo (cf. SHULHAN ARUCH), lived in the Kabbalist community of Safed, Palestine.

ASHKENAZIM, Jews of the central European tradition, as opposed to Sefardim, Jews of the Spanish tradition, from whom they differ in ritual and in their pronunciation of Hebrew.

BILU, a student Zionist group which in 1882, with the aid of the Lovers of Zion, began immigrating to Palestine.

HACHAM, *wise man, sage.*

IBN EZRA, c. 1092–1167, scholar and poet in Spain, famous for his commentary on the Pentateuch.

IBN GABIROL, c. 1021–c. 1058, philosopher and poet in Spain.

JUDAH HA-LEVI, 1085–c. 1141, in Spain, usually considered the greatest post-biblical Hebrew poet.

KADDISH, prayer recited by mourners.

LILIENBLUM, Moses Leib, 1843–1910, early Zionist leader, member of the Lovers of Zion.

MASORAH, *tradition,* the system of critical notes on the external form of the biblical text.

MIDRASH, *exposition,* exegesis based on Scripture.

MINYAN, quorum of ten men necessary for a communal religious service.

MISHNAH, *repetition,* compilation of legal teachings made by Judah Ha-Nasi, about 220 C.E., which forms the basis of the Talmud.

MITZVAH, *commandment;* hence, a good deed.

Library
Western Wyoming Community College

MUSAF, an additional service on Sabbath and festivals, in substitution for the sacrificial offering made in the days of the Temple.

ROSH HA-SHANAH, New Year, ushers in the ten days of repentance which end with Yom Kippur.

SANINE, Russian novel by Mikhail Petrovich Artzybashev, 1878–1927, which created a sensation following its publication in 1907.

SEFARDIM, descendants of the Spanish Jewish community, expelled from Spain at the end of the 15th century (cf. ASHKENAZIM).

SHOFAR, *ram's horn,* blown during the service for the New Year.

SHULHAN ARUCH, *Arranged Table,* rabbinical code compiled by Joseph Karo, 1488–1575.

SUKKAH, *booth, tabernacle,* simple shelter lived in during the holiday of Sukkot, the Feast of Tabernacles.

SUSAN, Hebrew "Shoshanah," *rose* or *lily*, frequently associated with the people of Israel, e.g. Hosea 14:6: "I will be as the dew to Israel; he shall blossom as the lily."

TARGUM, Aramaic rendition of the Pentateuch.

TEFILLIN, *phylacteries.*

USSISHKIN, Menahem, 1863–1941, Zionist leader, headed opposition to the "Uganda project" for a Jewish state in Africa; president of the Jewish National Fund from 1922 until his death.

THE LIFE AND WORKS OF SHMUEL YOSEF AGNON

By NOÉ GRUSS

S. Y. AGNON's works, classics of modern Hebrew literature, are powerfully original in conception and style. They are also in perfect harmony with his life. His stories stem from a profound realism—yet they give the impression of mysticism and fantasy, and have roots in ancient and medieval religious literature.

To understand these apparent contradictions, we must look at Agnon's life from his earliest youth. And the first fact to understand is that Agnon's world includes his birthplace in what is now Poland; and Israel, where he lived for over half a century; and Germany, where he spent several years collecting tales of the rabbis and of the Hassidim, a Jewish mystical sect. In his work Agnon was able to draw his inspiration almost exclusively from what he saw with his own eyes.

He was born Shmuel Yosef Czaczkes on July 17, 1888, in Buczacz, a small township in Eastern Galicia, then under the Austro-Hungarian monarchy. His father, Shalom Mordechai Czaczkes, had received a rabbinical education and was steeped in medieval Hebrew poetry. The elder Czaczkes had been a disciple of the rabbi of Tchortkov, but he did not choose to earn his living as a rabbi and worked in the fur trade. Shmuel's mother, Esther, was an educated woman; she was fond of reading and had some knowledge of German literature. When young Czaczkes left home, at the age of nineteen, he was familiar with rabbinical, Hassidic and Haskalah traditions, which merged harmoniously in his mind and heart.

His mother tongue was Yiddish. Between the ages of three and nine he attended the local *heder* or Jewish elementary school, for instruction in the Bible and the Talmud. At home, his father introduced him to the religious writings of the Haggadah and the work of the philosopher Maimonides, and his mother acquainted him with German literature in Yiddish translation. Later, he was taught German by a private tutor and attended a secondary school. He never received any higher education, but spent much of his time studying the Talmud and learning about Hassidic literature, the secular Hebrew literature of his day and Scandinavian literature. At the age of eight he wrote a poem every day.

The first of his published poems, written in Yiddish, appeared in the *Yiddishes Wochenblatt* in 1903, on the day of his fifteenth birthday. A ballad entitled "Joseph Della Reyna," it dealt with the sixteenth-century Palestinian cabbalist who endeavored to hasten the coming of the Messiah by fasting and mortification. During the next six years Czaczkes wrote in both Yiddish and in Hebrew, but when he left for Palestine, in 1907, he gave up Yiddish and turned to Hebrew for good. Just before that time, Dr. Eleazar Rokeah, an ardent Zionist, had arrived in Buczacz to campaign for Zionism. Through his talent as a speaker Rokeah galvanized the Jews of Galicia, and as part of his activities he started a paper, the *Yiddisher Wecker*. Young Czaczkes became his main contributor.

In the *Yiddisher Wecker* he published poems attacking the social inequality that mars the harmony of the great Jewish festivals.

A ballad in Yiddish called *"Di Kabtsonim"* (The Poor Men), for example, takes place on a major Jewish holiday, the feast of Purim. A blind old man with his grandson as his guide leaves the town to try to beg a little money in the neighborhood. But it is a frosty winter's day; when they become too tired to walk any further, they stop to rest and are both frozen to death. Now, in most of the Jewish writings of the time the Sabbath and religious festivals were holy and never criticized—they were supposed to be days that united the whole Jewish people. Czaczkes abandoned this tradition, introducing a dissonant note into the literature. The Hebrew works of his youth also deal with the idea of social inequality. An example is found in the tale of *"Melech and Malkah,"* in which it is the Passover festival that is marred.

The same theme is also found in some of his later writings, where it takes on even more importance. In a series of works written in Hebrew, Czaczkes depicts the gulf between the ideal and reality, between truth and its semblance. The truth he has in mind is universal; it does not stem from any specific political or religious doctrine. In these early works, it is the truth of an adolescent boy longing to eradicate life's poverty, pain, and shame, yearning for justice, and endeavoring to unmask human hypocrisy. In all these objectives he is filled with the spirit of European romanticism.

In 1905, the editor Gershom Bader asked Czaczkes to come to the city of Lvov (now in the Ukraine), to work on the Hebrew review *Ha-Et* and a publication of the "popular calendar" in Yiddish. He contributed to both, and also wrote for the Yiddish daily *Tagblatt*. He remained in Lvov only two years, but during his stay there he worked to perfect his skill as a writer. What he wrote in those youthful days did not always come up to professional standards, and editors often refused his contributions. These failures taught him to be self-critical. Of his Hebrew writings between 1905 and 1908, only twenty tales are still extant, and these have remained little known, for they are scattered among various journals that are rarities today.

In 1907 Czaczkes returned to Buczacz, where he played an active part in politics during the election of members of the Austrian Parliament. Among those standing for election was the Jewish national candidate Nathan Birnbaum, and the election campaign was later depicted by Czaczkes in an autobiographical tale, *Binarenu u-vizkenenu* (Young and Old) in which he substitutes the name Davidsohn for Birnbaum. His political beliefs crystalized at about the same time. For a short time anarchism had a strong influence on his thought, but the events of the time—a pogrom at Bialystok, the death of the Zionist leader Theodor Herzl, the Zionist congresses and, to some extent, the defeat of Birnbaum—made him realize that Buczacz was no place for him. He decided to leave for Palestine in order to do himself what he considered essential for every Jew.

Thus, in 1907, Czaczkes left Buczacz for Palestine. First he made a final short visit to Lvov, where he met and made friends with the Hebrew writer and columnist Joseph Haim Brenner, subsequently the publisher of his first book in Jerusalem. Next he stopped in Vienna, where he stayed with relatives. His uncle there wanted to pay for him to continue his studies in Lvov, advising him not to proceed with his journey, but Czaczkes refused and went on to Palestine. There, to earn a living, he took several different kinds of work, including the secretaryship of various organizations. The first story he wrote in Palestine was "Agunot," which tells of the tragic love between a young artisan and a middle-class girl destined to marry someone else. Here, for the first time, Czaczkes used the pen name "Agnon," which contains the three root letters of the word "Agunot," meaning "a deserted soul" or, more fully, "a lost soul searching in vain for its kindred soul." This pen name, which he took for his surname in 1924, is well suited to the general subject matter of his works.

In Palestine, Agnon met some immigrants who had arrived with the Second Aliyah, or return to the Promised Land, most of them in Jaffa. But he was attracted most strongly to Jerusalem and its age-old customs, rather than the style of the new arrivals. He wrote stories for the Jerusalem paper *Ha-poel ha-tzair,* most notably a long tale entitled "May the Slopes Turn into Plains." Its effect on its readers was extraordinary—for the first time they were hearing the voice of the real Agnon. He had rid himself of romantic redundancies and the Gothic touches with which his earlier stories were overloaded and, in the words of one critic, had created "an artistic folk epic."

This is an appropriate point to discuss the language and style that distinguish Agnon from other Hebrew writers. Agnon wrote after the manner of the authors of Hassidic and popular religious books, who interrupted their main plots with moral tales, fables, legends, apparently irrelevant conversations, and Hassidic stories about their wonder-working rabbis and commentaries on the Bible. His language is that of the people, yet still of great literary merit, without any contradiction in terms. This double nature is actually a specific feature of the Hebrew language in the time of the Diaspora, or the dispersion of the Jews. Hebrew had fallen into disuse as a spoken language many centuries ago, but it lived on in the spheres of religion, education, literary creation, and custom. The Jews of the Diaspora studied the Bible and the Talmud, said prayers, sang hymns and recited poems. At the same time, they used Hebrew for business agreements, community records, wills, folk tales, and moral writings. The people even wove Hebrew terms into some foreign languages, using words and phrases that had been previously used only by scholars. The Hebrew of the Diaspora drew on all the Hebrew literary sources—the Bible, the Talmud, the Midrash. This is the language that Jewish authors have used over the centuries, and it was the language used by Agnon, for he had the required intellectual preparation. In modern Hebrew literature, however, it was a novelty. This innovation misled many readers and created a false image of Agnon; they were so spellbound by the magic of his style that the contents passed unnoticed.

For Agnon there was no conflict between the old holy language (*lashon qodesh*) and the new modern Hebrew (*ivrit*). His language was a prayer rather than a literary exercise and his style a product of piety rather than of art. This is why Agnon often seemed a mystic, for whom reality was of small account, and why he has so often been compared—rightly or wrongly—with Franz Kafka.

During the first stage of his career his realism was artless and direct; his subject matter was not obscured by language or style. But his style took a new turn with the publication of "May the Slopes Turn into Plains." Here, the specific nature of the style cloaks the complicated, tragic story of a husband and wife who are compelled to part. As the story takes place over a century in the past and the hero is a believer, Agnon depicts him in his natural environment, steeped in Jewishness, specific beliefs, and superstitions that are as real to him as was the mythological world of Olympus to the Greeks. Thus, it was natural for Agnon to use the language of Mishnah and the Midrash, thereby reviving popular style in Hebrew literature.

Seeking to broaden his knowledge, Agnon left Palestine for Germany in 1913. During that year he attended the Eleventh Zionist Congress in Vienna, traveled to Buczacz to see his father, who was ill, and returned again to the town to attend his father's funeral. The years 1913–1914 were spent in Berlin, Leipzig, Hamburg, and other German cities. He earned his living as a private tutor and worked for the periodical *Jüdischer Verlag* along with Aharon Eliasberg, the well-known translator of Yiddish literary works in German. Jointly they published books by Polish Jews. *Jüdischer Verlag* published Agnon's tales in Hebrew as well as in German translations.

Some of the people he met during this period became of great importance in his life. He was befriended by S. Schocken, who founded a publishing house in Germany, and later in Palestine and in America, becoming the main publisher of Agnon's works and his lifelong mentor. In 1917 he made the acquaintance of the philosopher Martin Buber, with whom he started to prepare a collection of Hassidic tales; Agnon was to make use of these later in his own writings. He also contributed to the periodical *Der Jude* under Buber's editorship. In 1920 he married Esther Marx, by whom he was to have two children, a daughter and a son.

Agnon had not forgotten that the purpose of his stay in Germany was to broaden his mind. He studied German and French literature. He also developed a passion for collecting books and manuscripts, and began to build up a large collection. When a publication commemorating the martyrdom of Buczacz in World War II appeared, it contained a list, compiled by Agnon, of seventy-five rare books written by men who came from there. Unfortunately, his collection was later destroyed in a fire.

In 1924 Agnon returned to Palestine with the firm intention of settling in Jerusalem. For him Jerusalem was the sun; its very stones were alive. Few people have known the city as well as he did, and he was closely bound up with it. Agnon once pictured himself in Jerusalem 2,000 years ago. He saw himself in the Temple, with his brother Levites, singing psalms. "But the Temple is destroyed," he wrote, "so I spend my time on the Bible, the Prophets, the Mishnah and the Haggadah, the Geonim and the commentators. I study the Torah and try to go deeply into the ideas of the Torah and its exegetes and, when I think about it all, my heart is very heavy. Of our old greatness nothing remains but written texts. This sadness penetrates me and fills my heart and I begin to tell stories like a man who has been driven from his father's house, builds himself a hut and sits there describing to everyone the palace in which he once lived." Thus Agnon relived the past history of his nation and wove into it his own present-day life, with due allowance for the changes wrought by time. He loved the past and had a positive attitude toward it. He fully and gladly accepted the written and oral tradition of the ages.

He was far from identifying himself with the whole of the past, however. This is clear from his works and his attitude toward art, including literature. An example is found in his views on the theater, as expressed in *Oreah Nata Lalun* ("A Guest for the Night," 1939). For Agnon there were two kinds of inspiration: a simple kind, from which most plays spring and which does not reflect the truth; and a higher inspiration, which distinguishes truth from falsehood. With the aid of that higher inspiration, Agnon was able to open every door. He even saw what was going on "behind the world's back." The ability to create and identify with a character while remaining sufficiently detached to observe him is one sure sign of genius in an author, and Agnon created a large number of characters.

What are Agnon's main works—or rather, what types of work did he create? Part of the answer lies in the setting of many of his tales. Deeply attached to the Jerusalem of old, Agnon realized that during the time between the Jews' departure from Jerusalem in olden days and their return there today, the city's incarnation existed somewhere through the ages. "Somewhere," for him, was the township of Buczacz.

Agnon was not responsible for introducing the *shtetl,* or Jewish township, into literature; it already figured in Yiddish literature in the writings of Sholem Asch and I. M. Weissenberg. But each of these authors had only devoted one work to it, while Agnon made it the subject of several. The most characteristic of his books in this respect is *Ha-Khnassat Kallah* (The Bridal Canopy, 1922), a great folk epic of eighteenth-century Galician Jewry, inspired by Hassidism. In construction it is reminiscent of the Arabian Nights, a collection of loosely knit tales, and the style changes with the subject. In addition to a wealth of folklore, the book contains some pungent satire; but the central character of Reb Yudel, though a figure of fun, symbolizes Jewish spirituality and idealism as Agnon sees it. This major work is comparable to Cervantes' *Don Quixote.*

For Agnon, Buczacz is a town with a noble past. In one story about the town, "The Book of Buczacz," Agnon shows us some pictures of his beloved birthplace. It also appears in the story *Bilvav Yamim* ("In the Heart of the Seas"), and again in "A Guest for the Night," where it has lost much of its luster during the years after World War I. Even here, however, he finds some interesting people at Buczacz. There are Reb Hayim, Dr. Milch, Yerusham, Rachel Freeman and, in particular, a group of pioneers on a farm preparing to go to Palestine. This brings us to another novel, *Tmol Shilshom* ("Only Yesterday," 1945), which takes place in the time of the second Aliyah. It is both a recollection of the recent past and a realistic chronicle, with countless details in the style of epic tales.

Tmol Shilshom is almost the only Palestinian novel containing no mention of the dreams of deliverance, Messianism, or miracles that are so common in other novels about Hassidim on their way to Palestine. It shows the country as it really is, contrasting the new, developing features with the old. It is a somber novel, full of sorrow, and meant to be read as a sharp satire on the faults committed by the old population and the new settlers. It shows the blemishes that mar Jerusalem, and Agnon seems convinced that this state of affairs is unalterable. This is why one well-known Israeli writer, Moshe Shamir, considers Agnon a great sceptic, a destroyer of illusions. He bases this view on several examples, but most particularly on *Tmol Shilshom* in which Agnon sees falsity everywhere, with disappointment and death as the only concrete truths. According to Shamir, Agnon also exposes the ridiculous side of those who fancy that they are building something. Shamir sees Agnon's greatness in the very fact that he unmasks, exposes, and lays bare all lies and hypocrisy.

An author of an earlier generation, A. J. Brawer, who knows Israel well, confirms the authenticity of Agnon's pictures. He notes that Agnon's art was not that of the photographer recording every feature of his subject, but of the painter suppressing detail in an attempt to express essentials. To relive the days of the second Aliyah, the days of hope for a new life and faith in a better future, we must read the Jerusalem and Jaffa papers, the hundreds of leaflets and pamphlets and the books of memoirs. They present us with a mass of personages and facts. But the atmosphere of those days, the birth of a new working class in Palestine, the construction of Tel Aviv, the organization of the first Kibbutz, the establishment of the first secondary schools—all this can be fully grasped in a reading of *Tmol Shilshom.*

His heroes' tragedy lies primarily in the fact that they have lost their home and are wandering in their new homeland like a band of exiles, torn from their native soil without as yet taking root in the desolate land to which they have come. Agnon believed that secular Zionism, by its insistence upon the reconstruction of the country, had made Palestine lose its holiness; he considered this was a cause of decadence. He did not fail to stress the relationship between the people already living in Palestine and the new pioneers, who felt humiliated because they had to ask for work. Agnon's ideal was the preservation of the holiness of the country along with the values of toil for which the pioneers had left their homes to build new ones.

All these problems find expression in characters and conflicts that Agnon brought to life in a masterly fashion. The hero of the novel, Isaac Krumer (in whom we can see Agnon himself), wavers between belief and disquiet. He reflects the tragedy of his generation, in which conflicting instincts swept man in different directions and caused the suffering that is inseparable from any search after truth. But Agnon left it to others to describe the ideal of the pioneers, though he was one himself. For his part, he merely wanted to bring home to the reader all the physical and moral difficulties that he faced and that, he believed, had to be overcome. Agnon dealt with social inequalities without acrimony or bitterness. He wrote: "The world is made up of successful people and nice people. The successful ones take everything; the others trust them and are consequently of no account."

Martin Buber wrote this of Agnon's style, "There is nothing shallow about his pathos; it is the expression of his innermost feelings just as the pulse is the manifestation of the heartbeat. No exaltation, but his books bring tears to our eyes and that is the best sign of real talent as a writer." Agnon's style is always original. He was not one of those writers who never think again about a poem or tale once it is written. He constantly came back to his heroes, for they lived in him. He expanded tales into novels, and incorporated earlier poems and tales in other novels. He removed some tales from new editions, and none of the editions of his complete works is identical with any other. A biographer of Agnon's, Ephraim Tsoref, explained Agnon's methods in the writer's own words: "I am never satisfied; I always feel I have to do better and better. People should never say 'I have finished.' Let none of my biographers or critics take any notice of the first editions of my tales. There are fundamental changes between the first and the last one."

He loved the world to which his heroes belonged because it was his own. "Some will read my books as they read fairy tales," he said, "others will learn something from them; personally, I believe in fairy tales." Deeply anchored as he was in Jewish life, his outlook might have been a narrow one, preventing him from feeling sympathy with his fellowmen. Actually nothing could be further from the truth; and it would, indeed, have been unnatural for a writer so deeply attached to man and with a faith that profound to shut himself up in the ivory tower of his own little world.

Agnon was shown the highest respect in Jerusalem; at one time, for example, the local authorities erected a sign near his home reading, "Quiet. Agnon is writing." Even before he received the Nobel Prize in 1966, honors and prizes were showered on him in his own country and, from his fiftieth birthday onward, each new decade in his life was marked by a public celebration. In 1946 he received the Ussishkin Prize; he gave half the prize money to a children's charity. He was twice awarded the Bialik Prize—in 1934 and in 1951. He twice (1954, 1958) won the Israel Prize, awarded by the state of Israel, and the University of Jerusalem conferred an honorary doctorate on him in 1958.

The Nobel Prize and subsequent world recognition came none too soon, for Agnon died in February, 1970, at the advanced age of eighty-two.

Noé Gruss is former principal of the Tel Aviv High School and a friend of Agnon.
Translated by Annie Jackson.

THE 1966 PRIZE

By KJELL STRÖMBERG

THE NOBEL PRIZE for Literature had not been divided between two people for nearly fifty years. In 1917, two Danish writers, Henrik Pontoppidan and Karl Gjellerup, were jointly honored; in 1904, Frédéric Mistral, the Provençal Homer, had to share the Prize with José Echegaray, the Spanish writer. Under the circumstances, nobody questioned the justice of this exceptional measure. According to the Swedish Academy's official report which was broadcast, the division of the 1966 Prize was justified because it was a question of "honoring two works of literature which, although divided by their language, are united by a spiritual relationship and which complete each other in celebrating the cultural patrimony of the Jewish people." And indeed, both Agnon and Nelly Sachs had become the poets most representative of the grandeur and suffering of their compatriots in the Diaspora.

The Prize was given to Agnon in particular "for his profoundly distinctive narrative art, with motifs from the life of the Jewish people." Although Nelly Sachs had something of a reputation in Sweden, the country of her adoption, where Agnon also had established good relations, each was relatively unknown to the international public, even though both their names had several times been mentioned in the forecasts for the Nobel Prize. It is true that Shmuel Yosef Agnon had been proposed for this high distinction on several occasions, dating from 1948. Long before this, the names of various Israeli writers had been proposed and discussed: Chaim Bialik in 1933, Sholem Asch in 1946, and above all the eminent philosopher-poet Martin Buber, professor at the University of Jerusalem. Buber's candidacy must have been taken into consideration seriously from 1954, when he became the great favorite of the late Secretary-General of the U.N., Dag Hammarskjöld, who was an influential member of the Swedish Academy. Buber would certainly have had the Prize, had he not died. It is permissible to suppose that Agnon was crowned in his place, insofar as he was Buber's spiritual heir; in any case, the two men had been united in a deep and fruitful friendship.

It was quite clear that the attention of the Swedish Academy had for long been directed to the new, rising literature of the Holy Land, which had at last been liberated from Turkish domination. One after another, the great Jewish writers of Eastern Europe were to go there, sometimes to settle, even before the Zionist state of Israel was created and formally recognized after World War II. This was the case with Martin Buber and also with Agnon: they both came from Polish Galicia, which up to 1919 formed part of the ancient monarchy of the Habsburgs.

Agnon's first contacts with Sweden and the Swedes were made with the help of the Grand Rabbi of Stockholm, Dr. Marcus Ehrenpreis. Through him, Agnon met Professor Fredrik Böök, a member of the Swedish Academy and one of the most influential critics in the country, who visited the Holy Land in 1924. Two years later, in 1926, with the help of Dr. Ehrenpreis, a collection of Agnon's stories was published in a Swedish translation. It did not pass unnoticed, thanks to an article that caused a stir, written by Fredrik Böök, in *Svenska Dagbladet,* an important daily newspaper of Stockholm. But the great critic was still a long way from dreaming of a Nobel Prize for this man who was quite young, who wore the ritual caftan and corkscrew curls, and whom he had met at the famous Wailing Wall. Nevertheless, a regular correspondence started between Agnon and Dr. Ehrenpreis, who invited his friend and fellow-Jew to visit Sweden. But in 1951, when Agnon decided to make the long journey, Ehrenpreis had just died: Agnon himself fell seriously ill, but he saw Böök again and through him made valuable friendships in the country's intellectual circles.

Agnon was certainly not ignorant of the fact that he had been suggested as a candidate for the Nobel Prize for the first time three years before by his friend Dr. Hugo Bergman, professor of philosophy at the University of Jerusalem. Unfortunately, it was not his old patron Fredrik Böök, but Per Hallström, a former permanent secretary of the Swedish Academy, who was asked to proceed with the examination of his work, which was mainly known through a few English and German translations. Hallström discerned in it a most interesting, even thrilling record of the intimate, and in particular the religious life of the Levite tribe of which the author was a member. But according to Hallström, this work lacked the great artistic inspiration which could have won for it the appreciation represented by a Nobel Prize. His examination ended in a kind of dismissal of the case.

Eighteen years later it was a very different tale when another study was made of Agnon's work by a poet and critic with Surrealist orientations, Artur Lundkvist, a newly elected academician. He too had read and greatly appreciated some of Agnon's stories published in a French translation in 1959, which at that time were the first and only works by Agnon to appear in France. He described the stories as "a sort of paradoxical union between Hamsun and Kafka, an archaizing modernism which renews and revives the past in an extraordinary way." Agnon's candidacy was now firmly established.

The news was out on October 18, 1966. There was a rush of journalists, a formal visit from the Minister for Culture to the modest country house, and telegrams of congratulation from former President Ben Gurion, President Eshkol, and the Minister for Foreign Affairs, Abba Eban: the venerable old man was no longer in any doubt as to what awaited him. An indiscretion on the part of the Swedish radio, which had approached the Israeli radio in order to prepare a joint program appropriate to the great day, had betrayed the secret which ought to have been jealously kept until after the final vote.

When the news was confirmed, "the greatest poet of Israel," as he was called by Ben Gurion in his message, became the object of the warmest tributes from Jewish communities and Zionist organizations in all the countries of the world. A religious service in honor of the laureate was organized in his synagogue at Talpiot. The *Jerusalem Post,* which devoted whole pages to the event, most particularly emphasized that among the political and literary notabilities who had presented their good wishes to the great Jewish writer, was Dr. Ludwig Erhard, the Chancellor of West Germany.

During the formal distribution of the Prizes in the Concert Palace of Stockholm, to everyone's surprise, Agnon appeared in evening dress instead of the caftan which had been expected: nevertheless he wore a small black skullcap firmly fixed on his head, which he kept on even when he greeted the King. It is true that his arrival in Stockholm very nearly created some seemingly insoluble problems. December 10th is the anniversary of the death of Alfred Nobel and the unalterable date for the celebrations: that year it happened to fall on a Saturday, the Jewish Sabbath, on which day the orthodox believers observe absolute inaction, interrupted only by obligatory prayers. Could Agnon then take part in the celebrations? After much hesitating and endless palaver, the problem was solved: in these high latitudes the winter sun sets at three o'clock, therefore the Sabbath would end before the beginning of the party, which was arranged for five o'clock in the afternoon. There was nothing therefore to prevent the presence of the laureate, who was obsessed with the fear of profaning the Sabbath. So Agnon was in a sparkling good humor, smiling at everyone throughout the evening. And although he spoke fluent German and passable English, he chose to make his acceptance speech in Hebrew.

Translated by Camilla Sykes.

Ivo Andrić

1961

"For the epic force with which he has traced themes and depicted human destinies from his country's history"

Illustrated by LAJOS SZALAY

PRESENTATION ADDRESS

By ANDERS ÖSTERLING

PERMANENT SECRETARY
OF THE SWEDISH ACADEMY

THE NOBEL PRIZE FOR LITERATURE has been awarded this year to the Yugoslav writer Ivo Andrić, who has been acknowledged in his own country as a novelist of unusual stature, and who in recent years has found an increasingly wide audience as more and more of his works have come to be translated.

He was born in 1892 of a family of artisans that had settled in Bosnia, a province still under Austrian rule when he was a child. As a young Serbian student he joined the national revolutionary movement, suffered persecution, and was imprisoned in 1914 when the war broke out. Nevertheless, he studied at several universities, finally obtaining his degree from Graz. For several years he served his country in the diplomatic service; at the outbreak of World War II he was the Yugoslav Ambassador in Berlin. Only a few hours after his return to Belgrade, the city was bombed by German planes. Forced to retreat during the German occupation, Andrić nevertheless managed to survive and to write three remarkable novels. These are generally called the Bosnian trilogy, although they have nothing in common but their historical setting, which is symbolized by the Crescent and the Cross. The creation of this work, in the deafening roar of guns and in the shadow of a national catastrophe whose scope then seemed beyond calculation, is a singularly striking literary achievement. The publication of the trilogy did not take place until 1945.

The epic maturity of these chronicles in novel form, especially of his masterpiece *Na Drini ćuprija* (*The Bridge on the Drina,* 1945), was preceded by a phase during which Andrić, speaking in the first person of the lyric poet, sought to express the harsh pessimism of his young heart. It is significant that in the isolation of his years in prison he had found the greatest consolation in Kierkegaard. Later, in the asceticism of strict self-discipline, he discovered the way that could lead him back to what he called "the eternal unconscious and blessed patrimony," a discovery that also signified the introduction into his work of the objective epic form which he henceforth cultivated, making himself the interpreter of those ancestral experiences that make a people conscious of what it is.

The Bridge on the Drina is the heroic story of the famous bridge which the vizier Nehmed Pasha had built during the middle of the sixteenth century near the Bosnian city of Višegrad. Firmly placed on its eleven arches of light-colored stone, richly ornamented, and raised in the middle by a superstructure, it proudly perpetuated the memory of an era throughout the following eventful centuries until it was blown up in World War I. The vizier had wanted it to be a passage that would unite East and West in the center of the Ottoman Empire. Armies and caravans would cross the Drina on this bridge, which for many generations symbolized permanence and continuity despite the fluctuations of history. This bridge became the scene for every important event in this strange corner of the world. Andrić's local chronicle is amplified by the powerful voice of the river, and it is, finally, a heroic and bloody act in world history that is played here.

In the following work, *Travnička hronika* (*Bosnian Story,* 1945), the action takes place at the time of the Napoleonic Wars. Here we witness the rivalry between the Austrian and French consuls in a desolated, old-fashioned city where a Turkish vizier has established his residence. We find ourselves in the midst of events which bring together tragic destinies. The discontent which stirs among the bazaars in the alleys of Travnik; the revolts of the Serbo-Croatian peasants; the religious wars between Mohammedans, Christians, and Jews—all of this contributes to create the atmosphere which after a century of tension was going to be rent by the lightning at Sarajevo. Again, Andrić's power is revealed in the breadth of his vision and the masterly control of his complex subject matter.

The third volume, *Gospodjica* (*The Woman from Sarajevo,* 1945), is different; it is a purely psychological study of avarice in its pathological and demoniac aspect. It tells the story of a merchant's daughter who lives alone in Sarajevo. Her bankrupt father had told her on his deathbed to defend her interests ruthlessly, since wealth is the only means of escape from the cruelties of existence. Although the portrait is strikingly successful, Andrić here confines himself to a subject that does not permit him a full display of his great narrative gifts. They are revealed fully, however, in a minor work that should receive at least a brief mention: *Prokleta avilija* (*Devil's Yard,* 1954). A story set in an Istanbul prison, it is as colorful in its pattern as an Oriental tale and yet realistic and convincing.

Generally speaking, Andrić combines modern psychological insight with the fatalism of the *Arabian Nights.* He feels a great tenderness for mankind, but he does not shrink from horror and violence, the most visible proof to him of the real presence of evil in the world. As a writer he possesses a whole network of original themes that belong only to him; he opens the chronicle of the world, so to speak, at an unknown page, and from the depth of the suffering souls of the Balkan slaves he appeals to our sensibility.

In one of his novellas, a young doctor recounting his experiences in the Bosnia of the 1920s says, "If you lie awake one whole night in Sarajevo you learn to distinguish the voices of the Sarajevian night. With its rich and firm strokes the clock of the Catholic cathedral marks the hour of two. A long minute elapses; then you hear, a little more feeble, but shrill, the voice of the Orthodox Church, which also sounds its two strokes. Then, a little more harsh and far away, there is the voice of the Beg Mosque clock; it sounds eleven strokes, eleven ghostly Turkish hours, counted after the strange division of time in those far-off regions. The Jews have no bell to toll their hours, and God alone knows what time it is for them, God alone knows the number indicated on the calendar of the Sephardims and the Ashkenazims. Thus, even in the deep of the night, when everybody sleeps, the world is divided; it is divided over the counting of the lost hours of a night that is coming to an end."

Perhaps this suggestive nocturnal atmosphere also gives a key to the chief problems that have dominated Andrić's work. The study of history and philosophy has inevitably led him to ask what forces, in the blows and bitterness of antagonisms and conflicts, act to fashion a people and a nation. His own spiritual attitude is crucial in that respect. Considering these antagonisms with a deliberate and acquired serenity, he endeavors to see them all in the light of reason and with a profoundly human spirit. Herein lies, in the last analysis, the major theme of all his work; from the Balkans it brings to the entire world a Stoic message, as our generation has experienced it.

Dear Sir—It is written on your diploma that the Nobel Prize has been bestowed upon you "for the epic force with which you have traced themes and depicted human destinies from your country's history." It is with great satisfaction that the Swedish Academy honors in you a worthy representative of a linguistic area which, up to now, has not appeared on the list of laureates. Extending to you our most sincere congratulations, I ask you to receive from the hands of His Majesty the King the Prize awarded to you.

ACCEPTANCE SPEECH

By IVO ANDRIĆ

IN CARRYING OUT the high duties entrusted to it, the Nobel Committee of the Swedish Academy has this year awarded the Nobel Prize for Literature, a signal mark of honor on the international scene, to a writer from a small country, as it is commonly called. In receiving this honor, I should like to make a few remarks about this country and to add a few considerations of a more general character about the storyteller's work to which you have graciously awarded your Prize.

My country is indeed a "small country between the worlds," as it has aptly been characterized by one of our writers, a country which, at breakneck speed and at the cost of great sacrifices and prodigious efforts, is trying in all fields, including the field of culture, to make up for those things of which it has been deprived by a singularly turbulent and hostile past. In choosing the recipient of this award you have cast a shining light upon the literary activity of that country, at the very moment when, thanks to a number of new names and original works, that country's literature is beginning to gain recognition through an honest endeavor to make its contribution to world literature. There is no doubt that your distinction of a writer of this country is an encouragement which calls for our gratitude; I am happy to have the opportunity to express this gratitude to you in this place and at this time, simply but sincerely.

It is a more difficult and more delicate task to tell you about the storyteller's work which you have honored with your Prize. In fact, when it comes down to a writer and his work, can we expect him to be able to speak of that work, when in reality his creation is but a part of himself? Some among us would rather consider the authors of works of art either as mute and absent contemporaries or as famous writers of the past, and think that the work of art speaks with a clearer and purer voice if the living voice of the author does not interfere. This attitude is neither uncommon nor particularly new. Even in his day Montesquieu contended that authors are not good judges of their own works. I remember reading with understanding admiration Goethe's rule: "The artist's task is to create, not to talk"; and many years later I was moved to find the same thought brilliantly expressed by the greatly mourned Albert Camus.

Let me then, as seems fitting to me, concentrate in this brief statement on the story and the storyteller in general. In thousands of languages, in the most diverse climes, from century to century, beginning with the very old stories told around the hearth in the huts of our remote ancestors down to the works of modern storytellers which are appearing at this moment in the publishing houses of the great cities of the world, it is the story of the human condition that is being spun and that men never weary of telling to one another. The manner of telling and the form of the story vary according to periods and circumstances, but the taste for telling and retelling a story remains the same: the narrative flows endlessly and never runs dry. Thus, at times, one might almost believe that from the first dawn of consciousness throughout the ages, mankind has constantly been telling itself the same story, though with infinite variations, to the rhythm of its breath and pulse. And one might say that after the fashion of the legendary and eloquent Scheherazade, this story attempts to stave off the executioner, to suspend the ineluctable decree of the fate that threatens us, and to prolong the illusion of life and of time.

Or should the storyteller by his work help man to know and to recognize himself? Perhaps it is his calling to speak in the name of all those who did not have the ability or who, crushed by life, did not have the power to express themselves. Or could it be that the storyteller tells his own story to himself, like the child who sings in the dark in order to assuage his own fear? Or finally, could the aim of these stories be to throw some light on the dark paths into which life hurls us at times and to tell us about this life, which we live blindly and unconsciously, something more than we can apprehend and comprehend in our weakness? And thus the words of a good storyteller often shed light on our acts and on our omissions, on what we should do and on what we should not have done. Hence one might wonder whether the true history of mankind is not to be found in these stories, oral or written, and whether we might not at least dimly catch the meaning of that history. And it matters little whether the story is set in the present or in the past.

Nevertheless, some will maintain that a story dealing with the past neglects, and to a certain degree turns its back on, the present. A writer of historical stories and novels could not in my opinion accept such a gratuitous judgment. He would rather be inclined to confess that he does not himself know very well when or how he moves from what is called the present into what we call the past, and that he crosses easily—as in a dream—the threshold of centuries. But in the end, do not past and present confront us with similar phenomena and with the same problems: to be a man, to have been born without knowing it or wanting it, to be thrown into the ocean of existence, to be obliged to swim, to exist; to have an identity; to resist the pressure and shocks from the outside and the unforeseen and unforeseeable acts—one's own and those of others—which so often exceed one's capacities? And what is more, to endure one's own thoughts about all this: in a word, to be human.

So it happens that beyond the imaginary demarcation line between past and present the writer still finds himself eye to eye with the human condition, which he is bound to observe and understand as best he can, with which he must identify, giving it the strength of his breath and the warmth of his blood, which he must attempt to turn into the living texture of the story that he intends to translate for his readers, in such a way that the result be as beautiful, as simple, and as persuasive as possible.

How can a writer arrive at this aim, by what ways, by what means? For some it is by giving free rein to their imagination, for others it is by studying with long and painstaking care the instructions that history and social evolution afford. Some will endeavor to assimilate the substance and meaning of past epochs, others will proceed with the capricious and playful nonchalance of the prolific French novelist who once said, "What is history but a peg to hang my novels on?" In a word, there are a thousand ways and means for the novelist to arrive at his work, but what alone matters and alone is decisive is the work itself.

The author of historical novels could put as an epigraph to his works, in order to explain everything to everyone, once and for all, the old saying: *"Cogitavi dies antiquos et annos aeternos in mente habui"* (I have pondered the days of yore and I have kept in mind the years of eternity). But with or without epigraph, his work, by its very existence, suggests the same idea.

Still, these are ultimately nothing but questions of technique, tastes, and methods, a fascinating intellectual pastime concerning a work or having vaguely to do with it. In the end it matters little whether the writer evokes the past, describes the present, or even plunges boldly into the future. The main thing is the spirit which informs his story, the message that his work conveys to mankind; and it is obvious that rules and regulations do not avail here. Each builds his story according to his own inward needs, according to the measure of his inclinations, innate or acquired, according to his conceptions and to the power of his means of expression. Each assumes the moral responsibility for his own story and each must be allowed to tell it freely. But, in conclusion, it is to be hoped that the story told by today's author to his contemporaries, irrespective of its form and content, should be neither tarnished by hate nor obscured by the noise of homicidal machines, but that it should be born out of love and inspired by the breadth of ideas of a free and serene human mind. For the storyteller and his work serve no purpose unless they serve, in one way or another, man and humanity. That is the essential point. And that is what I have attempted to bring out in these brief reflections inspired by the occasion and which, with your permission, I shall conclude as I began them, with the repeated expression of a profound and sincere gratitude.

THE BRIDGE ON THE DRINA

By IVO ANDRIĆ

Translated from the Serbo-Croat by Lovett F. Edwards[1]

1

For the greater part of its course the river Drina flows through narrow gorges between steep mountains or through deep ravines with precipitous banks. In a few places only the river banks spread out to form valleys with level or rolling stretches of fertile land suitable for cultivation and settlement on both sides. Such a place exists here at Višegrad, where the Drina breaks out in a sudden curve from the deep and narrow ravine formed by the Butkovo rocks and the Uzavnik Mountains. The curve which the Drina makes here is particularly sharp and the mountains on both sides are so steep and so close together that they look like a solid mass out of which the river flows directly as from a dark wall. Then the mountains suddenly widen into an irregular amphitheater whose widest extent is not more than about ten miles as the crow flies.

Here, where the Drina flows with the whole force of its green and foaming waters from the apparently closed mass of the dark steep mountains, stands a great clean-cut stone bridge with eleven wide sweeping arches. From this bridge spreads fanlike the whole rolling valley with the little oriental town of Višegrad and all its surroundings, with hamlets nestling in the folds of the hills, covered with meadows, pastures and plum-orchards, and crisscrossed with walls and fences and dotted with shaws and occasional clumps of evergreens. Looked at from a distance through the broad arches of the white bridge it seems as if one can see not only the green Drina, but all that fertile and cultivated countryside and the southern sky above.

On the right bank of the river, starting from the bridge itself, lay the center of the town, with the market-place, partly on the level and partly on the hillside. On the other side of the bridge, along the left bank, stretched the Maluhino Polje, with a few scattered houses along the road which led to Sarajevo. Thus the bridge, uniting the two parts of the Sarajevo road, linked the town with its surrounding villages.

Actually, to say "linked" was just as true as to say that the sun rises in the morning so that men may see around them and finish their daily tasks, and sets in the evening that they may be able to sleep and rest from the labors of the day. For this great stone bridge, a rare structure of unique beauty, such as many richer and busier towns do not possess ("There are only two others such as this

---

[1] *A note on pronunciation is printed on page 338.*

in the whole Empire," they used to say in olden times) was the one real and permanent crossing in the whole middle and upper course of the Drina and an indispensable link on the road between Bosnia and Serbia and further, beyond Serbia, with other parts of the Turkish Empire, all the way to Stambul. The town and its outskirts were only the settlements which always and inevitably grow up around an important center of communications and on either side of great and important bridges.

Here also in time the houses crowded together and the settlements multiplied at both ends of the bridge. The town owed its existence to the bridge and grew out of it as if from an imperishable root.

In order to see a picture of the town and understand it and its relation to the bridge clearly, it must be said that there was another bridge in the town and another river. This was the river Rzav, with a wooden bridge across it. At the very end of the town the Rzav flows into the Drina, so that the center and at the same time the main part of the town lay on a sandy tongue of land between two rivers, the great and the small, which met there and its scattered outskirts stretched out from both sides of the bridges, along the left bank of the Drina and the right bank of the Rzav. It was a town on the water. But even though another river existed and another bridge, the words "on the bridge" never meant on the Rzav bridge, a simple wooden structure without beauty and without history, that had no reason for its existence save to serve the townspeople and their animals as a crossing, but only and uniquely the stone bridge over the Drina.

The bridge was about two hundred and fifty paces long and about ten paces wide save in the middle where it widened out into two completely equal terraces placed symmetrically on either side of the roadway and making it twice its normal width. This was the part of the bridge known as the *kapia.* Two buttresses had been built on each side of the central pier which had been splayed out towards the top, so that to right and left of the roadway there were two terraces daringly and harmoniously projecting outwards from the straight line of the bridge over the noisy green waters far below. The two terraces were about five paces long and the same in width and were bordered, as was the whole length of the bridge, by a stone parapet. Otherwise, they were open and uncovered. That on the right as one came from the town was called the *sofa.* It was raised by two steps and bordered by benches for which the parapet served as a back; steps, benches and parapet were all made of the same shining stone. That on the left, opposite the *sofa,* was similar but without benches. In the middle of the parapet, the stone rose higher than a man and in it, near the top, was inserted a plaque of white marble with a rich Turkish inscription, a *tarih,* with a carved chronogram which told in thirteen verses the name of the man who built the bridge and the year in which it was built. Near the foot of this stone was a fountain, a thin stream of water flowing from the mouth of a stone snake. On this part of the terrace a coffee-maker had installed himself with his copper vessels and Turkish cups and ever-lighted charcoal brazier, and an apprentice who took the coffee over the way to the guests on the *sofa.* Such was the *kapia.*

On the bridge and its *kapia,* about it or in connection with it, flowed and developed, as we shall see, the life of the townsmen. In all tales about personal, family or public events the words "on the bridge" could always be heard. Indeed on the bridge over the Drina were the first steps of childhood and the first games of boyhood.

The Christian children, born on the

left bank of the Drina, crossed the bridge at once in the first days of their lives, for they were always taken across in their first week to be christened. But all the other children, those who were born on the right bank and the Moslem children who were not christened at all, passed, as had once their fathers and their grandfathers, the main part of their childhood on or around the bridge. They fished around it or hunted doves under its arches. From their very earliest years, their eyes grew accustomed to the lovely lines of this great stone structure built of shining porous stone, regularly and faultlessly cut. They knew all the bosses and concavities of the masons, as well as all the tales and legends associated with the existence and building of the bridge, in which reality and imagination, waking and dream, were wonderfully and inextricably mingled. They had always known these things as if they had come into the world with them, even as they knew their prayers, but could not remember from whom they had learnt them nor when they had first heard them.

They knew that the bridge had been built by the Grand Vezir, Mehmed Pasha, who had been born in the nearby village of Sokolovići, just on the far side of one of those mountains which encircled the bridge and the town. Only a Vezir could have given all that was needed to build this lasting wonder of stone (a Vezir—to the children's minds that was something fabulous, immense, terrible and far from clear). It was built by Rade the Mason, who must have lived for hundreds of years to have been able to build all that was lovely and lasting in the Serbian lands, that legendary and in fact nameless master whom all people desire and dream of, since they do not want to have to remember or be indebted to too many, even in memory. They knew that the *vila* of the boatmen had hindered its building, as always and everywhere there is someone to hinder building, destroying by night what had been built by day, until "something" had whispered from the waters and counseled Rade the Mason to find two infant children, twins, brother and sister, named Stoja and Ostoja, and wall them into the central pier of the bridge. A reward was promised to whoever found them and brought them hither.

At last the guards found such twins, still at the breast, in a distant village and the Vezir's men took them away by force; but when they were taking them away, their mother would not be parted from them and, weeping and wailing, insensible to blows and to curses, stumbled after them as far as Višegrad itself, where she succeeded in forcing her way to Rade the Mason.

The children were walled into the pier, for it could not be otherwise, but Rade, they say, had pity on them and left openings in the pier through which the unhappy mother could feed her sacrificed children. Those are the finely carved blind windows, narrow as loopholes, in which the wild doves now nest. In memory of that, the mother's milk has flowed from those walls for hundreds of years. That is the thin white stream which, at certain times of year, flows from that faultless masonry and leaves an indelible mark on the stone. (The idea of woman's milk stirs in the childish mind a feeling at once too intimate and too close, yet at the same time vague and mysterious like Vezirs and masons, which disturbs and repulses them.) Men scrape those milky traces off the piers and sell them as medicinal powder to women who have no milk after giving birth.

In the central pier of the bridge, below the *kapia,* there is a larger opening, a long narrow gateway without gates, like a gigantic loophole. In that pier, they say, is a great room, a gloomy hall, in which a black Arab lives. All the children know this. In their dreams and in their fancies he plays a great role. If he should appear to anyone, that man must die. Not a single child has seen him yet, for children do not die. But Hamid, the asthmatic porter, with bloodshot eyes, continually drunk or suffering from a hangover, saw him one night and that very same night he died, over there by the wall. It is true that he was blind drunk at the time and passed the night on the bridge under the open sky in a temperature of −15°C. The children used to gaze from the bank into that dark opening as into a gulf which is both terrible and fascinating. They would agree to look at it without blinking and whoever first saw anything should cry out. Open-mouthed they would peer into that deep dark hole, quivering with curiosity and fear, until it seemed to some anemic child that the opening began to sway and to move like a black curtain, or until one of them, mocking and inconsiderate (there is always at least one such), shouted "The Arab," and pretended to run away. That spoiled the game and aroused disillusion and indignation among those who loved the play of imagination, hated irony and believed that by looking intently they could actually see and feel something. At night, in their sleep, many of them would toss and fight with the Arab from the bridge as with fate until their mother woke them and so freed them from this nightmare. Then she would give them cold water to drink "to chase away the fear" and make them say the name of God, and the child, overtaxed with daytime childish games, would fall asleep again into the deep sleep of childhood where terrors can no longer take shape or last for long.

Up river from the bridge, in the steep banks of gray chalk, on both sides of the river, can be seen rounded hollows, always in pairs at regular intervals, as if cut in the stone were the hoofprints of some horse of supernatural size; they led downwards from the Old Fortress, descended the scarp towards the river and then appeared again on the farther bank, where they were lost in the dark earth and undergrowth.

The children who fished for tiddlers all day in the summer along these stony banks knew that these were hoofprints of ancient days and long dead warriors. Great heroes lived on earth in those days, when the stone had not yet hardened and was soft as the earth and the horses, like the warriors, were of colossal growth. Only for the Serbian children these were the prints of the hooves of Šarach, the horse of Kraljević Marko, which had remained there from the time when Kraljević Marko himself was in prison up there in the Old Fortress and escaped, flying down the slope and leaping the Drina, for at that time there was no bridge. But the Turkish children knew that it had not been Kraljević Marko, nor could it have been (for whence could a bastard Christian dog have had such strength or such a horse!) any but Djerzelez Alija on his winged charger which, as everyone knew, despised ferries and ferrymen and leaped over rivers as if they were watercourses. They did not even squabble about this, so convinced were both sides in their own belief. And there was never an instance of any one of them being able to convince another, or that any one had changed his belief.

In these depressions which were round and as wide and deep as rather large soup-bowls, water still remained long after rain, as though in stone vessels. The children called these pits, filled with tepid rainwater, wells and, without distinction of faith, kept the tiddlers there which they caught on their lines.

On the left bank, standing alone, immediately above the road, there was a fairly large earthen barrow, formed of some kind of hard earth, gray and almost like stone. On it nothing grew or blos-

somed save some short grass, hard and prickly as barbed wire. That tumulus was the end and frontier of all the children's games around the bridge. That was the spot which at one time was called Radisav's tomb. They used to tell that he was some sort of Serbian hero, a man of power. When the Vezir, Mehmed Pasha, had first thought of building the bridge on the Drina and sent his men here, everyone submitted and was summoned to forced labor. Only this man, Radisav, stirred up the people to revolt and told the Vezir not to continue with this work for he would meet with great difficulties in building a bridge across the Drina. And the Vezir had many troubles before he succeeded in overcoming Radisav for he was a man greater than other men; there was no rifle or sword that could harm him, nor was there rope or chain that could bind him. He broke all of them like thread, so great was the power of the talisman that he had with him. And who knows what might have happened and whether the Vezir would ever have been able to build the bridge, had he not found some of his men who were wise and skillful, who bribed and questioned Radisav's servant. Then they took Radisav by surprise and drowned him while he was asleep, binding him with silken ropes for against silk his talisman could not help him. The Serbian women believe that there is one night of the year when a strong white light can be seen falling on that tumulus direct from heaven; and that takes place sometime in autumn between the greater and lesser feasts of the Virgin. But the children who, torn between belief and unbelief, remained on vigil by the windows overlooking Radisav's tomb have never managed to see this heavenly fire, for they were all overcome by sleep before midnight came. But there had been travelers, who knew nothing of this, who had seen a white light falling on the tumulus above the bridge as they returned to the town by night.

The Turks in the town, on the other hand, have long told that on that spot a certain dervish, by name Sheik Turhanija, died as a martyr to the faith. He was a great hero and defended on this spot the crossing of the Drina against an infidel army. And that on this spot there is neither memorial nor tomb, for such was the wish of the dervish himself, for he wanted to be buried without mark or sign, so that no one should know who was there. For, if ever again some infidel army should invade by this route, then he would arise from under his tumulus and hold them in check, as he had once done, so that they should be able to advance no farther than the bridge at Višegrad. And therefore heaven now and again shed its light upon his tomb.

Thus the life of the children of the town was played out under and about the bridge in innocent games and childish fancies. With the first years of maturity, when life's cares and struggles and duties had already begun, this life was transferred to the bridge itself, right to the *kapia,* where youthful imagination found other food and new fields.

At and around the *kapia* were the first stirrings of love, the first passing glances, flirtations and whisperings. There too were the first deals and bargains, quarrels and reconciliations, meetings and waitings. There, on the stone parapet of the bridge, were laid out for sale the first cherries and melons, the early morning *salep* and hot rolls. There too gather the beggars, the maimed and the lepers, as well as the young and healthy who wanted to see and be seen, and all those who had something remarkable to show in produce, clothes or weapons. There too the elders of the town often sat to discuss public matters and common troubles, but even more often young men who only knew how to sing and joke.

There, on great occasions or times of change, were posted proclamations and public notices (on the raised wall below the marble plaque with the Turkish inscription and above the fountain), but there too, right up to 1878, hung or were exposed on stakes the heads of all those who for whatever reason had been executed, and executions in that frontier town, especially in years of unrest, were frequent and in some years, as we shall see, almost of daily occurrence.

Weddings or funerals could not cross the bridge without stopping at the *kapia.* There the wedding guests would usually preen themselves and get into their ranks before entering the market-place. If the times were peaceful and carefree they would hand the plum brandy around, sing, dance the *kolo* and often delay there far longer than they had intended. And for funerals, those who carried the bier would put it down to rest for a little there on the *kapia* where the dead man had in any case passed a good part of his life.

The *kapia* was the most important part of the bridge, even as the bridge was the most important part of the town, or as a Turkish traveler, to whom the people of Višegrad had been very hospitable, wrote in his account of his travels: "their *kapia* is the heart of the bridge, which is the heart of the town, which must remain in everyone's heart." It showed that the old masons, who according to the old tales had struggled with *vilas* and every sort of wonder and had been compelled to wall up living children, had a feeling not only for the permanence and beauty of their work but also for the benefit and convenience which the most distant generations were to derive from it. When one knows well everyday life here in the town and thinks it over carefully, then one must say to oneself that there are really only a very small number of people in this Bosnia of ours who have so much pleasure and enjoyment as does each and every townsman on the *kapia.*

Naturally winter should not be taken into account, for then only whoever was forced to do so would cross the bridge, and then he would lengthen his pace and bend his head before the chill wind that blew uninterruptedly over the river. Then, it was understood, there was no loitering on the open terraces of the *kapia.* But at every other time of year the *kapia* was a real boon for great and small. Then every citizen could, at any time of day or night, go out to the *kapia* and sit on the *sofa,* or hang about it on business or in conversation. Suspended some fifteen meters above the green boisterous waters, this stone *sofa* floated in space over the water, with dark green hills on three sides, the heavens, filled with clouds or stars above, and the open view down river like a narrow amphitheater bounded by the dark blue mountains behind.

How many Vezirs or rich men are there in the world who could indulge their joy or their cares, their moods or their delights in such a spot? Few, very few. But how many of our townsmen have, in the course of centuries and the passage of generations, sat here in the dawn or twilight or evening hours and unconsciously measured the whole starry vault above! Many and many of us have sat there, head in hands, leaning on the well-cut smooth stone, watching the eternal play of light on the mountains and the clouds in the sky, and have unraveled the threads of our small-town destinies, eternally the same yet eternally tangled in some new manner. Someone affirmed long ago (it is true that he was a foreigner and spoke in jest) that this *kapia* had had an influence on the fate of the town and even on the character of its citizens. In those endless sessions, the stranger said, one must search for the key to the inclination of many of our townsmen to reflection and dreaming and one of the main reasons for that melancholic serenity for which the inhabitants of the town are renowned.

In any case, it cannot be denied that the people of Višegrad have from olden times been considered, in comparison with the people of other towns, as easy-going men, prone to pleasure and free with their money. Their town is well placed, the villages around it are rich and fertile, and money, it is true, passes in abundance through Višegrad, but it does not stay there long. If one finds there some thrifty and economical citizen without any sort of vices, then he is certainly some newcomer; but the waters and the air of Višegrad are such that his children grow up with open hands and widespread fingers and fall victims to the general contagion of the spendthrift and carefree life of the town with its motto: "Another day another gain."

They tell the tale that Starina Novak, when he felt his strength failing and was compelled to give up his role as highwayman in the Romania Mountains, thus taught the young man Grujić who was to succeed him:

"When you are sitting in ambush look well at the traveler who comes. If you see that he rides proudly and that he wears a red corselet and silver bosses and white gaiters, then he is from Foča. Strike at once, for he has wealth both on him and in his saddlebags. If you see a poorly dressed traveler, with bowed head, hunched on his horse as if he were going out to beg, then strike freely, for he is a man of Rogatica. They are all alike, misers and tight-fisted but as full of money as a pomegranate. But if you see some mad fellow, with legs crossed over the saddlebow, beating on a drum and singing at the top of his voice, don't strike and do not soil your hands for nothing. Let the rascal go his way. He is from Višegrad and he has nothing, for money does not stick to such men."

All this goes to confirm the opinion of that foreigner. But none the less it would be hard to say with certainty that this opinion is correct. As in so many other things, here too it is not easy to determine what is cause and what effect. Has the *kapia* made them what they are, or on the contrary was it imagined in their souls and understandings and built for them according to their needs and customs? It is a vain and superfluous question. There are no buildings that have been built by chance, remote from the human society where they have grown and its needs, hopes and understandings, even as there are no arbitrary lines and motiveless forms in the work of the masons. The life and existence of every great, beautiful and useful building, as well as its relation to the place where it has been built, often bears within itself complex and mysterious drama and history. However, one thing is clear; that between the life of the townsmen and that bridge, there existed a centuries-old bond. Their fates were so intertwined that they could not be imagined separately and could not be told separately. Therefore the story of the foundation and destiny of the bridge is at the same time the story of the life of the town and of its people, from generation to generation, even as through all the tales about the town stretches the line of the stone bridge with its eleven arches and the *kapia* in the middle, like a crown.

2

Now we must go back to the time when there was not even a thought of a bridge at that spot, let alone such a bridge as this.

Perhaps even in those far-off times, some traveler passing this way, tired and drenched, wished that by some miracle this wide and turbulent river were bridged, so that he could reach his goal more easily and quickly. For there is no doubt that men had always, ever since they first traveled here and overcame the obstacles along the way, thought how to make a crossing at this spot, even as all travelers at all times have dreamed of a good road, safe traveling companions and a warm inn. Only not every wish bears fruit, nor has everyone the will and the power to turn his dreams into reality.

The first idea of the bridge, which was destined to be realized, flashed, at first naturally confused and foggy, across the imagination of a ten-year-old boy from the nearby village of Sokolovići, one morning in 1516 when he was being taken along the road from his village to far-off, shining and terrible Stambul.

Then this same green and awe-inspiring Drina, this mountain river "which often grew angry," clamored there between barren and naked, stony and sandy banks. The town even then existed, but in another form and of different dimensions. On the right bank of the river, on the crest of a precipitous hill, where now there are ruins, rose the well preserved Old Fortress, with widespread fortifications dating from the time of the flowering of the Bosnian kingdom, with casements and ramparts, the work of one of the powerful Pavlović nobles. On the slopes below this fortress and under its protection stood the Christian settlements, Mejdan and Bikovac, and the recently converted Turkish hamlet of Dušče. Down on the level ground between the Drina and the Rzav, where the real town later spread, were only the town meadows, with a road running through them, beside which was an old-fashioned inn and a few huts and water-mills.

Where the Drina intersected the road was the famous Višegrad ferry. That was a black old-fashioned ferryboat and on it a surly, slow old ferryman called Jamak, whom it was harder to summon when awake than any other man from the deepest sleep. He was a man of giant stature and extraordinary strength, but he had suffered in the many wars in which he had won renown. He had only one eye, one ear and one leg (the other was wooden). Without greeting and without a smile, he would moodily ferry across goods and passengers in his own good time, but honestly and safely, so that tales were told of his reliability and his honesty as often as of his slowness and obstinacy. He would not talk with the passengers whom he took across nor would he touch them. Men threw the copper coins that they paid for the crossing into the bottom of the black boat where they lay all day in the sand and water, and only in the evening would the ferryman collect them carelessly in the wooden scoop which he used to bale out the boat and take them to his hut on the river bank.

The ferry only worked when the current and height of the river were normal or a little higher than normal, but as soon as the river ran cloudy or rose above certain limits, Jamak hauled out his clumsy bark, moored it firmly in a backwater and the Drina remained as impassable as the greatest of oceans. Jamak then became deaf even in his one sound ear or simply went up to the Fortress to work in his field. Then, all day long, there could be seen travelers coming from Bosnia who stood on the farther bank in desperation, frozen and drenched, vainly watching the ferry and the ferryman and from time to time yelling long drawn summonses:

"O-o-o-o-o . . . Jama-a-a-k. . . ."

No one would reply and no one would appear until the waters fell, and that moment was decided by Jamak himself, dark and unrelenting, without discussion or explanation.

The town, which was then little more than a hamlet, stood on the right bank of the Drina on the slopes of the steep hill below the ruins of the one-time fortress, for then it did not have the size and shape it was to have later when the bridge was built and communications and trade developed.

On that November day a long convoy of laden horses arrived on the left bank of the river and halted there to spend the night. The aga of the janissaries, with armed escort, was returning to Stambul after collecting from the villages of eastern Bosnia the appointed number of Christian children for the blood tribute.

It was already the sixth year since the last collection of this tribute of blood, and so this time the choice had been easy and rich; the necessary number of healthy, bright and good-looking lads between ten and fifteen years old had been found without difficulty, even though many parents had hidden their children in the forests, taught them how to appear half-witted, clothed them in rags and let them get filthy, to avoid the aga's choice. Some went so far as to maim their own children, cutting off one of their fingers with an axe.

The chosen children were laden on to little Bosnian horses in a long convoy. On each horse were two plaited panniers, like those for fruit, one on each side, and in every pannier was put a child, each with a small bundle and a round cake, the last thing they were to take from their parents' homes. From these panniers, which balanced and creaked in unison, peered out the fresh and frightened faces of the kidnapped children. Some of them gazed calmly across the horses' cruppers, looking as long as they could at their native land, others ate and wept at the same time, while others slept with heads resting on the pack-saddles.

A little way behind the last horses in that strange convoy straggled, dishevelled and exhausted, many parents and relatives of those children who were being carried away forever to a foreign world, where they would be circumcized, become Turkish and, forgetting their faith, their country and their origin, would pass their lives in the ranks of the janissaries or in some other, higher, service of the Empire. They were for the most part women, mothers, grandmothers and sisters of the stolen children.

When they came too close, the aga's horsemen would drive them away with whips, urging their horses at them with loud cries to Allah. Then they would fly in all directions and hide in the forests along the roadsides, only to gather again a little later behind the convoy and strive with tear-filled eyes to see once again over the panniers the heads of the children who were being taken from them. The mothers were especially persistent and hard to restrain. Some would rush forward not looking where they were going, with bare breasts, and dishevelled hair, forgetting everything about them, wailing and lamenting as at a burial, while others almost out of their minds moaned as if their wombs were being torn by birth-pangs, and blinded with tears ran right onto the horsemen's whips and replied to every blow with the fruitless question: "Where are you taking him? Why are you taking him from me?" Some tried to speak clearly to their children and to give them some last part of themselves, as much as might be said in a couple of words, some recommendation or advice for the way. . . .

"Rade, my son, don't forget your mother. . . ."

"Ilija, Ilija, Ilija!" screamed another

woman, searching desperately with her glances for the dear well-known head and repeating this incessantly as if she wished to carve into the child's memory that name which would in a day or two be taken from him forever.

But the way was long, the earth hard, the body weak and the Osmanlis powerful and pitiless. Little by little the women dropped back exhausted by the march and the blows, and one after the other abandoned their vain effort. Here, at the Višegard ferry, even the most enduring had to halt for they were not allowed on the ferry and were unable to cross the water. Now they could sit in peace on the bank and weep, for no one persecuted them any longer. There they waited as if turned to stone and sat, insensible to hunger, thirst and cold, until on the farther bank of the river they could see once more the long drawn out convoy of horses and riders as it moved onward towards Dubrina, and tried once more to catch a last glimpse of the children who were disappearing from their sight.

On that November day in one of those countless panniers a dark-skinned boy of about ten years old from the mountain village of Sokolovići sat silent and looked about him with dry eyes. In a chilled and reddened hand he held a small curved knife with which he absent-mindedly whittled at the edges of his pannier, but at the same time looked about him. He was to remember that stony bank overgrown with sparse, bare and dull gray willows, the surly ferryman and the dry water-mill full of draughts and spiders' webs where they had to spend the night before it was possible to transport all of them across the troubled waters of the Drina over which the ravens were croaking. Somewhere within himself he felt a sharp stabbing pain which from time to time seemed suddenly to cut his chest in two and hurt terribly, which was always associated with the memory of that place where the road broke off, where desolation and despair were extinguished and remained on the stony banks of the river, across which the passage was so difficult, so expensive and so unsafe. It was here, at this particularly painful spot in that hilly and poverty-stricken district, in which misfortune was open and evident, that man was halted by powers stronger than he and, ashamed of his powerlessness, was forced to recognize more clearly his own misery and that of others, his own backwardness and that of others.

All this was summed up in that physical discomfort that the boy felt on that November day and which never completely left him, though he changed his way of life, his faith, his name and his country.

What this boy in the pannier was later to become has been told in all histories in all languages and is better known in the world outside than it is among us. In time he became a young and brave officer at the Sultan's court, then Great Admiral of the Fleet, then the Sultan's son-in-law, a general and statesman of world renown, Mehmed Pasha Sokolli, who waged wars that were for the most part victorious on three continents and extended the frontiers of the Ottoman Empire, making it safe abroad and by good administration consolidated it from within. For these sixty odd years he served three Sultans, experienced both good and evil as only rare and chosen persons may experience them, and raised himself to heights of power and authority unknown to us, which few men reach and few men keep. This new man that he had become in a foreign world where we could not follow even in our thoughts, must have forgotten all that he had left behind in the country whence they had once brought him. He surely forgot too the crossing of the Drina at Višegrad, the bare banks on which travelers shivered with cold and uncertainty, the slow and worm-eaten ferry, the strange ferryman, and the hungry ravens above the troubled waters. But that feeling of discomfort which had remained in him had never completely disappeared. On the other hand, with years and with age it appeared more and more often; always the same black pain which cut into his breast with that special well-known childhood pang which was clearly distinguishable from all the ills and pains that life later brought to him. With closed eyes, the Vezir would wait until that black knife-like pang passed and the pain diminished. In one of those moments he thought that he might be able to free himself from this discomfort if he could do away with that ferry on the distant Drina, around which so much misery and inconvenience gathered and increased incessantly, and bridge the steep banks and the evil water between them, join the two ends of the road which was broken by the Drina and thus link safely and forever Bosnia and the East, the place of his origin and the places of his life. Thus it was he who first, in a single moment behind closed eyelids, saw the firm graceful silhouette of the great stone bridge which was to be built there.

That very same year, by the Vezir's order and at the Vezir's expense, the building of the great bridge on the Drina began. It lasted five years. That must have been an exceptionally lively and important time for the town and the whole district, full of change and of events great and small. But for a wonder, in the town which remembered for centuries and discussed every sort of event, including all those directly connected with the bridge, not many details of the commencement of the operation were preserved.

The common people remember and tell of what they are able to grasp and what they are able to transform into legend. Anything else passes them by without deeper trace, with the dumb indifference of nameless natural phenomena, which do not touch the imagination or remain in the memory. This hard and long building process was for them a foreign task undertaken at another's expense. Only when, as the fruit of this effort, the great bridge arose, men began to remember details and to embroider the creation of a real, skillfully built and lasting bridge with fabulous tales which they well knew how to weave and to remember.

3

In the spring of that year when the Vezir had made his decision to build, his men arrived in the town to prepare everything necessary for the construction work on the bridge. There were many of them, with horses, carts, various tools and tents. All this excited fear and apprehension in the little town and the surrounding villages, especially among the Christians.

At the head of this group was Abidaga, who was responsible to the Vezir for building the bridge; with him was the mason, Tosun Effendi. (There had already been tales about this Abidaga, saying that he was a man who stopped at nothing, harsh and pitiless beyond measure.) As soon as they had settled in their tents below Mejdan, Abidaga summoned the local leaders and all the principal Turks for a discussion. But there was not much of a discussion, for only one man spoke and he was Abidaga. Those who had been summoned saw a powerfully built man, with green eyes and an unhealthy reddish face, dressed in rich Stambul clothes, with a reddish beard and wonderfully upturned moustaches in the Magyar fashion. The speech which this violent man delivered to the notables astonished them even more than his appearance: "It is more than likely that you have heard tales about me even before I came here and I know without asking that those tales could not have been pleasant or favorable. Probably you have heard that I demand work and obedience from everyone, and that I will beat and kill anyone who does not work as he should and does not obey without argument; that I do not know the meaning of 'I cannot' or 'There isn't any,' that wherever I am heads will roll at the slightest word, and that in short I am a bloodthirsty and hard man. I want to tell you that those tales are neither imaginary nor exaggerated. Under my linden tree there is no shade. I have won this reputation over long years of service in which I have devotedly carried out the orders of the Grand Vezir. I trust in God that I shall carry out this work for which I was sent and when at the completion of the work I go hence, I hope that even harsher and darker tales will go before me than those which have already reached you."

After this unusual introduction to which all listened in silence and with downcast eyes, Abidaga explained that it was a matter of a building of great importance, such as did not exist even in richer lands, that the work would last five, perhaps six, years, but that the Vezir's will would be carried out to the fineness of a hair and punctual to a minute. Then he laid down his first requirements and what he therefore expected from the local Turks and demanded from the *rayah*—the Christian serfs.

Beside him sat Tosun Effendi, a small, pale, yellowish renegade, born in the Greek islands, a mason who had built many of Mehmed Pasha's bequests in Stambul. He remained quiet and indifferent, as if he were not hearing or did not understand Abidaga's speech. He gazed at his hands and only looked up from time to time. Then they could see his big black eyes, beautiful and short-sighted eyes with a velvety sheen, the eyes of a man who only looks to his work and does not see, does not feel and does not understand anything else in life or in the world.

The notables filed out of the small stuffy tent, troubled and downcast. They felt as if they were sweating under their new ceremonial clothes and each one of them felt fear and anxiety taking root in him.

A great and incomprehensible disaster had fallen upon the town and the whole of the district, a catastrophe whose end could not be foreseen. First of all began the felling of the forests and the transport of the timber. So great a mass of scaffolding arose on both banks of the Drina that for long the people thought that the bridge would be built of wood. Then the earthworks began, the excavations, the revetting of the chalky banks. These were mostly carried out by forced labor. So everything went on until the late autumn, when work was temporarily stopped and the first part of the construction completed.

All this was carried out under Abidaga's supervision and that of his long green staff which has passed into legend. Whomever he pointed at with this staff, having noticed that he was malingering or not working as he should, the guards seized; they beat him on the spot and then poured water over his bleeding and unconscious body and sent him back to work again. When in late autumn Abidaga left the town, he again sent for the notables and told them that he was going away to another place for the winter, but that his eye would still be on them. All would be responsible for everything. If it were found that any part of the work had been damaged, if a single stick were missing from the scaffolding, he would fine the whole town. When they ventured to say that damage might be caused by floods, he replied coldly and without hesitation that this was their district and the river too was theirs as well as whatever damage it might cause.

All the winter the townsmen guarded the material and watched the construction works like the eyes in their head. And when with the spring Abidaga once again appeared, with Tosun Effendi, there came with them Dalmatian stonemasons, whom the people called "Latin masters." At first there were about thirty of them, led by a certain Mastro Antonio, a Christian from Ulcinj. He was a tall, handsome man of keen eye, bold glance and hooked nose, with fair hair falling to his shoulders and dressed like a noble in the western manner. His assistant was a Negro, a real Negro, a young and merry man whom the whole town and all the workmen soon nicknamed "the Arab."

If in the previous year, judging from the mass of scaffolding, it seemed as if Abidaga had intended to build the bridge of wood, it now seemed to everyone that he wanted to build a new Stambul here on the Drina. Then began the hauling of stone from the quarries which had already been opened up in the hills near Banja, an hour's walk from the town.

Next year a most unusual spring broke near the Višegrad ferry. Besides all that which sprang up and flowered every year at that time, there arose out of the earth a whole settlement of huts; new roads made their appearance and new approaches to the water's edge. Countless oxcarts and packhorses swarmed on all sides. The men from Mejdan and Okolište saw how every day, like a sort of harvest, there grew there by the river a restless swarm of men, beasts and building material of every kind.

On the steep banks worked the master stone-masons. The whole area took on a sort of yellowish color from the stone-dust. And a little farther along, on the sandy plain, local workers were slaking lime and moving, ragged and pale, through the white smoke which rose high from the kilns. The roads were torn to pieces by the overloaded carts. The ferry worked all day, taking from one bank to the other building material, overseers and workmen. Wading in the spring waters up to their waists, special workmen drove in piles and stakes and put in position gabions filled with clay, intended to break the current.

All this was watched by those who up till then had lived peacefully in their scattered houses on the slopes near the Drina ferry. And it would have been well for them had they been able only to watch, but the work soon became so extensive and its impetus so great that it drew into the whirlpool everything alive or dead, not only in the town but also from great distances away. With the second year the number of workers had grown to such an extent that they equaled all the male inhabitants of the town. All carts, all horses and oxen worked only for the bridge. Everything that could creep or roll was taken and pressed into service, sometimes paid but sometimes by force. There was more money than before, but high prices and shortages increased more rapidly than the money flowed in, so that when it reached men's hands it was already half eaten away. Even worse than the rise in prices and the shortages was the unrest, disorder and insecurity which now enveloped the town as a consequence of the incursion of so many workmen from the outer world. Despite all Abidaga's severity, there were frequent clashes among the workers, and many thefts from the gardens and courtyards. The Moslem women had to keep their faces veiled even when they went into their own yards, for the gaze of the countless workers, local and foreign, might come from anywhere and the Turks of the town kept the practices of Islam very strictly, the more so since they were all recently converted and there was scarcely one of them who did not remember either a father or a grandfather who was a Christian or a recently converted Turk. Because of this the older persons who followed the law of Islam were openly indignant and turned their backs on this chaotic mass of workers, draft animals, wood, earth and stone which grew ever larger and more complicated on both sides of the ferry and which, in the underpinning operations, broke into their streets, their courtyards and their gardens.

At first they had all been proud of the great bequest which the Vezir was to erect in their district. Then they had not realized, as they now saw with their own eyes, that these glorious buildings involved so much disorder and unrest, effort and expense. It was a fine thing, they thought, to belong to the pure ruling faith; it was a fine thing to have as a countryman the Vezir in Stambul, and still finer to imagine the strong, costly bridge across the river, but what was happening now in no way resembled this. Their town had been turned into a hell, a devil's dance of incomprehensible works, of smoke, dust, shouts and tumult. The years passed, the work extended and grew greater, but there was no end or thought of end to be seen. It looked like anything you like, but not a bridge.

So thought the recently converted Turks of the town and, in private among themselves, avowed that they were fed up to the teeth with lordship and pride and future glory and had had more than enough of the bridge and the Vezir. They only prayed Allah to deliver them from this disaster and restore to them and their homes their former peace and the quietness of their humble lives beside the old-fashioned ferry on the river.

All this affected the Turks, but even more it affected the Christian *rayah* of the whole Višegrad district, with this difference, that no one asked their opinion about anything, nor were they even able to express their indignation. It was now the third year since the people had been on forced labor for the new bridge, they themselves and all their horses and oxen. And that too not only for the local *rayah* but also all those from the nearby districts. Everywhere Abidaga's guards and horsemen seized the *rayah* from the villages and even the towns and drove them away to work on the bridge. Usually they surprised them while sleeping and pinioned them like chickens. Through all Bosnia, traveler told traveler not to go to the Drina, for whoever went there was seized, without question of who or what he was or where he was going, and was forced to work for at least a few days. The young men in the villages tried to run away into the forests, but the guards took hostages from their houses, often women, in place of those who fled.

This was the third autumn that the people had been forced to labor on the bridge and in no way could it be seen that the work was progressing or that the end of their misfortune was in sight. Autumn was already in full spate; the roads were breaking up from the rains, the Drina was rising and troubled, and the bare stubble full of slow-winged ravens. But Abidaga did not halt the work. Under the wan November sun the peasants dragged wood and stone, waded with bare feet or in sandals of freshly slaughtered hide along the muddy roads, sweating with strain or chilled by the wind, folding around themselves cloaks full of new holes and old patches, and knotting up the ragged ends of their single shirts of coarse linen, blackened by rain, mud and smoke, which they dared not wash lest they fall to pieces in the water. Over all of them hovered Abidaga's green staff, for Abidaga visited both the quarries at Banja and the works around the bridge several times each day. He was filled with rage and fury against the whole world because the days were growing shorter and the work had not progressed as quickly as he wished. In a heavy surcoat of Russian fur and high boots, he climbed, with red congested face, over the scaffolding of such piers as already arose from the waters, visited forges, barracks and workers' huts and swore at everyone he came across, overseers and contractors alike.

"The days are short. Always shorter. You sons of bitches, you are eating your bread for nothing!"

He burst out in fury, as if they were to blame because it dawned late and darkened early. Before twilight, that relentless and implacable Višegrad twilight, when the steep hills seemed to close in over the town and each night fell quickly, as heavy and deaf as the last, Abidaga's fury rose to its height; and having no one left on whom to vent his wrath, he turned it on himself and could not sleep for thinking of so much work not being done and so many people malingering and wasting time. He ground his teeth. He summoned the overseers and worked out how, from then on, it would be possible to make better use of the daylight and exploit the workers more effectively.

The people were sleeping in their huts and stables, resting and restoring their forces. But all did not sleep; they too knew how to keep vigil to their own profit and in their own manner. In a dry and spacious stable a fire was burning, or more exactly had been burning, for now only a few embers glowing in the half-lit space remained. The whole stable was filled with smoke and the heavy, sour smell of wet clothes and sandals and the exhalations of about thirteen human bodies. They were all pressed men, peasants from the neighborhood, Christian *rayah.* All were muddy and wet through, exhausted and careworn. They resented this unpaid and pointless forced labor while up there in the villages their fields awaited the autumn ploughing in vain. The greater number were still awake. They were drying their gaiters by the fire, plaiting sandals or only gazing at the embers. Among them was a certain Montenegrin, no one knew from where, whom the guards had seized on the road and had pressed for labor for several days, though he kept telling them and proving to them how wearisome and hard this work was for him and how his honor could not endure this work for slaves.

Most of the wakeful peasants, especially the younger ones, gathered around him. From the deep pocket of his cloak the Montenegrin drew out a *gusle,* a tiny primitive fiddle, clumsy and as small as the palm of a man's hand, and a short bow. One of the peasants went outside and mounted guard before the stable lest some Turk should chance to come along. All looked at the Montenegrin as if they saw him for the first time and at the *gusle* which seemed to disappear in his huge hands. He bent over, the *gusle* in his lap, and pressed its head under his chin, greased the string with resin and breathed heavily on the bow; everything was moist and slack. While he occupied himself with these petty tasks, calmly and self-confidently as if he were alone in the world, they all looked at him without a movement. At last the first notes wailed out, sharp and uneven. The excitement rose. The Montenegrin found the key and began to sing through his nose and accompany himself with the *gusle.*

Everyone was intent, awaiting the wonderful tale. Then, suddenly, after he had more or less attuned his voice to the *gusle,* the Montenegrin threw back his head proudly and violently so that his Adam's apple stood out in his scrawny neck and his sharp profile was outlined in the firelight, and sang in a strangled and constrained voice: A-a-a-a-a-a-a-a- and then all at once in a clear and ringing tone:

"The Serbian Tsar Stefan
Drank wine in fertile Prizren,
By him sat the old patriarchs,
Four of them, the old patriarchs;
Next them were nine bishops
And a score of three-tailed Vezirs
And the ranks of Serbian nobles.
Wine was served by Michael the cup-bearer
And on the breast of the sister Kandosia
Shone the light of precious stones . . ."

The peasants pressed closer and closer around the singer but without making the slightest noise; their very breathing could be heard. They half closed their eyes, carried away with wonder. Thrills ran up and down their spines, their backs straightened up, their breasts expanded, their eyes shone, their fingers opened and shut and their jaw muscles tightened. The Montenegrin developed his melody more and more rapidly, even more beautiful and bolder, while the wet and sleepless workmen, carried away and insensible to all else, followed the tale as if it were their own more beautiful and more glorious destiny.

Among the countless peasants pressed for hard labor was a certain Radisav from Unište, a small village quite close to the town. He was a smallish man, dark-faced, with restless eyes, a little bent, and walked quickly, spreading out his legs and moving his head and shoulders from left to right, right to left, as if sowing wheat. He was not as poor as he appeared to be, nor as simple as he made himself out. His family were known as the Heraci; they had good land and there were many males in the house, but almost the whole village had been converted to Islam over the past forty years so that they were lonely and isolated. This small, bowed Radisav had been scurrying about from one stable to the next these autumn nights "sowing" revolt and had insinuated himself among the peasants like an eel, whispering and counseling with one only at a time. What he said was roughly this:

"Brother, we have had enough of this. We must defend ourselves. You can see for yourself that this building work will be the death of all of us; it will eat us all up. Even our children will have to do forced labor on the bridge, if there are any of us left. For us this work means extermination and nothing less. A bridge is no good to the poor and to the *rayah,* but only for the Turks; we can neither raise armies nor carry on trade. For us the ferry is more than enough. So a few of us have agreed among ourselves to go by night, at the darkest hour, and break down and spoil as much as possible of what has been done, and to spread the rumor that it is a *vila,* a fairy, who is destroying the works at the bridge and who does not want any bridge over the Drina. We shall see if this will be of any help. We have no other way and something must be done."

There were, as always, some who were fainthearted and unreliable, who thought this to be a sterile idea; since the cunning and powerful Turks would not be turned away from their intention they would have to do forced labor even longer since God so willed. They should not make bad worse. But there were also those who felt that anything was better than to go on slaving and to wait until even the last rag of clothing fell from a man and the last ounce of strength be wasted by the heavy labor and Abidaga's short commons; and that they must follow anyone who was willing to go to extremes. These were for the most part young men, but there were also serious married men, with families, who agreed, though without enthusiasm or fire, and who said worriedly:

"Come and let's break it down; may his blood eat him up before he eats us up. And if that does not help. . . ."

And at that point they waved their hands in desperate resolution.

So in these first autumn days the rumor began to spread, first among the workers and then in the town itself, that the *vila* of the waters had intervened in the work on the bridge, that she destroyed and pulled down overnight what had been built by day and that the whole scheme would come to nothing. At the same time, inexplicable damage began to appear over night in the revetments and even in the masonry itself. The tools which the masons had up till then left on the piers began to get lost and disappear, the revetments to break down and be carried away by the waters.

The rumor that the bridge would never be finished spread far afield. Both Turks and Christians spread it and little by little it took form as a firm belief. The Christian *rayah* were jubilant, whispering it stealthily and soundlessly but from a full heart. The local Turks, who had earlier looked on the Vezir's building work with pride, began to wink disdainfully and wave their hands. Many of the converted Turks who, in changing faith, had not found what they had hoped for, but had continued to sit down to a meager supper and go about with patched elbows, heard the rumor and repeated with enjoyment the story of the great lack of success and found some sort of proud satisfaction in the thought that not even Vezirs could carry out everything they had a mind to do. It was already being said that the foreign *maestri* were preparing to leave and that there would be no bridge there where no bridge had ever been before and where it should never have been begun. All these tales blended and spread quickly.

The common people easily make up fables and spread them quickly, wherein reality is strangely and inextricably mixed and interwoven with legend. The peasants who listened at night to the *gusle* player said that the *vila* who was destroying the bridge had told Abidaga that she would not cease her work of destruction until twin children, Stoja and Ostoja by name, should be walled into the foundations. Many swore that they had seen the guards who were searching for such a pair of children in the villages (the guards were indeed going around the villages but they were not looking for children but listening for rumors and interrogating the people in order to try and find out who were those unknown persons who were destroying the bridge).

A short time before, it had happened that in a village above Višegrad a poor stuttering half-witted girl, who was a servant, became pregnant, she herself would not say, or could not say, by whom. It was a rare and almost unheard of event that a girl, and such a girl, should conceive and still more so that the father should remain unknown. The story was noised far abroad. In good time the girl gave birth, in some stable or other, to twins, both stillborn. The women from the village who helped her at the birth, which was exceptionally difficult, at once buried the children in a plum orchard. But on the third day after, the unfortunate mother got up and began to look for her children everywhere in the village. In vain they explained to her that the children had been born dead and had been buried. Finally, in order to be rid of her incessant questionings, they told her, or rather explained to her by gestures, that her children had been taken away to the town, down there where the Turks were building the bridge. Weak and distraught, she wandered down into the town and began to range around the ferry and the construction works, looking fearfully into the eyes of the men there and asking in incomprehensible stutterings for her children. The men looked at her in amazement or drove her away so that she should not hinder them at their work. Seeing that they did not understand what she wanted, she unbuttoned her coarse peasant shift and showed them her breasts, painful and swollen, on which the nipples had already begun to crack and showed all bloody from the milk that flowed from them irresistibly. No one knew how to help her and explain to her that her children had not been walled up in the bridge, for to all kind words and assurances, curses and threats, she only stuttered miserably and with sharp distrustful glances peered into every corner. Finally they gave up persecuting her and allowed her to wander about the construction work, avoiding her with a sorrowful compassion. The cooks gave her some of the worker's porridge which had got burned at the bottom of the cauldrons. They called her mad Ilinka and, after them, the whole town did so. Even Abidaga himself passed by her without cursing her, turning his head away superstitiously, and ordered that she be given alms. So she went on living there, a harmless idiot, by the construction works. And because of her the story remained that the Turks had walled her children into the bridge. Some believed it and others not, but none the less it was repeated all the more and noised afar.

Meanwhile the damage went on, now less now more, and parallel with it the rumors spread even more obstinately that the *vilas* would not permit a bridge to be built across the Drina.

Abidaga was furious. It enraged him that anyone could be found who dared to undertake anything against his work or his intentions despite his proverbial harshness which he cultivated as a special subject for pride. Also all these people disgusted him, the Moslems as much as the Christians; slow and unskilled in their work, they were quick enough for raillery and lack of respect and knew only too well how to find mocking and corrosive words for everything they did not understand or did not know how to do. He posted guards on both banks of the river. The damage to the earthworks then ceased, but damage to the construction work in the river itself continued. Only on moonlit nights was there no damage. That confirmed Abidaga, who did not believe in the *vila,* in his belief that this particular *vila* was not invisible and did not descend from on high. For a long time he would not, or could not, believe those who said it was due to peasant cunning, but now he was convinced that that was exactly what it was. And that excited him to still greater fury. But he none the less knew that he must appear calm and hide his fury if he wanted to snare these pests and finish once and for all with these tales about *vilas* and about stopping work on the bridge, which might become dangerous. He summoned the chief of the guards, a certain man from Plevlje, who had grown up in Stambul, a pale and unhealthy man.

The two men were instinctively hostile to one another, but at the same time were continually drawn together and came into conflict. Between them incomprehensible feelings of hatred, repulsion, fear and distrust were woven permanently. Abidaga, who was mild and pleasant towards no one, displayed an unconcealed repulsion towards this pale-faced renegade. All that he did or said drove Abidaga into a frenzy and provoked him to curse and humiliate him, but the more that the man from Plevlje abased himself and was obsequious, the greater grew Abidaga's repulsion. From the first day of their meeting the leader of the guards was superstitiously and terribly afraid of Abidaga and this fear became in time an oppressive nightmare which never left him. At every step and movement, often in his dreams, he would think: what will Abidaga say about this? In vain he tried to please him and do what he wished. Everything that came from him Abidaga accepted with disdain. And that incomprehensible hatred hampered and disconcerted the man from Plevlje and made him still stiffer and clumsier. He believed that, because of Abidaga, he would one day lose not only his job and his position, but also his head. Therefore he lived in a state of permanent agitation and passed from dull discouragement to a feverish and cruel zeal. When now, pale and stiff, he stood before Abidaga, the latter spoke to him in a voice hoarse with anger.

"Listen, blockhead, you are clever with these sons of sows, you know their language and all their monkey-tricks. Yet for all that you are incapable of finding out what scab it is who has dared to spoil the Vezir's work. That is because you are a scab yourself, the same as they are, and the only worse scab is whoever made you leader and a chief and has found nobody to reward you as you deserve. So I will do so, since there is no other. Know that I will put you under the earth so that you will not throw as much shadow as even the tiniest blade of grass. If all damage to the works does not cease within three days, if you do not catch whoever is doing this and do not put an end to all these silly stories about *vilas* and about stopping the work, then I will put you living on a stake on the highest part of the staging, that all may see you and take fright and get some sense into their heads. I swear this by my life and my faith, which I do not swear by lightly. Today is Thursday. You have till Sunday. Now go to the devil who sent you to me. Go! March!"

Even without this oath the man from Plevlje would have believed Abidaga's threat, for even in his dreams he used to shudder at his words and at his glance. Now he went out in one of his fits of panic-stricken terror and at once set desperately to work. He summoned his own men and, passing suddenly from dull torpor to mad rage, he began to curse them.

"Blind good-for-nothings!" raged the man from Plevlje, as if he were already placed alive upon the stake and yelling in the face of each of the guards. "Is it thus that you keep watch and look after the Sultan's interests? You are quick and lively enough when you go to the cooking pots, but when you are on duty your legs are leaden and your wits are dull. My face burns because of you. But you will do no more slacking in my employ. I will massacre all of you; not a single one of you will keep his head on his shoulders if in two days this business does not end and if you do not seize and kill these bastards. You have still two days to live. I swear it by my faith and the Koran!"

He went on shouting in this way for a long time. Then, not knowing what else to say to them or with what more to threaten them, he spat at them one by one. But when he had played himself out and freed himself from the pressure of his fear (which had taken the form of rage) he set to work at once with desperate energy. He spent the night cruising up and down the banks with his men. At one time during the night it seemed to them that something was knocking at that part of the staging which was farthest out in the river and they rushed thither. They heard a plank crack and a stone fall into the river, but when they got to the spot they indeed found some broken scaffolding and a part of the masonry torn away but no trace of the miscreants. Faced with that ghostly emptiness the guards shivered from superstitious fright and from the darkness and moisture of the night. They called to one another, peered into the blackness, waved lighted torches, but all in vain. The damage had been done again, and they who had done it had not been caught and killed, as though in very truth they were invisible.

The next night the man from Plevlje arranged his ambush better. He sent some of his men over to the farther bank also and when night fell he hid guards in the scaffolding right out to the end and he himself with two others sat in a boat which he had drawn unnoticed in the darkness to the left bank. Thence in a few strokes they could be at one of the two piers on which construction had begun. In this way he could fall on the miscreants from two sides, so that they could not escape unless they had wings or could go under water.

All that long cold night the man from Plevlje lay in the boat covered with sheepskins, tormented by the dark thoughts whirling in his head; would Abidaga really carry out his threat and take his life which, under such a chief, was in any case no life but only terror and torment? But along the whole of the construction works not a murmur could be heard except the monotonous lapping and lisping of the unseen waters. Thus it dawned and the man from Plevlje felt in all his stiffened body that his life was darkening and shortening.

On the next, the third and last night, there was the same vigil, the same arrangements, the same fearful listening. Midnight passed. The man from Plevlje was seized with a mortal apathy. Then he heard a slight splash and then, louder, a blow on the oak beams which were placed in the river and on which the staging rested. There was a sharp whistle. But the leader's boat had already moved. Standing upright, he peered into the darkness, waving his hands and shouting in a hoarse voice:

"Row, row. . . ."

The men, half awake, rowed vigorously, but a strong current caught the boat earlier than it should have. Instead of reaching the staging, the boat turned down river. They were unable to make way against the current and it would have swept them far away had not something unexpectedly checked them.

There, right in the middle of the main current, where there were neither beams nor scaffolding, their boat struck something heavy and wooden which echoed dully. Only then did they realize that on the scaffolding above them the guards were struggling with something. The guards, local renegades, were all shouting at once; they fell over one another in the darkness in a medley of broken and incomprehensible cries:

"Hold there, don't let go!"

"Hey, fellows, here!"

"It's me! . . ."

Between the shouts some heavy object or human body could be heard splashing into the water.

The man from Plevlje was for some moments uncertain where he was or what was happening, but as soon as he had come to his senses he began to pull with an iron hook at the end of a long pole at the beams on which his boat had struck and succeeded in pulling the boat upstream nearer and nearer the scaffolding. Soon he was up to the oak piles and, taking heart, shouted at the top of his voice:

"Lights! Light a torch there! Throw me a rope!"

At first no one answered. Then, after

much shouting, in which no one listened to or could understand anyone else, a weak torch glimmered uncertainly and fitfully above. This first spark of light only confused the eyes even more and mingled in an uneasy whirl, men, things and their shadows with the red reflections on the water. But then another torch flamed in another hand. The light steadied and men began to pull themselves together and recognize one another. Soon everything became clear and explicable.

Between the boat of the man from Plevlje and the scaffolding lay a small raft made of only three planks; at the front was an oar, a real raftsman's oar, only shorter and weaker. The raft was moored with a bark cord to one of the beams under the scaffolding and was held thus against the swift waters which splashed about it and tried with all their force to pull it away downstream. The guards on the staging helped their leader to cross the raft and climb up to them. All were haggard and out of breath. On the planks a Christian peasant was lying. His breast was heaving quickly and violently and his eyes starting out of his head, showed fear-stricken whites.

The oldest of the four guards explained to their excited leader that they had been keeping watch at various points on the staging. When they heard the sound of oars in the darkness, they had thought it was their leader's boat, but they had been clever enough not to show themselves and to wait and see what would happen. Then they saw two peasants who approached the piers and with some difficulty moored their raft to one of them. They let them climb up and come among them and then they attacked them with axes, overcame them and bound them. One, who had been struck unconscious by a blow from an axe, they had bound easily, but the other one, after pretending to be half-dead, had slipped from their grasp like a fish through the planks into the water. The frightened guard halted in his story and the man from Plevlje screamed:

"Who let him go? Tell me who let him go, or I shall chop you into small pieces, all of you."

The men stood silently and blinked at the red flickering light while their leader kept turning around as if searching the darkness, and shouting insults at them such as they had never heard him use by day. Then, suddenly, he started, leaned over the bound peasant as if over a precious hoard, and began to mutter through his teeth in a thin lachrymose voice:

"Guard him, guard him well! You bastards, if you let him go, not a single one of you will keep his head on his shoulders."

The guards crowded round the peasant. Two more hurried to join them, crossing the ferry from the farther bank. The man from Plevlje ordered them to bind the prisoner more securely. So they carried him like a corpse slowly and carefully to the bank. The man from Plevlje went with them, not looking where he was treading and never taking his eyes from the bound man. It seemed to him that he was growing in stature with every step, that only from that moment was he beginning to live.

On the bank new torches were lighted and began to flare up. The captive peasant was taken into one of the workmen's barracks where there was a fire, and was bound tightly to a post with ropes and chains taken from the hearth.

It was Radisav of Unište himself.

The man from Plevlje calmed down a little; he no longer screamed or swore, but he was unable to keep still. He sent guards along the banks to look for the other peasant who had leapt into the water, though it was clear that on so dark a night, if he had not drowned, it would be impossible to find or catch him. He gave order after order, went out, came in again and then once again went back, drunk with excitement. He began to interrogate the bound peasant, but soon left off doing that also. All that he did was only to master and conceal his nervousness, for in fact he had only one thought in his head; he was waiting for Abidaga. He had not long to wait.

As soon as he had slept out his first sleep Abidaga, as was his habit, waked shortly after midnight and, no longer able to sleep, stood by his window and looked out into the darkness. By day he could see from his balcony at Bikavac the whole river valley and all the construction works, with the barracks, mills, stables and all that devastated and littered space around them. Now in the darkness he sensed their presence and thought with bitterness how slowly the work was proceeding and how, sooner or later, this must reach the Vezir's ears. Someone would be sure to see to that. If no one else, then that smooth, cold and crafty Tosun Effendi. Then it might chance that he might fall into disgrace with the Vezir. That was what prevented him from sleeping, and even when he did fall asleep he trembled in his dreams. His food seemed poison to him, men seemed odious and his life dark when he even thought of it. Disgrace—that meant that he would be exiled from the Vezir's presence, that his enemies would laugh at him (Ah! Anything but that!), that he would be nothing and nobody, no more than a rag, a good for nothing, not only in the eyes of others but also in his own. It would mean giving up his hard won fortune or, if he managed to keep it, to eke it out stealthily, far from Stambul, somewhere in the obscure provinces, forgotten, superfluous, ridiculous, wretched. No, anything but that! Better not to see the sun, not to breathe the air. It would be a hundred times better to be nobody and to have nothing. That was the thought that always came back to him and several times a day forced the blood to beat painfully in his skull and his temples, but even at other times never completely left him but lay like a black cloud within him. That was what disgrace meant to him, and disgrace was possible every day, every hour, since everyone was working to bring it on him. Only he alone worked against it and defended himself; it was one man against everyone and everything. That had now lasted fifteen years, from the first time that the Vezir had entrusted him with a great and important task. Who could endure it? Who could sleep and be at peace?

Although it was a cold damp autumn night, Abidaga opened the casement and looked into the darkness, for the closed room seemed stifling to him. Then he noticed that there were lights and movements on the scaffolding and along the banks. When he saw that there were more and more of them, he thought that something unusual must have happened, dressed and woke his servant. Thus he arrived at the lighted stable just at the moment when the man from Plevlje no longer knew what further insults to use, whom to order and what to do to shorten the time.

The unexpected arrival of Abidaga completely bewildered him. So much had he longed for this moment, yet now that it had come he did not know how to profit from it as he had hoped. He stuttered in excitement and forgot all about the bound peasant. Abidaga only gazed through him disdainfully and went straight up to the prisoner.

In the stable they had built up a big fire to which the guards kept adding fresh faggots so that even the most distant corner was lit up.

Abidaga stood looking down at the bound peasant for he was much the taller man. He was calm and thoughtful. Everyone waited for him to speak, while he thought to himself; so this is the one with whom I have had to struggle and fight, this is what my position and my fate depended upon, this wretched half-witted renegade from Plevlje and the incomprehensible and obdurate opposition of this louse from the *rayah*. Then he shook himself and began to give orders and to question the peasant.

The stable filled with guards, and outside could be heard the voices of the awakened overseers and workmen. Abidaga put his questions through the man from Plevlje.

Radisav first said that he and another man had decided to run away and that therefore they had prepared a small raft and set off downstream. When they pointed out to him the senselessness of this story since it was impossible in the darkness to go down the turbulent river full of whirlpools, rocks and shoals, and that those who want to run away do not climb on the scaffolding and damage the works, he fell silent and only muttered sullenly:

"Well, I am in your hands. Do what you like."

"You will soon find out what we like," Abidaga retorted briskly.

The guards took away the chains and stripped the peasant to the buff. They threw the chains into the heart of the fire and waited. As the chains were covered with soot, their hands were blackened and great patches were left on themselves and on the half-naked peasant. When the chains were almost red hot, Merdjan the Gipsy came up and took one end of them in a long pair of tongs, while one of the guards took the other end.

The man from Plevlje translated Abidaga's words.

"Perhaps now you will tell the whole truth."

"What have I got to tell you? You know everything and can do what you like."

The two men brought the chains and wrapped them round the peasant's broad hairy chest. The scorched hair began to sizzle. His mouth contracted, the veins in his neck swelled, his ribs seemed to stand out and his stomach muscles to contract and relax as when a man vomits. He groaned from the pain, strained at the ropes which bound him and writhed and twisted in vain to lessen the contact of his body with the red hot iron. His eyes closed and the tears flowed down his cheeks. They took the chain away.

"That was only the beginning. Isn't it better to talk without that?"

The peasant only breathed heavily through his nose, and remained silent.

"Who was with you?"

"His name was Jovan, but I do not know either his house or his village."

They brought the chains again and the burning hair and skin sizzled. Coughing from the smoke and writhing from the pain, the peasant began to speak jerkily.

Those two alone had come to an agreement to destroy the work on the bridge. They thought that it had to be done and they had done it. No one else had known anything about it or had taken part in it. At first they had set out from the banks in various places and been quite successful, but when they saw that there were guards on the scaffolding and along the banks, they had thought of binding three planks together to make a raft and thus, unnoticed, approach the work from the river. That had been three days ago. On the first night they had nearly been caught. They only just got away. So the next night they had not gone out at all. When they tried again that same night with the raft, there had happened what had happened.

"That is all. So it was, and so we worked. Now do what you will."

"No, no, this is not what we want. Tell

us who made you do this! What you have suffered up till now is nothing to what you will get later on!"

"Well, do what you like."

Merdjan then came nearer with a pair of pincers. He knelt in front of the bound man and began to tear the nails off his naked feet. The peasant remained silent and clenched his teeth but a strange trembling shook his whole body up to the waist even though he was bound which showed that the pain must have been exceptionally great. After a few moments the peasant forced a few muttered words through his teeth. The man from Plevlje, who had been hanging on his every word and waiting eagerly for some sort of admission, made a sign with his hand to the gipsy to stop and at once asked:

"What was that? What did you say?"

"Nothing. I only said: why in the name of God do you waste your time torturing me?"

"Tell us who made you do it?"

"Who made me do it? Why, the devil."

"The devil?"

"The devil. Certainly that same devil who made you come here and build the bridge!"

The peasant spoke softly, but clearly and decisively.

The devil! A strange word, said so bitterly in so unusual a situation. The devil! The devil is certainly somewhere in this, thought the man from Plevlje, standing with bowed head as if the bound man were questioning him and not he the bound man. The words touched him on a sensitive spot and awoke in him all of a sudden all his anxieties and fears, in all their strength and terror, as if they had never been swept away by the capture of the culprit. Perhaps indeed all this, with Abidaga and the building of the bridge and this mad peasant, was the devil's work. The devil! Perhaps he was the only one to fear. The man from Plevlje shivered and shook himself. At that moment the loud and angry voice of Abidaga brought him to himself.

"What's the matter with you? Are you asleep, good-for-nothing?" shouted Abidaga, striking his right boot with his short leather whip.

The gipsy was still kneeling with the pincers in his hand and looking upwards with black shining eyes, frightened and humble, at the tall figure of Abidaga. The guards piled up the fire which was already roaring. The whole place shone; it was like a furnace but somehow solemn. What that evening had seemed a gloomy and undistinguished building all at once was transformed, became larger, widened out. In the stable and around it reigned a sort of solemn emotion and a special silence as there is in places where one extracts the truth, a living man is tortured or where fateful things occur. Abidaga, the man from Plevlje and the bound man moved and spoke like actors and all the others went on tiptoe with lowered eyes, not speaking save when forced to and then only in a whisper. Everyone wished to be somewhere else, only not to be in this place nor at this work, but since that was not possible, they all lowered their voices and moved as little as they could, as if to get as far away as possible from this affair.

Seeing that the interrogation was going slowly and did not give any hope of results, Abidaga with impatient movements and loud oaths went out of the stable. After him reeled the man from Plevlje, followed by the guards.

Outside it was growing light. The sun had not yet risen, but the whole horizon was clear. Deep among the hills the clouds lay in long dull purple bands and between them could be seen the clear sky almost green in color. Scattered patches of mist lay over the moist earth out of which peeked the tops of the fruit trees with sparse yellowish leaves. Still striking at his boot with his whip, Abidaga gave orders. The criminal should continue to be interrogated, especially about those who had helped him, but he should not be tortured beyond endurance lest he die. Everything must be made ready so that at noon that same day he should be impaled alive on the outermost part of the construction work at its highest point, so that the whole town and all the workers should be able to see him from the banks of the river; Merdjan was to get everything ready and the town-crier to announce the execution through all the quarters of the town, so that at midday all the people might see what happened to those who hindered the building of the bridge, and that the whole male population, both Turks and *rayah,* from children to old men, must gather on one or other of the banks to witness it.

The day which was dawning was a Sunday. On Sunday work went on as on any other day, but this day even the overseers were distrait. As soon as it was broad daylight, the news spread about the capture of the criminal, his torture and his execution which was to to take place at midday. The hushed and solemn mood of the stable spread over the whole area about the building works. The men on forced labor worked silently, each one avoided looking his neighbor in the eyes, and each man looked only to the work before him as if that were the beginning and the end of his world.

An hour before noon the people of the town, for the most part Turks, had collected on a level space near the bridge. Children were hoisted on to high blocks of building stone which were lying about. The workmen swarmed around the narrow benches where the meager rations which kept them alive were usually distributed. Chewing at them, they were silent and looked uneasily about them. A little later Abidaga appeared, accompanied by Tosun Effendi, Mastro Antonio and one or two of the more prominent Turks. All stood on a small dry hummock between the bridge and the stable where the condemned man was. Abidaga went once more to the stable, where he was told that everything was ready; lying there was an oak stake about eight feet long, pointed as was necessary and tipped with iron, quite thin and sharp, and all well greased with lard. On the scaffolding were the blocks between which the stake would be embedded and nailed, a wooden mallet for the impalement, ropes and everything else that was needed.

The man from Plevlje was distraught, his face earthen in color and his eyes bloodshot. Even now he was not able to endure Abidaga's flaming glances.

"Listen, you! If everything is not as it should be and if you disgrace me in public, neither you nor your bastard of a gipsy will ever appear before me again, for I will drown you both in the Drina like a pair of blind puppies."

Then, turning to the shivering gipsy, he said more kindly:

"You will get six grosh for the job, and another six if he stays alive till nightfall. See to it!"

The *hodja* called out from the main mosque in the market-place in a clear sharp voice. Uneasiness spread among the assembled people and a few moments later the door of the stable opened. Ten guards were drawn up in two ranks, five on either side. Between them was Radisav, barefooted and bareheaded, alert and stooping as ever, but he no longer "sowed" as he walked but marched strangely with short steps, almost skipping on his mutilated feet with bleeding holes where the nails had been; on his shoulders he carried a long white sharpened stake. Behind him was Merdjan with two other gipsies who were to be his helpers in the execution of the sentence. Suddenly from somewhere or other the man from Plevlje appeared on his bay and took his place at the head of the procession, which only had to go about a hundred paces to reach the first scaffolding.

The people craned their necks and stood on tiptoe to see the man who had hatched the plot and destroyed the building work. They were all astonished at the poor miserable appearance of the man they had imagined to be quite different. Naturally, none of them knew why he hopped in so droll a manner and took abrupt little steps, and none of them could see the burns from the chains which crossed his chest like great belts, for his shirt and cloak hid them. Therefore he seemed to all those there too wretched and too insignificant to have done the deed which now brought him to execution. Only the long white stake gave a sort of gruesome grandeur to the scene and kept everyone's eyes fixed on it.

When they reached the spot on the bank where the excavation work began, the man from Plevlje dismounted and with a sort of solemn and theatrical air gave the reins to a groom, then disappeared with the others in the steep muddy track which led down to the water's edge. A little later the people saw them again as they appeared in the same order on the staging, climbing upwards slowly and carefully. On the narrow passages made of planks and beams the guards closely surrounded Radisav and kept him very near them lest he should leap into the river. They dragged their way along slowly and climbed even higher till they reached the top. There, high above the water, was a boarded space about the size of a small room. On it, as on a raised stage, they took their places, Radisav, the man from Plevlje and the three gipsies, with the rest of the guards posted around them on the staging.

The people watching moved uneasily and shifted about. Only a hundred paces separated them from those planks, so that they could see every man and every movement, but could not hear words or distinguish details. The people and the workmen on the left bank were about three times farther away, and moved around as much as they could and made every effort to try to see and hear better. But they could hear nothing and what they could see seemed at first only too ordinary and uninteresting and at the end so terrible that they turned their heads away and many quickly went home, regretting that they had ever come.

When they ordered Radisav to lie down, he hesitated a moment and then, looking past the gipsies and guards as if they were not there, came close up to the man from Plevlje and said almost confidentially as if speaking to a friend, softly and heavily:

"Listen, by this world and the next, do your best to pierce me well so that I may not suffer like a dog."

The man from Plevlje started and shouted at him, as if defending himself from that too intimate approach:

"March, Vlach! You who are so great a hero as to destroy the Sultan's work now beg for mercy like a woman. It will be as it has been ordered and as you have deserved."

Radisav bent his head still lower and the gipsies came up and began to strip off his cloak and his shirt. On his chest the wounds from the chains stood out, red and swollen. Without another word the peasant lay down as he had been ordered, face downward. The gipsies approached and the first bound his hands behind his back; then they attached a cord to each of his legs, around the ankles. Then they pulled outwards and to the side, stretching his legs wide apart. Meanwhile Merdjan placed the stake on two small wooden chocks so that it pointed between the peasant's legs. Then he took from his belt a short broad knife, knelt beside the stretched-out man and leaned over him to cut away the cloth of his trousers and to widen the opening through which the stake would enter his body. This most terrible part of the bloody task was, luckily, invisible to the onlookers. They could only see the bound body shudder at the short and unexpected prick of the knife, then half rise as if it were going to stand up, only to fall back again at once, striking dully against the planks. As soon as he had finished, the gipsy leaped up, took the wooden mallet and with slow measured blows began to strike the lower blunt end of the stake. Between each two blows he would stop for a moment and look first at the body in which the stake was penetrating and then at the two gipsies, reminding them to pull slowly and evenly. The body of the peasant, spreadeagled, writhed convulsively; at each blow of the mallet his spine twisted and bent, but the cords pulled at it and kept it straight. The silence from both banks of the river was such that not only every blow but even its echo from somewhere along the steep bank could be clearly heard. Those nearest could hear how the man beat with his forehead against the planks, and, even more, another and unusual sound, that was neither a scream, nor a wail, nor a groan, nor anything human; that stretched and twisted body emitted a sort of creaking and cracking like a fence that is breaking down or a tree that is being felled. At every second blow the gipsy went over to the stretched-out body and leaned over it to see whether the stake was going in the right direction and when he had satisfied himself that it had not touched any of the more important internal organs he returned and went on with his work.

From the banks all this could scarcely be heard and still less seen, but all stood there trembling, their faces blanched and their fingers chilled with cold.

For a moment the hammering ceased. Merdjan now saw that close to the right shoulder muscles the skin was stretched and swollen. He went forward quickly and cut the swollen place with two crossed cuts. Pale blood flowed out, at first slowly then faster and faster. Two or three more blows, light and careful, and the iron-shod point of the stake began to break through at the place where he had cut. He struck a few more times until the point of the stake reached level with the right ear. The man was impaled on the stake as a lamb on the spit, only that the tip did not come through the mouth but in the back and had not seriously damaged the intestines, the heart or the lungs. Then Merdjan threw down the mallet and came nearer. He looked at the unmoving body, avoiding the blood which poured out of the places where the stake had entered and had come out again and was gathering in little pools on the planks. The two gipsies turned the stiffened body on its back and began to bind the legs to the foot of the stake. Meanwhile Merdjan looked to see if the man was still alive and carefully examined the face that had suddenly become swollen, wider and larger. The eyes were wide open and restless, but the eyelids were unmoving, the mouth was wide open but the two lips stiff and contracted and between them the clenched teeth shone white. Since the man could no longer control some of his facial muscles the face looked like a mask. But the heart beat heavily and the lungs worked with short, quickened breath. The two gipsies began to lift him up like a sheep on a spit. Merdjan shouted to them to take care and not shake the body; he himself went to help them. Then they embedded the lower, thicker end of the stake between two beams and fixed it there with huge nails and then behind, at the same height, buttressed the whole thing with a short strut which was nailed both to the stake and to a beam on the staging.

When that too had been done, the gipsies climbed down and joined the guards, and on that open space, raised a full eight feet upright, stiff and bare to the waist, the man on the stake remained alone. From a distance it could only be guessed that the stake to which his legs had been bound at the ankles passed right through his body. So that the people saw him as a statue, high up in the air on the very edge of the staging, high above the river.

A murmur and a wave of movement passed through the onlookers on the banks. Some lowered their eyes and others went quickly home without turning their heads. But the majority looked dumbly at this human likeness, up there in space, unnaturally stiff and upright. Fear chilled their entrails and their legs threatened to give way beneath them, but they were still unable to move away or take their eyes from the sight. And amid that terrified crowd mad Ilinka threaded her way, looking everyone in the eyes and trying to read their glances to find from them where her sacrificed and buried children were.

Then the man from Plevlje, Merdjan and a pair of guards went up to the impaled man and began to examine him more closely. Only a thin trickle of blood flowed down the stake. He was alive and conscious. His ribs rose and fell, the veins in his neck pulsed and his eyes kept turning slowly but unceasingly. Through the clenched teeth came a long drawn-out groaning in which a few words could with difficulty be distinguished.

"Turks, Turks, . . ." moaned the man on the stake, "Turks on the bridge . . . may you die like dogs . . . like dogs."

The gipsies picked up their tools and then, with the man from Plevlje, came down from the staging to the bank. The people made way for them and began to disperse. Only the children on the high blocks of stone and the bare trees waited a little longer, not knowing if this were the end or whether there would be more, to see what would happen next with that strange man who hovered over the waters as if suddenly frozen in the midst of a leap.

The man from Plevlje approached Abidaga and reported that everything had been carried out correctly and satisfactorily, that the criminal was still alive and that it seemed that he would go on living since his internal organs had not been damaged. Abidaga did not reply but only gave a sign with his hand to bring his horse and began to say goodbye to Tosun Effendi and Mastro Antonio. Everyone began to disperse. Through the market-place the town-crier could be heard announcing that the sentence had been carried out and that the same or a worse punishment awaited anyone who would do the like in future.

The man from Plevlje remained in perplexity on the level space which had now suddenly emptied. His servant held his horse and the guards waited for orders. He felt that he ought to say something but was not able to because of the wave of feeling that only now began to rise within him and choke him. Only now did he become conscious of all that he had forgotten since he had been too busy carrying out the sentence. He remembered Abidaga's threat that it would have been he who would have been placed upon the stake had he not succeeded in catching the criminal. He had escaped that horror, but only by a hair and only at the last moment. But things had turned out otherwise. The sight of that man, who was hanging, bound and still alive, over the river filled him with terror and also with a sort of painful joy that such a fate had not been his and that his body was still undamaged, was free and able to move. At that thought burning pains shot through his chest and spread into his legs and arms and forced him to move about, to smile and to speak, just to prove to himself that he was healthy, that he could move freely, could speak and laugh aloud, could even sing if he so wished, and not merely mutter useless curses from a stake, awaiting death as the only happiness which could still be his. His hands and arms moved to their own volition, his lips opened and from them flowed unwittingly a strangled laugh and a copious flow of words:

"Ha, ha, ha, Radisav, thou mountain *vila,* why so stiff? . . . Why not go on and undermine the bridge? . . . Why writhe and groan? Sing, *vila.* Dance, *vila!*"

Astonished and bewildered, the guards watched their leader dance with outstretched arms, heard him sing and choke with laughter and with strange words, saw the white foam oozing more and more from the corners of his lips. And his bay horse, in fear, cast sidelong glances at him.

4

All those who had been present at the execution of the sentence spread terrible reports through the town and the surrounding villages. An indescribable fear gripped the townsmen and the workers. Slowly and gradually a full consciousness of what had happened in their midst in the course of a short November day came home to them. All conversation centered on the man who, high up there on the scaffolding, was still alive on the stake. Everyone resolved not to speak of him; but what good was that when their thoughts turned continually to him and all glances centered on the spot?

The peasants coming from Banja carting stone in their bullock carts turned their eyes away and curtly ordered their oxen to make haste. The workers at work along the banks and on the staging called to one another in hushed voices and as little as they could. The overseers themselves, with their wooden staves in their hands, were subdued and less brutal. The Dalmatian stonemasons clenched their jaws, turned their backs on the bridge and struck angrily with their chisels which in the universal stillness sounded like a flock of woodpeckers.

Twilight came quickly and the workers hurried to their hovels in the wish to get as far as possible from the staging. Before it was quite dark, Merdjan and a trusted servant of Abidaga once more climbed the staging and definitely confirmed that Radisav was even then, four hours after the sentence had been carried out, alive and conscious. Consumed with fever, he rolled his eyes slowly and painfully, and when he saw the gipsy below him, he began to groan more loudly. In this groaning, which showed his life was ebbing, it was possible to distinguish only a few isolated words:

"The Turks . . . the Turks . . . the bridge!"

Having satisfied themselves, they returned to Abidaga's house at Bikavac, telling everyone whom they met on their way that the criminal was still alive; and since he ground his teeth and spoke well and clearly from the stake there was every hope that he would live until noon the next day. Abidaga too was satisfied and gave orders that Merdjan was to be paid his promised reward.

That night everything living in the town and about the bridge slept in fear. Or rather those who could slept but there were many to whom sleep would not come.

The next day which was a Monday dawned a sunny November morning. There was not an eye in the whole town or about the building work that did not turn towards that intricate criss-cross of beams and planks over the waters, at the farther end of which, upright and apart, was the man on the stake. Many who, on waking, had thought that they had dreamed all that had taken place the day before upon the bridge, now rose and with fixed eyes looked at the continuance of this nightmare which remained there stark in the sun.

Among the workers there was still that hush of the day before, filled with pity and bitterness. In the town there was still that whispering and anxiety. Merdjan and that same servant of Abidaga's climbed up the scaffolding once more and examined the condemned man; they spoke to each other, lifted their eyes and looked upward into the face of the peasant and then, suddenly, Merdjan pulled at his trousers. From the way in which they made their way downwards to the bank and walked silently through the men at work, everyone realized that the peasant had at last died. Those who were Serbs felt a certain easing of the spirit, as at an invisible victory.

Now they looked more boldly up at the scaffolding and the man who had been condemned. They felt as if fate, in their continual wrestling and measuring of forces with the Turks, had now inclined to their side. Death was the greatest trump in the game. Mouths till then contracted in fear now began to open. Muddy, wet, unshaven and pale, rolling great blocks of Banja stone with pinewood levers, they halted for a moment to spit on their palms and say to each other in hushed voices:

"May God pardon him and have mercy upon him!"

"Ah, the martyr! It is hard for such as we!"

"Don't you see that he has become a saint?"

And everyone glanced up at the dead man who stayed there as upright as if he had been marching at the head of a company. Up there, so high, he no longer seemed terrible or pitiful to them. On the other hand, it was now clear to all of them how he was exalted and set apart. He no longer stood on the earth, his hands held to nothing, he did not swim, did not fly; he no longer had any weight. Freed from all earthly ties and burdens, he was no longer a prey to troubles; no one could do anything more against him, neither rifle nor sword, nor evil thoughts, nor men's words, nor Turkish courts. Naked to the waist, with arms and legs bound, his head thrown back against the stake, that figure no longer seemed to bear any likeness to a human body which grows and then rots away, but seemed to be raised on high, hard and imperishable as a statue which would remain there forever.

The men on forced labor turned and crossed themselves stealthily.

In Mejdan the women hurried through the courtyards to whisper to each other for a moment or so and weep, and then at once rushed back to see if the luncheon had burned. One of them lighted an ikon-lamp. Quickly, in all the houses ikon-lamps hidden away in the corners of the rooms began to glow. The children, blinking in this solemn atmosphere, looked at the brightness and listened to the broken and incomprehensible sentences of their elders: "Defend us, O Lord, and protect us!," "Ah, martyr, he is chosen before God as if he had built the greatest of churches!," "Help us, O Lord, Thou Holy One, drive away the enemy and do not let him rule longer over us!"; and incessantly asked who was the martyr and who was building a church and where. The small boys were especially inquisitive. Their mothers hushed them:

"Be quiet, my soul. Be quiet and listen to mother. As long as you are alive keep away from those accursed Turks."

Before it began to darken, Abidaga once more went around the construction work and, satisfied with the result of this terrible example, ordered that the peasant be taken down from the stake.

"Throw the dog to the dogs!"

That night, which fell suddenly as soft and moist as spring, there began an incomprehensible murmuring, a coming and going among the workers. Even those who had not wanted to hear of destruction and resistance were now ready to make sacrifices and do all that they could. The man on the stake had become an object of general attention as if he had been holy. Some hundreds of exhausted men, moved by an inner force made up of pity and ancient custom, instinctively joined in an effort to get the corpse of the martyred man, to prevent it from being profaned and to give it Christian burial. After cautious whispered consultations in the huts and stables, the men of forced labor collected among themselves the considerable sum of seven grosh with which to bribe Merdjan. To carry out this work they chose three of the craftiest among them and succeeded in getting in touch with the executioner. Wet and tired from their labors, the three peasants bargained, slowly and cunningly, going round and round the point. Frowning, scratching his head and stuttering intentionally, the oldest of the peasants said to the gipsy:

"Well, it's all over now. It was so fated. Still, you know it is a human being, one of God's creations . . . it shouldn't . . . you know what I mean . . . it shouldn't be eaten by beasts or torn to bits by dogs."

Merdjan, who knew well enough what was in the wind, defended himself, more sorrowfully than obstinately.

"No. Don't even speak of it. You'll get me well roasted. You don't know what a lynx that Abidaga is!'

The peasant was troubled, frowned and thought to himself: "He is a gipsy, a thing without cross or soul, one cannot call him either friend or brother, and one cannot take his word by anything in heaven or earth," and held his hand in the shallow pocket of his cloak tightly grasping the seven grosh.

"I know that very well. We all know that it is not easy for you. Only, no one can blame you. Here we have got together four grosh for you which, as we see it, should be enough. . . ."

"No, no, my life is dearer to me than all the treasure in the world. Abidaga would never let me live; that one sees everything, even when he is asleep. I am dead at the mere thought of it!"

"Four grosh, even five, but that's all we can do! We could even find that much," went on the peasant, paying no heed to the gipsy's laments.

"I dare not, I dare not. . . ."

"Very well then. . . . Since you have got your orders to throw the . . . the body . . . to the . . . to the dogs, you will throw it. But what happens after that is none of your affair, nor will anyone ask you about it. So you see if we, for example, should take that . . . that body . . . and should bury it somewhere according to our law but, let us say, stealthily so that not a living soul will know . . . then you will, for example, say next day that the dogs have . . . have carried away that . . . that body. No one will be any the worse and you will have got your share. . . ."

The peasant spoke carefully and with circumspection, only he halted with a strange uneasiness before the word "body". . . .

"Am I to lose my head for five grosh? No, no, n-o-o-."

"For six," added the peasant calmly.

The gipsy drew himself up, spread out his arms, and assumed an expression of moving sincerity, as only men who do not distinguish truth from lies can do. He stood before the peasant as though he were the judge and the peasant the criminal.

"Let it be on my head, since that is my fate, and let my *chai* remain a widow and my children beggars; if you give me seven grosh, take the body away, but no one must see and no one must know."

The peasant shook his head, regretting deeply that this scab must get everything right down to the last farthing, as if the gipsy had been able to see into his closed fist!

Then they came to an agreement, down to the last detail. Merdjan was to bring the corpse, when he had taken it from the scaffolding, to the left bank of the river and there, as soon as it grew dark, was to throw it down on a stony patch near the road, so that it could be seen both by Abidaga's servants and by anyone who might be passing by. The three peasants would be hidden in a thicket, a little farther on. As soon as darkness fell, they would take the corpse, carry it away and bury it, but in a hidden place and without any visible trace, so that it would seem quite likely that the dogs had dragged it away overnight and eaten it. Three grosh were to be paid in advance and four more when the job was finished.

That same night everything was carried out according to the agreement.

At twilight Merdjan brought the corpse and threw it on the roadside. (It no longer resembled that body which all had looked at for the past two days, upright and stiff upon the stake; this was once again the old Radisav, small and bowed, only now without blood or life.) Then he went back at once with his assistants by the ferry to the town on the other bank. The peasants waited in the thicket. One or two late workers passed, and a Turk on his way home to the town. Then the whole countryside became quite still and dark. Dogs began to appear, those powerful, mangy, hungry, cowardly curs without masters or homes. The peasants concealed in the undergrowth threw stones at them and drove them away. They ran with tails between their legs but only for twelve paces or so from the corpse where they waited to see what would happen next. Their eyes could be seen glowing and shining. When it was clear that night had really fallen and there was no longer any likelihood that anyone else would come along, the peasants came out of their hiding place carrying a pick and shovel. They had also brought two planks with them on which they placed the corpse and so carried it away. There in a gully caused by the spring and autumn rains rushing down the hill into the Drina, they removed the larger stones which formed the bed of a dry watercourse, and dug out a deep grave quickly, silently, without words and without noise. In it they placed the cold, stiff, twisted body. The oldest of the peasants leaped into the pit, crossed himself carefully a few times, lit first a piece of tinder and then a small candle of twisted wax, shielding the light with his two hands; he placed it above the head of the dead man and crossed himself, repeating three times quickly and aloud, "In the Name of the Father, the Son and the Holy Spirit." The two men with him crossed themselves in the darkness above. The peasant then made a movement with his hands over the dead man as if pouring from his empty hand the unseen wine and said twice, softly and reverently:

"Peace with the saints, O Christ, for the soul of Thy slave."

Then he whispered a few more words, disconnected and incomprehensible, but sounding like prayers solemn and reverent, while the two men above the grave crossed themselves continually. When he had ended, they lowered the two planks so that they formed a sort of roof over the dead man. Then the peasant crossed himself once more, extinguished the candle and climbed out of the grave. Then, slowly and carefully, they replaced the earth in the grave, treading it down well so that no swelling could be seen. When that was done, they put back the stones, like the bed of the stream, across the freshly dug earth, crossed themselves once more and went back home, making a wide detour so as to rejoin the road at a point as far away as possible.

That night there fell a dense soft rain without wind, and in the morning that dawned the whole river valley was filled with milky mist and a heavy moisture. In a sort of white resplendence which now rose and now fell, the sun could be seen somewhere struggling with the mists which it was unable to pierce. All was ghostly, new and strange. Men suddenly appeared out of the mist and equally suddenly were lost in it. In such weather, early in the morning, there passed through the market-place a simple country cart and on it two guards watching the man from Plevlje, their leader until the day before, bound and under arrest.

From the previous day, when in the access of unexpected emotion at finding himself still alive and not on the stake he had begun to dance before them all, he had never calmed down. All his muscles twitched, he could no longer keep still, but was constantly tormented by the irresistible urge to prove to himself and show others that he was still healthy, whole and capable of movement. At intervals he would remember Abidaga (that was the black spot in his new joy!) and would fall into a dark reverie. But while he was in this mood, fresh forces would collect within him which drove him irresistibly to wild and spasmodic movements like a madman. He would get up again and begin to dance, spreading out his arms, clicking his fingers and twisting like a dancer, showing by sudden and lively actions that he was not on the stake and gasping to the rhythm of his dance:

"See . . . see . . . I can do this . . . and that . . . and that! . . ."

He refused to eat and would suddenly break off every conversation that he began and start to dance, affirming childishly at every movement:

"See, see, I can do this . . . and this . . . !"

When that night they finally decided to tell Abidaga what had happened, he replied coldly and abruptly:

"Take the madman to Plevlje and let them keep him chained up in his own house there, so that he does not play the fool round here. He was not the man for a job like that!"

So was it done. But as their leader was unable to keep still, his guards were forced to bind him to the cart in which he was sitting. He wept and defended himself and as long as he was able to move any part of his body, he struggled and shouted: "See, see!" Finally they had to bind his arms and his legs, so that now he sat in the cart upright like a sack of wheat swaddled in ropes. But, since he was no longer able to move, he began to imagine that they were impaling him on the stake and writhed and resisted with desperate cries:

"No me, not me! Catch the *vila!* No, Abidaga!"

From the last houses on the outskirts of the town, people rushed out excited by his cries, but the cart with the guards and the sick man was swiftly lost to sight in the thick mist along the Dobruna road through which the sun could just be glimpsed.

The unexpected and pitiable departure of the man from Plevlje instilled still greater fear into men's bones. It began to be whispered that the condemned peasant had been innocent and that this had preyed on the mind of the man from Plevlje. Among the Serbs in Mejdan the women began to tell how the *vilas* had buried the dead body of the hapless Radisav below Butkovo Stijene and how at night a plenteous light fell upon his grave, thousands and thousands of lighted candles which flamed and quivered in a long line reaching from heaven to earth. They had seen them through their tears.

All sorts of things were whispered and believed, but fear was stronger than all else.

Work on the bridge was carried on quickly, smoothly and without interruption or hindrance. It went on somehow or other until the beginning of December when an unexpectedly hard frost came, against which even Abidaga's power could do nothing.

There were unheard-of frosts and blizzards in that first half of December. The stones froze into the ground and the wood cracked. A fine crystalline snow covered everything, tools and whole huts, and the next day a capricious wind would drive it to another side and bury another part. Work ceased of itself and the fear of Abidaga paled and finally disappeared. Abidaga tried to fight against it for some days but finally gave way. He dismissed the workers and stopped the work. In the midst of the heaviest snowfall he rode away with his men. That same day Tosun Effendi set out on a peasant's sleigh heaped with straw and blankets, and after him Mastro Antonio, in the opposite direction. And all that camp of forced laborers dispersed into the villages and the deep valleys without a sound and as imperceptibly as water soaked up by the earth. The building works remained like a discarded toy.

Before setting out Abidaga again summoned the leading Turks. He was depressed by his angry impotence and told them, as in the previous year, that he left everything in their hands and that theirs was the responsibility.

"I am going away but my eyes remain here. Take heed; better that you cut off a score of disobedient heads than that a single nail of the Sultan's should be lost. As soon as spring breaks I shall be here once more and shall call everyone to account."

The leaders promised everything as they had the year before and dispersed to their homes, filled with anxiety and wrapped in their cloaks, caps and shawls, thanking God to themselves that God had given winter blizzards to the world and had in that way shown that His power was able to put a limit to the power of the mighty.

But when spring broke again, it was not Abidaga who came, but a new representative of the Vezir, Arif Beg, together with Tosun Effendi. What he had so much feared had happened to Abidaga. Someone, someone whom he knew well and had worked near him, had sent to the Grand Vezir detailed and accurate reports of his work on the Višegrad bridge. The Vezir had been accurately informed that for those two years between two and three hundred workmen had been summoned for forced labor every day without a single para of pay and very often bringing their own food, and that Abidaga had taken the Vezir's money for himself (the amount of money that he had up till then managed to embezzle was also reckoned). He had covered up his dishonesty, as is so often the case in life, by excessive zeal and exaggerated severity, so that the people of the whole district, not only the *rayah* but also the Turks, instead of giving thanks for this great bequest, cursed both the hour when it had been begun and the man for whom it was being built.

Mehmed Pasha, who had been struggling all his life with the peculations and dishonesty of his officials, had ordered his unworthy servant to reimburse the whole sum and take what remained of his fortune and his harem and go at once to a small town in Anatolia, and never to let himself be heard of again unless he wanted a worse fate to befall him.

Two days after Arif Beg, Mastro Antonio also arrived from Dalmatia with the first workers. Tosun Effendi presented him to the new chief, and on a warm sunny April day they inspected the construction works and settled the order for the first work. After Arif Beg had withdrawn, leaving the other two alone on the bank, Mastro Antonio looked attentively at the face of Tosun Effendi who, even on so sunny a day, was huddled up in a wide black mantle.

"This is quite another sort of man. Thanks be to God! I only ask myself who was so smart and so brave as to inform the Vezir and have that animal removed?"

Tosun Effendi only looked straight in front of him and said quietly:

"There is no doubt, this one is better."

"It must have been someone who knew Abidaga's affairs well and who had access to the Vezir and enjoyed his trust."

"Certainly, certainly, this one is better," replied Tosun Effendi without looking up and wrapping his mantle even more closely around him.

So the work began under the new chief, Arif Beg.

He was, indeed, quite a different sort of man. Exceptionally tall, stooping, bald, with salient cheekbones and slit-like black laughing eyes, the people at once nicknamed him Misir-Baba—Old Baldie. Without shouting, without a staff, without big words or visible effort, he gave orders and set everything in order good-humoredly and casually with confident authority; he never overlooked anything or lost track of anything. But he also brought with him a feeling of strict attention to everything that was the Vezir's will or order, but like a calm, normal and honest man who had nothing to be afraid of and nothing to conceal, so that he had no need to frighten or persecute anyone. The work went on at the same speed (since speed was what the Vezir wanted), faults were punished with similar severity, but unpaid forced labor was stopped from that day. All the workers were paid and received rations in flour and salt, and all went quicker and better than in Abidaga's time. Also, mad Ilinka vanished; during the winter she had disappeared somewhere into the villages.

The construction work grew and extended.

It could now be seen that the Vezir's bequest was not for a bridge only, but also for a *han* or caravanserai, in which travelers from afar who intended to cross the bridge could find shelter for themselves, their horses and their goods should they arrive at nightfall. On Arif Beg's order the construction of this caravanserai was commenced. At the entry to the market-place, 200 paces from the bridge, just where the road to Mejdan began to rise steeply, there was a level space on which until then the Wednesday stock-market had been held. On this level space the building of the new *han* began. Work went on slowly, but from the very start it could be seen that it would be a solid and grandiose building conceived on a grand scale. The people scarcely even noticed how, slowly but surely, a great stone *han* was rising, for their attention was wholly centered on the building of the bridge.

What was now being done on the Drina was so complicated, all the work so interlocked and complex, that the loungers in the town, who watched the building work from the two banks as if it were some natural phenomenon, could no longer follow it with understanding. There were always fresh embankments and trenches running in various directions, and the river was divided and split up into side-currents and backwaters and its main course moved from one to another. Mastro Antonio brought from Dalmatia especially skilled cordwainers and collected all the hemp even from the districts around. In special buildings the master-workmen twisted ropes of exceptional strength and thickness. Greek carpenters, according to designs of their own or those drawn up by Tosun Effendi, built huge wooden cranes with pawls, erected them on rafts and thus, with these ropes, raised even the heaviest blocks of stone and transported them to the piers which, one by one, began to rise out of the bed of the river. The transport of each one of these huge blocks from the banks to its position in the foundations of the bridge-piers lasted four days.

Watching all this, day after day, year after year, the townspeople began to lose count of time and of the real intentions of the builders. It seemed to them that the construction had not moved an inch forward but was becoming more and more complicated and involved in auxiliary and subsidiary workings, and the longer it lasted the less it looked like what it was intended to be. Men who do not work themselves and who undertake nothing in their lives easily lose patience and fall into error when judging the work of others. The Višegrad Turks again began to shrug their shoulders and wave their hands when they talked of the bridge. The Christians remained silent, but watched the building work with secret and hostile thoughts, wishing for its failure as for that of every Turkish undertaking. It was about this time that the *iguman* of the monastery as Banja near Priboj wrote on the last blank page of one of his sacred books: "Be it known that about this time Mehmed Pasha undertook the building of a bridge over the Drina at Višegrad. And great oppression fell upon the Christian people with hard labor. From the sea came master-masons. For three years they built and many *aspers* were spent in vain. They divided the waters into two and into three but they were unable to complete the bridge."

Years passed; summer and autumn, winter and spring, followed one another; the workers and the master-masons came and went. Now the whole Drina was conquered, not by the bridge but by the wooden scaffoldings which looked like a complicated and senseless conglomeration of pine beams and planks. From both banks rose high wooden cranes fastened on firmly fixed rafts. On both sides of the river fires smoked, on which lead was being melted in order to be poured into the holes in the stone blocks binding them invisibly to one another.

At the end of the third year occurred one of those accidents without which great buildings are rarely completed. The central pier, which was a little higher and wider at the top than the others, since on it the *kapia* was to rest, was just being completed. During the transportation of a great stone block, work suddenly came to a stop. The workmen swarmed about the great rectangular stone which, held by thick ropes, hung above their heads. The crane had not been able to lift it accurately over its place. Mastro Antonio's assistant, the Arab, rushed impatiently to the spot and began with loud angry cries (in that strange composite language which had been evolved in the course of years between these men from all parts of the world) to give orders to those handling the crane on the waters below. At that moment, for no known reason, the ropes gave way and the block fell, first by one corner and then with its full weight onto the excited Arab who had not even troubled to look above his head but only down at the water. By a strange chance the block fell exactly into position, but in its fall it caught the Arab and crushed the whole lower part of his body. Everyone began to rush around, to give the alarm, to shout for help. Mastro Antonio arrived quickly. The young Negro, after his first unconsciousness, had come to himself; he groaned through clenched teeth and looked, sad and frightened, into Mastro Antonio's eyes. Frowning and pale, Mastro Antonio gave orders to summon the workmen, bring tools and try to lift the block. But all was in vain. A flow of blood suddenly poured out, the young man's breath came short and his eyes glazed over. Within half an hour he died, feverishly clutching Mastro Antonio's hands in his.

The Arab's funeral was a solemn event which was long remembered. All the Moslem males turned out to escort him and each for a few paces carried the bier on which lay only the upper half of the young body, for half had remained under the stone block. Mastro Antonio raised over his grave a fine memorial, made of the same stone from which the bridge was built. The death of this young man, whom he had befriended as a child living in poverty in Ulcinj, where a few Negro families still lived, had shaken him. But the work did not cease even for a moment.

That year and the next the winter was mild and work went on until mid-December. The fifth year of the work began. Now that wide irregular circle of wood, stone, auxiliary equipment and all sorts of material began to contract.

On the level space beside the Mejdan road the new *han,* freed from its scaffolding, already stood. It was a large building, constructed of the same sort of stone of which the bridge was made. Work was still going on both inside and out, but already from a distance it could be seen how much it excelled in size, the harmony of its lines and the solidity of its construction, anything that had ever been built or even thought of in the town. That building of clear, yellowish stone, with its roof of dark red tiles and a row of finely carved windows, seemed to the townsmen a thing unheard of, which from now on must become an integral part of their everyday life. Built by a Vezir, it looked as though only Vezirs could inhabit it. The whole building shone with a sense of grandeur, taste and luxury which bewildered them.

About the same time all that formless mass of crisscross beams and supports over the river began to be reduced in size and to thin out and through it emerged, more and more clearly, the bridge itself, of lovely Banja stone. Individual workers and small groups were still employed on jobs which seemed to the people senseless and unconnected with the main construction, but by now it was clear even to the most doubting of the townsmen that out of all this work the bridge itself rose, to a single design and a faultless reckoning, over and above all these individual jobs. First the lesser arches, both in height and in span, which were nearest to the banks appeared and then, one by one, the others were revealed until even the last of them was freed of its scaffolding, showing the whole bridge with all its eleven arches, perfect and wondrous in its beauty, like a new and strange feature in the townsmen's eyes.

Quick to respond to good or evil, the people of Višegrad were now ashamed of their doubts and lack of belief. They no longer tried to conceal their wonder or to restrain their enthusiasm. Passage across the bridge was not yet permitted, but they collected on both banks, especially on the right one where the market-place and the greater part of the town were, and watched the workers passing across it and how they worked at smoothing the stones of the parapet and the raised seats of the *kapia*. The Višegrad Turks watched this work by another's hand at another's expense to which for a full five years they had given every sort of name and prophesied the worst of futures.

"*Ama,* but I always told you," a little Moslem *hodja* from Dušče said excitedly and gleefully, "that nothing escapes the Sultan's hand and that these men of sense would finally put up what they had in mind, but you kept saying: they won't do this, or they can't do that. Now you see they have built it, and what a bridge they have built, what convenience and what beauty!"

Everyone approved his words, though no one really remembered when he said them, and they all knew very well that he too had ridiculed the building and the man who had been building it. All of them were sincerely enraptured.

"Eh, fellows, fellows, see what is rising here, in this town of ours!"

"See how great is the Vezir's power and foresight. Wherever he turns his eyes there is profit and blessing."

"Yet all this is nothing," added the gay and lively little *hodja,* "there will be still finer things. You see how they are grooming and decorating it like a horse for a fair."

So they competed in expressions of enthusiasm, searching for new, better and more high-flown words of praise. Only Ahmedaga Sheta, the rich grain merchant, a sullen man and a miser, still looked askance at the work and those who praised it. Tall, yellow and wizened, with black piercing eyes and thin lips that looked as if they were glued together, blinking in the fine September sun, he alone did not renounce his earlier opinion (for certain men are filled with unreasonable hate and envy greater and stronger than anything that other men can imagine). To those who enthusiastically praised the greatness and permanence of the bridge, saying that it was stronger than any fortress, he retorted disdainfully:

"Just wait till the floods, one of our real Višegrad floods! Then you will see what will be left of it!"

All of them argued bitterly with him and praised those who had been working on the bridge, especially Arif Beg, who with the smile of a great lord always on his lips had created such a work as though it had been child's play. But Sheta was firmly determined not to acknowledge anything of anyone:

"Yes, indeed. But if it had not been for Abidaga with his green staff and his tyranny and oppression, I ask you what could Old Baldie have done to finish the bridge despite his smile and his hands clasped behind his back?"

Offended at the universal enthusiasm as if it had been a personal insult, Sheta departed angrily to his shop, to sit in his usual place where he could see neither sun nor bridge, nor hear the murmur and the movement of the excited throng.

But Sheta was an isolated example. The joy and enthusiasm of the citizens continued to grow and spread to the surrounding villages. In the early days of October, Arif Beg ordered a great feast for the completion of the bridge. This man of lordly manners, of unrelenting severity and strict honesty, who had spent all the monies confided to him for the purpose for which they were intended and had kept nothing for himself, was regarded by the people as the chief personage in this achievement. They spoke more of him than of the Vezir himself. So his feast turned out rich and brilliant.

The overseers and workers received gifts in money and clothing and the feast, in which anyone who wished could take part, lasted two days. The Vezir's health was celebrated in meat and drink, in music, dancing and song; horse and foot races were arranged, and meat and sweetstuffs divided among the poor. On the square which linked the bridge with the market-place, *halva* was cooked in cauldrons and served piping hot to the people. That *halva* even got as far as the villages around the town and whoever ate it wished good health to the Vezir and long life to his buildings. There were children who went back fourteen times to the cauldrons until the cooks, recognizing them, drove them away with their long wooden spoons. One gipsy child died after eating too much hot *halva.*

Such things were long remembered and spoken about when tales were told of the creation of the bridge, the more so since, it seems, generous Vezirs and honest officials in later years died out and such feasts became rarer and at last completely unknown, until in the end they passed into legend with the *vilas,* with Stoja and Ostoja and similar wonders.

While the feast lasted, and in general all those early days, the people crossed the bridge countless times from one bank to the other. The children rushed across while their elders walked slowly, deep in conversation or watching from every point the new views open to them from the bridge. The helpless, the lame and the sick were brought on litters, for no one wanted to be left out or renounce their share in this wonder. Even the least of the townsmen felt as if his powers were suddenly multiplied, as if some wonderful, superhuman exploit was brought within the measure of his powers and within the limits of everyday life, as if besides the well-known elements of earth, water and sky, one more were open to him, as if by some beneficent effort each one of them could suddenly realize one of his dearest desires, that ancient dream of man—to go over the water and to be master of space.

The Turkish youths formed a round dance, a *kolo,* around the cauldrons of *halva* and then led the dance across the bridge, since it seemed to them that they were flying and not treading the solid earth. The dance wound round in circles about the *kapia,* the dancers beating their heels and stamping on the new flagstones as if to test the stoutness of the bridge. Around that winding, circling *kolo* of young bodies tirelessly leaping up and down in the same rhythm, the children played, running in and out between the dancing feet as if through a moving fence, standing in the center of this *kolo* which was being danced for the first time in their lives on that bridge about which there had been so much talk for years, and even on the *kapia,* wherein, it was said, the unlucky Arab was imprisoned and showed himself of nights. Enjoying the young men's *kolo,* they were none the less overcome by that fear which the Arab himself, when he had been alive and working on the bridge, had always instilled into the children of the town. On that high, new and strange bridge, it seemed to them that they had long forsaken their mothers and their homes and were wandering in lands of black people, marvelous buildings and strange dances; they trembled, but were unable to keep their thoughts from the Arab or to abandon the wonderful new *kapia.* Only some fresh marvel could have distracted their attention.

A certain Murat, known as "the dumb one," a dim-witted youth from the noble family of Turković from Nezuke, who was often the butt of the town, suddenly climbed on to the stone parapet of the bridge. There were shrieks from the children, startled cries from the older people, but the idiot, as though under a spell, with outstretched arms and head flung back, went along the narrow stones, step by step, as though he were not flying above the waters and the depths but taking part in a wonderful dance. Parallel with him walked a crew of urchins and nondescripts urging him on. On the farther side of the bridge his brother Aliaga waited for him and spanked him like a small child.

Many people went far down the river, half an hour's walk, to Kalata or Mezalin, and looked thence at the bridge, standing out white and delicate with its eleven arches, like a strange arabesque on the green waters amid the dark hills.

About this time too a great white plaque was brought, with an engraved inscription, and built into the *kapia,* into that wall of reddish stone which rose a good six feet from the parapet of the bridge. The people gathered around the inscription and looked at it until some seminarist or koranic student was found who would, with more or less ability, for a coffee or a slice of watermelon or even for the pure love of Allah, read the inscription as best he could.

A hundred times those days they spelled out the verses of the *tarih,* written by a certain Badi, which gave the name and title of the man who had made the bequest as well as the fortunate year 979 AH, that is to say 1571 in the Christian calendar, when it was completed. This Badi for good money wrote easy and sonorous verses and knew well how to foist them upon great men who erected or restored great buildings. Those who knew him (and who were somewhat envious of him) used to say mockingly that the vault of heaven was the one and only building on which there was not a *tarih* from Badi's pen. But he, despite all his fine earnings, was a poor famished devil continually at odds with that special sort of penury that often goes with verse writing like a kind of curse and which no amount of pay or salary can assuage.

Because of their literary shortcomings, their thick heads and lively imaginations, each of the local scholars read and interpreted in his own way Badi's *tarih* on the stone plaque which, as every text once revealed to the public, stood there, eternal on the eternal stone, always and irrevocably exposed to the looks and interpretations of all men, wise or foolish, evil or well-intentioned. Each one of these listeners remembered those lines which best suited his ear and his temperament. So what was there, engraved on the hard stone in the sight of all men, was repeated from mouth to mouth, often changed and corrupted into nonsense.

On the stone was written:

"See how Mehmed Pasha, the greatest among the wise and great of his time,
Mindful of the testament of his heart, by his care and toil
Has built a bridge over the River Drina,
Over this water, deep and swift-flowing.
His predecessors had not been able to put up anything.
I pray that by the Mercy of Allah this bridge will be firm
And that its existence will be passed in happiness
And that it will never know sorrow.
For in his lifetime he poured out gold and silver for his bequest
And no man can say that fortune has been wasted
Which has been spent to such an end.
Badi, who has seen this, when the bridge was completed gave this *tarih.*
'May Allah bless this building, this wonderful and beautiful bridge.' "

But at last the people had eaten their fill and had wondered enough, walked enough and had listened to the verses of the inscription to their hearts' content. The nine days' wonder became a part of their everyday life and they crossed the bridge hurriedly, indifferently, anxiously, absent-mindedly as the tumultuous waters that flowed beneath it, as if it were only one of the countless roads that they and their beasts trod beneath their feet. And the plaque with the inscription fell as silent as any other stone.

Now the road from the left bank of the river was directly connected with that end of the road on the level space on the farther side. Gone was the dark, worm-eaten ferry with its eccentric ferryman. Far below the last arches of the bridge there remained that sandy rock and the steep banks equally difficult to ascend or descend and on which travelers had waited so despairingly and had called so vainly from one bank to the other. All that, together with the stormy river, had been surmounted as if by magic. Men now passed far above, as if on wings, straight from one high bank to the other, along the wide strong bridge which was as firm and lasting as a mountain and which echoed under horses' hooves as if it were made only of a thin plaque of stone.

Gone too were those wooden water-mills and the hovels in which travelers in case of need had spent the night. In their place stood the firm and luxurious caravanserai which received the travelers who daily grew more numerous. They entered the *han* through a wide gateway of harmonious lines. On each side was a large window with a grille, not of iron but carved in a single block of limestone. In the wide rectangular court was space for merchandise and baggage and around it were ranged the doors of thirty-six rooms. Behind, under the hillside, were the stables; to general amazement they too were of stone, as if built for the Sultan's stud. There was not such another *han* from Sarajevo as far as Adrianople. In it every traveler might remain for a day and a night and receive, free of all cost, fire, shelter and water for himself, his servants and his beasts.

All this, as the bridge itself, was the bequest of the Grand Vezir, Mehmed Pasha, who had been born more than sixty years before up there behind the mountains in the hillside village of Sokolovići, and who in his childhood had been taken away with a crowd of other Serbian peasant boys as blood tribute to Stambul. The expenses for maintaining the caravanserai came from the *vakuf,* the religious endowment, which Mehmed Pasha had founded from the rich properties seized in the newly-conquered territories of Hungary.

Thus many troubles and inconveniences disappeared with the erection of the bridge and the foundation of the *han.* There disappeared too that strange pain which the Vezir in his childhood had brought from Bosnia, from the Višegrad ferry; those dark shooting pains which from time to time had seemed to cut his breast in two. But it was not fated that Mehmed Pasha should live without those pangs or long enjoy in his thoughts his Višegrad bequest. Shortly after the final completion of the work, just when the caravanserai had begun to work properly and the bridge to become known to the world, Mehmed Pasha once again felt the "black knife" in his breast. And that for the last time.

One Friday, when he went with his suite to the mosque, a ragged and half-demented dervish approached him with his left hand stretched out for alms. The Vezir turned and ordered a member of his suite to give them. But the dervish then drew a heavy butcher's knife from his right sleeve and violently stabbed the Vezir between the ribs. His suite cut the dervish down, but the Vezir and his murderer breathed their last at the same moment. The dead assassin, big, red-faced, lay with outstretched arms and legs as if still exalted by the impulse on his senseless blow; and beside him the Grand Vezir, with his robe unbuttoned on his chest and his turban flung far away. In the last years of his life he had grown thin and bowed, almost withered and coarser in feature. And now with half-bared chest, bareheaded, bleeding, twisted and crumpled, he looked more like an ageing and battered peasant of Sokolovići than the dignitary who until a short time before had administered the Turkish Empire.

Months and months passed before the reports of the Vezir's assassination reached the town and then not as a clear and definite fact but as a secret whisper which might or might not have been true. For in the Turkish Empire it was not permitted to spread reports or to gossip about bad news and tragic events even when they had taken place in a nearby country, much less so when they took place on its own soil. Furthermore, in this case, it was in no one's interest to talk much about the Grand Vezir's death. The party of his adversaries, which had at last succeeded in overthrowing him, hoped that with his solemn funeral every livelier memory of him would also be buried. And Mehmed Pasha's kin, collaborators and supporters in Stambul had for the most part no objection to saying as little as possible about the one-time Grand Vezir, for in this way their own chances of conciliating the new rulers and having their own past overlooked were increased.

But the two fine buildings on the Drina had already begun to exercise their influence on trade and communications, on the town of Višegrad and the whole country around, and they went on doing so without regard for the living or the dead, for those who were rising or those who were falling. The town soon began to move downwards from the hillside to the water's edge and expand and develop more and more about the bridge and around the caravanserai, which the people called the Stone Han.

Thus was born the bridge with its *kapia* and so the town developed around it. After that, for a period of more than 300 years, its role in the development of the town and its significance in the life of the townspeople were similar to that which we have described above. And the significance and substance of its existence were, so to speak, in its permanence. Its shining line in the composition of the town did not change, any more than the outlines of the mountains against the sky. In the changes and the quick burgeoning of human generations, it remained as unchanged as the waters that flowed beneath it. It too grew old, naturally, but on a scale of time that was much greater not only than the span of human existence but also than the passing of a whole series of generations, so that its ageing could not be seen by human eye. Its life, though mortal in itself, resembled eternity for its end could not be perceived.

5

The first century passed, a time long and mortal for men and for many of their works, but insignificant for great buildings, well conceived and firmly based, and the bridge with its *kapia* and the nearby caravanserai stood and served as they had on their first day. So too would a second century have passed over them, with its changes of seasons and human generations, and the buildings would have lasted unchanged; but what time could not do, the unstable and unpredictable influence of faraway affairs did.

At that time, at the end of the seventeenth century, much was sung, spoken and whispered about Hungary, whence the Turkish armies after a hundred years of occupation were about to withdraw. Many Bosnian *spahis* (landowners who held their lands on military tenure) had left their bones on Hungarian soil, defending their properties in the battles preceding the withdrawal. They were, it might be thought, the lucky ones for many of the other *spahis* returned as bare as a finger to their former Bosnian homeland, where there awaited them sparse soil and a straitened and penurious life after the rich lordliness and spaciousness of life on the great Hungarian estates. The far-off and uncertain echo of all this penetrated as far as Višegrad, but no one there could ever have imagined that distant Hungary, a land of legend, could have any connection with the real, everyday life of the town. But with the Turkish retreat from Hungary there remained outside the frontiers of the Empire also those properties of the *vakuf* (the religious endowment) from the revenues of which the caravanserai at Višegrad was maintained.

Both the people of the town and the travelers who had made use of the Stone Han for the past 100 years had become accustomed to it and had never even considered by what means it had been maintained, how the revenues had been founded, or from what source they came. All had made use of it, profiting by it as from a blessed and fertile roadside orchard which was both nobody's and everybody's; they repeated mechanically "peace to the Vezir's soul" but did not stop to think that the Vezir had died 100 years before, nor did they ask who now preserved and defended the imperial lands and the *vakuf*. Who could ever have dreamed that the affairs of the world were in such dependence upon one another and were linked together across so great a distance? So at first no one in the town even noticed that the income of the *han* had dried up. The attendants worked and the *han* received travelers as before. It was thought that the money for its upkeep had been delayed, as had happened before. But the months passed and even the years, and the money did not come. The *mutevelia* (the administrator of the bequest), Dauthodja Mutavelić, for the people so called him after his appointment and the nickname stuck, applied to everyone he could think of, but received no reply. The travelers had to look after their own needs and cleaned up the *han* as much as they found necessary for their own convenience, but as each one went his way he left behind manure and disorder for others to clean up and put right, even as he himself had tidied up whatever he had found dirty and in disorder. But after each traveler there remained just a little more dirt than he himself had found.

Dauthodja did all that he could to save the *han* and keep it going. First he spent his own money and then he began to borrow from his relatives. So he patched things up from year to year and kept the precious building in its former beauty. To those who reproached him for ruining himself trying to preserve what could not be preserved, he replied that he was investing the money well for he gave it as a loan to God and that he, the *mutevelia,* should be the last to desert this bequest which it seemed all others had deserted and abandoned.

This wise and godfearing, stubborn and obstinate man, whom the town long remembered, allowed no one to turn him from his vain effort. Working devotedly, he had long become reconciled to the idea that our destiny on this earth lies in the struggle against decay, death and dissolution and that man must persevere in this struggle, even if it were completely in vain. Sitting before the *han* which was falling into dissolution before his eyes, he replied to all those who tried to dissuade him or pitied him:

"There is no need to feel sorry for me. For all of us die only once, whereas great men die twice, once when they leave this world and a second time when their lifework disappears."

When he was no longer able to pay day-laborers, he himself, old as he was, rooted up the weeds around the *han* with his own hands and carried out minor repairs to the building. So it was that death overtook him one day when he had climbed up to repair a cracked slate on the roof. It was natural that a small town *hodja* could not maintain what a Grand Vezir had founded and which historical events had sentenced to disaster.

After Dauthodja's death the *han* rapidly began to fall into ruins. Signs of decay appeared everywhere. The gutters began to crack and to smell nasty, the roof to let in the rains, the doors and windows the winds, and the stables to be choked with manure and weeds. But from without the perfect building still looked unchanged, calm and indestructible in its beauty. Those great arched windows on the ground floor, with grilles as delicate as lace cut in soft stone from a single block, looked peacefully out upon the world, but the simpler windows on the floor above already showed signs of poverty, neglect and internal disorder. Little by little travelers began to avoid spending the night in the town or, if they did, stayed at Ustamujić's inn and paid for their night's lodging. They came more and more rarely to the caravanserai, even though they had not to pay but only to wish peace to the Vezir's soul. At last, when it became clear that the money would never come, everyone abandoned any pretense to care for the building, even the new *mutevelia,* and the caravanserai stayed mute and deserted and fell into ruin and disrepair as do all buildings in which no one lives and which no one looks after. Wild grasses, weeds and thistles grew around it. Ravens nested on the roof and crows gathered there in dense black flocks.

Thus before its time and unexpectedly forsaken (all such things seem to happen unexpectedly) the Vezir's Stone Han began to disintegrate and fall to pieces.

But if the caravanserai, due to unusual circumstances, was forced to betray its mission and fall into ruin before its time, the bridge, which needed neither supervision nor maintenance, remained upright and unchanged, linking the two banks and bearing across the river burdens dead and alive, as it had in the first days of its existence.

In its walls the birds nested and in the invisible cracks opened by time grew little tufts of grass. The yellowish porous stone of which the bridge was built hardened and contracted under the alternate influence of moisture and of heat. Eternally beaten by the winds which blew up and down the river valley, washed by the rains and dried by the fierce heats of summer, that stone in time turned white with the dull whiteness of parchment and shone in the twilight as if lighted from within. The great and frequent floods, which were a heavy and continual menace to the town, were unable to do anything against it. They came every year, in spring and autumn, but all were not dangerous and fateful to the town beside the bridge. Every year, once or perhaps twice, the Drina rose in tumult and its muddied waters roared down, bearing through the arches of the bridge torn-up fences from the fields, uprooted stumps of trees, and dark earthy waters filled with leaves and branches from the riverside forests. The courtyards, gardens and storerooms of the houses nearest the river suffered. But everything ended there. At irregular intervals of between twenty and thirty years came great floods which were afterwards remembered as one remembers insurrections or wars and were long used as a date from which to reckon time, to calculate the ages of citizens or the term of men's lives ("Five or six years before the great flood. . . ." "During the great flood. . . .").

After these great floods little movable property remained in that larger part of the town which lay on the low sandy strip between the Drina and the Rzav.

Such a flood threw the whole town several years back. That generation spent the rest of its life in repairing the damage and the misfortune left by the "great flood." To the end of their lives men, talking among themselves, recalled the terror of that autumn night when, in the chill rain and hellish wind, to the light of an occasional lantern, they would take out their goods, each from his own shop, and carry them to higher ground at Mejdan and there store them in the shops and warehouses of others. When the next day, in the cloudy dawn, they looked down from the hillside on the town that they loved as strongly and as unconsciously as their own blood, and saw the darkened muddied waters rushing through the streets at roof level, they would try to guess whose house it was from which the foaming waters were noisily tearing the roof plank by plank and whose house still remained upright.

On feast days and festivals and during the nights of Ramazan the gray-haired toilworn and anxious fathers of families would grow lively and talkative when the conversation turned to the greatest and hardest event of their lives, to the "great flood." After the interval of fifteen or twenty years in which they had once more restored their fortunes and their homes, the flood was recalled as something great and terrible, near and dear to them; it was an intimate bond between the men of that generation who were still living, for nothing brings men closer together than a common misfortune happily overcome. They felt themselves closely bound by the memory of that bygone disaster. They loved to recall memories of the hardest blow dealt them in their lives. Their recollections were inexhaustible and they repeated them continually, amplified by memory and repetition; they looked into one another's eyes, sclerotic and with yellowing whites, and saw there what the younger men could not even suspect. They were carried away by their own words and drowned all their present everyday troubles in the recollection of those greater ones which they had experienced so long ago.

Sitting in the warm rooms of their homes through which that flood had at one time passed, they recounted for the hundredth time with special enjoyment moving and tragic scenes. And the more harrowing and painful the recollection the greater pleasure was there in recollecting it. Seen through tobacco smoke or a glass of plum brandy, such scenes were often transformed by distance and imagination, magnified and embellished, but not one of them ever noticed that this was so and would have sworn that it had in fact so happened, for they all shared in this unconscious exaggeration.

Thus there still lived a few old men who remembered the last "great flood," about which they could still speak among themselves, repeating to the younger men that there were no longer such disasters as in time past, but no such blessings and good living either.

One of the very greatest of all these floods, which occurred in the second half of the eighteenth century, was especially long remembered and became the subject of countless tales.

In that generation, as the older men later said, there was practically no one who remembered the last great flood well. None the less, on those rainy autumn days all were on the alert, knowing that "the waters were hostile." They emptied the warehouses closest to the river and wandered by night, by the light of lanterns, along the banks to listen to the roar of the waters, for the older men affirmed that they could tell by some special moaning of the waters whether the flood to come would be one of those ordinary ones which visited the town every year and caused minor damage, or whether it would be one of those, happily rare, which flooded both the bridge and the town and carried away everything that was not on firm foundations. Next day the Drina did not rise and the town that night slept soundly, for men were tired out from lack of sleep and the excitement of the night before. So it was that the waters deceived them. That night the Rzav rose suddenly in a manner never before remembered and, red with mud, piled up at its confluence with the Drina. Thus the two rivers overwhelmed the whole town.

Suljaga Osmanagić, one of the richest Turks in the town, then owned a thoroughbred Arab horse, a chestnut of great value and beauty. As soon as the reinforced Drina began to rise, two hours before it overflowed into the streets, this chestnut began to neigh and did not calm down until it had awakened the stable-boys and its owner and until they had taken it out of its stall which was beside the river. So the greater part of the inhabitants were awakened. Under the chill rain and the raging wind of the dark October night began a flight and a saving of all that could be saved. Half-dressed, the people waded up to their knees, carrying on their backs their wakened and complaining children. At every moment dull crashes could be heard when the tree stumps which the Drina washed down from the flooded forests struck against the piers of the stone bridge.

Up at Mejdan, which the waters had never in any circumstances been able to reach, windows were all alight and flickering lanterns danced and quivered in the darkness. All the houses were open to welcome those who had suffered and who came drenched and despondent with their children or their most precious belongings in their arms. In the stables burned fires by which those unable to find a place in the houses could dry themselves.

The leading merchants of the town, after they had placed the people in the houses, Turkish in Turkish homes and Christian and Jewish in Christian homes, gathered in the great ground-floor room of Hadji Ristič's house. There were the *mukhtars* (the Moslem leaders) and the *kmets* (the Christian headmen) of all the quarters, exhausted and wet to the skin, after having wakened and moved to safe quarters all their fellow citizens. Turks, Christians and Jews mingled together. The force of the elements and the weight of common misfortune brought all these men together and bridged, at least for this one evening, the gulf that divided one faith from the other and, especially, the *rayah* from the Turks: Suljaga Osmanagić, Petar Bogdanović, Mordo Papo, the big, taciturn and witty parish priest Pop Mihailo, the fat and serious Mula Ismet, the Višegrad *hodja,* and Elias Levi, known as Hadji Liacho, the Jewish rabbi well known even far beyond the town for his sound judgment and open nature. There were about ten others, from all three faiths. All were wet, pale, with clenched jaws, but outwardly calm; they sat and smoked and talked of what had been done to save the people and of what still remained to be done. Every moment younger people entered, streaming with water, who reported that everything living had been taken to Mejdan and to the fortress and put in houses there, Turkish and Christian, and that the waters down in the valley were still rising and invading street after street.

As the night passed—and it passed slowly and seemed enormous, growing greater and greater like the waters in the valley—the leaders and rich men of the town began to warm themselves over coffee and plum brandy. A warm and close circle formed, like a new existence, created out of realities and yet itself unreal, which was not what it had been the day before nor what it would be the day after, but like a transient island in the flood of time. The conversation rose and strengthened and changed subject. They avoided speaking of past floods known only in tales, but spoke of other things that had no connection with the waters and with the disaster which was at that moment taking place.

Desperate men make desperate efforts to appear calm and indifferent, almost casual. By some tacit superstitious agreement and by the unwritten but sacred laws of patronal dignity and business order which have existed since olden times, each considered it his duty to make an effort and at that moment at least externally to conceal his fear and his anxieties in face of a disaster against which he could do nothing and to talk in a light tone about unrelated things.

But just as they began to grow calm in this conversation and to find in it a moment of forgetfulness, and thereby the rest and energy that they would need so greatly in the day to come, a man entered, bringing with him Kosta Baranac. That young merchant was wet through, muddied to the knees and dishevelled. Dazzled by the light and confused by the numbers present, he looked at them as if in a dream, wiping the water from his face with his open hand. They made room for him and offered him plum brandy, which he was unable to raise to his lips. His whole body shivered. A whisper ran through the room that he had tried to leap into the dark current that now flowed in a sandy torrent immediately above the spot where his barns and granaries had been.

He was a young man, a recent settler, who had been brought to the town twenty years before as an apprentice, but had later married into a good family and become a merchant. A peasant's son, he had in the last few years by daring speculation and ruthless exploitation become rich, richer than many of the leading families of the town. But he was not used to loss and was unable to support disaster. That autumn he had bought large quantities of plums and walnuts, far beyond his real resources, reckoning that in winter he would be able to control the price of both dried plums and walnuts and so clear his debts and make a good profit, as he had done in previous years. Now he was ruined.

Some time was to pass before the impression made on them by the sight of this ruined man could be dispelled, since all of them, some more some less, had been hit by this flood and only by inborn dignity had they been able to control themselves better than this upstart.

The oldest and most prominent among them once again turned the conversation to casual matters. They began to tell long stories of former times, which had no sort of connection with the disaster that had drawn them hither and surrounded them on all sides.

They drank hot plum brandy and embarked on recollections of earlier days, about the eccentric characters of the town and every kind of strange and unusual event. Pop Mihailo and Hadji Liacho set the example. When the talk inevitably returned to earlier floods, they recalled only what was pleasant or comical, or at least seemed so after so many years, as if they wanted to cast a spell upon the waters and to defy the flood.

They talked of Pop Jovan, who had once been parish priest here, who his parishioners had said was a good man but did not have "a lucky hand" and that God had paid little heed to his prayers.

At the time of the summer droughts which often ruined the whole harvest, Pop Jovan had regularly led a procession and read the prayers for rain, but the only result was still greater drought and stifling heat. When one autumn, after such a dry summer, the Drina began to rise and threaten a general flood, Pop

Jovan had gone out to the banks, collected the people, and began to read a prayer that the rain should cease and the waters recede. Then a certain Jokić, a drunkard and ne'er-do-well, reckoning that God always did exactly the opposite from what Pop Jovan prayed for, shouted:

"Not that one, father! Read the summer one, the one for rain; that will help the waters dry up."

Fat and well-fed Ismet Effendi spoke of his predecessors and their struggles with the floods. At one of these disasters long ago a pair of the Višegrad *hodjas* went out to read a prayer to stay the disaster. One of these *hodjas* had a house in the lower part of the town, the other one on the hillside where the waters could not reach. The first to read was the *hodja* from the house on the hillside but the waters showed no sign of receding. Then a gipsy whose house was already half disintegrated in the waters shouted:

"*Ama,* fellows, let the *hodja* from the market-place, whose house is under water like ours, read. Can't you see that that fellow from the hill only reads with half his heart?"

Hadji Liacho, red-faced and smiling, with riotous tufts of white hair showing from under his unusually shallow fez, laughed at everything and said mockingly to the priest and *hodja*:

"Don't talk too much about prayers against floods, or else our people might remember and drive all three of us out in this downpour to read prayers for them."

So they ranged story against story, all insignificant in themselves but each with a meaning for them and their generation though incomprehensible to others; harmless recollections which evoked the monotonous, pleasant yet hard life of the townsmen, their own life. Though all these things had changed long ago they still remained closely bound up with their lives, although far from the drama of that night which had brought them together in that fantastic circle.

Thus the town's leaders, accustomed from childhood to misfortunes of every kind, dominated the night of the great flood and found enough strength in themselves to jest in face of the disaster which had come upon them and thus mastered the misery that they were not able to avoid.

But within themselves they were all greatly anxious and each of them, beneath all the jokes and laughter at misfortune, as if under a mask, turned over and over in his mind anxious thoughts and listened continually to the roar of the waters and the wind from the town below, where he had left all that he possessed. The next day in the morning, after a night so spent, they looked down from Mejdan to the plain below where their houses were under water, some only half submerged and others covered to the roof. Then for the first and last time in their lives they saw their town without a bridge. The waters had risen a good thirty feet, so that the wide high arches were covered and the waters flowed over the roadway of the bridge which was hidden beneath them. Only that elevated part on which the *kapia* had been built showed above the surface of the troubled waters which flowed about it like a tiny waterfall.

But two days later the waters suddenly fell, the skies cleared and the sun broke through, as warm and rich as it does on some October days in this fertile land. On that lovely day the town looked pitiable and terrible. The houses of the gipsies and the poorer folk on the banks were bent over in the direction of the current, many of them roofless and with the mud and clay of their walls washed away, displaying only a black trellis of willow branches so that they looked like skeletons. In the unfenced courtyards the houses of the richer townsmen gaped open with staring windows; on each a line of reddish mud showed how deeply it had been flooded. Many stables had been washed away and granaries overturned. In the lower shops there was mud to the knees, and in that mud all the goods that had not been taken away in time. In the streets were whole trees rooted up and brought there by the waters from no one knew where, and the swollen corpses of drowned animals.

That was their town, to which they must now descend and go on with their lives. But between the flooded banks, above the waters which still raged noisily, stood the bridge, white and unchanged in the sun. The waters now reached halfway up the piers and the bridge seemed as if it were in some other and deeper river than that which usually flowed beneath it. Along the parapet still remained deposits of mud which had now dried and were cracking in the sun, and on the *kapia* was piled up a whole heap of small branches and rubbish from the river. But all that in no way altered the appearance of the bridge, which alone had passed through the flood unaltered and emerged from it unscathed.

Every man in the town set to work at once to repair the damage and no one had time to think of the meaning of the victory of the bridge, but going about his affairs in that ill-fated town in which the waters had destroyed or at least damaged everything, he knew that there was something in his life that overcame every disaster and that the bridge, because of the strange harmony of its forms and the strong and invisible power of its foundations, would emerge from every test unchanged and imperishable.

The winter which then began was a hard one. Everything that had been stored in courtyards and barns, wood, wheat, hay, the flood had carried away; houses, stables and fences had to be repaired and fresh goods had to be obtained on credit to replace those which had been destroyed in warehouses and shops. Kosta Baranac, who had suffered more than any, because of his overbold speculations with plums, did not outlive the winter, but died of mortification and shame. He left his young children almost penniless and a number of small but widespread debts in all the villages. He was recalled in the memory of the town as a man who had overtaxed his strength.

But by the next summer the recollection of the great flood had begun to pass into the memory of the older men, where it would live long, while the younger people sat singing and talking on the smooth white stone *kapia* over the water which flowed far below them and accompanied their songs with its murmurings. Forgetfulness heals everything and song is the most beautiful manner of forgetting, for in song man feels only what he loves.

So, on the *kapia,* between the skies, the river and the hills, generation after generation learned not to mourn overmuch what the troubled waters had borne away. They entered there into the unconscious philosophy of the town; that life was an incomprehensible marvel, since it was incessantly wasted and spent, yet none the less it lasted and endured "like the bridge on the Drina."

6

As well as floods there were also other onslaughts on the bridge and its *kapia.* They were caused by the development of events and the course of human conflicts; but they could do even less than the unchained waters to harm the bridge or change it permanently.

At the beginning of last century Serbia rose in revolt. This town on the very frontier of Bosnia and Serbia had always been in close connection and permanent touch with everything that took place in Serbia and grew with it "like a nail and its finger." Nothing that happened in the Višegrad district—drought, sickness, oppression or revolt—could be a matter of indifference to those in the Užice district, and vice versa. But at first the affair seemed distant and insignificant; distant, because it was taking place on the farther side of the Belgrade *pashaluk,* insignificant since rumors of revolt were no sort of novelty. Ever since the Empire had existed there had been such rumors, for there is no rule without revolts and conspiracies, even as there is no property without work and worry. But in time the revolt in Serbia began to affect the life of the whole Bosnian *pashaluk* more and more, and especially the life of this town which was only an hour's march from the frontier.

As the struggle in Serbia grew, more and more was demanded from the Bosnian Turks. They were asked to send men to the army and to contribute to its equipment and supply. The army and the commissariat sent into Serbia passed to a great extent through the town. That brought in its train expenses and inconveniences and dangers not only for the Turks, but especially for the Serbs who were suspected, persecuted and fined in those years more than ever before. Finally, one summer, the revolt spread to these districts. Making a detour around Užice, the insurgents came to within two hours' march of the town. There, at Veletovo, they destroyed Lufti Beg's fortified farmhouse by cannon fire and burned a number of Turkish houses at Crniče.

There were in the town both Turks and Serbs who swore that they had heard with their own ears the rumbling of "Karageorge's gun" (naturally with completely opposite feelings). But even if it were a matter for doubt whether the echo of the Serb insurrectionists' gun could be heard as far as the town, for a man often thinks that he can hear what he is afraid of or what he hopes for, there could be no doubt about the fires which the insurgents lit by night on the bare and rocky crest of Panos between Veletovo and Gostilje, on which the huge isolated pines could be counted from the town with the naked eye. Both Turks and Serbs saw the fires clearly and looked at them attentively, although both pretended not to have noticed them. From darkened windows and from the shadows of dense gardens, both took careful note of when and where they were lighted and extinguished. The Serbian women crossed themselves in the darkness and wept from inexplicable emotion, but in their tears they saw reflected those fires of insurrection even as those ghostly flames which had once fallen upon Radisav's grave and which their ancestors almost three centuries before had also seen through their tears from that same Mejdan.

Those flickering and uneven flames, scattered along the dark background of the summer night, wherein skies and mountains merged, seemed to the Serbs like some new constellation in which they eagerly read bold presentiments and, shivering, guessed at their fate and at coming events. For the Turks they were the first waves of a sea of fire which was spreading there in Serbia and which, even as they watched, splashed against the mountains above the town. In those summer nights the wishes and the prayers of both circled around those flames, but in different directions. The Serbs prayed to God that these saving flames, like those which they had always carried in their hearts and carefully concealed, should spread to these mountains, while the Turks prayed to Allah to halt their progress and extinguish them, to frustrate the seditious designs of the infidel and restore the old order and the peace of the true faith. The nights were filled with prudent and passionate whisperings in which pulsed invisible waves of the most daring dreams and wishes, the most improbable thoughts and plans which triumphed and broke in the blue darkness overhead. Next day at dawn, Turks and Serbs went out to work and met one another with dull and expressionless faces, greeted one another and talked together with those hundred or so commonplace words of provincial courtesy which had from times past circulated in the town and passed from one to another like counterfeit coin which none the less makes communication both possible and easy.

When, soon after the feast of St. Elias, the fires disappeared from Panos and the revolt was pushed back from the Užice district, once again neither the one side nor the other showed their feelings. And it would really be difficult to say what were the true feelings of either side. The Turks were gratified that the revolt was now far away from them and hoped that it would be entirely extinguished and would end there where all godless and evil enterprises ended. But none the less that gratification was incomplete and overshadowed for it was hard to forget so close a danger. Many of them for long after saw in their dreams those fantastic insurgent fires like a shower of sparks on all the hills around the town or heard Karageorge's gun, not as a distant echo but as a devastating cannonade which brought ruin with it. The Serbs, however, as was natural, remained disillusioned and disappointed after the withdrawal of the fires on Panos but in the depth of their hearts, in that true and ultimate depth which is revealed to no one, there remained the memory of what had taken place and the consciousness that what has once been can be again; there remained too hope, a senseless hope, that great asset of the downtrodden. For those who rule and must oppress in order to rule must work according to reason; and if, carried away by their passions or driven by an adversary, they go beyond the limits of reasonable action, they start down the slippery slope and thereby reveal the commencement of their own downfall. Whereas those who are downtrodden and exploited make equal use of their reason and unreason for they are but two different kinds of arms in the continual struggle, now underground, now open, against the oppressor.

In those times the importance of the bridge as the one sure link between the Bosnian *pashaluk* and Serbia was greatly increased. There was now a permanent military force in the town, which was not disbanded even in the long periods of truce, and which guarded the bridge over the Drina. To carry out this task as well as possible with the minimum of labor, the soldiers began to erect a wooden blockhouse in the center of the bridge, a monstrous erection crude in shape, position, and the material of which it was made (but all the armies of the world put up, for their own special aims and momentary needs, buildings such as this which, later on, from the point of view of normal peaceful life appear both absurd and incomprehensible). It was a real two-storied house, clumsy and hideous, made of rough beams and unplaned planks, with a free passage like a tunnel beneath it. The blockhouse was raised up and rested on stout beams, so that it straddled the bridge and was supported only at its two ends on the *kapia,* one on the left and the other on the right terrace. Beneath it there was a free passage for carts, horses and pedestrians, but from above, from the floor on which the guards slept and to which led an uncovered stairway, it was possible to inspect all who passed, to examine papers and baggage and, at any moment, should the need arise, to stop them.

That indeed altered the appearance of the bridge. The lovely *kapia* was concealed by the wooden structure which squatted over it with its wooden beams like some sort of gigantic bird.

The day the blockhouse was ready it still smelled strongly of resinous wood and steps echoed in its emptiness. The guards at once took up their quarters. By dawn on the first day the blockhouse, like a trap, already claimed its first victim.

In the low and rosy sun of early morning there collected beneath it the soldiers and a few armed townsmen, Turks, who mounted guard around the town by night and so helped the army. In the midst of this group stood a little old man, a vagabond religious pilgrim, something between a monk and a beggar, but mild and peaceful, somehow clean and sweet in his poverty, easy and smiling despite his white hair and lined face. He was an eccentric old fellow named Jelisije from Čajniče. For many years he had been wandering about, always mild, solemn and smiling, visiting churches and monasteries, religious meetings and festivals; he prayed, did penance and fasted. Earlier the Turkish authorities had paid no attention to him and regarded him as a feeble-minded and religious man, letting him go where he would and say what he liked. But now, due to the insurrection in Serbia, new times had come and harsher measures prevailed. A few Turkish families had arrived in the town whose property had been destroyed by the insurgents; they spread hatred and called for vengeance. Guards were everywhere. Supervision was intensified, the local Turks were anxious, filled with rancor and ill-will and looked on everyone bloodthirstily and with suspicion.

The old man had been traveling along the road from Rogatica and by bad luck was the first traveler on the day when the blockhouse had been completed and the first guards had taken up their posts there. In fact he had chosen the very worst time, for the day had not fully dawned. He bore before him, as a man carries a lighted candle, a sort of thick stick decorated with strange signs and letters. The blockhouse swallowed him up like a spider does a fly. They interrogated him curtly. They demanded who he was, what he was doing and whence he came, and commanded him to explain the decorations and writing on his staff. He replied freely and openly, even to questions that had not been asked him, as if speaking before the Last Judgment of God and not before a group of evil Turks. He said that he was no one and nothing, a traveler on this earth, a transient in a transient world, a shadow in the sun, but that he passed his few and short days in prayer and in going from monastery to monastery, until he had visited all the holy places, all the bequests and the tombs of the Serbian tsars and nobles. As to the signs and letters on his staff they represented the times of Serbian freedom and greatness, past and future. For, said the old man, smiling gently and timidly, the day of resurrection was coming soon and, judging from what he had read in books and from what might be seen on the earth and in the skies, it was now quite near. The kingdom was reborn, redeemed by trials and founded on truth.

"I know that it is not pleasant, gentlemen, for you to have to listen to these things and that I should not even speak of them before you, but you have stopped me and told me that I should tell you the whole truth, wherever it may lead. God is truth and God is One! And now, I beg you, let me go on my way for I am due today at Banja, at the Monastery of the Holy Trinity."

The interpreter Shefko translated, struggling in vain to find in his poor knowledge of the Turkish language equivalents for abstract ideas. The Captain of the Guard, a sickly Anatolian, still only half awake, listened to the confused and disconnected words of the translator and from time to time threw a glance at the old man who, without fear or evil thoughts, looked back at him and confirmed with his eyes that everything was just as the interpreter had said, though he knew not a word of Turkish. Somewhere in the back of his mind it was clear to the Captain that this man was some sort of half-witted infidel dervish, a good-natured and harmless madman. And in the old man's staff, which they had already cut through in several places thinking that it was hollow and that messages were concealed in it, they found nothing. But in Shefko's translation the old man's words seemed suspicious, smelled of politics and seditious intent. The Captain, for his part, would have let this poor dim-witted creature go his way, but the rest of the soldiers and civil guards had gathered together there and were listening to the interrogation. There was his sergeant Tahir, an evil man, sullen and rheumy-eyed, who had already several times slandered him to his chief and accused him of lack of care and severity. Then too there was that Shefko, who in his translation was obviously putting the worst possible construction on the old man's exalted phrases and who loved to stick his nose into everything and carry tales even when there was nothing in them, and was ever ready to give or to confirm an evil report. Then too there were those Turks from the town, volunteers, who went their rounds sullenly and self-importantly, arrested suspicious characters and interfered needlessly in his official duties. They were all there. And all of them, these days, were as if drunk with bitterness, from desire for vengeance and longed to punish or kill whomsoever they could, since they could not punish or kill those whom they wished. He did not understand them, nor did he approve of them, but he saw that they were all agreed that the blockhouse must have its victim this first morning. He suspected that because of their intoxication of bitterness he might be the one to suffer if he opposed their wishes. The thought that he might have unpleasantness because of this mad old fool seemed to him intolerable. And the old man with his tales of the Serbian Empire would not in any case get very far among the Turks of the district who, these days, were like a swarm of angry bees. Let the troubled waters carry him away, even as they had brought him here. . . .

As soon as the old man had been bound and the Captain was preparing to go into the town so as not to have to watch the execution, some Turkish policemen and a few civilians appeared, leading a poorly dressed Serbian youth. His clothing was torn and his face and hands scratched. This was a certain Mile, a poor devil from Lijesko, who lived quite alone in a water-mill at Osojnica. He might have been nineteen at most, strong and bursting with health.

That morning before sunrise Mile placed some barley in the mill to be ground and then opened the big millrace and went into the forest to cut wood. He brandished his axe and cut the soft alder branches like straw. He enjoyed the morning freshness and the ease with which the wood fell before his axe. His own movements were a pleasure to him. But his axe was sharp and the thin wood too frail for the force that was in him. Something within him swelled his breast and drove him to shout aloud at each movement. His cries became more and more frequent and connected. Mile who, like all men of Lijesko, had no ear and no idea of how to sing, sang and shouted in the thick and shady forest. Without thinking of anything and forgetting where he was, he began to sing what he had heard others singing.

At that time, when Serbia had risen in revolt, the people had made of the old song:

"When Alibeg was a young beg
A maiden bore his standard . . ."

a new song:

"When Karageorge was a young beg
A maiden bore his standard . . ."

In that great and strange struggle, which had been waged in Bosnia for centuries between two faiths, for land and power and their own conception of life and order, the adversaries had taken from each other not only women, horses and arms but also songs. Many a verse passed from one to the other as the most precious of booty.

This song, then, was one recently sung among the Serbs, but stealthily and in secret, in closed houses, at family feasts or in distant pastures where a Turk might not set foot for years at a time and where a man, at the price of loneliness and poverty in the wilds, might live as he wished and sing what he liked. And it was just this song that Mile, the mill attendant, had thought fit to sing in the forest just below the road along which the Turks of Olujac and Orahovac passed on their way to the market in the town.

Dawn had just touched the crests of the mountains and there, in that shady place, it was still quite dark. Mile was all wet with the dew but warm from a good night's sleep, hot bread and work. He brandished his axe and struck the slender alder near its root but the tree only bent and bowed like a young bride who kisses the hand of the *"kum"* who leads her to marriage. The alder was sprinkled with cold dew like a fine rain and remained bent, for it could not fall because of the thickness of the greenery around. Then he cut off the green branches with his axe in one hand as if playing. While he was doing this he sang at the top of his voice pronouncing certain of the words with enjoyment. "Karageorge" was something vague but strong and daring; "maiden" and "standard" were also things unknown to him, but things which in some way answered to his most intimate dreams; to have a girl of his own and to bear a standard. In any case there was a sweetness in pronouncing such words. And all the strength within him drove him on to pronounce them clearly and countless times over. His utterance of them seemed to renew his strength making him repeat them still more loudly.

So sang Mile at the break of day until he had cut and trimmed the branches for which he had come. Then he went down the wet slope dragging his fresh burden behind him. There were some Turks in front of the mill. They had tethered their horses and were waiting for someone. There were ten of them. He felt himself again, as he had been before he set out to get the wood, clumsy, ragged and embarrassed, without Karageorge before his eyes, without a girl or a standard near him. The Turks waited until he had put down his axe, then fell on him from all sides and after a short struggle bound him with a halter and took him to the town. On their way they beat him and kicked him in the groin, asking him where was his Karageorge now and saying evil words about his girl and his standard.

Under the blockhouse on the *kapia* where they had just bound the half-witted old man some of the town ne'er-do-wells had joined the soldiers even though it had only just dawned. Among them were a number of refugees from Serbia whose homes had been burned down. All were armed and wore a solemn expression as though a great event or a

decisive battle were in question. Their emotion rose with the rising sun. The sun rose rapidly, amid shining mists down there on the skyline above Goleš. The Turks waited for the terrified youth as if he had been a revolutionary leader, though he was ragged and miserable and had been brought from the left bank of the Drina where there was no insurrection.

The Turks from Olujac and Orahovac, exasperated by the arrogance which they were unable to believe was not intentional, bore witness that the young man had been singing in a provocative manner beside the road songs about Karageorge and the infidel fighters. He, frightened, in wet rags, scratched and beaten, his eyes filled with emotion that made him seem to squint, watched the Captain as if he were hoping for salvation from him. As he came rarely to the town he had not known that a blockhouse was being erected on the bridge; therefore everything seemed to him strange and unreal as if he had wandered in his sleep into a strange town filled with evil and dangerous men. Stuttering and keeping his eyes on the ground, he swore that he had never sung anything and had never struck a Turk, that he was a poor man, who looked after the water-mill, that he was cutting wood and did not know why he had been brought here. He shivered from fear and was really unable to understand what had happened and how, after that exalted mood down there by the freshness of the stream, he had suddenly found himself bound and beaten here on the *kapia,* the center of all interest, before so many people to whom he had to answer. He had himself quite forgotten that he had ever sung even the most innocent of songs.

But the Turks stood by their words; that he had been singing insurrectionist songs at the moment they had been passing and that he had resisted them when they wanted to bind him. Each of them confirmed this on oath to the Captain who interrogated them:

"Do you swear by Allah?"

"I swear by Allah."

"Is that the truth?"

"That is the truth."

So thrice repeated. Then they put the young man beside Jelisije and went to waken the headsman who, it seemed, slept very soundly. The old man looked at the youth who, confused and ashamed, blinked since he was not used to being the center of attention in broad daylight on the bridge surrounded by so many people.

"What is your name?" the old man asked.

"Mile," said the youth humbly, as if he were still replying to the Turkish questions.

"Mile, my son, let us kiss," and the old man leaned his gray head on Mile's shoulder. "Let us kiss and make the sign of the Cross. In the Name of the Father and of the Son and of the Holy Ghost. In the Name of the Father and of the Son and of the Holy Ghost. Amen."

So he crossed himself and the youth in words only, for their hands were bound, quickly, for the executioner had already arrived.

The headsman, who was one of the soldiers, rapidly finished his task and the first comers, who descended the hills because of market day and went across the bridge, could see the two heads placed on fresh stakes on the blockhouse and a bloodstained place, sprinkled with gravel and smoothed down, on the bridge where they had been beheaded.

Thus the blockhouse began its work.

From that day onwards all who were suspected or guilty of insurrection, whether caught on the bridge itself or somewhere on the frontier, were brought to the *kapia*. Once there they rarely got away alive. The heads of those connected with the revolt, or simply those who were unlucky, were exposed on stakes placed around the blockhouse and their bodies thrown from the bridge into the Drina if no one appeared to ransom the headless corpse.

The revolt, with shorter or longer periods of truce, lasted for years and in the course of those years the number of those thrown into the river to drift down to "look for another, better and more reasonable land" was very great. Chance had decreed, that chance that overwhelms the weak and unmindful, that these two simple men, this pair from the mass of unlearned, poverty-stricken and innocent, should head the procession, since it is often such men who are first caught up in the whirlpool of great events and whom this whirlpool irresistibly attracts and sucks down. Thus the youth Mile and the old man Jelisije, beheaded at the same moment and in the same place, united as brothers, first decorated with their heads the military blockhouse on the *kapia*, which from then onwards, as long as the revolt lasted, was practically never without such decoration. So these two, whom no one before then had ever seen or heard of, remained together in memory, a memory clearer and more lasting than that of so many other, more important victims.

So the *kapia* disappeared under this bloodstained blockhouse of ill repute and with it vanished also all meetings, conversations, songs and enjoyment. Even the Turks passed that way unwillingly while only those Serbs who were forced, crossed the bridge hastily and with lowered heads.

Around the wooden blockhouse, whose planks with time became first gray and then black, was quickly created that atmosphere that always surrounds buildings in permanent use by the army. The soldiers' washing hung from the beams and rubbish was tipped from the windows into the Drina, dirty water and all the refuse and filth of barrack life. On the white central pier of the bridge remained long dirty streaks which could be seen from afar.

The job of headsman was for long always carried out by the same soldier. He was a fat and dark-skinned Anatolian with dull yellowish eyes and negroid lips in a greasy and earthen-colored face, who seemed always to be smiling, with the smile of a well-nourished and good-humored man. He was called Hairuddin and was soon known to the whole town and even beyond the frontier. He carried out his duties with satisfaction and conscientiousness; and certainly he was exceptionally swift and skillful at them. The townsmen used to say that he had a lighter hand than Mushan the town barber. Both old and young knew him, at least by name, and that name excited awe and curiosity at the same time. On sunny days he would sit or lie all day long on the bridge in the shade under the wooden blockhouse. From time to time he would rise to inspect the heads on the stakes, like a market-gardener his melons. Then he would lie down again on his plank in the shade, yawning and stretching himself, heavy, rheumy-eyed and good-humored, like an ageing sheepdog. At the end of the bridge, behind the wall, the children gathered inquisitively and watched him timidly.

But when his work was in question, Hairuddin was alert and precise to the minutest detail. He disliked anyone to interfere with his work, a thing which happened more and more often as the insurrection developed. When the insurgents burned some of the villages above the town, the anger of the Turks passed all measure. Not only did they arrest all insurgents and spies, or those whom they considered such, and brought them to the

Captain on the bridge, but in their rancor they even wanted to take part in the execution of the sentence.

Thus one day dawn revealed the head of the Višegrad parish priest, that same Pop Mihailo who had found strength to joke with the *hodja* and the rabbi on the night of the great flood. In the general fury against the Serbs he had been killed, even though innocent, and the gipsy children stuck a cigar in his dead mouth.

Hairuddin strongly disapproved of such actions and prevented them whenever he was able.

When one day the fat Anatolian died unexpectedly of anthrax a new headsman, in truth far less skillful, continued his work and went on doing so for several years, and until the revolt in Serbia had died down there were always two or three heads exposed on the *kapia*. In such times people quickly grow hardened and insensible. They soon became so accustomed to them that they passed them by indifferently and paid no more heed to them, so that they did not at once notice when they ceased to be exhibited.

When the situation in Serbia and on the frontier died down, the blockhouse lost its importance and its reason for existence. But the guard went on sleeping there, although the crossing of the bridge had long been free and without supervision. In every army things change slowly and in the Turkish army more slowly than in any other. And so it would have remained for God alone knows how long had not a fire broken out one night because of a forgotten candle. The blockhouse was made of resinous planks and was still warm after the heat of the day. It burned to its foundations, that is to say down to the flagstones of the *kapia*.

The excited people of the town watched the huge blaze which lit up not only the bridge but also the mountains around, and was reflected in wavering red light on the surface of the river. When morning broke, the bridge again appeared in its former shape freed from the clumsy wooden monstrosity which had for years concealed its *kapia*. The white stones were tarnished and sooty, but the rains and snows soon washed them clean again. Thus nothing remained of the blockhouse and the bloody events connected with it save a few bitter memories which paled and finally disappeared with that generation, and one oak beam which had not been burned as it was fixed into the stone steps of the *kapia*.

So the *kapia* once again became for the town what it had formerly been. On the left terrace as one came from the town a coffee brewer once again lit his brazier and set out his utensils. Only the fountain had suffered, for the snake's head from which the water had flowed had been crushed. The people once again began to dally on the *sofa* and pass the time there in conversation, in business deals or in drowsy time-wasting. On summer nights the young men sang there in groups or sat there solitary suppressing their love-yearning or giving way to that vague desire to go out into the distant world to do great deeds and take part in great events which so often torments young people brought up in a narrow milieu. After a score or so of years a new generation grew up which did not even remember the deformed wooden carcass of the blockhouse or the harsh cries of the guard stopping travelers by night, or Hairuddin or the exposed heads which he had cut off with such professional skill. Only some of the old women, driving away the urchins who came to steal their peaches, would shout in loud and angry curses:

"May God send Hairuddin to cut your hair for you! May your mother recognize your head on the *kapia!*"

But the children who ran away over

the fences could not understand the real sense of these curses, though they knew, naturally, that they meant nothing favorable.

Thus the generations renewed themselves beside the bridge and the bridge shook from itself, like dust, all the traces which transient human events had left on it and remained, when all was over, unchanged and unchangeable.

7

Time passed over the bridge by years and decades. Those were the few decades about the middle of the nineteenth century in which the Turkish Empire was consumed by a slow fever. Measured by the eye of a contemporary, those years seemed comparatively peaceful and serene, although they had their share of anxieties and fears and knew droughts and floods and epidemics and all manner of exciting events. Only all these things came in their own time, in short spasms amid long lulls.

The border between the two *pashaluks* of Bosnia and Belgrade, which passed just above the town, began in those years to become ever more sharply defined and to take on the appearance and significance of a state frontier. That changed the conditions of life for the whole district and for the town also, influenced trade and communications, and the mutual relations of Turks and Serbs.

The older Turks frowned and blinked in incredulity, as if they wished to drive away this unpleasant apparition. They threatened and discussed and then for months at a time forgot all about the matter, until harsh reality would once again remind them and alarm them once more.

Thus, one spring day one of the Turks from Veletovo, up there on the frontier, sat on the *kapia* and with deep emotion told the leading Turks gathered there what had been happening at Veletovo.

Sometime in the winter, the man from Veletovo said, there had appeared above their village the ill-famed Jovan Mičić, the *serdar* of Ruyan, who had come from Arilje with armed men and begun to inspect and mark out the frontier. When they asked him what he intended to do and why he was there, he replied arrogantly that he had to give account to no one, least of all to Bosnian renegades, but if they really wanted to know he had been sent there by the Prince Miloš to find out where the frontier was to run and how much was to be included in Serbia.

"We thought," said the man from Veletovo, "that the Vlach was drunk and did not know what he was saying, for we have long known him as a bandit and a rascal. So we refused to let him stay and then forgot all about him. But not more than two months later he came again, this time with a whole company of Miloš' soldiers and a delegate of the Sultan, a soft pale fellow from Stambul. We could not believe our eyes. But the delegate confirmed everything. He lowered his eyes in shame, but he confirmed. Thus, he said, it had been ordered by Imperial decree that Miloš should administer Serbia in the Sultan's name and that the frontier should be marked out, to know exactly to what point his authority stretched. When the delegate's men began to drive in stakes along the crest below Tetrebica, Mičić came and pulled them up and threw them aside. The mad Vlach (may the dogs eat his flesh!) flew at the delegate, shouted at him as if he were a subordinate and threatened him with death. That, he said, was not the frontier; the frontier had been fixed by the Sultan and the Russian Tsar who had given a *ferman* to Prince Miloš. It now ran along the Lim down as far as the Višegrad bridge and thence down the Drina; thus all this land is part of Serbia. This too, he said, is only for a certain time; later it will have to be advanced. The delegate had great trouble in convincing him and then they fixed the frontier above Veletovo. And there it remains, at least for the present. Only from then on we have been filled with doubt and a sort of fear, so that we do not know what to do or where to turn. We have discussed all this with the people of Užice, but they too do not know what has happened nor what to expect. And old Hadji-Zuko who has twice been to Mecca and is now more than ninety years old says that before a generation has passed the Turkish frontier will be withdrawn right to the Black Sea, fifteen days' march away."

The leading Turks of Višegrad listened to the man from Veletovo. They seemed calm to all outward appearance, but inwardly they were shaken and confused. They squirmed unintentionally at his words and caught hold of the stone seat with their hands, as if some powerful and invisible force were shaking the bridge beneath them. Then, mastering themselves, they sought words to lessen and diminish the importance of this event.

They did not like unfavorable news or heavy thoughts or serious and despondent conversations on the *kapia,* but they could see for themselves that this boded no good; nor could they deny what the man from Veletovo had said or find words to calm and reassure him. So they could scarcely wait for the peasant who had brought this unpleasant news to return to his village in the mountains. That, naturally, would not lessen the anxiety but it would remove it far from them. And when in fact the man went away, they were only too pleased to be able to return to their usual habits, and to go on sitting peacefully on the *kapia* without conversations which made life disagreeable and the future terrifying, and to leave it to time to soften and ease the weight of the events which had taken place over there behind the mountains.

Time did its work. Life went on, to all appearances unchanged. More than thirty years passed since that conversation on the *kapia.* But those stakes which the Sultan's delegate and the *serdar* of Ruyan had planted struck root and brought forth fruit, late-ripening but bitter to the Turks. The Turks had now to abandon even the last towns in Serbia. One summer day the bridge at Višegrad was burdened with a pitiable procession of refugees from Užice.

It was on one of those hot days with long pleasant twilights on the *kapia* when the Turks from the market-place filled both the terraces over the water. On such days melons were brought there on donkey back. The ripe canteloupes and watermelons had been cooled all day long and in the early evening people would buy and eat them on the *sofa.* Usually two of them would bet whether the inside of a certain watermelon were red or white. Then they would cut it open and whoever lost paid for it and they would eat it together, with talk and loud jokes.

The day's warmth still beat up from the stone terraces but with the twilight there was a cool refreshing air from the water. The middle of the river shone, and near the banks under the willows it turned a shadowy dull green. All the hills around were reddened by the sunset, some strongly and others scarcely touched. Above them, filling the whole south-western part of that amphitheater which could be seen from the *kapia,* were summer mists of continually changing color. These mists are among the most beautiful sights to be seen in summer on the *kapia.* As soon as the daylight grows strong and the sun leaps up, they appear behind the mountains like thick white silvery-gray masses, creating fantastic landscapes, irregular cupolas and countless strange buildings. They remain thus all day long, heavy and unmoving above the hills surrounding the town which swelters in the sun. The Turks who in early evening sat on the *kapia* had those mists always before their eyes like white silken Imperial tents which in their imagination evoked vague shapes of wars and forays and pictures of strange and immeasurable power and luxury, till darkness extinguished and dispersed them and the skies created fresh magic from the stars and moonlight.

Never could the wonderful and exceptional beauty of the *kapia* be better felt than at that hour on such summer days. A man was then as if in a magic swing; he swung forth over the earth and the waters and flew in the skies, yet was firmly and surely linked with the town and his own white house there on the bank with its plum orchard about it. With the solace of coffee and tobacco, many of those simple citizens, who owned little more than those houses and the few shops in the market-place, felt at such times the richness of the world and the illimitability of God's gifts. Such a bridge, lovely and strong, could offer all this to men and would continue to offer it for centuries to come.

This was just such an evening, an evening filled with chatter and laughter and jokes among themselves and the passers-by.

The sprightliest and loudest jokes centered on a short but powerful young man of strange appearance. This was Salko Ćorkan, One-eyed Salko.

Salko was the son of a gipsy woman and some Anatolian soldier or officer who had at some time been stationed in the town and had left it before this unwanted son had been born. Shortly afterwards, his mother too had died and the child had grown up without anyone of his own. The whole town fed him; he belonged to everybody and nobody. He did odd jobs about the shops and houses, carried out tasks which no one else would do, cleaned the cesspools and street channels, and buried anything that had died or had been brought down by the waters. He had never had a house or occupation of his own. He ate whatever he happened to find, still standing or walking about, slept in attics, and dressed in parti-colored rags given him by others. While still a child he had lost his left eye. Eccentric, good-humored, merry and a drunkard, he often worked for the townsmen for a word or a joke instead of pay.

Around Salko had gathered a number of merchants' sons, young men who laughed at him and played crude jokes on him.

The air smelled of fresh melons and roasting coffee. From the great flagstones, still warm from the day's heat, and sprinkled with water, rose moist and scented the special smell of the *kapia* which filled men with freedom from care and evoked lively fancies.

It was the moment between day and night. The sun had set but the great star which rose over Moljevnik had not yet appeared. In such a moment, when even the most ordinary thing took on the appearance of a vision filled with majesty, terror and special meaning, the first refugees from Užice appeared on the bridge.

The men were for the most part on foot, dusty and bowed, while the women wrapped in their veils were balanced on small horses with small children tied to the saddle-bags or to boxes. Now and again a more important man rode a better horse, but with lowered head and at a funereal pace, revealing even more clearly the misfortune which had driven them hither. Some of them were leading a single goat on a short halter. Others carried lambs in their laps. All were silent; even the children did not cry. All that could be heard was the beat of horseshoes and footsteps and the monotonous chinking of wooden and copper vessels on the overloaded horses.

The appearance of this overtired and destitute procession damped the gaiety on the *kapia.* The older people remained seated on the stone benches, while the younger stood up and formed living walls on both sides of the *kapia* and the procession passed between them. Some of the townsmen only looked compassionately at the refugees and remained silent, while others greeted them with *"merhaba,"* tried to stop them and offer them something. They paid no attention to the offers and scarcely responded to the greetings, but hurried on to reach their post for the night at Okolište while it was still light.

In all there were about 120 families. More than 100 families were going on to Sarajevo where there was a chance of being settled, while fifteen were to stay in the town; they were for the most part those who had relatives there.

One only of these dog-tired men, poor in appearance and apparently alone, stopped for a moment on the *kapia,* drank his fill of water and accepted an offered cigar. He was white all over from the dust of the road, his eyes shone as if in fever and he was unable to keep his glance fixed on any single object. Vigorously puffing out smoke, he looked around him with those shining disagreeable glances, without replying to the timid and humble questions of individuals. He only wiped his long moustaches, thanked them curtly and with that bitterness which overtiredness and a feeling of being outcast leaves in a man he muttered a few words looking at them with one of those sudden unseeing glances.

"You sit here at your ease and do not know what is happening behind Staniševac. Here we are fleeing into Turkish lands, but where are you to flee when, together with us, your turn will come? None of you knows and none of you ever thinks of it."

He suddenly ceased. Even the little he said was much for those who till then had been so carefree, and yet little enough for his own bitterness which would not allow him to stay silent yet at the same time prevented him from expressing himself clearly. It was he himself who cut short the heavy silence by saying farewell and hurrying away to catch up with the rest of the procession. All stood up to shout good wishes after him.

All that evening the mood on the *kapia* remained heavy. All were silent and downcast. Even Salko sat dumb and motionless on one of the stone steps surrounded by the husks of the watermelons he had eaten for a bet. Depressed and silent he sat there with downcast looks, absent-mindedly, as though he were not looking at the stone before him but at something far distant which he could scarcely perceive. The people began to disperse earlier than usual.

But next day everything was as it had always been, for the townsmen did not like to remember evil and did not worry about the future; in their blood was the conviction that real life consists of calm periods and that it would be mad and vain to spoil them by looking for some other, firmer and more lasting life that did not exist.

In those twenty-five years in the middle of the nineteenth century the plague raged twice at Sarajevo and the cholera once. When this happened the town kept regulations which, according to tradition, had been given by Mohammed himself to the faithful for their guidance in the event of an epidemic: "While the Pestilence rages in some place do not go there, for you may become infected, and if you are already in the place where it rages then do not depart from that place lest you infect others." But since men do not observe even the most salutary of regulations, even when they derive from the Apostle of God himself, if not forced to do so by "the power of the authorities," then the authorities on the occasion of every "plague" limited or completely stopped all travel and postal communications. Then life on the *kapia* changed its aspect. The people of the town, busy or at leisure, thoughtful or singing, disappeared, and on the empty *sofa,* as in times of war or revolution, once again sat a guard of several gendarmes. They stopped all travelers coming from the direction of Sarajevo and waved them back with their rifles or shouted loudly to them to retreat. The post they accepted from the messenger but with every measure of precaution. A small fire of "aromatic woods" was lit on the *kapia* and produced an abundant white smoke. The gendarmes took each individual letter in a pair of tongs and passed it through this smoke. Only such "purified" letters were sent onward. Goods they did not accept at all. But their main task was not with letters but with living men. Every day a few arrived, travelers, merchants, bearers of news, tramps. A gendarme awaited them at the entry to the bridge and from a distance signaled with his hand that they might not go farther. The traveler would halt, but begin to argue, to justify himself and explain his case. Each of them considered that it was absolutely necessary to let him into the town and each of them swore that he was healthy and had had no connection with the cholera which was there somewhere in Sarajevo. During these explanations the travelers would edge little by little halfway across the bridge and approach the *kapia.* There, other gendarmes would take their part in the conversation and as they talked at several paces' distance they all shouted loudly and waved their arms. Those gendarmes also joined in who sat all day on the *kapia* sipping plum brandy and eating garlic; their service gave them this right for it was believed that both these were good antidotes against infection, and they made abundant use of their privilege.

Many a traveler would grow tired of pleading with and trying to convince the gendarmes and would return downcast, his work unfinished, along the Okolište road. But some were more persistent and persevering and remained there on the *kapia* hoping for a moment of weakness or inattention or some mad and lucky chance. If it so happened that the leader of the town gendarmes, Salko Hedo, were there, then there was no likelihood that the traveler would achieve anything. Hedo was that true conscientious official who does not really see or hear whomever he talks to and who only considers him in so far as it is necessary to find the place for him set out by the regulations in force. Until he had done this he was deaf and blind and when he had done it he became dumb as well. In vain the traveler would implore or flatter:

"Salik-Aga, I am healthy. . . ."

"Well then, go in health whence you came. Get along, out of my sight. . . ."

There was no arguing with Hedo. But if some of the younger gendarmes were alone, then something might still be done. The longer the traveler stood on the bridge and the more he shouted and talked with them, told all his troubles, why he had set out and all the problems of his life, the more personal and familiar he seemed to become and less and less like a man who might have cholera. In the end, one of the gendarmes would offer to take a message for him to whomever he wished in the town. This was the first step towards yielding. But the traveler knew that the message would never be delivered for the gendarmes, always suffering from a hangover or half drunk as they were, remembered things with difficulty and delivered messages inside out. Therefore he went on indefinitely with his conversation, implored, offered bribes, called upon God and his soul. All this he did until the gendarme whom he had marked down as the most lenient remained alone on the bridge. Then the business was finished somehow or other. The soulful gendarme would turn his face to the raised wall as if to read the ancient inscription on it, with his hands behind his back and the palm of his right hand extended. The persevering traveler would put the agreed sum of money into the gendarme's palm, glance right and left, and then slide across the other half of the bridge and become lost in the town. The gendarme went back to his post, chewed a head of garlic and washed it down with plum brandy. This filled him with a certain gay and carefree resolution and gave him fresh strength to keep vigil and guard the town from cholera.

But misfortunes do not last forever (this they have in common with joys) but pass away or are at least diminished and become lost in oblivion. Life on the *kapia* always renews itself despite everything and the bridge does not change with the years or with the centuries or with the most painful turns in human affairs. All these pass over it, even as the unquiet waters pass beneath its smooth and perfect arches.

8

It was not only the wars, pestilences and migrations of the times which broke against the bridge and interrupted life on the *kapia*. There were also other exceptional events which gave their name to the year in which they took place and were long remembered.

Left and right of the *kapia* in both directions, the stone parapet of the bridge had long become smooth and somewhat darker than the rest. For hundreds of years the peasants had rested their burdens on it when crossing the bridge, or idlers had leaned shoulders and elbows upon it in conversation while waiting for others or when, solitary and leaning on their elbows, they looked in the depths below them at the waters as they went foaming swiftly past, always new and yet always the same.

But never had so many idle and inquisitive people leaned on the parapet and watched the surface of the water, as if to read in it the answer to some riddle, as in the last days of August that year. The water was clouded by the rains though it was only towards the end of summer. In the eddies below the arches a white foam formed, which moved in circles with twigs, small branches and rubbish. But the leisurely and leaning townsmen were not really looking at the waters which they had always known and which had nothing to tell them; but on the surface of the water and in their own conversations they searched for some sort of explanation for themselves and tried to find there some visible trace of an obscure and cruel destiny which, in those days, had troubled and surprised them.

About that time an unusual thing had taken place on the *kapia* which would long be remembered and which was not likely to happen again as long as the bridge and the town on the Drina existed. It had excited and shaken the townspeople and the story of it had passed beyond the town itself, to other places and districts, to become a legend.

This was, in fact, a tale of two Višegrad hamlets, Velje Lug and Nezuke. These two hamlets lay at the extreme ends of that amphitheater formed about the town by the dark mountains and their green foothills.

The great village of Stražište on the north-eastern side of the valley was the nearest to the town. Its houses, fields and gardens were scattered over several foothills and embowered in the valleys between them. On the rounded flank of one of these hills lay about fifteen houses, buried in plum orchards and surrounded on all sides by fields. This was the hamlet of Velje Lug, a peaceful, rich and beautiful Turkish settlement on the slopes. The hamlet belonged to the village of Stražište, but it was nearer to the town than to its own village center, for the men of Velje Lug could walk down to the marketplace in half an hour, had their shops there and did business in the town like the ordinary townsmen. Between them and the townsmen there was indeed little or no difference save perhaps that their properties were more solid and lasting for they stood on the firm earth, not subject to floods, and the men there were more modest and did not have the bad habits of the town. Velje Lug had good soil, pure water and handsome people.

A branch of the Višegrad family of Osmanagić lived there. But even though those in the town were richer and more numerous, it was generally considered that they had "degenerated" and that the real Osmanagićs were those of Velje Lug whence the family had come. They were a fine race of men, sensitive and proud of their origin. Their house, the largest in the district, showing up white on the hillside just below the crest of the hill, turned towards the southwest; it was always freshly whitewashed, with a roof of blackened thatch and fifteen glazed windows. Their house could be seen from afar and was the first to catch the eye of a traveler coming to Višegrad and the last that he saw on leaving it. The last rays of the setting sun behind the Liještan ridge rested there and shone on the white and shining face of this house. The townsmen were long accustomed to look at it from the *kapia* in the early evening and see how the setting sun was reflected from the Osmanagić windows and how the light left them one after the other. As the sun set and the town was in shadow its last rays, falling on one of the windows, as it broke through the clouds, would shine for a few moments longer like a huge red star over the darkened town.

Also well known and esteemed in the town was the head of that house, Avdaga Osmanagić, a bold and fiery man in private life as in business. He had a shop in the market, a low twilit room in which maize, dried plums or pinecones lay scattered over planks and plaited mats. Avdaga only did a wholesale trade, therefore his shop was not open every day, but regularly on market days and throughout the week according to the needs of business. In it was always one of Avdaga's sons, while he himself usually sat on a bench before it. There he chatted with customers or acquaintances. He was a big and imposing man, ruddy in appearance, but with pure white beard and moustaches. His voice was harsh and throaty. For years he had suffered cruelly from asthma. Whenever he grew excited in conversation and raised his voice, and that was a frequent occurrence, he would suddenly choke, his neck tendons stand out, his face grow red and his eyes fill with tears, while his chest creaked, wheezed and echoed like a storm on the hills. When the fit of choking had passed he would pull himself together, take a deep breath and go on with the conversation where he had left off, only in a changed thin voice. He was known in the town and the surroundings as a man of harsh words, but generous and brave. So he was in everything, even in business, though often to his own hurt. Often by a bold word he would reduce or raise the price of plums or maize even when this was not to his own advantage, only to spite some avaricious peasant or rapacious merchant. His word was universally listened to and accepted in the market-place, though it was known that he was often hasty and personal in his judgments. When Avdaga came down from Velje Lug and sat before his shop he was rarely alone, for men liked to listen to his talk and wanted to hear his opinion. He was always open and lively, ready to speak out and defend what others considered was best passed over in silence. His asthma and attacks of heavy coughing would interrupt his conversation at any moment, but for a wonder this did not spoil it but made it seem the more convincing and his whole manner of expressing himself had a sort of heavy and painful dignity, which it was not easy to resist.

Avdaga had five married sons and an only daughter, who was the youngest of his children and just ripe for marriage. She was called Fata and it was known of her that she was exceptionally beautiful and the very image of her father. The whole town and to some extent even the whole district discussed the question of her marriage. It has always been the case with us that at least one girl in every generation passes into legend and song because of her beauty, her qualities and her nobility. So she was in those few years the goal of all desires and the inaccessible example; imagination flared up at mention of her name and she was surrounded by the enthusiasm of the men and the envy of the women. She was one of those outstanding persons set apart by nature and raised to dangerous heights.

This daughter of Avdaga resembled her father not only in face and appearance but also in quickness of wit and the gift of words. The youths who, at weddings or meetings, sought to win her by cheap flattery or embarrass her by daring jests, knew this well. Her wit was no less than her beauty. Therefore, in the song about Fata the daughter of Avdaga (songs about such exceptional beings spring up of themselves spontaneously) it was sung:

"Thou art wise as thou art lovely,
Lovely Fata Avdagina . . ."

So they sang and spoke in the town, but there were very few who had the courage to ask for the hand of the girl from Velje Lug. And when they had one and all been rejected, a sort of vacuum was created about Fata, an enchanted circle, made of hatred and envy, of unacknowledged desires and of malicious expectation, such a circle as always surrounds beings with exceptional gifts and an exceptional destiny. Such persons, of whom much is said and sung, are rapidly borne away by that especial destiny of theirs and leave behind them, instead of a life fulfilled, a song or a story.

Thus it often happens among us that a girl who is much spoken of remains for that very reason without suitors and "sits out," whereas girls who in no way measure up to her marry quickly and easily. This was not destined for Fata, for a suitor was found who had the audacity to desire her and the skill and endurance to attain his ends.

In that irregular circle formed by the Višegrad valley, exactly on the opposite side from Velje Lug, lay the hamlet of Nezuke.

Above the bridge, not quite an hour's walk upstream, amid that circle of dark mountains whence, as from a wall, the Drina breaks out in a sudden curve, there was a narrow strip of good and fertile land on the stony river bank. This was formed by the deposits brought down by the river and by the torrents which came down from the precipitous slopes of the Butkovo Rocks. On it were fields and gardens and, above them, steep meadows with sparse grass which lost themselves on the slopes in rugged stone crops and dark undergrowth. The whole hamlet was the property of the Hamzić family, who were also known by the name of Turković. On one half lived five or six families of serfs and on the other were the houses of the Hamzić brothers, with Mustajbeg Hamzić at their head. The hamlet was remote and exposed, without sun but also without wind, richer in fruit and hay than in wheat. Surrounded and shut in on all sides by steep hills, the greater part of the day it was in shadow and in silence, so that every call of the shepherds and every movement of the cowbells was heard as a loud and repeated echo from the hills. One path only led to it from Višegrad. When one crossed the bridge coming from the town and left the main road which turned to the right down river, one came upon a narrow stone track to the left across a patch of waste and stony ground up the Drina along the water's edge, like a white selvedge on the dark slopes which ran down to the river. A man on horse or on foot going along that path, when seen from the bridge above, seemed as if he were going along a narrow tree trunk between the water and the stone, and his reflection could be seen following him in the calm green waters.

That was the path which led from the town to Nezuke and from Nezuke there was no way on, for there was nowhere to go. Above the houses, in the steep slopes overgrown with sparse forest, two deep white watercourses had been cut, up which the shepherds climbed when they took the cattle to their mountain pastures.

There was the great white house of the eldest Hamzić, Mustajbeg. It was in no way smaller than the Osmanagić house at Velje Lug, but it was different in that it was completely invisible in that hollow alongside the Drina. Around it grew fifteen tall poplars in a semicircle, whose murmur and movement gave life to that spot so shut in and difficult of access. Below this house were the smaller and humbler houses of the remaining pair of Hamzić brothers. All the Hamzićs had many children and all were fair-skinned, tall and slender, taciturn and reserved, but well able to hold their own in business, united and active in all their affairs. Like all the richer people at Velje Lug, they too had their shops in the town where they brought for sale everything that they had produced at Nezuke. At all times of the year, they and their serfs swarmed and climbed like ants along that narrow stony track beside the Drina bringing produce to the town or returning, their business concluded, with money in their pockets, to their invisible village among the hills.

Mustajbeg Hamzić's great white house awaited the visitor as a pleasant surprise at the end of that stony track that seemed as if it led nowhere. Mustajbeg had four daughters and one son, Nail. This Nailbeg of Nezuke, only son of a noble family, was among the first to cast an eye on Fata of Velje Lug. He had admired her beauty at some wedding or other through a half-opened door, outside which a group of young men had been hanging like a bunch of grapes. When he next had the chance of seeing her, surrounded by a group of her friends, he had essayed a daring jest:

"May God and Mustajbeg give you the name of young bride!"

Fata gave a stifled giggle.

"Do not laugh," said the excited youth through the narrow opening of the door, "even that marvel will take place one day."

"It will indeed, when Velje Lug comes down to Nezuke!" replied the girl with another laugh and a proud movement of her body, such as only women like her and of her age can make, and which said more than her words and her laugh.

It is thus that those beings especially gifted by nature often provoke their destiny, boldly and thoughtlessly. Her reply to young Hamzić was repeated from mouth to mouth, as was everything else that she said or did.

But the Hamzićs were not men to be put off or discouraged at the first difficulty. Even when it was a question of minor matters, they did not come to a conclusion hastily so how much less in such a question as this. An attempt made through some relations in the town had no better success. But then old Mustajbeg Hamzić took into his own hands the matter of his son's marriage. He had always had common business dealings with Osmanagić. Avdaga had recently had some serious losses, due to his explosive and proud character, and Mustajbeg had helped him and supported him as only good merchants can help and support one another in difficult moments; simply, naturally and without unnecessary words.

In these cool half-lit shops and on the smooth stone benches before them were settled not only matters of commercial honor but also human destinies. What happened between Avdaga Osmanagić and Mustajbeg Hamzić, how did Mustajbeg came to ask for the hand of Fata for his only son Nail, and why did the proud and upright Avdaga "give" the girl? No one will ever know. No one will ever know either exactly how the matter was thrashed out up there at Velje Lug between the father and his lovely only daughter. There could, naturally, be no question of any opposition on her part. One look filled with pained surprise and that proud and inborn movement of her whole body, and then mute submission to her father's wishes, as it was and still is everywhere and always among us. As if in a dream, she began to air, to complete and to arrange her trousseau.

Nor did a single word from Nezuke filter out to the outer world. The prudent Hamzićs did not ask other men to confirm their successes in empty words. They had achieved their wish and, as always, were content with their success. There was no need of anyone else to share in their satisfaction, even as they had never asked for sympathy in their failures and their misfortunes.

But none the less people talked of this widely and unthinkingly, as is the habit of men. It was told throughout the town and the country around that the Hamzićs had got what they wanted, and that the lovely, proud and clever daughter of Avdaga, for whom no suitor good enough had been found in all Bosnia, had been outplayed and tamed; that none the less "Velje Lug would come to Nezuke" even though Fata had publicly proclaimed that it would not. For people love to talk about the downfall and humiliation of those who have been exalted too much or have flown too high.

For a month the people savored the event and drank in tales of Fata's humiliation like sweet water. For a month they made preparations at Nezuke and at Velje Lug.

For a month Fata worked with her friends, her relations and her servants on her trousseau. The girls sang. She too sang. She even found strength to do that. And she heard herself singing, though she still thought her own thoughts. For with every stroke of her needle she told herself that neither she nor her needlework would ever see Nezuke. She never forgot this for an instant. Only, thus working and thus singing, it seemed to her that it was a long way from Velje Lug to Nezuke and that a month was a long time. At night it was the same. At night when, with the excuse that she had some work to finish, she remained alone there opened before her a world rich and full of light, of joyful and unlimited change.

At Velje Lug the nights were warm and fresh. The stars seemed low and dancing, as though bound together by a white shimmering radiance. Standing before her window, Fata looked out at the night. Through all her body she felt a calm strength, overflowing and sweet, and every part of her body seemed a special source of strength and joy, her legs, her hips, her arms, her neck and above all her breasts. Her breasts, full and large but firm, touched the frame of the window with their nipples. And in that place she felt the whole hillside with all that was on it, houses, outbuildings, fields, breathing warmly, deeply, rising and falling with the shining heavens and the expanse of the night. With that breathing the wooden frame of the window rose and fell, touching the tips of her breasts, leaving them once more for some vast distance and then returning once again to touch them, then rising and falling again and again.

Yes, the world was great, the world was limitless even by day when the valley of Višegrad quivered in the heat and one could almost hear the wheat ripening and when the white town was strung out along the green river, framed by the straight lines of the bridge and the dark mountains. But at night, only at night, the skies grew alive and burst open into infinity and the power of that world where a living being is lost, and has no longer the sense of what he is, where he is going or what he wishes or what he must do. Only there one lived truly, serenely and for long; in that space there were no longer words that bound one tragically for one's whole life, no longer fateful promises or situations from which one could not escape, with the brief time that flows and flows onward inexorably, with death or shame as the only outcome. Yes, in that space it was not as it is in everyday life, where what has once been said remains irrevocable and what has been promised inescapable. There everything was free, endless, nameless and mute.

Then, from somewhere below her, as from afar, could be heard a heavy, deep and stifled sound:

"A-a-a-aah, kkkh . . . A-a-a-aaah . . . kkkkh!"

Down on the ground floor Avdaga was struggling with his nightly attack of coughing.

She heard the sound and could see her father clearly, almost as if he were there before her, as he sat and smoked, sleepless and tormented by his cough. She could see his big brown eyes, as well known as a dear landscape, eyes which were just like her own, save that they were shadowed by old age and bathed in a tearful yet laughing shimmer, eyes in which for the first time she had seen the inevitability of her fate on that day she was told that she had been promised to Hamzić and that she must finish her preparations within a month.

"Kkha, kkha, kkha, Aaaaah!"

That ecstasy of a moment before at the beauty of the night and the greatness of the world was suddenly extinguished. That perfumed breath of the earth ceased. The girl's breasts tightened in a brief spasm. The stars and the expanse disappeared. Only fate, her cruel and irrevocable fate on the eve of its realization, was being completed and accomplished as the time passed in the stillness of that immobility and that void which remained beyond the world.

The sound of coughing echoed from the floor below.

Yes, she both saw and heard him as if he were standing beside her. That was her own dear, powerful, only father with whom she had felt herself to be one, indivisibly and sweetly, ever since she had been conscious of her own existence. She felt that heavy shattering cough as if it had been in her own breast. In truth it had been that mouth that had said yes where her own had said no. But she was at one with him in everything, even in this. That yes of his she felt as if it were her own (even as she felt too her own no). Therefore her fate was cruel, unusual, immediate, and therefore she saw no escape from it and could see none, for none existed. But one thing she knew. Because of her father's yes, which bound her as much as her own no, she would have to appear before the *kadi* with Mustajbeg's son, for it was inconceivable to think that Avdaga Osmanagić did not keep his word. But she knew too, equally well, that after the ceremony her feet would never take her to Nezuke, for that would mean that she had not kept her own word. That too was inconceivable, for that too was the word of an Osmanagić. There, on that point of no return, between her no and her father's yes, between Velje Lug and Nezuke, somewhere in that most inescapable impasse, she must find a way out. That was all she thought of now. No longer the expanses of the great rich world, not even the whole route from Velje Lug to Nezuke, but only that short and pitiful little scrap of road which led from the courthouse in which the *kadi* would marry her to Mustajbeg's son, as far as the end of the bridge where the stony slope led down to the narrow track which led to Nezuke and on which, she knew for a certainty, she would never set foot. Her thoughts flew incessantly up and down that little scrap of road, from one end to the other, like a shuttle through the weave. They would fly from the courthouse, across the market-place to the end of the bridge, to halt there as before an impassable abyss, and then back across the bridge, across the market-place to the courthouse. Always thus; back and forward, forward and back! There her destiny was woven.

And those thoughts which could neither remain still nor were able to find a way out, more and more often halted at the *kapia,* on that lovely and shining *sofa,* where the townspeople sat in conversation and the young men sang, and beneath which roared the deep swift green waters of the river. Then, horrified at such a way of escape, they would fly once again, as if under a curse, from one end of the journey to the other and, without finding any other solution, would stop there once again on the *kapia.* Every night her thoughts more and more often halted there and remained there longer. The very thought of that day, when in fact and not only in her thoughts she must go along that way and find her way out before she reached the end of the bridge, brought with it all the terror of death or the horror of a life of shame. It seemed to her, helpless and forsaken, that the very terror of that thought must remove or at least postpone that day.

But the days passed, neither fast nor slow, but regular and fateful and with them came at last the day of the wedding.

On that last Thursday in August (that was the fateful day) the Hamzićs came on horseback for the girl. Covered with a heavy new black veil, as if under a suit of armor, Fata was seated on a horse and led into the town. Meanwhile, in the courtyard, horses were loaded with the chests containing her trousseau. The marriage was announced in the courthouse before the *kadi.* So was kept the word by which Avdaga gave his daughter to Mustajbeg's son. Then the little procession set out on the way to Nezuke where the formal wedding ceremonies had been prepared.

They passed through the market-place, a part of that road without escape which Fata had covered so often in her thoughts. It was firm, real and everyday, almost easier to traverse than in her imagination. No stars, no expanse, no father's muffled cough, no desire for time to go more quickly or more slowly. When they reached the bridge, the girl felt once more, as in the summer nights before her window, every part of her body strongly and separately, and especially her breasts in a light constriction as if in a corselet. The party arrived on the *kapia.* As she had done so many times in her thoughts those last nights, the girl leaned over and in a whisper begged the youngest brother who was riding beside her to shorten her stirrups a little, for they were coming to that steep passage from the bridge down to the stony track which led to Nezuke. They stopped, first those two and then, a little farther on, the other wedding guests. There was nothing unusual in this. It was not the first nor would it be the last time that a wedding procession halted on the *kapia.* While the brother dismounted, went around the horse and threw the reins over his arm, the girl urged her horse to the very edge of the bridge, put her right foot on the stone parapet, sprang from the saddle as if she had wings, leaped over the parapet and threw herself into the roaring river below the bridge. The brother rushed after her and threw himself at full length on the parapet, managing to touch with his hand the flying veil but was unable to hold it. The rest of the wedding guests leaped from their horses with the most extraordinary cries and remained along the stone parapet in strange attitudes as if they too had been turned to stone.

That same day rain fell before evening, abundant and exceptionally cold for the time of year. The Drina rose and grew angry. Next day the yellowish flood waters threw Fata's corpse on to a shoal near Kalata. There it was seen by a fisherman who went at once to notify the police chief. A little later the police chief himself arrived with the *muktar,* the fisherman and Salko Corkan. For without Salko nothing of this sort could ever take place.

The corpse was lying in soft wet sand. The waves moved it to and fro and from time to time their cloudy waters washed over it. The new black veil which the waters had not succeeded in pulling off had been turned back and thrown over her head; mingled with her long thick hair it formed a strange black mass beside the white lovely body of the young girl from which the current had torn away the thin wedding garments. Frowning and with set jaws Salko and the fisherman waded out to the shoal, caught hold of the naked girl and, embarrassed and carefully, as if she were still alive, took her to the bank from the wet sand in which she had already begun to sink, and there at once covered her with the wet and mud bespattered veil.

That same day the drowned girl was buried in the nearest Moslem graveyard, on the steep slope below the hill on which Velje Lug was built. And before evening the ne'er-do-wells of the town had collected in the inn around Salko and the fisherman with that unhealthy and prurient curiosity which is especially developed among those whose life is empty, deprived of every beauty and lacking in excitement and events. They toasted them in plum brandy and offered them tobacco in order to hear some detail about the corpse and the burial. But nothing helped. Even Salko said nothing. He smoked continuously and with his one bright eye looked at the smoke which he blew as far away as possible from him with strong puffs. Only those two, Salko and the fisherman, looked at one another from time to time, lifted their little flasks in silence as if pledging something invisible and drained them at a gulp.

Thus it was that that unusual and unheard of event took place on the *kapia*. Velje Lug did not go down to Nezuke and Avdaga's Fata never became the wife of a Hamzić.

Avdaga Osmanagić never again went down into the town. He died that same winter, suffocated by his cough, without speaking a word to anyone of the sorrow that had killed him.

The next spring Mustajbeg Hamzić married his son to another girl, from Brankovići.

For some time the townspeople talked about the incident and then began to forget it. All that remained was a song about a girl whose beauty and wisdom shone above the world as if it were immortal.

9

Some seventy years after the Karageorge insurrection war broke out again in Serbia and the frontier reacted by rebellion. Once more Turkish and Serbian houses flamed on the heights, at Žlijeba, Gostilje, Crniće and Veletovo. For the first time after so many years the heads of decapitated Serbs again appeared on the *kapia*. These were thin-faced short-haired peasant heads with bony faces and long moustaches, as though they were the same as those exposed seventy years before. But all this did not last long. As soon as the war between Serbia and Turkey ended, the people were again left in peace. It was, in truth, an uneasy peace which concealed many fearful and exciting rumors and anxious whisperings. More and more definitely and openly was there talk of the entry of the Austrian army into Bosnia. At the beginning of the summer of 1878 units of the regular Turkish army passed through the town on their way from Sarajevo to Priboj. The idea spread that the Sultan would cede Bosnia without a struggle. Some families made ready to move into the Sanjak, among them some of those who thirty years before, not wishing to live under Serbian rule, had fled from Užice and who were now once again preparing to flee from another and new Christian rule. But the majority stayed, awaiting what was to come in painful uncertainty and outward indifference.

At the beginning of July the *mufti* of Plevlje arrived with a small body of men, filled with a great resolve to organize resistance in Bosnia against the Austrians. A fair-headed serious man of calm appearance but fiery temperament, he sat on the *kapia* where, one lovely summer's day, he summoned the Turkish leaders of the town and began to incite them to fight against the Austrians. He assured them that the greater part of the regular army would remain in Bosnia despite its orders and would join with the people to oppose the new conqueror, and called on the young men to join him and the townspeople to send provisions to Sarajevo. The *mufti* knew that the people of Višegrad had never had the reputation of being enthusiastic fighters and that they preferred to live foolishly rather than to die foolishly, but he was none the less surprised at the lukewarm response that he encountered. Unable to control himself any longer he threatened them with the justice of the people and the anger of God, and then left his assistant Osman Effendi Karamanli to go on convincing the people of Višegrad of the need for their participation in a general insurrection.

During the discussions with the *mufti*, the greatest resistance had been shown by Alihodja Mutevelić. His family was one of the oldest and most respected in the town. They had never been noted for their fortune, but rather for their honesty and openness. They had always been reckoned obstinate men, but not susceptible to bribes, intimidation, flattery or any other consideration of lower type. For more than 200 years the oldest member of their family had been the *mutevelia,* the guardian and administrator of Mehmed Pasha's foundation in the town. He looked after the famous Stone Han near the bridge. We have seen how, after the loss of Hungary, the Stone Han lost the revenues on which it depended for its upkeep and by force of circumstances became a ruin. Of the Vezir's foundation there remained only the bridge, a public benefit which did not require special maintenance and brought in no revenue. So there remained for the Mutevelićs only their family name as a proud memorial of the calling which they had honorably carried out for so many years. That calling had in fact ceased at the time when Dauthodja had succumbed in his struggle to maintain the Stone Han, but the pride had remained and with it the traditional custom that the Mutevelić family was called upon above all others to look after the bridge and that it was in some way responsible for its fate, since the bridge was an integral part of the great religious foundation which the family had administered and which had so pitiably dried up. Also by long established custom one of the Mutevelić family went to school and belonged to the *ulema,* the learned body of the Moslem clergy. Now it was Alihodja. Otherwise the family had greatly diminished both in numbers and property. They now had only a few serfs and a shop, which they had kept for a long time past, in the best position in the market-place, quite close to the bridge. Two elder brothers of Alihodja had died in the wars, one in Russia and the other in Montenegro.

Alihodja himself was still a young man, lively, healthy and smiling. Like a real Mutevelić he held contrary opinions in everything, defending them tenaciously and sticking to them obstinately. Because of his outspoken nature and independence of his thought he was frequently at odds with the local *ulema* and the Moslem notables. He had the title and rank of *hodja* but neither carried out any of the duties of that office nor received any income from that calling. In order to be as independent as possible, he himself looked after the shop which had been left by his father.

Like the majority of the Višegrad Moslems, Alihodja too was opposed to any armed resistance. But in his case there could be no question of cowardice or religious lukewarmness. He loathed the foreign Christian power and all that it would bring with it as much as the *mufti* or any of the insurgents. But seeing that the Sultan had in fact left Bosnia at the mercy of the Schwabes (for so they called the Austrians) and knowing his fellow-citizens, he was opposed to any disorganized popular resistance which could only end in disaster and make their misfortune the greater. When once this idea was firmly implanted in his mind, he preached it openly and defended it with spirit. On this occasion too he kept on asking awkward questions and made sarcastic comments which greatly disconcerted the *mufti.* Thus unintentionally he sustained among the people of Višegrad, who in any case would not have been so swift to battle or much inclined to make sacrifices, a spirit of open resistance against the *mufti's* warlike intentions.

When Osman Effendi Karamanli remained in the town to continue his discussions with the people, he found himself faced with Alihodja. Those few begs and agas who swallowed their words and measured their phrases and who in fact were in complete agreement with Alihodja left it to the sincere and ebullient *hodja* to come into the open and enter into conflict with Karamanli.

Thus early one evening the leading Višegrad Turks were sitting on the *kapia,* cross-legged in a circle. In the center was Osman Effendi, a tall thin pale man. Every muscle of his face was unnaturally set, his eyes were feverish and his forehead and cheeks marked all over with scars like an epileptic. Before him stood the *hodja,* reddish in face and small in stature, yet somehow impressive, asking more and more questions in his thin reedy voice. What forces had they? Where were they to go? With what means? How? What for? What will happen in case of failure? The cold and almost mischievous pedantry with which the *hodja* treated the matter only served to conceal his own anxiety and bitterness at the Christian superiority and the evident weakness and disorder of the Turks. But the hot-headed and somber Osman Effendi was not the man to notice or understand such things. Of violent and uncontrolled temper, a fanatic with overstrung nerves, he quickly lost patience and control and attacked the *hodja* at every sign of doubt or wavering as if he were a Schwabe. This *hodja* irritated him and he replied to him only with generalities and big words. The main thing was not to allow the foe to enter the country without resistance, and whoever asked too many questions only hindered the good work and aided the enemy. In the end, completely beside himself, he replied with scarcely concealed disdain to every question of the *hodja:* "The time has come to die," "We will lay down our lives," "We shall all die to the last man."

"But," broke in the *hodja,* "I understood that you wanted to drive the Schwabes out of Bosnia and that was the reason why you were collecting us. If it is only a question of dying, then we too know how to die, Effendi, even without your assistance. There is nothing easier than to die."

"Ama, I can see that you will not be one of those who die," broke in Karamanli, harshly.

"I can see that you will be one," answered the *hodja* sarcastically, "only I do not see why you ask for our company in this senseless attempt."

The conversation then degenerated into an open quarrel in which Osman Effendi referred to Alihodja as a renegade, one of those traitors whose heads, like the Serbs', should be exposed on the *kapia,* while the *hodja* imperturbably went on splitting hairs and demanding proofs and reasons, as if he had not even heard those threats and insults.

Indeed it would have been hard to find two worse negotiators or more unsuited contestants. Nothing more could have been expected of them than increasing general anxiety and the creation of one quarrel the more. That was to be regretted, but there was nothing to be done about it, for such moments of social upset and great inevitable change usually throw up just such men, unbalanced and incomplete, to turn things inside out or lead them astray. That is one of the signs of times of disorder.

None the less this barren quarrel was a boon to the begs and agas for the question of their participation in the insurrection remained unanswered and they themselves were not compelled to take sides at once. Quivering with rage and shouting insults at the top of his voice, Osman Effendi left the next day with a few of his men to follow the *mufti* to Sarajevo.

The news which arrived in the course of the month only served to confirm the agas and begs in their opportunist view that it would be better to preserve their town and their homes. By mid-August the Austrians entered Sarajevo. A little later there was a disastrous clash on Glasinac, which was also the end of all resistance. Remnants of the routed Turkish bands began to descend the steep road from Lijeska through Okolište. Among them were some regular soldiers who despite the Sultan's order had joined the resistance movement of the local insurgents on their own account. The soldiers only asked for bread and water and the way on to Uvac, but the insurgents were bitter and angry men whom the rout had not broken. Blackened, dusty and in rags, they replied curtly to the questions of the peaceable Višegrad Turks and made ready to dig trenches and defend the bridge.

Alihodja was again to the fore; he pointed out indefatigably and regardless of consequences that the town could not be defended and that resistance was senseless since the "Schwabes had already swept through Bosnia from end to end." The insurgents knew that well enough themselves but did not want to acknowledge it, for these well-fed and well-clothed men who had saved their houses and properties by keeping wisely and cravenly far from the revolt irritated and provoked them. With them came that same Osman Effendi Karamanli, as if out of his mind, paler and thinner than ever, even more frenzied and warlike. He was one of those men for whom failure has no meaning. He spoke of resistance in any place and at any price and continually of the need to die. Before his furious ardor everyone retreated or withdrew, save only Alihodja. He proved to the aggressive Osman Effendi, without the slightest malice, coldly and brutally, that what had happened to the revolt was exactly what he had foreseen a month ago on this very *kapia*. He recommended him to leave with his men as quickly as possible for Plevlje and not to make bad worse. The *hodja* was now less aggressive, even to a certain extent compassionate towards this Karamanli as towards a sick man. For within himself, beneath all his outward obstinacy the *hodja* was greatly shaken by the approaching misfortune. He was unhappy and embittered as only a true-believing Moslem could be who sees that a foreign force is approaching inexorably, before whose onslaught the ancient order of Islam could not long survive. That hidden rancor could be felt in his own words even against his will.

To all Karamanli's insults he replied almost sadly:

"Do you think, Effendi, that it is easy for me to be alive to await the coming of the Schwabes to our land? As if we did not know what is in store for us in the times to come? We know where it hurts us and what we are losing; we know it only too well. If you came here to tell us this, you should not have returned here. Indeed there was no need for you to come from Plevlje at all. For, as I see, you do not understand matters. Had you done so, you would not have done what you have done or said what you have said. This is a worse torment, Effendi, than you can think; nor do I know a remedy for it, but I know that what you suggest is not a remedy."

But Osman Effendi was deaf to everything that did not accord with his deep and sincere passion for resistance and he hated this *hodja* as much as the Schwabes against whom he had revolted. So is it always when an overwhelming enemy is near and a great defeat certain. In every society appear fratricidal hatreds and mutual quarrels. Not finding anything fresh to say, he went on calling Alihodja a traitor, ironically recommending him to get baptized before the Schwabes came.

"My ancestors were not baptized, nor will I be. I, Effendi, have no wish either to be baptized with a Schwabe or to go to war with an idiot," the *hodja* replied calmly.

All the leading Višegrad Turks were of the same opinion as Alihodja, but all did not think it discreet to say so, especially so harshly and uncompromisingly. They were afraid of the Austrians who were coming but they were also afraid of Karamanli who with his men had taken over control of the town. Therefore they shut themselves up in their houses or withdrew to their properties outside the town, and when they could not avoid meeting Karamanli and his men they looked away or replied with equivocal phrases looking for the most convenient pretext and the safest way of extricating themselves.

On the level space in front of the ruins of the caravanserai Karamanli held open court from morning to evening. A motley crowd was always about him, his own men, chance passers-by, those who came to beg something from the new master of the town and travelers whom the insurgents brought more or less by force in front of their leader. And Karamanli talked incessantly. Even when he was talking to one man he shouted as if he were addressing hundreds. Still paler, he rolled his eyes, in which the whites had noticeably yellowed, and white foam gathered at the corners of his lips. One of the townsmen had told him of the Moslem tradition about Sheik Turhania who had died there long ago defending the passage of the Drina against an infidel army and now rested in his grave on the farther bank just above the bridge, but who without doubt would rise again the moment the first infidel soldier stepped on to the bridge. He seized on this legend, feverishly and passionately, expounding it to the people as a real and unexpected aid.

"Brothers, this bridge was a Vezir's bequest. It is written that an infidel force shall never cross it. It is not we alone who are to defend it but also this 'holy one' whom rifles cannot hit nor swords cut. Should the foe come, he will rise from his grave and will stand in the center of the bridge with outstretched arms; and when the Schwabes see him their knees will tremble, and their hearts fail so that they will not even be able to run away. Turkish brothers, do not disperse but all follow me to the bridge."

So Karamanli shouted to the crowd. Standing stiffly in his black shabby cloak, stretching out his arms and showing how the "holy one" would stand, he looked exactly like a tall thin black cross with a turban on top.

This the Višegrad Turks knew even better than Karamanli, for every one of them had heard and told this legend countless times in his childhood, but they none the less showed not the least desire to mingle fact with legend or reckon on the help of the dead since nothing could be expected of the living. Alihodja, who had not moved far from his shop, but to whom the people told all that was said or done before the Stone Han, only waved his arms sorrowfully and compassionately.

"I knew that that idiot would not leave either the living or the dead in peace. *Allah selamet olsun!* May God help us!"

But Karamanli, helpless before the real enemy, turned all his fury against Alihodja. He threatened, he shouted and swore that before he was forced to leave the town he would nail the obstinate *hodja* to the *kapia* like a badger to await the Schwabes in that way, since he did not want to fight or to allow others to do so.

All this bickering was cut short by the appearance of the Austrians on the Lijeska slopes. Then it was seen that the town really could not be defended. Karamanli was the last to leave the town, abandoning on the raised level space before the caravanserai both the iron cannons that he had dragged there. But before he left he carried out his threat. He ordered his servant, a smith by profession, a man of giant size but with the brain of a bird, to bind Alihodja and to nail him by the right ear to that oak beam wedged between two stone steps on the *kapia,* which was all that remained of the former blockhouse.

In the general crush and confusion which reigned in the market-place and around the bridge, all heard that order given in a loud voice but no one even dreamed that it would be carried out in the form in which it was given. In such circumstances all sorts of things, brave words and loud curses, can be heard. So too it was in this case. At first sight the thing seemed inconceivable. It was to be considered a threat or an insult or something of the sort. Nor did Alihodja himself take the matter very seriously. Even the smith himself who had been ordered to carry it out and who was busy spiking the guns hesitated and seemed to think it over. But the thought that the *hodja* must be nailed to the *kapia* was in the air and the suspicious and embittered townsmen turned over in their minds the prospects and probabilities of such a crime being carried out or not carried out. Would it be, or would it not be? At first the majority of them thought the affair to be, as indeed it was, senseless, ugly and impossible. But in moments of general excitement, something has to be done, something big and unusual, and that was the only thing to be done. Would it be—or would it not be? The possibility seemed stronger and became every moment and with every movement more probable and more natural. Why not? Two men already held the *hodja* who did not defend himself overmuch. They bound his hands behind his back. But all this was still far from so mad and terrible a reality. But it was coming nearer and nearer. The smith, as if suddenly ashamed of his weakness and indecision, produced from somewhere or other the hammer with which a short time before he had been spiking the guns. The thought that the Schwabes were so to speak already here, half an hour's march from the town, gave him the resolution to bring the matter to a head. And with this same painful thought the *hodja* obstinately maintained his indifference to everything, even towards that mad, undeserved and shameful punishment to which they had condemned him.

So in a few moments there took place what in any one of those moments would have seemed impossible and incredible. There was no one who would have considered that this deed was good or possible, yet everyone to some extent played his part in the fact that the *hodja* found himself on the bridge nailed by his right ear to a wooden beam which was on the *kapia;* and when everyone fled in all directions before the Schwabes who were coming down the slopes into the town, the *hodja* remained in this strange but comic position, forced to kneel motionless since every movement, even the slightest, was exceedingly painful and threatened to tear off his ear, which seemed to him as heavy and as large as a mountain. He cried out, but there was no one to hear him or release him from his painful situation for everything living had hidden in the houses or scattered into the villages for fear, partly of the Schwabes who were coming and partly of the insurgents who were leaving. The town seemed dead and the bridge as empty as if death had swept it clean. There was neither living nor dead to defend it, only on the *kapia* the motionless Alihodja crouched down with his head stuck to the beam, groaning with pain but even in this position thinking up fresh proofs against Karamanli.

The Austrians approached slowly; from the farther bank their patrols had seen the two cannons in front of the caravanserai and they at once halted to await the arrival of their mountain guns. About midday they fired a few shells from the shelter of a little wood at the deserted caravanserai. They damaged the already ruined *han* and destroyed those exceptionally fine window grilles, each cut from a single piece of soft stone. Only after they had got the range and overturned the two Turkish cannons and seen that they were abandoned and that no one replied did the Schwabes cease their fire and begin to approach the bridge and the town with every precaution. Some Magyar *honveds* approached the *kapia* slowly with their rifles at the ready. They halted in uncertainty before the huddled *hodja* who in fear of the shells, which had whistled and grumbled above his head, had for a moment forgotten the pain from his nailed ear. When he saw the hated soldiers with their rifles trained on him, he began to utter piteous and prolonged sobs, since that was a language that everyone understood. This prevented him from being shot. Some of them continued their slow advance step by step across the bridge while others remained by him looking at him more closely and unable to understand his position. Only when a hospital orderly arrived did they find a pair of pliers, carefully extracted the nail, one of those used for shoeing horses, and released Alihodja. So stiff and exhausted was he that he collapsed on the stone step, groaning and sobbing. The orderly dressed his ear with some sort of liquid which stung. Through his tears the *hodja* as if in a strange dream looked at the broad white band on the soldier's left arm and on it a large regular cross in red material. Only in fever could such repulsive and terrible sights be seen. This cross swam and danced before his eyes and filled his whole horizon like a nightmare. Then the soldier bound up his wound and fixed his turban over the bandage. His head thus bandaged, and as if broken in his loins, the *hodja* dragged himself to his feet and remained so for some moments leaning on the stone parapet of the bridge. With difficulty he collected himself and regained his calm.

Opposite him, on the far side of the *kapia,* beneath the Turkish inscription in the stone, a soldier had affixed a large white paper. Though his head was throbbing with pain the *hodja* could not restrain his curiosity and looked at that white placard. It was a proclamation by General Filipović, in Serbian and Turkish, addressed to the population of Bosnia and Herzegovina on the occasion of the entry of the Austrian army into Bosnia. Screwing up his right eye, Alihodja spelled out the Turkish text, but only those sentences printed in large letters:

"People of Bosnia and Herzegovina!

"The Army of the Emperor of Austria and King of Hungary has crossed the frontier of your country. It does not come as an enemy to take the land by force. It comes as a friend to put an end to the disorders which for years past have disturbed not only Bosnia and Herzegovina but also the frontier districts of Austria-Hungary.

* * *

"The King-Emperor could no longer see how violence and disorder ruled in the neighborhood of his dominions and how misery and misfortune knocked at the frontiers of his lands.

"He has drawn the attention of the European States to your position and at a Council of the Nations it has been unanimously decided that Austria-Hungary shall restore to you the peace and prosperity that you have so long lost.

"His Majesty the Sultan who has your good at heart has felt it necessary to confide you to the protection of his powerful friend the King-Emperor.

* * *

"The King-Emperor decrees that all sons of this land shall enjoy the same rights before the law and that the lives, faith and property of all shall be protected.

* * *

"People of Bosnia and Herzegovina! Put yourselves with confidence under the protection of the glorious standards of Austria-Hungary. Welcome our soldiers as friends, submit yourselves to the authorities and return to your occupations. The fruits of your toil will be protected."

The *hodja* read haltingly, sentence by sentence. He did not understand every word, yet every word caused him pain, a special sort of pain completely distinct from those pains which he felt in his wounded ear, in his head and in his loins. Only now, from these words, these "imperial words," was it at once clear to him that everything was ended for them, all that was his and theirs, ended in some strange fashion once and for all; eyes go on seeing, lips speaking, man goes on living but life, real life, exists no more. A foreign tsar had put his hand on them and a foreign faith ruled. That emerged clearly from those big words and obscure commands, and still more clearly from that leaden pain in his breast which was fiercer and harder to bear than any human pain that could be imagined. It was not thousands of fools like that Osman Karamanli who could do anything or change anything (thus the *hodja* continued to argue within himself). "We shall all die," "We must die." What was the use of all that hullabaloo when, here and now, there had come for a man a time of disaster in which he could neither live nor die, but rotted like a stake in the earth and belonged to whomever you wished but not himself. That was the great misery which the Karamanlis of all sorts did not see and could not understand and which by their lack of understanding they made even heavier and more shameful.

Deep in his thoughts Alihodja slowly left the bridge. He did not even notice that the Austrian red-cross man was accompanying him. His ear did not pain him as much as that leaden and bitter pain which had risen in his breast after reading "the imperial words." He walked slowly and it seemed to him that never again would he cross to the farther bank, that this bridge which was the pride of the town and ever since its creation had been so closely linked with it, on which he had grown up and beside which he had spent his life, was now suddenly broken in the middle, right there at the *kapia;* that this white paper of the proclamation had cut it in half like a silent explosion and that there was now a great abyss; that individual piers still stood to right and to left of this break but that there was no way across, for the bridge no longer linked the two banks and every man had to remain on that side where he happened to be at this moment.

Alihodja walked slowly, immersed in these feverish visions. He seemed like a seriously wounded man and his eyes continually filled with tears. He walked hesitantly as if he were a beggar who, ill, was crossing the bridge for the first time and entering a strange unknown town. Voices aroused him. Beside him walked some soldiers. Among them he saw that fat, good-natured, mocking face of the man with a red cross on his arm who had taken out the nail. Still smiling, the soldier pointed to his bandage and asked him something in an incomprehensible language. The *hodja* thought that he was offering to help him and at once stiffened and said sullenly:

"I can myself. . . . I need no one's help."

And with a livelier and more determined step he made his way home.

10

The formal and official entry of the Austrian troops took place the following day.

No one could remember such a silence as then fell on the town. The shops did not even open. The doors and windows of the houses remained shuttered though it was a warm sunny day towards the end of August. The streets were empty, the courtyards and gardens as if dead. In the Turkish houses depression and confusion reigned, in the Christian houses caution and distrust. But everywhere and for everyone there was fear. The entering Austrians feared an ambush. The Turks feared the Austrians. The Serbs feared both Austrians and Turks. The Jews feared everything and everyone since, especially in times of war, everyone was stronger than they. The rumbling of the previous day's guns was in everyone's ears. But even if men were now only listening to their own fear, no one living that day would have dared to poke his nose out of doors. But man has other masters. The Austrian detachment which had entered the town the day before had routed out the police chief and gendarmes. The officer in command of the detachment had returned his sword to the police chief and ordered him to continue his duties and maintain order in the town. He told him that at one hour before noon next day the commandant, a colonel, would arrive and that the leading men of the town, that was to say the representatives of the three faiths, were to be there to meet him when he entered the town. Gray and resigned, the police chief at once summoned Mula Ibrahim, Husseinaga the schoolmaster, Pop Nikola, and the rabbi David Levi and informed them that as "recognized notables" they must await the Austrian commandant next day at noon on the *kapia,* must welcome him in the name of the citizens and accompany him to the market-place.

Long before the appointed time the four "recognized notables" met on the deserted square and walked with slow steps to the *kapia.* Already the assistant chief of police, Salko Hedo, with the aid of a gendarme, had spread out a long Turkish carpet in bright colors to cover the steps and the middle of the stone seat on which the Austrian commandant was to sit. They stood there together for some time, solemn and silent, then seeing that there was no trace of the commandant along the white road from Okolište, they looked at one another and as if by common consent sat down on the uncovered part of the stone bench. Pop Nikola drew out a huge leather tobacco pouch and offered it to the others.

So they sat on the *kapia* as they had once done when they were young and carefree and like the rest of the young people wasted their time there. Only now they were all advanced in years. Pop Nikola and Mula Ibrahim were old, and the schoolmaster and the rabbi in the prime of life. They were all in their best clothes, filled with anxiety both for themselves and for their flocks. They looked at one another closely and long in the fierce summer sun, and each seemed to the others grown old for his years and worn out. Each of them remembered the others as they had been in youth or childhood, when they had grown up on this bridge, each in his own generation, green wood of which no one could tell what would be.

They smoked and talked of one thing while turning another over in their minds, glancing every moment towards Okolište whence the commandant upon whom everything depended was to come and who could bring them, their people and the whole town, either good or evil, either peace or fresh dangers.

Pop Nikola was undoubtedly the most calm and collected of the four, or at least seemed so. He had passed his seventieth year but was still fresh and strong. Son of the celebrated Pop Mihailo whom the Turks had beheaded on this very spot, Pop Nikola had passed a stormy youth. He had several times fled into Serbia to take refuge there from the hatred and revenge of certain Turks. His indomitable nature and his conduct had often given occasion both for hatred and revenge. But when the troublous years had passed, Pop Mihailo's son had settled down in his old parish, married, and calmed down. Those times were long ago and now forgotten. ("My character has changed long ago and our Turks have become peaceable," Pop Nikola would say in jest.) For fifty years now Pop Nikola had administered his widespread, scattered and difficult frontier parish calmly and wisely, without other major upheavals and misfortunes than those which life brings normally in its train, with the devotion of a slave and the dignity of a prince, always just and equitable with Turks, people and leaders.

Neither before him nor after him in any class of men or in any faith was there a man who enjoyed such general respect and such a reputation among all the townspeople without distinction of faith, sex or years, as this priest whom everyone called "granddad." He represented for the whole town the Serbian church and all that the people called or regarded as Christianity. The people looked on him as the perfect type of priest and leader so far as this town in these conditions could imagine one.

He was a man of great stature and exceptional physical strength, not over literate but of great heart, sound common sense and a serene and open spirit. His smile disarmed, calmed and encouraged. It was the indescribable smile of a man who lives at peace with himself and with everything around him; his big green eyes contracted into narrow slits whence flashed golden sparks. And so he remained in old age. In his long overcoat of fox-fur, with his great red beard just beginning to turn gray with the years and which covered his whole chest, with his enormous hood beneath which his flowing hair was plaited into a pigtail, he walked through the market-place as if he had indeed been the priest of this town beside the bridge and all this mountainous district, not for fifty years only and not for his church only, but from time immemorial, from those times when the people were not divided into their present faiths and churches. From the shops on both sides of the market-place the merchants greeted him, whatever their faith. Women stood to one side and waited with bowed head for "granddad" to pass. The children (even the Jewish ones) left off their play and stopped shouting and the oldest among them, solemnly and timidly, would come up to the enormous hand of "granddad" to feel it for a moment on their shaven heads and faces heated by play, and hear his merry and powerful voice fall upon them like a good and pleasant dew:

"God grant you life! God grant you life, my son!"

This token of respect towards "granddad" had become a part of the ancient and universally recognized ceremonial in which generations of the townsfolk had grown up.

But even in Pop Nikola's life there was one shadow. His marriage had remained childless. That was, without doubt, a heavy blow but no one could recall having heard a bitter word or seen a regretful glance either from him or from his wife. In their house they always maintained at their own expense at least two children belonging to some of their relatives in the villages. These they would look after until they married, and then find others.

Next to Pop Nikola sat Mula Ibrahim, a tall, thin, dried-up man with a sparse beard and pendulant moustaches. He was not much younger than Pop Nikola, had a large family and a fine property left him by his father, but he was so slipshod, thin and timid, that he seemed with his blue childlike eyes more like some hermit or some poor and pious pilgrim than the *hodja* of Višegrad, descendant of many *hodjas*. Mula Ibrahim had one affliction: he stuttered in his speech, long and painfully ("A man must have nothing to do before he can talk with Mula Ibrahim," the townsmen used to say in jest). But Mula Ibrahim was known far around for his goodness and generosity. Mildness and serenity breathed out of him and at the first meeting men forgot his outward appearance and his stutter. He attracted all who were overburdened by illness, poverty or any other misfortune. From the most distant villages men came to ask advice of Mula Ibrahim. Before his house there was always a crowd to see him, and men and women often stopped him in the street to seek his advice. He never refused anyone and never handed out expensive charms or amulets as other *hodjas* did. He would sit down at once in the first patch of shade or on the first stone, a little to the side; the man would then tell all his troubles in a whisper. Mula Ibrahim would listen attentively and sympathetically, then say a few good words to him, always finding the best possible solution for his troubles, or would thrust his thin hand into the deep pocket of his cloak, taking care not to be overseen by anyone, and slip a few coins into his hand. Nothing was difficult or repugnant or impossible to him if it were a question of helping some Moslem. For that he could always find time and money. Nor did his stutter hinder him in this, for when whispering with his co-religionist in misfortune he forgot to stutter. Everyone went away from him if not completely consoled, then at least momentarily relieved, for it could be seen that he felt their misfortunes as if they were his own. Continually surrounded with every sort of trouble and need and never thinking of himself, he none the less, or so it seemed, passed his whole life healthy, happy and rich.

The Višegrad schoolmaster, Hussein Effendi, was a smallish plump man, well dressed and well cared for. He had a short black beard carefully trimmed in a regular oval about his pink and white face with round black eyes. He had been well educated and knew a good deal, but pretended to know much more and deceived himself that he knew even more. He loved to talk and to have an audience. He was convinced that he spoke well and that led him to speak a lot. He expressed himself carefully and affectedly with studied gestures, holding his arms up a little, both at the same height, with white soft hands with pinkish nails, shadowed by short black hairs. When speaking he behaved as if he were in front of a mirror. He had the largest library in the town, a bound chest full of books kept carefully locked, which had been bequeathed him by his teacher, the celebrated Arap-hodja, and which he not only conscientiously preserved from dust and moth but even on rare occasions read. But the mere knowledge that he had so great a number of such valuable books gave him repute among men who did not know what a book was, and raised his value in his own eyes. It was known that he was writing a chronicle of the most important events in the history of the town. Among the citizens this gave him the fame of a learned and exceptional man, for it was considered that by this he held in some way the fate of the town and of every individual in it in his hands. In actual fact that chronicle was neither extensive nor dangerous. In the last five or six years, since the schoolmaster had first begun this work, only four pages of a small exercise book had been filled. For the greater number of the town's events were not considered by the schoolmaster as of sufficient importance to warrant entry into his chronicle and for that reason it remained as unfruitful, dry and empty as a proud old maid.

The fourth of the "notables" was David Levi, the Višegrad rabbi, grandson of that famous old rabbi Hadji Liacho who had left him as inheritance his name, position and property but nothing of his spirit and his serenity.

He was pale and puny, with dark velvety eyes and melancholy expression. He was inconceivably timid and silent. He had only recently become rabbi and had married not long before. In order to seem bigger and more important he wore a wide rich suit of heavy cloth and his face was overgrown with beard and whiskers, but beneath all this one could discern a weak sickly body and the childish oval of his face peered out fearfully from the black sparse beard. He suffered terribly whenever he had to appear in public and take his part in discussions and decisions, always feeling himself to be weak and undeveloped.

Now all four of them sat in the sun and sweated under their formal clothes, more moved and anxious than they wished to show.

"Let's light another one. We've time, by the soul of my grandmother! He's no bird to fly down to the bridge," said Pop Nikola, like a man who has long learned how to conceal with a jest his own and others' thoughts and fears.

All looked at the Okolište road and then went on smoking.

The conversation flowed slowly and carefully, forever coming back to the imminent welcome to the commandant. All were agreed that it was Pop Nikola who should greet him and bid him welcome. With half-closed eyes and brows furrowed so that his eyes became those two golden-studded slits that formed his smile, Pop Nikola looked at the three others long, silently and intently.

The rabbi was quivering with fright. He had hardly strength to puff the smoke away from him but let it linger in his moustaches and beard. The schoolmaster was no less scared. All his eloquence and his dignity as a man of learning had vanished suddenly the day before. He was very far from realizing how disconsolate he looked and how greatly he was scared, for the high opinion which he had of himself did not allow him to believe anything of the sort. He tried to deliver one of his literary addresses with his studied gestures that explained everything, but his fine hands only fell into his lap and his words became mixed up and halting. Even he himself wondered where his customary dignity had vanished, and vainly tormented himself trying to recover it, as something to which he had long been accustomed and which now, when he needed it most, had somehow deserted him.

Mula Ibrahim was somewhat paler than usual but otherwise calm and collected. He and Pop Nikola looked at one another from time to time as if they understood one another by their eyes alone. They had been close acquaintances since youth and good friends, insofar as one could speak of friendship between a Turk and a Serb in times as they then were. When Pop Nikola in his youthful years had had his "troubles" with the Višegrad Turks and had had to fly for refuge, Mula Ibrahim, whose father had been very influential in the town, had been of some service to him. Later, when more peaceful times had come and relations between the two faiths had become more bearable and the two of them were already grown men, they had made friends and called one another "neighbor" in jest, for their houses were at opposite ends of the town. On occasions of drought, flood, epidemic or other misfortune they found themselves working together, each among men of their own faith. Otherwise, whenever they met at Mejdan or Okolište, they greeted one another and asked after one another's health, as priest and *hodja* never did elsewhere. Then Pop Nikola would often point with his pipestem at the town beside the river and say half in jest:

"All that breathes or creeps or speaks with human voice down there is either your or my responsibility."

"It is so, neighbor," Mula Ibrahim would stutter in reply, "indeed they are."

(And so the townsmen who could always find time to mock at everyone and everything would say of men who lived in friendship: "They are as close as the priest and the *hodja*"; and this saying became a proverb with them.)

These two now understood one another perfectly though they did not exchange a word. Pop Nikola knew how hard it was for Mula Ibrahim and Mula Ibrahim knew that it was not easy for the priest. They looked at one another as they had done so many times before in their lives and on so many different occasions, as two men who had on their souls that double burden of the town, the one for those who crossed themselves, the other for those who bowed down in the mosque.

At that moment the sound of trotting was heard and a Turkish gendarme hurried up on a scraggy pony. Scared and out of breath, he shouted at them from a distance like a town-crier.

"Here he is; the one on the white horse!"

The police chief too arrived, always calm, always amiable, always silent.

Dust rose from along the Okolište road.

These men, born and brought up in this remote district of Turkey, the rotten-ripe Turkey of the nineteenth century, had naturally never had the chance of seeing the real, powerful and well-organized army of a great power. All that they had been able to see till then had been the incomplete, badly fed, badly clothed and badly paid units of the Sultan's *askers* or, which was even worse, the Bosnian irregulars, the *bashibazouks,* recruited by force, undisciplined and fanatic. Now for the first time there appeared before them the real "power and force" of an Empire, victorious, glistening and sure of itself. Such an army dazzled them and checked the words in their throats. At the first sight of the saddlery and the tunic-buttons another world could be sensed behind these hussars and *jaegers* in parade kit. Their astonishment was great and the impression profound.

First rode two trumpeters on two fat bays, then a detachment of hussars on black horses. The horses were well groomed and moved like girls with short tidy steps. The hussars, all young and fresh, with waxed moustaches, in red shakos and yellow frogged tunics, seemed rested and vigorous as if they had just come out of barracks. Behind them rode a group of six officers led by a colonel. All eyes were fixed on him. His horse was larger than the others, a flea-bitten gray with a very long and curved neck. A little behind the officers came the infantry detachment, *jaegers,* in green uniforms, with a panache of feathers on their leather caps and white bands across their chests. They shut out everything save themselves and seemed like a moving forest.

The trumpeters and hussars rode past the priest and the police chief, halted on the market-place, and drew up along the sides.

The men on the *kapia,* pale and shaken, stood in the center of the bridge facing the officers. One of the younger officers spurred his horse up to the colonel and said something to him. All slowed down. A few paces in front of the "notables" the colonel suddenly halted and dismounted, as did the officers behind him as if by order. The soldiers whose duty it was to hold the horses hurried up and led them a few paces back.

As soon as his foot touched the ground, the colonel seemed another man. He was a small, undistinguished, overtired, unpleasant and aggressive man, behaving as if he alone had fought for all of them. Only now could it be seen that he was simply dressed, dishevelled and ungroomed, in contrast to his pale-faced smartly-uniformed officers. He was the image of a man who drives himself mercilessly, who continually overtaxes himself. His face was flushed, his beard untrimmed, his eyes troubled and anxious, his tall helmet a little on one side and his crumpled uniform seemingly too big for his body. He was wearing cavalry boots of soft unpolished leather. Walking with legs apart like a horseman he came closer, swinging his riding-crop. One of the officers spoke to him, pointing out the men ranged before him. The colonel looked at them shortly and sharply, the angry glance of a man continually occupied with difficult duties and great dangers. It was at once evident that he did not know how to look in any other way.

At that moment Pop Nikola began to speak in a calm deep voice. The colonel looked up and fixed his gaze on the face of the big man in the black cloak. That broad serene mask of a biblical patriarch held his attention for a moment. It may be that he did not understand, or that he pretended not to listen to, what the old man was saying, but that face could not go unnoticed. Pop Nikola spoke fluently and naturally, addressing himself more to the young officer who was to translate his words than to the colonel himself. In the name of all the faiths here present, he assured the colonel that they, and their people, were willing to submit themselves to the coming authorities and would do all that was in their power to maintain peace and order as the new authorities demanded. They asked the army to protect them and their families and make a peaceful life and honest toil possible for them.

Pop Nikola spoke shortly and ended abruptly. The nervous colonel did not have any excuse to lose patience. But all the same he did not wait for the end of the young officer's translation. Brandishing his riding-crop, he interrupted him in a harsh and uneven voice:

"Good, good! All those who behave themselves will be protected. Peace and order must be maintained everywhere. It must be, whether they like it or not."

Then, shaking his head, he moved onward without a glance or a greeting. The "notables" moved aside. The colonel passed them, followed by the officers and the orderlies with the horses. None of them paid the least attention to the "notables" who remained alone on the *kapia.*

All of them were disillusioned. For the day before, and all through the previous night, in which not one of them had slept much, each had asked himself a hundred times what that moment would be like when they had to welcome the commandant of the Imperial Army on the *kapia.* They had imagined him in every sort of way, each according to his nature and intelligence, and had been ready for the worst. Some of them had already seen themselves carried away immediately to exile in faraway Austria, never again to see their homes or their town. Others remembered the stories about Hairuddin who at one time used to cut off heads on this very *kapia.* They had imagined in every possible way, save that in which it had actually happened, the meeting with that small but curt and bad-tempered officer to whom war was life, who did not think of himself or pay any heed to others, but saw all men and all lands only as a subject or an occasion for war and conflict, and who behaved as if he were waging war on his own account and in his own name.

So they stood, looking at one another in uncertainty. Each of their looks seemed to say dumbly: "We have got out of this alive. Have we really gone through the worst? What is still in store for us and what must be done?"

The police chief and Pop Nikola were the first to come to themselves. They came to the conclusion that the "notables" had done their duty and that nothing more was left for them to do but to go home and tell the people not to be frightened and run away, but to take good care what they did. The others, without blood in their faces or thoughts in their heads, accepted this conclusion as they would have accepted any other, since they themselves were in no state to come to any conclusion.

The police chief, whom nothing could ruffle, went about his duties. The gendarme rolled up the long multicolored carpet which had not been fated to receive the visit of the commandant, with Salko Hedo standing beside him as cold and unfeeling as Fate. Meanwhile the "notables" dispersed each in his own way and each in his own direction. The rabbi hurried off with tiny steps in order to get home as soon as possible and feel again the warmth and protection of the family circle in which his mother and his wife lived. The schoolmaster left more slowly, deep in thought. Now that everything had passed so unexpectedly well and easily, though harshly and unpleasantly enough, it seemed to him quite clear that there had never been any real reason for panic and it seemed to him that he had never in fact been afraid of anyone. He thought only what importance this event should have in his chronicle and how much space should be devoted to it. A score of lines should be enough. Perhaps even fifteen, or maybe less. The nearer he got to his house the more he reduced the number. With every line spared it seemed to him that he saw all around him diminished in importance while he, the schoolmaster, became greater and more important in his own eyes.

Mula Ibrahim and Pop Nikola walked together as far as the slope leading to Mejdan. They both remained silent, astonished and discouraged at the appearance and bearing of the Imperial colonel. Both were hastening to get home as soon as possible and foregather with their families. At the point where their paths diverged, they stood and looked at one another for a moment in silence. Mula Ibrahim rolled his eyes and moved his lips as if continually chewing over some word that he was unable to utter. Pop Nikola, who had once more recovered his smile of golden sparks which encouraged both himself and the *hodja,* uttered his own and the *hodja's* thought:

"A bloody business, this army, Mula Ibrahim!"

"You are right, a b-b-b-bloody business," stuttered Mula Ibrahim raising his arms and saying farewell with a movement of his head.

Pop Nikola went back to his house by the church, slowly and heavily. His wife who was waiting for him asked no questions. She at once took off his boots, took his cloak and removed the hood from the thick sweaty mass of red and gray hair. He sat down on a low divan. On its wooden arm a glass of water and a lump of sugar were ready waiting. After refreshing himself and lighting a cigar he closed his eyes wearily. But in his inmost thoughts still flashed the image of that colonel, like a flash of lightning that dazzles a man and fills his whole field of vision so that nothing else may be seen and yet it is impossible to look away from it. The priest puffed his smoke far away from him with a sigh and then spoke quietly as if to himself:

"A strange sort of bastard, on my grandmother's soul!"

From the town could be heard a drum and then a bugle of the *jaeger* detachment, gay and penetrating, a new and unusual melody.

11

Thus the great change in the life of the town beside the bridge took place without sacrifices other than the martyrdom of Alihodja. After a few days life went on again as before and seemed essentially unchanged. Even Alihodja himself plucked up his courage and opened his shop near the bridge like all the other traders, save that now he wore his turban slightly tipped to the right so that the scar on his wounded ear could not be seen. That "leaden weight" which he had felt in his chest after seeing the red cross on the arm of the Austrian orderly and reading the "Imperial words" had not actually vanished, but it had become quite small like the bead of a rosary, so that it was possible to live with it. Nor was he the only one who felt such a weight.

So began the new era under the occupation which the people, unable to prevent, considered in their hearts to be temporary. What did not pass across the bridge in those first few years after the occupation! Yellow military vehicles rumbled across it in long convoys bringing food, clothing and furniture, instruments and fittings hitherto unheard of.

At first only the army was to be seen. Soldiers sprang up, like water from the earth, behind every corner and every bush. The market-place was full of them, but they were also in every part of the town. Every minute of the day some frightened woman would scream, having unexpectedly come across a soldier in her courtyard or in the plum-orchard behind her house. In dark blue uniforms, tanned by two months of marching and fighting, glad that they were alive and eager for rest and enjoyment, they sauntered through the town and the country around. Few of the citizens went to the *kapia* for now it was always full of soldiers. They would sit there, singing in various languages and buying fruit in their blue leather-peaked caps with a yellow metal cockade on which was cut the imperial initials FJI.

But when autumn came the soldiers began to move away. Slowly and imperceptibly there seemed fewer and fewer of them. There remained only the gendarme detachments. These requisitioned houses and prepared for a long stay. At the same time officials began to arrive, civil servants with their families and, after them, artisans and craftsmen for all those trades which up till then had not existed in the town. Among them were Czechs, Poles, Croats, Hungarians and Austrians.

At first it seemed that they had come by chance, as if driven by the wind, and as if they were coming for a short stay to live more or less the same life as had always been lived here, as though the civil authorities were to prolong for a short time the occupation begun by the army. But with every month that passed the number of newcomers increased. However, what most astonished the people of the town and filled them with wonder and distrust was not so much their numbers as their immense and incomprehensible plans, their untiring industry and the perseverance with which they proceeded to the realization of those plans. The newcomers were never at peace; and they allowed no one else to live in peace. It seemed that they were resolved with their impalpable yet ever more noticeable web of laws, regulations and orders to embrace all forms of life, men, beasts and things, and to change and alter everything, both the outward appearance of the town and the customs and habits of men from the cradle to the grave. All this they did quietly without many words, without force or provocation, so that a man had nothing to protest about. If they encountered resistance or lack of understanding, they at once stopped, discussed the matter somewhere out of sight and then changed only the manner and direction of their work, still carrying out whatever was in their minds. Every task that they began seemed useless and even silly. They measured out the waste land, numbered the trees in the forest, inspected lavatories and drains, looked at the teeth of horses and cows, asked about the illnesses of the people, noted the number and types of fruit-trees and of different kinds of sheep and poultry. (It seemed that they were playing games, so incomprehensible, unreal and futile all these tasks of theirs appeared to the people.) Then all that they had carried out with so much care and zeal vanished somewhere or other as if it had been lost without trace or sound. But a few months later, sometimes even a year later, when the whole thing had been completely forgotten by the people, the real sense of these measures which had seemed so senseless was suddenly revealed. The *mukhtars* of the individual quarters would be summoned to the *konak* (the administrative center) and told of a new regulation against forest felling, or of the fight against typhus, or the manner of sale of fruit and sweetmeats, or of permits for the movement of cattle. Every day a fresh regulation. With each regulation men saw their individual liberties curtailed or their obligations increased, but the life of the town and the villages, and of all their inhabitants as a mass, became wider and fuller.

But in the homes, not only of the Turks but also of the Serbs, nothing was changed. They lived, worked and amused themselves in the old way. Bread was still mixed in kneading troughs, coffee roasted on the hearth, clothes steamed in coppers and washed with soda which hurt the women's fingers; they still spun and wove on tambours and hand-looms. Old customs of *slavas* (patronal feats), holidays and weddings were kept up in every detail and as for the new customs which the newcomers had brought with them there were only whispers here and there as of something far off and incredible. In short, they lived and worked as they had always done and as in most of the houses they would continue to work and live for another fifteen or twenty years after the occupation.

But on the other hand the outward aspect of the town altered visibly and rapidly. Those same people, who in their own homes maintained the old order in every detail and did not even dream of changing anything, became for the most part easily reconciled to the changes in the town and after a longer or shorter period of wonder and grumbling accepted them. Naturally here, as always and everywhere in similar circumstances, the new life meant in actual fact a mingling of the old and the new. Old ideas and old values clashed with the new ones, merged with them or existed side by side, as if waiting to see which would outlive which. People reckoned in florins and kreutzers but also in grosh and para, measured by arshin and oka and drams but also by meters and kilos and grams, confirmed terms of payment and orders by the new calendar but even more often by the old custom of payment on St. George's or St. Dimitri's day. By a natural law the people resisted every innovation but did not go to extremes, for to most of them life was always more important and more urgent than the forms by which they lived. Only in exceptional individuals was there played out a deeper, truer drama of the struggle between the old and the new. For them the forms of life were indivisibly and unconditionally linked with life itself.

Such a man was Shemsibeg Branković of Crnče, one of the richest and most respected begs in the town. He had six sons, of whom four were already married. Their houses comprised a whole small quarter surrounded by fields, plum-orchards and shrubberies. Shemsibeg was the undisputed chief, the strict and silent master of this community. Tall, bent with years, with a huge white gold-embroidered turban on his head, he only came down to the market to pray in the mosque on Fridays. From the first day of the occupation he stopped nowhere in the town, spoke to no one and would not look about him. Not the smallest piece of clothing or costume, not a new tool or a new word was allowed to enter the Branković house. Not one of his sons had any connection with the new authorities and his grandchildren were not allowed to go to school. All the Branković community suffered from this; among his sons there was dissatisfaction at the old man's obstinacy but none of them dared to oppose him by a single word or a single glance. Those Turks from the market-place, who worked and mingled with the newcomers, greeted Shemsibeg when he passed through the market with a dumb respect in which was mingled fear and admiration and an uneasy conscience. The oldest and most respected Turks of the town often went to Crnče as if on a pilgrimage to sit and talk with Shemsibeg. Those were meetings of men who were determined to persevere in their resistance to the end and were unwilling to yield in any way to reality. These were, in fact, long sessions without many words and without real conclusions.

Shemsibeg sat and smoked on a red rug, cloaked and buttoned up in summer as in winter, with his guests around him. Their conversation was usually about some new incomprehensible and sinister measure of the occupation authorities, or of those Turks who were more and more accommodating themselves to the new order. Before this harsh and dignified man, they all felt the need to give vent to their bitterness, their fears and their uncertainties. Every conversation ended with the questions: where is all this leading and where will it stop? Who and what were these strangers who, it seemed, did not know the meaning of rest and respite, knew neither measure nor limits? What did they want? With what plans had they come? What was this restlessness which continually drove them on, like some curse, to new works and enterprises of which no one could see the end?

Shemsibeg only looked at them and for the most part remained silent. His face was darkened, not by the sun, but by his inner thoughts. His glance was hard, but absent and as if lost. His eyes were clouded and there were whitish-gray circles around the black pupils as in an ageing eagle. His big mouth, with scarcely perceptible lips, was firmly set but moved slowly as if he were always turning over in his mind some word which he did not pronounce.

None the less, men left him with a feeling of comfort, neither calmed nor consoled, but touched and exalted by his firm and hopeless intransigence.

Whenever Shemsibeg went down to the market-place on Fridays, he was met with some fresh change in men or buildings which had not been there the Friday before. In order not to have to look at it, he kept his eyes fixed on the ground but there, in the drying mud of the streets, he saw the marks of horses' hooves and noticed how alongside the broad rounded Turkish shoes the sharp-pointed bent Austrian horseshoes were becoming more and more common. So that even there in the mud his gaze read the same merciless judgment that he read everywhere in men's faces and in the things about him, a judgment of time which would not be halted.

Seeing that there was nowhere to rest his eyes, Shemsibeg ceased altogether to come down into the market. He withdrew completely to his Crnče and sat there, a silent but strict and implacable master, severe towards all but most of all towards himself. The oldest and most respected Turks of the town continued to visit him there, regarding him as a sort of living saint (among them, in particular, Alihodja). At last, in the third year of the occupation, Shemsibeg died without ever having been ill. He passed away without ever pronouncing that bitter word which was forever on the tip of his old lips and never again setting foot in the market-place, where all men had set out on the new ways.

Indeed the town changed rapidly in appearance, for the newcomers cut down trees, planted new ones in other places, repaired the streets, cut new ones, dug drainage canals, built public buildings. In the first few years they pulled down in the market-place those old and dilapidated shops which were out of line and which, to tell the truth, had up till then inconvenienced no one. In place of those old-fashioned shops with their wooden drop-counters, new ones were built, well sited, with tiled roofs and metal rollers on the doors. (Alihodja's shop too was destined to be a victim of these measures, but the *hodja* opposed it resolutely, took the affair to law, contested it and dragged it on in every possible way until at last he succeeded, and his shop remained just as it was and just where it was.) The market-place was leveled and widened. A new *konak* was erected, a great building intended to house the law courts and the local administration. The army, too, was working on its own account, even more rapidly and inconsiderately than the civil authorities. They put up barracks, cleared waste land, planted and changed the appearance of whole hills.

The older inhabitants could not understand, and wondered; just when they thought that all this incomprehensible energy had come to an end, the newcomers started some fresh and even more incomprehensible task. The townsmen stopped and looked at all this work, but not like children who love to watch the work of adults but as adults who stop for a moment to watch children's games. This continual need of the newcomers to build and rebuild, to dig and to put back again, to put and modify, this eternal desire of theirs to foresee the action of natural forces, to avoid or surmount them, no one either understood or appreciated. On the other hand all the townsmen, especially the older men, saw this unhealthy activity as a bad omen. Had it been left to them the town would have gone on looking as any other little oriental town. What burst would be patched up, what leaned would be shored up, but beyond that no one would needlessly create work or make plans or interfere in the foundations of buildings or change the aspect which God had given to the town.

But the newcomers went on with their tasks, one after the other, quickly and logically, according to unknown and well-prepared plans, to the even greater wonder and astonishment of the townsfolk. Thus unexpectedly and quickly came the turn of the dilapidated and abandoned caravanserai, which was always regarded as an integral part of the bridge, even as it had been 300 years before. In fact what had been known as the Stone Han had long ago become completely ruined. The doors had rotted, those lace-like grilles of soft stone on the windows broken, the roof had fallen into the interior of the building and from it grew a great acacia and a welter of nameless shrubs and weeds, but the outer walls were still whole, a true and harmonious rectangle of stone still standing upright. In the eyes of the townspeople, from birth to death, this was no ordinary ruin but the completion of the bridge, as much an integral part of the town as their own houses, and no one would ever have dreamed that the old *han* could be touched or that it was necessary to change anything about it that time and nature had not already changed.

But one day its turn came too. First engineers who spent a long time measuring the ruins, then workmen and laborers who began to take it down stone by stone, frightening and driving away all sorts of birds and small beasts which had their nests there. Rapidly the level space above the market-place by the bridge became bald and empty and all that was left of the *han* was a heap of good stone carefully piled.

A little more than a year later, instead of the former caravanserai of white stone, there rose a high, massive two-storied barracks, washed in pale-blue, roofed with gray corrugated iron and with loopholes at the corners. Soldiers drilled all day on the open space and stretched their limbs or fell head first in the dust like suppliants to the loud shouts of the corporals. In the evening the sound of incomprehensible soldiers' songs accompanied by an accordion could be heard from the many windows of the ugly building. This went on until the penetrating sound of the bugle with its melancholy melody, which set all the dogs of the town howling, extinguished all these sounds together with the last lights in the windows. So disappeared the lovely bequest of the Vezir and so the barracks, which the people true to ancient custom went on calling the Stone Han, commenced its life on the level by the bridge in complete lack of harmony with all that surrounded it.

The bridge now remained completely isolated.

To tell the truth, things were happening on the bridge too, where the old unchanging customs of the people clashed with the innovations which the newcomers and their way of life brought with them, and in these clashes all that was old and local was always forced to give way and adapt itself.

As far as the local people were concerned, life on the *kapia* went its way as of old. Only it was noticed that now Serbs and Jews came more freely and in greater numbers to the *kapia* and at all times of day, paying no heed as they once had done to the habits and privileges of the Turks. Otherwise all went on as before. In the daytime merchants sat there waiting for the peasant women and buying from them wool, poultry and eggs, and beside them the lazy and idle who moved from one part of the town to another in keeping with the movements of the sun. Towards evening other citizens began to arrive and the merchants and workers gathered there to talk a little or to remain silent for a time looking at the great green river bordered by dwarf willows and sandbanks. The night was for the young. They had never known, nor did they know now, any limits for the time that they stayed on the bridge nor for what they did there.

In that night-time life of the *kapia* there were, at least at first, changes and misunderstandings. The new authorities had introduced permanent lighting in the town. In the first years of the occupation they put lanterns on green standards, in which petrol lamps burned, in the main streets and at the crossroads. The lanterns were cleaned, filled and lit by big Ferhat, a poor devil with a house full of children, who until then had been a servant in the municipality. He discharged the petards announcing Ramazan and carried out similar jobs, without any fixed or certain wages. The bridge too was lighted at several points, including the *kapia*. The standard for this lantern was fixed to that oak beam which was all that remained of the former blockhouse. This lantern on the *kapia* had to endure a long struggle with the local jokers, with those who loved to sing in the darkness or to smoke and chat on the *kapia* as also with the destructive impulses of the young men in whom love-yearning, solitude and plum brandy mingled and clashed. That flickering light irritated them and so countless times both the lantern and the lamp inside were smashed to pieces. There were many fines and sentences because of that lantern. At one time a special police agent was told to keep an eye on the light. So the nightly visitors now had a living witness, even more unpleasant than the lantern. But time exercised its influence and the new generation grew accustomed to it and so reconciled to its existence that they gave free vent to their night feelings under the weak light of the municipal lantern, and no longer threw at it whatever came to hand, sticks, stones or anything else. This reconciliation was made so much the easier because on moonlit nights, when the *kapia* was most visited, the lantern was generally not lit.

Only once a year the bridge had to experience a great illumination. On the eve of August 18th every year, the Emperor's birthday, the authorities decorated the bridge with garlands and lines of young pine trees and, as darkness fell, lit strings of lanterns and fairy-lights; hundreds of army ration tins, filled with lard and fat, flamed in long rows along the parapet of the bridge. They lit up the center of the bridge, leaving the ends and the piers lost in the darkness, so that the illuminated part seemed as if floating in space. But every light quickly burns out and every feast comes to an end. By the next day the bridge was once again what it had always been. Only in the eyes of some of the children there remained a new and unusual picture of the bridge under the short-lived play of light, a bright and striking vision, but short and transient as a dream.

Besides permanent lighting, the new authorities also introduced cleanliness on the *kapia,* or more exactly that special sort of cleanliness that accorded with their ideas. The fruit peelings, melon seeds and nutshells no longer remained for days on the flagstones until the rain or the wind carried them away. Now a municipal sweeper brushed them up every morning. But that irritated no one, for men quickly become accustomed to cleanliness even when it forms no part of their needs or habits; naturally on condition that they personally do not have to observe it.

There was still one more novelty which the occupation and the newcomers brought with them; women began to come to the *kapia* for the first time in its existence. The wives and daughters of the officials, their nursemaids and servants would stop there to chat or come to sit there on holidays with their military or civil escorts. This did not happen very often, but none the less it was enough to disturb the older men who came there to smoke their pipes in peace and quiet over the water, and disconcerted and confused the younger ones.

There had, naturally, always been a link between the *kapia* and the women in the town, but only in so far as the menfolk gathered there to pass compliments to the girls crossing the bridge or to express their joys, pains and quarrels over women and find relief from them on the *kapia*. Many a lonely man would sit for hours or even days singing softly to himself "for my soul only," or wreathed in tobacco smoke, or simply watching the swift waters in silence, paying tribute to that exaltation to which we must all pay due and from which few escape. Many a contest between rivals was settled there, many love intrigues imagined. Much was said or thought about women and about love, many passions were born and many extinguished. All this there was, but women had never stopped or sat on the *kapia,* neither Christian nor, still less, Moslem. Now all that was changed.

Now on Sundays and holidays on the *kapia* could be seen cooks tightly laced and red in the face, with rolls of fat overflowing above and below their corsets in which they could scarcely breathe. With them were their sergeants in well-brushed uniforms, with shining metal buttons and riflemen's pompons on their chests. And on working days at dusk, officers and civil servants strolled there with their wives, halted on the *kapia,* chatted in their incomprehensible language, strolled about at their ease and laughed loudly.

These idle, laughing women were a cause of scandal to all, some more some less. The people wondered and felt insulted for a time and then began to grow accustomed to them, as they had grown accustomed to so many other innovations, even though they did not approve them.

In fact it could be said that all these changes on the bridge were insignificant, fleeting and superficial. The many and important changes which had taken place in the spirits and habits of the citizens and in the outward appearance of the town seemed as though they had passed by the bridge without affecting it. It seemed that the white and ancient bridge, across which men had passed for three centuries, remained unchanged without trace or mark even under the "new Emperor" and that it would triumph over this flood of change and innovation even as it had always triumphed over the greatest floods, arising once more, white and untouched, from the furious mass of troubled waters which had wanted to flow over it.

12

Now life on the *kapia* became even livelier and more varied. A large and variegated crowd, locals and newcomers, old and young, came and went on the *kapia* all day long until a late hour of the night. They thought only of themselves, each one wrapped up in the thoughts, moods and emotions which had brought him to the *kapia*. Therefore they paid no heed to the passers-by who, impelled by other thoughts and by their own cares, crossed the bridge with lowered heads or absent glances, looking neither to right nor left and paying no attention to those seated on the *kapia*.

Among such passers-by one was certainly Milan Glasičanin of Okolište. He was tall, thin, pale and bowed. His whole body seemed transparent and without weight, yet attached to leaden feet, so that he swayed and bent in his walk like a church banner held in a child's hands during the procession. His hair and moustaches were gray, like those of an old man, and his eyes were always lowered. He did not notice that anything had changed on the *kapia* or among the people gathered there, and passed among them almost unnoticed by those who came there to sit, to dream, to sing, to trade, to chat or simply to waste time. The older men had forgotten him, the younger men did not recall him and the newcomers had never known him. But none the less his fate had been closely bound up with the *kapia,* at least judging from what was said about him or whispered in the town ten or twelve years before.

Milan's father, Nikola Glasičanin, had settled in the town about the time when the insurrection in Serbia was at its height. He had bought a fine property at Okolište. It was generally believed that he had fled from somewhere or other with a large but ill-gotten fortune. No one had any proof of this and everyone only half believed it. But no one ever definitely denied it. He had married twice but none the less had few children. He had brought up one child only, his son Milan, and left him all that he possessed, whether open or hidden. Milan, too, had only a single son, Peter. His property would have been sufficient and he would have left that to his son after his death had he not had one vice, only one, but that an overwhelming passion—gambling.

The real townsmen were not gamblers by nature. As we have seen, their passions were other and different; an immoderate love of women, an inclination to alcohol, song, lounging and idle dreamings beside their native river. But man's capacities are limited, even in such matters. Therefore their vices often clashed with one another, contradicted one another and often completely canceled one another out. This did not mean that in the town there were not men addicted to this vice, but the actual number of gamblers was always few in comparison with other towns, and for the most part they were strangers or newcomers. Anyhow, Milan Glasičanin was one of them. From his earliest youth he had been entirely given over to gambling. When he could not find the company he needed in the town, he would go to nearby districts whence he would return, either weighed down with money like a merchant from a fair or with empty pockets, without watch or chain, tobacco pouch or rings, but always pale and washed out like a sick man.

His habitual place was in Ustamujić's inn at the far end of the Višegrad market. There, in a narrow windowless room where a candle burned day and night, could always be found three or four men to whom gambling was dearer than anything else on earth. In that room, shut off from the world, they would crouch in the tobacco smoke and stale air, with bloodshot eyes, dry mouths and quivering hands. They met there frequently, day or night, slaves to their passion like martyrs. In that little room Milan passed a great part of his youth and there left a good part of his strength and property.

He had not been much more than thirty when that sudden and to most people inexplicable change took place in him, which cured him forever of his driving passion but at the same time altered his whole way of life and completely transfigured him.

One autumn, some fourteen years before, a stranger had come to the inn. He was neither young nor old, neither ugly nor handsome, a man of middle age and medium height, silent and smiling only with his eyes. He was a man of business, entirely wrapped up in the affairs for which he had come. He passed the night there and at dusk entered that little room in which the gamblers had been shut up since early afternoon. They greeted him with distrust but he behaved so quietly and meekly that they did not even notice when he too began to put small stakes on the cards. He lost more than he won, frowned uncertainly and with an unsure hand took some silver money from an inner pocket. After he had lost a considerable sum, they had to give him the deal. At first he dealt slowly and carefully, then more swiftly and freely. He played without showing his feelings but was prepared to stake the limit. The pile of silver coins before him grew. One by one, the players began to drop out. One offered to stake a gold chain on a card, but the newcomer refused coldly, saying that he played for money only.

About the time of the last prayer the game broke up, for no one had any ready money left. Milan Glasičanin was the last, but in the end he too had to withdraw. The newcomer politely took his leave and retired to his own room.

Next day they played again. Again the stranger alternately lost and won, but always won more than he lost, so that once again the townsmen were left without ready money. They looked at his hands and his sleeves, watched him from every angle, brought fresh cards and changed places at the table, but all to no purpose. They were playing that simple but ill-famed game called *otuz bir* (thirty-one) which they had all known from childhood, but none the less they were not able to follow the newcomer's mode of play. Sometimes he drew twenty-nine and sometimes thirty, and sometimes he stood pat at twenty-five. He accepted every stake, the smallest as well as the greatest, overlooked the petty irregularities of individual players as if he had not noticed them, but denounced more serious ones curtly and coldly.

The presence of this newcomer at the inn tormented and irritated Milan Glasičanin. He was in any case at the time feverish and washed out. He swore to himself that he would play no more, but come again, and again lost his last coin, returning home filled with gall and shame. The fourth and fifth evenings he managed to control himself and remained at home. He had dressed and prepared his ready money but none the less stood by his resolution. His head felt heavy and his breath came in fits and starts. He ate his supper in haste, scarcely knowing what he was eating. Finally he went out, smoked, walked up and down in front of his house several times, and looked at the silent town in the clear autumn night. After he had walked thus for some time, he suddenly saw a vague figure going along the road who turned and stopped before his house.

"Good evening, neighbor!" shouted the unknown. Milan knew the voice. It was the stranger from the inn. Clearly the man had come to see him and wanted to talk to him. Milan came up to the fence.

"Why didn't you come to the inn tonight?" the stranger asked casually, calm and indifferent.

"I was not in the mood today. Are the others there?"

"There is no one left. They all left earlier than usual. Come along and let's have a hand together."

"It is too late, and there's nowhere to go."

"Let us go down and sit on the *kapia*. The moon will soon be rising."

"But it is not the right time," Milan objected. His lips were dry and his words seemed as if another had spoken them.

The stranger went on waiting, certain that his suggestion would be accepted.

And, in fact, Milan unlatched his gate and followed the man, as though his words and thoughts and efforts had all given way before that calm power which drew him on and from which he could not free himself, however much he felt humiliated by this stranger who roused in him resistance and revulsion.

They descended the slope from Okolište quickly. A large and waxing moon was rising behind Staniševac. The bridge seemed endless and unreal, for its ends were lost in a milky mist and the piers merged into the darkness; one side of each pier and of each arch was brightly lit while the other remained the deepest shadow. These moonlit and darkened surfaces were broken and cut into sharp outlines, so that the whole bridge seemed like a strange arabesque created by a momentary play of light and darkness.

On the *kapia* there was not a living soul. They sat down. The stranger took out a pack of cards. Milan started to say how unsuitable this was, that they could not see the cards well and could not distinguish the money, but the stranger paid no attention to him. They began to play.

At first they still exchanged an occasional word, but as the game grew faster they fell silent. They only rolled cigarettes and lit them one after the other. The cards changed hands several times, only to remain finally in the hands of the stranger. The money fell soundlessly on the stones which were covered by a fine dew. The time had come, which Milan knew so well, when the stranger drew a two to twenty-nine or an ace to thirty. His throat contracted and his gaze clouded. But the face of the stranger, bathed in moonlight, seemed calmer than usual. In not quite an hour Milan no longer had any ready money. The stranger proposed that he should go home and get some more and said that he would accompany him. They went there and returned and went on with the game. Milan played as if dumb and blind, guessing at the cards and showing by signs what he wanted. It almost seemed as if the cards between them had become incidental, a pretext in this desperate and unrelenting duel. When he again ran out of money, the stranger ordered him to go home and bring some more, while he himself remained on the *kapia* smoking. He no longer thought it necessary to accompany him, for he could no longer imagine that Milan would not obey, or play a trick on him and remain at home. Milan obeyed, went without argument and returned humbly. Then the luck suddenly changed. Milan won back all that he had lost. The knot in his throat tightened more and more under the stress of emotion. The stranger began to double the stakes and then to treble them. The game grew more and more swift, more and more intense. The cards flew between them weaving a web of gold and silver. Both were silent. Only Milan breathed excitedly, sweating and feeling chilled alternately in the mild moonlit night. He played, dealt and covered his cards, not from the pleasure of the game but because he had to. It seemed to him that this stranger wanted to draw out of him not only all his money, ducat by ducat, but also the marrow from his bones and the blood from his veins, drop by drop, and that his strength and his will-power were leaving him with every new loss in the game. From time to time he stole a glance at his opponent. He expected to see a satanic face with bared teeth and eyes like red-hot coals, but on the contrary he still saw before him the stranger's ordinary face with the intent expression of a man working at an everyday task, hastening to finish the work in hand which was neither easy nor pleasant.

Once more Milan rapidly lost all his ready money. Then the stranger proposed staking cattle, land and property.

"I wager four good Hungarian ducats against your bay with its saddle. Is it a deal?"

"I agree."

So the bay went, and after it two packhorses, then cows and calves. Like a careful and meticulous merchant, the stranger numbered all the beasts in Milan's stables by name and set down accurately the value of each head, as if he had been born and reared in the house.

"Here are thirteen ducats for that field of yours you call *salkusha*. Have I your word?"

"You have."

The stranger dealt. Milan's five cards totaled twenty-eight.

"More?" asked the stranger calmly.

"One," muttered Milan in a scarcely audible voice and all his blood rushed to his heart.

The stranger slowly turned a card. It was a two, a lucky draw. Milan muttered indifferently through closed teeth.

"Enough."

He closed his cards, concealing them feverishly. He tried to make his voice and expression indifferent, to prevent his opponent from guessing how he stood.

Then the stranger began to draw for himself, with open cards. When he got to twenty-seven he stopped and looked Milan in the eyes, but Milan looked away. The stranger turned another card. It was a two. He sighed quickly, scarcely audibly. It seemed that he would stand pat at twenty-nine and the blood began to flow back to Milan's head in a joyful presentiment of victory. Then the stranger started, expanded his chest and threw back his head so that his eyes and forehead shone in the moonlight and turned up another card. Another two. It seemed impossible that three twos should turn up one after the other, but so it was. On the turned-up card Milan seemed to see his field, ploughed and harrowed as it was in spring when it was at its best. The furrows whirled about him as in delirium, but the calm voice of the stranger recalled him to himself.

"*Otuz bir!* The field is mine!"

Then came the turn of the other fields, then both houses and then the oak grove at Osojnica. They invariably agreed on the values. Sometimes Milan would win and would snatch up the ducats. Hope shone before him like gold but after two or three unlucky hands he was again without money and again began staking his property.

When the game had swept away everything like a torrent both players stopped for a moment, not to take breath for both of them it seemed feared to do so, but to consider what else they could wager. The stranger was calm like a conscientious worker who has finished the first part of his task and wants to hasten on with the second. Milan remained tense as if turned to ice; his blood was beating in his ears and the stone seat beneath him rose and fell. Then the stranger suggested in that monotonous, even, somewhat nasal voice:

"Do you know what, friend? Let us have one more turn at the cards, but all for all. I will wager all that I have gained tonight and you your life. If you win, everything will be yours again just as it was, money, cattle and lands. If you lose, you will leap from the *kapia* into the Drina."

He said this in the same dry and business-like voice as he had said everything else, as if it were a question of the most ordinary wager between two gamblers absorbed by their play.

So it has come to losing my soul or saving it, thought Milan and made an effort to rise, to extricate himself from that incomprehensible whirlpool that had taken everything from him and even now drew him on with irresistible force, but the stranger sent him back to his place with a glance. As if they had been playing at the inn for a stake of three or four grosh he lowered his head and held out his hand. They both cut. The stranger cut a four and Milan a ten. It was his turn to deal and that filled him with hope. He dealt and the stranger asked for a complete new hand.

"More! More! More!"

The man took five cards and only then said: "Enough!" Now it was Milan's turn. When he reached twenty-eight he stopped for a second, looking at the cards in the stranger's hand and at his enigmatic face. He was unable to get any idea at how many the stranger had stopped, but it was exceedingly likely that he had more than twenty-eight; firstly, because all evening he had never stopped at low scores and secondly, because he had five cards. Summoning the last of his strength, Milan turned over one more card. It was a four; that meant thirty-two. He had lost.

He looked at the card but was unable to believe his eyes. It seemed to him impossible that he should have lost everything so quickly. Something fiery and noisy seemed to course through him, from his feet to his head. Suddenly everything became clear; the value of life, what it meant to be a man and the meaning of his curse, that inexplicable passion to gamble with friends or strangers, with himself and with all around him. All was clear and light as if the day had dawned and he had only been dreaming that he had gambled and lost, but everything was at the same time true, irrevocable and irreparable. He wanted to make some sound, to groan, to cry out for help, even were it only a sigh, but he could not summon up enough strength.

Before him the stranger stood waiting.

Then, all of a sudden, a cock crowed somewhere on the bank, high and clear, and immediately after, a second. It was so near that he could hear the beating of its wings. At the same time the scattered cards flew away as if carried off by a storm, the money was scattered and the whole *kapia* rocked to its foundations. Milan closed his eyes in fear and thought that his last hour had come. When he opened them again he saw that he was alone. His opponent had vanished like a soap bubble and with him the cards and the money from the stone flags.

An orange-colored moon swam on the horizon. A fresh breeze began to blow. The roar of waters in the depths became louder. Milan tentatively fingered the stone on which he was sitting, trying to collect himself, to remember where he was and what had happened; then he rose heavily and as if on someone else's legs moved slowly homeward to Okolište.

Groaning and staggering, he scarcely reached the door of his house before he fell like a wounded man, striking the door heavily with his body. Those in the house, wakened by the noise, carried him to bed.

For two months he lay in fever and delirium. It was thought that he would not survive. Pop Nikola came and consecrated the holy oils. None the less he recovered and got up again, but as a different man. He was now a man old before his time, an eccentric who lived in a world apart, who spoke little and associated with other men as little as possible. On his face, which never smiled, was an expression of painful and concentrated attention. He concerned himself only with his own house and went about his own business, as if he had never heard of company or of cards.

During his illness he had told Pop Nikola all that had happened that night on the *kapia,* and later he told it all to two good friends of his, for he felt that he could not go on living with that secret on his mind. The people heard the rumors of what had happened but, as if what had actually happened had been a small matter, they added further details and elaborated the whole story, and then, as is usually the case, turned their attention elsewhere and forgot all about Milan and his experience. So what was left of the one-time Milan Glasičanin lived, worked and moved among the townsfolk. The younger generation only knew him as he was in their time and never suspected that he had been different. And he himself seemed to have forgotten everything. When, descending from his house to the town, he crossed the bridge with his heavy slow sleepwalker's step, he passed by the *kapia* without the least emotion, even without any memory of it. It never even crossed his mind that the *sofa* with its white stone seats and carefree crowd could have any connection with that terrible place, somewhere at the ends of the earth, where he had one night played his last game, staking on a deceiving card all that he possessed, even his own life in this world and the next.

Often Milan asked himself if all that night episode on the *kapia* had been only a dream which he had dreamed as he lay unconscious before the door of his house, the consequence and not the cause of his illness. To tell the truth, both Pop Nikola and those two friends in whom he had confided were more inclined to regard the whole of Milan's tale as a hallucination, a fantasy which had appeared to him in a fever. For none of them believed that the devil played *otuz bir* or that he would take anyone he wished to destroy to the *kapia.* But our experiences are often so heavy and clouded that it is no wonder that men justify themselves by the intervention of Satan himself, considering that this explains them or at least makes them more bearable.

But whether true or not, with the devil's help or without it, in dream or in fact, it was sure that Milan Glasičanin, since he had lost his health and his youth and a large sum of money overnight, had by a miracle been finally liberated forever from his vice. And not only that. To the story of Milan Glasičanin was added yet another tale of yet another destiny, whose thread started also from the *kapia.*

The day after the night when Milan Glasičanin (in dream or in waking) had played his terrible final game on the *kapia* dawned a sunny autumn day. It was a Saturday. As always on Saturdays, the Višegrad Jews, merchants with their male children, were gathered on the *kapia.* At leisure and in formal dress, with satin trousers and woolen waistcoats, with dull red shallow fezzes on their heads, they strictly observed the Sabbath Day, walking beside the river as if looking for someone in it. But for the most part they sat on the *kapia,* carrying on loud and lively conversations in Spanish, only using Serbian when they wanted to swear.

Among the first to arrive on the *kapia* that morning was Bukus Gaon, the eldest son of the pious, poor and honest barber, Avram Gaon. He was sixteen and still had not found permanent work or a regular occupation. The young man, unlike all the other Gaons, was somewhat scatter-brained and this had prevented him from behaving reasonably and settling down to a trade, and drove him to look for something higher and better for himself. When he wanted to sit down, he looked to see if the seat was clean. It was while doing this that he saw, in a crack between two stones, a thin line of shining yellow. That was the shine of gold, so dear to men's eyes. He looked more closely. There could be no doubt; a ducat had somehow fallen there. The young man looked around him, to see if anyone was watching, and searched for something to pry loose the ducat which laughed at him from its hiding place. Then suddenly he remembered that it was Saturday and that it would be a shame and a sin to do any kind of work. Excited and embarrassed, he went on sitting on that spot and did not move until noon. When it was time for lunch and all the Jews, old and young, had gone home, he found a thick barley stalk and, forgetting the sin and the holy day, carefully pried the ducat loose from between the stones. It was a real Hungarian ducat, thin and weighing no more than a dead leaf. He was late for lunch. When he sat down at the sparse table around which all thirteen of them (eleven children, father and mother) were sitting, he did not hear how his father scolded him and called him a lazy wastrel who could not even be in time for lunch. His ears hummed and his eyes were dazzled. Before him opened those days of unheard-of luxury of which he had often dreamed. It seemed to him that he was carrying the sun in his pocket.

Next day, without much reflection, Bukus went to Ustamujić's inn and edged his way into that little room where at almost any time of the day or night the cards were in play. He had always dreamed of doing this, but had never had enough money to dare to go in and try his luck. Now he was able to realize his dream.

There he passed several hours filled with anguish and emotion. At first they had all greeted him with disdain and mistrust. When they saw him change the Hungarian ducat they at once thought that he had stolen it from someone but they agreed to accept him and his stake (for if gamblers questioned the origin of every stake, the game would never begin). But then fresh miseries commenced for the beginner. Whenever he won, the blood rushed to his head and his eyes clouded with sweat and heat. When he made a rather greater loss it seemed to him that he stopped breathing and his heart died. But despite all his torments, each of which seemed insoluble, he none the less left the inn that evening with four ducats in his pocket. Though he was broken and feverish with emotion as if he had been beaten with fiery rods, he walked proud and erect. Before his glowing imagination opened far and glorious prospects which threw a glittering sheen over his poverty and swept away the whole town down to its foundations. He walked with a solemn pace as though drunk. For the first time in his life he was able to feel not only the shimmer and the sound of gold but also its weight.

That same autumn, though still young and green, Bukus became a gambler and a vagabond and left the family home. Old Gaon shriveled up from shame and grief for his eldest son, and the whole Jewish community felt the misfortune as if it had been its own. Later he left the town and went out into the world with his evil gambler's destiny. And nothing more was ever heard of him for all those fourteen years. The cause of all that, they said, was that "devil's ducat" which he had found on the *kapia* and had pried loose on the Sabbath Day.

13

It was the fourth year of the occupation. It seemed as if everything had somehow or other calmed down and "was working." Even if the sweet peace of Turkish times had not been restored, at least order had been established according to the new ideas. But then there were once more troubles in the land, fresh troops arrived unexpectedly and a guard was once again mounted on the *kapia*. This was the way of it.

The new authorities that year began recruiting in Bosnia and Herzegovina. This provoked great agitation among the people, especially the Turks. Fifty years before, when the Sultan had introduced the *nizam* (the first Turkish regular army), clothed, drilled and equipped in the European manner, they had revolted and waged a series of small bloody wars, for they would not wear the infidel clothing and put on belts which crossed over the chest and so created that hated symbol of the cross. Now they had to put on the same odious "tight clothing" and that, furthermore, in the service of a foreign ruler of another faith.

In the first years after the occupation, when the authorities had begun numbering houses and taking a census of the population, these measures had already excited mistrust among the Turks and stirred up undefined but deeply felt misgivings.

As always in such cases, the most learned and respected of the Višegrad Turks met stealthily to discuss the significance of these measures and the attitude they should adopt towards them.

One May morning these leaders gathered on the *kapia* as if by chance and occupied all the seats on the *sofa*. Peacefully drinking their coffee and looking straight in front of them, they talked in whispers of the new and suspicious measures of the authorities. They were all ill at ease about the new ideas, the very nature of which was contrary to their ideas and habits, for each of them considered this interference by the authorities in his personal affairs and his family life as an unnecessary and incomprehensible humiliation. But no one knew how to interpret the real sense of this numbering, nor could suggest how it could best be resisted. Among them was Alihodja who otherwise rarely came to the *kapia,* for his right ear always throbbed painfully when he happened to look at those stone steps leading up to the *sofa*.

The Višegrad schoolmaster, Husseinaga, a learned and loquacious man, interpreted, as the most competent among them to do so, what this noting down of houses by number and this counting of men and children might mean.

"This has, it seems, always been an infidel custom; thirty years ago, if not more, there was a Vezir in Travnik, a certain Tahirpasha Stambolija. He was one of the converted, but false and insincere. He remained a Christian in his soul, as he had once been. He kept, it is said, a bell beside him and when he wanted to call one of his servants he would ring this bell like a Christian priest until someone answered. It was this Tahirpasha who began to number the houses in Travnik and on each house he nailed a tablet with the number (it was for this reason that he was known as 'the nailer'). But the people rebelled and collected all those tablets from the houses, made a pile of them and set fire to it. Blood was about to flow for this, but luckily a report of this reached Stambul and he was recalled from Bosnia. May all trace of him be abolished! Now this is something of the same sort. The Schwabes want to have registers of everything, even our heads."

They all stared straight in front of them and listened to the schoolmaster who was well known to prefer recounting long and detailed stories of the past to giving his own opinion shortly and clearly on what was taking place in the present.

As always, Alihodja was the first to lose patience.

"This does not concern the Schwabes' faith, Muderis Effendi; it concerns their interests. They are not playing and do not waste their time even when they are sleeping but look well to their own affairs. We cannot see today what all this means, but we shall see it in a month or two, or perhaps a year. For, as the late lamented Shemsibeg Branković used to say: 'The Schwabes' mines have long fuses!' This numbering of houses and men, or so I see it, is necessary for them because of some new tax, or else they are thinking of getting men for forced labor or for their army, or perhaps both. If you ask me what we should do, this is my opinion. We have not got the army to rise at once in revolt. That God sees and all men know. But we do not have to obey all that we are commanded. No one need remember his number nor tell his age. Let them guess when each one of us was born. If they go too far and interfere with our children and our honor, then we shall not give way but will defend ourselves, and then let it be as God wills!"

They went on discussing the unpalatable measures of the authorities for a long time, but in the main they were in agreement with what Alihodja had recommended: passive resistance. Men concealed their ages or gave false information, making the excuse that they were illiterate. And as for women no one even dared to ask about them, for that would have been considered a deadly insult. Despite all the instructions and threats of the authorities the tablets with the house numbers were nailed upside down or hidden away in places where they were invisible. Or else they immediately white-washed their houses and, as if by chance, the house number was white-washed too.

Seeing that the resistance was deep-seated and sincere, though concealed, the authorities turned a blind eye, avoiding any strict application of the laws with all the consequences and disputes which would inevitably have ensued.

Two years passed. The agitation about the census had been forgotten when the recruitment of young men, irrespective of faith and class, was actually put into force. Open rebellion broke out in Eastern Herzegovina, in which not only Turks but also Serbs took part. The leaders of the rebels tried to establish ties with foreign countries, especially with Turkey, and claimed that the occupation authorities had gone beyond the powers granted them at the Berlin Congress and that they had no right to recruit in the occupied districts which still remained under nominal Turkish suzerainty. In Bosnia there was no organized resistance, but the revolt spread by way of Foča and Goražda to the borders of the Višegrad district. Individual insurgents or the remnants of routed bands tried to seek refuge in the Sanjak or in Serbia, crossing the bridge at Višegrad. As always in such circumstances, in addition to the rebellion, banditry began to flourish.

So once more, after so many years, a guard was mounted on the *kapia*. Though it was winter and heavy snow had fallen, two gendarmes kept watch on the *kapia* day and night. They stopped all unknown or suspected persons crossing the bridge, interrogated them and inspected their belongings.

A fortnight later a detachment of *streifkorps* appeared in the town and relieved the gendarmes on the *kapia*. The *streifkorps* had been organized when the rebellion in Herzegovina had begun to assume serious proportions. They were mobile storm troops, picked men equipped for action in difficult terrain, and made up of well-paid volunteers. Among them were men who had responded to the first call-up with the occupation troops and did not want to return to their homes, but remained to serve in the *streifkorps*. Others had been seconded from the gendarmerie to the new mobile units. Finally, there were also a certain number of local inhabitants who served as informers and guides.

Throughout that winter, which was neither short nor mild, a guard of two *streifkorps* men kept watch on the bridge. Usually the guard consisted of one stranger and one local man. They did not build a blockhouse, as the Turks had done during the Karageorge insurrection in Serbia. There was no killing or cutting off of heads. But none the less this time, as always when the *kapia* was closed, there were unusual events which left their trace on the town. For hard times cannot pass without misfortune for someone.

Among the *streifkorps* men who mounted guard on the *kapia* was a young man, Gregor Fedun, a Ruthenian from Eastern Galicia. This young man was in his twenty-third year, of gigantic stature but childlike mind, strong as a bear but modest as a girl. He had almost completed his military service when his regiment was sent to Bosnia. He had taken part in fighting at Maglaj and on the Glasinac Mountains and had then spent eighteen months on garrison duty in Eastern Bosnia. When his time was up, he had not wanted to go back to his Galician town of Kolomea and to his father's house which was rich in children but in little else. He was in Pest with his group when the call for volunteers to enroll in the *streifkorps* was made. As a soldier who knew Bosnia through several months of fighting, Fedun was accepted at once. He was sincerely glad at the thought that he was again to see the Bosnian townships and hamlets where he had spent both hard and pleasant days, of which his memory recalled the days of hardship as more beautiful and lively even than the pleasant ones. He melted with joy and was filled with pride, imagining the faces of his parents, brothers and sisters when they received the first silver florins which he would send them from his ample *streifkorps* pay. Above all he had the good fortune not to be sent into Eastern Herzegovina where the fighting with the insurgents was tiring and often very dangerous, but to the town on the Drina where his duties consisted of patroling and guard-keeping.

There he spent the winter, stamping his feet and blowing on his fingers on the *kapia* in the clear frosty nights, when the stones cracked in the frost and the sky paled above the town so that the large autumn stars became tiny, wicked little candles. There he awaited the spring and watched its first signs on the *kapia:* that dull, heavy booming of the ice on the Drina which a man feels deep down in his entrails, and that sullen soughing of some new wind which has howled all night through the naked forests on the mountains close pressed above the bridge.

The young man mounted guard in his turn and felt how the spring, with all its signs on the earth and on the waters, was slowly entering into him also, flooding his whole being and troubling his senses and his thoughts. He kept watch and hummed all the Ruthenian songs which were sung in his own country. As he sang it seemed to him, more and more every spring day, as if he were waiting for someone on that exposed and windy spot.

At the beginning of March, headquarters sent an order to the detachment guarding the bridge to double their precautions since, according to reliable information, the notorious brigand Jakov Čekrlija had crossed from Herzegovina into Bosnia and was now hiding somewhere near Višegrad whence, in all likelihood, he would try to reach either the Serbian or the Turkish frontier. The *streifkorps* men on guard were given a personal description of him, with the comment that the brigand, though physically small and insignificant, was very strong, daring and exceptionally cunning, and had already several times succeeded in escaping and outwitting the patrols that had surrounded him.

Fedun had listened to this warning when making his report, and had taken it seriously as he did all official communications. But he had considered it to be unnecessarily exaggerated, since he could not imagine how anyone could cross unperceived that ten paces which constituted the width of the bridge. Calm and unworried he passed several hours, by day and by night, on the *kapia*. His attention was indeed doubled, but it was not taken up with the appearance of Jakov, of whom there was neither sight nor sound, but with those countless signs and portents by which spring announced its arrival on the *kapia.*

It is not easy to concentrate all one's attention on a single object when one is twenty-three years old, when one's body is quivering with strength and life and when around one, on all sides, spring is burgeoning, shining and filling the air with perfume. The snow was melting in the ravines, the river ran swift and gray as smoked glass, the wind which blew from the north-east brought the breath of snow from the mountains and the first buds to the valleys. All this intoxicated and distracted Fedun as he paced out the space from one terrace to the other or, when on night duty, leaned against the parapet and hummed his Ruthenian songs to the accompaniment of the wind. By day or by night the feeling that he was waiting for someone never left him, a feeling tormenting and yet sweet, and which seemed to find confirmation in all that was taking place around him, in the waters, the earth and the sky.

One day about lunchtime a Turkish girl passed the guard. She was of the age when Turkish girls, not yet veiled in the heavy *feridjah,* no longer go with uncovered faces but wrap themselves in a large thin shawl which conceals the whole body, the hair and the hands, chin and forehead, but still leaves uncovered a part of the face: eyes, nose, mouth and cheeks. She was in the short phase between childhood and womanhood when the Moslem girls show innocently and gaily their still childish and yet womanly features which, perhaps even the next day, will be covered forever by the *feridjah.*

There was not a living soul on the *kapia.* Fedun's fellow guard was a certain Stevan of Prača, one of the peasants attached to the *streifkorps.* He was a man of a certain age, by no means averse to plum brandy, who sat drowsing, contrary to regulations, on the stone *sofa.*

Fedun looked at the girl timidly and cautiously. Around her floated her gaily-colored shawl, waving and shimmering in the sunlight as if alive, moving with the gusts of wind and in rhythm with the girl's pace. Her calm lovely face was closely and tightly framed by the stretched weave of the shawl. Her eyes were downcast but flickering. So she passed before him and disappeared across the bridge into the market.

The young man paced more briskly from one terrace to the other and kept an eye fixed on the market-place. Now it seemed to him that he really had someone for whom to wait. After half an hour—the noonday lull was still unbroken on the bridge—the Turkish girl returned from the market and again crossed before the troubled youth. This time he looked at her a little longer and more boldly, and what was even more wonderful she too looked at him, a short but candid glance, with a sort of half-smile, almost cunningly but with that innocent cunning with which children get the better of one another at their games. Then she swayed away again, moving slowly but none the less vanishing quickly from his sight, with a thousand bends and movements of the wide shawl wrapped about her young but sturdy figure. The oriental design and lively colors of the shawl could long be seen between the houses on the farther bank.

Only then did the young man wake from his reverie. He stood in the same place and in the same position as he had been at the moment when she had passed before him. With a start he fingered his rifle and looked around him with the sensation of a man who has let slip his opportunity. Stevan was still dozing in the deceptive March sun. It seemed to the young man that both of them had in some way failed in their duty and that a whole army platoon could have passed by them without him being able to say how many of them there were, or what significance they might have had for himself or for others. Ashamed of himself, he woke Stevan in exaggerated zeal and they both remained on guard until their relief arrived.

All that day, both when he was off duty and while he was mounting guard, the picture of the young Turkish girl passed like a vision countless times through his mind. Next day, once again about noon when there were very few people on the bridge, she again crossed. Fedun again saw that face framed in the brightly-colored shawl. All was as it had been the day before. Only their glances were longer, livelier and bolder, almost as if they were playing a game together. Stevan was again drowsing on the stone bench and later, as he always did, swore that he had not been asleep and that even when he was at home in bed he could not close an eye. On the way back the girl seemed almost ready to stop, looked the *streifkorps* boy straight in the eyes while he muttered a couple of vague and unimportant words, feeling as he did so that his legs failed him through emotion and forgetting completely where he was.

Only in dreams do we dare so much. When the girl was once more lost to sight on the farther bank the young man shivered with fright. It was incredible that a young Turkish girl should think of looking at an Austrian soldier. Such an unheard-of and unprecedented thing could only happen in dreams, in dreams or in spring on the *kapia*. He knew very well that nothing in this land or in his position was as scandalous and as dangerous as to touch a Moslem woman. They had told him that when he had been in the army and again in the *streifkorps*. The punishment for such daring was a heavy one. There had been some who had paid with their lives at the hands of the insulted and infuriated Turks. All that he knew, and most sincerely desired to keep the orders and regulations, but none the less he acted contrary to them. The misfortune of unlucky men lies in just this, that those things which for them are impossible and forbidden become in a moment easy and attainable, or at least appear so. Yet when once such things are firmly fixed in their desires they seem once again as they were, unattainable and forbidden, with all the consequences that they have for those who, despite everything, still attempt them.

On the third day too, about noon, the Turkish girl appeared. And as it is in dreams all took place as he would have wished, like a unique reality to which all else was subordinate. Stevan was again drowsing, convinced and always ready to convince others that he had not closed an eye; there were no passers-by on the *kapia*. The young man spoke again, muttering a few words, and the girl slowed her pace and replied, equally timidly and vaguely.

The dangerous and incredible game went on. On the fourth day the girl in passing, choosing a moment when there was no one on the *kapia,* asked in a whisper when he would next be on guard. He told her that he would be on duty on the *kapia* again at dusk.

"I will bring my old grandmother to the market-place, where she is to spend the night, and I will return alone," whispered the girl without stopping or turning her head, but darting a provocative and eloquent glance at him. And in each of those very ordinary words was the hidden joy that she would soon see him again.

Six hours later Fedun was once more on the *kapia* with his sleepy comrade. After the rain a chill twilight had fallen which seemed to him full of promise.

Passers-by became fewer and fewer. Then on the road from Osojnica the Turkish girl appeared, wrapped in her shawl, its colors dimmed by the twilight. Beside her walked an old, bowed Turkish woman bundled up in a thick black *feridjah.* She walked almost on all fours, supporting herself by a staff in her right hand and holding on to the girl with her left.

They passed by Fedun. The girl walked slowly, accommodating her pace to the slow walk of the old crone whom she was leading. Her eyes, made larger by the shadows of early dusk, now gazed boldly and openly into the young man's as if they could not look away from him. When they disappeared into the market-place, a shiver passed through the youth and he began to pace with more rapid steps from one terrace to the other as if he wanted to make up for what he had lost. With an excitement that was almost fear he waited for the girl's return. Stevan was dozing.

"What will she say to me when she passes?" thought the youth. "What shall I say to her? Will she perhaps suggest meeting somewhere at night in a quiet spot?" He quivered with delight and the excitement of danger lay in that thought.

A whole hour passed thus, waiting, and the half of another, and still the girl did not return. But even in that waiting there was delight. His eagerness rose with the falling darkness. At last, instead of the girl, his relief came. But this time not only the two *streifkorps* men who were to remain there on guard but also the sergeant-major Draženović in person. A strict man with a short black beard, he ordered Fedun and Stevan in a sharp and strident voice to go to the dormitory as soon as they reached barracks and not to leave it until further orders. The blood rushed to Fedun's face at the idea that he was in some way to blame.

The huge chill dormitory with twelve regularly spaced out beds was empty. The men were all at supper or in the town. Fedun and Stevan waited, troubled and impatient, thinking things over and making vain guesses why the sergeant-major had been so stern and had so unexpectedly confined them to barracks. After an hour, when the first of the soldiers began to come in to sleep, a corporal burst in and ordered them loudly and harshly to follow him. From everything about him, the two felt that the severity against them was increasing and that all this presaged no good. As soon as they left the dormitory they were separated and questioned.

The night wore on. Even the last lights in the town were extinguished, but the windows of the barracks still blazed with light. From time to time there was a ring at the main gates, the clink of keys and the thud of heavy doors. Orderlies came and went, hurrying through the dark and sleeping town between the barracks and the *konak,* where lamps also burned on the first floor. It could be seen from all these signs that something unusual was afoot.

When, about eleven o'clock at night, they brought Fedun into the sergeant-major's office, it seemed to him that days and weeks had passed from those moments on the *kapia.* On the table burned a metal oil-lamp with a shade of green porcelain. By it was seated the major Krčmar. The light fell on his arms up to the elbows, but the upper half of his body and his head were in shadow cast by the green shade. The young man knew that pale, full, almost womanly face, clean-shaven, with fine moustaches and dark rings around the eyes. The soldiers feared the slow heavy words of this big placid officer. There were few of them who could endure for long the gaze of those large gray eyes, and who did not stammer when replying to his questions, in which each word was softly yet separately, distinctly and clearly enunciated from the first to the last syllable as at school or in the theater. A little away from the table stood the sergeant-major Draženović. The whole upper part of his body also was in shadow and only his hands were strongly illuminated, hanging limply at his side; on one finger glistened a heavy gold ring.

Draženović opened the interrogation:

"Tell us how you passed the time between five and seven o'clock while you were with assistant *streifkorps* private Stevan Kalacan on guard duty on the *kapia?*"

The blood rushed to Fedun's head. Every man passed his time as best he could, but no one had ever thought that he would later have to answer for it before some strict judge and give account of everything that had taken place, to the minutest detail, to the most hidden thoughts and the last minute. No one, least of all when one is twenty-three years old and that time has been spent on the *kapia* in spring. What was he to answer? Those two hours on guard had passed as they had always done, as they had done the day before and the day before that. But at that moment he could not remember anything everyday and usual which he could report. Only incidental, forbidden things rose in his memory, things that happen to everyone but which are not told to one's superiors; that Stevan had dozed as usual; that he, Fedun, had exchanged a few words with an unknown Turkish girl, that then, as dusk was falling, he had sung softly and fervently all the songs of his own country awaiting the girl's return and with it something exciting and unusual. How hard it was to reply, impossible to tell everything but embarrassing to remain silent. And he must hurry, for time was passing and that only increased his confusion and embarrassment. How long had his silence lasted already?

"Well?" said the major. Everyone knew that "well" of his, clear, smooth and forceful like the sound of some strong, complex and well-oiled machine.

Fedun began to stammer and get confused as though he felt himself guilty from the very start.

The night wore on, but the lamps were not extinguished either in the barracks or in the *konak*. Interrogations, evidence and the confrontation of witnesses followed one another. Others who had mounted guard on the *kapia* that day were also interrogated. But it was clear that the net was closing around Fedun and Stevan and, in their interrogation, about the old Turkish woman whom a young girl had taken across the bridge.

It seemed to the young man as if all the magical and inextricable responsibilities that he had felt in his dreams were falling on his shoulders. Before dawn he was confronted with Stevan. The peasant closed his eyes cunningly and spoke in a forced voice, continually harking back to the fact that he was an illiterate man, a peasant, and sheltering himself from all responsibility by always referring to "that Mr. Fedun" as he insisted on calling his companion on guard.

That's the way to answer, the young man thought to himself. His entrails were crying out from hunger and he himself was trembling all over from emotion though it was still not clear to him what this was all about and where exactly lay the question of his guilt or innocence. But morning brought complete explanation.

All through that night a fantastic round-dance whirled about him; in its center was the major, cold and implacable. Himself dumb and unmoving, he allowed no one else to be silent or at peace. In bearing and appearance he no longer seemed like a man, but like duty embodied, the terrible ministrant of justice inaccessible to weakness or sentiment, gifted with supernatural strength and immune from the ordinary human needs of food, rest or sleep. When dawn broke, Fedun was once again brought before the major. There was now in the office, besides the major and Draženović, an armed gendarme and a woman who, at first sight, seemed unreal to the young man. The lamp had been extinguished. The room, facing north, was cold and in semi-darkness. The young man felt as if this were a continuation of his dream of the night before which refused to pale and vanish even in the light of day.

"Is that the man who was on guard?" Draženović asked the woman.

With a great effort which caused him pain Fedun only then looked full at her. She was the Moslem girl of the day before, only bareheaded without her shawl and with her heavy chestnut plaits wrapped around her head. She was wearing brightly colored Turkish trousers, but the rest of her dress, blouse, sash and bolero, was that of the Serbian girls from the villages on the high plateau above the town. Without her shawl, she seemed older and sturdier. Her face seemed different, her mouth large and bad-tempered, her eyelids reddened and her eyes clear and flashing as if the shadows of the day before had fled from them.

"It is," the woman replied indifferently in a hard voice which was as new and unusual to Fedun as her present appearance.

Draženović went on asking her how many times in all she had crossed the bridge, what she had said to Fedun and he to her. She replied for the most part precisely, but proudly and indifferently.

"Good, Jelenka, and what did he say to you the last time you crossed?"

"He said something but I don't know exactly what, for I was not listening but only thinking how I could get Jakov across."

"You were thinking of that?"

"Of that," answered the woman unwillingly. She was clearly worn out and did not want to say more than she must. But the sergeant-major was inexorable. In a threatening voice which betrayed his conviction that he must be answered without argument he forced the woman to repeat all that she had said at her first interrogation at the *konak*.

She defended herself, shortened and skipped various bits of her earlier evidence, but he always checked her and by sharp and skillful questioning made her go back over it all again.

Little by little the whole truth was laid bare. Her name was Jelenka and she came from the village of Tasić in Upper Lijeska. Last autumn the *haiduk* Jakov Čekrlija had come into her district to pass the winter hidden in a stable above her village. They had brought him food and clothing from her house. For the most part it had been she who had brought it. They had liked the look of each other and had become lovers. When the snow began to melt and the *streifkorps* squads came more frequently, Jakov had decided to cross into Serbia at all costs. At that time of year the Drina was hard to cross even if it had not been patroled and there had not been a permanent guard on the bridge. She had gone with him, determined to help him even at the risk of her life. They had first descended to Lijeska and then to a cave above Okolište. Earlier, on Glasinac, Jakov had obtained some Turkish women's clothes from some gipsies; a *feridjah,* Turkish trousers and a shawl. Then she, on his instructions, began to cross the bridge at a time when there were not many Turks about, since one of them might ask who was that unknown girl, and in order that the guard might grow accustomed to her. Thus she crossed three days running, and then decided to take Jakov with her.

"And why did you take him across

when this particular soldier was on guard?"

"Because he seemed to me the softest of them."

"So?"

"So."

At the sergeant-major's insistence the woman continued. When everything had been prepared, Jakov had wrapped himself in the *feridjah* and just as it was beginning to get dark she took him disguised as her old grandmother across the bridge past the guard. The guard had noticed nothing, for this young man was looking at her and not at the old woman, while the other, older guard was sitting on the *sofa* dozing.

When they got to the market-place, they had taken the precaution of not going right across it, but had used the side-streets. It was this had proved their undoing. They had lost their way in the town, which neither of them knew, and instead of coming out at the bridge across the Rzav and thus joining the road which led from the town towards both frontiers, they had found themselves in front of a Turkish café, just as some people were coming out. One of them was a Turkish gendarme, born in the town. This closely wrapped up old woman and the girl whom he had never seen before seemed suspect to him, and he followed them. He kept them in sight as far as the Rzav. Then he came nearer to ask them who they were and where they were going. Jakov, who had been watching him attentively through his face-veil, considered that the moment had come to flee. He threw off his *feridjah,* and pushed Jelenka at the gendarme so violently that they both lost their footing ("for he is small and insignificant to look at, but as strong as the earth and courageous above all other men"). She, as she calmly and clearly confessed, tangled herself with the legs of the gendarme. By the time that the gendarme had freed himself of her, Jakov had already rushed across the Rzav as if it had been a stream, though the water was above his knees, and was lost in the willow clumps on the farther side. Then they had taken her to the *konak,* beaten and threatened her, but she had nothing more to say and would say nothing more.

In vain the sergeant-major tried evasive questions, flatteries and threats to get something more out of the girl, to learn from her about others who helped or sheltered bandits, or about Jakov's further intentions. All this had not the slightest effect on her. She had spoken freely enough of what she wanted to tell but despite all Draženović's efforts they could not get a word out of her about what she did not want to tell.

"It would be better for you to tell us all you know than for us to question and torture Jakov who has surely by now been caught on the frontier."

"Caught who? Him? Ha, ha!"

The girl looked at the sergeant-major with pity, as at a man who does not know what he is talking about, and the right corner of her upper lip rose disdainfully. In fact the movement of this upper lip, which looked like a writhing leech, expressed her feelings of anger, disdain or pride, whenever those feelings grew more than she could express in words. That writhing movement gave for a moment to her otherwise beautiful and regular face a troubled and unpleasant expression. Then with some quite childlike and fervent expression completely in contrast to that ugly writhing she looked out of the window as a peasant looks at a field when he wants to gauge the influence of the weather on the harvest.

"God help you! It's dawn now. From last night till now he has had time to get across all Bosnia, not merely to cross a frontier only an hour or two's march away. I know that much. You can beat me and kill me, I came with him for that, but him you will never see again. Don't even dream of it! Ha!"

Her upper lip writhed and lifted and her whole face seemed suddenly older, more experienced, bold and ugly. And when that lip suddenly ceased to writhe, her face again took on that childlike expression of bold and innocent daring.

Not knowing what more to do, Draženović looked at the major, who gave a sign to send the girl away. Then he resumed the interrogation of Fedun. This could no longer be either long or hard. The young man admitted everything and had nothing to put forward in his own defense, not even what Draženović himself had hinted at in his questions. Not even the major's words which contained a merciless and implacable judgment, but in which none the less there was restrained pain because of their own severity, could wake the youth from his torpor.

"I had always considered you, Fedun," Krčmar said in German, "a serious young man, conscious of your duties and of your aim in life, and I had thought that one day you would become a perfect soldier, a credit to our unit. But you have been blinded by the first female animal to run in front of your nose. You have behaved like a weakling, like one to whom serious work cannot be entrusted. I am forced to hand you over to court-martial. But whatever its sentence may be, your greatest punishment will be to know that you have not shown yourself worthy of the confidence placed in you and that at the right moment you were unable to behave at your post like a man and a soldier. Now go."

Not even these words, heavy, curt, carefully enunciated, could bring anything fresh to the young man's mind. He felt all that already. The appearance and speech of that woman, the bandit's mistress, the behavior of Stevan and the whole course of that short enquiry had suddenly revealed to him in its true light his thoughtless, naïve and unpardonable spring fever on the *kapia*. The major's words only seemed to him to place the official seal on all that; they were more necessary to the major himself, in order to satisfy some unwritten but eternal demand for law and order, than to Fedun. As before a prospect of unsuspected grandeur, the young man found himself faced with a knowledge that he could not grasp; the meaning of a few moments of forgetfulness in an evil hour and in a dangerous place. Had they been lived through and remained unknown, there on the *kapia,* they would have meant nothing at all; one of those youthful pranks later told to friends during dull patrol duties at night. But thus, reduced to a question of definite responsibility, they meant everything. They meant more than death, they meant the end of everything, an unwanted and unworthy end. There would be no more full and frank explanations either to himself or to comrades. There would be no more letters from Kolomea, no more family photographs, no money orders such as he had sent home with pride. It was the end of one who has deceived himself and allowed others to deceive him.

Therefore he found not a word to reply to the major.

The supervision over Fedun was not particularly strict. They gave him breakfast, which he ate as though with someone else's mouth, and ordered him to pack up his personal effects, hand in his arms and all government property and be ready to leave at ten o'clock accompanied by a gendarme by the postal courier for Sarajevo, where he would be handed over to the garrison court.

While the young man was taking down his things from the shelf above his bed, those of his comrades who were still in the dormitory tiptoed out, closing the door carefully and silently behind them.

Around him grew that circle of loneliness and deep silence which is always formed around a man whom ill fortune has struck, as around a sick animal. First he took off its hooks the black tablet on which his name, rank, detachment number and unit were written in oil colors in German and placed it on his knees, with the writing down. On the black back of the tablet the young man scribbled hastily with a scrap of chalk: "All that I leave please send to my father at Kolomea. I send greetings to all my comrades and beg my superiors to pardon me. G. Fedun." Then he looked once more through the window, relishing that little piece of the outside world that he was able to see through its narrow frame. Then he took down his rifle, loaded it with a single charge of ball still sticky with grease. Then he took off his shoes and with a penknife cut his stocking over his big toe, lay down on the bed, wrapped his arms and legs around the rifle so that the top of the barrel was pressed firmly beneath his chin, shifted his right leg so that the hole in his stocking fitted over the trigger and pressed. The sound of the shot rang through the barracks.

After a great decision, everything becomes simple and easy. The doctor came. A Commission of Enquiry was held and attached to its findings a record in duplicate of Fedun's interrogation.

Then arose the question of Fedun's burial. Draženović was ordered to go to Pop Nikola and discuss the matter with him; could Fedun be buried in the graveyard even though he had taken his own life, and would the priest agree to conduct the service, for the deceased was by faith a Uniate.

In the last year Pop Nikola had suddenly grown old and weak in his legs, so he had taken as assistant for his great parish Pop Joso, a taciturn and nervous sort of man, thin and black as a spent match. In the previous few months, he had carried out almost all the duties of the priest and the services in the town and villages, while Pop Nikola, who could only move with difficulty, dealt mainly with what he could do at home or in the church next to his house.

By the major's order, Draženović went to Pop Nikola. The old man received him lying on a divan; by him stood Pop Joso. After Draženović had explained the circumstances of Fedun's death and the question of his burial, both priests remained silent for a moment. Seeing that Pop Nikola did not speak, Pop Joso began first, timidly and uncertainly; the matter was exceptional and unusual, there were difficulties both in the canons of the church and in established custom, but if it could be shown that the suicide had not been of sound mind then something might be done. But then Pop Nikola sat up on his hard and narrow couch, covered with an old and faded rug. His body once again assumed that monumental form which it had once had when he walked through the marketplace and was greeted on all sides. The first word that he said illuminated his broad and still ruddy face, with his huge moustaches which tangled in his beard and his heavy almost white eyebrows, thick and bushy, the face of a man who has learned from birth how to think independently, to give his opinion sincerely and to defend it well.

Without hesitation and without big words he answered both priest and sergeant-major directly:

"Now that the misfortune has happened, there is nothing more to be done about it. Who with a sound mind would ever raise his hand against himself? And who would dare to take it on his soul to bury him as if he were without faith, somewhere behind a fence and without a priest? But you, sir, go and give orders that the dead man be prepared and we shall bury him as soon as we can. In the graveyard, most certainly! I will sing his requiem. Later, if ever some priest of his law should happen to pass this way, let him add or alter as he wishes, should he not find everything to his liking."

When Draženović had left, he turned once more to Pop Joso, who was astonished and humiliated.

"How could we forbid a Christian to be buried in the graveyard? And why should I not sing his requiem? Isn't it enough that he had bad luck when he was alive? There, on the other side, let those ask about his sins who will ask all the rest of us about ours."

Thus the young man who had made his mistake on the *kapia* remained forever in the town. He was buried the following morning. Pop Nikola sang the requiem, assisted by the sacristan Dimitrije.

One by one his comrades of the *streifkorps* filed past the grave and each threw on it a handful of earth. While two sextons worked rapidly, they stood there a few seconds longer as if waiting for orders, looking across to the far side of the river where, close to their own barracks, rose a straight white column of smoke. There, on the level patch of grass above the barracks, they were burning the bloodstained straw from Fedun's mattress.

The cruel fate of the young *streifkorps* boy, whose name no one ever remembered and who had paid with his life for a few spring moments of inattention and emotion on the *kapia,* was one of those incidents for which the townspeople had much understanding and long remembered and repeated. The memory of that sensitive and unlucky youth lasted far longer than the guard on the *kapia.*

By next autumn the insurrection in Herzegovina had fizzled out. A few of the more important leaders, Moslems and Serbs, fled to Montenegro or Turkey. There remained only a few *haiduks* who in fact never had much real connection with the insurrection about conscription but had worked for themselves. Then those too were either captured or driven away. Herzegovina was pacified. Bosnia gave recruits without resistance. But the departure of the first recruits was neither simple nor easy.

Not more than 100 young men were taken from the entire district, but on the day they were mustered before the *konak,* peasants with their bags and a few townsmen with their wooden chests, it seemed as if there were plague and uproar in the town. Many of the recruits had been drinking steadily from early morning and mixing their drinks. The peasants were in clean white shirts. There were few who had not been drinking and these sat near their belongings, drowsing behind a wall. The majority were excited, flushed with drink and sweating in the heat of the day. Four or five boys from the same village would embrace, and then put their heads close together and swaying like a living forest begin a harsh and long-drawn chanting as if they were the only people in the world.

"Oy my mai-ai-ai-ai-den! O-o-o-y!"

A far greater commotion than that made by the recruits themselves was made by the women, mothers, sisters and other relatives of the young men, who had come from distant villages to say farewell, to see them for the last time, to weep, to wail and to give them some last gift or final sign of love. The square near the bridge was packed with women. They sat there as if turned to stone, talked among themselves and from time to time wiped away their tears with the fringes of their kerchiefs. In vain it had been earlier explained to them in their villages that the young men were going neither to war nor to slavery, but that they would serve the Emperor in Vienna, and be well fed, well clothed and well shod; that after a term of two years they would return home, and that young men from all the other parts of the Empire served in the army, and that they served for a three-year term. All that passed over their heads like the wind, foreign and completely incomprehensible. They listened only to their instincts and would only be guided by them. These ancient and inherited instincts brought tears to their eyes and a wail to their throats, forced them persistently to follow as long as they could and try to get a last glance at him whom they loved more than life and whom an unknown Emperor was carrying off into an unknown land, to unknown trials and tasks. In vain even now the gendarmes and officials from the *konak* went among them and assured them that there was no reason for such exaggerated grief, and advised them not to block the way nor rush after the recruits and create trouble and disorder, for they would all return hale and hearty. But it was all in vain. The women listened to them, agreed to all they said dully and humbly and then returned once more to their tears and wailing. It seemed as if they loved their tears and their wailing as much as they loved those for whom they wept.

When the time came to move and the young men were drawn up in four ranks in the correct manner and moved across the bridge, a crowding and rushing began in which even the most equable of gendarmes could hardly retain his composure. The women ran and tore themselves from the hands of the gendarmes in order to be beside someone of their own, pushing and overturning one another. Their wails were mingled with cries, entreaties and last-moment recommendations. Some of them even ran in front of the line of recruits whom four gendarmes were keeping in file and fell under their feet, clutching at their bare breasts and shouting:

"Over my body! Over my body!"

The men lifted them up with difficulty, carefully disentangling boots and spurs from dishevelled hair and disordered skirts.

Some of the recruits, ashamed, tried by angry gestures to make the women return home. But most of the young men sang or shouted, increasing the general disorder. The few townsmen among them, pale with emotion, sang together in the town manner:

"In Sarajevo and Bosnia
Every mother mourns
Who has sent her son
As a recruit for the Emperor. . . ."

This song created even greater weeping.

When, somehow or other, they crossed the bridge towards which the whole convoy was headed and took the Sarajevo road, all the townspeople were awaiting them, drawn up on each side of the road, in order to see the recruits and to weep for them as if they were being taken away to be shot. There were many women there too who wept for every one of them although none of their own relations was among those who were going. For every woman has some reason to weep and weeping is sweetest when it is for another's sorrow.

But little by little the ranks along the road became sparser. Even some of the peasant women gave up. The most persistent were the mothers who ran around the convoy as though they were fifteen years old, leaped the ditch at the side of the road from one side to the other and tried to outwit the gendarmes and stay as long as possible close to their sons. When they saw that, the young men themselves, pale with emotion and a sort of embarrassment, turned and shouted:

"Get along home when I tell you!"

But the mothers went on for long, blind to all save the sons that were being taken from them and listening to nothing save their own weeping.

But even these troublous days passed. The people dispersed to their villages and the town again grew calm. When letters and the first photographs from the recruits in Vienna began to arrive, everything became easier and more tolerable. The women wept for long over those letters and photographs, but more gently and more calmly.

The *streifkorps* was disbanded and left the barracks. For a long time there had been no guard on the *kapia* and the townsfolk went on sitting there as they had done before.

Two years quickly pass. That autumn the first recruits returned from Vienna, clean, close-cropped and well-fed. The people clustered around them as they told tales of army life and of the greatness of the cities they had seen, their talk interlarded with strange names and unfamiliar expressions. At the next call-up there was less weeping and agitation.

Generally speaking, everything became easier and more normal. Young men grew up who no longer had any clear or lively memory of Turkish times and who had to a great extent accepted the new ways. But on the *kapia* they still lived according to the ancient custom of the town. Without regard for the new fashions of dress, new professions and new trades, the townspeople still went on meeting there as they had done for centuries past, in those conversations which had always been and still were a real need of their hearts and their imaginations. The recruits went to their service without uproar and without commotion. The *haiduks* were mentioned only in old men's tales. The *streifkorps* was forgotten as completely as that earlier Turkish guard when there had been a blockhouse on the *kapia.*

14

Life in the town beside the bridge became more and more animated, seemed more and more orderly and fuller, assuming an even pace and a hitherto unknown balance, that balance towards which all life tends, everywhere and at all times, and which is only rarely, partially and temporarily achieved.

In the far-off cities unknown to the townsmen whence at that time the power and administration over these districts originated, there was—in the last quarter of the nineteenth century—one of those short and rare lulls in human relationships and social events. Something of that lull could be felt even in these remote districts, just as a great calm at sea may be felt even in the most distant creeks.

Such were those three decades of relative prosperity and apparent peace in the Franz-Josef manner, when many Europeans thought that there was some infallible formula for the realization of a centuries-old dream of full and happy development of individuality in freedom and in progress, when the nineteenth century spread out before the eyes of millions of men its many-sided and deceptive prosperity and created its *fata morgana* of comfort, security and happiness for all and everyone at reasonable prices and even on credit terms. But to this remote Bosnian township only broken echoes penetrated of all this life of the nineteenth century, and those only to the extent and in the form in which this backward oriental society could receive them and in its own manner understand and accept them.

After the first years of distrust, misunderstanding and hesitation, when the first feeling of transience had passed, the town began to find its place in the new order of things. The people found order, work and security. That was enough to ensure that here too life, outward life at least, set out "on the road of perfection and progress." Everything else was flushed away into that dark background of consciousness where live and ferment the basic feelings and indestructible beliefs of individual races, faiths and castes, which, to all appearances dead and buried, are preparing for later far-off times unsuspected changes and catastrophes without which, it seems, people cannot exist and above all the peoples of this land.

The new authorities, after the first misunderstandings and clashes, left among the townspeople a definite impression of firmness and of permanence (they were themselves impregnated with this belief without which there can be no strong and permanent authority). They were impersonal and indirect and for that reason more easily bearable than the former Turkish rulers. All that was cruel and grasping was concealed by the dignity and glitter of traditional forms. The people still feared the authorities but in much the same way as they feared sickness and death and not as one fears malice, misery and oppression. The representatives of the new authority, military as well as civil, were for the most part newcomers to the land and unskillful in their dealings with the people and were themselves of little importance, but with every step they made they felt themselves to be part of a greater mechanism and that behind each one of them stood more powerful men and greater organizations in long rows and countless gradations. That gave them a standing which far surpassed their own personality and a magic influence to which it was easier to submit. By their titles which appeared to be great, by their calm and their European customs, they aroused among the people, from whom they so greatly differed, feelings of confidence and respect and did not excite envy or real criticism, even though they were neither pleasant nor loved.

On the other hand, after a certain time, even these newcomers were unable to avoid completely the influence of the unusual oriental milieu in which they had to live. Their children introduced the children of the townspeople to strange phrases and foreign names, brought with them new games and toys, but equally they easily picked up from the local children the old songs, ways of speech, oaths and the traditional games of knuckle-bones, leap-frog and the like. It was the same with the grown-ups; they too brought a new order, with unfamiliar words and habits, but at the same time they too accepted every day something of the speech and manner of life of the older inhabitants. It is true that the local people, especially the Christians and Jews, began to look more and more like the newcomers in dress and behavior, but the newcomers themselves did not remain unchanged or untouched by the milieu in which they had to live. Many of these officials, the fiery Magyar or the haughty Pole, crossed the bridge with reluctance and entered the town with disgust and, at first, were a world apart, like drops of oil in water. Yet a year or so later they could be found sitting for hours on the *kapia,* smoking through thick amber cigarette-holders and, as if they had been born in the town, watching the smoke expand and vanish under the clear sky in the motionless air of dusk; or they would sit and wait for supper with the local notables on some green hillock, with plum brandy and snacks and a little bouquet of basil before them, conversing leisurely about trivialities or drinking slowly and occasionally munching a snack as the townsmen knew how to do so well. There were some among these newcomers, officials or artisans, who married in the town and had decided never to leave it.

But for none of the townspeople did the new life mean the realization of what they felt deep down within themselves and had always desired; on the contrary all of them, Moslems and Christians alike, had taken their place in it with many and definite reservations, but these reservations were secret and concealed, whereas life was open and powerful with new and apparently great possibilities. After a longer or shorter period of wavering, most of them fell in with the new ideas, did their business, made fresh acquisitions, and lived according to the new ideas and customs which offered greater scope and, it seemed, gave greater chances to every individual.

Not that the new existence was in any way less subject to conditions or less restricted than in Turkish times, but it was easier and more humane, and those conditions and restrictions were now far away and skillfully enforced, so that the individual did not feel them directly. Therefore it seemed to everyone as if the life around him had suddenly grown wider and clearer, more varied and fuller.

The new state, with its good administrative apparatus, had succeeded in a painless manner, without brutality or commotion, to extract taxes and contributions from the local people which the Turkish authorities had extracted by crude and irrational methods or by simple plunder; and, moreover, it got as much or more, even more swiftly and surely.

Even as the gendarmes, in their own time, had replaced the soldiers and after the soldiers had come the officials, so now, after the officials, came the merchants. Felling began in the forests and brought with it foreign contractors, engineers and workers, and provided varied sources of gain for the ordinary people and traders, with changes in dress and speech. The first hotel was built, of which we shall have much to say later. Canteens and workshops sprang up which had not been known hitherto. Besides the Spanish-speaking Jews, the Sephardi, who had been living in the town for hundreds of years, for they had first settled there about the time when the bridge had been built, there now came the Galician Jews, the Ashkenazi.

Like fresh blood, money began to circulate in hitherto unknown quantities and, which was the main thing, publicly, boldly and openly. In that exciting circulation of gold, silver and negotiable paper, every man could warm his hands or at least "gladden his eyes," for it created even for the poorest of men the illusion that his own bad luck was only temporary and therefore the more bearable.

Earlier too there had been money and rich people, but these last had been rare and had concealed their money like a snake its legs and had revealed their superiority only as a form of power and protection, difficult both for themselves and for those about them. Now wealth, or what passed as such and was so named, was openly displayed in the form of pleasure and personal satisfaction, therefore the mass of the people could see something of its glitter and its gleanings.

So it was with all else. Pleasures which up till then had been stolen and concealed could now be purchased and openly displayed, which increased their attraction and the number of those who sought them. What had earlier been unattainable, far off and expensive (forbidden by law or all-powerful custom) now became, in many cases, possible and attainable to all who had or who knew.

Many passions, appetites and demands which till then had been hidden in remote places or left completely unsatisfied could now be boldly and openly sought and fully or at least partially satisfied. In fact even in that there was greater restriction, order and legal hindrance; vices were punished and enjoyments paid for even more heavily and dearly than before, but the laws and methods were different and allowed the people, in this as in all else, the illusion that life had suddenly become wider, more luxurious and freer.

There were not many more real pleasures nor, certainly, more happiness but it was undoubtedly easier to come by such pleasures and it seemed that there was room for everyone's happiness. The old inborn partiality of the people of Višegrad for a carefree life of enjoyment found both support and possibilities of realization in the new customs and the new forms of trading and profit brought by the newcomers. Immigrant Polish Jews with their numerous families based all their business on that. Schreiber opened what he called a "general store," Gutenplan a canteen for the soldiers, Zahler ran a hotel, the Sperling brothers set up a soda-water factory and a photographer's "atelier" and Zveker a jeweler's and watchmaker's shop.

After the barracks which had replaced the Stone Han, Municipal Offices were built of the stone that remained, with local administrative offices and courts. After these, the largest building in the town was the Zahler Hotel. It was built on the river bank just beside the bridge. That right bank had been supported by an ancient retaining wall which shored up the bank on both sides of the bridge and had been built at the same time. So it happened that both to left and right of the bridge stretched two level spaces, like two terraces above the water. On these open spaces, which were called racecourses by the people of the town, children had played from generation to generation. Now the local authorities took over the left-hand "racecourse," put a fence round it and made a sort of municipal botanical garden. On the right-hand one the hotel was built. Until then the first building at the entry to the market-place had been Zarije's inn. It was "in the right place," for the tired and thirsty traveler on entering the town from across the bridge must first light on it. Now overshadowed by the great building of the new hotel, the low old inn seemed every day lower and more humiliated as if it had sunk into the earth.

Officially the new hotel had been given the name of the bridge beside which it had been built. But the townspeople named everything according to their own special logic and according to the real significance it had for them. Over the entrance of the Zahler Hotel the inscription "Hotel zur Brücke," which a soldier skilled in the trade had painted in large letters, quickly faded. The people called it "Lotte's Hotel" and the name stuck. For the hotel was run by the fat and phlegmatic Jew, Zahler, who had a sickly wife, Deborah, and two little girls, Mina and Irene, but the real proprietress was Zahler's sister-in-law Lotte, a young and very pretty widow with a free tongue and a masculine energy.

On the top floor of the hotel were six clean and well-furnished guest-rooms and on the ground floor two public rooms, one large and one small. The large one was patronized by the humbler clients, ordinary citizens, noncommissioned officers and artisans. The smaller one was separated from the larger by large frosted-glass doors on one of which was written EXTRA and on the other ZIMMER. That was the social center for officials, officers and the richer townspeople. One drank and played cards, sang, danced, held serious conversations and closed business deals, ate well and slept well in clean sheets at Lotte's. It often happened that the same group of begs, merchants and officials would sit from dusk until dawn and still go on until they collapsed from drink and lack of sleep or grew so tired over their cards that they could no longer distinguish them (they no longer played hidden away secretly in that dark stuffy cubby-hole at Ustamujić's inn). Those who had drunk too much or had lost all they had Lotte would see off the premises and then turn to welcome fresh and sober guests eager for drink and play. No one knew and no one ever asked when that woman rested, when she slept or ate and when she found time to dress and freshen herself up. For she was always there (or at least so it seemed) at everyone's beck and call, always amiable, always the same and always bold and discreet. Well built, plump, with ivory-white skin, black hair and smouldering eyes, she had a perfectly assured manner of dealing with guests, who would spend freely but were often aggressive and crude when overcome by drink. She would talk sweetly, boldly, wittily, sharply, flatteringly with all of them, smoothing them down. Her voice was hoarse and uneven but could at moments become a sort of deep and soothing cooing. She spoke incorrectly, for she never learned Serbian well, in her own piquant and picturesque language in which the cases were never right and the genders uncertain, but which in tone and meaning was entirely in keeping with the local way of expression. Every client had her at his disposal to listen to all his troubles and desires in recompense for the money he spent and the time he wasted. But these two things, spending money and wasting time, were all he could be sure of; everyone thought there would be more to it, whereas in fact there was not. For two generations of the rich spendthrifts of the town Lotte was a glittering, expensive and cold *fata morgana* who played with their senses. Those rare individuals who had supposedly got something out of her, but who were quite unable to say what or how much, were the subject of local stories.

It was no simple matter to know how to deal with the rich and drunk townsmen in whom unsuspected and coarse desires were often aroused. But Lotte, that untiring and cold woman of chilled passions, quick intelligence and masculine heart tamed every fury, silenced every demand of uncontrolled men by the inexplicable play of her perfect body, her great cunning and her no less great daring, and always succeeded in maintaining the necessary distance between herself and them, which only served to inflame their desires and increase her own value. She played with these uncontrolled men in their coarsest and most dangerous moments of drunkenness and rage, like a torero with a bull, for she quickly got to know the people with whom she had to deal and easily found the key to their apparently complex demands and all the weak points of those cruel and sensual sentimentalists. She offered them everything, promised much and gave little, or rather nothing at all. For their desires were, of their very nature, such as never could be satisfied and in the end they had to content themselves with little. With most of her guests she behaved as if they were sick men who from time to time had passing crises and hallucinations. In fact it could be said that despite her trade, which of its nature was neither pleasant nor particularly chaste, she was an understanding woman of kind nature and compassionate heart who could help and console whoever had spent more than he should on drinks or had lost more than he should at cards. She sent them all mad, for they were naturally mad, deceived them for they wanted to be deceived and, finally, took from them only what they had already been determined to throw away and lose. In fact she earned very much, took good care of her money and in the first few years had already managed to accumulate a considerable fortune, but she also knew how to "write off" a debt magnanimously and to forget a loss without a word. She gave to beggars and the sick and with much tact and care helped rich families who had fallen into destitution, orphans and widows from better houses, all those "ashamed poor" who did not know how to beg and were embarrassed at accepting alms. All this she did with the same skill as she showed in running the hotel and controlling the drunken, lustful and aggressive guests, taking from them all that she could, giving them nothing and yet never refusing them finally or completely.

Men who knew the world and its history often thought that it was a pity that fate had given this woman so narrow and undistinguished a part to play. Had her fate not been what or where it was, who knows what this wise and humane woman, who did not think only of herself and who, predatory yet unselfish, beautiful and seductive but also chaste and cold, ran a small town hotel and emptied the pockets of petty Casanovas, could have been or could have given to the world. Perhaps she would have been one of those famous women of whom history tells and who have controlled the destinies of great families, of courts or states, always turning everything to good.

At that time, about 1885, when Lotte was at the height of her powers, there were rich men's sons who spent days and nights in the hotel, in that special room with doors of milky frosted glass. In the early evening they would drowse there, beside the stove, forgetting in dreams or fatigue where they were or why they were sitting there or what they were waiting for. Profiting by this lull, Lotte would withdraw into a little room on the first floor intended for the potboys, which she had converted into her "office" where she allowed no one to enter. That tiny room was heaped up with every kind of furniture, with photographs and objects of gold, silver and crystal. There too, hidden behind a curtain, was Lotte's green steel safe and her little desk which was quite invisible beneath a pile of papers, bills, receipts, accounts, Austrian newspapers, cuttings about the money market and lottery lists.

In that tiny overcrowded and stuffy room, whose only window, smaller than any other in the building, looked directly and at short range on to the smallest arch of the bridge, Lotte spent her spare moments and lived that second, hidden part of her life which belonged to her alone.

In it Lotte, in those hours of stolen freedom, read money market reports and studied prospectuses, wrote up accounts, answered letters from banks, made decisions, gave instructions, dealt with bank deposits and made fresh payments. To all those downstairs and to the world in general this was an unknown side of Lotte's work, the true and invisible part of her life. There she cast aside the smiling mask and her face grew hard and her glance sharp and somber. From this room she corresponded with her very numerous relatives, the Apfelmaiers of Tarnovo, her married sisters and brothers, various nephews and nieces and all the hordes of Jewish poor from Eastern Galicia, now scattered throughout Galicia, Austria and Hungary. She controlled the destinies of a whole dozen Jewish families, entered into the minutest details of their lives, arranged their marrying and giving in marriage, sent healing to the sick, warned and admonished the workshy and spendthrift and praised the thrifty and industrious. She resolved their family quarrels, gave counsel in cases of misunderstanding and doubt, and incited all of them to a more understanding, better and more dignified way of life and at the same time made this more possible and easier for them. For with each of her letters she sent a money order for a sum sufficient to ensure that her counsels were listened to and her advice followed and that certain spiritual or bodily needs be satisfied or shortages avoided. In this raising of the standard of the whole family and the setting of each individual member on his feet, she found her sole real satisfaction and a reward for all the burdens and renunciations of her life. With each member of the Apfelmaier family who rose even a single step in the social scale, Lotte felt that she too rose and in that found her reward for her hard work and the force to struggle onward.

Sometimes it happened that when she came up from the *Extrazimmer* so exhausted or disgusted that she had not even the strength to write or to read letters and accounts she simply went to the little window to breathe the fresh air from the river. Then her gaze would fall on that strong and graceful arch of stone, which filled the entire view, and the swift waters beneath. At dusk or dawn, in sunshine, winter moonlight or the soft light of the stars, that arch was always the same. Its two sides swept upwards, met at a sharp apex and supported one another in perfect and unwavering balance. As the years rolled on that became her only and familiar view, the dumb witness to whom this Jewess with the two faces turned in the moments when she demanded rest and freshness and when in her trade and her family trials, which she always solved for herself, she came to a dead center and a point where there was no way out.

But such restful moments never lasted long for it always happened that they were interrupted by some cry from the café below; or new clients demanding her presence or some drunkard, awakened and ready for renewed onslaughts, shouting for more drinks, for the lamps to be lighted, for the orchestra to come, and always calling for Lotte. Then she would leave her lair and, carefully locking the door with a special key, go down to welcome the guests, or by her smile and her special vocabulary to smooth down the drunkard like a newly awakened child and to help him to a chair where he could recommence his nightly session of drinking, conversation, song and spending.

Down below everything went wrong when she was not there. The guests squabbled among themselves. A beg from Crnče, young, pale and haggard, spilled every drink brought to him, retorted to everything said to him and insisted on picking quarrels with the staff or the guests. Save for a few short intervals, he had been drinking in the hotel for days past, and lusting after Lotte, but he had drunk so much and longed so greatly that it was clear that some deeper, much greater misery unknown even to himself was driving him on, something greater than his unrequited love for, and unreasonable jealousy of, the lovely Jewess from Tarnovo.

Lotte went up to him fearlessly, easily and naturally.

"What is it, Eyub? What are you making such a noise about?"

"Where have you been? I want to know where you have been . . . ," stammered the drunkard in a voice already appeased and looking at her as if she were a vision. "They are giving me some sort of poison to drink. They are poisoning me, but they do not know that I . . . if I . . ."

"Sit down, sit down quietly," the

woman consoled him, with her white perfumed hands playing just in front of the young beg's face. "Sit down. I will get you bird's milk to drink if you want it. I will get it for you myself."

She called the waiter and gave an order in German.

"Don't talk that lingo which I don't understand in front of me; all this *firtzen-fürtzen,* for I . . . well you know me. . . ."

"I know, I know, Eyub: I know no one better than you, Eyub, but you I know. . . ."

"Hm! Who have you been with? Tell me!"

The conversation between the drunken man and the sober woman maundered on without end or meaning, without sense or conclusion, beside bottles of some expensive wine and two glasses; one, Lotte's, always full and the other, Eyub's, continually filled and emptied.

While the young spendthrift stuttered and muttered on in his thick drunkard's voice about love, death, hopeless yearning and similar matters which Lotte knew by heart, for they were the stock in trade of every local drunkard, she rose, went over to the other tables at which sat the other guests who met regularly every evening in the hotel.

At one table was a group of young worthies who had only just begun to frequent the cafés and drink, town snobs for whom Zarije's inn was too boring and too ordinary and who were still intimidated by the hotel. At the others were officials, strangers, with an officer or two who had abandoned the officers' mess for that day and come down to the civilian hotel with the aim of touching Lotte for a quick loan. At a third were the engineers who were building the first forest railway for the export of timber.

In a corner reckoning something sat Pavle Ranković, one of the young but richer merchants and some Austrian or other, a contractor for the railway. Pavle was in Turkish style dress with a red fez which he did not take off in the café. His small eyes looked like two lighted slits, black and thin in his pale face, but which could widen and become unusually large and diabolically merry in exceptional moments of joy or triumph. The contractor was in a gray sports suit with high yellow laced boots which reached to his knees. The contractor was writing with a gold pencil attached to a silver chain, and Pavle with a short stub which some wood dealer, a military contractor, had left behind in his shop five years before when buying nails and hinges. They were concluding an agreement for the feeding of the workers on the line. Completely wrapped up in their tasks, they multiplied, divided and added; they ranged rows of figures, one set visible, on paper, by which each hoped to convince and deceive the other, and another, invisible and in their heads, closely and quickly reckoned, in which each for himself sought for hidden possibilities and profits.

For each of these guests Lotte found the right words, a full smile or even a silent glance full of understanding. Then she returned once more to the young beg who was again beginning to become uneasy and aggressive.

In the course of that night, throughout the whole drinking bout, with all its noisy, yearning, lachrymose or coarse phases, which she knew so well, Lotte would find a few moments in which she could go back once again to her room and in the milky light of the porcelain lamp continue her rest or her correspondence, until downstairs some scene would begin again or until they called her down.

Tomorrow was another day, just such another with the same scene of drunken spending and for Lotte the same anxieties

which she must meet with a smiling face and the same task which always seemed an easy yet desperate game.

It seemed incomprehensible and inexplicable how Lotte could manage the quantity and variety of tasks which she carried out day after day and which demanded of her more cunning than a woman has and more strength than any man could muster. But none the less she was able to finish everything, never complaining, never explaining anything to anyone, never speaking about any task which she had just finished or which still awaited her. Despite all that she always managed to find an hour or two every day for Alibeg Pašić. He was the only man whom the town believed had won Lotte's sympathy, genuinely and independently of any source of profit. But he was also the most reserved and taciturn man in the town. The eldest of the four Pašić brothers, he had never married (in the town it was believed that this was because of Lotte), never took part in business or public life. He never drank to excess or went into cafés with men of his own age. He was always of the same mood, universally amiable and restrained towards all, without distinction. Quiet and reserved, he did not avoid society or conversation, yet no one ever remembered any opinion expressed by him or ever repeated anything that he had said. He was sufficient unto himself and completely satisfied with what he was and what he seemed in the eyes of others. He himself had no need to be or to seem in any way different from what he was and no one expected him or asked him to be anything else. He was one of those men who bear their social position as some heavy and noble calling which completely fills their lives; an inborn, great and dignified position justified by itself alone and which cannot be explained, nor denied nor imitated.

With the guests in the large hall Lotte had little contact. That was the job of the waitress Malčika and the *"zahlkelner"* Gustav. Malčika was a shrewd Hungarian girl well known to the whole town who looked like the wife of some lion tamer, and Gustav, a small, reddish Czech-German of irascible nature, bloodshot eyes, bow legs and flat feet. They knew all the guests and all the townspeople; they knew who were or were not good payers, their habits when drunk, whom to receive coldly and whom to welcome cordially and whom not to allow to enter at all for "he was not for this hotel." They took care that the guests should drink a lot and should pay regularly, but that everything should end smoothly and well since it was Lotte's motto: "Nur kein Skandal!" If sometimes, exceptionally, it so happened that someone went unexpectedly berserk in his cups or, after already getting drunk at some less reputable café, should force his way into the room, then Milan the servant appeared, a tall broad-shouldered and hairy man from Lika, of gigantic strength, a man who spoke little and did all the odd jobs. He was always correctly dressed as a hotel servant (Lotte saw to that). He was always in his shirtsleeves, with a brown waistcoat and white shirt, with a long apron of green cloth, with sleeves rolled back summer and winter to show his huge forearms as hairy as two brushes, and with finely waxed moustaches and black hair stiff with perfumed military pomade. Milan was the man who extinguished every scandal at its very conception.

There was a long-established and consecrated tactic for this disagreeable and undesired operation. Gustav kept the furious and drunken guest in conversation until Milan came up behind him; then the *zahlkelner* suddenly moved out of the way and Milan seized the drunkard from behind, one arm round his waist and the other round his neck, so swiftly and skillfully that no one was ever able to see what "Milan's grip" really was. Then even the strongest of the town ne'er-do-wells flew like a ragdoll through the doors which Malčika held open at just the right moment, and through them into the street. At the same moment Gustav threw his hat, stick and anything else he had with him after him and Milan put the whole weight of his body and clanged down the metal shutter over the door. All this was over in the twinkling of an eye, in close co-operation and smoothly, and almost before the other guests could turn to look, the unwelcome visitor was already in the street and could, if he were really maddened, beat a few times with knife or stone on the roller-blind as the marks on it showed. But that was not a scandal in the hotel but in the street, a matter for the police who in any case always had a man on patrol in front of the hotel. It had never happened to Milan, as had been the case in other cafés, that the guest knocked anyone down or rushed through the rooms breaking tables and chairs or clung with arms and legs to the door so that afterwards not even a yoke of oxen could drag him away. Milan never brought any excessive zeal or bad humor to his task, no love of fighting or personal prejudice; therefore he finished the matter swiftly and perfectly. A minute after the expulsion he was back at his work in the kitchen or pantry as if nothing had happened. Gustav only went, as if by chance, through the *Extrazimmer* and looking at Lotte, who sat at some table with the better guests, suddenly closed both eyes which meant that something had happened but that everything was now settled. Then Lotte, without stopping her conversation or ceasing to smile, also blinked quickly and imperceptibly, which meant:

"All right, thank you; keep an eye on it!"

There remained only the question of what the expelled guest had drunk or broken. That sum Lotte wrote off in Gustav's accounts when they made up the accounts for the day, which they did late at night behind a red screen.

15

There were many ways by which the turbulent and skillfully expelled guest, if he were not immediately taken to prison from outside the hotel, could recover his spirits and his strength after the unpleasantness that had befallen him. He could totter to the *kapia* and refresh himself there in the cool breeze from the waters and the surrounding hills; or he could go to Zarije's inn which was only a little farther on, in the main square, and there freely and without hindrance grind his teeth, threaten and curse the invisible hand that had so painfully and definitely thrown him out of the hotel. There, after the solid citizens and artisans who had only come to drink their "evening nip" or chat with their fellows had dispersed, there was no scandal, nor could there be, for everyone drank as much as he liked or as much as he could pay for, everyone did and said what he liked. There was no question of asking a guest to spend money and drink up and at the same time behave as if he was sober. Though if anyone went beyond due measure there was always the solid and taciturn Zarije himself whose scowling and bad-tempered face discouraged even the most rabid drunkards and brawlers. He quietened them with a slow movement of his heavy hand and a few words in his gruff voice:

"Hey you there! Drop it! Enough of your fun and games!"

But even in that old-fashioned inn where there were no separate rooms or waiters, for there was always some fellow or other from the Sanjak to serve the drinks, new habits mingled wondrously with the old.

Withdrawn into the farthest corners the notorious addicts of plum brandy sat silent. They were lovers of shadow and silence, sitting over their plum brandy as if it were something sacred, hating movement and commotion. With burned-out stomachs, inflamed livers and disordered nerves, unshaven and uncared for, indifferent to everything else in the world and a burden even to themselves, they sat there and drank and, while drinking, waited until that magical light which shines for those completely given over to drink should at last burst upon them, that joy for which it is sweet to suffer, to decay and finally to die, but which unfortunately appears more and more rarely and shines more and more weakly.

The most noisy and talkative were the beginners, for the most part sons of local worthies, young men in those dangerous years which mark the first steps on the road to ruin, paying that tribute which all must pay to the vices of drink and idleness, some for shorter, others for longer periods. Most of them did not remain long on this road but turned away from it, founded families and devoted themselves to thrift and labor, to the daily life of a citizen with vices suppressed and passions moderated. Only an insignificant minority, accursed and preordained, continued on that road forever, choosing alcohol instead of life, that shortest and most deceptive illusion in this short and deceptive life; they lived for alcohol and were consumed by it, until they became sullen, dull and puffy like those who sat in the corners in the shadows.

Since the new ways of life began, without discipline or consideration, with more lively trade and better wages, as well as Sumbo the Gipsy who had accompanied all the townsmen's orgies for the past thirteen years with his *zurla,* or peasant clarinet, there now came often to the inn Franz Furlan with his accordion. He was a thin reddish man with a gold earring in his right ear, a wood-carver by profession, but too great a lover of wine and music. The soldiers and foreign workmen loved to listen to him.

It often happened that a *guslar* (a player on the one-stringed fiddle) could also be found there, usually some Montenegrin, thin as a hermit, poorly dressed but proud in bearing, famished but ashamed, proud but forced to accept alms. He would sit for some time in a corner, noticeably withdrawn, ordering nothing and looking straight in front of him, pretending to notice nothing and to be indifferent to everything. None the less it could be seen that he had other thoughts and intentions than his appearance revealed. Within him wrestled invisibly many contrary and irreconcilable feelings, especially the contrast between the greatness that he felt in his soul and the misery and weakness of what he was able to express and reveal before others. Therefore he was always a little confused and embarrassed. Proudly and patiently he waited for someone to ask for a song from him and then hesitantly took his *gusle* out of his bag, breathed on it, looked to see if his bow had been slackened by damp, and tuned up, all the while quite clearly wanting to attract as little attention as possible to these technical preliminaries. When he first passed the bow across the string it was still a wavering sound, uneven as a rutted road. But just as somehow or other one passes such a road, so he too through his nose with closed mouth began softly to accompany the sound and complete and harmonize it with his voice. When at last the two sounds merged into a single melancholy even note which wove an accompaniment for his song, the miserable singer changed as if by magic and all his troubled hesitation disappeared, his inner contradictions calmed and all his outer cares forgotten. The *guslar* suddenly raised his head, like a man who throws off the mask of humility, no longer having need to conceal who and what he was, and began unexpectedly in a strong voice his introductory verses:

"The sprig of basil began to weep,
O gentle dew, why fall you not upon me?"

The guests, who until then had pretended not to notice and had been chatting together, all fell silent. At these first verses all of them, Turks and Christians alike, felt the same shiver of undefined desire, of thirst for that dew which lived in themselves as in the song, without distinction or difference. But when immediately afterwards the *guslar* continued softly:

"But it was not the sprig of basil . . ."

and lifting the veil from his metaphor began to enumerate the real desires of Turks and Serbs concealed behind these words of dew and basil, there arose divided feelings among the listeners which led them along opposing paths according to what each felt within himself and what each desired or believed. But none the less, by some unwritten rule, they all quietly listened to the end of the song and, patient and enduring, did not reveal their mood, but only looked into the glasses before them where, on the shining surface of the plum brandy, they seemed to see the victories so desired, the fights, the heroes, the glory and the glitter, such as existed nowhere in the world.

It was liveliest in the inn when the younger men, sons of rich local worthies, sat down to drink. Then there was work for Sumbo and Franz Furlan and Ćorkan the One-Eyed and Šaha the Gipsy.

Šaha was a squinting gipsy woman, a bold virago who drank with anyone who could pay, but never got drunk. No orgy could be imagined without Šaha and her meaty jokes.

The men who made merry with them changed, but Ćorkan, Sumbo and Šaha were always the same. They lived on music, jokes and plum brandy. Their work lay in the time-wasting of others and their reward in others' spendings. Their true life was at night, especially in those unusual hours when healthy and happy men are asleep, when plum brandy and hitherto restrained instincts create a noisy and glittering mood and unexpected enthusiasms which are always the same yet seem always new and unimaginably beautiful. They were close-mouthed paid witnesses before whom everyone dared to show himself as he really was, or in the local expression "to show the blood beneath the skin," without having afterwards either to repent or be ashamed; with them and in their presence everything was permitted which would be considered scandalous by the rest of the world and at home would be sinful and impossible. All these rich, respected fathers and sons of good families could, in their name and to their account, be for a moment what they did not dare show themselves, at least at certain times and at least in a part of their being. The cruel could mock at them or beat them, the cowards could shout insults at them, the prodigal could reward them generously; the vain bought their flattery, the melancholic and moody their jokes and pleasantries, the debauched their boldness or their services. These were an eternal but unrecognized need of the townsmen whose spiritual lives were stunted and deformed. They were rather in the position of artists in a milieu where art is unknown. There are always such people in a town, singers, jesters, buffoons, eccentrics. When one of them grew threadbare or died, another replaced him, for besides the notorious and well known there developed fresh ones to shorten the hours and make gay the lives of new generations. But much time would have to pass before such another appeared as Salko Ćorkan the One-Eyed.

When, after the Austrian occupation, the first circus had come to the town Ćorkan had fallen in love with the tightrope walker and because of her had behaved so madly and eccentrically that he had been beaten and sent to prison, and the local worthies who had heedlessly led him astray and encouraged him to lose his head had had to pay heavy fines.

Some years had passed since then, the people had grown accustomed to many things and the arrival of strange players, clowns and conjurers no longer excited such universal and contagious sensation as had the first circus, but Ćorkan's love for the dancer was still remembered.

For a long time he had wasted his strength in doing odd jobs by day and by night helping the local begs and rich men to forget their cares in drinking and brawling. So it went from generation to generation. As some sowed their wild oats and withdrew, got married and settled down, other and younger ones who wanted to sow theirs took their places. Now Ćorkan was washed out and old before his time; he was far more often in the inn than at work and lived not so much from what he earned as from free drinks and snacks given him by the customers.

On rainy autumn nights the guests in Zarije's inn were overcome by boredom. Their thoughts came slowly and were all concerned with melancholy and unpleasant matters; speech came with difficulty and sounded empty and irritating, faces were cold, absent or mistrustful. Not even plum brandy could enliven and improve their mood. On a bench in a corner of the inn Ćorkan drowsed overcome by fatigue, the moist heat and the first glasses of plum brandy; it was raining cats and dogs.

Then one of the sullen guests at the main table mentioned, as if by chance, the dancer from the circus and Ćorkan's unhappy love. They all glanced at the corner but Ćorkan did not budge and pretended to go on dozing. Let them say what they liked; he had firmly decided that very morning, after a heavy night's drinking, not to reply to their jeering and mocking and not to let them play crude jokes on him as some of them had done the night before in that very inn.

"I believe that they still write to each other," said one.

"So you see, the bastard writes love-letters to one while another is on her knees to him here!" retorted another.

Ćorkan forced himself to remain indifferent but the conversation irritated and excited him as if the sun were burning his face; his only eye seemed as if it forced itself to open and all the muscles of his face stretched into a happy laugh. He was no longer able to maintain his motionless silence. At first he waved his hand in a casual and indifferent gesture and then said:

"All that is over, over long ago."

"All over, is it? What a wretch this fellow Ćorkan is! One girl is pining away for him somewhere far away while another is going mad for him here. One is all over, this one here will soon be the same and then it will be the turn of a third. What sort of a fellow are you, you wretch, to turn their heads one after the other?"

Ćorkan leaped to his feet and approached the table. He had forgotten his drowsiness and fatigue and his decision not to be drawn into conversation. With hand on heart he assured the guests that it had not been his fault and that he was not so great a lover and seducer as they made out. His clothes were still damp and his face streaked and dirty, for the color of his cheap red fez ran, but it was lighted up with a smile of alcoholic bliss. He sat down near the table.

"Rum for Ćorkan!" shouted Santo Papo, a fat and greasy Jew, son of Mente and grandson of Morde Papo, leading hardware merchants.

Ćorkan had recently begun to drink rum instead of plum brandy whenever he could get hold of it. The new drink was as if made for such as he; it was stronger, quicker in effect and pleasantly different from plum brandy. It came in small flasks of two *decis* each, with a label showing a young mulatto girl with luscious lips and fiery eyes with a wide straw hat on her head, great golden earrings and the inscription beneath: Jamaica. (That was something exotic for a Bosnian in the last stages of alcoholism bordering on delirium. It was made in Slavonski Brod by the firm of Eisler, Sirowatka and Co.) When he looked at the picture of the young mulatto girl, Ćorkan also felt the fire and aroma of the new drink and at once thought that he would never have been able to know this earthly treasure had he died even a year before. "And how many such wonderful things there are in this world!" He felt deeply moved at this thought and therefore always waited for a few pensive moments before he opened a bottle of rum. And after the satisfaction of that thought came the delight of the drink itself.

This time too he held the bottle before his face as if conversing with it unheard. But he who had first managed to draw him into conversation asked him sharply:

"Why are you dreaming about that girl, you wretch; are you going to take her as your wife or play about with her as you did with all the others?"

The girl in question was a certain Paša from Dušče. She was the prettiest girl in the town, poor and fatherless, a seamstress as was also her mother.

During the countless picnics and drinking bouts of the past year the young bachelors had talked and sung much about Paša and her inaccessible beauty. Listening to them Ćorkan had gradually and imperceptibly become enthusiastic too, he himself did not know how or why. So they began to tease him about her.

One Friday they took Ćorkan with them for *ašikovanje* (to flirt with the town girls in the Turkish manner) when from behind the courtyard gates or the window lattices muffled giggles could be heard and the whispering of the unseen girls within. From one courtyard where Paša and her friends lived a sprig of tansy was thrown over the wall and fell at Ćorkan's feet. He hesitated in confusion, not wanting to tread on the flower and undecided whether to pick it up. The youths who had brought him clapped him on the back and congratulated him that Paša had chosen him from so many and had shown him greater attention than anyone else had ever obtained from her.

That night they had gone drinking beside the river under the walnut trees at Mezalin and continued until dawn. Ćorkan sat beside the fire, solemn and withdrawn, now joyous, now pensive. That night they would not let him serve the drinks or busy himself preparing coffee and snacks.

"Don't you know, fellow, the meaning of a sprig of tansy thrown by a girl?" said one of them. "It means that Paša is telling you: I am pining away for you like this plucked flower; but you neither ask for my hand nor allow me to go to another. That is what it means."

They all began to talk to him about Paša, so lovely, so chaste, alone in the world, waiting for the hand that should pluck her, and that the hand for which she was waiting was Ćorkan's and his alone.

They pretended to get angry and shouted loudly; how did she come to cast her eye on Ćorkan? Others defended him. As Ćorkan went on drinking he came almost to believe in this marvel, only to reject it at once as an impossibility. In conversation he insisted that she was not the girl for him, and defended himself against their jeers by saying that he was a poor man, that he was growing old and not very attractive, but in his moments of silence he let his thoughts dwell on Paša, her beauty and the joy that she would bring, heedless whether such joy were possible for him or not. In that wonderful summer night which with the plum brandy and the songs and the fire burning on the grass seemed endless, everything was possible or at least not completely impossible. That the guests were mocking and ridiculing him he knew; gentlemen could not live without laughter, someone had to be their buffoon, it always had been and always would be. But if all this were only a joke, his dream of a marvellous woman and an unattainable love, of which he had always dreamed and still dreamed today, was no joke. There was no joke in those songs in which love was both real and unreal and woman both near and unattainable as in his dream. For the guests all that too was a joke, but for him it was a true and sacred thing which he had always borne within himself and which had become real and indubitable, independent of the guests' pleasure, of wine and of song, of everything, even of Paša herself.

All this he knew well and yet easily forgot. For his soul would melt and his mind flow like water.

So Ćorkan, three years after his great love and the scandal about the pretty German tight-rope walker, fell into a new and enchanted love and all the rich and idle guests found a fresh game, cruel and exciting enough to give them cause for laughter for months and years to come.

That was in midsummer. But autumn and winter passed and the game about Ćorkan's love for the beautiful Paša filled the evenings and shortened the days for the merchants from the market-place. They always referred to Ćorkan as the bridegroom or the lover. By day, overcome by the night's drinking and lack of sleep, when Ćorkan did odd jobs in the shops, fetching and carrying, he was surprised and angered that they should call him so, but only shrugged his shoulders. But as soon as night came and the lamps were lit in Zarije's inn, someone would shout "Rum for Ćorkan!" and another sing softly as if by chance:

"Evening comes and the sun goes down:
On thy face it shines no longer. . . ."

then suddenly everything changed. No more burdens, no more shrugging of shoulders, no more town or inn or even Ćorkan himself as he was in reality, snuffling, unshaven, clothed in rags and cast-off clothing of other men. There existed a high balcony lit by the setting sun and wreathed in vines, with a young girl who looked for him and waited for the man to whom she had thrown a sprig of tansy. There was still, to be true, the coarse laughter around him and the crude jests, but they were all far away, as in a fog, and he who sang was near him, close by his ear:

"If I could grow warm again
In the sunlight that you bring me. . . ."

and he warmed himself in that sun, which had set, as he had never been warmed by the real sun which rose and set daily over the town.

"Rum for Ćorkan!"

So the winter nights passed. Towards the end of that winter Paša got married. The poor seamstress from Dušče, in all her beauty of not quite nineteen years, married Hadji Omer who lived behind the fortress, a rich and respected man of fifty-five—as his second wife.

Hadji Omer had already been married more than thirty years. His wife came from a famous family and was renowned for her cleverness and good sense. Their property behind the fortress was a whole settlement in itself, progressive and rich in everything. His shops in the town were solidly built and his income assured and large. All this was not so much due to the peaceable and indolent Hadji Omer, who did little more than walk twice a day to the town and back, as to his able and energetic, always smiling wife. Her opinion was the last word on many questions for all the Turkish women of the town.

His family was in every way among the best and most respected in the town, but the already ageing couple had no children. For long they had hoped. Hadji Omer had even made the pilgrimage to Mecca and his wife had made bequests to religious houses and given alms to the poor. The years had passed, everything had increased and prospered, but in this one most important matter they had received no blessing. Hadji Omer and his good wife had borne their evil fortune wisely and well but there could be no longer any hope of children. His wife was in her forty-fifth year.

The great inheritance which Hadji Omer was to leave behind him was in question. Not only his and his wife's numerous relations had concerned themselves in this matter, but to some extent the whole town also. Some had wanted the marriage to remain childless to the end, while others had thought it a pity that such a man should die without heirs and that his goods should be dispersed among the many relations, and had therefore urged him to take a second, younger wife while there was still a chance of heirs. The local Turks were divided into two camps on the question. But the matter was settled by the barren wife herself. Openly, resolutely and sincerely, as in everything she did, she told her undecided husband:

"The good God has given us everything, all thanks and praise to Him, concord and health and riches, but He has not given us what he gives to every poor man; to see our children and to know to whom to leave what shall remain after us. That has been my bad fortune. But even if I, by the will of God, must bear this, there is no reason why you should do so. I see that the whole market-place is concerning itself with our troubles and urging you to marry again. Well, since they are trying to marry you off, then it is I who want to arrange your marriage for you, for no one is a greater friend to you than I."

She then told him her plan; as there was no longer any likelihood that they two could ever have children, then he must bring to their home, beside her, a second wife, a younger one, by whom he might still be able to have children. The law gave him that right. She, naturally, would go on living in the house as "the old *hadjinica*" and see that everything was done properly.

Hadji Omer long resisted and swore that he asked no better companion than she, that he did not need a second wife, but she stuck to her opinion and even informed him which girl she had chosen. Since he must marry in order to have children, then it were best that he take a young, healthy and pretty girl of poor family who would give him healthy heirs and, while she was alive, would be grateful for her good fortune. Her choice fell on pretty Paša, daughter of the seamstress from Dušče.

So it was done. At the wish of his older wife and with her assistance, Hadji Omer married the lovely Paša and eleven months later Paša gave birth to a healthy boy. So the question of Hadji Omer's inheritance was settled, the hopes of many relations were extinguished and the mouths of the market-place sealed. Paša was happy and "the old *hadjinica*" satisfied, and the two lived in Hadji Omer's house in concord like mother and daughter.

That fortunate conclusion of the question of Hadji Omer's heir was the beginning of Ćorkan's great sufferings. That winter the principal amusement of the idle guests in Zarije's inn was Ćorkan's sorrow at Paša's marriage. The unfortunate lover was drunk as he had never been before; the guests laughed till they cried. They all toasted him and each one of them got good value for his money. They mocked him with imaginary messages from Paša, assuring him that she wept night and day, that she was pining for him, not telling anyone the real reason for her sorrow. Ćorkan was in a frenzy, sang, wept, answered all questions seriously and in detail and bewailed the fate which had created him so unprepossessing and poor.

"Very well, Ćorkan, but how many years younger are you than Hadji Omer?" one of the guests would begin the conversation.

"How do I know? And what good would it do me even if I were younger?" Ćorkan answered bitterly.

"Eh, if I were to judge by heart and youth, then Hadji Omer would not have what he has, nor would our Ćorkan be sitting where he is," broke in another guest.

It did not need much to make Ćorkan tender and sentimental. They poured him rum after rum and assured him that not only was he younger and handsomer and more suitable for Paša but that, after all, he was not so poor as he thought or as he seemed. In the long nights these idle men over their plum brandy thought up a whole history; how Ćorkan's father, an unknown Turkish officer, whom no one had ever seen, had left a great property somewhere in Anatolia to his illegitimate son in Višegrad as sole heir, but that some relations down there had stayed the execution of the will; that now it would only be necessary for Ćorkan to appear in the rich and distant city of Brusa to counter the intrigues and lies of these false heirs and recover what rightly belonged to him. Then he would be able to buy up Hadji Omer and all his wealth.

Ćorkan listened, went on drinking and only sighed. All that pained him but at the same time did not stop him from sometimes thinking of himself so, and behaving as a man who has been cheated and robbed both in this town and over there somewhere in a distant and beautiful land, the homeland of his supposed father. Those around him pretended to make preparations for his journey to Brusa. Their jokes were long, cruel and worked out to the smallest detail. One night they brought him a supposedly complete passport, and with coarse jokes and roars of laughter pulled Ćorkan into the center of the inn and turned him round and examined him, in order to inscribe his personal characteristics on it. Another time they calculated how much money he would need for his trip to Brusa, how he would travel and where he would spend his nights. That too passed a good part of the long night.

When he was sober Ćorkan protested; he both believed and disbelieved all he was told, but he disbelieved more than he believed. When he was sober he believed, in fact, nothing at all but as soon as he was drunk he behaved as though he believed it all. For when alcohol got a grip on him he no longer asked himself what was true and what was a lie. The truth was that, after the second little bottle of rum, he already seemed to feel the scented air from distant and unattainable Brusa and saw, a lovely sight, its green gardens and white houses. He had been deceived, unfortunate in everything from birth, in his family, his property and his love; wrong had been done to him, so great a wrong that God and men were alike his debtors. It was clear that he was not what he appeared to be or as men saw him. The need to tell all those around him tormented him more with every glass, though he himself felt how hard it was to prove a truth that was to him clear and evident, but against which cried out all that was in him and about him. After the first glass of rum, he explained this to everyone, all night long, in broken sentences and with grotesque gestures and drunkard's tears. The more he explained the more those around him joked and laughed. They laughed so long and heartily that their ribs and their jaws ached from that laughter, contagious, irresistible and sweeter than any food or drink. They laughed and forgot the boredom of the winter night, and like Ćorkan drank themselves silly.

"Kill yourself!" shouted Mehaga Sarač who by his cold and apparently serious manner best knew how to provoke and excite Ćorkan. "Since you have not been man enough to seize Paša from that weakling of a Hadji Omer, then you oughtn't to live any longer. Kill yourself, Ćorkan; that is my advice."

"Kill yourself, kill yourself!" wailed Ćorkan. "Do you think I haven't thought of that? A hundred times I have gone to throw myself into the Drina from the *kapia* and a hundred times something held me back."

"What held you back? Fear held you back, full breeches, Ćorkan!"

"No, no. It was not fear, may God hear me, not fear!"

In the general uproar and laughter Ćorkan leaped up, beat his breast and tore a piece of bread from the loaf before him and thrust it under the cold and immobile face of Mehaga.

"Do you see this? By my bread and my blessing, it was not fear, but . . ."

Suddenly someone began to hum in a low voice:

"On thy face it shines no longer. . . ."

Everyone picked up the song and drowned Mehaga's voice shouting at Ćorkan.

"Kill . . . kill . . . your—self . . . !"

Thus singing they themselves fell into that state of exaltation into which they had tried to drive Ćorkan. The evening developed into a mad orgy.

One February night they had thus awaited dawn, driving themselves mad with their victim Ćorkan, and themselves victims of his folly. It was already day when they came out of the inn. Heated with drink, with veins swollen and crackling, they went to the bridge which at the time was coated with a fine layer of ice.

With shouts and gusts of laughter, paying no heed to the few early passers-by, they bet among themselves; who dares to cross the bridge, but along the narrow stone parapet shining under the thin coating of ice.

"Ćorkan dares!" shouted one of the drunkards.

"Ćorkan? Not on your life!"

"Who daren't? I? I dare to do what no living man dares," shouted Ćorkan beating his breast noisily.

"You haven't the guts! Do it if you dare!"

"I dare, by God!"

"Ćorkan dares!"

"Liar!"

These drunkards and boasters shouted each other down, even though they could scarcely keep their feet on the broad bridge, staggering, teetering and holding on to one another for support.

They did not even notice when Ćorkan climbed on to the stone parapet. Then, suddenly, they saw him floating above them and, drunk and dishevelled as he was, begin to stand upright and walk along the flagstones on the parapet.

The stone parapet was about two feet wide. Ćorkan walked along it swaying now left now right. On the left was the bridge and on the bridge, there beneath his feet, the crowd of drunken men who followed his every step and shouted words at him which he scarcely understood and heard only as an incomprehensible murmur; and on the right a void, and in that void somewhere far below, the unseen river; a thick mist floated upwards from it and rose, like white smoke, in the chill morning air.

The few passers-by halted, terrified, and with wide-open eyes watched the drunken man who was walking along the narrow and slippery parapet, poised above the void, waving his arms frantically to retain his balance. In that company of drunkards a few of the more sober who still had some common sense watched the dangerous game. Others, not realizing the danger, walked along beside the parapet and accompanied with their cries the drunken man who balanced and swayed and danced above the abyss.

All at once, in his dangerous position, Ćorkan felt himself separated from his companions. He was now like some gigantic monster far above them. His first steps were slow and hesitating. His heavy clogs kept slipping on the stones covered with ice. It seemed to him that his legs were failing him, that the depths below attracted him irresistibly, that he must slip and fall, that he was already falling. But his unusual position and the nearness of great danger gave him strength and hitherto unknown powers. Struggling to maintain his balance, he made more and more little jumps and bent more and more from his waist and knees. Instead of walking he began to dance, he himself did not know how, as free of care as if he had been on a wide green field and not on that narrow and icy edge. All of a sudden he felt himself light and skillful as a man sometimes is in dreams. His heavy and exhausted body felt without weight. The drunken Ćorkan danced and floated above the depths as if on wings. He felt as if a gay strength flowed through his body which danced to an unheard music and that gave him security and balance. His dance bore him onward where his walk would never have borne him. No longer thinking of the danger or the possibility of a fall, he leaped from one leg to the other and sang with outstretched arms as if accompanying himself on a drum.

"Tiridam, tiridam, tiritiritiritiridam,
tiridam, tiridam. . . ."

Ćorkan sang and himself beat out the rhythm to which dancing surefootedly he made his dangerous crossing. His legs bent at the knees and he moved his head to left and right.

"Tiridam, tiridam . . . hai . . .
hai. . . ."

In that unusual and dangerous position, exalted above all the others, he was no longer Ćorkan the One-Eyed, the butt of the town and the inn. Below him there was no longer that narrow and slippery stone parapet of that familiar bridge on which he had countless times munched his bread and, thinking of the sweetness of death in the waves beneath, had gone to sleep in the shade of the *kapia*.

No, this was that distant and unattainable voyage of which they had spoken every night at the inn with coarse jokes and mockery and on which now, at last, he had set out. This was that glorious long-desired path of great achievements and that in the distance at the end of it was the imperial city of Brusa with its real riches and his legitimate heritage, the setting sun and the lovely Paša with his son; his wife and his child.

So, dancing in a sort of ecstasy, he passed the parapet around the *sofa* and then the second half of the bridge. When he came to the end he leaped down and looked confusedly about him, in wonder that he had once again landed on the hard and familiar Višegrad road. The crowd which till then had accompanied him with encouragement and jokes welcomed him. Those who had halted in fear rushed up. They began to embrace him, to clap him on the back and on his faded fez. All of them shouted together:

"*Aferim*, bravo, Ćorkan, our falcon!"

"Bravo, hero!"

"Rum for Ćorkan!" yelled Santo Papo in a raucous voice with a Spanish accent, thinking that he was in the inn.

In this general uproar and commotion someone proposed that they stay together and not go home, but go on drinking in honor of Ćorkan's exploit.

Those children who were then in their eighth and ninth years and were that morning hurrying across the frozen bridge to their distant school stopped and stared at the unusual sight. They opened their mouths in astonishment and little clouds of steam rose from them. Tiny, muffled up, with slates and schoolbooks under their arms, they could not understand this game of the grown-ups, but for the rest of their lives they would remember, together with the lines of their own bridge, the picture of Ćorkan the One-Eyed, that man so well known to them who now, transfigured and light, dancing daringly and joyously as if transported by magic, walked where it was forbidden to walk and where no one ever dared to go.

16

A score of years had passed since the first yellow Austrian military vehicles had crossed the bridge. Twenty years of occupation—that is a long sequence of days and months. Each such day and month, taken by itself, seemed uncertain and temporary, but all of them taken together constituted the longest period of peace and material progress that the town ever remembered, the main part of the life of that generation which at the moment of the occupation had just come to years of discretion.

These were years of apparent prosperity and safe gains, even though small, when mothers speaking of their sons said: "May he live and be healthy and may God grant him easy bread!," and when even the wife of tall Ferhat, the eternal poor man, who lit the municipal street lamps and received for his work the wage of twelve florins a month, said with pride: "Thanks be to God, even my Ferhat has become an official."

The last years of the nineteenth century, years without upheavals or important events, flowed past like a broad calm river before reaching its unknown mouth. Judging from them, it seemed as if tragic moments had ceased to disturb the life of the European peoples or that of the town beside the bridge. In so far as they took place now and again in the world outside, they did not penetrate to Višegrad and were far-off and incomprehensible to its townspeople.

Thus, one summer day after so many years, there once more appeared on the *kapia* a white official notice. It was short and this time framed in a heavy black border, and announced that Her Majesty the Empress Elizabeth had died in Geneva, the victim of a dastardly assassination by an Italian anarchist, Lucchieni. The announcement went on to express the disgust and profound sorrow of all the peoples of the great Austro-Hungarian Monarchy and called on them to rally still more closely around the throne in loyal devotion and thereby afford the greatest consolation to the ruler whom fate had so heavily bereaved.

The announcement was pasted up below the white plaque with the Turkish inscription, as had at one time been the proclamation of General Filipović about the occupation, and all the people read it with emotion since it concerned an Empress, a woman, but without any real understanding or deep sympathy.

For a few evenings there were no songs or noisy gatherings on the *kapia* by order of the authorities.

There was only one man in the town whom this news deeply affected. He was Pietro Sola, the only Italian in the town, a contractor and builder, stone-mason and artist, in short a man of all tasks and the specialist of the town. Maistor-Pero, as the whole town called him, had come at the time of the occupation and had remained in the town, marrying a certain Stana, a poor girl of not too savory a reputation. She was reddish, powerful, twice as big as Maistor-Pero and was considered a woman of sharp tongue and heavy hand with whom it was better not to quarrel. Maistor-Pero himself was a small, bent, good-natured man with mild blue eyes and pendent moustaches. He worked well and earned much. In time he had become a real townsman only, like Lotte, he was never able to master the language and the pronunciation. Because of his skillful hands and gentle nature he was loved by the whole town and his athletically powerful wife led him through life strictly and maternally, like a child.

When, returning home from work gray with stonedust and streaked with paint, Maistor-Pero read the announcement on the *kapia,* he pulled his hat down over his eyes and feverishly bit on the thin pipe which was always between his teeth. He explained to the more serious and respected citizens whom he met that he, although an Italian, had nothing in common with this Lucchieni and his dastardly crime. The people listened to him, consoled him and assured him that they believed him and that, furthermore, they had never even thought anything of the sort about him. None the less, he went on explaining to everyone that he was ashamed to be alive, that he had never even killed a chicken in his life how much less a human being, and that a woman and so great a personage. In the end his timidity became a real mania. The townspeople began to laugh at Maistor-Pero's worries, his zeal and his superfluous assurances that he had nothing in common with anarchists and murderers. The urchins of the town at once made up a cruel game. Hidden behind some fence they would shout at Maistor-Pero: "Lucchieni!" The poor devil defended himself from these shouts as from a swarm of wasps, pulled his hat down over his eyes and fled home to bewail his fate and weep on the broad lap of his Stana.

"I am ashamed, I am ashamed," sobbed the little man, "I can't look anyone in the face."

"Get along, you old fool, what have you to be ashamed of? That an Italian has murdered the Empress? Let the Italian king be ashamed of that! But who are you and what have you done to be ashamed of?"

"I am ashamed to be alive," wailed Maistor-Pero to the woman, who shook him and tried to instill a little strength and resolution into him and to teach him to walk through the market-place with head held high, not lowering his gaze before anyone.

Meanwhile the older men sat on the *kapia* with stony faces and downcast looks and listened to the most recent news, with details of the murder of the Austrian Empress. The news was no more than an excuse for a discussion on the fate of crowned heads and great men. Surrounded by a group of respectable, inquisitive and unlettered Turkish merchants, the Višegrad schoolmaster Hussein Effendi was holding forth on who and what were anarchists.

The schoolmaster was just as stiff and solemn, clean and neat, as he had been twenty years before when awaiting the arrival of the first Schwabes with Mula Ibrahim and Pop Nikola, both of whom had long been lying in their respective graveyards. His beard was already gray but just as carefully trimmed and rounded, his whole smooth face calm and peaceful, for men with a rigid understanding and hard heart age slowly. The high opinion which he had always had of himself had grown even greater in these last twenty years. It may be said in passing that the case of books on which his reputation as a learned man rested to a great extent was still largely unread, and his chronicle of the town had grown in these twenty years by four pages only, for the older the schoolmaster grew he esteemed himself and his chronicle more and more and the events around him less and less.

Now he spoke in a low voice, slowly as if reading from some obscure manuscript and in a dignified manner, solemnly and severely, using the fate of the infidel Empress only as a pretext which did not in any way enter into the real sense of his interpretation. According to this interpretation (and that too was not his own, for he had found it in the good old books inherited from his one-time teacher, the famous Arap-hodja) those now known as anarchists had always existed and would always exist while the world lasted. Human life was so ordered—and God, the One, the Merciful and Compassionate, had so ordained—that for every dram of good there were two drams of evil and there could be no goodness on this earth without hatred and no greatness without envy, even as there was not even the smallest object without its shadow. That was particularly true of famous people. Beside each one of them, alongside their glory, was also their executioner waiting for his chance and who seized it, sometimes earlier, sometimes later.

"Take for example our countryman Mehmed Pasha who has long been in Paradise," said the schoolmaster and pointed to the stone plaque above the proclamation, "who served three Sultans and was wiser than Asaf and who by his power and piety erected even this stone on which we are sitting and who too died by the knife. Despite all his power and wisdom he was unable to escape his appointed hour. Those whom the Grand Vezir hindered in their plans, and they were a great and powerful party, found a way to arm and suborn a mad dervish to kill him, and that just at the moment when he was entering the mosque to pray. With his shabby dervish cloak on his back and a rosary in his hand the dervish barred the way of the Vezir's suite and humbly and hypocritically asked for alms, and when the Vezir was about to put his hand in his pocket to give them to him, the dervish stabbed him. And so Mehmed Pasha died as a martyr to the faith."

The men listened and blowing the smoke of their cigarettes far from them looked now at the stone plaque with the inscription, now at the white placard bordered by a black line. They listened attentively, though not one of them fully understood every word of the schoolmaster's interpretation. But, looking through their cigarette smoke into the distance, beyond the inscription and the placard, they seemed to see somewhere in the world another and different life, a life of great ascents and sudden falls, in which greatness mingled with tragedy and which in some manner maintained a balance with this peaceful and monotonous existence of theirs on the *kapia*.

But those days passed too. The old order returned to the *kapia* with its usual loud conversations, jokes and songs. Discussions about anarchists ceased; the announcement of the death of that foreign and little-known Empress changed under the influence of sun, rain and dust until at last the wind tore it away and it floated in fragments down river into the void.

For a little longer the ragamuffins of the town shouted "Lucchieni" after Maistor-Pero without knowing themselves what they meant nor why they did so, but solely from that childish need to tease and torment weak and sensitive creatures. They shouted, and then ceased to shout having found some other amusement. Stana of Mejdan contributed not a little to this result by mercilessly beating two of the most obstreperous of the urchins.

After a couple of months no one mentioned the Empress's death or anarchists any longer. That life at the end of the century, which seemed tamed and domesticated forever, concealed everything beneath its wide and monotonous course and left among men the feeling that a century was opening of peaceful industry leading into some distant and unattainable future.

That unceasing and irresistible activity to which the foreign administrators seemed condemned and with which the townspeople were with difficulty reconciled, though they had just this to thank for their livelihood and their prosperity, changed many things in the course of those twenty years, in the outward appearance of the town and in the costume and habits of its citizens. It was natural that it would not stop short of the ancient bridge which looked eternally the same.

It was in 1900, the close of that happy century and the beginning of the new, which in the feelings and opinions of many was to be even happier, that engineers came to examine the bridge. The people were already accustomed to such things; even the children knew what it meant when these men in leather overcoats, with breast-pockets stuffed with varicolored pencils, began to prowl about some hill or some building. It meant that something would be demolished, built, dug up or changed. Only no one was able to imagine what they could be doing with the bridge which to every living soul in the town meant a thing as eternal and unalterable as the earth on which they trod or the skies above them. But the engineers inspected it, measured it and took notes; then they went away and the matter was forgotten. But about midsummer, when the river was at its lowest, contractors and workmen suddenly began to arrive and erect temporary leantos to store their tools near the bridge. Already the rumor spread that the bridge was to be repaired, and complicated scaffolding was erected near the piers and on the bridge itself windlass lifts were set up; by their help the workers moved up and down the piers as on some narrow wooden balcony and stopped at places where there was a hole or where tufts of grass had grown out of the stonework.

Every hole was plugged, the grasses plucked out and the birds' nests removed. When they had finished this task, work began on the waterlogged foundations of the bridge. The current was checked and its course altered so that the blackened and corroded stone could be seen, together with an occasional oak beam, worn away but petrified by the waters in which it had been placed 330 years before. The indefatigable lifts lowered cement and gravel, load after load, and the three central piers which were the most exposed to the strong current and the most corroded were filled in at the bases as a rotten tooth is filled at its root.

That summer there were no sessions on the *kapia* and the customary life around the bridge was suspended. The bridge was crowded with horses and carts bringing sand and cement. The shouts of the workmen and the orders of the foremen echoed from all sides. On the *kapia* itself a wooden toolshed was erected.

The townsmen watched the work on the great bridge, astonished and perplexed. Some made a jest of it, others only waved their arms and went their way, and to all of them it seemed that the foreigners were doing this work, as they did all other work, only because they must work at something. Work for them was a necessity and they could not do otherwise. No one said this, but everybody thought it.

All those who had been accustomed to pass their time on the *kapia* now sat outside Lotte's hotel, Zarije's inn or in front of the wooden door-shutters of the shops near the bridge. There they drank coffee and told stories, waiting until the *kapia* should be free again and that attack on the bridge should pass, as a man waits for the end of a shower or some other inconvenience.

In front of Alihodja's shop which was sandwiched between the Stone Han and Zarije's inn, where the bridge could be seen from an angle, two Turks sat from early morning, two hangers-on in the market-place, chatting about everything and more especially about the bridge.

Alihodja listened to them in ill-humored silence, pensively watching the bridge which was swarming with workmen like ants.

In those twenty years the *hodja* had married three times. Now he had a wife much younger than himself and malicious tongues said that that was the reason he was always ill-humored until noon. By these three wives he had fourteen children. His house was filled with a noisy crowd all day long and in the market-place they said in jest that the *hodja* did not know all his own children by name. They even told a story of how one of his numerous brood met the *hodja* in a side-street and took his hand to kiss it, but the *hodja* only stroked his head and asked: "God give you good health, son! And whose may you be?"

To the eye the *hodja* had not changed greatly; only he was now plumper and redder in the face. He no longer moved so briskly and went home up that steep slope to Mejdan more slowly than before, for his heart had been troubling him for some time, even when he was asleep. He had therefore gone to the district doctor, Dr. Marovski, the only one of the newcomers whom he recognized and respected. The doctor gave him some drops which did not cure his ills, but helped him to bear them, and from him Alihodja learned the Latin name for his complaint: *angina pectoris.*

Alihodja was one of the few local Turks who had accepted none of the novelties and changes which the newcomers had brought, either in dress, in customs, in speech or in methods of trade and business. With that same bitter obstinacy with which he had at one time stood out against useless resistance, he had for years stood out against everything that was Austrian and foreign and against everything that was gathering impetus around him. For that reason he sometimes came into conflict with others and had had to pay fines to the police. Now he was a little tired and disillusioned, but he was essentially just the same as he had been when he had argued with Karamanli on the *kapia,* obstinate in everything and at all times; save that his proverbial freedom of speech had turned to sharpness and his fighting spirit into a sullen bitterness which even the most daring words could not express and which was calmed and extinguished only in silence and in solitude.

With time the *hodja* had fallen more and more into a sort of calm meditation in which he had no need of anyone else and found all men hard to endure. Everyone, the idle merchants of the market-place, his customers, his young wife and all that horde of urchins which filled his house with noise, irritated him. Before the sun rose he fled from his house to his shop which he opened before any of the other merchants. There he carried out his morning devotions. There his lunch was brought to him. And when, during the day, conversation, visitors and business bored him, he put up the wooden shutters and withdrew into a tiny closet behind the shop which he called his coffin. That was a secret place, narrow, low and dark; the *hodja* almost filled it when he crawled in. He had there a small stool covered with a rug on which he could sit with crossed legs, a few shelves with empty boxes, old scales and all sorts of rubbish for which there was no room in the shop. In that narrow dark hole the *hodja* could hear through the thin walls of his shop the hum of life in the market-place, the sound of horses' hooves and the cries of the sellers. All that came to him as from another world. He could hear too some of the passers-by who stopped before his closed shop and made malicious jokes and comments about him. But he listened to them calmly, for to him these men were dead and had not realized it; he knew and forgot them in the same moment. Hidden behind those few planks, he felt himself completely protected from all that this life could bring him, this life which in his opinion had long become rotten and proceeded along evil ways. There the *hodja* shut himself in with his thoughts on the destiny of the world and the course of human affairs, and forgot all else, the market-place, his worries about debts and bad tenants, his too young wife whose youth and beauty had suddenly turned into a stupid and malicious ill-humor, and that brood of children which would have been a heavy burden on an Emperor's treasury and about which he thought only with horror.

After he had recovered his spirits and rested there, the *hodja* would again take down his shutters as if he had just come back from somewhere.

So now he listened to the empty chatter of his two neighbors.

"You see now how the times are and the gifts of God; time eats away even stone like the sole of a shoe. But the Schwabes will not have it so and at once mend what is damaged," philosophized one of them, a well-known lazybones from the market-place, as he sipped Alihodja's coffee.

"While the Drina is the Drina the bridge will be the bridge. Even if they had not touched it, it would last its appointed time. All this expense and all this trouble will serve them nothing," said the other guest, of the same occupation as the first.

They would have dragged on their idle chatter indefinitely had not Alihodja interrupted.

"And I tell you that no good will come of their interfering with the bridge. You will see, nothing good will come of all this restoration. What they repair today they will tear down again tomorrow. The late lamented Mula Ibrahim used to tell me that he had learned from ancient books that it is a great sin to meddle with living water, to turn its course aside or change it, were it even for a day or an hour. But the Schwabes do not feel themselves alive unless they are hammering or chiseling something or other. They would turn the whole world upside down if they could!"

The first of the idlers tried to show that, when all was said and done, it was not so bad that the Schwabes should repair the bridge. If it did not prolong its life it would at any rate do it no harm.

"And how do you know that they will do it no harm?" the *hodja* broke in angrily. "Who told you? Don't you know that a single word can destroy whole cities; how much more then such a babel! All this earth of God's was built upon a word. If you were literate and educated, as you are not, then you would know that this is not a building like any other, but one of those erected by God's will and for God's love; a certain time and certain men built it, and another time and other men will destroy it. You know what the old men say about the Stone Han; there was none other like it in the Empire. Yet who destroyed it? Had it been a question of its solidity and the skill of its construction it would have lasted a thousand years; yet it has melted away as if it had been made of wax and now on the place where it was the pigs grunt and the Schwabes' trumpet sounds."

"But, as I think, I believe . . ." the idler replied.

"You believe wrongly," interrupted the *hodja*. "According to your ideas nothing would ever have been built and nothing destroyed. That has never occurred to you. But I tell you that all this is not good, it foretells evil, for the bridge and for the town and for all of us who are looking at it with our own eyes."

"He is right. The *hodja* knows best what the bridge is," broke in the other idler, maliciously recalling Alihodja's one-time martyrdom on the *kapia*.

"You needn't think I don't know," said the *hodja* with conviction and at once began quite calmly to tell one of his stories at which the townsfolk used to mock, but to which they loved to listen time and time again.

"At one time my late lamented father heard from Sheik Dedije and told me as a child how bridges first came to this world and how the first bridge was built. When Allah the Merciful and Compassionate first created this world, the earth was smooth and even as a finely engraved plate. That displeased the devil who envied man this gift of God. And while the earth was still just as it had come from God's hands, damp and soft as unbaked clay, he stole up and scratched the face of God's earth with his nails as much and as deeply as he could. Therefore, the story says, deep rivers and ravines were formed which divided one district from another and kept men apart, preventing them from traveling on that earth that God had given them as a garden for their food and their support. And Allah felt pity when he saw what the Accursed One had done, but was not able to return to the task which the devil had spoiled with his nails, so he sent his angels to help men and make things easier for them. When the angels saw how unfortunate men could not pass those abysses and ravines to finish the work they had to do, but tormented themselves and looked in vain and shouted from one side to the other, they spread their wings above those places and men were able to cross. So men learned from the angels of God how to build bridges, and therefore, after fountains, the greatest blessing is to build a bridge and the greatest sin to interfere with it, for every bridge, from a tree trunk crossing a mountain stream to this great erection of Mehmed Pasha, has its guardian angel who cares for it and maintains it as long as God has ordained that it should stand."

"So it is, so it is, by God's will!" the two idlers marveled humbly.

So they passed their time in conversation, as the days passed and the work went on there on the bridge, whence they could hear the squeaking of carts and the pounding of machines mixing sand and cement.

As always, in this discussion too, the *hodja* had the last word. No one wanted to press an argument with him to the end, least of all those two idle and empty-headed fellows who drank their coffee there and knew well that the next day also they would have to pass a good part of their long day in front of his shop.

So Alihodja talked to everyone who stopped before the shutters of his shop, whether on business or just making a call. They all listened to him with mocking curiosity and apparent attention, but no one in the town shared his opinions or had any understanding of his pessimism or his forebodings of evil, which he himself was unable to explain or to support by proof. Furthermore they had for long been accustomed to look on the *hodja* as an eccentric and an obstinate man who now, under the influence of ripening years, difficult circumstances and a young wife, saw the black side of everything and gave everything a special and ill-omened significance.

The townspeople were, for the most part, indifferent to the work on the bridge, as they were towards everything which the newcomers had been doing for years in and about the town. Only the children were disappointed when they saw that the workmen with their wooden ladders went in through that black opening in the central pier, that "room" in which by universal childish belief the Arab lived. From this place the workmen brought out and tipped into the river countless baskets of birds' droppings. And that was all. The Arab never appeared. The children made themselves late for school, waiting vainly for hours for the black man to emerge from his darkness and strike the first workman in his path, strike him so strongly that he would fly from his moving scaffolding in a great curve into the river. They were furious that this had not happened, and some of the urchins tried to say that it had happened already, but they did not sound convincing and all their "words of honor" were to no purpose.

As soon as the repair work on the bridge was finished, work began on a water supply. Till then the town had had wooden fountains of which only two on Mejdan gave pure spring water; all the others, down on the level, were connected with water from the Drina or the Rzav and ran cloudy whenever the water of those two rivers was cloudy, and dried up altogether during the summer heats when the river level fell. Now engineers found that this water was unhealthy. The new water was brought right from the mountains on the other side of the Drina, so that the pipes had to be taken across the bridge into the town.

Once again there was noise and commotion on the bridge. Flagstones were raised and a channel dug for the conduits. Fires burned on which pitch was boiled and lead melted. Hemp was plaited into ropes. The townspeople watched the work with distrust and curiosity as they had always done before. Alihodja was irritated by the smoke which drifted across the square to his shop, and spoke disdainfully of the "new" unclean water which passed through iron pipes so that it was not fit to drink or for ablutions before prayer and which not even horses would drink if they were still of the good old breed that they once were. He laughed at Lotte who brought the water into her hotel. To everyone willing to listen he proved that the waterworks were only one of the signs of the approaching evil which sooner or later would fall upon the town.

However, next summer, the water supply was installed, even as so many earlier works had been introduced and completed. Clean and abundant water, which was no longer dependent either on drought or flood, flowed into the new iron fountains. Many brought the water into their courtyards and some even into their houses.

The same autumn the building of the railway began. That was a much longer and more important task. At first it did not seem to have any connection with the bridge. But that was only apparent.

This was the narrow-gauge railway described in newspaper articles and official papers as the "eastern railway." It was to link Sarajevo with the Serbian frontier at Vardište and the boundary of the Turkish-held Sanjak of Novi Pazar at Uvce. The line ran right through the town which was the most important station on it.

Much was said and written about the political and strategic significance of this line, of the impending annexation of Bosnia and Herzegovina, of the further aims of Austro-Hungary through the Sanjak to Salonica and all the complicated problems connected with them. But in the town all these things still seemed completely innocent and even attractive. There were new contractors, fresh hordes of workmen and new sources of gain for many.

This time everything was on a grand scale. The building of the new line, 166 kilometers long, on which were about 100 bridges and viaducts and about 130 tunnels, cost the state seventy-four million crowns. The people spoke of this great number of millions and then looked vaguely into the far distance as if trying in vain to see there this great mountain of money which went far beyond any calculation or imagining. "Seventy-four millions!" repeated many of them knowingly as if they could count them on the palm of their hand. For even in this remote little town where life in two-thirds of its forms was still completely oriental, men began to become enslaved by figures and to believe in statistics. "Something less than half a million, or to be accurate 445,782.12 crowns per kilometer." So the people filled their mouths with big figures but thereby neither became richer nor wiser.

During the building of the railway, the people for the first time felt that the easy, carefree gains of the first years after the occupation existed no longer. For some years past the prices of goods and everyday necessities had been leaping upward. They leaped upward but never fell back and then, after a shorter or a longer period, leaped up again. It was true there was still money to be made and wages were high, but they were always at least twenty per cent less than real needs. This was some mad and artful game which more and more embittered the lives of more and more people, but in which they could do nothing for it depended on something far away, on those same unattainable and unknown sources whence had come also the prosperity of the first years. Many men who had grown rich immediately after the occupation, some fifteen or twenty years before, were now poor and their sons had to work for others. True, there were new men who had made money, but even in their hands the money played like quick-silver, like some spell by which a man might easily find himself with empty hands and tarnished reputation. It became more and more evident that the good profits and easier life which they had brought had their counterpart and were only pieces in some great and mysterious game of which no one knew all the rules and none could foresee the outcome. And yet everyone played his part in this game, some with a smaller some with a greater role, but all with permanent risk.

In the summer of the fourth year the first train, decorated with green branches and flags, passed through the town. It was a moment of great popular rejoicing. The workmen were served with a free luncheon with great barrels of beer. The engineers had their pictures taken around the first locomotive. All that day travel on the railway was free ("One day free and a whole century for money," mocked Alihodja at those who took advantage of this first train).

Only now, when the railway had been completed and was working, could it be seen what it meant for the bridge and its role in the life of the town. The line went down to the Drina by that slope below Mejdan, cut into the hillside, circumvented the town itself and then went down to the level ground by the farthest houses near the bank of the Rzav, where the station was. All traffic, both passengers and goods, with Sarajevo and beyond Sarajevo to the rest of the western world, now remained on the right bank of the Drina. The left bank, and with it the bridge, was completely paralyzed. Only those from the villages on the left bank now went across the bridge, peasants with their little overburdened horses and bullock carts or wagons dragging timber from distant forests to the station.

The road which led upwards from the bridge across Lijeska to Semeć and thence across the Glasinac and Romania ranges to Sarajevo, and which had at one time echoed to the songs of the drovers and the clatter of packhorses, began to be overgrown with grass and that fine green moss which gradually accompanies the decline of roads and buildings. The bridge was no longer used for traveling, farewells were no longer said on the *kapia* and men no longer dismounted there to drink the stirrup-cups of plum brandy "for the road."

The packhorse owners, their horses, the covered carts and little old-fashioned fiacres by which men at one time traveled to Sarajevo remained without work. The journey no longer lasted two whole days with a halt for the night at Rogatica, as up till now, but a mere four hours. That was one of those figures which made men stop and think, but they still spoke of them without understanding and with emotion, reckoning up all the gains and savings given them by speed. They looked with wonder at the first townsmen who went one day to Sarajevo, finished their business, and returned home again the same evening.

Alihodja, always mistrustful, pigheaded, plain-spoken and apart in that as in all else, was the exception. To those who boasted of the speed with which they could now finish their business and reckoned how much time, money and effort they had saved, he replied ill-humoredly that it was not important how much time a man saved, but what he did with it when he had saved it. If he used it for evil purposes then it had been better he had never had it. He tried to prove that the main thing was not that a man went swiftly but where he went and for what purpose and that, therefore, speed was not always an advantage.

"If you are going to hell, then it is better that you should go slowly," he said curtly to a young merchant. "You are an imbecile if you think that the Schwabes have spent their money and brought their machine here only for you to travel quickly and finish your business more conveniently. All you see is that you can ride, but you do not ask what the machine brings here and takes away other than you yourself and others like you. That you can't get into your head. Ride then, my fine fellow, ride as much as you like, but I greatly fear that all your riding will lead only to a fall one of these fine days. The time will come when the Schwabes will make you ride where you don't want to go and where you never even dreamed of going."

Whenever he heard the engine whistle as it rounded the bend on the slope behind the Stone Han, Alihodja would frown and his lips would move in incomprehensible murmurs and, looking out slantwise from his shop at the unchanging bridge, he would go on elaborating his former idea; that the greatest buildings are founded by a word and that the peace and existence of whole towns and their inhabitants might depend upon a whistle. Or so at least it seemed to this weakened man who remembered much and had grown suddenly old.

But in that as in all else Alihodja was alone in his opinions like an eccentric and a dreamer. In truth the peasants too found it hard to grow accustomed to the railway. They made use of it, but could not feel at ease with it and could not understand its ways and habits. They would come down from the mountains at the first crack of dawn, reaching the town about sunrise, and by the time they reached the first shops would begin asking everyone they met:

"Has the machine gone?"

"By your life and health, neighbor, it has gone long ago," the idle shopkeepers lied heartlessly.

"Really gone?"

"No matter. There'll be another tomorrow."

They asked everyone without stopping for a moment, hurrying onwards and shouting at their wives and children who lagged behind.

They arrived at the station running. One of the railwaymen reassured them and told them that they had been misinformed and that there were still three good hours before the departure of the train. Then they recovered their breath and sat down along the walls of the station buildings, took out their breakfasts, ate them, and chatted or dozed, but remained continually alert. Whenever they heard the whistle of some goods engine they would leap to their feet and bundle their things together, shouting:

"Get up! Here comes the machine!"

The station official on the platform cursed them and drove them out again:

"Didn't I just tell you that it was more than three hours before the train comes? What are you rushing for? Have you taken leave of your senses?"

They went back to their old places and sat down once more, but still suspicious and distrustful. At the first whistle or even only at some uncertain noise they once more leaped to their feet and crowded on to the platform, only to be repulsed once more to wait patiently and listen attentively. For however much the officials told them and explained to them, they could not get it into their heads that the "machine" was not some sort of swift, mysterious and deceitful contraption invented by the Schwabes which slipped away from anyone inattentive enough to wink an eye and which had only one idea in its mind: how to cheat the peasant and leave without him.

But all these things, the peasants' stupidity and Alihodja's bad-tempered grumbling, were things of no importance. The people laughed at them and at the same time soon grew accustomed to the railway as they had to everything else that was new, easy and pleasant. They still went out to the bridge and sat on the *kapia* as they had always done, and crossed it on their everyday affairs, but they traveled in the direction and manner imposed on them by the new times. Quickly and easily they grew reconciled to the idea that the road across the bridge no longer led to the outside world and that the bridge was no longer what it once had been: the link between East and West. Better to say, most of them never thought about it.

But the bridge still stood, the same as it had always been, with the eternal youth of a perfect conception, one of the great and good works of man, which do not know what it means to change and grow old and which, or so it seemed, do not share the fate of the transient things of this world.

17

But there, beside the bridge, in the town bound to it by fate, the fruits of the new times were ripening. The year 1908 brought with it great uneasiness and a sort of obscure threat which thenceforward never ceased to weigh upon the town.

In fact this had begun much earlier, about the time of the building of the railway line and the first years of the new century. With the rise in prices and the incomprehensible but always perceptible fluctuations of government paper, dividends and exchanges, there was more and more talk of politics.

Till then the townspeople had concerned themselves exclusively with what was near to them and well known, with their gains, their pastimes and, in the main, only with questions of their family and their homes, their town or their religious community, but always directly and within definite limits, without looking much ahead or too far into the past. Now, however, more and more frequently in conversation questions arose which lay farther away, outside this narrow circle. In Sarajevo religious and national organizations and parties were founded, Serbian and Moslem, which immediately set up their sub-committees in Višegrad. New papers were started in Sarajevo and began to arrive in the town. Reading rooms and choral societies were founded; first Serbian, then Moslem and finally Jewish. Students from the secondary schools and the universities at Vienna and Prague returned to their homes in the vacations and brought with them new books, pamphlets and a new manner of expression. By their example they showed to the younger townsfolk that they did not always have to keep their mouths shut and keep their thoughts to themselves as their elders had constantly believed and affirmed. Names of new organizations began to come into the conversation, religious and national, on wide bases and with bold aims, and finally workers' organizations also. Then the word "strike" was heard in the town for the first time. The young apprentices became more serious. In the evenings on the *kapia* they carried on conversations incomprehensible to others and exchanged little paper-backed pamphlets with such titles as: "What is socialism?," "Eight hours of work, eight hours of rest, eight hours of self-improvement" and "Aims and ways of the world proletariat."

There was talk to the peasants on the agrarian problem, the relations between serfs and landowners, of Turkish feudal landholding. The peasants listened, looking a little aside with imperceptible movements of their moustaches and little frowns, as if trying to remember all that was said in order to think it over later, either alone or in discussion with their fellows.

There were plenty of citizens who continued to keep a discreet silence and who rejected such novelties and such boldness of thought and language. But there were many more, especially among the younger ones, the poor and the idle, who accepted all this as a joyful confirmation which corresponded to their inner needs long kept silent, and brought into their lives that something great and exciting which had up till then been lacking. When reading speeches and articles, protests and memoranda issued by party or religious organizations, each one of them had the feeling that he was casting off chains, that his horizon was widening, his thoughts freed and his forces linked with those of men more distant and with other forces never thought of until then.

Now they began to look at one another from a point of view they had never before taken. In short, it seemed to them, in this matter also, that their life had become more expansive and richer, that the frontiers of the impermissible and the impossible had moved back and that there opened before them prospects and possibilities such as had never before existed, even for him who until then had never possessed them.

In actual fact, even now they had nothing new nor were they able to see anything better, but they were able to look beyond the everyday life of the town, and that gave them the exciting illusion of space and power. Their habits had not changed, their ways of life and the forms of mutual relations remained the same, only that in the time-honored ritual of sitting idly over coffee, tobacco and plum brandy, bold words and new methods of conversation had been introduced. Men began to leave their old associates and form new groups, to be repelled or attracted according to new criteria and new ideas, but under the stress of old passions and ancestral instincts.

Now too, external events began to find their echo in the town. First there were the dynastic changes of 1903 in Serbia and then the change of régime in Turkey. The town which was right on the Serbian frontier and not far from the Turkish boundaries, linked by deep and invisible bonds to one or other of these two lands, felt these changes, lived them and interpreted them, although nothing of all that was thought and felt about them was ever said publicly or talked of openly.

The activities and pressure of the authorities began to be felt more openly in the town, first the civil authorities and then the military as well. And that in quite a new form; at first they had paid attention to who did what and how he behaved, and now they inquired about who thought what and how he expressed his opinions. The number of gendarmes in the surrounding villages along the frontier was gradually increased. A special Information Officer, a man from the Lika, arrived at the local headquarters. The police arrested and fined youths for imprudent declarations or for singing prohibited Serbian songs. Suspected foreigners were deported; and differences of opinion led to arguments and quarrels among the citizens themselves.

With the introduction of the railway traveling became quicker and the transport of goods easier, and somehow at about the same time events too quickened their pace. The townspeople did not notice this, for the quickening was gradual and all of them were involved in it. They became accustomed to sensations; exciting news was no longer something rare and unusual but an everyday food and a real need. The whole of life seemed to be hastening somewhere, suddenly speeded up, as a freshet quickens its pace before it breaks into rapids, rushes over steep rocks and becomes a cascade.

Only four years had passed since the arrival of the first train in the town when, one October morning, a huge white proclamation was posted on the *kapia*, beneath the plaque with the Turkish inscription. It was put up by the municipal official Drago. At first only the idlers and children gathered around it and then, later, the rest of the citizens. Those who knew how to read deciphered the proclamation, spelling it out and halting at the foreign expressions and unfamiliar phrasing. The others listened in silence and with downcast eyes and after listening for a while dispersed without looking up, stroking their beards and moustaches as if to brush away words which had never been spoken.

After the noon prayer Alihodja too came, placing a bar across his shop front as a sign that the shop was closed. This time the proclamation was not written in Turkish also, so that the *hodja* could not read it. A boy was reading the proclamation aloud, quite mechanically, as if at school.

"PROCLAMATION
to the People of Bosnia and Herzegovina.

"We, Franz Joseph, Emperor of Austria, King of Bohemia etc. and Apo-apo-apo-stolic King of Hungary, to the inhabitants of Bosnia and Herzegovina: When a gen-gener-generation ago Our Armies crossed the frontiers of Your lands. . . ."

Alihodja felt his right ear tingling beneath his white turban and, as if it had been the day before, his quarrel with Karamanli flashed before his eyes, the outrage then committed on him, the red cross which swam before his eyes filled with tears, while the Austrian soldier carefully extracted the nail, and the white placard with the proclamation then addressed to the people.

The youth went on:

"An ass-ass-assurance was then given You that they had not come as enemies but as Your friends with the avowed intention of rooting out all the evils which had for years op-op-oppressed You.

"That word given to You in that crit-critical moment . . ."

Everyone shouted at the inexpert reader who, blushing and embarrassed, slipped away into the crowd. In his place came some unknown man in a leather jacket, who seemed as if he were only waiting for his chance, who began to read quickly and fluently as if it were a prayer that he already knew by heart.

"That word given to You in that critical moment has been honestly kept. Our Government has always seriously concerned itself and worked to maintain peace and order, to lead Your Fatherland towards a happier future.

"And We, to Our great joy, dare freely to say: the seed which has been sown in the furrows of the soil so prepared has produced a rich harvest. You too must feel those facts as a blessing; that in place of violence and tyranny have come order and security, that work and life have developed continuously, that the ennobling influence of its work has multiplied opportunities for culture and that under the protection of a regular administration every man may enjoy the fruits of his labors.

"It is the solemn duty of all of Us to continue along this way.

"Having this aim constantly before Our eyes, We hold that the time has come to give the inhabitants of these two lands a fresh proof of Our faith in their political maturity. In order to raise Bosnia and Herzegovina to a higher level of political life, We have decided to grant constitutional institutions—such as will answer to their present conditions and their common interests—to both these lands and to give in this manner a legal basis for the representation of their wishes and interests.

"Let Your voices also be heard when in the future decisions will be made touching the affairs of Your country which will have, as it has had up till now, its separate administration.

"But the first necessary condition for the introduction of this national constitution is the clear and indubitable definition of the legal position of both these lands. Starting from this principle and bearing in mind those bonds which in olden times existed between Our glorious predecessors on the Throne of Hungary and these lands, We extend Our rights of sovereignty over Bosnia and Herzegovina and We desire that these lands accept the order of succession which is valid for Our House.

"Thus the inhabitants of both lands will become participators in all these benefits which will assure them the lasting consolidation of those bonds which, up to the present, have linked them to Us. The new state of affairs will be the guarantee that culture and prosperity will continue to find a sure home in Your country.

"Bosnians and Herzegovinians!

"Among the countless cares which surround Our Throne, that which We shall have for Your material and moral prosperity will not be the least. The supreme conception of the equality of all before the law, the participation in the making of laws and the administration of the country, an equal protection afforded to all faiths, languages and national characteristics—all these supreme benefits You will enjoy in full measure.

"The freedom of the individual and the good of the community will be the guiding star of Our Government for both these lands. . . ."

With mouth half open and head lowered, Alihodja listened to these words, for the most part unfamiliar or unknown to him, and even those words which were not of themselves unfamiliar became in that context in some manner queer and incomprehensible. "Seed . . . sown in the furrows of the soil so prepared . . . first and necessary condition for the introduction of this local constitution; clear and indubitable definition of legal position . . . guiding star of Our Government!" Yes, those were the "Imperial words" once again! Each one of them opened before the *hodja's* inner vision now some distant, extraordinary and dangerous horizon, now some sort of curtain which fell, black and leaden, just before his eyes. So, first one thing and then the other; either he saw nothing or he saw something that he did not understand and which presaged no good. In this life nothing is impossible and every wonder possible. It could even happen that a man might listen carefully and yet understand nothing in detail while at the same time, when all those details were taken together, he could realize completely and understand perfectly! That seed, that star, those cares about the throne; all those things might just as well have been in some foreign language, yet none the less the *hodja,* or so it seemed to him, could understand what they intended to mean and what they wished to convey. These Emperors had for the past thirty years shouted across the lands and cities and over the heads of the peoples; yet every word in every proclamation of every Emperor was pregnant with meaning. For these countries were broken into fragments and in these countries heads rolled because of these words. So they spoke of "seed . . . stars . . . cares of the throne" lest they call things by their real names and speak what was the fact; that lands and provinces and, with them, living men and their habitations passed from hand to hand like small change; that a well-intentioned true-believing man could no longer find peace on this earth, no more than he could find the little he needed for this short life; that his position and his goods changed independently of himself and contrary to his wishes and his best intentions.

Alihodja listened and he had continually the impression that these words were the same words of thirty years ago; he felt the same leaden heaviness in his breast, the same message that the Turkish times were ended and that "the Turkish candle was burned out," but that it was necessary to repeat them for they would not understand or realize them, but deceived themselves and pretended to know nothing of them.

"You will therefore show Yourselves worthy of the confidence placed in You, so that the noble harmony existing between ruler and people, that most precious gage of all state progress, will always accompany Our common labors.

"Given in our Royal and Capital City of Budapest.

Franz Joseph."

The man in the leather jacket suddenly ceased reading and shouted unexpectedly:

"Long live His Majesty the Emperor!"

"Long life," shouted tall Ferhat, the municipal lamplighter, as if by order.

All the others dispersed at the same moment in silence.

Before dark that day the great white proclamation was torn down and thrown into the Drina. The next day some Serbian youths were arrested on suspicion and a fresh copy of the white proclamation was put up on the *kapia* and a local gendarme posted there to guard it.

Whenever a government feels the need of promising peace and prosperity to its citizens by means of a proclamation, it is time to be on guard and expect the opposite. Towards the end of October, the army began to arrive, not only by train but also along the old deserted road. As it had done thirty years before, it came down the steep slope from Sarajevo and crossed the bridge into the town, with arms and commissariat. There were units of all kinds except cavalry. All the barracks were full. They camped under canvas. Fresh units were continually arriving, stayed a few days in the town and were then posted to the villages along the Serbian frontier. The soldiers were mainly reservists, of various nationalities, with plenty of money. They made their minor personal purchases in the shops and bought fruit and sweetmeats at the street-corners. Prices leaped. Hay and oats completely disappeared. Fortifications began to be built on the hills surrounding the town. And on the bridge itself a very strange task began. In the middle of the bridge, just beyond the *kapia* as one came from the town to go to the left bank of the Drina, workmen specially brought for the job began to drill a hole about a yard square in one of the piers. The spot where they worked was concealed under a green tent, from beneath which continual hammering could be heard as they went deeper and deeper. The stone excavated was at once thrown over the parapet into the river. But however much the work was concealed, it was soon known in the town that the bridge was being mined, that is to say that a deep opening was being dug through one of the piers, right to the foundations, and that explosives would be placed in it in case war broke out and it was found necessary to destroy the bridge. Long iron ladders led down into the opening and when everything was finished an iron manhole cover was placed over it. Within a few days this cover could no longer be distinguished from the stones and dust. Carts passed over it, horses trotted by, and the townsmen hurried on their business without giving a thought to the mine and the explosives beneath. Only the children on their way to school halted for a moment at this spot, tapped inquisitively at that iron cover, trying to guess what was beneath it. They made up tales of some Arab hidden in the bridge, and argued among themselves about what an explosive was, what it did and whether it could ever destroy so great a building.

Among the grown-ups, only Alihodja prowled around and gazed somberly and suspiciously both at the green tent while the work was going on and at the iron cover which remained on the bridge after it had been finished. He listened to all that was said or whispered; that a hole as deep as a well had been made in that pier and explosives placed in it, and that it was connected by an electrical lead to the bank so that the commandant could at any time of the day or night destroy the bridge right in the middle as though it were made of sugar and not of stone. The *hodja* listened, shook his head, thought it over by day when he retired to his "coffin" and by night in bed when he should have been asleep; now he believed, now he rejected such an idea as mad and godless, but he worried about it continually so that even in his sleep the one-time *mutevelis* of Mehmed Pasha's *vakuf* appeared before him and asked him severely what all this was and what were they doing to the bridge. He turned his troubles over and over in his mind. He did not want to ask anyone in the market, considering that for a long time past there had been no one with whom a sensible man could consult or converse reasonably, since all the people had either lost their senses and their reputations or were just as embittered and confused as he himself was.

None the less, he soon found an opportunity to learn more about it. One of the Branović begs from Crnče, Muhamed, who had done his army service in Vienna, had stayed there as a long-service man and been promoted to sergeant-major (he was the grandson of that Shemsibeg who after the occupation had shut himself up in Crnče and died of sorrow, and who was still quoted by the older Turks as an unattainable example of moral grandeur and logic). Muhamed-beg had that year come home on leave. He was a big tall man of reddish complexion, dressed in an impeccable dark-blue uniform with yellow rank-badges, red piping and little silver stars on his lapel, with white kid-gloves on his hands and red fez on his head. Courteous, smiling, irreproachably clean and neat, he walked in the market-place, his long sword tapping gently on the cobbles, greeting everyone amiably and confidently like a man who has eaten the bread of the Emperor, who has no doubt of his own importance or any reason to be afraid of others.

When this Muhamed-beg came to his shop, asked about his health and sat down to drink a cup of coffee, Alihodja took the opportunity of asking him, as an "imperial man" who lived far from the town, for an explanation of the cares that oppressed him. He told him what the trouble was, what had been done on the bridge and what they were saying in the town, and asked him if such a thing were possible and whether they could plan the destruction of a bequest of such universal benefit as this one.

As soon as he had heard what was in question, the sergeant-major suddenly became serious. His broad smile disappeared and his ruddy clean-shaven face took on a wooden expression as if he were on parade at the moment of the command: attention. He was silent for a moment as if in indecision and then replied in a sort of hushed voice.

"There is something in all you say. But if you really want my advice, then it is best not to inquire about this or speak of it, for it comes under the head of military preparedness, official secrets and so forth and so on."

The *hodja* hated all the new expressions and especially that "and so forth and so on." It was not only that the words grated on his ears, but he felt clearly that, in the speech of these strangers, it took the place of an unspoken truth and that all that had been said before meant nothing at all.

"In the name of God, don't stuff me up with their . . . 'and so forth and so on,' but tell me and explain, if you can, what they are doing to the bridge. There can be no secret about that. In any case what sort of a secret is that, if even the schoolchildren talk about it?" the *hodja* interrupted angrily. "What has the bridge to do with their war?"

"It has, Alihodja; it has very much to do with it," said Branković, once again smiling.

And he explained to Alihodja amiably but a little condescendingly, as if speaking to a child, that all this was provided for in the rules of the service, that this was the duty of engineers and bridge-builders, and that in the Imperial Army everyone knew only his own job and did not concern himself in the affairs of some other branch.

The *hodja* listened to him, listened and watched, but did not understand very much. Finally, he could no longer hold himself in.

"All that is very fine, my fine fellow, but do they know that this is a Vezir's bequest, built for the good of his soul and the glory of God and that it is a sin to take even a stone from it?"

The sergeant-major only waved his hands, shrugged his shoulders, pursed his lips and closed his eyes, so that his whole face assumed a crafty and obsequious expression, unmoving, blind, deaf, such as men can only achieve by long years of practice in old-fashioned and decaying administrations in which discretion has long degenerated into insensibility and obedience into cowardice. A page of white unsullied paper is eloquent compared with the dumb caution of such a face. A moment later, the Emperor's man opened his eyes, let fall his hands, composed his face and once again resumed his usual appearance of confidence and serenity in which Viennese good-humor and Turkish courtesy met and mingled like two waters. Changing the subject and praising with well-chosen words the *hodja's* health and youthful appearance, he took his leave with the same inexhaustible amiability with which he had come. The *hodja* remained confused and uncertain in himself but in no way less troubled than he had been before. Lost in his thoughts he looked out from his shop at the shining loveliness of that first day of March. Opposite him, a little to the side, stood the eternal bridge, everlastingly the same; through its white arches could be seen the green, sparkling, tumultuous waters of the Drina, so that they seemed like some strange diadem in two colors which sparkled in the sun.

18

The tension known to the outside world as "the annexation crisis," which had thrown its ill-omened shadow over the bridge and the town beside it, rapidly subsided. Somewhere out there, by diplomacy and discussions between the interested parties, a peaceful solution had been found.

The frontier, always so inflammable, for once did not flare up. The army which had filled the town and the frontier villages in the first days of spring began to withdraw. But as always the changes which the crisis had brought remained after it had passed. The permanent garrison in the town was much larger than it had been before. The bridge remained mined. But no one gave it a thought except Alihodja Mutevelić. The piece of land on the left flank of the bridge above the ancient retaining wall, which had been the town park, was taken over by the military authorities. The fruit trees in the center of the park were cut down and a fine building erected. That was the new officers' mess, for the former mess, a small one-storied building up at Bikavac, was now too small for the increased number of officers. So that now, on the right side of the bridge was Lotte's hotel and on the left the officers' mess, two white almost identical buildings and between them the square, surrounded by shops and, on a small rise above the square, the great barracks which the people still called the Stone Han in memory of Mehmed Pasha's caravanserai which had once been there but had now disappeared without trace.

Prices, which had leaped up the previous autumn because of the large number of soldiers, remained unchanged, with much greater likelihood of further rises than of returning to their former level. That year a Serbian and a Moslem bank were opened. The people made use of money orders like medicines. Now everybody incurred debts more freely. But the more money a man had the more he needed. Only to those who spent more than they gained did life seem easy and good. But the merchants and businessmen were worried. Terms of payment became shorter than ever. Good and reliable customers were fewer and fewer. The number of articles whose price was higher than the people could afford to pay was ever greater. Business was on a small scale, and cheaper and cheaper types of goods were in demand. Only bad payers bought freely. The only sure and safe business was army contracting or work for some government institution, but not everyone could get it. State taxes and municipal dues became larger and more numerous; the strictness of the collectors increased. One could feel from afar the unhealthy fluctuations of the exchanges. The profits which arose from them went into unseen hands, while the losses reached even the most remote corners of the monarchy and struck the retail traders, both as sellers and consumers.

The general feeling in the town was neither more serene nor more calm. That sudden slackening of tension did not result in a real appeasement either among the Serbs or the Moslems; it left to the first a concealed disillusionment, to the second distrust and fear of the future. The expectation of great events began to grow once more, without visible reason or direct cause. The people hoped for something or were afraid of something (in actual fact some hoped while others feared) and looked on everything in the light of those hopes and fears. In a word, men's hearts were disturbed, even among the simple and illiterate, especially among the younger people, and no one was any longer satisfied with the monotonous sort of life which had dragged on for years. Everyone wanted more, asked for better or trembled in fear of worse. The older people still regretted that "sweet tranquillity" which in Turkish times had been regarded as the main aim of existence and the most perfect expression of public and private life, and which had still existed in the first decades of the Austrian administration. But there were few of these. All the others demanded an animated, noisy and exciting life. They wanted sensations or the echo of sensations or at least variety, noise and excitement which would give the illusion of sensation. That desire changed not only the state of men's minds but even the external appearance of the town. Even that time-honored and established life on the *kapia,* that life of quiet conversation and peaceful meditations, simple jokes and lovesick songs between the waters, the sky and the mountains, began to change.

The coffee merchant obtained a gramophone, a clumsy wooden box with a big tin trumpet in the shape of a bright blue flower. His son changed the records and the needles and was continually winding this raucous contraption which echoed from both banks and made the *kapia* quiver. He had been forced to get it in order not to be left behind by his competitors, for now gramophones could be heard not only at meetings and in the reading rooms but even in the humblest cafés where the guests sat under a lime tree, on the grass or on brightly-lit balconies, and talked with few words and in low voices. Everywhere the gramophone ground and churned out Turkish marches, Serbian patriotic songs or arias from Viennese operettas, according to the tastes of the guests for whom it played. For men would no longer go where there was neither noise, glitter nor movement.

Newspapers were read avidly, but superficially and hastily; everyone looked only for the sensational news printed in large type on the front page. There were few who read the articles or the news in small type. All that took place was accompanied by clamor and the brilliance of big words. The younger people did not think that they had lived that day if by the evening their ears were not singing or their eyes had not been dazzled by what they had heard or seen in the course of the day.

The *agas* and *effendis* of the town came to the *kapia,* serious and outwardly indifferent, to listen to the latest news about the Turco-Italian war in Tripoli. They listened avidly to all that was written in the papers about the heroic young Turkish major, Enver Bey, who beat the Italians and defended the Sultan's lands like a descendant of the Sokollis or the Kuprulus. They frowned at the raucous music of the gramophone, which prevented their thinking, and, without showing it, trembled deeply and sincerely for the fate of the distant Turkish province in Africa.

It chanced that just then Pietro the Italian, Maistor-Pero, returning from work clothed in his linen overall, white with stone-dust and stained with paint and turpentine, crossed the bridge. He had grown old and bent and even more humble and timid. As at the time when Lucchieni assassinated the Empress, it seemed, by some logic incomprehensible to him, that he was again guilty of something which his Italian fellow-countrymen, with whom for many years he had had no contact, had done somewhere in the outer world. One of the Turkish youths shouted:

"So you want Tripoli, you bastard! You there, I mean!" and made obscene gestures at him.

But Maistor-Pero, bent and tired, with his tools under his arm, only pulled his hat further over his eyes, feverishly bit on his pipe-stem and hurried home to Mejdan.

There his Stana was waiting for him. She too had grown older and had lost some of her physical strength, but she was still a formidable and outspoken woman. He complained bitterly to her about the young Turks who said things they should not have said and had asked him about Tripoli, which until a few days ago he had not even known existed. But Stana, as always, would not understand him or console him, but went on saying that it was he himself who was at fault and even deserved to have insults shouted at him.

"If you were a real man, which you are not, you would have hit their ugly phizzes with your chisel or your hammer. Then those ragamuffins would not even think of jeering at you but would get to their feet when you cross the bridge."

"Eh, Stana, Stana," said Maistor-Pero good-humoredly and a little sadly, "how could a man hit another in the face with a hammer?"

So those years passed in a succession of greater or lesser sensations, or in the constant need of them. So it came to the autumn of 1912; then 1913 with the Balkan wars and the Serbian victories. By a strange exception, just these things which were of such great importance to the fate of the bridge and the town and all who lived in it came silently and almost unnoticed.

Flushed with red at sunrise and sunset,

golden at midday, the October days passed over the town, which was waiting for the maize crop and the new season's plum brandy. It was still pleasant to sit on the *kapia* in the noonday sun. Time, it seemed, was holding its breath over the town. It was just then that it happened.

Even before the literates in the town could find their way through the contradictory newspaper reports, the war between Turkey and the four Balkan States had already broken out and followed the well-worn paths across the Balkans. Before the people had fully grasped the sense and import of this war it was practically over as a result of the victories of the Serbian and Christian armies; all was ended far from Višegrad, without fires on the frontiers, without the grumble of the guns and without heads on the *kapia*. As it had been with trade and money, so it was with those more important things also; everything happened far away and unbelievably quickly. Somewhere far away in the world the dice had been thrown, the battles fought, and it was there that the fate of each one of the townsfolk was decided.

But if the outward appearance of the town remained peaceful and unchanged, these events stirred up in the minds of men whole tempests of the greatest enthusiasm and the deepest depression. As in the case of everything else that had happened in the world in recent years, they were looked on in the town with diametrically opposed feelings by the Serbs and the Moslems; only in their intensity and depth were they perhaps equal. These events surpassed all the hopes of the one; all the fears of the others appeared justified. Those desires which for hundreds of years had flown before the slow pace of history could now no longer keep pace with it but outdistanced it by some fantastic flight along the road to the most daring realization.

Everything that the town could see or feel directly of that fateful war took place incredibly simply and with the swiftness of an arrow.

At Uvce where the frontier between Austro-Hungary and Turkey followed the little river Uvac, and where a wooden bridge separated the Austrian gendarmerie barracks from the Turkish blockhouse, the Turkish officer with his small guard crossed to the Austrian side. There, he broke his sword with a theatrical gesture on the parapet of the bridge and surrendered to the Austrian gendarmes. At that moment the gray-clad Serbian infantry came down from the hills. They replaced the old-fashioned *askers* along the whole frontier between Bosnia and the Sanjak. The triangle between Austria, Turkey and Serbia disappeared. The Turkish frontier which only the day before had been about nine miles from the town was suddenly withdrawn more than 600 miles, somewhere far beyond Jedrene (Adrianople).

So many and such important changes, carried out in so short a time, shook the town to its foundations.

For the bridge on the Drina this change was fateful. The railway link with Sarajevo had, as we have seen, reduced its connection with the West and now, in a moment, its connection with the East also ceased. In fact the East, which had created it and which had up to the day before still been there, greatly shaken and weakened no doubt, but still as permanent and real as sky and land, had now vanished like an apparition. Now the bridge in reality no longer linked anything save the two parts of the town and those dozen or so villages on one or the other side of the Drina.

The great stone bridge which, according to the ideas and the pious intentions of the Grand Vezir from Sokolovići, was meant to link the two parts of the Empire, and "for the love of God" make easier the passage from West to East and from East to West, was now in fact cut off from both East and West and abandoned like a stranded ship or a deserted shrine. For three whole centuries it had endured and experienced everything and, unchanging, had truly served its purpose, but human needs had altered and world conditions changed; now its task had betrayed it. By its size, its solidity and its beauty, armies might pass across it and caravans follow one another for centuries to come, but thus, by the eternal and unforeseen play of human relations, the Vezir's bequest suddenly found itself abandoned and, as if by some magic spell, outside the main stream of life. The present role of the bridge in no way corresponded to its eternally young appearance and its gigantic but harmonious proportions. But it still stood the same as when the Grand Vezir had seen it in his inward vision behind closed eyes and as when his masons had built it; powerful, beautiful and enduring, beyond all possibility of change.

It needed time, it needed effort, before the townspeople understood all that has been said here in a few lines and what had in fact taken place in a few months. Not even in dreams did frontiers change so quickly or go so far away.

All that had lain quiescent in men, as ancient as that bridge and equally dumb and motionless, now suddenly came alive and began to influence their everyday life, their general mood and the personal fate of every individual.

The first summer days of 1913 were rainy and oppressive. On the *kapia* by day sat the Moslems of the town, morose and disconsolate, about a dozen elderly men grouped around a younger one who read to them from the newspapers, interpreting foreign expressions and unusual names and explaining the geography. All smoked peacefully and gazed unwaveringly in front of them but could not completely conceal that they were anxious and shaken. Hiding their emotion, they bent over the map which showed the future partition of the Balkan Peninsula. They looked at the paper and saw nothing in those curving lines, but they knew and understood everything, for their geography was in their blood and they felt biologically their picture of the world.

"Who will get Uskub (Skoplje)?" asked one old man, apparently indifferently, to the youth who was reading.

"Serbia."

"Uh!"

"And who will get Salonica?"

"Greece."

"Uh! Uh!"

"And Jedrene?" asked another in a low voice.

"Bulgaria, probably."

"Uh! Uh! Uh!"

These were not loud and mournful wailings, like women or weaklings, but deep and stifled sighs which were lost with the tobacco smoke which drifted through their moustaches into the summer air. Many of these old men had passed their seventieth year. In their childhood, the Turkish power had stretched from the Lika and the Kordun right to Stambul and from Stambul to the uncertain desert frontiers of far-off and illimitable Arabia (that Turkish power had been the great, indivisible and indestructible unity of the Moslem faith, all that part of the terrestrial globe where the muezzin called the faithful to prayer). They remembered that well, but they also remembered how, later on, in the course of their lives, that Turkish power had withdrawn from Serbia into Bosnia and then from Bosnia into the Sanjak. And now, now they lived to see that power like some fantastic ocean tide suddenly withdraw and pass away somewhere far out of sight, while they remained here, deceived and menaced, like seaweed on dry land, left to their own devices and their own evil fate. All this came from God and was, without doubt, envisaged in the ordinances of God, but it was hard for men to understand; their breath came short, their consciousness was troubled, they felt as if the solid earth was being drawn irresistibly away from under their feet as if it were a carpet, and how frontiers which should have been firm and lasting had become fluid and shifting, moving away and lost in the distance like the capricious rivulets of spring.

With such thoughts and feelings the old men sat on the *kapia* and listened vaguely to all that the newspapers wrote. They listened silently though the words in which the papers spoke of kingdoms and states seemed to them mad, impudent and out of place, and their whole manner of writing as something godless, contrary to the eternal laws and the logic of life, something which would "get no better" and with which no decent or honorable man could become reconciled. Above their heads floated clouds of tobacco smoke, and in the skies cruised white, fleecy clouds of a rainy summer, casting quick broad shadows on the earth.

At night on the *kapia* youths from the Serbian houses sat till the small hours, singing loudly and provocatively the song about the Serbian gun and no one came to fine or punish them. Among them could often be noticed students from the universities or secondary schools. They were mostly thin, pale youths with long hair and black shallow hats with wide brims. That autumn they came very often, though the school year had already commenced. They came by train from Sarajevo with instructions and recommendations, passed the night here on the *kapia,* but were no longer in the town at dawn next day for the young men of Višegrad sent them on by underground routes to Serbia.

With the summer months, at the time of the school holidays, the town and the *kapia* became lively with schoolboys and students, born in the town and returning to their homes. They influenced the whole life of the town.

At the end of June a group of students from the Sarajevo secondary school arrived in the town and in the first half of July students of law, medicine and philosophy from the Universities of Vienna, Prague, Graz and Zagreb, began to arrive one by one. With their arrival even the outward aspect of the town began to change. Their young faces could be seen in the market-place and on the *kapia* and they were easily distinguishable by their bearing, their speech and their clothes from the established customs and unchanging clothing of the townspeople. They wore clothes of dull colors and the latest cut. This was the "Glöckenfaçon" then considered the height of fashion and the best of taste in all Central Europe. On their heads they wore soft Panama hats with turned-down brims and ribbons of six different but discreet colors; on their feet wide American shoes with sharply turned up toes. Most of them carried very thick bamboo canes and in the lapels of their coats they wore metal Sokol badges or those of some student organization.

The students brought with them new words and jokes, new dances from the balls of the previous winter, and especially new books and pamphlets, Serbian, Czech and German.

It had happened earlier too, in the first years of the Austrian occupation, that young men from the town had gone away to study, but not in such large numbers nor inspired by this sort of spirit. In those first few decades a few of them had finished at the Teachers' Train-

ing College at Sarajevo, and two or three had even read philosophy at Vienna, but these had been rare exceptions, modest youths who had passed their examinations quietly and without advertisement and once their studies had been completed had been lost in the gray and countless ranks of the state bureaucracy. But for some time past the number of students from the town had suddenly increased. By the help of national cultural institutions even peasants' sons and the children of petty artisans went to the university. The spirit and character of the students themselves changed.

These were no longer those one-time students of the first years after the occupation, mild and timid youths devoted to their studies in the closest sense of the word. But neither were they the ordinary town dandies and goodfellows of an earlier time, future landowners and shopkeepers who at a certain period in their lives wasted their excess of youth and strength on the *kapia* till their families said of them: "Marry him off and stop his squalling!" These were a new sort of young men, educated in various cities and states and under various influences. From the great cities, from the universities and schools which they attended, these young men came back intoxicated with that feeling of proud audacity with which his first and incomplete knowledge fills a young man, and carried away by ideas about the rights of peoples to freedom and of individuals to enjoyment and dignity. With every summer vacation they brought back with them free-thinking views on social and religious questions and an enthusiastically revived nationalism which recently, especially after the Serbian victories in the Balkan wars, had grown to a universal conviction and, in many of these youths, to a fanatical desire for action and personal sacrifice.

The *kapia* was the main scene of their meetings. They would meet there after supper. In the darkness, under the stars or in the moonlight, above the boisterous river, echoed their songs, jests, noisy conversation and endless arguments, new, bold, naïve, sincere and unselfconscious.

With the students were also their childhood friends who had studied with them in the local elementary school, but had remained in the town as apprentices, shop assistants or clerks in the municipal offices. There were two types. Some were satisfied with their destiny and the life of the town in which they would pass their days. They looked with curiosity and sympathy at their educated comrades, admired them and never thought of comparing themselves with them, and, without the slightest jealousy, followed their development and their career. There were others who were dissatisfied with life in the town to which they were condemned by force of circumstances and who longed for something that they considered higher and better and which had escaped them, becoming every day farther away and more inaccessible. Though they used to meet together with their student comrades, these youths usually kept apart from their educated fellows either by some crude form of irony or by their unfriendly silence. They could not take part as equals in their conversations. Therefore, constantly tormented by their feeling of inferiority, they now exaggerated and stressed in conversation their crudeness and ignorance by comparison with their more fortunate comrades or, from the height of their ignorance, mocked at all that they could not understand. In either case, envy breathed out of them as an almost visible and tangible force. But youth easily bears with even the worst instincts, and lives and moves freely and easily among them.

There had been and there would be again starlight nights on the *kapia* and rich constellations and moonlight, but there had never been, and God alone knows whether there would be again, such young men who in such conversations and with such feelings and ideas would keep vigil on the *kapia*. That was a generation of rebel angels, in that short moment while they still had all the power and all the rights of angels and also the flaming pride of rebels. These sons of peasants, traders or artisans from a remote Bosnian township had obtained from fate, without any special effort of their own, a free entry into the world and the great illusion of freedom. With their inborn small-town characteristics, they went out into the world, chose more or less for themselves and according to their own inclinations, momentary moods or the whims of chance, the subject of their studies, the nature of their entertainments and the circle of their friends and acquaintances. For the most part they were unable, or did not know how, to seize and make use of what they succeeded in seeing, but there was not one of them who did not have the feeling that he could take what he wished and that all that he took was his. Life (that word came up very often in their conversations, as it did in the literature and politics of the time, when it was always written with a capital letter), Life stood before them as an object, as a field of action for their liberated senses, for their intellectual curiosity and their sentimental exploits, which knew no limits. All roads were open to them, onward to infinity; on most of those roads they would never even set foot, but none the less the intoxicating lust for life lay in the fact that they could (in theory at least) be free to choose which they would and dare to cross from one to the other. All that other men, other races, in other times and lands, had achieved and attained in the course of generations, through centuries of effort, at the cost of lives, of renunciations and of sacrifices greater and dearer than life, now lay before them as a chance inheritance and a dangerous gift of fate. It seemed fantastic and improbable but was none the less true; they could do with their youth what they liked, and give their judgments freely and without restriction; they dared to say what they liked and for many of them those words were the same as deeds, satisfying their atavistic need for heroism and glory, violence and destruction, yet they did not entail any obligation to act nor any visible responsibility for what had been said. The most gifted among them despised all that they should have learned and underestimated all that they were able to do, but they boasted of what they did not know and waxed enthusiastic at what was beyond their powers to achieve. It is hard to imagine a more dangerous manner of entering into life or a surer way towards exceptional deeds or total disaster. Only the best and strongest among them threw themselves into action with the fanaticism of fakirs and were there burned up like flies, to be immediately hailed by their fellows as martyrs and saints (for there is no generation without its saints) and placed on pedestals as inaccessible examples.

Every human generation has its own illusions with regard to civilization; some believe that they are taking part in its upsurge, others that they are witnesses of its extinction. In fact, it always both flames up and smolders and is extinguished, according to the place and the angle of view. This generation which was now discussing philosophy, social and political questions on the *kapia* under the stars, above the waters, was richer only in illusions; in every other way it was similar to any other. It had the feeling both of lighting the first fires of one new civilization and extinguishing the last flickers of another which was burning out. What could especially be said of them was that there had not been for a long time past a generation which with greater boldness had dreamed and spoken about life, enjoyment and freedom and which had received less of life, suffered worse, labored more hardly and died more often than had this one. But in those summer days of 1913 all was still undetermined, unsure. Everything appeared as an exciting new game on that ancient bridge, which shone in the moonlight of those July nights, clean, young and unalterable, strong and lovely in its perfection, stronger than all that time might bring and men imagine or do.

19

Just as one warm summer night in August is like another, so the discussions of these schoolboys and students on the *kapia* were always the same or similar.

Immediately after a good supper hurriedly eaten (for the day had passed in bathing and basking in the sun) they arrived one by one on the *kapia*. There was Janko Stiković, son of a tailor from Mejdan, who had already been studying natural science at Graz for two years. He was a thin young man with sharp features and smooth black hair, vain, sensitive, dissatisfied with himself but even more with everyone about him. He read much and wrote articles under a penname which was already well known in revolutionary youth papers published in Prague and Zagreb. He also wrote poems and published them under another penname. He was preparing a book of them which was to be published by *Zora,* the Nationalist Edition. He was also a good speaker and a fiery debater at students' meetings. Velimir Stevanović was a healthy, well-built youth, an adopted child of uncertain parentage; he was ironic, down to earth, thrifty and industrious; he had completed his medical studies at Prague. There was Jacov Herak, son of the good-natured and popular Višegrad postman, a small, dark law student, of piercing eyes and swift words, a socialist of polemical spirit, who was ashamed of his kind heart and concealed every trace of emotion. Ranko Mihailović was a taciturn and good-natured youth who was studying law at Zagreb and was already thinking of a career as a civil servant. He took little part and that half-heartedly in his comrades' arguments and discussions on love, politics, views on life and social conditions. On his mother's side he was the great-grandson of that Pop Mihailo whose head, with a cigar stuck between its lips, had been put on a stake and exposed on that very *kapia.*

There were also a few Sarajevo secondary school students who listened avidly to their older colleagues and their tales of life in the great cities, and with the imagination that whips up the vanity and hidden desires of children thought of everything as even greater and more beautiful than it really was or ever could be. Among them was Nikola Glasičanin, a pale stiff youth who because of poverty, poor health and lack of success had had to leave the secondary school after the fourth class and return to the town and accept a post as clerk to a German timber exporting firm. He came from a decayed landowning family at Okolište. His grandfather, Milan Glasičanin, had died a short time after the occupation, in the Sarajevo lunatic asylum, after gambling away in his youth the greater part of his property. His father, Peter, a sickly creature without will, force or reputation, had died some time ago. Now Nikola spent all day long on the river bank with the workmen who poled the heavy pine logs and made them into rafts. He measured the cubic meterage of the wood and afterwards, in the office, entered it in the books. This monotonous task among such people, without ideals and without wider views, he felt as a torture and a humiliation, and the absence of any likelihood of being able to change his social status or get on in the world had created of the sensitive youth a man old before his time, bilious and taciturn. He read much in his spare time, but that spiritual food did nothing to give him force or exalt him, for everything in him took a sour turn. His bad luck, his loneliness and his suffering opened his eyes and sharpened his senses to many things, but even the most beautiful thoughts and most precious knowledge could only discourage and embitter him the more, for they threw an even stronger light on his lack of success and his lack of prospects in the town.

There was also Vlado Marić, a locksmith by trade, a merry and good-humored man whom his colleagues from the higher schools loved and invited, as much for his strong and lovely baritone as for his simple-heartedness and goodness. This vigorous young man with his locksmith's cap on his head was one of those humble men who are always sufficient to themselves and do not think of comparing themselves with others, but calmly and thankfully accept whatever life offers to them and give simply and naturally all they can.

There were also the two local schoolmistresses, Zorka and Zagorka, both born in the town. All the youths competed for their favors and around them played that naïve, complicated, brilliant and tormenting game of love. In their presence the discussions raged like a court of love in earlier centuries; because of them young men would later sit on the *kapia* smoking in the darkness and solitude or singing with others after an evening spent drinking somewhere else; because of them there were hidden enmities between comrades, badly concealed jealousies and open quarrels. About ten o'clock the girls would go home; but the young men remained for long, though the mood on the *kapia* slackened and the rival eloquence diminished.

Stiković, who usually took the lead in these discussions, that evening sat silent, smoking. He was troubled and out of humor with himself, but he concealed it as he always concealed all his true feelings, though he never succeeded in concealing them completely. That afternoon he had had his first rendezvous with the schoolmistress Zorka, an attractive girl with a full figure, pale face and fiery eyes. On Stiković's insistence, they had been able to do the most difficult of all things in a small town; that is for a youth and a girl to meet in a hidden place where no one could see them or know anything about it. They had met in her school which was deserted at that time because of the holidays. He had gone in from one street, through the garden, and she from another by the main entrance. They had met in a dimly-lit, dusty room piled almost to the ceiling with benches. It is thus that the passion of love is often compelled to look for remote and ugly places. They could neither sit nor lie down. Both of them were embarrassed and awkward. Too full of desire, too impatient, they embraced and mingled on one of those benches which she knew so well, without looking at or noticing anything around them. He was the first to recover. Abruptly, without transition, as young men do, he stood up to arrange his clothing and go away. The girl burst into tears. Their disillusion was mutual. When he had more or less calmed down he went out, almost as if escaping, by a side door.

At home he met the postman who had brought the youth-paper with his article "The Balkans, Serbia and Bosnia-Herzegovina." Reading the article again turned his thoughts away from the incident of a few moments before. But even in that he found reason for dissatisfaction. There were printers' errors in the article and some of the sentences sounded silly to him; now, when it was no longer possible to make alterations, it seemed to him that many things could have been better expressed, more clearly and more concisely.

The same evening they sat on the *kapia* discussing his article in the presence of Zorka herself. His principal adversary was the talkative and aggressive Herak who looked at everything and criticized everything from an orthodox socialist viewpoint. The others only intervened in the discussion from time to time. The two schoolmistresses remained silent, preparing an unseen wreath for the victor. Stiković defended himself weakly, firstly because he himself now saw many weaknesses and illogicalities in his own article, though he would never admit this before his colleagues; and secondly because he was troubled by the memory of the afternoon in the dusty and stuffy classroom, a scene which now seemed to him both comic and ugly but which had long been the aim of his most intense desires and his most ardent feelings towards the pretty schoolmistress. She herself was sitting there in the summer darkness looking at him with shining eyes. He felt like a debtor and a criminal and would have given much not to have been in the school that day and not to be here with her now. In such a mood, Herak seemed to him like an aggressive gadfly from whose attacks he could only defend himself with difficulty. It seemed to him that he must answer not only for his article but also for all that had happened that day in the school. Above all he wanted to be alone, somewhere far away, so that he could think calmly of something other than the article or the girl. But self-love drove him on to defend himself. Stiković quoted Cvijić and Štrosmajer, Herak Kautsky and Babel.

"You are putting the cart before the horse," shouted Herak, analyzing Stiković's article. "It is not possible for the Balkan peasant, plunged in poverty and every sort of misery, to found a good and lasting state organization. Only the preliminary economic liberation of the exploited classes, the peasants and the workers, that is to say the greater number of the people, can create real conditions for the formation of independent states. That is a natural process and the road we all must take, and in no way the other way round. Therefore both national liberation and unification must be carried out in the spirit of socialist liberation and renascence. Otherwise it will happen that the peasant, worker and ordinary citizen will introduce their pauperism and their slavish mentality, like a mortal contagion, into the new state formations and the small number of exploiters will instil into them their parasitical, reactionary mentality and their anti-social instincts. Therefore enduring states or a healthy society cannot exist."

"All that is foreign book-learning, my good fellow," answered Stiković, "which vanishes before the living impetus of awakened nationalist forces among the Serbs and then among the Croats and Slovenes also, though tending to one aim. Things do not come to pass according to the forecasts of German theoreticians but advance in complete accord with the deep sense of our history and our racial destiny. From Karageorge's words: "Let each kill his Turkish chief" the social problem in the Balkans has always solved itself by the way of national liberation movements and wars. It all moves beautifully logically, from the less to the great, from the regional and tribal to the national and the formation of the State. Were not our victories at Kumanovo and on the Bregalnica also the greatest victories of progressive thought and social justice?"

"That remains to be seen," broke in Herak.

"Who does not see it now, will never see it. We believe . . ."

"You believe, but we believe nothing, but want to be convinced by actual proofs and facts," answered Herak.

"Surely the disappearance of the Turks and the weakening of Austro-Hungary as the first step towards her annihilation are really the victories of small, democratic peoples and enslaved classes in their aspiration to find a place in the sun?" Stiković developed his idea.

"If the realization of nationalist aims brings with it the creation of social justice, then in the Western European states which have for the most part achieved all their nationalist ideals and are in that matter satisfied, there should no longer be any major social problems, or movements, or conflicts. Yet we see that that is not so. On the contrary."

"And I keep telling you," Stiković answered weariedly, "that without the creation of independent states on the basis of national unity and modern conceptions of personal and social liberty, there can be no talk of 'social liberation.' For, as some Frenchman once said, politics come first. . . ."

"The stomach comes first," interrupted Herak.

The others too became heated and the naïve students' discussion became a youthful squabble with everyone talking at once and interrupting one another and which, at the first quips, degenerated into laughter and shouting.

That was a welcome excuse for Stiković to break off the argument and remain silent, without having to give the impression of a withdrawal or a defeat.

After Zorka and Zagorka who went home about ten o'clock, escorted by Velimir and Ranko, the others too began to disperse. At last only Stiković and Nikola Glasičanin were left.

These two were about the same age. At one time they had gone to school together and had shared the same lodgings in Sarajevo. They knew one another down to the last detail and just for that reason they could neither of them make up his mind whether they really liked one another. With the years the distance between them naturally became wider and harder to bridge. Every vacation they met again here in the town and each took the other's measure and looked on the other as an inseparable enemy. Now the beautiful and wayward schoolmistress Zorka had also come between them. In the long months of the previous winter she had gone about with Glasičanin who had never concealed, or been able to conceal, that he was in love. He had plunged head over heels in love with all the fire that embittered and dissatisfied persons can put into such an emotion. But as soon as the summer months came and the students began to appear, the sensitive Glasičanin was unable to avoid seeing the interest that the schoolmistress showed in Stikovič. For that reason the old tension between them, which had always been kept hidden from others, had greatly increased. All this vacation they had not once been alone together as they were now.

Now that chance had so arranged it, the first thought of each of them was to separate as soon as possible without conversation which could only be unpleasant for both. But some ridiculous consideration, known only to youth, prevented them from doing as they wished. But in this embarrassment chance again helped them and lessened at least for a moment the heavy silence that oppressed them.

In the darkness could be heard the voices of two youths who were walking on the bridge. They were moving slowly and just then halted by the *kapia* behind the angle of the parapet, so that Stiković and Glasičanin could not see them, or be seen by them, from their seat on the *sofa*. But they could hear every word and the voices were well known to them. They were two of their younger comrades, Toma Galus and Fehim Bahtijarević. These two kept themselves a little apart from the group which comprised most of the other students and which gathered every evening on the *kapia* around Stiković and Herak, for, although younger, Galus was a rival of Stiković both as a poet and as a nationalist speaker. He did not like Stiković nor admire him, while Bahtijarević was exceptionally silent, proud and reserved as befitted a true grandchild of a family of begs.

Toma Galus was a tall youth with red cheeks and blue eyes. His father, Alban von Galus, the last descendant of an ancient family of the Burgenland, had come to the town as a civil servant immediately after the occupation. He had been for twelve years a forestry inspector and now lived in the town on pension. At the very beginning, he had married the daughter of one of the local landowners, Hadji Toma Stanković, a robust and full-blown young woman of dark skin and strong will. They had had three children, two daughters and one son, all of whom had been christened into the Serbian Orthodox Church and had grown up like real townsmen's children and grandchildren of Hadji Toma.

Old Galus, a tall and formerly a very handsome man, with a pleasant smile and masses of thick white hair, had long become a real townsman, "Mr. Albo," whom the younger generation could not think of as a foreigner and a newcomer. He had two passions which harmed no one; hunting and his pipe, and had made many old and true friends, both among the Serbs and among the Moslems, throughout the whole district who shared his passion for the chase. He had completely assimilated many of their customs as if he had been born and bred among them, especially their habit of cheerful silence and calm conversation, so characteristic of men who are passionate smokers and who love hunting, the forests and life in the open.

Young Galus had matriculated that year at Sarajevo and that autumn was due to go on to Vienna to study. But in the matter of these studies there was a division of opinion in the family. The father wanted his son to study technical sciences or forestry and the son wanted to study philosophy. For Toma Galus only resembled his father in appearance and all his desires led him in a completely opposite direction. He was one of those good scholars, modest and exemplary in everything, who pass all their examinations with ease as if playing at them, but whose real and sincere interests are taken up with satisfying their somewhat confused and disordered spiritual aspirations outside school and outside the official curriculum. These are students of serene and simple heart but of uneasy and inquisitive spirit. Those difficult and dangerous crises of the life of the senses and emotions through which so many other younger men of their age pass, are almost unknown to them, therefore they find difficulty in stilling their spiritual anxieties and very often remain all their lives dilettantes, interesting eccentrics without stable occupation or definite interests. As every young man must not only fulfil the eternal and natural demands of youth and maturity and also pay tribute to the current spiritual moods and fashions of his time, which for the moment reign among youth, Galus too had written verses and was an active member of the revolutionary nationalist student organizations. He had also studied French for five years as an optional subject, taken an interest in literature and, more especially, philosophy. He read passionately and indefatigably. The main body of reading of the young men at school in Sarajevo at that time consisted of works from the well-known and enormous German publishing list *Reclams Universal-Bibliotek*. These small, cheap booklets with yellow covers and exceptionally small print were the main spiritual food available to the students of that time; from them they could become acquainted not only with German literature, but with all the more important works in world literature in German translation. From them Galus drew his knowledge of modern German philosophers, especially Nietzsche and Stirner, and in his walks in Sarajevo along the banks of the Miljačka held endless discussions about them with a sort of cold passion, in no way linking his reading with his personal life, as so many youths often do. This type of young scholar just through his examinations, ripened too early and overloaded with all kinds of varied, chaotic and uncoordinated knowledge, was not rare among the students of that time. A modest youth and a good student, Galus knew the freedom and the unrestraint of youth only in the daring of his thoughts and the exaggerations of his reading.

Fehim Bahtijarević was a townsman on his mother's side only. His father had been born in Rogatica and was now *kadi* (Moslem judge) there, but his mother was from the great local family of Osmanagić. From his earliest childhood he had passed a part of the summer vacation in the town with his mother and her relatives. He was a slender youth, graceful and well formed, fine-boned but strong. Everything about him was measured, restrained, controlled. The fine oval of his face was sunburned, his skin browned with light touches of a dark bluish shade, his movements few and abrupt; his eyes were black with blue shadings in the whites and his glance burning but without sparkle. He had thick eyebrows which met, and a fine black down on his upper lip. Such faces are reminiscent of Persian miniatures.

That summer he too had matriculated and he was now waiting to get a state grant to study oriental languages in Vienna.

The two young men were continuing some conversation begun earlier. The subject was Bahtijarević's choice of studies. Galus was proving to him that he would be making a mistake in taking up oriental studies. In general Galus spoke much more, and more animatedly, than his companion for he was accustomed to be listened to and to lay down the law, while Bahtijarević spoke shortly, like a man who has his own fixed ideas and feels no need to convince anyone else. Like most young men who have read much, Galus spoke with a naïve satisfaction in words, picturesque expressions and comparisons, and with a tendency to generalize, whereas Bahtijarević spoke dryly, curtly, almost indifferently.

Hidden in the shadows and reclining on the stone seats, Stiković and Glasičanin remained silent as if they had tacitly agreed to listen to the conversation of their two comrades on the bridge.

Finishing the conversation about studies, Galus said belligerently:

"In that you Moslems, you begs' sons, often make a mistake. Disconcerted by the new times, you no longer know your exact and rightful place in the world. Your love for everything oriental is only a contemporary expression of your 'will to power'; for you the eastern way of life and thought is very closely bound up with a social and legal order which was the basis of your centuries of lordship. That is understandable. But it in no way means that you have any sense for orientalism as a study. You are orientals but you are making a mistake when you think that you are thereby called upon to be orientalists. In general you have not got the calling or the true inclination for science."

"Really!"

"No, you haven't. And when I say that, I am not saying anything insulting or offensive. On the contrary. You are the only nobles in this country, or at least you were; for centuries you have enlarged, confirmed and defended your privileges by sword and pen, legally, religiously and by force of arms; that has made of you typical warriors, administrators and landowners, and that class of men nowhere in the world worries about abstract sciences but leaves them to those who have nothing else and can do nothing else. The true studies for you are law and economics, for you are men of practical knowledge. Such are men from the ruling classes, always and everywhere."

"You mean that we should remain uneducated?"

"No, it does not mean that, but it means that you must remain what you are or, if you like, what you have been; you must, for no one can be at the same time what he is and the contrary of what he is."

"But we are no longer a ruling class today. Today we are all equal," Bahtijarević broke in once more with a touch of irony, in which was both bitterness and pride.

"You are not, naturally you are not. The conditions which at one time made you what you were have changed long ago, but that does not mean that you can change with the same speed. This is not the first, nor will it be the last, instance of a social caste losing its reason for existence and yet remaining the same. Conditions of life change but a class remains what it is, for only so can it exist and as such it will die."

The conversation of the two unseen youths broke off for a moment, stifled by Bahtijarević's silence.

In the clear June sky, above the dark mountains on the horizon, the moon appeared. The white plaque with the Turkish inscription suddenly shone in the moonlight, like a dimly lit window in the blue-black darkness.

Bahtijarević then said something, but in so low a voice that only disjointed and incomprehensible words reached Stiković and Glasičanin. As so often in young men's discussions, in which changes of subject are rapid and bold, the conversation was now about another matter. From the study of oriental languages, they had now passed on to the content of the inscription on the white plaque before them and to the bridge and he who built it.

Galus's voice was the louder and more expressive. While agreeing with Bahtijarević's praises of Mehmed Pasha Soković and the Turkish administration of his times, which had made possible the building of such a bridge, he now developed his nationalist views on the past and present of the people, their culture and civilization (for in such student discussions each follows his own train of thought).

"You are right," said Galus. "He must have been a man of genius. He was not the first nor the last man of our blood who distinguished himself in the service of a foreign empire. We have given hundreds of such men, statesmen, generals and artists, to Stambul, Rome and Vienna. The sense of our national unification in a single, great and powerful modern state lies just in that. Our own forces should remain in our own country and develop there and make their contribution to general culture in our name and not from foreign centers."

"Do you really think that those 'centers' arose by chance and that it is possible to create new ones at will whenever and wherever one likes?"

"Chance or not, that is no longer the question; it is not important how they arose, but it is important that today they are disappearing, that they have flowered and decayed, that they must make way for new and different centers, through which young and free nations, appearing for the first time on the stage of history, can express themselves directly."

"Do you think that Mehmed Pasha Sokolović, had he remained a peasant's child up there yonder at Sokolović, would have become what he became and would, among other things, have built this bridge on which we are now talking?"

"In those times, certainly, he would not. But, when you come to think of it, it was not hard for Stambul to put up such buildings, when it took from us, and from so many other subject peoples, not only property and money, but also our best men and our purest blood. If you stop to think what we are and how much has been stolen from us through the centuries, then all these buildings are merely crumbs. But when we finally achieve our national freedom and our independence, then our money and our blood will be ours alone, and will stay ours. Everything will be solely and uniquely for the improvement of our own national culture, which will bear our mark and our name and which will be mindful of the happiness and prosperity of all our people."

Bahtijarević remained silent, and that silence, like the most lively and eloquent speech, provoked Galus. He raised his voice and continued in a sharper tone. With all his natural vivacity and all the vocabulary then prevalent in nationalist literature, he set out the plans and aims of the revolutionary youth movement. All the living forces of the race must be awakened and set in action. Under their blows the Austro-Hungarian monarchy, that prison of the peoples, would disintegrate as the Turkish Empire had disintegrated. All the anti-national and reactionary forces which today hinder, divide and lull to sleep our national forces will be routed and trampled underfoot. All this can be done, for the spirit of the times in which we live is our strongest ally, for all the efforts of all the other small and oppressed nations support us. Modern nationalism will triumph over religious diversities and outmoded prejudice, will liberate our people from foreign influence and exploitation. Then will the national state be born.

Galus then described all the advantages and beauties of the new national state which was to rally all the Southern Slavs around Serbia as a sort of Piedmont on the basis of complete national unity, religious tolerance and civil equality. His speech mixed up bold words of uncertain meaning and expressions that accurately expressed the needs of modern life, the deepest desires of a race, most of which were destined to remain only desires, and the justified and attainable demands of everyday reality. It mingled the great truths which had ripened through the generations but which only youth could perceive in advance and dare to express, with the eternal illusions which are never extinguished but never attain realization, for one generation of youth hands them on to the next like that mythological torch. In the young man's speech there were, naturally, many assertions which could not have stood up to the criticism of reality and many suppositions which could not, perhaps, have borne the proof of experience, but in it too was that freshness, that precious essence which maintains and rejuvenates the tree of humanity.

Bahtijarević remained silent.

"You will see, Fehim," Galus enthusiastically assured his friend as if it were a matter of the same night or the next morning, "you will see. We shall create a state which will make the most precious contribution to the progress of humanity, in which every effort will be blessed, every sacrifice holy, every thought original and expressed in our own words, and every deed marked with the stamp of our name. Then we will carry out work which will be the result of our free labor and the expression of our racial genius, put up buildings in comparison with which all that has been done in the centuries of foreign administration will appear like silly toys. We will bridge greater rivers and deeper abysses. We will build new, greater and better bridges, not to link foreign centers with conquered lands but to link our own lands with the rest of the world. There cannot be any doubt any longer. We are destined to realize all that the generations before us have aspired to; a state, born in freedom and founded on justice, like a part of God's thought realized here on earth."

Bahtijarević remained silent. Even Galus's voice lowered in tone. As his ideas became more exalted, his voice became lower and lower, hoarser and hoarser, till it became a strong and passionate whisper and was finally lost in the great silence of the night. At last both young men were silent. But none the less Bahtijarević's silence seemed a thing apart, heavy and obstinate in the night. It seemed like an impassable wall in the darkness which by the very weight of its existence resolutely rejected all that the other had said, and expressed its dumb, clear and unalterable opinion.

"The foundations of the world and the bases of life and human relationships in it have been fixed for centuries. That does not mean that they do not change, but measured by the length of human existence they appear eternal. The relation between their endurance and the length of human existence is the same as the relation between the uneasy, moving and swift surface of a river and its stable and solid bed whose changes are slow and imperceptible. The very idea of the change of these 'centers' is unhealthy and unacceptable. That would be as if someone wished to change and measure the sources of great rivers or the sites of mountains. The desire for sudden changes and the thought of their realization by force often appear among men like a disease and gain ground mainly in young brains; only these brains do not think as they should, do not amount to anything in the end and the heads that think thus do not remain long on their shoulders. For it is not human desires that dispose and administer the things of the world. Desire is like a wind; it shifts the dust from one place to another, sometimes darkens the whole horizon, but in the end calms down and falls and leaves the old and eternal picture of the world. Lasting deeds are realized on this earth only by God's will, and man is only His blind and humble tool. A deed which is born of desire, human desire, either does not live till realization or is not lasting; in no case is that good. All these tumultuous desires and daring words under the night sky on the *kapia* will not change anything basically; they will pass, beneath the great and permanent realities of the world and will be lost where all desires and winds are stilled. In truth great men and great buildings rise and will rise only where they are appointed to arise in God's thought, in their right place independent of empty transient desires and human vanity."

But Bahtijarević did not utter a single one of these words. Those who, like this Moslem youth of noble family, carry their philosophy in their blood, live and die according to it, do not know how to express it in words, or feel the need to do so. After this long silence Stiković and Glasičanin only saw one or other of the pair of unseen comrades throw a cigarette stub over the parapet and watched it fall like a shooting star in a great curve from the bridge into the Drina. At the same time they heard the two friends slowly and softly moving away towards the market-place. The sound of their footsteps was soon lost.

Alone once more, Stiković and Glasičanin started and looked at one another as though they had only just met.

In the pale moonlight their faces showed in bright and dark surfaces sharply defined, so that they seemed much older than in fact they were. The glow from their cigarettes had a sort of phosphorescence. Both were depressed. Their reasons were quite different, but the depression was mutual. Both had the same wish; to get up and go home. But both seemed as if nailed to the stone seats still warm from the day's sunlight. The conversation of that pair of young comrades which they by chance overheard had been welcome to them as a postponement of their own conversation and mutual explanation. But now it could no longer be avoided.

"Did you hear Herak and his arguments?" Stiković spoke first, referring to the evening's discussion, and at once felt the weakness of his position.

Glasičanin, who for his part felt the momentary advantage of his position as arbiter, did not reply at once.

"I ask you," went on Stiković impatiently, "in these days to speak of class struggle and recommend small measures, when it is clear to every last man among us that national unity and liberation carried out by revolutionary methods is the most pressing aim of our community! Why, that is downright silly!"

His voice held both a question and an appeal. But again Glasičanin did not reply. In the hush of that revengeful and vindictive silence, the sound of music came to them from the officers' mess on the river bank. The ground-floor windows were wide open and brightly lit. A violin was playing with a piano accompanying it. It was the military doctor, Regimentsarzt Balas, who was playing, accompanied by the wife of the commander of the garrison, Colonel Bauer. They were practicing the second movement of Schubert's Sonatina for violin and piano. They played well together but before they were halfway through the piano was ahead and the violinist stopped playing. After a short silence, during which they were doubtless arguing about the disputed passage, they began again. They practiced together almost every evening and played until late at night, while the Colonel sat in another room playing endless games of *preference* or simply dozing over Mostar wine and tobacco while the younger officers joked among themselves at the expense of the enamored musicians.

Between Madame Bauer and the young doctor a complicated and difficult story had in fact been building up for months. Not even the keenest-eyed among the officers had been able to decide on the real nature of the relationship. Some said that the tie between them was wholly spiritual (and naturally laughed at it), while others said that the body had its due share in the matter also. The two were, however, inseparable, with the full fatherly approval of the Colonel who was a good-natured man, already blunted by long service, the weight of years, wine and tobacco.

The whole town looked on these two as a couple. Otherwise, the whole officers' mess lived a completely isolated life, without any connection with the local people and citizens or even the foreign officials. At the entrance to their parks, filled with beds of rare flowers laid out in circles and stars, a notice announced impartially that it was forbidden to bring dogs into the parks and that civilians were not allowed to enter. Their pleasures and their duties were alike inaccessible to all who were not in uniform. Their whole life was in fact that of a huge and completely exclusive caste, which cherished its exclusiveness as the most important aspect of its power and which beneath a brilliant and stiff exterior concealed all that life gave to other men of greatness and poverty, sweetness and bitterness.

But there are things which by their very nature cannot remain hidden, which break down every barrier however strong and cross even the most strictly guarded frontier. "There are three things which cannot be hidden," say the Osmanlis, "and these are: love, a cough and poverty." This was the case with this pair of lovers. There was not an old man or a child, man or woman, in the town who had not come across them on one of their walks on unfrequented paths around the town, lost in conversation and completely blind and deaf to everything about them. The shepherds were as used to them as to those pairs of beetles that can be seen in May on the leaves by the wayside, always two by two in loving embrace. They were to be seen everywhere; along the Drina and the Rzav, by the ruins of the old fortress, on the road leading from the town, or around Stražište, and at any time of the day. For time is always short to lovers and no path long enough. They sometimes rode or drove in a light carriage, but for the most part walked, and walked at that pace usual to two persons who exist only one for the other, and with that characteristic gait which shows that they are indifferent to everything in the world save what each has to say to the other.

He was a Hungarianized Slovak, son of a civil servant and educated at state expense, young and genuinely musical. He was ambitious but over-sensitive about his origins which prevented him from feeling at ease with the Austrian or Hungarian officers from rich and famous families. She was a woman in her forties, eight years older than he. She was tall and blond, already a little faded but her skin was still a clear pink and white. With her large shining dark-blue eyes, in appearance and bearing she looked like one of those portraits of queens which so enchant young girls.

Each of them had personal, real or imagined but deep, reasons for dissatisfaction with life. Furthermore they had one great reason in common; both felt themselves to be unhappy and like outcasts in this town and this society of officers, for the most part frivolous and empty-headed. So they clung to one another feverishly like two survivors of a shipwreck. They lost themselves in one another and forgot themselves in long conversations or, as now, in music.

Such was the invisible pair whose music filled the troubled silence between the two youths.

A few moments later the music which had been pouring into the peaceful night again ran into difficulties and stopped for a time. In the silence that followed, Glasičanin began to speak in a wooden sort of voice, picking up Stiković's last words.

"Silly? There was much that was silly in that whole discussion, if we look at it fairly."

Stiković suddenly took the cigarette from his lips, but Glasičanin went on slowly but resolutely to express views which were clearly not based on that night only but which had long troubled him.

"I listen carefully to all these discussions, both those between you two and other educated people in this town; also I read the newspapers and reviews. But the more I listen to you, the more I am convinced that the greater part of these spoken or written discussions has no connection with life at all and its real demands and problems. For life, real life,

I look at from very close indeed; I see its influence on others and I feel it on myself. It may be that I am mistaken and that I do not know how to express myself well, but I often think that technical progress and the relative peace there is now in the world have created a sort of lull, a special atmosphere, artificial and unreal, in which a single class of men, the so-called intellectuals, can freely devote themselves to idleness and to the interesting game of ideas and 'views on life and the world.' It is a sort of conservatory of the spirit, with an artificial climate and exotic flowers but without any real connection with the earth, the real hard soil on which the mass of human beings move. You think that you are discussing the fate of these masses and their use in the struggle for the realization of higher aims which you have fixed for them, but in fact the wheels which you turn in your heads have no connection with the life of the masses, nor with life in general. That game of yours becomes dangerous, or at least might become dangerous, both for others and for you yourselves."

Glasičanin paused. Stiković was so astonished by this long and considered exposition that he had not even thought of interrupting him or answering him. Only when he heard the word "dangerous" he made an ironical gesture with his hand. That irritated Glasičanin who continued even more animatedly.

"For heaven's sake! Listening to you, one would think that all questions were settled happily, all dangers forever removed, all roads made smooth and open so all we have to do is to walk along them. But in life there is nothing solved, or which can easily be solved, or even has any chance of being solved at all. Everything is hard and complicated, expensive and accompanied by disproportionately high risk; there is no trace either of Herak's bold hopes or of your wide horizons. Man is tormented all his life and never has what he needs, let alone what he wants. Theories such as yours only satisfy the eternal need for games, flatter your own vanity, deceive yourself and others. That is the truth, or at least that is how it appears to me."

"It is not so. You have only to compare various historical periods and you will see the progress and meaning of man's struggle and therefore also the 'theory' that gives sense and direction to that struggle."

Glasičanin at once took this to be an allusion to his interrupted schooling and as always in such a case quivered inwardly.

"I have not studied history. . . ." he began.

"You see. If you had studied it, you would see. . . ."

"But neither have you."

"What? That is . . . well, yes, of course I have studied. . . ."

"As well as natural sciences?"

His voice quivered vindictively. Stiković was embarrassed for a moment and then said in a dead sort of voice:

"Oh well, if you really want to know, there it is; besides natural sciences, I have been taking an interest in political, historical and social problems."

"You are lucky to have had the chance. For as far as I know, you are an orator and an agitator also, as well as being a poet and a lover."

Stiković smiled unnaturally. That afternoon in the deserted schoolroom passed through his mind as a distant but irritating thing. Only then he realized that Glasičanin and Zorka had been close friends until his arrival in the town. A man who does not love is incapable of feeling the greatness of another's love or the force of jealousy or the danger concealed in it.

The conversation of the two young men changed without transition into that bitter personal quarrel that had from the very beginning been hovering in the air between them. Young people do not try to avoid quarrels, even as young animals easily take part in rough and violent games among themselves.

"What I am and what I do is none of your business. I don't ask you about your cubes and your tree-trunks."

That spasm of anger which always gripped Glasičanin at any mention of his position made him suffer.

"You leave my cubes alone. I live from them, but I don't trick people with them. I deceive no one. I seduce no one."

"Whom do I seduce?" broke in Stiković.

"Anyone who will let you."

"That is not true."

"It is true. And you know it is true. Since you force me to speak, then I will tell you."

"I am not inquisitive."

"But I will tell you, for even leaping about tree-trunks all day long a man may still see something and learn how to think and feel. I want to tell you what I think about your countless occupations and interests and your daring theories and your verses and your loves."

Stiković made a movement as if to rise but none the less remained where he was. The piano and violin from the officers' mess had resumed their duet some time ago (the third movement of the Sonatina, gay and lively) and their music was lost in the night and the roar of the river.

"Thank you. I have heard all that from others more intelligent than you are."

"Oh no! Others either do not know you or lie to you or think as I do but keep silent. All your theories, all your many spiritual occupations, like your loves and your friendships, all these derive from your ambition, and that ambition is false and unhealthy for it derives from your vanity, only and exclusively from your vanity."

"Ha, ha!"

"Yes. Even that nationalist idea which you preach so ardently is only a special form of vanity. For you are incapable of loving your mother or your sister or your own blood brother, so how much less an idea. Only from vanity could you be good, generous, self-sacrificing. For your vanity is the main force that moves you, the only thing you revere, the one and only thing that you love more than yourself. One who doesn't know you might easily be mistaken, seeing your force and your industry, your devotion to the nationalist ideal, to science, to poetry or to any other great aim which is above personal feelings. But you cannot in any case serve it for long or remain with it for long, for your vanity will not let you. The moment your vanity is no longer in question, everything becomes meaningless to you. You do not want anything and would not even move a finger to obtain it. Because of it you will betray yourself, for you are yourself the slave of your own vanity. You do not know yourself how vain you are. I know your very soul and I know that you are a monster of vanity."

Stiković did not reply. At first he had been surprised at the considered and passionate outburst of his comrade who now suddenly appeared to him in a new light and an unexpected role. Therefore that caustic, even speech which at first irritated and insulted him, now seemed interesting and almost pleasant. Individual phrases had, it is true, hit home and hurt, but on the whole all that sharp and profound exposure of his character had flattered and pleased him in a special sort of way. For to tell a young man that he is a monster merely means to tickle his pride and his self-love. In fact he wanted Glasičanin to continue this cruel probing into his inner self, that clear projection of his hidden personality, for in it he found only one more proof of his exceptional superiority. His eyes fell on the white plaque opposite him which shone in the moonlight. He looked straight at the incomprehensible Turkish inscription as if he were reading it and trying to decipher the deeper sense of what his friend beside him had been saying penetratingly and consideredly.

"Nothing is really important to you and, in fact, you neither love nor hate, for to do either you must at least for a moment stand outside yourself, express yourself, forget yourself, go beyond yourself and your vanity. But that you cannot do; nor is there anything for which you would do so even were you able. Someone else's sorrow cannot move you, how much less hurt you; not even your own sorrow unless it flatters your vanity. You desire nothing and you find joy in nothing. You are not even envious, not from goodness but from boundless egoism, for you do not notice the happiness or unhappiness of others. Nothing can move you or turn you from your purpose. You do not stop at anything, not because you are brave, but because all the healthy impulses in you are shriveled up, because save for your vanity nothing exists for you, neither blood ties nor inward considerations, neither God nor the world, neither kin nor friend. You do not esteem even your own natural capacities. Instead of conscience it is only your own wounded vanity that can sting you, for it alone, always and in everything, speaks with your mouth and dictates your actions."

"Is this an allusion to Zorka?" Stiković suddenly asked.

"Yes, if you like, let us talk of that too. Yes, because of Zorka also. You do not care a jot for her. It is only your inability to stop and restrain yourself before anything which momentarily and by chance is offered you and which flatters your vanity. Yes, that is so. You seduce a poor, muddled and inexperienced schoolmistress just as you write articles and poems, deliver speeches and lectures. And even before you have completely conquered them you are already tired of them, for your vanity becomes bored and looks for something beyond. But that is your own curse too, that you can stop nowhere, that you can never be sated and satisfied. You submit everything to your vanity but you are yourself the first of its slaves and its greatest martyr. It may well be that you will have still greater glory and success, a greater success than the weakness of some love-crazed girl, but you will find no satisfaction in any one thing, for your vanity will whip you onwards, for it swallows everything, even the greatest successes and then forgets them immediately, but the slightest failure or insult it will remember forever. And when everything is withered, broken, soiled, humiliated, disintegrated and destroyed about you, then you will remain alone in the wilderness you have yourself created, face to face with your vanity and you will have nothing to offer it. Then you will devour yourself, but that will not help you, for your vanity accustomed to richer food will despise and reject you. That is what you are, though you may seem different in the eyes of most men and though you think differently of yourself. But I know."

Glasičanin ceased suddenly.

The freshness of the night could already be felt on the *kapia* and the silence spread, accompanied by the eternal roar of the waters. They had not even noticed when the music from the bank had ceased. Both youths had completely forgotten where they were and what they were doing. Each had been carried away by his own thoughts as only youth can be. The jealous and unhappy "cube-measurer" had spoken only of what he had so many times thought over passionately, deeply and intensely, but for which he had never before been able to find suitable words and expressions and which that night had come easily and eloquently, bitterly and exaltedly. Stiković had listened, motionlessly looking at the white plaque with the inscription as if it had been a cinema screen. Every word had hit home. He felt every harsh comment but he no longer found in all that this scarcely visible friend beside him had said any insult or any danger. On the other hand, it seemed to him that with every word of Glasičanin he grew, and that he flew on invisible wings, swift and unheard, exulting and daring, high above all men on this earth and their ties, laws and feelings, alone, proud and great, and happy or with some feeling akin to happiness. He flew above everything. That voice, those words of his rival, were only the sound of the waters and the roar of an invisible, lesser world far below him: it mattered little to him what it was, what it thought and what it said, for he flew above it as a bird.

The momentary silence of Glasičanin seemed to bring them both to their senses. They did not dare to look at one another. God alone knows in what form the quarrel would have continued had there not appeared on the bridge a crowd of drunkards coming from the marketplace, shouting loudly and singing snatches of songs. Loudest among them was a tenor who sang in falsetto an ancient song:

"Thou art wise as thou art lovely,
Lovely Fata Avdagina! . . ."

They recognized the voices of a number of young merchants' and landowners' sons. Some were walking slowly and sedately, others wavered and tottered. From their noisy jests it could be concluded that they had come from "Under the Poplars."

More than fifteen years earlier, even before the building of the railway had begun, a certain Hungarian and his wife had settled in the town. He was called Terdik and his wife Julka. She spoke Serbian for she had been born in Novi Sad. It soon became known that they had come with the intention of opening a business in the town for which the local people had no name. They opened it on the outskirts of the town, under the tall poplars which grew on the Stražište slopes, in an old Turkish house which they completely rebuilt.

This was the town's house of shame. All day long the windows remained shuttered. As dusk fell a white acetylene lamp was lit in the doorway which burned there all night. Songs and the tinkle of an automatic piano echoed from the ground floor. Young men and dissolute idlers bandied about among themselves the names of the girls whom Terdik had brought and kept there. At first there were four of them: Irma, Ilona, Frieda and Aranka.

Every Friday "Julka's girls" could be seen going in two cabs up to the hospital for their weekly inspection. They were heavily rouged and powdered, with flowers in their hats and with long-handled sunshades with streamers of floating lace. When these cabs went by, the women of the town hustled their daughters out of sight and averted their eyes with mixed feelings of shame, disgust and pity.

When work began on the railway and there was an influx of money and workers, the number of girls was increased. Besides the old Turkish house, Terdik built a new "planned" one with a red-tiled roof which could be seen from afar. There were three rooms; the general room, the *extra-zimmer* and the officers' salon. In each of them were different prices and different guests. At "Under the Poplars," as it was known in the town, the sons and grandsons of those who had once drunk at Zarije's inn, or later at Lotte's, could leave their inherited or hard-won money. The grossest practical jokes, the most notorious quarrels, wild drinking parties and sentimental dramas took place there. Many personal and family misfortunes had their origins in that house.

The center of that group of drunkards who had spent the first part of the night "Under the Poplars" and had now come to cool off on the *kapia* was a certain Nikola Pecikoza, a silly good-natured youth whom they made drunk and on whom they played their jokes.

Before the drunkards reached the *kapia* they halted by the parapet. A loud and drunken argument could be heard. Nikola Pecikoza bet two liters of wine that he could walk along the stone parapet to the end of the bridge. The bet was taken and the young man climbed on to the parapet and set out with arms outspread, placing one foot carefully before the other like a sleepwalker. When he reached the *kapia* he noticed the two late visitors; he said nothing to them but humming some song and wavering in his drunkenness continued on his dangerous way, while the merry party accompanied him. His great shadow in the weak moonlight danced on the bridge and broke into fragments on the opposite parapet.

The drunkards passed by in a frenzy of disconnected shouts and stupid comments. The two young men rose and, without saying goodnight, each went his own way to his own house.

Glasičanin disappeared into the darkness towards the left bank where was the path which led to his house up at Okolište. Stiković made his way with slow steps in the opposite direction towards the market-place. He walked slowly and irresolutely. He did not want to leave that place which was lighter and fresher than in the town. He halted by the parapet. He felt the need to catch hold of something, to lean on something.

The moon had set behind the Vidova Gora. Leaning on the stone parapet at the end of the bridge, the young man looked long at the huge shadows and few lights of his native town as if he now saw it for the first time. Only two windows were still lighted in the officers' mess. The music could no longer be heard. Probably the unhappy lovers were there, the doctor and the colonel's lady, holding their discussions on music and on love or about their personal fates which would not permit them to be at peace with themselves or with one another.

From the spot where Stiković was now standing he could see that one window was still lighted in Lotte's hotel. The young man looked at those lighted windows on each side of the bridge as if he expected something from them. He was tired out and melancholy. The vertiginous walk of that idiot Pecikoza suddenly reminded him of his earliest childhood, when on his way to school he had seen in the mist of a winter's morning the squat figure of Čorkan dancing on that same parapet. Every memory of his childhood aroused sorrow and uneasiness in him. That sentiment of fateful and exalted greatness and universal flight above everyone and everything which Glasičanin's bitter and fiery words had excited in him was now lost. It seemed to him that he had suddenly fallen from the heights and that he was crawling on the darkened earth with everyone else. The memory of what had happened with the schoolmistress, and should not have happened, tormented him as if someone else had done it in his name; so too did the article which now seemed to him weak and full of faults, as if another had written it and had published it in his name and against his will. He thought of the long conversation with Glasičanin which now all of a sudden seemed to him full of malice and hate, of bitter insults and real perils.

He shivered inwardly and from the chill which arose from the river. As if suddenly awakened he noticed that the two windows in the officers' mess were no longer lighted. The last guests were leaving the building. He could hear the clink of their swords as they crossed the darkened square and the sound of loud, artificial chatter. The young man regretfully left the parapet and, looking at the solitary window still alight in the hotel, the last light in the sleeping town, made his way slowly towards his simple house up there at Mejdan.

20

The only lighted window in the hotel, which remained as the last sign of life that night in the town, was that small window on the first floor where Lotte's room was. Even at night Lotte sat there at her overladen table. It was just as it had been earlier, more than twenty years before, when she had come to this little room to snatch a moment of respite from the bustle and noise of the hotel. Only now everything downstairs was dark and quiet.

At ten o'clock that night Lotte had withdrawn to her room to sleep. But before she lay down she went over to the window to breathe in the freshness from the river and to take a last glance at that arch of the bridge which was the only and eternally the same view from her window. Then she remembered some old account and sat down to look for it. Once she began looking through her accounts she became absorbed and remained for more than two hours at her table.

Midnight had long passed while Lotte, wakeful and absorbed, entered figure after figure and turned paper after paper.

Lotte was tired. In the daytime, in conversation and at work, she was still animated and talkative, but at night when she was alone she felt all the weight of her years and her fatigue. She had grown old. Of her onetime beauty only traces remained. She had grown thinner and yellow in the face; her hair was without luster and was growing thin on her scalp, and her teeth, once shining and strong, were yellow and showed gaps. The glance of her black and still shining eyes was hard and at times sad.

Lotte was tired, but not with that blessed and sweet tiredness which follows heavy work and great gains, such as at one time had driven her to search for rest and respite in that room. Old age had come upon her and the times were no longer good.

She would not have been able to express in words, nor could she explain it to herself, but she felt at every step that the times were out of joint, at any rate for one who had always kept only her own good and that of her family before her eyes. When, thirty years before, she had come to Bosnia and begun work there, life had seemed all of a piece. Everyone was moving in the same direction as she was; work and family. Everyone was in his right place and there was a place for everyone. And over everyone reigned one order and one law, an established order and a strict law. So had the world then appeared to Lotte. Now everything had changed and was topsy-turvy. Men were divided and separated without, it seemed to her, rhyme or reason. The law of profit and loss, that divine law which had always controlled human activities, seemed as if it were no longer valid, for so many men worked, spoke or wrote about things of which she could not see the aim or the sense and which could only end in misfortune and damage. Life was bursting asunder, was crumbling, was disintegrating. It seemed to her that the present generation attached more importance to its views on life than to life itself. It seemed to her mad and completely incomprehensible, yet it was so. Therefore life was losing its value and wasting away in mere words. Lotte saw this clearly and felt it at every step.

Her business affairs, which at one time had seemed to gambol before her eyes like a flock of spring lambs, now lay inert and dead like the great tombstones in the Jewish cemetery. For the past ten years the hotel had done little business. The forests around the town had been cut down and felling was moving farther and farther away, and with it the best of the hotel's customers and the greater part of its profits. That shameless and insolent boor, Terdik, had opened his house "under the poplars" and enticed away many of Lotte's guests, offering them easily and immediately all that they had never been able to get in her hotel however much they paid. Lotte had long revolted against this unfair and shameless competition and said that the last days had come, those days in which law and order existed no longer or the chance of making an honest living. At first she had bitterly referred to Terdik as "the whoremaster"; but he had brought her before the courts and Lotte had been sentenced to pay a fine for defamation of character. But even now she never referred to him by any other term, though she took care before whom she was speaking. The new officers' mess had its own restaurant, a cellar of good wines and its own guestrooms where distinguished visitors could be put up. Gustav, the sullen and badtempered but skillful and reliable Gustav, had left the hotel after many years of service and opened his own café in the most frequented part of the market-place, and so instead of a colleague he had become a competitor. The choral society and the various reading-rooms which had been opened in the town in the past few years had their own cafés and attracted many guests.

There was no longer the former animation either in the main room or, still less, in the *extra-zimmer*. An occasional unmarried civil servant had his lunch there, read the newspapers and took coffee. Alibeg Pašić, the taciturn and impassioned friend of Lotte's youth, still went there every afternoon. Still as careful and discreet as ever, both in speech and actions, still correct and carefully dressed, he had grown gray and ponderous. His coffee was served with saccharine because of the severe diabetes from which he had been suffering for years. He smoked quietly and, silent as ever, listened to Lotte's chatter. When the time came he rose just as quietly and silently and went home to Crnče. There was also another daily visitor, Lotte's neighbor Pavle Ranković. He had long left off wearing national costume and now wore the "tight" civilian dress, but he still stuck to his shallow red fez. He always wore a starched shirt with a stiff collar, and cuffs on which he noted down figures and accounts. He had long ago succeeded in taking over the leading place in the Višegrad trading community. His position was by now consolidated and assured, but not even he was without his cares and difficulties. Like all the older men who had a certain amount of property he was bewildered by the new times and the clamorous onrush of new ideas and new ways of life, thought and expression. All these things were embraced for him by the single word "politics." It was those "politics" that confused and angered him and embittered those years which should have been years of respite and satisfaction after so much work and thrift and renunciation. He in no way wanted to stand aside or withdraw himself from the majority of his fellow countrymen, but at the same time he had no wish to come into conflict with the authorities with whom he wished to remain at peace and at least outwardly in agreement. But that was difficult, almost impossible, to achieve. He could not even understand his own sons as he should. Like all the rest of the younger generation they were simply baffling and incomprehensible to him; yet many other people either from necessity or weakness followed their example. Their bearing, behavior and actions seemed to Pavle rebellious as if they thought that to live and die in present conditions was no better than to spend their lives like brigands in the mountains. Young people did not think what they said, paid no heed to what they did, did not count the cost and were careless in their work; they ate their bread without stopping to think whence it came and talked, talked, talked, "baying at the moon" as Pavle expressed it in his arguments with his sons.

This way of thinking without limits, this speech without consideration, and this life without calculation and hostile to every calculation, drove Pavle, who had worked all his life by and with calculation, to frenzy and desperation. He was filled with fear whenever he heard or saw them; it seemed to him that they imprudently and irresponsibly hacked away at the very foundations of life, at all that was dearest and most sacred to him. When he asked them for an explanation which would convince and reassure him they replied disdainfully and haughtily with vague and high-sounding words; freedom, future, history, science, glory, greatness. His skin crawled at all these abstract words. Therefore he liked to sit and drink coffee with Lotte, with whom he could talk about business and events, always based on a sure and admitted calculation, very different from the "politics" and the big, dangerous words that questioned everything, explained nothing and affirmed nothing. During the conversation he often took out his pencil stub, not that of twenty-five years back but one just as shiny and almost equally invisible, and put all that was said to the infallible and irrefutable proof of figures. They often recalled in their talk some long-ago happening, or some jest in which nearly all the participants were now dead, and then Pavle, bowed with cares, would go to his shop in the marketplace and Lotte remained alone with her worries and her accounts.

Lotte's personal speculations were in no better shape than the hotel's business. In the first years after the occupation it had been enough to buy any share in any enterprise and one could be sure that the money was well invested and the only question that could arise was the amount of the profit. But at that time the hotel had only just started work and Lotte had neither the ready money at her disposal nor the credit which she later enjoyed. When she had achieved both money and credit the state of affairs on the exchanges had completely changed. One of the most serious of the cyclic crises had hit the Austro-Hungarian Monarchy at the end of the nineteenth and the beginning of the twentieth century. Lotte's stocks and shares began to play like dust in a high wind. She would weep with rage when she read the most recent quotations each week in the Vienna *Merkur*. All the profits of the hotel, which at that time was still doing good business, were not enough to cover the losses caused by the general decline in values. At that time too she had had a severe nervous breakdown which lasted a full two years. She was almost mad with pain. She chatted to people without hearing what they said or thinking what she herself was saying. She looked them full in the face but did not see them but the small-print columns of the *Merkur* which were to bring her good or evil luck. Then she began to buy lottery tickets. Since everything was in any case only a game of chance, she might as well do it properly. She had lottery tickets from every country. She even succeeded in getting hold of a quarter share in a ticket of the great Spanish Christmas Lottery whose first prize amounted to fifteen million pesetas. She prayed God for a miracle and that her ticket should draw the first prize. But she never won anything.

Seven years before, Lotte's brother-in-law Zahler had gone into partnership with a couple of wealthy men on pension and founded the "Modern Milk Cooperative" in the town. Lotte provided three-fifths of the capital. Business on a large scale was envisaged. It was reckoned that the initial successes, which could not fail to eventuate, would attract capital from outside the town and even outside Bosnia. But just at the moment when the enterprise was in its critical phase the annexation crisis took place. This destroyed every hope of attracting fresh capital. These frontier districts became so unsafe that capital already invested in them began to flee. The Cooperative went into liquidation after two years, with the total loss of all the invested capital. Lotte had to mortgage her best and safest shares, like those of the Sarajevo Brewery and the Solvaj Soda Factory at Tuzla, to cover the deficit.

Parallel with these financial misfortunes and allied to them were family troubles and disappointments. It was true that one of Zahler's daughters, Irene, had married unexpectedly well (Lotte had provided the dowry). But the elder daughter, Mina, remained. Embittered by the marriage of her younger sister and unfortunate in her suitors she had become before her time a vinegary and sharp-tongued old maid to whom life at home and work in the hotel seemed even heavier and more unbearable than in fact they were. Zahler who had never been lively or quick-witted grew even more ponderous and indecisive and lived at home like a dumb but good-natured guest from whom there was neither harm nor profit. Zahler's wife, Deborah, though sickly and in advanced years, had given birth to a son, but the boy was backward and rickety. He was now ten years old and still could not speak clearly or stand upright, but expressed himself in vague sounds and crawled about the house on his hands and knees. But this miserable creature was so pitiable and good and clung so desperately to his Aunt Lotte, whom he loved far more than his mother, that Lotte, despite all her worries and duties, looked after him, fed him, dressed him and sang him to sleep. With this cretin ever before her eyes, her heart contracted at the idea that business was now so bad that there was not enough money to send him to the famous doctors in Vienna or into some institution, and at the thought that the days of miracles were past and that such creatures could not grow healthy by God's will or by man's good works and prayers.

Lotte's Galician dependents, whom she had educated or given in marriage during the good years, also caused her no little worry and disappointment. Some among them had founded families, extended their business and acquired property. Lotte got regular news from them, letters filled with respect and gratitude and regular reports of the progress of their families. But the Apfelmaiers to whom Lotte had given a start in life, had educated or provided homes for, did not help her or take any responsibility for new relatives born and growing up in poverty in Galicia but, once settled in distant cities, only bothered about themselves and their own children. For them the greater part of their success lay in forgetting Tarnow and the cramped and wretched circumstances in which they had grown up and from which they had had the luck to liberate themselves, as quickly and as completely as possible; and Lotte herself was no longer able to set aside money as she had once done to give that black poverty of Tarnow its chance in life. She never went to sleep or woke now without the thought that someone of hers in Tarnow was forever sunk in the slough of hopeless poverty, condemned forever to ignorance and filth, in that shameful poverty which she knew so well and which she had fought against all her life.

Even among those whose lot she had already improved there was reason enough for complaint and dissatisfaction. Even the best among them had turned from the right path and made mistakes after their first successes and most shining hopes. One niece, a gifted pianist, who by Lotte's help and encouragement had completed her studies at the Vienna Conservatoire, had poisoned herself a few years earlier at the time of her first and best successes; no one knew why.

One of her nephews, Albert, Lotte's pride and the hope of the family, had completed all his studies, both at secondary school and university, with outstanding success and only because he was a Jew had not received his diploma *"sub auspiciis regis"* or obtained the Imperial signet as Lotte had secretly hoped. None the less, Lotte had imagined him at least as a leading lawyer in Vienna or Lwow, since being a Jew he could not become a senior civil servant which would best have accorded with her ambitions. In such dreams she reaped the reward for all her sacrifices for his education. But there too she had had to suffer a painful disillusionment. The young doctor of law went into journalism and became a member of the Socialist Party, and of that extremist wing which became notorious in the Vienna general strike of 1906. Lotte had to read with her own eyes in the Viennese newspapers that "during the cleaning up in Vienna of subversive foreign elements the well-known Jewish agitator Dr. Albert Apfelmaier has been expelled, after first purging a sentence passed against him of twenty days' imprisonment." That, in the language of the town, meant the same as if he had been a *haiduk,* a brigand. A few months later Lotte received a letter from her dear Albert in which he told her that he was emigrating to Buenos Aires.

In those days she could not find peace even in her own room. With the letter in her hand she went to her sister and brother-in-law and desperately, senselessly, flew into a passion with her sister Deborah who could only weep. She shouted with rage:

"What is to become of us? I ask you, what is to become of us, when no one knows how to make his way and stand up for himself? Unless they are propped up they all fall. What is going to happen to us? We are accursed, that is all there is to it."

"Gott, Gott, Gott," wailed poor Deborah with tears flowing down her cheeks, naturally quite unable to answer Lotte's questions. Nor did Lotte herself find an answer but clasped her hands and lifted her eyes to heaven, not weeping and frightened like Deborah, but furious and despairing.

"He has become a Socialist! A Soc - ial - ist! Isn't it enough that we are Jews, but he must be that as well! O Great and Only God, how have I sinned that You must punish us thus? A Socialist!"

She wept for Albert as though he were dead and then never spoke of him again.

Three years later one of her nieces, sister of that same Albert, married well in Pest. Lotte took charge of the trousseau and took a leading part in the moral crisis that this marriage provoked in the great Apfelmaier family of Tarnow, rich only in children and an unsullied religious tradition. The man whom this niece was to marry was a rich speculator on the Bourse, but a Christian and a Calvinist, and he made it a condition that the girl should be converted to his faith. The relatives all opposed this but Lotte, with the interest of the whole family in mind, said that it was hard to keep afloat with so many persons in the boat and that it was sometimes necessary to throw something overboard for the salvation of all the rest. She supported the girl and her word was decisive. The girl was baptized and married. Lotte hoped that with the help of her new relative she would be able to introduce at least one of those cousins or nephews now of suitable age into the business world of Pest. But bad luck had it that the rich Pest speculator died in the first year of marriage. The young wife went almost mad with grief. Months passed and her great grief did not lessen. The young widow had now been living in Pest for four years, given over to her unnatural grief which amounted to a mild form of madness. The great, richly furnished apartment was swathed in black cloth. She went every day to the cemetery, sat by her husband's grave and read softly and devotedly to him the list of market quotations for the day from beginning to end. To all suggestions made that she should awake from the lethargy into which she had fallen she answered softly that the dead man had loved that above all and that it had been the sweetest music he had ever known.

Thus many destinies of all kinds accumulated in that little room. These were many accounts, many doubtful bills, many others written off and expunged forever in that great, many-sided bookkeeping of Lotte's; but the great principle of work remained the same. Lotte was tired but she was not discouraged. After every loss or failure, she would call on her resources, set her teeth and go on with the struggle. In recent years she had been fighting a rearguard action but she went on struggling with the same aim before her eyes and with the same resolution as she had shown when she made money and went forward in the world. She was the "man" of that household and "Aunt Lotte" to the whole township. There were still many both in the town and in the outside world who waited for her aid, her advice or at least her encouragement, and who did not ask and could not imagine that Lotte was tired. But she was really tired, more than anyone suspected and more than she herself knew.

The little wooden clock on the wall struck one. Lotte rose with difficulty, her hands on her hips. She carefully extinguished the great green lamp on the wooden side-table and with the short steps of an old woman, steps she used only when she was in her own room and even then only when going to bed, she went to lie down.

There was complete and universal darkness over the sleeping town.

21

It is now 1914, the last year in the chronicle of the bridge on the Drina. It came as all earlier years had come, with the quiet pace of winter but with the sullen roar of ever new and ever more unusual events which piled upon one another like waves.

So many years had passed over the town and so many more would still pass over it. There had been, and there still would be, years of every sort, but the year 1914 will always remain unique. So at least it seemed to those who lived through it. To them it seemed that never would they be able to speak of all that they had seen then of the course of human destinies, however much, still concealed by time and events, might be said or written about it later. How could they explain and express those collective shudders which suddenly ran through all men and which from living beings were transmitted to inert objects, to districts and to buildings? How could they describe that swirling current among men which passed from dumb animal fear to suicidal enthusiasm, from the lowest impulses of bloodlust and pillage to the greatest and most noble of sacrifices, wherein man for a moment touches the sphere of greater worlds with other laws? Never can that be told, for those who saw and lived through it have lost the gift of words and those who are dead can tell no tales. Those were things which are not told, but forgotten. For were they not forgotten, how could they ever be repeated?

In that summer of 1914, when the rulers of human destinies drew European humanity from the playing fields of universal suffrage to the already prepared arena of universal military service, the town of Višegrad provided a small but eloquent example of the first symptoms of a contagion which would in time become European and then spread to the entire world. That was a time on the limits of two epochs in human history whence one could more easily see the end of that epoch which was closing than the beginning of that new one which was opening. Then one sought for a justification for violence and found some name borrowed from the spiritual treasury of the past century for savagery and bloodlust. All that took place still had the outer semblance of dignity and the attraction of novelty, a terrible, short-lived and inexpressible charm which later disappeared so completely that even those who then felt it so strongly could no longer evoke its memory.

But these are all things which we recall only in passing and which poets and scientists of coming ages will investigate, interpret and resurrect by methods and manners which we do not suspect and with a serenity, freedom and boldness of spirit which will be far above ours. Probably they will succeed in finding an explanation even for that strange year and will give it its true place in the history of the world and the development of humanity. But here it is unique for us, for above all that was the fatal year for the bridge on the Drina.

The summer of 1914 will remain in the memory of those who lived through it as the most beautiful summer they ever remembered, for in their consciousness it shone and flamed over a gigantic and dark horizon of suffering and misfortune which stretched into infinity.

That summer did in fact begin well, better than so many earlier summers. The plums ripened as they had not done for long before, and the wheat promised a good harvest. After ten years or so of troubles and commotions, the people hoped for at least a lull and a good year which would recompense in every way for the harms and misfortunes of earlier years. (The most deplorable and tragic of all human weaknesses is undoubtedly our total incapacity for seeing into the future, which is in sharp contrast to so many of our gifts, our skills and our knowledge.)

Sometimes there is such a year when the heat of the sun and the moisture of the earth combine, and the whole Višegrad valley trembles from the superabundance of its force and the universal urge towards fecundity. The earth swells and everything in it bursts vigorously into buds and leaves and blossoms and brings forth fruit a hundredfold. That breath of fertility could easily be seen quivering like a warm blue cloud over every furrow and every heap of earth. The cows and goats walked with hindlegs astraddle and moved with difficulty because of swollen and brimming udders. The fish in the river which every year at the beginning of summer came in shoals down the Rzav to spawn at its mouth were in such numbers that the children scooped them out of the shallows in buckets and threw them on the bank. The porous stone of the bridge became softer and as if it were alive swelled with the force and abundance which beat upwards from the soil and hovered over the whole town in the heat of the dog-days in which everything breathed more quickly and matured more vigorously.

Such summers were not frequent in the Višegrad valley. But when one occurred, men forgot all the bad days that had been and did not even think of the misfortunes which might still be in store, but lived with the threefold intensity of the life of the valley upon which the blessings of fertility had fallen, themselves only a part in that game of moisture and heat and ripening juices.

Even the peasants who always found occasion to complain of something had to agree that the year had fruited well, but to every word of praise they added the qualification: "If this weather holds. . . ." The merchants of the market-place threw themselves headlong into business like bees into the cups of flowers. They scattered into the villages around the town to make deposit payments on wheat in the ear and plums still in blossom. The peasants, bewildered by this invasion of eager buyers, as well as by the large and exceptional yield, stood beside their fruit trees already bending under the weight of fruit or beside the fields which were like waves in the wind, and could not be sufficiently prudent and restrained to deal with the townsmen who had taken the trouble to come to visit them. That prudence and restraint gave their faces a shuttered and anxious expression, twin of that mask of woe worn by peasant faces in years of bad harvest.

When the merchants were rich and powerful, it was the peasants who came to them. On market days the shop of Pavle Ranković was always full of peasants in need of ready money. So too was the shop of Santo Papo who had for long been the leading figure among the Višegrad Jews, for even despite the fact that banks, mortgage banks and other credit facilities had long existed in the town, the peasants, especially the older ones, liked to commit themselves in the old-fashioned way with the merchants from whom they bought their goods and with whom their fathers before them had contracted obligations.

Santo Papo's shop was one of the highest and most solid in the Višegrad market. It was built of stone, with thick walls and a floor of stone flags. The heavy doors and window-shutters were of wrought iron and there were thick close grilles on the tall and narrow windows.

The front part of the building served as a shop. Along the walls were wooden shelves filled with enamel ware. From the ceiling, which was exceptionally high, so that it was lost in the gloom, hung lighter goods: lanterns of all sizes, coffee-pots, traps, mouse-traps and other objects of twisted wire. All these hung in great bunches. Around the long counter were piled boxes of nails, sacks of cement, plaster and various paints; hoes, shovels and mattocks without handles were strung on wire in heavy garlands. In the corners were large tin containers with paraffin, turpentine and lamp-black. It was cool there even in the height of summer and even at noon was dark and gloomy.

But most of the stock was in the rooms behind the shop, through a low entry with iron doors. The heavy goods were kept there: iron stoves, crowbars, ploughshares, picks and other large tools. They were all piled up in great heaps so that one could only walk between the piled goods along the narrow paths as if between high walls. Perpetual darkness reigned there and no one entered save with a lantern.

A chill dank air of stone and metal, which nothing could warm or disperse, exuded from the thick walls, stone ceiling and piled up iron. That air in a few years transformed the lively and red-cheeked apprentices into silent, pale and puffy assistants, but made them skillful and thrifty. It was undoubtedly harmful also to the generations of shopkeepers but it was at the same time sweet and dear to them since it meant the feeling of property, the thought of gain and the source of riches.

The man who now sat in the front part of the cool, half-lit shop at a small table beside a great green Wertheim safe in no way resembled that turbulent and vivacious Santo who had once, thirty years before, had his own special way of shouting "Rum for Čorkan!" The passage of years and the work in the shop had changed him. Now he was heavy and ponderous and yellow in the face; dark rings about his eyes stretched halfway down his cheeks; his eyes had grown weak, those black and protruding eyes which now peered out from behind spectacles with thick lenses and metal rims, with a severe and yet timid expression. He still wore his cherry-colored fez as a last remnant of his one-time Turkish costume. His father, Mente Papo, a wizened and bald old man in his eighties, was still in reasonable health though his sight was failing. He would come to the shop on sunny days. With his watery eyes which seemed to be melting away behind thick spectacles he would look at his son seated by the safe and his grandson at the counter, breathe in that aroma of his shop and then return home at a slow pace, his right hand resting on the shoulder of his ten-year-old great-grandson.

Santo had six daughters and five sons, most of them married. His eldest son, Rafo, already had grown-up children who helped the father in the shop. One of Rafo's sons, who bore his grandfather's name, was at the Sarajevo secondary school. He was a pale, short-sighted and slender youth who at the age of eight had known perfectly how to recite the poems of the patriotic poet Zmaj, but otherwise was not good at his studies, did not like to go to the synagogue or help in his grandfather's shop during the holidays and said that he was going to become an actor or something equally famous and unusual.

Santo sat bowed over the huge, worn and greasy counter with an alphabetical ledger, and in front of him, on an empty nailbox, squatted the peasant Ibro Čemanović of Uzavnica. Santo was reckoning up how much Ibro already owed him and therefore how much and on what conditions he could obtain a fresh loan.

"Sinquenta, sinquenta i ocho . . . sinquenta i ocho, sesienta i tres . . . ," Santo whispered, reckoning in Ladino Spanish.

The peasant watched him with anxious anticipation as if watching an incantation and not listening to the account which he already knew to the last *para* and which ran through his head even when he was asleep. When Santo finished and announced the amount of the loan with interest, the peasant murmured slowly: "Will that be so . . . ?" merely to gain time enough to compare his own reckoning with Santo's.

"So it is, Ibraga, and in no way different," replied Santo in the formula time-honored in such cases.

After they had agreed on the state of present indebtedness, the peasant had to demand a fresh loan and Santo to make clear the likelihood and the conditions. But that was no rapid or easy task. A conversation developed between them, similar in the minutest detail to the conversations which, ten years ago or more, also before the harvest, had been held in this same spot between the father of Ibro from Uzavnica and Santo's father, Mente

Papo. The main subject of the conversation would be broached in a torrent of words which meant nothing in themselves and which seemed entirely superfluous and almost senseless. Anyone uninitiated, looking at them and listening to them, might easily have thought that the talk had nothing to do with money or a loan, or at least so it often appeared.

"The plums are well forward and brought forth much fruit among us, even more than in any other district," said Santo. "It has been years since there was such a crop."

"Yes, thanks be, they have borne well enough; if Allah permits the weather to hold there will be fruit and bread. One cannot deny it. Only who knows what the price will be," said the anxious peasant, rubbing his thumb along the seam of his heavy green cloth trousers and looking at Santo out of the corner of his eye.

"There is no way of telling that now, but we shall know by the time you bring them to Višegrad. You know the saying, the price is in the owner's hands."

"Yes, that is so. If Allah allows them to ripen and mature," the peasant again qualified.

"Without God's will, naturally, there is no gathering nor reaping; however much man looks to what he has sown, it will avail him nothing if he have not God's blessing," broke in Santo, raising his hand to heaven to show whence that blessing should come, somewhere high above those heavy blackened rafters of the shop from which hung peasant lanterns of all sizes and bundles of other goods.

"It will avail nothing, you are right," sighed Ibro. "A man sows and plants but it is just as if, by the Great and Only God, he had thrown it all into the water; one digs, hoes, prunes and picks, but no! If it is not so written there will be no blessing on it. But if God decides to give us a good harvest then no one will lack and a man may clear himself of debt and then become indebted once more. Only let him keep his health!"

"Ah, yes. Health is the main thing. Nothing is as important as health. So is man's life; give him everything and take health from him and it is as if he were given nothing," affirmed Santo, turning the conversation in that direction.

Then the peasant also expressed his views on health, which were just as general and commonplace as Santo's. For a moment it seemed as if the whole conversation would be lost in futilities and generalizations. But at a favorable moment, as if by some ancient ritual, he returned to the opening question. Then began the bargaining for a new loan, over the amount, the interest, the terms and the methods of payment. They discussed it for long, now vivaciously, now quietly and anxiously, but in the end they came to an agreement. Then Santo rose, took a bunch of keys on a chain from his pocket and without removing them from the chain, unlocked the safe which began by creaking, opened slowly and solemnly and then, like all large safes, closed with a fine metallic noise like a sigh. He counted out the money to the peasant, down to the copper *hellers,* all with the same care and attention, with a solemnity that seemed a little sad. Then in a changed and more animated voice:

"Well, is that all right by you, Ibraga? Are you satisfied?"

"Yes, by God," the peasant replied quietly and pensively.

"May God send you blessing and profit! Till we meet again in good health and good friendship," said Santo, now quite lively and gay; and he sent his grandson to the café across the way for two coffees, "one bitter, one sweet."

A second peasant was already awaiting his turn in front of the shop bound on the same errand and similar reckonings.

With these peasants and their reckoning about the coming harvest and the gathering of the plums, the warm and heavy breath of an exceptionally fruitful year penetrated into the twilit gloom of Santo's shop. The green steel safe sweated from it and Santo stretched the collar around his fat, soft, yellowish neck with his forefinger and wiped the steam off his spectacles with a handkerchief.

So did summer begin.

But none the less at the very beginning of that year of blessing there fell a tiny shadow of fear and sorrow. In the early spring, at Uvac, a small place on the former Turco-Austrian frontier and the new Serbo-Austrian border, a typhus epidemic broke out. As the place was on the frontier and two cases had occurred in the gendarmerie station, the Višegrad military doctor, Dr. Balas, went there with one male nurse and the necessary medicines. The doctor skillfully and resolutely did all that was necessary to isolate the sick, and himself undertook their treatment. Of fifteen who had been taken ill only two died and the epidemic was limited to the village of Uvac and stamped out at its source. The last man to take ill was Dr. Balas himself. The inexplicable manner in which he had caught the disease, the shortness of his illness, the unexpected complications and sudden death, all bore the stamp of genuine tragedy.

Because of the danger of infection the young doctor had to be buried at Uvac. Madame Bauer with her husband and a few other officers attended the funeral. She gave some money for a tombstone of roughly hewn granite to be erected over the doctor's grave. Immediately afterwards she left both the town and her husband and it was rumored that she had gone to some sanatorium near Vienna. This was the story current among the girls in the town; the older people, as soon as the danger had passed and the measures against the epidemic ceased, forgot both the doctor and the colonel's lady. Inexperienced and uneducated, the town girls did not know exactly what the word sanatorium meant, but they had known very well what it meant when two persons walked about the paths and foothills as the doctor and the colonel's wife had done until lately. Pronouncing that strange word in their confidential discussions about the unhappy pair, they loved to imagine that sanatorium as some sort of mysterious, distant and melancholy place in which beautiful and sinful women expiated their forbidden loves.

The exceptionally lovely and fruitful summer grew and matured over the fields and summits around the town. In the evening the windows of the officers' mess, over the river and by the bridge, were lighted and wide open as in the previous year, only the sound of the piano and the violin no longer came from them. Colonel Bauer sat at his table with a few of his senior officers, good-humored, smiling and sweating from the effects of the red wine and the heat of the summer.

The young men sat on the *kapia* on warm nights and sang. It was nearly the end of June and the students were shortly expected to arrive, as they did every year. On such nights on the *kapia* it seemed as if time had stopped, while life flowed on endless, rich and easy and one could not foresee how long it would continue thus.

At that time of the night the main streets were illuminated, for the town had had electric light since spring that year. About a year earlier an electrically driven sawmill had been built on the river bank about a mile from the town and beside it a factory for extracting turpentine from pine refuse; it also produced resin. This factory had made an agreement with the municipality to light the town streets from its private power station. So the green lamp-standards with their petroleum lights disappeared, and with them tall Ferhat who used to clean and light them. The main street which stretched the whole length of the town, from the bridge to the new quarter, was lit by powerful lamps of white milky glass, while the sidestreets which branched off to right and left and meandered around Bikavac or climbed upwards to Mejdan and Okolište were lighted by ordinary bulbs. Between these lines of similar lights stretched long irregular patches of darkness. These were courtyards or large gardens on the slopes.

In one of these dark gardens Zorka the schoolmistress was sitting with Nikola Glasičanin.

The dissension which had arisen between these two last year, when Stiković had appeared at the time of the vacation, had lasted for long, right up to the beginning of the new year. Then, as every winter, preparations for the Festival of St. Sava had been begun in the Srpski Dom. A concert and a play were being prepared. Both Zorka and Glasičanin took part and returning home after the rehearsals they had spoken together for the first time since the previous summer. At first their talks had been short, reserved and distant. But they did not stop seeing one another, for young people prefer even the most bitter and hopeless of lovers' quarrels to the boredom and loneliness of a life without the play and thoughts of love. Somewhere in the course of their endless arguments they had made peace, they themselves knew not how or when. Now, on these warm summer nights, they met regularly. From time to time the figure of the absent Stiković rose between them and the whole pointless argument flamed up again, but it did not drive them apart, while every reconciliation drew them closer and closer together.

Now they sat in the warm darkness on the stump of an old walnut tree and wrapped in their own thoughts looked down at the big and little lights of the town along the river which roared monotonously. Glasičanin, who had been talking for a long time, was now silent for a moment. Zorka, who had been silent all evening, remained silent as only women know how when they are disentangling their love troubles in their minds, those troubles which are more intimate and more important to them than anything else in life.

About this time last year, when Stiković had first appeared on the scene, Zorka had thought that an endless paradise of happiness had opened before her, in which perfect affinity of feelings and unity of thought and desires had the sweetness of a kiss and the duration of a human existence. But that illusion had not lasted long. However inexperienced and enraptured she may have been, she could not fail to notice that this man quickly took fire but equally quickly burned out, according to his own ideas, without any consideration for her and without any connection with those things which she considered greater and more important than either herself or him. He had left her almost without saying goodbye. She had been left a prey to indecision from which she suffered as from a hidden wound. The letter which had come from him had been perfectly phrased, a perfect example of literary skill, but as measured as a counsel's opinion and as clear and as transparent as an empty glass jar. In it he had spoken of his love, but as if the pair of them had already been a century in their graves, like persons famous and long dead. To her warm and vivid reply came his card: "In the tasks and anxieties which harass and annoy me I think of you as of a peaceful Višegrad night, filled with the sound of the river and the perfume of unseen grasses." And that was all. In vain she tried to remember when she had heard the sound of the river and sensed the perfume of those unseen grasses. They existed only on his postcard. Certainly she did not remember them, even as he, it seemed, did not remember anything that had taken place between them. Her mind darkened with the thought that she had been deceived and that he had deceived her, and then consoled herself with something that she herself did not understand and which was less likely than a miracle. "It is not possible to understand him," she thought to herself, "he is strange and cold, selfish, moody and capricious, but perhaps all exceptional men are like that." In any event what she felt was more like suffering than love. Her inner flinching and the break that she felt in the depths of her being made it seem to her that the whole burden of that love which he had provoked lay upon her alone, and that he was lost somewhere far in the fog and the distance which she dared not call by its real name. For a woman in love, even when she has lost all her illusions, cherishes her love like a child she has not been destined to bear. She hardened her heart and did not reply to his card. But after a silence of two months another card arrived. It was written from some high mountain in the Alps: "At a height of 2,000 meters, surrounded by people of various tongues and nationalities, I look at the boundless horizon and think of you and last summer." Even for her years and her little experience that was enough. Had he written: "I did not love you, I do not love you now, nor will I ever be able to love you," it could have been no clearer or more painful to her. For when all was said and done, it was love that was in question, not far-off memories or how many meters above sea-level a man was writing, nor what people were around him nor what languages they spoke. And there was nothing about love!

A poor girl and an orphan, Zorka had grown up in Višegrad with some relations. After she had finished her studies at the Teachers' Training College at Sarajevo, she had been posted to Višegrad and had returned to the house of the well-to-do but simple folk to whom she felt in no way attached.

Zorka had grown thin and pale and had withdrawn into herself, but she had confided in no one, and did not reply to his Christmas message of greetings, which was equally short, cold and faultless in style. She wanted to come to terms with her own grief and shame without anyone's help or consolation but, weak, discouraged, young, ignorant and inexperienced, she became more and more involved in that inextricable net of real events and great desires, of her own thoughts and his incomprehensible and inhuman behavior. Had she been able to ask anyone or to take anyone's advice, it would certainly have been easier for her but shame held her back. Even so it often seemed to her that the whole town knew about her disappointment and that mocking and malicious glances seemed to burn into her as she walked through the market-place. Neither men nor books gave her any explanation; and she herself did not know how to explain anything. If he really did not love her why had there been all that comedy of passionate words and vows during the vacation last year? What had been the reason for that episode on the school bench, which could only be justified and defended by love, without which it fell into the mud of unbearable humiliation? Was it possible that there were men who respected themselves and others so little that they would enter lightheartedly into such a game? What drove them on if not love? What did his burning glances, his warm and halting breath, his passionate kisses mean? What could they mean, if not love? But it was not love! She saw that now, better and more clearly than she would have liked. But she could not resign herself truly and lastingly to such a thought (who has ever been able to resign themselves completely to it?). The natural conclusion of all these internal conflicts was the thought of death which always lurks on the frontiers of every dream of happiness. To die, thought Zorka, to slip from the *kapia* into the river as if by chance, without letters or farewells, without admissions or humiliations. "To die" she thought to herself in the last moments before going to sleep and on recovering consciousness in the morning, in the midst of the most lively conversations and beneath the mask of every smile. Everything in her said and repeated those words—"to die! to die!"—but one does not die, but lives with that insupportable thought within one.

Comfort came from the source she least of all expected. Some time about the Christmas vacation her hidden torment reached its height. Such thoughts and such unanswered questions destroy one even more than an illness. Everyone noticed changes for the worse in her and worried about her, her relatives, her headmaster, a merry man with many children, and her friends, advising her to see a doctor.

Good luck had it that just at this time were the rehearsals for the St. Sava festivities and that, after so many months, she again talked with Glasičanin. Up till then he had avoided every meeting or conversation with her. But that goodwill that usually reigns at these naïve but sincere dramatic and musical shows in small places, and then the clear cold nights as they returned home, saw to it these these two young estranged persons should draw closer to one another. Her need to lessen her torment drove her on and his love, deep and sincere, drove him.

Their first words were naturally cold, defiant, double-edged, and their conversations long explanations without issue. But even those brought solace to the girl. For the first time she could talk with a living being about her inner, shameful wretchedness without having to confess its most shameful and painful details. Glasičanin spoke to her of it long and animatedly but with warmth and consideration, saving her pride. He did not express himself more harshly about Stiković than was inevitable. His explanation was such as we have already heard that night on the *kapia*. It was short, sure and unsparing. Stiković was a born egoist and a monster, a man who could love no one and who as long as he lived, himself tormented and unsatisfied, would torture all those whom he deceived and who were near to him. Glasičanin did not speak much of his own love, but it was evident in every word, every glance and every movement. The girl listened to him, remaining silent for the most part. After every such conversation she felt more serene, more at peace with herself. For the first time after so many months she had moments of respite from her internal storms and for the first time succeeded in looking at herself as other than an unworthy being. For the young man's words, filled with love and respect, showed her that she was not irretrievably lost and that her despair was only an illusion even as her dream of love the previous summer had been only an illusion. They had taken her out of that gloomy world in which she had already begun to lose herself and sent her back to living human reality, where there was healing and aid for everyone, or nearly everyone.

Their talks continued even after the St. Sava celebrations. The winter passed and after it the spring. They saw one another almost every day. In time the girl came to herself, grew stronger and healthier, and was transformed, quickly and naturally, as only youth can be. So too passed that fruitful and uneasy summer. People were already accustomed to regard Zorka and Glasičanin as a couple who were "walking out."

It was true that the long speeches of Glasičanin to which she had at first listened avidly, drinking them in like medicine, were now less interesting. At times this need for mutual confession and confidence weighed on her. She asked herself with genuine wonder how this closeness between them had come about, but then she remembered that last winter he had "saved her soul" and, mastering her boredom, listened to him like a good debtor, as carefully as she could.

That summer night his hand was over hers (that was the ultimate limit of his modest daring). Through that contact the warm richness of the night penetrated him also. In such moments it was fully clear to him how much treasure was hidden in this woman and at the same time he felt how the bitterness and dissatisfaction of his life were being transformed into fruitful power sufficient to take two people to even the most distant goal, if love bound them and sustained them.

Filled with those feelings in the darkness he was no longer the everyday Glasičanin, a minor clerk of the great Višegrad enterprise, but quite another man, strong and self-confident, who controlled his own life freely and far-sightedly. For a man filled with a great, true and unselfish love, even if it be on one side only, there open horizons and possibilities and paths which are closed and unknown to so many clever, ambitious and selfish men.

He spoke to the woman beside him.

"I do not think I am mistaken; if for no other reason, then just because I should never be able to deceive you. While some talk and rave and others do business and make gains, I follow everything and watch everything and I see more and more clearly that there is no sort of life here. For a long time there will be neither peace nor order nor profitable work. Not even Stiković, not even Herak, can create them. On the other hand, everything will get worse. We must get away from here, as from a house that is falling down. These countless and uneasy saviours who pop up at every step are the best proof that we are heading for a catastrophe. Since we cannot help, we can at least save ourselves."

The girl remained silent.

"I have never spoken to you about this, but I have thought often and much, and have even done a little. You know that Bogdan Djurović, my friend from Okolište, has now been in America for three years. I have been in correspondence with him since last year. I showed you the photograph he sent me. He has asked me to come over there and has promised me a safe job at a good wage. I know that it is not a simple matter to do all this, but I do not think it is impossible. I have thought everything over and calculated everything. I will sell the little property I have up there at Okolište. If you will say yes, we will get married as soon as possible and leave for Zagreb without saying anything to anyone. There is a company there which arranges for emigrants to get to America. We could wait there until Bogdan sends us an affidavit. In the interval we could learn English. If we are not successful, perhaps because of my military service, then we will cross over into Serbia and leave from there. I will arrange everything to make it as easy as possible for you. In America we will both work. There are Serbian schools there where you could teach. I would easily find work there, for over there all jobs are open and unrestricted. We will be free and happy. I will arrange everything, if only you would . . . if only you would agree."

The young man stopped. By way of answer she put both her hands on his. In that he felt the expression of a great gratitude. But her answer was neither yes nor no. She thanked him for all his trouble and attention and for his boundless goodness and, in the name of that goodness, asked for a month before she gave him a definite answer; until the end of the school year.

"Thank you, Nikola, thank you! You are good to me!" she whispered, pressing his hands.

From the *kapia* below rose the sound of young men singing. They were Višegrad youths, perhaps also some students from Sarajevo. In a fortnight the university students were due to arrive. Until then she would not be able to come to any decision. Everything made her suffer, most of all the goodness of this man, but at that moment she would not have been able to say "yes" even if she were to be cut to pieces. She no longer hoped for anything save to see once more "that man who can love no one." Once more, and then let be what would! Nikola would wait; that she knew.

They rose and, hand in hand, went slowly down the slope which led towards the bridge whence the singing came.

22

On Vidovdan the Serbs held their regular outing at Mezalin. Under the dense walnut-trees, at the meeting of the two rivers Drina and Rzav, on the high green banks, tents were put up in which drinks were on sale and before which lambs were turning on spits over slow fires. Families who had brought their lunch with them sat in the shade. Below a canopy of fresh branches an orchestra was already playing. On the well-beaten open space there had been a *kolo* since morning. Only the youngest and idlest were dancing, those who had come here directly after morning service, straight from the church. The real general outing only began in the afternoon. But the *kolo* was already lively and enthusiastic, better and more vigorous than it would be later on when the crowd came, and married women, unsatisfied widows and young children began to take part and when everything was transformed into a single long and gay, but haphazard and disconnected, garland. That shorter *kolo* in which more young men than girls were taking part was fast and furious, like a thrown lasso. Everything around it seemed to be moving, swaying to the rhythm of the music, the air, the thick crowns of the trees, the white summer clouds and the swift waters of the two rivers. The earth trembled under it and around it and seemed only to be trying to adapt its movement to the movements of the young bodies. Young men ran in from the main road to take their places in the *kolo,* but the girls restrained themselves and stood for a time watching the dancing as if counting the beats and waiting for some secret impulse in themselves; then they would suddenly leap in to the *kolo* with lowered heads and slightly bended knees as if eagerly leaping into cold water. The powerful current passed from the warm earth into the dancing feet and spread along the chain of warm hands; on that chain the *kolo* pulsed like a single living thing, warmed by the same blood and carried away by the same rhythm. The young men danced with heads thrown back, pale and with quivering nostrils, while the young girls danced with reddened cheeks and modestly downcast eyes, lest their glances betray the passion with which the dance had filled them.

At that moment, when the outing had only just begun, a number of gendarmes appeared at the edge of the meadow, their black uniforms and weapons shining in the afternoon light. There were more of them than was usual for the patrol which regularly visited fairs and

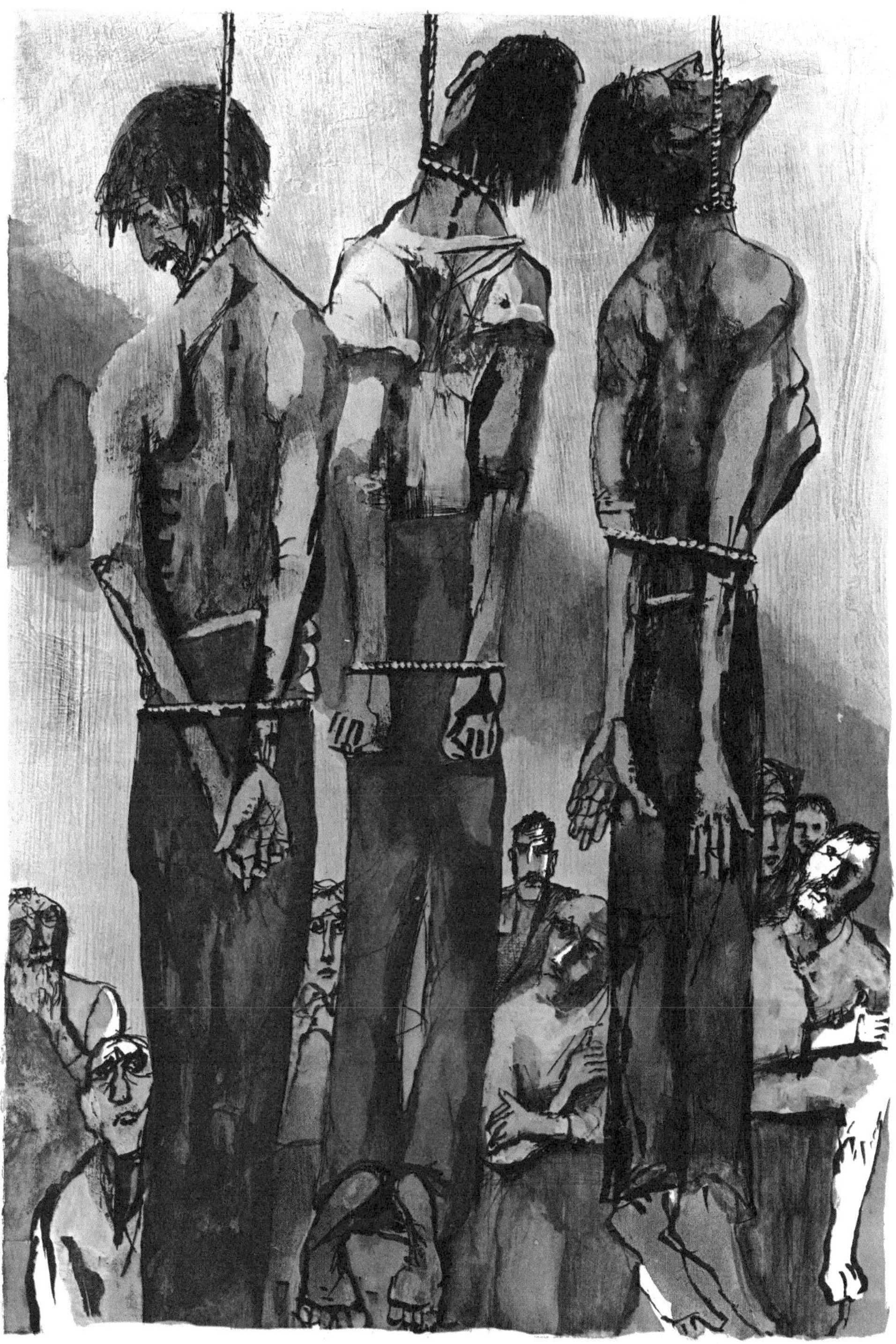

outings. They went straight to the canopy where the musicians were playing. One after the other, irregularly, the players ceased. The *kolo* wavered and stopped. Young men's cries of protest could be heard. The dancers stood hand in hand. Some were so carried away and filled with the rhythm that they went on dancing where they were, waiting for the music to begin again. But the players rose in haste and wrapped up their trumpets and their violins. The gendarmes went on farther, to the tents and the families sitting on the grass. Everywhere the sergeant said his piece, in a low harsh voice, and like some magic charm the gaiety faded away, the dancing ceased and conversations were broken off. Whomever they approached left the place where he had been till then, forgot whatever he was doing, gathered up his things as quickly as possible and left. The last to disperse was the *kolo* of youths and girls. They did not want to abandon their dancing and could not get it into their heads that this was really the end of the gaiety and the outing. But when they saw the white face and bloodshot eyes of the sergeant of gendarmes even the most obstinate slunk away.

Disillusioned and perplexed, the people trailed back from Mezalin along the wide, white road; the farther they went into the town the more they heard vague and frightened whispers about the assassination that morning at Sarajevo and the death of the Archduke Franz Ferdinand and his wife and the persecution of the Serbs which was generally expected. In front of the Municipal Offices they came upon the first group of arrested men, among them the young priest Mihailo, being taken to prison.

So the second part of that summer day, which should have been a festival, was transformed into a bewildered, bitter and frightened expectation.

On the *kapia,* instead of a festival mood and the gaiety of men released from work, there was the silence of the dead. A guard had already been mounted. A soldier in a new uniform paced slowly from the *sofa* to the spot where the iron manhole covered the way down into the mined pier. He marched these five or six paces incessantly, and at each turn his bayonet glinted in the sun like a signal. The next day, beneath the plaque with the Turkish inscription, a white official notice appeared on the wall, printed in large letters and surrounded by a thick black border. It announced the news of the assassination and death in Sarajevo of the Crown Prince and expressed the indignation roused by this evil deed. None of the passers-by stopped to read it, but passed in front of the notice and the guard as quickly as possible with lowered heads.

From that time onward the guard remained on the bridge. The whole life of the town was suddenly interrupted, like the *kolo* at Mezalin and that July day which should have been a day of festivity.

The days to come were strange, filled with the avid reading of newspapers, of whispers, of fear and defiance, the arrests of Serbs and suspect travelers and the rapid reinforcement of military measures on the frontiers. The summer nights passed, but without song, without meetings of young men on the *kapia* and without the whispering of couples in the darkness. In the town mainly soldiers were to be seen. At nine o'clock at night when the buglers sounded the melancholy notes of the Austrian last-post in the cantonments at Bikavac and in the great barracks by the bridge, the streets were almost entirely deserted. Those were bad times for young lovers eager to meet and have private conversations. Every evening Glasičanin passed Zorka's house. She was sitting at an open window on the ground-floor. There they talked, but only for a short time, since he was in haste to cross the bridge and return to Okolište before nightfall.

So it happened that evening also. Pale, hat in hand, he begged the girl to come out to the gate for he had something private to tell her. After some hesitation she came. Standing on the threshold of the courtyard she was now level with the youth who spoke excitedly in a scarcely audible whisper.

"We have decided to flee. This evening. Vlado Marić and two others. I think that we have foreseen everything and that we shall get across. But if not . . . if something should happen. Zorka!"

The young man's whisper ceased. In her wide-open eyes he saw fear and embarrassment. He was deeply moved as if he regretted that he had spoken to her and come to say goodbye.

"I thought it better to tell you."

"Thank you! Then there is nothing of our . . . nothing of America!"

"No, not 'nothing.' Had you consented when I suggested a month ago that we should finish the matter at once, then perhaps we might already be far away from here. But perhaps it is better this way. Now you can see what the position is. I must go with my friends. The war is here already and there is need for all of us in Serbia. I must, Zorka, I must. It is my duty. If I come out of all this alive and if we become free, then it may no longer be necessary to go across the sea to America, for we shall have our own America here, a land in which a man may work hard and honestly and live well and freely. There will be a life in it for both of us, if only you will consent. It will depend on you. I will . . . I will think of you over there, and you, and you . . . sometimes . . ."

Words failed him and he suddenly put up his hand and quickly stroked her rich chestnut hair. That had always been his greatest desire and now, like a condemned man, he felt permitted to fulfil it. The girl withdrew in fright and he remained with his hand in the air. The gate shut silently and a moment later Zorka appeared at the window, pale, with wide-open eyes and feverishly twisting fingers. The young man came close up to the window, drew his head back and revealed his face, laughing, carefree, almost handsome. As if afraid to see what would happen next, the girl drew back into the room which was already dark. There she sat down on her bed, bent her head and began to weep.

At first she wept quietly and then more and more unrestrainedly with a feeling of heavy, universal hopelessness. The more she wept, the more reason she found to weep as everything around her seemed more and more hopeless. There was no way out, no solution; never would she be able to love, truly and as he deserved, that good and honest Nikola who was going away; never would she live to see the day when that other one, who could love no one, should love her. Never again would she see those lovely, happy days which she had passed only last year in this town. Not a single one of the Serbs would ever succeed in coming alive out of that dark circle of mountains, nor would see America, nor would create here a land where, so they said, a man could work hard and live freely. Never!

Next day the news spread that Vlado Marić, Glasičanin and a few other young men had fled to Serbia. All the other Serbs with their families, and all that they had, remained in that overheated valley as in a trap. Every day the atmosphere of danger and menace could be felt to be growing denser over the town. Then, in the last days of July, the storm burst over the frontier, a storm which would in time spread to the whole world and decide the fate of so many lands and cities, as well as that of the bridge on the Drina.

Only then began the real persecution of the Serbs and all those connected with them. The people were divided into the persecuted and those who persecuted them. That wild beast, which lives in man and does not dare to show itself until the barriers of law and custom have been removed, was now set free. The signal was given, the barriers were down. As has so often happened in the history of man, permission was tacitly granted for acts of violence and plunder, even for murder, if they were carried out in the name of higher interests, according to established rules, and against a limited number of men of a particular type and belief. A man who saw clearly and with open eyes and was then living could see how this miracle took place and how the whole of a society could, in a single day, be transformed. In a few minutes the business quarter, based on centuries of tradition, was wiped out. It is true that there had always been concealed enmities and jealousies and religious intolerance, coarseness and cruelty, but there had also been courage and fellowship and a feeling for measure and order, which restrained all these instincts within the limits of the supportable and, in the end, calmed them down and submitted them to the general interest of life in common. Men who had been leaders in the commercial quarter for forty years vanished overnight as if they had all died suddenly, together with the habits, customs and institutions which they represented.

The day after the declaration of war on Serbia a *schutzkorps* squad began to patrol the town. This squad, hastily armed and intended to assist the authorities in their hunt for Serbs, was made up of gipsies, drunkards and other persons of ill repute, mainly those who for long had been at odds with society and the law. A certain Huso Kokošar, a gipsy without honor or definite occupation, who had lost his nose in early youth as a result of a shameful disease, led the dozen or so ne'er-do-wells armed with old-fashioned Werndl rifles with long bayonets, and lorded it over the market-place.

Faced with this threat, Pavle Ranković, as President of the Serbian Church and School Community, went with a number of other leading members to the sub-prefect Sabljak. Sabljak was a pale, puffy man, completely bald, born in Croatia, who had only recently been appointed to Višegrad. Now he was excited and he had not slept well; his eyelids were reddened and his lips dry and bloodless. He was wearing high boots and in the lapel of his huntsman's coat wore some badge in two colors: black and yellow. He received them standing and did not offer them seats. Pavle, yellow in the face, his eyes like two thin black slits, spoke in a hoarse unfamiliar voice:

"Sir, you see what is going on and what is being prepared, and you know that we, Serbs and citizens of Višegrad, have not wanted this."

"I know nothing, sir," the Prefect curtly interrupted him in a voice harsh with vexation, "and I want to know nothing. We have other, more important, things to do now than listen to speeches. That is all I have to say to you!"

"Sir," Pavle began again calmly as if trying by his own calm to moderate even this irritable and angry man, "we have come to offer you our services and to assure you. . . ."

"I have no need of your services and there is nothing for you to assure me about. You have shown at Sarajevo what you can do. . . ."

"Sir," continued Pavle resolutely and with unchanged voice, "we would have liked within the limits of the law . . ."

"So! Now you remember the law! To what laws have you the effrontery to appeal . . . ?"

"The laws of the state, Sir, which apply to all."

The Prefect suddenly became serious as if he had calmed down a little. Pavle at once took advantage of this moment of calm.

"Sir, permit us to ask you whether we may be sure that our lives and property and those of our families will be respected, and if not, what we should do?"

The Prefect spread out his hands, palms upward, shrugged his shoulders, closed his eyes and convulsively shut his thin, pale lips.

Pavle knew only too well this characteristic gesture, pitiless, blind-deaf-dumb, which state officials adopt in important moments and saw at once that it was no use going on talking. The Prefect, after lowering his hands, looked up and said more gently:

"The military authorities will advise everyone what they must do."

Now it was Pavle's turn to spread out his hands, close his eyes and shrug his shoulders for a moment, and then say in a deep, changed voice:

"Thank you, Sir."

The representatives bowed stiffly and clumsily. Then they filed out like condemned men.

The market-place was filled with aimless movement and secret consultations.

In Alihodja's shop were sitting a number of prominent Turks, Nailbeg Turković, Osmanaga Šabanović and Suljaga Mezildjić. They were pale and worried, with that heavy, fixed expression which can always be seen on the faces of those who have something to lose when faced with unexpected events and important changes. The authorities had called on them to place themselves at the head of the *schutzkorps*. Now they had, as if by chance, met here to discuss, without being overheard, what they ought to do. Some were for accepting, others for holding back. Alihodja, red in the face, excited, with the old light in his eyes, resolutely opposed any idea of participation in the *schutzkorps*. He addressed himself especially to Nailbeg who was for taking up arms since they, as leading citizens, should place themselves at the head of the Moslem volunteer detachments instead of a bunch of gipsies.

"I will never mix myself up in their affairs as long as I am alive. And you, if you had any sense, would not do so either. Can't you see that these Vlachs are only making use of us and that, in the end, it will all come back on our own heads?"

With the same eloquence as he had once used in opposing Osman Effendi Karamanli on the *kapia* he showed them that there was nothing good "for the Turkish ear" on either side and that every intervention on their part could only be harmful.

"For a long time past no one has asked us about anything or paid the least heed to our opinions. The Schwabes entered Bosnia and neither Sultan nor Kaiser asked: 'By your leave, begs and gentlemen.' Then Serbia and Montenegro, until yesterday our serfs, rose in revolt and took away half the Turkish Empire and still no one ever thought about us. Now the Kaiser attacks Serbia and once again no one asks us anything, but only gives us rifles and trousers to make us Schwabe decoy ducks and tells us to hunt the Serbs lest they should tear their own trousers climbing Šargan. Can't you get that into your heads? Since no one has ever asked us about so many important things over so many years, this sudden favor is enough to make one burst one's ribs laughing. I tell you; there are big things at stake and it is best for him who does not get himself mixed up in them more than he must. Here on the frontier they have already come to grips and who knows how far it will spread? There must be someone behind this Serbia. It could not be otherwise. But you, up at Nezuke, have a mountain in front of your windows and can see no farther than its stones. Better give up what you have begun; don't go into the *schutzkorps* and don't persuade others to go. Better go on milking the dozen serfs you have left while they still bring you in something."

All were silent, serious and motionless. Nailbeg too was silent. He was obviously offended, though he concealed it. Pale as a corpse, he was turning over some decision in his mind. Save for Nailbeg, Alihodja had undecided them and cooled their ardor. They smoked and silently watched the endless procession of military wagons and laden packhorses crossing the bridge. Then, one by one, they rose and made their farewells. Nailbeg was the last. To his sullen greeting, Alihodja once more looked him in the eyes and said almost sadly:

"I see that you have made up your mind to go. You too want to die, and are afraid lest the gipsies get in first. But remember that long ago old men said: 'The time has not come to die but to let it be seen of what stuff a man is made.' These are such times."

The square between the *hodja's* shop and the bridge was crammed with carts, horses, soldiers of all kinds and reservists coming to report. From time to time the gendarmes would lead a group of bound men across it; Serbs. The air was filled with dust. Everyone yelled at the top of his voice and moved about more quickly than the occasion demanded. Faces were flushed and running with sweat; curses could be heard in all languages. Eyes were shining with drink and from sleepless nights and that troubled anxiety which always reigns in the presence of danger and bloody events.

In the center of the square, directly facing the bridge, Hungarian reservists in brand-new uniforms were hewing some beams. Hammers sounded and saws were busy cutting. Around them a group of children had gathered. From his shop window Alihodja watched two beams being set upright. Then a mustachioed Hungarian reservist scrambled up them and placed a third horizontally across the top. The crowd pressed around them as if *halva* were being given away, forming a living circle around the gallows. Most of them were soldiers, but there were also some Turkish village wastrels and gipsies from the town. When all was ready a way was made through the crowd and a table was brought and two chairs for the officer and his clerk. Then the *schutzkorps* brought first two peasants and then a townsman. The peasants were village serfs from the frontier villages of Pozderčić and Kamenica and the townsman a certain Vajo, a man from the Lika, who had long ago come to the town as a contractor and had married there. All three were bound, haggard and covered with dust. A drummer was standing by, waiting to give a roll on his drums. In the general flurry and commotion the noise of the drum sounded like distant thunder. Silence fell on that circle around the gallows. The officer, a Hungarian reserve lieutenant, read in a harsh voice the sentences of death in German; they were then translated by a sergeant. All three had been sentenced to death by a summary court, for witnesses had declared on oath that they had seen them giving light-signals by night towards the Serbian frontier. The hanging was to be carried out publicly on the square facing the bridge. The peasants were silent, blinking as if in perplexity. Vajo, the man from Lika, wiped the sweat from his face and in a soft sad voice swore that he was innocent and with frenzied eyes looked around him for someone to whom he could still say it.

Just at that moment when the sentence was about to be carried out there burst through the crowd of onlookers a soldier, small and reddish, with legs bowed like an X. It was Gustav, the one-time *zahlkelner* in Lotte's hotel and now a café-owner in the lower market-place. He was in a new uniform with a corporal's stripes. His face was flushed and his eyes more bloodshot than usual. Explanations began. The sergeant began to hustle him away but the bellicose café-owner held his ground.

"I have been an intelligence agent here for fifteen years, in the confidence of the highest military circles," he shouted in German in a drunken voice. "Only the year before last in Vienna I was promised that I could hang two Serbs with my own hands when the time came. You don't know with whom you have to deal. I have earned my right to . . . and now you . . ."

There were murmurs and whispers in the crowd. The sergeant stood in perplexity not knowing what to do. Gustav became even more aggressive and demanded that two of the condemned men be handed over to him so that he could hang them personally. Then the lieutenant, a thin dark man with the manner of a gentleman, as despairing as if he were himself one of the condemned men, without a drop of blood in his face, rose. Gustav, even though drunk, stood to attention but his thin red moustaches quivered and his eyes rolled to left and right. The officer came close to him and thrust his head into that flushed face as if he would spit on it.

"If you don't get out of here at once, I will give orders for you to be bound and taken to prison. Tomorrow you will report to the officer of the day. Do you understand? Now get out! March!"

The lieutenant had spoken in German with a Hungarian accent, quite softly, but so sharply and exasperatedly that the drunken café-owner at once thought better of it and was lost in the crowd, incessantly repeating his military greeting and muttering vague words of excuse.

Only then did the attention of the crowd return to the condemned men. The two peasants, fathers of families, behaved exactly alike. They blinked and frowned from the sun and the heat of the crowd around them as if that were all that was troubling them. But Vajo in a weak and tearful voice asserted his innocence, that his competitor was responsible for the charge, that he had never done any military service and never in his life known that one could make signals with lights. He knew a little German and desperately linked word with word, trying to find some convincing expression to halt this mad torrent which had swept him away the day before and which now threatened to sweep him off this earth, innocent though he was.

"Herr Oberleutnant, Herr Oberleutnant, um Gottes willen. . . . Ich, unschuldiger Mensch . . . viele Kinder. . . . Unschuldig! Lüge! Alles Lüge! . . ." (Lieutenant, in God's name. . . . I am innocent . . . many children . . . innocent! Lies! . . . All lies!). Vajo chose his words as if searching for those which were right and could bring salvation.

The soldiers had already approached the first peasant. He quickly took off his cap, turned towards Mejdan where the church was and rapidly crossed himself twice. With a glance, the officer ordered them to finish with Vajo first. Then the desperate man from Lika, seeing it was now his turn, raised his hands to heaven imploringly and shouted at the top of his voice:

"Nein! Nein! Nicht, um Gottes willen! Herr Oberleutnant, Sie wissen . . . alles ist Lüge. . . . Gott! . . . Alles Lüge!"

But the soldier had already seized him by his legs and waist and lifted him on to the trestles under the rope.

Breathlessly the crowd followed all that happened as if it were some sort of game between the unlucky contractor and the lieutenant, burning with curiosity to know who would win and who lose.

Alihodja, who had up till then only heard meaningless voices and had no idea of what was happening in the center of that circle of densely packed onlookers, suddenly saw the panic-stricken face of Vajo above their heads and at once leaped up to shut his shop though there was a specific order of the military authorities that all places of business must remain open.

Fresh troops kept arriving in the town and after them munitions, food and equipment, not only by the overcrowded railway line from Sarajevo but also by the old carriage road through Rogatica. Horses and carriages crossed the bridge day and night and the first thing to meet their eyes was the three hanged men on the square. As the head of the column usually became wedged in the overcrowded streets, this meant that the bulk of the column had to halt there on the bridge or in the square beside the gallows until those in front had extricated themselves. Covered with dust, red-faced and hoarse from furious shouting, the sergeants passed on horseback between the carts and laden packhorses, making desperate signals with their hands and swearing in all the languages of the Austro-Hungarian Monarchy and by all the sacred things of all recognized confessions.

On the fourth or fifth day, early in the morning, when the bridge was again crammed with supply vehicles which crawled slowly towards the crowded market-place, a sharp and unusual whistling was heard over the town and in the center of the bridge, not far from the *kapia* itself, a shell burst on the stone parapet. Fragments of stone and iron struck horses and men. There was a rush of men, a rearing of horses and a general flight. Some fled forward into the market-place, others back along the road whence they had come. Immediately afterwards three more shells fell, two in the water and one more on the bridge among the press of men and horses. In a twinkling of an eye the bridge was deserted; in the emptiness so created could be seen, like black spots, dead horses and men. The Austrian field artillery from the Butkovo Rocks tried to get the range of that Serbian mountain battery which was spraying the scattered supply columns on both sides of the bridge with shrapnel.

From that day on, the mountain battery from Panos continually pounded the bridge and the nearby barracks. A few days later, again early in the morning, a new sound was heard from the east, from somewhere on Goleš. This sound was more distant but deeper, and incendiary shells fell even more frequently over the town. These were howitzers, two in all. The first shots fell in the Drina, then on the open space before the bridge where they damaged the houses around, Lotte's hotel and the officers' mess, and then regular salvos began to center on the bridge and the barracks. Within an hour the barracks was on fire. The mountain battery from Panos sprinkled with shrapnel the soldiers trying to put out the fire. Finally, they left the barracks to its fate. In the heat of the day it burned as if made of wood, and shells fell from time to time into the burning mass and destroyed the interior of the building. So for the second time the Stone Han was destroyed and became once again a pile of stones.

After that the two howitzers from Goleš continually and regularly aimed at the bridge and especially the central pier. The shells fell sometimes in the river, right and left of the bridge, sometimes smashed to pieces against the massive stone piers and sometimes hit the bridge itself, but none of them hit the iron manhole over the opening which led into the interior of the central pier which held the explosive charge for mining the bridge.

In all that ten-days-long bombardment no major damage was done to the bridge. The shells struck against the smooth piers and rounded arches, ricocheted and exploded in the air without leaving other marks on the stone than light, white, scarcely perceptible scratches. The fragments of shrapnel bounced off the smooth firm stone like hail. Only those shells which actually hit the roadway left little holes in the gravel but these could hardly be seen save when one was on the bridge itself. Thus in all this fresh storm which had burst over the town, overturning and tearing up by the roots its ancient customs, sweeping away living men and inanimate things, the bridge remained white, solid and invulnerable as it had always been.

23

Because of the continual bombardment all movement across the bridge ceased by day; civilians crossed freely and even individual soldiers scurried across, but as soon as a slightly larger group began to move they were sprayed by shrapnel from Panos. After a few days a certain regularity was established. The people took note of when the fire was strongest, when less and when it ceased altogether, and finished their more urgent tasks accordingly, so far as the Austrian patrols would let them.

The mountain battery from Panos fired only by day, but the howitzers from behind Goleš fired at night also and tried to hinder troop movements and the passage of supplies on both sides of the bridge.

Those citizens whose houses were in the center of the town, near the bridge and the road, moved with their families to Mejdan or other sheltered and distant quarters, to stay with relatives or friends and take refuge from the bombardment. Their flight, with their children and their most necessary household goods, recalled those terrible nights when the "great flood" came upon the town. Only this time men of different faiths were not mingled together or bound by the feeling of solidarity and common misfortune, and did not sit together to find help and consolation in talk as at those times. The Turks went to the Turkish houses and the Serbs, as if plague-stricken, only to Serbian homes. But even though thus divided and separated, they lived more or less similarly. Crushed into other people's houses, not knowing what to do, with time hanging on their hands, and filled with anxious and uneasy thoughts, idle and empty-headed like refugees, in fear of their lives and in uncertainty about their property, they were tormented by differing hopes and fears which, naturally, they concealed.

As in earlier times during the "great floods" the older people both among the Turks and the Serbs tried to cheer up those with them by jokes and stories, by an affected calm and an artificial serenity. But it seemed that in this sort of misfortune the old tricks and jokes no longer served, the old stories palled and the witticisms lost flavor and meaning, and it was a slow and painful process to make new ones.

At night they crowded together to sleep, though in fact no one was able to close an eye. They spoke in whispers, although they themselves did not know why they did so when every moment there was above their heads the thunder of the guns, now Serbian, now Austrian. They were filled with fear lest they should be "making signals to the enemy" although no one knew how such signals could be made nor what they in fact meant. But their fear was such that no one even dared to strike a match. When the men wanted to smoke they shut themselves up in suffocating little rooms without windows, or covered their heads with counterpanes, and so smoked. The moist heat strangled and throttled them. Everyone was bathed in sweat, but all doors were fastened and all windows closed and shuttered. The town seemed like some wretch who covers his eyes with his hands and waits for blows from which he cannot defend himself. All the houses seemed like houses of mourning. For whoever wished to remain alive had to behave as though he were dead; nor did that always help.

In the Moslem houses there was a little more life. Much of the old warlike instincts remained but they had been awakened in an evil hour, embarrassed and pointless in face of that duel going on over their heads in which the artillery of the two sides, both Christian, were taking part. But there too were great and concealed anxieties; there too were misfortunes for which there seemed no solution.

Alihodja's house under the fortress had been turned into a Moslem religious school. To the crowd of his own children had been added the nine children of Mujaga Mutapdžić; only three of these were grown up and all the rest small and weak ranged one after the other differing by an ear. In order not to have to watch them or to call them at every moment into the courtyard, they had been shut up with Alihodja's children in a large room and there their mothers and elder sisters dealt with them amid a continual flurry and fusillade of cries.

This Mujaga Mutapdić, known as the "man from Užice," was a recent comer to the town (we shall see a little later why and how). He was a tall man in his fifties, quite gray, with a great hooked nose and heavily lined face; his movements were abrupt and military. He seemed older than Alihodja although he was in fact ten years younger. He sat in the house with Alihodja, smoked incessantly, spoke little and seldom and was wrapped up in his own thoughts whose burden was expressed in his face and his every movement. He could not remain long in any one place. Every so often he would rise and go outside the house and from the garden watch the hills around the town, on both sides of the river. He stood thus with head raised, watching carefully as if for signs of bad weather. Alihodja, who never allowed him to remain alone, tried to keep him in conversation and followed him.

In the garden, which was on a steep slope but was large and beautiful, the peace and fecundity of the summer days reigned. The onions had already been cut and spread out to dry; the sunflowers were in full bloom and around their black and heavy centers the bees hummed. At the edges the small flowerets had already gone to seed. From that elevated place one could see the whole town spread out below on the sandy spit of land between the two rivers, Drina and Rzav, and the garland of mountains around, of unequal height and varied shapes. On the level space around the town and on the steep foothills scraps and belts of ripe barley alternated with areas of still green maize. The houses shone white and the forests that covered the mountains seemed black. The measured cannon fire from the two sides seemed like salutes, formal and harmless, so great was the extent of the earth and the sky above it in the serenity of the summer day which had only just begun.

The sight loosened the tongue even of the care-filled Mujaga. He thanked Ali-hodja for his kind words and told him the story of his own life, not that the *hodja* did not already know it, but Mujaga felt that here in the sunlight he could lessen the tension that gripped and strangled him. He felt that his fate was being decided here and now on this summer's day by every roar of the guns from one side or the other.

He had been not quite five years old when the Turks had had to leave the Serbian towns. The Osmanlis had left for Turkey but his father, Sulaga Mutapdić, still a young man, but already respected as one of the leading Turks of Užice, had decided to cross into Bosnia whence his family had come in olden times. He had piled the children into baskets and with all the money which in such circumstances he had been able to get for his house and lands he had left Užice forever. With a few hundred other Užice refugees he had crossed into Bosnia where there was still Turkish rule, and settled with his family in Višegrad where a branch of the family had once lived. There he passed ten years and had just begun to consolidate his position in the market when the Austrian occupation had taken place. A harsh and uncompromising man, he had thought it not worth his while to fly from one Christian rule only to live under another one. So, a year after the arrival of the Austrians, he had left Bosnia with his whole family, together with a few other families who had not wished to pass their lives "within the sound of the bell," and settled in Nova Varoš in the Sanjak. Mujaga had then been a young man of little over fifteen. There Suljaga had gone on with his trading and there the rest of the children had been born. But he was never able to forget all he had lost in Užice, nor could he get on with the new men and different manner of life in the Sanjak. That was the reason for his early death. His daughters, all pretty and of good reputation, had married well. His sons took over and extended the small inheritance left them by their father. But just when they had married and had begun to take deeper root in their new country came the Balkan Wars of 1912. Mujaga had taken part in the resistance put up by the Turkish army against the Serbs and Montenegrins. The resistance was short but it was neither weak nor unsuccessful in itself, but none the less, as if by some charm, his fate, like that of the war itself and of many thousands of men, was not decided there but somewhere far away, independent of any resistance, strong or weak. The Turkish army evacuated the Sanjak. Not willing to await an adversary from whom he had already fled as a child from Užice and whom he had now resisted without success, and having nowhere else to go, Mujaga decided to return to Bosnia under that same rule from which his father had fled. So now, for the third time a refugee, he had come with his whole family to the town in which he had passed his childhood.

With a little ready money and with the help of the Višegrad Turks, some of whom were his relatives, he had managed to build up a small business over the last two years. But it was not easy for, as we have seen, times were hard and insecure, and profits difficult to make even for those whose position was assured. He had been living on his capital while waiting for better and more peaceful times. Now, after only two years of the hard life of a refugee in the town, this storm had broken in which he could do nothing and could not even think of what to do next; the only thing left to him was to follow its course anxiously and await fearfully its outcome.

It was of this that the two men were now talking, softly, intermittently and disconnectedly, as one speaks of things already well-known and which can be looked at from the end, the beginning or any point in the middle. Alihodja, who liked and greatly respected Mujaga, tried to find some words of solace or consolation, not because he thought that anything would help, but because he felt it his duty in some way to partake in the misfortune of this honorable and unfortunate man and true Moslem. Mujaga sat and smoked, the very image of a man whom fate has loaded too heavily. Great beads of sweat broke out on his forehead and temples, stood there some time until they grew big and heavy, then shone in the sun and overflowed like a stream down his lined face. But Mujaga did not feel them nor brush them away. With dull eyes he looked at the grass in front of him and, wrapped up in his own thoughts, listened to what was happening within himself which was stronger and louder than any words of consolation or the most vigorous bombardment. From time to time he moved his hand a little and murmured something or other which was far more a part of his own inward conversation than any reply to what was being said to him or what was taking place around him.

"This has come upon us, my Alihodja, and there is no way out. The One God sees that we, my father (peace be to him) and myself, have done everything we could to remain in the pure faith and the true way of life. My grandfather left his bones in Užice and today we do not even know where he is buried. I myself buried my father in Nova Varoš and I do not know if by now the Vlachs are pasturing their cattle over his grave. I had thought that I at least would die here, where the muezzin still calls, but now it seems that it is written that our seed will be extinguished and that no one knows where his grave will be. Can it be that God's wishes are so? Only now I see that there is no way out. The time has come of which it is said that the only way left for the true faith is to die. For what can I do? Shall I go with Nailbeg and the *schutzkorps* and die with a Schwabe rifle in my hands, shamed both in this and in the next world? Or shall I wait and sit here until Serbia shall come, and wait once more for all that we fled from as refugees fifty years ago?"

Alihodja was about to utter some words of encouragement that might provide a little hope, but he was interrupted by a salvo from the Austrian battery on the Butkovo Rocks. It was immediately answered by the guns from Panos. Then those behind Goleš opened fire. They were firing low, directly over their heads, so that the shells wove a web of sound above them that catches at a man's entrails and tightens the blood-vessels until they hurt. Alihodja rose and suggested that they take refuge under the balcony, and Mujaga followed him like a sleepwalker.

In the Serbian houses huddled around the church at Mejdan there were, on the other hand, no regrets for the past or fears for the future; there was only the fear and burden of the present. There was a sort of special, dumb astonishment, that feeling which always remains among people after the first blows of a great terror, with arrests and killings without order or justice. But beneath this consternation everything was the same as it had been earlier, the same expectant waiting as before, more than a hundred years ago, when the insurgents' fires had burned on Panos, the same hope, the same caution and the same resolution to bear everything if it could not be otherwise, the same faith in a good result somewhere at the end of all ends.

The grandchildren and great-grandchildren of those who from this same hillside, shut up in their houses, anxious and frightened but moved to the depths of their being, had listened intently trying to hear the feeble echo of Karageorge's gun on the hillside above Veletovo, now listened in the warm darkness to the thunder and rumble of the heavy howitzer shells passing above their heads, guessing from the sound which were Serbian and which Austrian, calling them endearing nick-names or cursing them. All this while the shells were flying high and falling on the outskirts of the town, but when they were aimed low at the bridge and the town itself everyone fell suddenly silent for then it seemed to them, and they would have sworn to it, that in that complete silence, in the midst of so much space around them, both sides were aiming only at them and the house in which they were. Only after the thunder and roar of a nearby explosion had died away, they would begin talking again, but in changed voices, assuring one another that the shell which had fallen quite close was of a particularly devilish kind, worse than any other.

The merchants from the market-place had for the most part taken refuge in the Ristić house. It was immediately above the priest's house, but larger and finer, sheltered from the artillery fire by the steep slopes of the plum-orchards. There were few men but many women, whose husbands had been arrested or taken as hostages, who had taken refuge here with their children.

In this rich and extensive house lived old Mihailo Ristić with his wife and daughter-in-law, a widow who had not wanted to marry again or return to her father's house after the death of her husband, but remained there with the two old people to bring up her children. Her eldest son had fled to Serbia two years before and been killed as a volunteer on the Bregalnica. He had been eighteen years old.

Old Mihailo, his wife and daughter-in-law served their unusual guests as if they were at a family feast, a *slava*. The old man especially was untiring. He was bareheaded, which was unusual, for as a rule he never took off his red fez. His thick gray hair fell over his ears and forehead and his huge silvery moustaches, yellow at the roots from tobacco, surrounded his mouth like a perpetual smile. Whenever he noticed that anyone was frightened or more melancholy than the others, he would go up to him, talk to him and offer him plum brandy, coffee and tobacco.

"I can't, *kum* Mihailo. I thank you like a father, but I can't; it hurts me here," protested a young woman, pointing to her white and rounded throat.

She was the wife of Peter Gatal of Okolište. A few days before Peter had gone to Sarajevo on business. There he had been caught by the outbreak of war and from that time onward his wife had had no news of him. The army had driven them out of their house, and now she and her children had taken refuge with old Mihailo, to whom her husband's family had long been related. She was broken down with worry about her husband and her abandoned home. She wrung her hands, sobbing and sighing alternately.

Old Mihailo never took his eyes off her and kept near her always. That morning it had been learned that Peter, on his way back from Sarajevo by train, had been taken as a hostage to Vardište and there, after a false alarm of a revolt, had been shot in mistake. That was still being kept from her, and old Mihailo was doing his best to prevent anyone suddenly and inadvisedly telling her. Every few moments the woman would rise and try to go into the courtyard and look towards Okolište, but Mihailo prevented her and talked her out of it by every possible means, for he knew very well that the Gatal house in Okolište was already in flames and he wanted to spare the unfortunate woman this sight at least.

"Come, Stanojka, come, my lamb. Just a little glass. This is not plum brandy, but a real balm and cure for all ills."

The woman drank it meekly. Old Mihailo went on offering food and drink to everyone present and his untiring and irresistible hospitality forced them all to take heart. Then he went back to Peter's wife. The plum brandy had in fact loosened the constriction in her throat. Now she was calmer and only gazed pensively in front of her. Mihailo would not leave her side, but went on talking to her as to a child, telling her how all this too would pass and her Peter come back from Sarajevo alive and well, and they would all go home again to their house at Okolište.

"I know Peter. I was at his christening. They talked about that christening for a long time. I remember it as if it had been today. I was a young man then, just ripe for marriage, when I went with my father, who was *kum* to Janko's children, to christen that Peter of yours."

He told the tale of the christening of Peter Gatal which everyone already knew but which in these strange hours seemed as if new to them.

The men and women drew closer to listen, and in listening forgot their danger and paid no attention to the sound of the guns as old Mihailo told his tale.

In the good times of peace, when the famous Pop Nikola was priest in the town, Janko Gatal of Okolište, after many years of marriage and a whole succession of daughters, had a son. On the first Sunday after the birth, they brought the child to be christened and besides the joyous father and the *kum,* a number of relatives and neighbors came too. Even on the way down from Okolište they stopped often and had a nip from the *kum's* big flat flask of plum brandy. When on crossing the bridge they came to the *kapia,* they sat down for a short rest and another nip. It was a cold day in late autumn and there was no coffee maker on the *kapia,* nor had the town Turks come there to sit and drink coffee. Therefore the people of Okolište sat down as if they were at home, opened their bags of food and began a fresh flask of plum brandy. Toasting one another cordially and eloquently, they forgot all about the baby and the priest who was to christen it after the service. As in those days—the seventies of last century—there were still no bells, and dared not be, the merry party did not notice the passing of time and that the service had long been finished. In their conversations, wherein they boldly and at great length mingled the future of the baby with the past of its parents, time had no longer any importance or any measure. Several times the conscience of the *kum* smote him and he suggested that they should move on, but the others silenced him.

"Well, friends, let us go and finish what we have to do, by the law and the Christian faith," muttered the *kum.*

"Why the hurry, in God's name; no one in this parish has ever stayed unchristened," answered the others and each offered him a drink from his flask.

The father too at one time tried to hurry them on, but in the end the plum brandy silenced and reconciled them all. His wife who up till then had been holding the baby in her arms which were blue from cold, now put it down on the stone seat and wrapped it in a colored shawl. The baby was as quiet as if it were in its cradle, now sleeping, now opening its eyes inquisitively as if to take part in the general gaiety ("One can see that he is a true townsman," said the *kum.* "He loves good company and fun.")

"Your health, Janko," shouted one of the neighbors. "May your son be lucky and live long. God grant that he do you honor among the Serbs in all good and prosperity. God grant that. . . ."

"How would it be if we got on with the christening?" interrupted the father.

"Don't worry about the christening," they all cried and once more passed around the flask of plum brandy.

"Ragib Effendi Borovac has never been christened either, but you see what a fellow he is; his horse bends under him," shouted one of the neighbors amid general laughter.

But if time had lost all meaning for the men on the *kapia,* it had not done so for Pop Nikola, who had till then been waiting in front of the church, but by this time had grown angry. He wrapped his fox-skin cape about him and marched down from Mejdan into the town. There someone told him that the men with the child were on the *kapia.* He went there to give them a good browbeating, as he well knew how, but they welcomed him with so much heartfelt and sincere respect, with such solemn excuses and warm wishes and good words that even Pop Nikola, who was a hard and severe man, but a real townsman at heart, gave way and accepted a drink from a flask and some snacks. He bent over the baby and called it little baby names, while the child looked up calmly at the huge face with its big blue eyes and broad reddish beard.

It was not quite true, as they said, that the little one was christened then and there on the *kapia,* but it is true that they stayed there a long time talking, drinking and proposing many toasts. It was not until late in the afternoon that the whole gay company made its way up to Mejdan and the church was opened and the *kum,* stuttering and unsure of his words, renounced the devil in the name of the new townsman.

"It was so we christened *kum* Peter, may he remain safe and sound. He has now passed his fortieth year and as you see has lacked for nothing," old Mihailo ended.

Everyone accepted another coffee and a glass of plum brandy, forgetting the reality of the moment which might sweep them all away. All talked more freely and easily. Somehow it now seemed clear to them that there were other things in life, more joyful and human things, than this darkness, fear and murderous shooting.

So the night passed and with it life went on, filled with danger and suffering but still clear, unwavering and true to itself. Led on by ancient inherited instinct they broke it up into momentary impressions and immediate needs, losing themselves completely in them. For only thus, living each moment separately and looking neither forward nor back, could such a life be borne and a man keep himself alive in hope of better days.

So the day broke. That meant only that the artillery fire became more intense and the senseless and incomprehensible game of war continued. For in themselves days no longer had either name or sense; time had lost all meaning and value. Men knew only how to wait and to tremble. Save for that, words, work and movements had all become automatic.

So, or similarly, did men live in the steep quarters below the Fortress and at Mejdan.

Below, in the market-place itself, few citizens had remained. From the first day of the war there had been an order that all shops must remain open so that the soldiers in passing could make minor purchases, and even more to prove to the citizens that the war was far away and presented no danger to the town. That order had remained in force, no one knew why, even now during the bombardment, but everyone found some good excuse to keep his shop closed for the greater part of the day. Those shops which were near the bridge and the Stone Han, like those of Pavle Ranković and Alihodja, were closed all day for they were too exposed to the bombardment.

So too, Lotte's hotel was completely deserted and closed, its roof had been damaged by shell-fire and the walls pitted with shrapnel.

Alihodja only came down from his house on the hill once or twice a day to see if everything were in order, and then returned home.

Lotte and her whole family had left the hotel on the first day after the bombardment of the bridge began. They crossed to the left bank of the Drina and took refuge there in a large new Turkish house. The house was some way from the road, sheltered in a hollow and surrounded by dense orchards from which only its red roof emerged. Its owners with all his family had gone to the villages.

They had left the hotel at dusk, when as a rule there was a complete lull in the bombardment. Of the staff, the only one who remained was the loyal and unchanging Milan, an old bachelor but always immaculately turned out. For a long time past there had been no one for him to throw out of the hotel. All the others, as often happens in such circumstances, had fled as soon as the first shell whistled over the town. As always, in this transplantation also, Lotte had controlled and arranged everything, personally and without opposition. She decided what was most necessary and most valuable to take with them, and what to leave behind, what each should wear, who was to carry Deborah's crippled and feeble-minded son, who was to look after Deborah herself, weeping and sickly, and who take care of the portly Mina, who was out of her mind from fear. So, taking advantage of the darkness of the hot summer night, all of them—Lotte, Deborah, Zahler and Mina—crossed the bridge with their few belongings and the sickly child on a pushcart, with their cases and bundles in their hands. After thirty years the hotel was now for the first time completely closed and remained without a living soul in it. Darkened, damaged by the shell-fire, it already looked like a ruin. They too, as soon as they made their first steps across the bridge, aged or weak, crippled or fat, bow-legged or unaccustomed to walking, suddenly seemed like Jewish refugees who had been walking all the roads of the world in search of refuge.

So they crossed to the farther bank and came to the big Turkish house to spend the night. There too Lotte arranged everything and put everything in order, their refugee luggage and themselves. But when it was time for her to lie down in that strange half-empty room, without her things and her papers with which she had spent her life, her heart failed her and for the first time since she had been conscious of her own existence, her forces all at once gave way. Her scream echoed through the empty Turkish house, something that no one had ever heard or suspected could exist. Lotte's weeping was terrible, heavy and stifled like that of a man, uncontrolled and uncontrollable. The whole family was overcome with astonishment. At first there was an almost religious silence and then a general weeping and wailing. For them the breakdown of Aunt Lotte's forces was a heavier blow than the war itself and the flight and the loss of home and property, for with her it was possible to surmount and overcome everything but without her they could think of nothing and do nothing.

When the next day dawned, a brilliant summer day, filled with the singing of birds, with rosy clouds and heavy dew, instead of the one-time Lotte, who up to the day before had controlled the destinies of all her family, there remained huddled on the floor a weak old Jewess who could not look after or care for herself, who shivered from reasonless fear and who wept like a child, not knowing how to say of what she was afraid or tell what it was that pained her. Then another miracle took place. That old, cumbersome, drowsy Zahler, who even in his youth had never had a will of his own but had been content to let Lotte guide him as she did all the rest of the family, who in fact had never been young, now revealed himself as the real head of the family, with much wisdom and resolution, capable of making the necessary decisions and with enough force to put them into practice. He consoled and looked after his sister-in-law like a sick child and took care of everyone as she had done right up to the day before. He went down into the town during a lull in the bombardment and brought necessary food, goods and clothing from the deserted hotel. He found a doctor somewhere and brought him to the sick woman. The doctor diagnosed that the sick old woman had had a complete nervous breakdown, and said that she should be taken somewhere else as quickly as possible, outside the area of military operations, and prescribed some drops. Zahler arranged with the military authorities to get a cart and transport the whole family first to Rogatica and then to Sarajevo. It was only necessary to wait a day or two until Lotte was fit to travel. But Lotte lay as if paralytic, wept at the top of her voice and muttered in her picturesque and mangled language disconnected words of utter desperation, fear and repulsion. Deborah's unlucky child crawled around her on the bare floor, looked inquisitively into his aunt's face and called to her with those incomprehensible cries which Lotte had once understood so well and to which she did not now reply. She refused to eat anything or to see anyone. She suffered terribly from strange hallucinations of purely physical suffering. Sometimes it seemed to her that two planks beneath her suddenly opened like a trapdoor and that she fell between them into an unknown abyss and that, save for her own screams, there was nothing to save her and support her. At other times it seemed to her that she had in some way become huge, but light and very strong, as if she had giant's legs and powerful wings and ran like an ostrich, but with steps longer than from Višegrad to Sarajevo. The seas and rivers splashed under her tread like puddles, and towns and villages cracked under her steps like gravel and glass. That made her heart beat fiercely and her breath come in gasps. She did not know where that winged race would take her nor where it would stop, she only knew that she was escaping from those deceiving planks which opened beneath her with the speed of lightning. She knew that she trod down and left behind her a land in which it was not good to stay and that she stepped over villages and great towns in which men lied and cheated with words and figures. When their words became involved and their figures entangled, they at once changed their game, as a conjuror changes his scene, and contrary to all that had been said or was expected, guns and rifles advanced with other, new men with bloodshot eyes with whom there could be no conversation, no compromise and no agreement. Faced with this invasion she was suddenly no longer a powerful and giant bird that ran, but a weak, defenseless poor old woman on the hard floor. And these people came in hordes, in thousands, in millions; they shot, they cut throats, they drowned people, they destroyed without mercy or reason. One of them was bending over her; she could not see his face but felt the point of his bayonet pressed on that spot where the ribs separate and a person is softest.

"Ah . . . a . . . a . . . a . . . aah! No, don't! Don't!" Lotte woke with a shriek and tore pieces out of the thin gray shawl that covered her.

The little cretin squatted there, leaning against the wall, and watched her with his black eyes in which was more curiosity than fear or sympathy. Mina burst in from the next room, reassured Lotte, wiped the cold sweat from her face and gave her water to drink into which she carefully numbered the drops of valerian.

The long summer day over the green valley seemed endless, so that one could not remember when it had dawned or believe that it would ever be dusk. Here in the house, it was warm but not oppressive. Steps echoed in the house; other citizens kept arriving from the town or some soldier or officer wandered about. There was food and fruit in abundance. Milan brewed coffee continually. It might all have seemed like some extended festival visit to the villages, had it not been for Lotte's despairing scream which broke out from time to time and the sullen thunder of the guns which sounded in that sheltered hollow like howls of rage which showed that all was not well with the world, that universal and individual misfortune was nearer and greater than it seemed in the wide serenity of the day.

That was what war had done to Lotte's hotel and its occupants.

Pavle Ranković's shop was also shut. On the second day of the war Pavle, with other prominent Serbs, had been taken as a hostage. Some of them were at the station where they answered with their lives for the peace, order and regular communication of the line, while others were not far from the bridge, in a small wooden shed at the far end of the square where on market days the municipal scales were kept and where the local *octroi* was paid. There too the hostages had to answer with their lives, should anyone destroy or damage the bridge.

Pavle was sitting there on a café chair. With hands on knees and bowed head, he looked the perfect picture of a man who, exhausted after some great effort, had sat down for a moment's rest, but he had been sitting there motionless in the same position for several hours. At the door two soldiers, reservists, sat on a pile of empty sacks. The doors were shut and the shed was dark and oppressively hot. When a shell from Panos or Goleš whistled overhead, Pavle swallowed and listened to hear where it fell. He knew that the bridge had been mined and thought of that continually, asking himself whether one such shell could ignite the explosives should it penetrate to the charge. At every change of guard he listened to the non-commissioned officer giving instructions to the soldiers: "At the least attempt to damage the bridge, or at any suspicious sign that such a thing is being prepared, this man must be killed at once." Pavle had got used to listening to these words calmly as if they did not refer to him. The shells and shrapnel, which occasionally exploded so near the shed that gravel and pieces of metal struck the planks, disturbed him more. But what tormented him most of all were his long, his endless and unbearable, thoughts.

He kept thinking what was to happen to him, to his house and his property. The more he thought, the more everything seemed like a bad dream. In what other way could all that had happened to him in the last few days be explained? The gendarmes had taken away his two sons, students, on the first day. His wife had remained at home, alone with her daughters. The great warehouse at Osojnica had been burned down before his eyes. His serfs from the nearby villages had probably been killed or dispersed. All his credits over the whole district—lost! His shop, the most beautiful shop in the whole town, only a few paces from where he was now, had been shut and would probably be pillaged, or set on fire by the shells. He himself was sitting in the semi-darkness of this shed, responsible with his life for something that in no way depended on him; for the fate of that bridge.

His thoughts whirled in his head; tumultuous and disordered as never before, they crossed and mingled and were extinguished. What sort of connection had he with that bridge, he who all his life had paid no attention to anything save his work and his family? It was not he who had mined it, nor had he bombarded it. Not even when he had been an apprentice and unmarried, had he ever sat on the *kapia* and wasted his time in singing and idle jokes, like so many Višegrad youths. All his life passed before his eyes, with many details which he had long ago forgotten.

He remembered how he had come from the Sanjak as a fourteen-year-old boy, hungry and in shabby peasant sandals. He had struck a bargain with old Peter to serve him for one suit of clothes, his food and two pairs of sandals annually. He had looked after the children, helped in the shop, drawn water and groomed the horses. He had slept under the stairs in a dark, narrow cupboard without windows where he could not even lie down at full length. He had endured this hard life and, when he was eighteen, had gone into the shop "on salary." His place had been taken by another village boy from the Sanjak. In the shop he had got to know and understand the great idea of thrift, and had felt the fierce and wonderful passion in the great power that thrift gave. For five years he had slept in a little room behind the shop. In five years he had never once lit a fire or gone to sleep with a candle beside him. He had been twenty-three when Peter himself had arranged a marriage for him with a good and well-to-do girl from Čajniče. She had been a merchant's daughter and now both of them saved together. Then came the time of the occupation and with it livelier trade, easier gain and lower expenses. He made good use of the profits and avoided the expenses. Thus he was able to get a shop and began to make money. At that time it was not difficult. Many then made money easily and lost it even more easily. But what was made was hard to keep. He had kept his and every day made more. When these last years came and with them unrest and "politics," he, though already advanced in years, had tried to understand the new times, to stand up to them and adapt himself to them, and to go through them without harm and without shame. He had been Vice-President of the Municipality, President of the Religious Community, President of the Serbian Choral Society "Concord," main shareholder of the Serbian Bank and member of the executive committee of the local Agricultural Bank. He had tried his best, according to the rules of the market-place, to make his way wisely and honestly between the contrary influences which increased daily, without allowing his own interests to suffer, without being regarded with suspicion by the authorities or brought to shame before his own people. In the eyes of the townsmen he passed for an inimitable example of industry, common sense and circumspection.

Thus, for more than a half of a normal human existence he had worked, saved, worried and made money. He had taken care not to hurt a fly, been civil to all and looked only straight ahead of him, keeping silent and making money in his own way. And here was where it had led him; to sit between two soldiers like the lowest of brigands and wait until some shell or infernal machine should damage the bridge and, for that reason, to have his throat cut or be shot. He began to think (and that pained him most of all) that he had worked and worried and ill-used himself all in vain, that he had chosen the wrong path and that his sons and all the other "youngsters" had been right, and that times had come without measures or calculations or which had some sort of new measures and different calculations; in any case his own calculations had been shown to be inaccurate and his measures short.

"That's the way of it," said Pavle to himself, "that's the way; everyone teaches you and urges you to work and to save, the Church, the authorities and your own common sense. You listen and live prudently, in fact you do not live at all, but work and save and are burdened with cares; and so your whole life passes. Then, all of a sudden, the whole thing turns upside down; times come when the world mocks at reason, when the Church shuts its doors and is silent, when authority becomes mere brute force, when they who have made their money honestly and with the sweat of their brows lose both their time and their money, and the violent win the game. No one recognizes your efforts and there is no one to help or advise you how to keep what you have earned and saved. Can this be? Surely this cannot be?" Pavle asked himself continually, and without finding any answer went back to the point whence his thought had started—the loss of all that he possessed.

Try as he might to think of something else, he could not succeed. His thoughts returned continually to the point where they had started. Time crept by with mortal slowness. It seemed to him that the bridge over which he had crossed thousands of times but had never really looked at, now lay with all its weight on his shoulders like some inexplicable and fateful burden, like a nightmare but in a sleep from which there was no awakening.

Therefore Pavle went on sitting there, huddled on his chair with bowed head and shoulders. He felt the sweat oozing from every pore under his thick starched shirt, collar and cuffs. It fell in streams from under his fez. He did not wipe it away but let it stream down his face and fall in heavy drops to the floor and it seemed to him that it was his life that was draining away and was leaving him.

The two soldiers, middle-aged Hungarian peasants, remained silent and ate bread and ham sprinkled with paprika; they ate slowly, cutting off with a small penknife first a piece of bread and then a slice of ham as if they were in their own fields. Then they took a mouthful of wine from an army canteen and lit their short pipes. Puffing away, one of them said softly:

"Eh, I have never seen a man sweat so much."

Then they went on smoking in complete silence.

But it was not only Pavle who sweated such bloody sweat and lost himself in that sleep from which there is no awakening. In those summer days, on that little piece of earth between the Drina and the dry frontier, in the town, in the villages, on the roads and in the forests, everywhere men sought death, their own or others," and at the same time fled from it and defended themselves from it by all the means in their power. That strange human game which is called war became more and more intense and submitted to its authority living creatures and material things.

Not far from that municipal shed a detachment of an unusual army was resting. The men were in white uniforms with white tropical helmets on their heads. They were Germans, the so-called Skadar detachment. Before the war they had been sent to Skadar (Scutari in Albania) where they were to maintain law and order together with detachments from other nations, as part of an international army. When war broke out, they had received orders to leave Skadar and place themselves at the disposal of the nearest Austrian Army command on the Serbian frontier. They had come the evening before and were now resting in the hollow which separated the square from the market-place. There, in a sheltered corner, they awaited the order to attack. There were about 120 of them. Their captain, a plump reddish man who suffered from the heat, had just been cursing at the gendarmerie sergeant Danilo Repac, cursing him as only a senior officer of the German army can curse, noisily, pedantically and without any sort of consideration. The captain was complaining that his soldiers were dying of thirst, that they had not even the most necessary supplies, since all the shops nearby, which were probably full of everything, were shut despite the order that all shops were to remain open.

"What are you here for? Are you gendarmes or dolls? Must I die here with all my men? Or must I break open the shops like a robber? Find the owners at once and make them sell us provisions and something worth drinking! At once! Do you understand what that means? At once!"

At every word the captain grew more and more flushed. In his white uniform, his close-shaven head red as a poppy, he seemed to burn with anger like a torch.

Sergeant Repac, astounded, only blinked and went on repeating:

"I understand, sir. At once. I understand. At once!"

Then, passing suddenly from his cataleptic stiffness to frenzied action, he turned and hurried from the market-place. It seemed as if the sergeant, approaching too close to that captain flaming with anger, had himself been touched by that flame, which made him run, curse, threaten and beat all around him.

The first living being whom he met in the course of his mad rush was Alihodja, who had just come down from his house to cast an eye on his shop. Looking closely at the once familiar *"wachtmeister"* Repac, now completely changed, rushing towards him, the astonished *hodja* asked himself whether this savage and maddened man was really the same *"wachtmeister"* whom he had watched for years, calm, dignified and human, passing in front of his shop. Now this somber and infuriated Repac looked at him with new eyes which no longer recognized anyone and saw only their own fear. The sergeant at once began to shout, repeating what only a short time ago he had heard from the German captain.

"God in heaven, I ought to hang all of you! Weren't you ordered to keep your shops open? For your sake, I have had to . . ."

And before the astonished *hodja* was able to utter a word, he slapped him hard on the right cheek so that his turban slid from his right ear to his left.

Then the sergeant rushed frenziedly on to open other shops. The *hodja* set his turban straight, let down his door-shutter and sat on it, almost out of his mind from astonishment. Around the shop crowded a swarm of strange-looking soldiers in white uniforms such as he had never seen before. It seemed to the *hodja* as if he were dreaming. But in these times when slaps fell from heaven he no longer felt really astonished at anything.

So the whole month passed, in preliminary bombardment of the bridge and in the firing from the surrounding hills, in suffering and violence of every kind, and in the expectation of worse misfortunes. In the first days the greater number of the citizens had already left the town which now lay between two fires. By the end of September the complete evacuation of the town began. Even the last officials were withdrawn, by night along the road which led over the bridge, for the railway line had already been cut. Then the army was withdrawn little by little from the right bank of the Drina. There remained only a small number of defense squads, a few engineers' units and some gendarme patrols, until the orders came for them too to retire.

The bridge remained as if under sentence of death, but none the less still whole and untouched, between the two warring sides.

24

During the night the sky clouded over as if it were autumn; the clouds clung to the tops of the mountains and lingered in the valleys between them. The Austrians had taken advantage of the darkness of the night to effect the withdrawal of even the last detachments. Already before dawn they were all not only on the right bank of the Drina but on the heights behind the Liješte chain, out of sight and out of range of the Serbian guns.

At daybreak there was a fine, almost autumnal, rain. In that rain the last patrols visited houses and shops in the vicinity of the bridge to see if there were anyone still in them. Everything was as if dead; the officers' mess, Lotte's hotel, the ruined barracks and those three or four shops at the entrance to the market-place. But in front of Alihodja's shop they came upon the *hodja* who had just come down from his house and let down his door-shutter. The gendarmes, who knew the *hodja* as an eccentric, warned him most seriously to shut his shop at once and leave the market-place, for any longer stay in the vicinity of the bridge was most "dangerous to life" and strictly forbidden. The *hodja* looked at them as if they were drunk and did not know what they were saying. He wanted to reply that life had been dangerous for a long time past and that everyone was more or less dead already and only waiting his turn to be buried, but he thought better of it, taught by the bad experience of the last few days, and merely told them calmly and naturally that he had only come to take something from the shop and would return home at once. The gendarmes, who were evidently in a hurry, warned him once more that he should move away as soon as possible, and went on across the square to the bridge. Alihodja watched them marching away, their footfalls inaudible in the dust which the morning rain had turned to a thick, damp carpet. He was still watching them as they crossed the bridge, half concealed by the stone parapet, so that he could see only their heads and shoulders and the long bayonets on their rifles. The first rays of sunlight struck on the heights of the Butkovo Rocks.

All their orders were like this, severe, important and yet basically senseless, thought Alihodja, and smiled to himself like a child who has outwitted his teacher. He lifted the door-shutter enough to let him get inside and then let it fall, so that from the outside the shop appeared to be shut. Alone in the darkness, he wriggled his way into that little room behind the shop where he had so often taken refuge from the obtrusive world, from conversations that poisoned and bored him, from his family and from his own worries. He sat down on the small hard chair and crossed his legs under him and sighed. His inner self was still troubled by outward impressions, but he soon became calm and balanced again. The narrow room quickly filled with the warmth of his body and the *hodja* felt that sweetness of solitude, peace and forgetfulness which made of the close, dark, dusty little room a place of endless paradisiacal gardens with green banks between which murmured invisible waters.

In the darkness and closeness of this narrow space he could still feel the freshness of the morning rain and the sunrise outside. Outside there was an unusual silence which, for a wonder, was not broken by a single shot, a single voice or footfall. Alihodja was flooded with a feeling of happiness and gratitude. These few planks, he thought to himself, were enough, with God's help, to shelter and save a true believer, like some wonder ship, from every misery and care to which there seemed no solution and from the guns with which the two enemies, both infidel and each worse than the other, were fighting their duel over his head. There had not been such a calm since the opening of hostilities, the *hodja* thought joyously, and silence is sweet and good; with it returned, at least for a moment, a little of that real human life which had recently grown weaker and weaker and which, under the thunder of the infidel guns, had completely disappeared. Silence is for prayer; it is itself like a prayer.

At that moment the *hodja* felt the stool under him rise upward and lift him like a toy; his "sweet" silence was shattered and suddenly transformed into a dull roar and a great smashing that filled the air, tore at the eardrums and became universal and unbearable. The shelves on the wall opposite cracked and the things on them leaped at him as he at them. Ah, shrieked the *hodja:* or rather he only thought that he shrieked for he himself no longer had voice or hearing, even as he no longer had any place on the earth. Everything was deafened by sound, shattered, torn up by the roots and whirled about him. Improbable as it seemed, he felt as if the little tongue of land between the two rivers on which the town was built had been plucked out of the earth with a terrific noise and thrown into space in which it was still flying; that the two rivers had been torn out of their beds and drawn upward to the skies, only to fall once more with all their mass of waters into the void, like two waterfalls which had not yet been halted or broken. Was not this *kiyamet,* that last Day of Judgment of which books and learned men spoke, in which this lying world would be burned up in the twinkling of an eye, like one stubs out a spark? But what need had God, whose glance was enough to create and to extinguish worlds, with such a chaos? This was not divine. But if not, how had human hands such power? How could he, so astonished, so deceived, so overwhelmed by this terrible blow which seemed to destroy, break up and suffocate everything down to man's very thought, give an answer to this? He did not know what power it was that bore him up, he did not know where he was flying nor where he would stop, but he knew that he, Alihodja, had always and in everything been right. Ah, shrieked the *hodja* once again, but this time with pain for that same force that had lifted him up now threw him roughly and violently back again, but not to the place where he had been but to the floor between the wooden wall and the overturned stool. He felt a dull blow on his head and a pain under his knees and in his back. Now he could tell only by ear, like a sound separate and distinct from the universal thundering, that something heavy had struck the roof of the shop and that, there behind the partition, had begun a clashing and breaking of wooden and metal objects as if all the things in the shop had come alive, were flying about and colliding in mid-air. But Alihodja had already lost consciousness and lay motionless in his little room, as if it were indeed his coffin.

Outside it was by now full day.

He could not have said even approximately how long he lay there. What roused him out of his deep unconsciousness was a light and at the same time the sound of voices. He came to himself with difficulty. He knew very well that he was lying there in complete darkness and yet through the narrow entrance a ray of light reached him from the shop. He remembered how the world had been filled with sound and uproar in which a man's hearing was deafened and his entrails melted within him. Now there was silence once more, but no longer like that silence that had seemed to him so sweet before the cataclysm that had thrown him down where he was now, but like some evil sister of it. How deep was this silence he best realized by some weak voices which, as if from a great distance, were shouting his name.

Realizing that he was alive and still in his little room, the *hodja* extricated himself from the mass of objects that had fallen on top of him from the shelves, and rose, groaning continually and uttering cries of pain. Now he could hear the voices from the street clearly. He went down and crawled through the narrow opening into the shop. It was littered with fallen and broken objects, all in the full light of day. The shop was wide open, for the door-shutter, which he had left leaning but unlocked, had been knocked over by the blast.

In the chaos and disorder of scattered goods and damaged objects that lay in the center of the shop was a heavy stone about the size of a man's head. The *hodja* looked up. Clearly the stone had flown through the air, breaking through the weak roof of wooden shingles. Alihodja looked again at the stone, white and porous, smooth and clean-cut on two sides but sharp and crudely broken on the other two. "Ah, the bridge!" thought the *hodja* but the voices from the street summoned him even more loudly and peremptorily and would not let him think.

Bruised and still only half-conscious, the *hodja* found himself face to face with a group of five or six young men, dusty and unshaven, in gray uniforms with forage-caps on their heads and peasant sandles on their feet. All were armed and wore crossed bandoliers filled with small, shining bullets. With them was Vlado Marić the locksmith, but without his usual cap, wearing a fur hat and with the same cartridge belts across his chest. One of the men, clearly the leader, a young man with thin black moustaches and a regular face with fine features and fiery eyes, at once addressed the *hodja.* He was carrying his rifle over his shoulder like a hunter and had a thin hazel switch in his right hand.

"Hey, you! Do you usually leave your shop wide open? If anything is missing you will say that my soldiers have pillaged it. Do you expect me to look after your goods for you?"

The man's face was calm, almost without expression, but his voice was angry and the switch in his hand was raised threateningly. Vlado Marić came up and whispered to him.

"Very well, then. Perhaps he is a good and honest man, but if I find he has left his shop yawning wide open again, he will not get off so easily."

The armed men went on their way.

"Those are the others," said the *hodja* to himself, looking after them. "Why should they light on me as soon as they came into the town? It seems that nothing can change in this town without the whole lot falling on my head!"

He stood in front of his damaged shop, mouth open, with heavy head and broken body. Before him lay the square which, in the early morning sun, looked like a battlefield, scattered with large and small bits of stone, tiles and broken branches. His gaze turned to the bridge. The *kapia* was there where it had always been, but just beyond the *kapia* the bridge stopped short. There was no longer any seventh pier; between the sixth and the eighth yawned a gulf through which he could see the green waters of the river. From the eighth pier onward the bridge once more stretched to the farther bank, smooth and regular and white, as it had been yesterday and always.

The *hodja* blinked his eyes several times in unbelief; then he closed them. Before his inward sight appeared the memory of those soldiers whom he had seen six years before, concealed beneath a green tent, digging at that very pier, and he recalled the picture of that iron manhole which in later years had covered the entrance into the mined interior of the pier, and also the enigmatic yet eloquent face of Sergeant-Major Branković, deaf, blind and dumb. He started and opened his eyes again, but everything in front of him remained just as it was before; the square, scattered with large and small blocks of stone, and the bridge without one of its piers and a yawning gulf between two roughly broken arches.

Only in dreams could one see and experience such things. Only in dreams. But when he turned away from this improbable sight, there stood before him his shop with the great stone, a tiny part of that seventh pier, among his scattered goods. If it was a dream, it was everywhere.

Further down the square he could hear shouting, loud words of command in Serbian and steps hurriedly drawing nearer. Alihodja rapidly put up his door-shutter, locked it with a great padlock and began to make his way home, uphill.

Earlier too it had happened to him that while he was thus going uphill his breath had failed him and he had felt his heart beating where it should not have been. For a long time past, from his fiftieth year, he had found the hill on which his house was built steeper and steeper and the way home longer and longer. But never so long as it was today when he wanted to get away from the market-place as quickly as possible and get home as soon as he could. His heart was beating as it should not have, his breath failed him and he was forced to halt.

Down below there, it seemed, they were singing. Down below there, too, was the ruined bridge, horribly, cruelly cut in half. There was no need for him to turn (and he would not have turned for anything in the world) to see the whole picture: in the distance the pier cut short like a gigantic tree-trunk and scattered in a thousand pieces and the arches to left and right of it brutally cut short. The broken arches yawned painfully towards one another across the break.

No, not for anything would he have turned round. But he could not go forward, uphill, for his heart stifled him more and more and his legs refused to obey him. He began to breathe more and more deeply, slowly, in measure, each time more deeply. That had always helped him before. It helped him now. His chest seemed to grow easier. Between the measured deep breathing and the beating of his heart he established a sort of balance. He began to walk once more and the thought of home and bed stimulated and drove him on. He walked painfully and slowly and before his eyes, as if it moved along in front of him, was the whole scene with the ruined bridge. It was not enough to turn one's back on a thing for it to cease to goad and torment one. Even when he shut his eyes he could still see it.

Yes, thought the *hodja* more animatedly, for he was now breathing a little more easily, now one can see what all their tools and their equipment really meant, all their hurry and activity. (He had always been right, always, in everything and despite everybody. But that no longer gave him any satisfaction. For the first time it did not really matter. He had been only too right!) For so many years he had seen how they had always been concerning themselves with the bridge; they had cleaned it, embellished it, repaired it down to its foundations, taken the water supply across it, lit it with electricity and then one day blown it all into the skies as if it had been some stone in a mountain quarry and not a thing of beauty and value, a bequest. Now one could see what they were and what they wanted. He had always known that but now, now even the most stupid of fools could see it for himself. They had begun to attack even the strongest and most lasting of things, to take things away even from God. And who knew where it would stop! Even the Vezir's bridge had begun to crumble away like a necklace; and once it began no one could hold it back.

The *hodja* halted again. His breath failed him and the slope suddenly grew steeper before him. Again he had to calm his heartbeats with deep breathing. Again he succeeded in recovering his breath, felt himself revive and walked on more quickly.

So be it, thought the *hodja.* If they destroy here, then somewhere else someone else is building, Surely there are still peaceful countries and men of good sense who know of God's love? If God had abandoned this unlucky town on the Drina, He had surely not abandoned the whole world that was beneath the skies? They would not do this forever. But who knows? (Oh, if only he could breathe a little more deeply, get a little more air!) Who knows? Perhaps this impure infidel faith that puts everything in order, cleans everything up, repairs and embellishes everything only in order suddenly and violently to demolish and destroy, might spread through the whole world; it might make of all God's world an empty field for its senseless building and criminal destruction, a pasturage for its insatiable hunger and incomprehensible demands? Anything might happen. But one thing could not happen; it could not be that great and wise men of exalted soul who would raise lasting buildings for the love of God, so that the world should be more beautiful and man live in it better and more easily, should everywhere and for all time vanish from this earth. Should they too vanish, it would mean that the love of God was extinguished and had disappeared from the world. That could not be.

Filled with his thoughts, the *hodja* walked more heavily and slowly.

Now they could clearly be heard singing in the market-place. If only he had been able to breathe in more air, if only the road were less steep, if only he were able to reach home, lie down on his divan and see and hear someone of his own about him! That was all that he wanted now. But he could not. He could no longer maintain that fine balance between his breathing and his heartbeats; his heart had now completely stifled his breath, as had sometimes happened to him in dreams. Only from this dream there was no awakening to bring relief. He opened his mouth wide and felt his eyes bulging in his head. The slope which until then had been growing steeper and steeper was now quite close to his face. His whole field of vision was filled by that dry, rough road which became darkness and enveloped him.

On the slope which led upwards to Mejdan lay Alihodja and breathed out his life in short gasps.

Note on the Pronunciation of Serbo-Croat Names

Andrić's novel is published both in the Cyrillic and Latin (Croat) alphabets. I have used the Croatian spelling throughout. The language is strictly phonetic. One sound is almost always designated by one letter or (in Croat) combination of letters.

Generally speaking, the foreigner cannot go far wrong if he uses "continental" vowels and English consonants, with the following exceptions:

c is always ts, as in ca*ts*.

č is ch as in *ch*urch.

ć is similar but softer, as t in the Cockney pronunciation of tube.

Many family names end in ć. For practical purposes, the foreigner may regard č and ć as the same.

dj is the English j in judge—the English j in fact.

dž is practically the same, but harder. It is usually found in words of Turkish origin.

j is always soft, the English y.

r is sometimes a vowel, strongly rolled. Hence such strange looking words as vrh (summit).

š is sh as in *sh*ake.

z is zh as z in azure.

Other variations do not occur in this book. In a few cases I have left the conventionally accepted English spelling, instead of insisting pedantically on Serbo-Croat versions: e.g. Sanjak (Serbo-Croat: Sandžak), Belgrade (Serbo-Croat: Beograd), etc. In the case of purely Turkish names, I have sometimes transliterated them phonetically, as the Croat version is equally arbitrary.

The use of the original names retains dignity and flavor. Attempts to adapt them to English phonetics (in itself an ungrateful task) results in such monstrosities as Ts(e)rnche—for Crnče.

LOVETT F. EDWARDS

THE LIFE AND WORKS OF IVO ANDRIĆ

By VLADIMIR DEDIJER

FEW Yugoslav writers have opened up the problem of the absurd in life as much as Ivo Andrić has in his novels and short stories, especially in his chief work, *Na Drini Ćuprija* (*The Bridge on the Drina*).

How does Andrić interpret the absurd? Is it metaphysical or is it created by social conditions? Is it grounded only in the discontent of man with himself or in his discontent with the milieu around him—or in both? Does Andrić believe in the unchanged nature of man, of his inner turbulence, or does he believe that the unrest of loneliness is a result of the external human restlessness and the efforts of human beings to attain the impossible and the absolute?

During his childhood Andrić drank deeply of the folklore philosophies of his native Bosnia. The South Slav tribal forms of social organization survived in Bosnia into modern times, as in a deep freeze, unlike those in most parts of Europe. When the independent Bosnian state, along with the whole of the Balkan peninsula, was conquered in 1463 by the Turks, the new rulers did not interfere much in the internal life of the peasantry. Although after the conquest almost half of the population in Bosnia was deported to slavery in other parts of the Ottoman Empire, the rest were left to live under their own tribal social organization. The new rulers demanded strict allegiance to the state, and prompt fulfillment of all obligations toward it, but left the culture of the South Slavs alone. This way of life survived in Bosnia until modern times, even after the end of the sovereignty of the Ottoman Empire in 1908, when the Hapsburg Emperor Franz Joseph proclaimed that he was the new master of Bosnia.

Ivo Andrić was born in the Bosnian town of Travnik, in a family of artisans, in 1892. When he went to primary school in 1899, over ninety per cent of the Bosnian population was illiterate. Communication among the peasantry and to a great extent in towns, both in times of happiness and of sorrow, was oral. Andrić remembered from his early childhood legends and lyric and epic folklore poetry. He studied at the Sarajevo high school in the turbulent days prior to World War I. It was in this town that the pistol shots of the young schoolboy Gavrilo Princip rang out—Princip was a friend of Andrić—that not only announced the death of Franz Ferdinand, the heir apparent of the Austro-Hungarian Empire, but also the outbreak of the most destructive war in the history of mankind until then.

Before 1914, Andrić had established a reputation as a gifted poet, and he had published several poems in the leading literary magazines of Sarajevo and Zagreb. Ivo Andrić had nothing to do with the conspiracy that took the Archduke's life but he was president of a literary club of young revolutionaries called the Young Bosnians. He was arrested immediately after the outbreak of the war and was jailed until its end. When he came out, he published two collections of poetical prose, *Ex Ponto* and *Nemiri* (Turbulences, 1919).

At last free from foreign domination, the various South Slavs formed a common state under the name of Yugoslavia, literally, the land of the South Slavs. Ivo Andrić was now able to continue his history studies, first at the University of Zagreb, then at the University of Krakow in Poland, and he finally took his degree in ethnology at Graz University in Austria. As a scholar Andrić tried to rationalize the folkloric culture of Bosnia and to discover the reasons for its survival through the ages; he had a gifted ear, and was able to hear and understand the meaning of the delicate tones from long past times. In *Ex Ponto,* he speaks of "the blessed inheritance of our grandfathers, who left their bodies in the old tombs, but strong virtues in the foundations of our souls."

In the diplomatic service of the new Yugoslav government Andrić found a shelter in which to brood, read, and observe other countries and cultures. His stay in Spain was of particular importance for his development as a writer. Instead of poetry or poetical prose, he concentrated on short stories, publishing three collections of them, under the direct title *Pripovetke* (*Stories,* 1924, 1931, and 1938). The literary critics recognized almost unanimously that a great writer had appeared in Yugoslav literature.

As a diplomat, Andrić achieved his highest post as Yugoslav Ambassador in Berlin, on the very eve of the outbreak of World War II, which saw the invasion of Yugoslavia by the Germans and their allies in April 1941. In the summer of 1941 an uprising broke out in Yugoslavia. The German authorities asked the leading writers, scientists, and businessmen of Serbia to sign a proclamation denouncing the rebellion. Many put their names on that piece of paper; among the few who declined was Ivo Andrić. When the German messenger, who knew Andrić personally, rang the bell of his apartment, Andrić defiantly told him to tell his masters that he would not come to sign the enemy proclamation.

The rest of the war Andrić spent at his home, taking no part in public life. He kept writing his masterpieces, the novels *The Bridge on the Drina* and *Travnička hronika* (*Bosnian Story*), and *Gospodjica* (*The Woman from Sarajevo*) all of which were published immediately after the liberation of Belgrade in 1945.

In 1951 Andrić published *Prokleta Avlija* (*Devil's Yard*) in the review *Nova Misao* (New Thought), whose editors were Milovan Djilas, Skender Kulenović, Bora Drenovac, and others. This was a denunciation of the authoritarian state with its suppression of those who fight for social justice and freedom. Since 1951 he has not published any major work, but he is still writing actively and living in Belgrade.

Although Andrić did not fashion his writing after a model or a fixed literary pattern, he was profoundly influenced by the philosophy of Serb writers, whose roots went into the folklore wisdom of the South Slavs. Among the most important of these writers was the Prince Bishop of Montenegro, Petar Petrović-Njegoš (1793–1851). In his epics the symbol of heroism, one of the basic elements of folklore, was combined with the idea of martyrdom. He developed his own concept of permanent rebellion. He did not find the origin of the right to resistance against a tyrant only in the divine law, outside and above nature, but he sought its justification also in human society as such—in the constant state of restlessness of the South Slav peasantry against the Ottoman rule, particularly in the declining decades of the old Empire. As we shall see later, Andrić's concept of martyrdom was greatly influenced by Njegoš.

Andrić was even more influenced by Marko Miljanov (1833–1901), a Montenegrin shepherd of the clan Kuči, from the border of Albania, who later became its chief and won the battle of Fundina, the decisive Montenegrin victory in the 1876–1877 war against the Turks. In this battle 4,000 Montenegrins killed more than 9,000 Turkish soldiers. Although Marko Miljanov spent most of his life fighting as a *hajduk,* a popular defender of Christians against Turkish oppression, attacking the feudal lords and applying a kind of agrarian terrorism, in his writing (he learned to write at the age of 50) he showed no trace of enmity toward his enemies, the Turks and the Albanians. He found dignity in material poverty and held distaste for any power structure. He emphasized that both Montenegrins and Albanians when locked in a life and death struggle took care not to violate each other's dignity.

What are the folklore philosophies, cherished by generations of the rebellious South Slav peasantry, which so obsessed Njegoš, Miljanov, and Andrić? In her much esteemed 1963 essay on Njegoš's epic *Luča Mikrokozma,* Ethica Anica Savić-Rebac described the often deeply hidden popular currents as "the ancient subconscious traditions, the epitome of the ancient Balkans, heroic and mystic, the Balkans of fighting and *agones,* from the Hellenic features of Eastern Christianity and medieval Bogomilism, the dualistic sect of the Neo-Manichaeans, and the slow penetration of the efforts of the Byzantine culture." Both for students of social psychology and of the history of ideas in literature a tempting question is whether the dualistic, antimaterialistic ideas of Bogomilism could have survived among the South Slavs up to modern times. In particular, are these dualistic ideas present in *The Bridge on the Drina* and other works?

The first task is to define the main features of the Bogomil belief, its relationship with other Neo-Manichaeans variations in the Middle Ages, and to see what their doctrines had in common.

No doubt the various sects sprang from the dualistic teachings of Manes, a Persian philosopher (third century A.D.) who combined in his doctrine Christian, Persian, and even Buddhist elements. In opposition to the good god, the God of Light, the god of the spiritual, there exists the bad god, the God of Darkness, the god of the material world. In the world around us, the bad world, there exists the incarnated evil which can be overcome only by a spiritual renaissance. Manes divided his disciples among *perfecti,* the elected ones, and the *auditores,* the ordinary ones. The duty of the elected ones was to abstain from everything material as evil. They did not possess any private property. Even the prolongation of the species by the *perfecti* was regarded as a sin. They did not marry, had no intercourse with women, and declined the use of meat or eggs. Those among the *auditores* who felt that they could become martyrs, like the *perfecti,* were received in their ranks.

With the deepening crisis of the feudal order in the eleventh century, the Manichaean doctrine found fertile ground. For them, the Christian Church, having under its control a greater part of the feudal estates in France, Germany, and Italy, abounding in wealth and preoccupied with temporal affairs, was the servant of the evil god, the Synagogue of Satan. The Neo-Manichaeans were antagonized by the sale of the sacraments, simony, and favoritism; the abuse of Papal and episcopal jurisdiction; the neglect of preaching and the giving of indulgences. The Neo-Manichaeans attacked the whole system of government, both ecclesiastical and civil. This was the firm basis of all Neo-Manichaean sects in Europe, and the Popes were obliged to organize the Inquisition and to undertake oppressions in France from 1204 to 1229. The Church adopted the death penalty for heresy: Albigensians, Cathars, and Waldenses were massacred in the name of Christianity.

Among the Neo-Manichaean sects there existed many doctrinal variations. Manichaean social egalitarianism fitted the tribal forms of social organization of Bosnian society, but Bosnian Bogomilism had its own specifics. It was already in existence at the end of the eleventh century and was the religion of the Bosnian feudal state until that state's fall to the Turks at the end of the fifteenth century. Several campaigns headed by the kings of Hungary could not destroy the Bosnian heresy. No Roman Catholic cathedral was built under the rule of the Bosnian Bogomil kings.

The doctrines of the Bogomils are known primarily through the documents of their persecutors, both from the east and the west. In the archives of the Vatican there exists a 1461 document citing the main "prejudices" of the Bosnian Manichaeans: 1. There exist two Gods, of which one is the God of the Supreme Good and the other of the Supreme Bad. 2. There exist two basic principles of life: the spiritual one, anti-material one, and the material one, the evil one. The first one is called the God of Light and the other the God of Darkness. Among other "prejudices" the Vatican document cites: "the Roman Church is excommunicated by the Bosnians"; "they condemn the building of churches"; "they deny any authority of the Church."

Some historians, like F. Heer, are of the opinion that the Bogomil sects survived up to modern times as underground movements. Heer thinks that "the secret fraternities of the nineteenth century and early twentieth century in the Balkans which played their part in determining the course of the First and Second World Wars had their roots in the militant Bogomilism." He also holds that the whole character of the Balkan rebellious militant underground societies can be understood only in the light of Bogomilism. The first of Heer's theses is debatable. There are no primary historical sources to prove a direct link between the Bogomils and heretical sects in the Balkan society of later times. His other thesis, that some Bogomil teachings survived in the later centuries in folklore, is more acceptable, particularly if one analyzes the recorded epic and lyric poetry of Bosnian folklore.

Under the strict control of the Moslem feudal-tenure system, the Bosnian peasantry lived lethargically for long years before bursting into rebellion. As Ottoman rule with its outdated institutions continued, restlessness increased. In the nineteenth century alone there were more than twenty peasant uprisings in Bosnia. In the 1875–1878 rebellion, over 200,000 Bosnians—more than one-fourth the population—had to leave their homes, never to return. During World War I Bosnia and other South Slav lands lost 1,900,000 people, one out of every six.

In World War II, when Andrić was writing *The Bridge on the Drina,* another 1,700,000 South Slavs perished. So Andrić's chief work is basically a chronicle of violent mass death. Andrić describes his native Bosnia as "a darkened valley of death," in which real life consists of cease-fires between wars to the death and states that "it is foolish and in vain to disturb those rare truces, looking for some other, more stable, more secure life which does not exist." In his symbolic story *Devil's Yard,* the central prison of the Ottoman Empire in Istanbul is the material world itself: "Nobody's here by accident. Once a man has crossed into the Yard he's guilty. He's done some wrong, even if only in his sleep. If it's not that, then his mother's mind was on some wickedness when she carried him."

Death has many meanings for Andrić. It is, first, the great equalizer between the rich and the poor, between the powerful and the weak. Death is also a way for a man to show his real values. The martyr peasant Radisav from Unište, who had dared to sabotage the building of the vizier's bridge, and many others like him all through *The Bridge on the Drina* are examples of not only how much a man can suffer, but also how much a man can endure under intolerable conditions. In his concept of martyrdom Andrić accepts a Marko Miljanov dictum: "Martyrdom is the expression of a conscious, morally integral being, individual and collective, a victory over the changeable in life, a creative self-assurance of man." Andrić speaks about the duty to endure even when it seems that the outcome of the struggle is completely hopeless: Life is an uncomprehensible marvel, because it spends itself all the time, it destroys itself, but nevertheless it endures and it holds strongly as the bridge on the Drina."

Yet Andrić does not describe the struggle between good and evil in black and white. Few writers have portrayed the painful process of the identification of the victim with the aggressor, the so-called social mimicry acted out by the oppressed in Bosnian society in order to live. He does not condemn them, but describes their philosophy of co-optation by the warnings through the ages of the elders to the rebellious youth that "they should not force evil to become even worse than it is." And he distinguishes between those who make virtue of their moral prostitution and those who do not. He portrays with sympathy the Franciscan friars who apply all the artistry of Nicodemus (the Pharisee leader who dared to see Jesus only in the night) in order to save their faith and their integrity, despite some compromises with the superior force of the authorities.

Andrić's idea of *nemiri od vijeka,* "turbulences through the centuries," his own concept of permanent rebellion, is traceable like a red thread through all his writings. Perhaps it is expressed most vividly in a short story called "Priča iz Japana" (A Story from Japan):

> Among the Three Hundred and Fifty conspirators banished under the rule of the Empress Au-Ung, was the poet Mori Ipo.
>
> He spent three years on the smallest of the Seven Isles in a hut made of reeds. But when the Empress fell ill and her power started to fade, he, like the majority of the Three Hundred and Fifty, succeeded in returning to the capital city Jedo. He lived on the outskirts of the city in a wing of a temple.
>
> The citizens, sickened with the bloodthirsty tyranny of the mad and cruel Empress, grew to love the poet more and more, and the Three Hundred and Fifty were his inseparable companions. His short verses about heroism and death were passed secretly from hand to hand, and his kind smile often settled the disputes of his comrades.
>
> It happened that the Empress died unexpectedly from the poison of gen-

eral hatred. Her corrupt chamberlains ran away, and she lay ugly and swollen in the deserted palace, and there was no one to bury her.

The Three Hundred and Fifty conspirators quickly assembled and took power. Among themselves they divided the ranks and honors and began to rule over the unified Empire on the Seven Isles.

When the first ceremonial meeting was convened in the palace of the late Empress, after the count-up of the Three Hundred and Fifty, it was discovered that one of them was missing. And when the list of conspirators was read aloud, it was found that the poet Mori Ipo was absent. They refused to deliberate without him and at once a slave with a rickshaw was dispatched for him. After a time the slave returned with the empty rickshaw. He had been told that Mori Ipo had gone and that he had left a written message for the Council of the Three Hundred and Fifty. The oldest in the Council took the folded paper and handed it to the Chief of State Learned Ones, Who began to read aloud:

"Mori Ipo extends his greetings to his comrade conspirators, at this hour of departure!

"Deep thanks from my heart, comrades of mine, for the common sufferings and for our common faith and victory. I beg you humbly to forgive me because I cannot share with you authority as I shared the struggle. Poets—unlike other men—are faithful only in the hour of calamity and leave those who enjoy well-being. We poets are born for struggle; we are passionate hunters, but we do not eat the prey. A thin and almost invisible fence divides us; it is not as keen as the edge of the sword but nevertheless it is just as lethal. Without damage to my soul I could not cross this line, because we can endure everything but authority. This is the reason I am leaving you, my comrade conspirators. I am going to see if there is somewhere a thought which has not yet been realized or a cause unfulfilled, but if any calamity of danger should befall our Empire of the Seven Isles and the need comes for struggle and aid, then seek me out."

At that moment the chairman of the Council, who was a little deaf, interrupted the reading, and with the impatience of an old man and with disapproval in his voice, said:

"No calamity could befall the Empire during the just and enlightened rule of the Three Hundred and Fifty."

All the counselors nodded, and the older ones smiled with disdain and pity. What nonsense! The reading was discontinued and the bill on customs duty on imports was taken up instead.

Only the Chief of the State Learned Ones read the poet's message to the end, but to himself, and then he wrapped it up and deposited it in the Archives of the former Empress.

It was in this story that a young Andrić opened his dialogue with the absurd, a dialogue which he continued in his masterpiece, *The Bridge on the Drina.*

Vladimir Dedijer, a Yugoslav historian, philosopher, and politician, is a nephew of Andrić and author of a recent book on Tito's relationship with Stalin.

THE 1961 PRIZE

By KJELL STRÖMBERG

WHEN Ivo Andrić, the Serbo-Croat novelist and poet, won the Nobel Prize for Literature in 1961, there were about fifty other nominations. Particularly in his favor was the fact that he was a Yugoslav, and no Yugoslav had ever won the Prize.

Andrić was proposed for the first time in 1958 by the professional association of Yugoslav writers at the same time as his compatriot Miroslav Krléja, a poet who like so many others had progressed from unrestrained individualism to orthodox communism. Ivo Andrić had almost won the Nobel Prize two years later when his name had been put forward by an influential member of the Swedish Academy. He was narrowly edged out that year by St. John Perse who had the influential backing of Dag Hammarskjöld, then Secretary General of the United Nations.

The following year the Secretary-General was himself posthumously to receive the Nobel Prize for Peace, awarded by the Nobel Committee of the Storting, the Norwegian parliament. And that same year the Swedish Academy gave the Nobel Prize for Literature to Ivo Andrić "for the epic force with which he has traced themes and depicted human destinies from his country's history."

Like St.-John Perse, Ivo Andrić is a former diplomat. *The Bridge on the Drina,* which made him famous in his own country, has gone on to be translated into about twenty languages. So Andrić joins the long line of novelists from the small Slav countries, like Stéfan Zeromsky in Poland and Aloïs Jérasek in Czechoslovakia who, inspired by Tolstoy and his classic *War and Peace,* have exalted the virtues and the prowess of their countrymen, who for so long were subjugated to others.

Eyvind Johnson, who was himself the author of a remarkable series of historical novels, examined Andrić's works for the Nobel Committee of the Swedish Academy. He felt that the *Chronicle of Travnik,* an account of the period of the Napoleonic wars is markedly influenced by Stendhal in tone and treatment, was a considerable contribution to European literature, while *The Bridge on the Drina* proves Andrić to be "a storyteller in the style of the *Thousand and One Nights.*" Andrić was also strongly influenced by popular oriental tradition. The Committee's chairman notes that this oriental characteristic of exuberant and yet orderly fantasy is considerably stronger in his last big novel, *The Accursed Court,* "from the artistic point of view, the best composed and the most finished of anything I have read by this author."

It was in Belgrade as he returned from a walk in the public park overlooking the Danube that Andrić learned of the

Swedish Academy's decision from journalists outside his front door. His small four-room apartment, situated in a quiet street in the middle of Belgrade, was soon invaded by a crowd of visitors including government officials and many personal friends who all had come to congratulate him, while the journalists bombarded him with questions. The writer, who was about to enter his seventieth year, went to Stockholm to receive his Prize from the hands of King Gustavus Adolphus VI. After having been greeted as a worthy representative of his little country whose activities, both literary and diplomatic, had effectively served to throw a bridge between two worlds, the laureate enlarged upon this theme with eloquence in the speech he gave at the banquet.

Translated by Camilla Sykes.

Library
Western Wyoming Community College